Eva
the Adventuress

A Lost Novel of
Nellie Bly

Eva the Adventuress
by Nellie Bly

Originally published in the New York Family Story Paper and the London Story Paper

1889-1890

Transcribed by David Blixt and Syed Asad Nawazish

Edited by David Blixt

This edition copyright © 2021 David Blixt

Cover by Cathy Hunter

ISBN-13: 978-1944540555

Published by Sordelet Ink
www.sordeletink.com

Eva
the Adventuress

A Romance of a Blighted Life.

A Lost Novel of
Nellie Bly

Introduction by David Blixt

Sordelet ink

FOR MY OWN EVA,
AN ADVENTURESS IN THE
BEST SENSE OF THE WORD

NELLIE BLY.   EVA, THE ADVENTURESS

CONTENTS

THE LOST NOVELS OF NELLIE BLY

INTRODUCTION BY DAVID BLIXT

It was the first day of December, 2019, and like Alice, I was down a rabbit hole.

I was working on a short-story follow-up to *What Girls Are Good For*, my 2018 novel following the early career of groundbreaking undercover reporter Nellie Bly. My new story took place immediately after the exposé that made her a household name, her ten days spent as an inmate in the insane asylum on Blackwell's Island.

That experience had been turned into a book, *Ten Days In A Mad-House*, a terrific and horrifying read that remains hugely influential to this day (the nurses she describes were evidently the basis for Nurse Ratched in Ken Kesey's *One Flew Over The Cuckoo's Nest*). In order to catch up my readers on where the events of the story fell, I wanted to kick off with Bly receiving an offer from a publisher for that very book.

Trouble was, I had no idea how much money she was offered.

Fortunately, I knew the name of the original publisher, as well as the date of publication. But lacking a *Publisher's Weekly* to report book deals in 1887, I started following the paper trail of the publisher himself. I thought I might find a contract with another author, or perhaps some old balance sheets.

Instead I found something unexpected.

The lost novels of Nellie Bly.

ॐ

Bly's publisher was Norman L. Munro, brother of famed publisher George Munro. George was one of the pioneers of the Victorian-era wave of cheap books for the masses. Ten, fifteen, and twenty-five cent novels were gobbled up by a hungry audience, most of them women, and George Munro made a fortune feeding their appetite for every kind of story.

The brothers Munro were born and raised in Nova Scotia. After college, George moved to New York City and worked at the American News Company until he amassed enough capital to launch his own weekly publication, *The Fireside Companion*, in 1867. It was a smash, and the foundation of an international publishing empire.

Tagging along, Norman worked for his older brother until 1873, when he decided to go it alone and launched his own rival weekly, the *New York Family Story Paper*. Direct competition caused a rift between the siblings, who are said to have never spoken to each other again except through lawyers (when George began publishing cheap versions of classic books, Norman followed suit, naming his imprint, "Munro's Library." George filed a lawsuit over use of the family name, but the courts ruled for Norman, claiming he had as much right to the name Munro as George did).

While Norman never had the literary heft of his brother's imprint, he found success publishing "Irish" novels, "Indian" novels, romance novels, what have you. He published the Allan Quatermain adventures, and 25 short novels based on the life of French highwayman Claude Duval. In 1883 he launched another weekly, *Old Cap. Collier Library*, featuring detective stories with a rotating roster of main characters.

Then, in 1888, Norman had an instant bestseller in Nellie Bly's *Ten Days In A Mad-House*. He immediately asked her for another, and released *Six Months In Mexico* that same year, reprinting the articles Bly had written as the *Pittsburg Dispatch*'s foreign correspondent in Mexico. He clearly was making a fortune on Nellie Bly, reporter.

But Bly had other ambitions. She viewed reporting as a temporary job, a launching point for a broader literary career.

She wanted to be a novelist.

൙

Bly spent the three years after her cannon-blast debut in the pages of the *New York World* trying to top herself. She exposed the 'King of the Lobby' in Albany, outed a serial procurer of girls in Central Park, and interviewed the most notorious would-be murderess of the day. She kept putting herself in more and more peril in order to get a story. Why? Because the titillation of 'a girl in danger' sold papers—especially during the height of Ripper hysteria in London.

She reached the zenith of her fame by racing around the world in an attempt to best the fictional record of Jules Verne's character Phileas Fogg from *Around The World In Eighty Days*. She even got to meet Verne during her trip.

Bly was not alone in the phenomenon of "stunt girls," but thanks to that three-month race around the globe, she was by far the most famous. There were board games and trading cards based on her trip. Her face was known everywhere, and her ulster coat and cap were iconic.

But for Bly, stunt reporting had taken a toll. She'd begun to suffer terrible headaches. Stories that once would have fired her heart now left her cold. Celebrated and famous after her seventy-two-day girdling of the globe, she felt she had reached the peak of what newspaper reporting could offer her.

So when Norman Munro offered Bly a job writing for the *New York Family Story Paper*, she leapt at it. It's easy to understand why. Munro was offering her $40,000 over three years. Even for a star reporter, the most she could have been earning at the *World* was $5,000 a year. Munro's offer must have seemed a fortune.

Yet before signing, she cleverly insisted her contract allow her to return to reporting without giving up her new career. As she wrote to her friend Erasmus Wilson in August, 1890:

I sent you a newspaper the other day containing a notice of the very good contract I have made with Mr. Munro. It allows me to do reporting work. I had made up my mind never to work for a newspaper again but I can do serial stories for Mr. Munro and never go out of my own home. I am busy on one now entitled "New York by Night." You know all the great English novelists began in this way, so I hope. The woman who wrote "Bootles Baby" which has sold more than 500,000 copies and has been dramatized and played in every city in Europe and America has always been a writer for such story papers. And then Mrs. Burnett wrote for The Ledger until she made a hit as a novelist, so I feel encouraged.

Clearly Bly had high hopes for her literary career. Sadly, to that point, her record for fiction did not seem so very bright. Her first novel, *The Mystery of Central Park*, had been published a year earlier, first serially in the pages of the *World*, then in book form. The story was a murder-mystery loosely based on her 1888 exposé "Infamy of the Park."

While not nearly at the level of, say, Conan Doyle's recently-published *A Study In Scarlet*, Bly's short novel made use of her intimate knowledge of New York, and contained the same massive end-of-novel confession that Conan Doyle employed in his first two Sherlock Holmes novels. What's most fascinating about it are the links to both her own reporting and her own life (she berates a thinly-veiled version of her former beau, James Stetson Metcalfe, for being "brutal and unkind").

If Bly had been hoping to make a splash in this new career, alas, it was not to be. Of the four books released in Bly's name between 1888 and 1890, her one work of fiction was her least regarded. At the time, reviews of the novel were more reviews of Bly herself. A typical example:

> As a reporter, Bly has done much of the cleverest and most enterprising work known to the modern newspaper, and has a world-wide fame for sagacity, courage and spirited description of adventure. Her novel, we need not say, is bright, sparkling, and entertaining. (*Rochester Democrat and Chronicle, October 21, 1889*)

> "The Mystery of Central Park" is a well-written story, with a finely conceived plot. The story is told in "Nellie Bly's" own versatile way, and from the first to the last page holds the reader's attention. As a picture of the inside life of the great Metropolis, it should rank high. (*Indiana Democrat, October 31, 1889*)

Another contemporary review describes the novel as being "written in that sprightly style that characterizes her reporting and is rather better than the ordinary novel of this class." (*Philadelphia Enquirer, October 26, 1889*).

Talk about damning with faint praise.

Today *The Mystery of Central Park* is ridiculed for its stilted style, thin characters, and rather haphazard plot. Talking to Bly historians, I find everyone tends to shrug off her novels as an ill-fated endeavor, a bump on the road of her true career, reporting. Fair enough.

What strikes me about that first novel, though, is the story of the murder itself: an innocent girl becomes the kept woman of an unscrupulous and ambitious man. When he tires of her, rather than marry her as he promised, he murders her and leaves her body propped on a bench in Central Park.

While Bly did not yet have mastery of the art form, she was still Nellie Bly. She was still motivated by injustices against women.

She was still angry.

❧

It was Bly's anger that first appealed to the writer in me. Oh, I'd heard about her madhouse stay, and her race around the world. But it was only when I discovered how she got her first reporting job that I became captivated by her.

Reading an article entitled "What Girls Are Good For," twenty-year-old Elizabeth Cochrane was so angry at the premise—that women belonged at home, not in the workplace—that she penned a letter of protest to the *Pittsburg Dispatch*. We don't know what was in that letter, but it got her an interview, and eventually a job as a reporter. As women did not, as a rule, write under their own names, she was saddled with the *nom-de-plume* "Nellie Bly."

The day I read that story, I put aside all my other writing and for two years focused on Bly, getting to know her writing, her character, her contradictions, her charm, and her passion. It resulted in a novel, but I was well aware that Ms. Bly had not finished with me. So I pressed on to write the next part of her story.

Which brings us back to the Munro rabbit hole, hunting for what Bly was paid for her madhouse book.

I discovered that there was only one known issue of Munro's *New York Family Story Paper* containing part of a Nellie Bly novel—two chapters of something called *Eva The Adventuress*. That was one of only two titles Bly was known to have written. The other title, gleaned from that 1890 letter to Wilson, was *New York By Night*. Outside of those two, we knew nothing about Bly's fiction career writing for Munro's paper.

On my hunt for her remuneration, I followed links and read extracts about both brothers. In one biography I found a reference to another of Norman's publications, the *London Story Paper*. Evidently the New York edition was such a success that Norman created a mirror version of the paper across the pond, literally reproducing the New York edition six months later with no changes to the typesetting (which is why you find Christmas poems published in July).

Idly, I started hunting. At once I found searchable records of the *London Story Paper* at NewspaperArchive.com. So, buying a subscription, I plugged in the name "Nellie Bly" and hit return.

The results generated within seconds. Disbelieving, I stared at the screen.

There they were. The lost novels of Nellie Bly.

It took me hours that first day, collecting all the titles and putting them in order. When I was finished, I found I had eleven novels in all. More novels than any Bly historian had ever imagined she'd written.

The trouble was, half of the pages were completely illegible. Were the scans bad? Or did the original microfilm contain bad copies? It was near impossible to find out, as I quickly discovered there were only three library copies of the original microfilm in the entire world. One in London, one in Sydney, and one in Toronto.

So, in the break between Christmas and New Year's 2019, I drove to Toronto and spent a frantic day at the University of Toronto library. Yes, it was the original microfilm that was so faded. I discovered, however, that by zooming in close on the microfilm, I could get better resolution. Good enough to decipher every word. I took screenshots of each close-up and loaded them on a jump drive.

I walked out of the library blinking and aching, but certain I now had every word of Bly's lost novels. But what to do with them?

I approached a few agents, a few publishers. I was repeatedly told there was no interest for my discovery. This agreed with my attempts to sell my Nellie Bly novel two years earlier. I was told my novel about her life lacked "a hook." It was suggested to me that I make her a detective, or a vampire, or secretly a man (I kid you not).

So I enlisted several friends to help me transcribe these novels and determined to release them myself. You hold the fruits of our labor.

⟡

Thanks to this discovery, there's a small but significant change in our understanding of Bly's timeline. Before now, we only knew of four Bly books: three based on her reporting, and her lone novel. What we didn't know was that during 1889 she'd written another novel as well.

Eva The Adventuress is a bizarre yet gripping tale of a red-headed vixen wronged by everyone and eager for revenge. With her signature move of stabbing men in the chest but failing to kill them, Eva Scarlett is clearly based on the real-life, red-haired aspiring-murderess Eva Hamilton.

Nellie Bly interviewed Eva Hamilton in prison in early October, 1889. Bly must have been truly inspired, for she couldn't have had more than a month to finish her novel based on the fiery Eva. On November 14th Bly set off on her race around the world, and *Eva The Adventuress* had to have been complete before she left.

Since the race itself came as a surprise—she'd been pushing for over a year to make the trip, but the *World*'s editors only agreed a few days before she departed—Bly had probably been trying to shop the novel in the days before she left. But after the resounding thud *The Mystery Of Central Park* had created, Munro might've been wary of publishing it.

Things undoubtedly changed once the race had begun. Suddenly Bly's name was everywhere, blazoned across newspapers around the world. It was the kind of free advertising Munro would have been a fool not to utilize. Thus *Eva The Adventuress* started to run just before Christmas, on December 22, 1889, with the headline: *By Nellie Bly, Who is now attempting to make the circuit of the world in seventy-five days.*

We have no exact sales figures, but based on the huge jump in circulation of the *World*, and the incredible timeliness of both Nellie Bly and Eva Hamilton, the two most notorious women in New York, one can only imagine the bounty Munro reaped. Munro himself said that her story had increased circulation of the *Family Story Paper* by 50,000. He later claimed she had doubled his circulation. Munro's gambit had paid off.

It paid off for Bly, too. Finished, as she thought, with reporting, she parlayed her fame to gain a regular contract with Munro. Perhaps she told him she'd let him have the book about her trip if he put her on salary. However it happened, she had that amazing contract, being paid better than most men in either the reporting or the literary world. $40,000 over three years, to follow her dream.

Thus, from 1890 to 1895, Bly wrote serialized weekly novels in the pages of Munro's paper. Some are silly. Some are genuinely terrific. All of them are very much in line with the gothic pulp romances and mysteries of the era, filled with melodrama and cliffhanger endings.

Even more interesting are the number of themes and stories she resurrects, not just from her reporting days, but also from her own life. Again and again Blackwell's Island is referenced, and factory girls. Again and again, orphans figure prominently (though her mother still lived, Bly often referred to herself as an orphan. Her first published work for the *Dispatch* had been under the pen name "Lonely Orphan Girl").

And again and again she has a woman contemplate, or even attempt, suicide by throwing herself into the river. Because as she wrote these novels, Bly herself was in the midst of a severe depression, hardly able to leave her bed.

In 1889 she'd reported consulting seven doctors about her crippling headaches, to no avail. If she had hoped quitting the *World* would cure them, she was disappointed. Then in late 1890 she suffered a sprained or broken leg. Writing to Wilson in January, 1891, Bly reveals she is bedridden, and feeling hopeless:

> I would have answered your letter at once but I was trying to catch up with my work and its so tiresome writing in bed that I soon played out.

> I am glad, dear Q, that you always hope for the best. Life cannot be entirely cheerless while hope remains. It is a year since I have entertained such a feeling and, strange to say, I have not the least conception why I am, or should be, thus.

Two months later, in another letter to Wilson, she addresses her depression directly:

> I received your kind note some time ago and meant to answer it at once but I suddenly became a victim of the most frightful

depression that ever beset mortal (sic). *You can imagine how severe it is when I tell you that I have not done a stroke of work for four months. The doctor says it is my blood that is responsible for this languor and nervousness, still I am growing fat.*

Apparently reporting was her cure. After three years away, Bly returned to the pages of the *World* in November of 1893, picking up as if she'd never stopped. Munro would continue to publish her novels through June 1895, though he himself soon sold the business.

While her nonfiction books remained bestsellers, the eleven novels she'd written were never collected or reprinted. She seems to have given up on being a great novelist. After two more years as a reporter, she married a millionaire and settled into a life of leisure that would last nearly two decades, until lawsuits, poverty, and World War I forced her out of retirement and back to reporting. She died in 1922, writing and crusading to the very end.

Nellie Bly is rightly remembered for her reporting work, her early feminism, and her part in the rise of "stunt" journalism. She was also a canny industrialist, a generous employer, a devoted patron to many causes, a tireless fighter for the oppressed and dispossessed.

She was also a novelist.

Above all else, what I love about these books is the window they provide us into Bly's mind. Finding them has opened up a wealth of new insights into the clever, crusading, contradictory character that was Nellie Bly. I'm delighted to be able to share them.

I never did find out what she made from that first book, though.

I have made some editorial changes to Bly's work to ease modern reading, mostly consisting of removing extraneous commas before adverbs. I have occasionally merged paragraphs where the layout artist separated the same set of thoughts to fill space on the page. Sometimes I have changed an unharmonious verb tense—quite often when Bly is particularly excited about a scene she will lapse into present rather than past tense. If I thought this was conscious on her part, I would have left it as written. But it seems haphazard and accidental, the thing any editor would have picked up.

However, I have not altered a single particle of her stories themselves. Which leads to this caveat: these are products of their time. While certainly enlightened for her era, Bly engages in all the ethnic, cultural, and racial stereotypes of Victorian America. She pens descriptions and employs dialects for certain characters that are clearly offensive. Please read with care for yourself and forgiveness for her.

To that end, I have omitted one novel from this collection. In her seventh novel, *Dolly The Coquette*, Bly employed racial stereotypes all too common to her era. In particular she exploits at great length the racist trope of the Black "Mammy," a formerly enslaved woman devoted to a young white Southern girl (a trope Margaret Mitchell would make infamous in *Gone With The Wind*). In an age when we are still, as a culture, attempting to break free from exactly these hurtful and offensive racist tropes, I feel it would be irresponsible to publish it. While a possible curiosity to scholars, *Dolly* has no business being marketed as entertainment to the wider reading public. Like Disney's *Song Of The South*, it should remain in the vault as a product of a less progressive time.

It is important also to remember that these were serialized novels. I have left intact all of the insane cliffhangers Bly crafted for her readers, who normally got around three chapters per week. Therefore the melodrama is high to start, then lulls, then peaks, and so on. If it feels she's spinning her wheels, she's waiting for that next cliffhanger.

I want to draw attention to one of Bly's true talents—naming her characters. From Ruby Sharpe to Dimple Darlington, from Eva Scarlett to Amor Escandon, I truly love the names she invents.

For each volume I have added an afterword containing the articles from her time as a reporter that seemingly inspired part or all of each novel, from paper-box and shoe factories to Eva Hamilton and the "Infamy of the Park." The story is preceded by a biography of Bly that ran in the *London Story Paper*. I have also included selections of the art that accompanied the early chapters of these stories.

This novel in particular contains a hefty amount of extra material. As this is Bly's "ripped-from-the-headlines" novel, I have included dozens of newspaper stories about the real Eva Hamilton and the sensational headlines she provoked over the last decade of the 19th century.

ເ໐

I owe several people a world of thanks, most especially Judith West and Robert Kauzlaric, who are more involved in my writing career at times than they could ever have anticipated. Thanks, too, to Sarah Ann Leahy, Syed Asad Nawazish, Bharati Mohapatra, Eric Eilersen, Lauren Grace Thompson, Liz Wiley, Eryn O'Sullivan, Hope Newhouse, Tanya Dougherty, Barbara Figgins, Heidi Armbruster, Ian Geers, Wendy Huber, Mikaila Publes, and my mother, Jill Blixt.

Huge gratitude as well to Brooke Kroeger and Matthew Goodman, whose books about Bly remain the gold standard.

As ever, I could not attack my keyboard each day without the love and support of Janice, Dash, and Eva. I love you.

That's enough from me. I hope you enjoy the second Lost Novel of Nellie Bly: *Eva The Adventuress*.

— *David Blixt*
Chicago, 2021

Nellie Bly

NELLIE BLY

Nellie Bly is a descendant on her father's side of Lord Cochrane, the famous English admiral, and is closely connected with the present family, Lord and Lady Cochrane, at whose home Queen Victoria's daughter, the Princess Beatrice and her husband spent their honeymoon. In some characteristics Nellie Bly is said to closely resemble Lord Cochrane, who was noted for his deeds of daring, and who was never happy unless engaged in some exciting affair. Nellie Bly's great-grandfather Cochrane was one of a number of men who wrote a Declaration of Independence in Maryland near the South Mountains a long time before the historic Declaration of Independence was delivered to the world by our Revolutionary fathers. Her great-grandfather, on her mother's side, was a man of wealth, owning at one time almost all of Somerset Co., Pa. His name was Kennedy, and his wife was a nobleman's daughter. They eloped and fled to America. He was an officer, as were his two sons, in the Revolutionary War. Afterward he was sheriff of Somerset Co. repeatedly until old age compelled him to decline the office when then was considered one of power and importance. One of his sons, Thomas Kennedy, Nellie Bly's great-uncle, made a flying trip around the world, starting from and returning to New York, where his wife, a New York woman by birth, awaited his arrival. It took him three years to make the trip, and he returned in shattered health. He at once set about to write the history of his trip, but his health became so bad that he had to give up his task, and he was taken to his old home in Somerset, Pa., where he shortly died, a victim of consumption. He was buried there with the honors of war. Nellie Bly's father was a man of considerable wealth. He served for many years as judge of Armstrong Co., Pa. He lived on a large estate, where he raised cattle and had flour mills. The place took his name. It is called Cochrane's Mills. There Nellie Bly was born.

Being in reduced circumstances, owing to some family complications, after her father's death, and longing for excitement, she engaged to do special work for a Pittsburgh Sunday newspaper. She went for them to Mexico, where she remained six months, sending back weekly letters. After her return she longed for broader fields, and so came to New York. The story of her attempt to make a place for herself, or to find an opening, is a long one of disappointment, until at last she made a list of a number of daring and original ideas, which were submitted to a prominent editor. They were accepted, and she went to work.

Her first achievement was the exposure of the Blackwell's Island Insane Asylum, in which she spent ten days, and two days in the Bellevue Insane Asylum. The story created a great sensation, and she was called before the grand jury. An investigation was made, and her story proved true, so the grand jury recommended the changes she suggested, such as women physicians to superintend the bathing of the female insane inmates, better food and better clothing. On the strength of the story $3,000,000 a year increased appropriation was made for the benefit of the asylum.

Her next work of state interest was the story of her exposure of Ed Phelps, who was said to be the king of the Albany Lobby. For publishing this story she was summoned before an investigating committee, this time at Albany.

These two things alone made Nellie Bly's name known in other countries as well as this, and English and French journalists constantly noticed her work.

After three years' work on a New York paper she conceived the idea of making a trip around the world in less time than had been done by Phileas Fogg, the fictitious hero of Jules Verne's famous novel; but when she first planned the trip to do it in 58 days, it was not met with favor by her editor. When she did go, almost a year later, it was impossible to make close connections but she, however, was the first person to make an actual record, which was 72 days. On her return she was greeted by ovations all the way from San Francisco to New York such as were never granted the most illustrious persons of our country. Thousands of people fought for glimpses of her at the stations, and no President was ever greeted by as large crowds as welcomed her at Jersey City and New York.

Since then she has spent her time lecturing and writing a book describing her experience while flying around the world. Nellie Bly has received letters from all parts of the world, in all languages, congratulating her on her successful journey, and begging autographs. Papers in every country, even Japanese and Chinese, published accounts of her novel undertaking.

Nellie Bly at an early age already showed great literary ability in verse as well as in prose, and many poems were contributed by her to the Pittsburgh and New York papers. She has, so far, written two novels—"The Mystery of Central Park" and "Eva, the Adventuress"—the latter published some time ago in THE LONDON STORY PAPER. Her latest story—"New York By Night"—which will begin in two weeks, bids fair to be one of the greatest successes of her life. She has stopped all newspaper writing, and is under contract, at a large sum, to contribute exclusively to the columns of THE LONDON STORY PAPER.

Her portrait published herewith is an excellent likeness. Nellie Bly is unmarried, and resides with her mother.

London—March 28th, 1891

EDITOR'S NOTE: The description of Bly's professional career is basically accurate, though the refusal to name the paper that made her famous is perplexing.

As with much published about Bly's personal life, however, there is as much fiction as fact here. There is no evidence linking her family to British aristocracy, nor to any signers of any Declarations of Independence or Revolutionary War soldiers. This does not mean these facts should be entirely disregarded. The story about her great-uncle, for example, is entirely true.

WEALTH REVENGE

EVA THE ADVENTURESS

Eva
THE Adventuress

A Romance of a Blighted Life.

"EVA SARLETT, COME HERE!"

I

THE SCHOOL YARD FIGHT.

"Oft those whose cruelty make many mourn,
Do by the fires which they first kindle burn."

"COME, NOW, ALL YOU GIRLS form in line," called a girl in an imperious voice.

One after another they formed in line—merry-faced, happy-voiced school-children. The self-appointed leader, who maintained control over her playmates because she was better clad and louder voiced, busied about taking out a tall girl and placing her in front, or moving a short one back. When all were about placed to her liking, she suddenly caught a girl by the shoulder and pulled her from the ranks.

"Here, you, Eva Scarlett, you get out," she cried harshly, pushing the girl to one side and hastily closing up the vacancy in the line. "We don't want you playing with us; you're dirty trash. Now girls, start!"

In voices shrill and unmusical, these school-children, unmindful of the abject child, whose face crimsoned with mortification as she was cast from their company, began to sing:

> *"Lon-don Bridge is falling down;*
> *Falling down, falling down,*
> *Lon-don Bridge is falling down,*
> *My fair lady.*

> *"Here's a prisoner we have caught.*
> *We have caught, we have caught.*
> *Here's a prisoner we have caught,*
> *My fair lady.*

"Take a key and lock her up,
Lock her up, lock her up.
Take a key and lock tier up,
My fair lady."

She was not pretty, this girl who had been so insulted. If children were anything else than heartless at this age, they would have been moved to pity at the sight of the forlorn child.

The crimson brought to her checks by her deep mortification died away, leaving visible large freckles which were almost as brown as her eyes, and marred what beauty there might have been in her fair skin.

Thrown carelessly back from her face were masses of red hair as shaggy as if it had never known a brush or comb.

There was no frock as dirty on any child in that schoolyard as was hers.

Besides, it was ragged, and she had so out-grown it that her thin, shapeless legs looked really pathetic.

Deserted and forgotten, an outcast from what should have been her own kind, the poor unkempt child stood aloof, watching the other children at their merry game.

Her face grew so pale that the disfiguring freckles stood out as distinct as the marks on a coachdog.

Her thin legs trembled as violently as they would had the frigid air of the North Pole swept over them.

Her brown eyes were dry and bloodshot; but they were filled with a maddened hatred as they watched every movement of the scornful leader who had put upon her the stamp of inequality, and had cast her forth from among her schoolmates.

Who can tell what thoughts came into that child's brain as she stood alone on the greensward of the playground that day?

The after events—a long, wicked, miserable life—showed the result of one child's cruelty to another. That cruelty left a sting in the child's heart that lived as long as she lived, and the poison from the wound found lodgment in the heart of many an innocent being.

The school-bell clanged forth the closing of recess. At its first tap the girls broke line and with shrill cries rushed toward the building.

The imperious leader followed more slowly with a knot of admiring friends.

The noise of the other scholars was getting fainter and more indistinct as they disappeared into the school.

Eva Scarlett, who had stood motionless where she had been rudely pushed from among her playmates, suddenly rushed up to the little group that was slowly nearing the schoolroom and swiftly dealt her enemy a ringing blow in the face.

"There, take that!" she said with quiet fury.

The blood gushed forth, and the girl, with frightened, agonized cries, ran blindly toward the schoolroom.

Eva Scarlett made no move to escape the consequences of her own action, but quietly went into the schoolroom and sat down at her desk.

The school-mistress, who welcomed such events as causing a ripple in the dreadful monotony of her duties, did what she could to stop the flow of blood and to wash away the stains.

Meanwhile, the girls who had witnessed the unprovoked attack gave indignant and excited accounts of the blow as they hung about the teacher's chair, where the injured girl was being ministered to.

During the excitement the male part of the school were taking care of themselves generally, tossing paper balls and chalk, and darting from one desk to another.

Some of them would whisper, in audible tones, "You'll catch it, Reddy," to the girl who had been the cause of all the turmoil.

She paid no attention to any one. Wholly unmindful of all the school, she sat looking intently at her spelling-book.

When the injured leader, who was feeling very important over causing such a commotion, had been sent home to recuperate, the school-mistress tapped the bell on her desk for silence, and the scholars settled into an expectant calm.

They were all anxious to witness the punishment meted out to the ragged, mottle-faced culprit.

"Eva Scarlett, come here," called the school-mistress, in tones which almost intimated that she welcomed the duty before her.

"Won't you catch it, Reddy!" whispered a vicious boy, while others smiled in anticipation of the event.

Eva Scarlett slowly and steadily closed her book, and with unchanging face went up to the desk.

"Hold out your hands," commanded the school-mistress, taking up the rod of punishment, which occupied a prominent position on her desk.

"I won't," replied the girl stubbornly.

"You won't!" exclaimed the teacher, rising from her chair and grasping the girl's shoulder. "You dare defy me!" And then she brought the blows thick and fast down upon the thinly covered back.

The child cringed and shivered, but not a cry that would show the pain she bore escaped her lips.

After the whipping she was stood upon a chair with a dunce's cap upon her head, and remained there, much to the gratification and amusement of the other pupils, until school was dismissed.

When the scholars had gone, the teacher, after arranging her hair and putting on her hat, and gathering up her parasol and some papers, ordered Eva to get off the chair, to get her books and follow her.

Eva gathered up her few worn books, carefully placing her bits of pencils inside of them, because her pocket had holes in it. Putting a limp sun-bonnet on her head she followed the teacher out, waiting until she locked the door.

The scholars had all disappeared by this time, and these two walked through the country village in silence. There were some men lounging in front of some of the little store, where the people of the village did their shopping. The school-mistress walked past them with a conscious, lofty air, for hers was a position that commanded awe, if not respect, in that town, where ignorance held away.

Down a narrow alley, which was the outlet to many back yards, and the receptacle for the garbage of many homes, this teacher and pupil went.

Down to the end of it they went, where an old log cabin stood alone, shut in by a dilapidated fence that had lost more palings than it had saved.

On the other side of this old cabin was a wide public road. The cabin was neither picturesque nor comfortable. It had one small window in the side, and an open door, on the step of which sat a boy who resembled Eva Scarlett, except that his frame was yet slighter and thinner. His face wore a strange expression, but he seemed wholly lost in contemplation of the large brown seeds he was slowly picking from the heart of a sun-flower.

The school-mistress stopped at the door. Eva Scarlett walked in without inviting her to enter. Laying down her books, she said shortly to a woman who sat rocking a baby and reading a novel:

"Mam, the teacher wants you."

Mrs. Scarlett walked to the door, still holding the grunting babe to her bare breast.

"Mrs. Scarlett, I brought Eva home," the school-mistress began to explain, without waiting for the usual preliminaries exchanged at meeting. "She struck Lillian Cartwright in the face, knocking a tooth out and making her nose bleed. Lilly had not done anything to her, so I have suspended Eva for two weeks."

"Well, I never did see sich a child," began Mrs. Scarlett, more as a matter of show than feeling. "I'll wollop her, though, fer it, you mind me! Though I must say as I think that that there Lil Cartwright is a sassy thing. She hasn't got much to brag of, even if her pap is a boss."

The school-mistress, feeling she had done her duty, left, and Mrs. Scarlett went back into the log hut.

II

DEATH OF EVA'S ONLY FRIEND.

"Oh, breasts of pity void! t'oppress the weak,
To point your vengeance at the friendless head,
And with one mutual cry insult the fallen!"

"NOW, MISSIE, YOU KIN TURN in an' get supper fer your pap. He'll tend to you afore you go to bed," Mrs. Scarlett said as she went back to her monotonous rocking and perpetual novel.

Eva Scarlett made no reply. She knew it was useless.

If Mrs. Scarlett had any sense, she seldom made use of it. No matter what her children did, she never punished them unless she was in a bad humor; then she dealt out wholesale beatings that lasted until her next fit of ill-temper came on.

No one knew this better than her children. They were only quiet and submissive when Mrs. Scarlett's temper was ruffled. At other times they did much as they pleased without fear of punishment.

The Scarletts bore the worst name of any family in the small village where they lived. Bill Scarlett was the son of old Bill Scarlett, who had raised his family in dirt and ignorance, as, doubtless, he himself had been reared. When any little thing was missing in the village, people always whispered about the Scarlett being "light-fingered," but no open accusations were ever made. The male portion of the family never had any regular occupation or trade. They spent most of their time in hunting or lounging around the stores. Occasionally, when the streets needed fixing or there was a cellar or a grave to dig, the Scarletts were given the work.

The feminine portion of the family were noted for their laziness, filth, and wonderful breeding propensities. Fever, the outcome of their way of living, at last invaded the Scarlett family, and cut short their doleful existence. Bill

Scarlett was left, he and a sister, who had since married and moved to an adjoining town.

Bill, feeling the want of a family, soon after married. No difference how worthless a man is, he can always find some woman willing to take her chances with him.

His wife came from a family noted for their gossiping propensities and the regularity with which they all assumed the ties of paternity before that of matrimony.

Mrs. Scarlett in her days of bridehood did manage to keep her house clean and do her wash on Mondays, but as her family increased she became more careless, until now, while nursing her tenth child (happily four having died), she resigned her household cares to her children and the grace of God.

Eva Scarlett was the eldest; she was twelve, and she was given the main care of her sister "Sis" and two younger brothers, Jake and Bill, not counting the baby-boy that was hers to nurse when it pleased Mrs. Scarlett to hang on the fence and gossip with a neighbor, a thing she could do by the hour and feel refreshed thereby.

Marriage had in no wise changed Bill Scarlett. Lately, since oil had been struck near the limits of the village, he had been working about the wells steadier than he had ever worked before.

He still went on regular drunks Saturday evenings after pay. The neighbors claimed that this habit was the cause of his second son, Bill, being born a simpleton. Although Bill was in his sixth year when the events which I am relating occurred, he had never been weaned.

As long as there was a baby in the family, and it was but short durations between times, Bill stood at Mrs. Scarlett's knee and shared with the baby on her lap. At other times a bottle of warm milk satisfied him just as well.

Eva Scarlett was an awkward child, and slow at learning. The neighbors said that she was "only one better nor her brother," and her mother often told her she was "worse 'an Bill."

If she had any sense, she received little kindness to encourage it. Between her mother and her neighbors she had a very unhappy existence.

Still, she had never been openly insulted at school before that day. If the children did not like her, they at least coldly permitted her to join in their games.

Eva busied about setting the table. Slicing the bread, grinding the coffee, and making the cold potatoes and bacon ready to put on the fire.

When everything was done that could be done to the simple meal until the family made their appearance, Eva got her limp sun-bonnet from a peg on the back of the door, and fitting a lid to a dull, greasy tin-pail, started on her regular evening trip for milk to a farmhouse nearby.

"Take yer brother with yer," Mrs. Scarlett called, as Eva walked to the door.

She set down her pail without a word and got a shapeless straw hat from a peg near where her bonnet had hung. This she put on the head of the boy who sat so quietly in the doorway, tying it under his chin.

He evidently had sense enough to understand what it meant, for he rose to his feet and, taking hold of Eva's dress, walked along toward the gate with her.

A shaggy, honest-looking dog rose from his place among the bushes, and wagging his stumpy tail, joined this odd couple.

Strange-looking children they were, so unkempt and beggarly in appearance; the one with a peculiar, still expression, and the other with moody brows and burning eyes.

Silently they walked along the dusty highway, their bare feet raising little clouds of the soft, warm dust about them. The silent boy held tight his sister's dress, while he dragged his feet along as if he enjoyed the lightness of the dust.

Unmindful of all but her own sorrow, the girl walked along, tears gathering in her brown, burning eyes, and falling to the dusty road below. The shaggy dog would run on ahead and then return, jumping up against the weeping girl as if he would coax her to join him in a race, and so forget her trials.

After walking a ways, the boy pulled Eva's dress, and sat down on the grass that bordered the road, making a narrow green space between it and the moss-covered rail fence. Eva, knowing this meant weariness on the part of her brother, unchidingly sat down beside him.

Her tears fell faster now, and sometimes a hoarse sob choked in her throat. This child of poverty had never known any fondling, and she had learned early the art of self-repression. Her simple brother and her shaggy dog were the only ones that ever saw her tears.

The dog, conscious of what was unnoticed by the idiotic boy, crept into the unhappy girl's lap and licked her tear-stained cheeks. She wrapped her arms closely about him, and hid her face on his shaggy back

He was her only friend. He felt her sorrow, and his honest, loyal heart sympathized with her. And she loved him. He was the only one on earth who was always kind to her, who understood her, who would befriend her.

She got him when a pup from some boys who were trying to drown him. It was a bitter fight, but with scratched face and torn hair she came out victorious, and fled to her home with the wet, battered pup in her arms. She nursed and fed him; she loved him with all her life; she spent on him the devotion that was in her little heart, and found no outlet for a human being.

Wiping her tears away, Eva rose to her feet just as a light-topped wagon came around the bend in the road. At a glance she saw who it was, and with flashing eyes she stood proudly still to let them pass.

The wagon contained a woman, and Lillian Cartwright, the girl with whom Eva had quarreled at school, and a man sat in front with the driver.

"There she is, papa," cried the girl, who had her face bandaged. "That's Eva Scarlett."

The driver pulled up the horses and the man jumped angrily from the wagon. Eva, shaking like an aspen leaf, stepped in front of her idiotic brother as if to shield him as the man advanced toward her, whip in hand.

"You will beat my daughter, will you, you worthless hussy?" the man said, as he raised his whip and brought it down across the girl's shoulders.

"I'll kill you for this," Eva hissed between her grinding teeth.

Help was at hand for this friendless girl. Before she could speak another word, or receive another blow, the shaggy dog sprung madly at the man. The occupants of the wagon screamed, the man swore and fought with the dog, which was biting him frantically, unmindful of the whip with which the man attempted to beat him off.

Eva Scarlett laughed wickedly, but never moved to call off her faithful protector.

It was an uneven fight. The man beat the dog almost senseless with the butt end of the whip, and when he dropped exhausted to the road, the driver came up, unnoticed by Eva, and with a stone crushed out the humane dog's brains.

"Oh, you devils!" screamed Eva. "I'll kill you—I'll kill you for this!" and she knelt weeping over her dead pet, fondly caressing his shaggy wool.

The man, torn and bleeding, cursing the girl and dog, got into the wagon, which was driven away at a rapid speed, leaving a trail of dust in its wake.

Eva Scarlett, down in the blood-stained dust of the road, knelt over her dead dog, fondly caressing all that remained to her of him, while her simple brother sat on the grass close by, quietly pulling a daisy into shreds.

EVA'S DOG SPRANG AT THE MAN

III

PUNISHMENT BREEDS AN OATH OF VENGEANCE.

"But curses are like arrows shot upright,
And oftentimes on our own heads do light."

THE DAY PASSED VERY WEARILY for Eva Scarlett after the meeting on the public road.

When her first frantic grief at the death of her pet had become more calm, she had lifted her dead dog in her arms and carried him to her humble home.

She received a scolding for not doing her errand properly, and got no sympathy for her loss. They did not ask how her dog met his death, and she offered no explanations. His death meant so much to her, but what did others care for that?

With the heaviest heart she had ever known, and she had never carried a very light one, she laid her dead pet in his usual place under a currant bush. With the family comb, that had lost half its teeth, she smoothed his shaggy wool, and gathering what flowers the roadside and woods offered at that season of the year, she filled a box, and in that perfumed, flowered bed, laid the remains of all that was dear to her.

Her hands nailed it shut; her hands dug the simple grave at the foot of the apple-tree in the yard; her hands placed the box in the soft earth and covered it from sight.

When all was done, and a few flowers and a flat stone marked the grave, she went sadly back to the house and sat down on the door-step beside her simple brother, feeling that to her the world was void of all happiness.

Poor child! Life gave her very little.

"Mam, why isn't we like ither people?" she asked suddenly of Mrs. Scarlett, who sat rocking the baby by the window, and this time absently biting her finger nails instead of reading the novel that lay unfinished by her side.

"Ain't we as good as any of 'em?" Mrs. Scarlett asked, crossly.

"But we hain't got any carridge like most folks, and you hain't got any dresses like Mrs. Cartwright, and Mrs. Peebles, and all them wemen; and pap's pants have holes in 'em and patches on 'em, and his coat don't look like some men's; and we don't go to church, an' our house isn't big like other folks', an' we hain't got beds and carpets and pretty things same as they has," Eva said convincingly.

"Well, it ain't my fault, an' I think things air good enough for you anyhow," Mrs. Scarlett replied bitterly.

"Yes, mam, I know; but tell me why we ain't like them. Could I be like them if I tried?" asked Eva plaintively.

"There ain't no reason why not. I would have had things as nice as any of 'em if I hadn't married your pap. I took my pigs to a poor market, I kin tell you, for as fine a gal as I wez. Dan Cartwright was just crazy to have me, but I wouldn't have him, more fool fer it, fer now I could have been a-livin' in fashion instead of this 'ere," said Mrs. Scarlett fretfully.

"Oh, mam, could you have had Lil Cartwright's pap for your man?" asked Eva with a deep breath of rapture.

"Indeed an' I could have. He was just dying to have me, but I throwed him over for your pap. A fine gal I wez, too. I had more beaus thin eny gal in this town. I'll never raise a child that'll be my match in fine looks, I'll tell ye! I wouldn't be bad lookin' now if your pap didn't drink up all his pay and would give me something to dress on," said Mrs. Scarlett vainly, then fell to biting her nails again.

'Mam, do you think I could ever marry someone like that?' asked Eva earnestly.

"You hain't got my good looks to help you, but there's no telling! Susan Ridley warn't any better look-in' nor you when she married Dan Cartwright, and Sal Cooper, who married old Mike Buzard an' his money, which the Lord knows she tries to put all on her back, had no looks to brag on. A girl, if she's got sense, kin get mostly eny man she wants," Mrs. Scarlett finished sagely.

"Pap's comin', mam," Eva broke in warningly, getting up from the door-step so as not to interfere with the entrance of a tall, thin man who was walking unsteadily up from the gate, carrying a tin dinner-pail in his hand.

"I 'spose you've been drunk and lost yer job," Mrs. Scarlett said by the way of greeting as he came in the door.

"Yes, I've been sacked, but 'twarn't me that was to blame; it's that red-headed hussy of yourn," the man said, setting the pail on the floor and pulling off his shabby, dirty coat ere he sat down.

"YES I'VE BEEN SACKED!"

"She's as much yourn as mine," the woman said peevishly; "an' what's she been doin' anyhow to get you bounced?"

"She turned in an' whipped Cartwright's gal at school for one thing, and then she set her darned dog on Cartwright hisself last night on the township road. That's how her dog got killed; served him right, too. Cartwright's laid up with the bites, an' he sent word down that I was to be sacked, all on account of that red-headed hussy. I'll take it out of yer hide, mind me," he added, shaking his burly fist at Eva.

Leaving her under the threat of punishment, the husband and father wandered forth again. They knew what it meant. He would return still more intoxicated, and they would all have to bear the brunt of his brutish temper.

Eva busied about doing the little household duties and silently bearing the complaints and reproaches of her worthless mother.

She got supper for the little family, and afterward, pulling a trundle-bed from beneath the solitary large bed, prepared and put the children in it for their night's sleep.

Late into the night she sat with her mother, waiting Bill Scarlett's return.

The table, on which burned a tallow candle, was still set, and the simple meal was being kept warm in the oven for the absent one.

He came at last.

It was past midnight when they heard his unsteady step in the yard, and his muttered curses. Eva took the candle in her hand and opened the door, that the faint light might help guide him to his own threshold.

"The devil helps his own," he said with a curse, as he flung his hat down and Eva helped pull off his coat and boots.

He was not as drunk as usual, a thing for which they had reasons to be grateful.

"I told ye the devil helps his own," he repeated, as if wanting someone to deny his words. "Dan Cartwright struck three boomers to-day. They're all his own. Makes him worth millions, curse him! I 'spose yer a-wishin' yer'ed a-taken him fer yer man instead of drunken Bill Scarlett, hey?" leering at his wife. "Ye'ed be movin' to the city of New York to-morrow, an' ye'ed be wearin' fine duds an' jewelry an' ridin' in yer own carridge an' havin' gals and men to wait on ye hand and foot. Ha! ha! ha! Ye didn't think on that, did ye, when ye married Bill Scarlett? Well, I'm as good a man any day as Dan Cartwright," and Bill Scarlett made a pretense of drinking the coffee set before him.

"Is it true, mam?" asked Eva of Mrs. Scarlett, who was softly crying.

"Yer pap sez so," was the response.

"Will they have everything grand? Will Lily Cartwright have all she wants? Will she be rich and grand and happy?" she asked bitterly through her clinched teeth.

"Yes, an' we'll allus be beggars, just 'cause I married yer pap," the weeping woman replied reproachfully.

"But we won't, mam. Don't cry no more," said Eva, in a strong, clear voice, her eyes blazing. "I'll be rich, I swear it! If it takes my life. I swear I'll be rich, an' I'll make the Cartwright's bow down to me. I'll have revenge!"

"You! Yer freckled-faced, red-headed hussy!" said the drunken father scornfully, as he raised his head to look at his daughter.

"Yes, *me!*"—with emphasis; "mark my words," she cried prophetically, a smile so bitter upon her face that even her ignorant mother turned aside shiveringly. "They have everything now. I have nothing. But I'll bring them down, I'll conquer them, I'll have revenge—if it takes my life!"

IV

A FOOT-RACE FOR A KISS.

*"Teach not thy lip such scorn, for it was made
For kissing, lady, not for such contempt."*

*"Haste me to know it, that I with wings as swift
As meditation, or the thoughts of love,
May sweep to my revenge."*

"MAMMA, I WISH I COULD go away from home," said a girl, as she leaned her fair, young head back against the worn door-frame and sighed discontentedly.

It was the same girl, with all the wonderful changes two years bring to youth, in the same surroundings where she was born and reared.

The log hut was just as weather-beaten and dilapidated as it was two years ago, when Eva Scarlett was escorted home from school that memorable day by her teacher, but there was a clean muslin curtain at the small open window, the missing palings had been replaced, and freshly white-washed, the garden was grassy, except for a few old-fashioned flower beds, which were rich with perfume and color.

But the old hut and quaint garden were lost sight of when one caught a glimpse of the beautiful girl on the door-step, who had brought about what little change there was in her old home.

Beautiful beyond words! If was not all due to her masses of copper-colored hair, or to the dainty nose, or the sweetly-curved, fresh lips, or to the spotless complexion or fair young throat, or round, innocent, brown eyes.

There was something in those eyes, some deep, wistful expression that held attention and stirred the lazy blood of men.

There was something in the pose of that little bronze head and those perfect shoulders that made men feel respect, and women envy.

There was something in that proud, perfect smile that made men feel humble and obedient, and women spiteful.

But with all this beauty, subtle, magnetizing in its sweetness, the girl sat leaning wearily against the door, discontented, unhappy.

"Mamma, won't you say I may go?" she pleaded in a sweet, fretful voice as she watched the white clouds flitting by in the blue sky, wishing she could follow them far, far away.

"Yer pap won't let you go," replied Mrs. Scarlett, the same Mrs. Scarlett of two years ago.

"But I must go. I can't stay in this town any longer," Eva replied with quiet positiveness.

"This town's bin good enough fer yer pap an' me, an' you don't need to be stickin' up yer nose at it," Mrs. Scarlett replied angrily.

"You know, mam"—falling back on her childish term as she sat her sister down, who had made her way gradually from her mother's chair to the door, and now tried to crawl into Eva's lap—"you know I have no chance in this town. I want to do something,"—wistfully. "I want to get on in the world, and I can't here."

"Just because yer too big for yer boots! I'm sure you hain't got to go beggin' for a man if you want to get married. There's Bill Doty. He's got a good job, an' he'd make you a good man. Yer pap's friendly with Bill, an' so am I, an' you should be glad to get him," Mrs. Scarlett said with decision.

"Don't talk to me about marrying any man in this village," Eva cried vexedly. "I couldn't live if I did. I want a man that has seen the world, that wears fine clothes and has fine manners and plenty of money. There are none here of that kind, and how will I ever marry one unless I go away?"

"I got a man here, an' I guess they're good enough for you," said Mrs. Scarlett, as if that settled matters.

"But, mam, do you never think how different things would have gone if you had married someone else? There is Dan Cartwright. Oh, think, mam, if you had only married him!" Eva cried in rapture. "A grand house in New York, servants without number, beautiful dresses, grand parties, stylish friends! You would have been the grand, fashionable mother, with millions to command; and I—ah! I should have conquered the world—I should have been your fine daughter. But you didn't, and now—"

"You are right, Eva," Mrs. Scarlett said enviously, her tears beginning to fall. "But I married yer pap instead an' we'll allus be beggars."

"No, we won't," cried Eva sternly as she arose and hastily paced the uneven board floor of the hut.

"Mam, do you remember my oath?" she asked, coldly, as she stopped by her mother's chair. "I swore two years ago that I would have revenge on the Cartwrights. Ah! I haven't forgot," she said, striking one hand in the open palm of the other.

"I have studied hard, so to aid me in my purpose. I have been determined to grow beautiful. I have endured the envy and petty jealousies of these village women, all because I knew my day would come, when I can make them kiss the dust I walk in.

"You may have thought I forgot the insult put upon me by Lil Cartwright, or the beating from her father, and the death of my dog. Forget!" she cried, gritting her teeth—"never till I die!

"I have dreamed of my revenge, mam," she continued, in a low, deep voice; "I have lain awake nights and swore over and over to myself that I would be revenged. I have planned it all out, and it doesn't mean that I should marry a penniless country clod-hopper, and spend the remainder of my days in this village. Oh, no—no!

"And I have beauty, mam—every man's glance tells me so, and every woman's hatred and jealousy confirm it. Do you think beautiful city women are more beautiful than those in the country?" she asked, anxiously. "I have tried so hard to make myself attractive. I have read all about grand people, and I'm sure I can act as well as they do anywhere. Oh, mam, if I could only go to the city!"

"Well, you can't, so that settles it. After me raisin' you an' taken' care of you, you would go away an 'leave me to take care of all these children," Mrs. Scarlett said fretfully. "I don't think the baby will live anyhow, an' it's better for the innocent lamb to be taken now afore it knows what a lazy pap an' heartless sister it has."

"Oh, very well, mamma; I'll go for the milk now," said Eva, glad to change the subject. "I'll not talk about going away if you stop urging me to marry. These village men know that I will have none of them, and will not permit their rough attentions even if I am only Bill Scarlett's daughter. So there now!"

And Eva closed the argument by putting on her hat and taking a tin-pail that was now so bright and shining that she could see her pretty, dimpled face in it.

"Ain't you goin' to take Billy with you," her mother called after her as she was half to the gate.

"Not this time," she called back. "He is very happy playing under the apple-tree, and I won't disturb him."

Eva Scarlett wanted to be alone. She enjoyed these long walks to the farmhouse for milk because they gave her an opportunity to dream.

Ah! What dreams that girl of fifteen had.

She did not walk the dusty roads now. She had bright, new shoes and

"STUCK UP THING! SHE'LL COME TO NO GOOD END!"

she was careful of them, they were so hard to get.

She traveled a roundabout way through the woods to the farmhouse, but her own thoughts always kept the walk from seeming long or dull.

On to the heart of the wood she went, over the leaf-covered path, pulling loose from a briar here, jumping over a fallen log there, plucking a wild flower now; happy with her own thoughts of revenge, smiling at their promises, though vague of fulfillment.

Two women had been gossiping at a gate as she started from the village.

When she passed them the one said audibly as she drew her skirts aside:

"Stuck up thing, she'll come to no good end; even if she does carry that red head of hers so high."

Eva laughed and went on. What cared she? She had heard bitter things since she was born, and they failed to cut her now. Was she not beautiful? Was she not bright?

"The spiteful cats!" she said laughingly, as she stopped to look at herself in the shining side of her tin pail, and then laughed again at the strange reflection of her own pretty face.

"Wait until the man comes that I will marry. I'll have revenge on all of them. My hero shall bring me wealth and position, and then, Lil Cartwright, beware! Oh, I shall pay the insult back a thousand-fold. If my hero, my deliverer, would only come, or I could go in search of him, that I might the sooner fly on the powerful wings of wealth to revenge and victory."

Poor girl. She was to get her wish in a way she little dreamed of. It was near her, very near, even while she stood idly dreaming.

"I was waitin' for you," said a gruff voice, and Eva dropped the contemplation of herself in the tin pail to look at the man who addressed her.

"Well, Bill Doty, what do you want?" she asked cuttingly, her curved lips curled in scorn.

"I want to know when you'll marry me?" he said boldly.

"Never," she replied, hiding her excitement under a quiet voice.

"Well, I say you will. Your pap says so, too," he answered doggedly.

"I shall certainly please myself in such matters," she said, still quietly, as she started to pass and go on her way.

"You're tossin' a high head," he said, catching hold of her arm.

She stopped for a moment to still the beatings of her heart. She was determined her voice should be steady, but she felt so contaminated by his touch that she could hardly resist the temptation to slap his face.

"How dare you touch me, you low coward?" she said, in that low, deep voice, peculiar to her in moments of intense anger.

"Ha, ha! I'll do more. I'll kiss you, an' I'll bet I'm the first man in the village that's able to say he got a kiss from pretty Eva Scarlett," the low fellow said with a chuckle of satisfaction.

Eva silently dealt him a stinging blow in the face with her bright tin pail. In his surprise he loosened his hold, allowing her to jerk from his grasp.

The moment she was freed she started to run, and with an oath the baffled brute gave pursuit. Speedily she ran, but the man, robbed of his prey, ran faster.

Steadily he gained on her; she could almost feel his hot breath!

The color fled from her cheeks and lips, she could almost feel his grasp upon her arm; she felt she was lost; still there was no escape; still she ran, when—her foot caught in a trailing vine, and she fell down helpless!

"God have mercy!" she cried, appealing even when she lost hope.

But help came even as she prayed. She heard a hoarse cry, and felt a heavy body fall almost at her feet.

Breathless, she turned her great frightened eyes, and saw the ruffian who had insulted her lying still on the dead leaves, while over him stood a man. Handsome, tall, and strong, with a face of beauty, and a bearing of pride. The hero of her dreams—her deliverer!

"He has come," she thought, and she closed her eyes faintly, as she would had she gazed too long at the midday sun.

V

GOOD BYE TO CHERISHED HOPES.

"Let no one say that there is need
Of time for love to grow;
Ah. No! The love that kills, indeed.
Dispatches at a blow."

Ah, me!
The world is full of meetings such as this—
A thrill, a voiceless challenge and reply—
and sudden partings after.

"ARE YOU HURT!" THE HANDSOME stranger asked anxiously as he bent over Eva Scarlett, who had once again opened her eyes, but still lay prone upon the dry leaves, where she had fallen.

"No, I am not hurt. I was frightened and awkward," she said with a faint, apologetic smile.

He held out his hands to help her rise, his glance speaking the most ardent admiration for the sweet, dimpled, upturned face, with its wide, dark eyes, in which fright was slowly dying away.

Frankly and fearlessly she gave him both little hands, as a child does when It wants to be taken up.

Gently he raised her to her feet, his fingers clinging warmly to her long, cool, slender ones.

Somehow, her hands trembled—it may have been still from fright.

"He's all right," he reassured her with a smile, seeing her glance anxiously toward her fallen foe. Who, even as she looked, opened his eyes and stared about in a dazed, unseeing manner.

"Come, let us go away from here and avoid further trouble," said the stranger, picking up his rifle from where it had been dropped on the ground.

Eva Scarlett felt a warm thrill of delight that he had asked her to go with him, even if it was only to the edge of the wood.

Without a word to, or another glance at the man who lay on the ground before her, she walked away with her handsome rescuer.

"I suppose I should thank you for knocking that man down," she said shyly, after walking some distance in silence.

"Don't," he said, smiling down into her deep, brown eyes in such a fond, protecting way that it brought a warm flush to her cheeks. "I thought you wanted it done, so I did it,"—carelessly.

"Oh, yes, certainly. I—I couldn't do it myself, so I slapped his face with my tin pail and ran," she said quite seriously.

"Poor duffer! He was well punished between us, wasn't he, now?" he asked, laughing again at her words.

"He deserved it, the scoundrel!" Era said vindictively.

"I'll wager you the rascal was doing no more than any man would want to do. Oh, my pretty child"—laughing at her startled, upturned eyes—"a pretty face is as irresistible to the boor as to the gentleman. Tell me, am I wrong? Did he not want a kiss?"

"Yes, and he got a blow in the face instead," she answered hotly, her brown eyes flashing. "He asked me to marry him, the impudent cur! And when I refused, he caught me and tried to kiss me."

"Ah, so! I am glad I knocked him down," he said, while his eyes wandered from the girl's exquisite face to her neat but cheap dress, her glossy, coarse shoes and her rough, straw hat.

"I was hunting to-day, with poor success," he continued, smiling slightly, "and just happened along the path when I saw what I thought was a beautiful fancy of my brain, or an escaped fairy, who, with her hair streaming loose in the wind, came flying breathlessly down the most romantic and picturesque woodland path it was ever my good fortune to see. I stepped back so as not to interrupt her flight, when lo! The fairy tripped and fell at my feet, just as I saw a great, ugly, black demon ready to grasp her, so I laid down my gun, jumped from behind the tree, felled the demon and—captured the fairy!"

They both laughed heartily over his version of the affair, and Eva began to be conscious of a little painful strain about her heart, when she remembered that the way was short, and they would have to part at the end of the walk.

"Do you live in the village?" the hunter asked, resting slightly on his rifle as he stopped at the edge of the wood.

"Yes, all my life I have lived here," Eva answered, with a longing in her voice that did not escape her questioner.

"Do your usual evening walks lie in this direction?" he boldly asked.

"Yes; I carry our daily milk from Cowen's farmhouse to my home every evening about this time," she answered, hoping that he would note the fact and not forget her.

"If he would only love me," she thought, "he could deliver me from misery; he could help me on to revenge!"

Confident of her beauty, hopeful in her strong determination, she felt, if she could only see him again, she could win his love. She must! She would!

Strange, misguided child. Rich in beauty and ability, wholly without training and knowledge of the world, her life was swayed by a craving for revenge on those who had injured her.

"After the affair of to-night, will you not fear the long walk through the wood?" he asked anxiously.

"Not since I found a protector there," she said coquettishly.

He looked at her inquiringly, and then turned away from the gaze of her deep, magnetic eyes with a flush on his sun-burned cheek.

"Good-bye!" he said, holding out his strong, firm hand.

She put her hand in his; she looked, at him with her longing soul in her eyes; her fresh, curved lips trembled.

"Good-bye," she whispered, tremulously.

It was hard to kill the hope that had sprung into her heart at first sight of him; it was hard to have the wish that he would be her deliverer shattered by a single word—good-bye.

He released her hand, and removing his hat, stood motionless at the edge of the wood, while Eva Scarlett, blinded with hot tears, walked unsteadily toward the village.

VI

HIDDEN IN A HOLLOW TREE.

*"Blood, though it sleeps a time, yet never dies.
The gods on murderers fix revengeful eyes."*

"A long, long kiss, a kiss of youth and love."

"DID YOU HEAR THE NEWS, Mrs. Scarlett?"

Mrs. Scarlett, who was walking lazily about Eva's flower-beds, lifted her head at this challenge, and caught a glimpse of a woman balanced on the lower board of the fence.

"I never hear nothin' that's goin' on any more," Mrs. Scarlett replied in the tone of a martyr, making her way more rapidly than was her custom to the fence, the dividing line between her home and her neighbor's.

"Well, it's jist awful," the neighbor said, with an evident relish at being the first to spread the news, and still being anxious to retain the surprising news as long as possible.

"I jist said to Widow Jones, who stopped in to tell me, that jist as like as not we'd all be killed in our beds some of these nights, if things ain't fixed so honest folks can walk the streets without being murdered!"

"Murdered! My sakes alive!" gasped Mrs. Scarlett, almost losing her hold of the fence, over which she was half hanging, at this startling information.

"'Yes,' sez I 'murdered!' 'In cold blood?' sez Widow Jones; 'and' sez I, 'something hez to be done to put a stop to the wickedness this world is comin' to.'"

"Do say! An' who was murdered? Did you hear?" Mrs. Scarlett gasped.

"Why, yes, I heard all about it. 'Twas no one more nor less than Bill Doty."

"Bill Doty! Do say!" poor Mrs. Scarlett gasped, unhappy at losing a prospective son-in-law.

"Yes, an' he's as honest a man as is in this town, and quiet too. Nobody can say anything agin Bill Doty, 'cept that he's the worst to hisself when he drinks too much."

"Who killed him? Did you hear?" Mrs. Scarlett asked, the tears rolling down her cheeks, while her idiotic son, Bill, pulled at the skirts of her gown and peeped through the cracks in the fence.

"No one kin tell yet. Widow Joneses' son was goin' through Owens' woods this noon when he came across Bill Doty lyin' all still an' white. He thought Bill was drunk, an' he tried to wake him, when Bill groaned horrible-like, an' Widow Joneses son found Bill was out of his mind an' didn't know nobody, so be ran back to town an' some men went out an' carried poor Bill into his boardin' house, an' they've had all the doctors, an' they say Bill won't live till night."

"Oh, he ain't dead then?" Mrs. Scarlett said, brightening up.

"He's jist as good as dead the doctors say, an' they've started some men out to hunt for his murderer. If they find him they'll make short work of him, I kin tell you; but I must go now to see Mrs. Woods; maybe she hadn't heard the news."

The village gossip got down from the fence and started in opposite directions, both eager to spread the news.

"Ev—Ev, I never did hear anything worse," Mrs. Scarlett gasped, going into the hut where Eva, having finished the morning's work, was intent on a book.

Eva regarded her mother silently as she sunk breathlessly into a chair.

She was used to these breathless outbursts of her mother after holding a *séance* on the back fence with some of her neighbors.

"You'd never guess it till yer dyin' day. If you had only taken my advice, you'd a bin a widow now."

And Mrs. Scarlett, with the reaction of her own feelings, began to cry feebly.

"What do you mean?" Eva asked sharply, the color leaving her face.

"Bill Doty's bin killed. They found him dyin' in Owens' woods, an' the doctors sez he'll be dead afore night. If you hed only listened to me you might be cheerin' the poor fellow's last moments."

"Are you sure he is dying?" Eva asked sternly, her wide-open eyes filled with horror.

"All the doctors in the town are tendin' him, an' there ain't any mistake about it," Mrs. Scarlett said positively.

Eva Scarlett arose and hastily put on her little straw hat. Her face was colorless and her eyes had a strained, frightened expression.

The meeting in the wood with Bill Doty, the insult, her avenger and rescuer, were secrets locked in her own breast.

She had never received any sympathy from her family, and she had learned early to keep her secrets to herself.

When she had returned to her home the evening before without the tin pail, or milk, she'd explained that she had tripped and fallen, and by doing so had knocked the bottom out of the pail.

With a few cross words about her carelessness, the matter dropped, and Eva went early to her rough bed in the loft, as it was known, where she lay awake until morning, building air castles.

The handsome stranger, who had so timely defended her, filled a prominent place in her castle building.

Since she had thirsted for revenge, he had always had been in her dreams. Now she had seen him and she felt sure, although he had bidden her good-bye, that, in the eternal shuffle, fate would cast them together again.

Happy in this thought, expectantly nervous for the evening, that she might retrace the path where they had met, Eva was trying to kill time that passed too slowly for her when her mother brought her the startling news that her rude admirer was dying.

She felt like a murderer as she rushed from her humble home, heedless of the questions of her startled mother.

On she rushed to the house where Bill Doty lay dying.

She minded not the curious looks of the curious, gossiping crowd that swarmed about the gate.

"Well, Eva Scarlett, what brings you here?" asked a rough but kindly village doctor who met her at the door.

"I want to see Bill Doty. Is he really dying, doctor?" she asked, her voice strained and unnatural.

"I am afraid so, Eva," the doctor replied gravely. "He recovered consciousness long enough to give a pretty good description of his assailant. Why, Eva, girl, what is wrong?" the doctor asked, as he caught her swaying form.

"Nothing. I couldn't believe he was murdered; you don't believe it, do you? Why, what would any one kill Bill Doty for?" Eva asked pathetically.

"That's what no one understands. Bill had no enemies as anyone knows of, and after he described who hit him, he soon became unconscious again, and so we could not learn the motive of the assault," the doctor explained.

"What did he say the man—the one who hit him—looked like?" Eva asked hesitatingly, longing to know the worst.

"He said he did not belong to this town, and that he was a hunter, as far as he could understand. If you want to see Bill, I'll go and see if you can come in," the doctor added obligingly, going in to prepare the way.

As soon as the doctor was out of sight she fled from the house.

She did not want to see the dying man now. She had learned all she had come for, and she fled with a numbing fear in her heart, not for herself, but for her protector.

What could she do to save him? If she had only asked him where he lived, she might now have been able to warn him of his danger.

But she was helpless. She knew where to go to him, and if those rough men who formed the searching posse should meet him, she felt they were equal to any desperate deed in their angried state. A stranger was an unusual thing in their midst, so it is not surprising that the villagers expected before night to lay hands on the murderer.

"Mother, I am going to take the milk-bucket now, because I want to hunt some Indian root for my flower-beds," said Eva when she reached her home.

"I guess she's takin' Bill's death more to heart than I thought she would," Mrs. Scarlett thought; and so she raised no objections.

The sun shone bright in the sky when Eva reached the entrance to the wood, where a few short hours ago she had bidden good-bye to the stranger who had protected her.

She was determined to protect him now.

He had said good-bye; still she expected to meet him. She felt he would be waiting for her when the hour came for her to travel that way for milk. And if he waited, the searching parties were almost as sure as she was to meet him. If she could only find him first to warn him to fly!

She almost ran along the path where the day before she had walked leisurely, happy in the contemplation of her dreams and her beauty.

Self was forgotten now, even her long-planned revenge dwindled away in the face of the danger that threatened the man whom she felt was more to her than the entire world.

"If I could only find him!" she half cried as she ran along past the place where yesterday she had met him.

"If I could only find him!" And then she stopped, like a deer brought to bay, trembling in every limb.

Holding her breath, she listened to the low crackling of the fallen twigs and underbrush, and the wisping sound of the dry leaves. It meant the approach of some being, animal or man, she knew not which.

Her large eyes filled with a strange light, and she stood motionless as a carved figure, when in the distance before her she saw a party of the organized searchers passing cautiously along. Steadily, silently, determinedly, they moved on until lost to view in the thickness of the foliage.

"They are hunting for him—they may find him first!" she cried in desperation, and she crept along the path again, afraid now to make the least noise.

Again came the sound of footsteps on the dry leaves and twigs. It was near a spot that she knew well. A little ways off from the path, where now she stood motionless listening to those signs of approaching steps, was a large tree. At its base she had once built a fire. That fire had eaten a hole in the tree large enough to admit a man, and had hollowed the tree in such a manner that Eva, in her childhood days, ever after made use of it as her "cave-house."

With a swift, gliding movement, she went toward the tree and concealed herself in the hollow in its trunk.

Slyly she looked out as the footsteps drew nearer.

Nearer, nearer—then with a little muffled cry and a movement as swift as a hawk's, she darted from her retreat and regained the woodland path.

"Well, my fairy—" began the stranger, for it was he she saw.

"Don't speak!" she commanded in an awed whisper, grasping his hand firmly in hers. "Come with me—hurry!"

With an expression half amusement half pleasure at indulging the pretty girl, he obeyed.

"Get in there," Eva said, pointing to the hollow in the tree.

He obeyed again, still looking amused.

"Now, my fairy," he said, sitting down on a short log that had been put here by Eva for one of her imaginary chairs, when the tree had been her "cave house," "now, tell me what all these hushed whispers mean?" he continued, drawing her down on the log beside him.

"You haven't been to town? You know nothing?" she asked, looking at him wistfully.

"Some things, but probably not very much," he answered lightly, pinching her cheek.

"Bill Doty is dying," she said sternly, pulling herself away from him.

"Indeed! And who is Bill Doty, may I ask?" said he, carelessly holding a lighted match to the cigarette he had just put in his mouth.

"Bill Doty is the man you knocked down yesterday. The doctors say he'll be dead before night," she whispered impressively.

"By Jove! Do you mean it?" he asked, becoming serious in a moment.

"Yes, yes; and the town men are searching for you. They say they will lynch you," she sobbed, clinging, half frightened, to his arm.

"It was not intentional," he said gravely, throwing down his unsmoked cigarette.

"How do they know who did it?" he asked suddenly. "Did you tell?"

"Never a word," she said, indignantly. "They found Bill this morning where we left him. He was unconscious, but he regained consciousness

long enough to partially describe you. As soon as I heard the news I went
to his house and found out everything from the doctor. Then I got my
milk bucket, and telling mother I was going to hunt Indian root, I came in
search of you," she explained, and he patted her trembling hands as if to
silently assure her of his appreciation of her goodness.

"You must leave at once," she whispered huskily. "I saw the searchers
not very far from here as I came along. If they find you they will—"

"Don't," he said with a faint smile, putting the tips of his fingers to her
rosy lips. "They shall not find me, my fairy; I will escape them in some
way."

"But how? They are in the wood at this very moment searching for you,"

Eva cried apprehensively.

The stranger sat silent after this information. Even if he could clear himself, he had no desire to be brought to trial—he doubted the lynching part—for murder, or whatever they might choose to make it. He was silent now, because he was trying to plan some way to escape the searching party.

"Now, my fairy, with your aid, I'll outwit them some way," he said, quite cheerfully. "You go out, look for the searchers; if you do not see them, but find the way clear going toward the farmhouse where you get the milk, come quickly back and report to me, and I will make my escape. Do you think you can do this?" he asked earnestly.

"Yes. Yes. You saved me yesterday; I'll save you to-day. Stay quiet here until I return."

And with one long, wistful look she started to leave him.

"You will be very quiet and not venture out until I return?" she asked, anxiously, as she hesitated near the entrance to the tree.

"I am your prisoner until you release me," he replied laughingly, and with a flush of pride she started on her exploring expedition.

Cautiously she ran swiftly along, her bright eyes glancing in every direction for the enemy.

She forgot that if she released him she lost him, and her heart swelled with happiness when she proved the way was clear.

Tireless, she ran back toward the place where she had left him, joyfully carrying to him the hope of escape.

Just as she came to the tree where he was concealed she glanced back, and to her dismay saw a group of men approaching in her direction.

"Ha!" she cried, darting inside, and pulling a heavy branch before the opening.

"They are coming this way," she whispered, her brown eyes wild with fright and her face as white as death.

He clasped her close in his arms, as though both to protect and encourage her, and so, without speaking, they sat listening to the crunching of the twigs, the sound of which came nearer and nearer, she with her eyes, wild with fear, fixed upon his handsome face, that had lost every vestige of color.

"If they find you, I'll swear I killed him," she whispered savagely as she gritted her little white teeth.

"You must not," he whispered back sternly. "You would ruin us both. If they find me I will deny it, and you must not, if you want to save my life, say you ever saw me."

She nodded her head in reply.

Closer came those sounds. They could even hear the gruff voices of the men as they came on.

Opposite the tree, on the path where, a while before, she found the handsome stranger, the searchers stopped for a moment.

The hearts of those two, so near the searchers, beat even more rapidly than before, and he held her close in his arms, as if her nearness gave him hope.

A moment, that seemed as if it would never pass to the prisoners, and then the searchers walked on.

"I shall go after them," Eva whispered as a quick thought came to her. "I shall meet them and I will tell them I saw the man I think they are searching for, and I'll lead them off in another direction. While I do this, you make your escape," she explained in a quick whisper.

"Splendid!" he whispered back approvingly; "and so we part, my fairy?"

"Save yourself and I will be happy," she whispered, tears coming to her eyes.

"Would you like to leave here—would you come to me if I should send for you? But, there, don't answer, child. Let me kiss you once. It is good-bye, my fairy," he said tenderly, looking down into the pure face that was raised trustingly to his own.

A long—long kiss, a kiss of admiration and gratefulness, met by a kiss of love and misery.

"Be very careful. Farewell;" and she was gone.

VII

TAKEN PRISONER AT LAST.

*"How disappointment tracks
The steps of hope."*

*"When sorrows come, they come not single spies,
But in battalions.*

THERE WERE NO TEARS NOW, except those in her heart. With dry eyes and a set determination on her pallid face, Eva Scarlett ran swiftly along the way the searchers had gone before.

Her forced quiet covered an aching heart filled with despair. She loved him, and they had parted! Like the Aztecs, she had long dreamed of and waited for the god who was to come and deliver her from the bondage of poverty.

He had come. In build and manners, and dress and looks, he was the hero of her dreams. Unworldly and childlike in her perfect belief that her prayer had been answered, she bestowed on him, unasked, her love.

But they had parted, and she had no regret for her own suffering if she could only save him from the hands of the rough village men.

She saw them now. There they were on in advance, still infused with a dogged determination to hunt down the man who had assaulted their friend and neighbor.

Brawls and drunkenness were everyday occurrences about the oil wells in their section, but murder was an unusual thing, and they enjoyed the novelty and excitement of it.

Eva Scarlett, moving as soft and quiet as a panther, took a rapid cut around through the wood managing so as to come out in advance of the men.

The heavy beatings of her heart almost smothered her as she stood waiting for them to approach.

"Have you found any trace of the person you are hunting?" she asked, with the freedom peculiar to village maids who know the citizens of their town as they know their own family.

"We didn't have any luck till we met Sam Dougherty's boy. He said he saw a man with a gun comin' along Owens' path, but that boy's a liar! I guess he never saw nobody. We didn't find him anyhow, and if he had been along Owens' path we'ed a-got him," the foremost man explained readily as he mopped his heated face.

Eva's heart fluttered painfully. How short a time ago had she dragged him from Owens' path to the hollow of the tree!

"I saw a stranger 'way over there," pointing in the direction they faced. "I was hunting Indian root when I saw him."

"What'd he look like?" another man asked, the rest moving up closer, eagerly waiting for Eva's answer.

"I can't tell very well," she said, with white lips, those lips that had kissed him farewell so fondly. "I know he was a stranger, and he had a gun, and looked frightened, and when he saw me he went away as if he did not want to be looked at."

The committee exchanged knowing and satisfied looks. Ah! They were on his track now.

There was some discussion for a few moments, and then it was unanimously decided to go the way where Eva had seen the strange hunter.

"I will lead you, I will show you," she said, a faint flush touching the pallor of her cheek. "Come, hurry this way, and you will surely find him."

Her willing feet almost kept the men on a run, so ready was she to aid in hunting the assassin down.

"Further apart, further apart," she was saying, half frantically, as she urged the men on to greater speed.

"Here, where the underbrush is thickest," she said breathlessly, having placed a long distance between them and the man she wished to save. "Here, he rushed in among the underbrush, trying to get out of sight."

"Let them hunt," she said savagely as they separated and quietly moved about, peering into the thick foliage where the birds built their nests and snakes hid from sight.

"He is free now," she thought exultingly. Standing still, she joyfully watched the flight of startled birds and the waving of the bushes that indicated the presence of the searchers.

"He will escape. The fools! They doubted a boy's truthful statement, and eagerly accepted my lie," she thought, and a little heartless chuckle escaped her lips, in which the color was slowly returning.

Sitting down on the ground, she idly picked up the fallen leaves that lay in boundless profusion about her, piercing one with the stem of another, until she had formed a long trail of richly-colored leaves.

"How will it end?" she wondered, miserably. "I can't go back to my wretched life as I did before I met him. Only yesterday and it seems years!

"Am I to be balked now, just because one man sees fit to die? Served him right," she thought, her heart growing hard at the recollection of the insult. "Fool! His insult brought me face to face with—with a man I love; but his death separates me from him. I would have met him anyway. He was in my path. It was Fate. If only that poor fool had not come between us. He deserves to die.

"He has escaped now, and he'll forget me," she cried, bitterly. "I will have to live and die here without getting my revenge on the Cartwrights. It's hard, hard! All my life I have been cursed with something. I'd rather die than live this life any longer."

Then she fell to watching the moving bushes, too miserable for thought.

When the sun had gone down, the tired men gave up their fruitless search, and they, with common consent, wended their way back to the village and dinner.

Eva went with them, satisfied that her ruse had been successful.

Mrs. Scarlett and her children were busy at their evening meal when Eva returned. Dispirited and exhausted she sat down with them, partially explained her absence to her mother, who felt a scant satisfaction that her daughter, though late, had realized the wisdom of her mother's choice, and cared enough to aid in the search for Bill Doty's assailant.

"Bill's livin' yet," Mrs. Scarlett said as Eva choked down some food.

"He may not die," Eva answered quietly.

"They're waitin' on him. He'll never git over it." Mrs. Scarlett was positive.

"I suppose pap's drunk again," Eva said suddenly as Mrs. Scarlett ordered her son Jake to get and light the candle.

"Like as not. He hain't been home all day," Mrs. Scarlett replied, slapping the pinching fingers of her nursing babe.

When supper was finished, Eva placed the remaining food in the oven to keep it warm for her father. Then she washed the few heavy dishes.

There was not much work to do about their plain home, but what there was fell mainly on Eva, who uncomplainingly performed the disagreeable task.

Several hot tears fell down and were lost in the dishpan, but otherwise Eva was silent and unmoved.

Her mother was too excited over the events of the day to attempt reading, so she sat in her rocking chair near the table rocking her babe and absently biting her finger nails.

Sis and Jake were leaning on the partially-set table looking at a book, and Bill, the simpleton, in a high chair, watched them all with strange, bright eyes, much as might a curious dog.

"Ev, I hear like people runnin'," Mrs. Scarlett said nervously.

Eva was too deep in her own unhappy thoughts to care for the fancies of her mother, so she made no reply.

"Ev, I heard a yell. Open the door an' see if you kin see anything," Mrs. Scarlett said after a few moments.

"There's nothing," Eva answered, drying her hands on her apron before obeying her mother.

She opened the door and looked out into the darkness, carelessly at first and then intently.

"What is it?" her mother asked, but she made no reply.

Off in the darkness she could distinguish forms still darker running excitedly, all in the one direction.

A nameless fear caught her heart-strings.

That direction was a little to the right of her home, where stood but one thing—the old log fort house that had been the first building in this old and non-progressive town. The only public officials in the town were the justice of the peace and the sheriff. The old fort-house was now the jail, where drunks and such minor offenders were often locked up overnight.

"Everybody is running toward the fort," she said hoarsely.

"They've caught the murderer, then!" Mrs. Scarlett cried excitedly, and not without satisfaction, as she dropped her babe, which began to cry, and rushed to the door.

"I will see," Eva said excitedly, and hatless she ran out into the darkness.

She joined some straggling runners, and on they went to the fort.

A curious scene she saw.

On a barrel beside the doorstep stood the justice talking to the crowd of people whose forms, but not features, were visible in the dim light of the lantern held uplifted by a man who stood near the speaker.

"As the judge of this town," he said, his arm uplifted in an exhortation style, "I want you all, men and women, to go to your homes. The prisoner we have here must be tried according to the law, and, as lawful citizens,

you'll all want this done, especially as our injured friend is still living, and while there's life there's hope. Everything is made secure, and the prisoner will be kept in the fort, while the sheriff and a trusty citizen will keep guard. I hope the law-abiding citizens of this town will not linger about, or in any wise interfere with the duty of these men."

With this, the justice carefully descended from the barrel, and the man lowered his lantern, making the crowd look darker.

There was an attempt to cheer the remarks made by the renowned branch of the law, but it was faint.

With a great deal of grumbling the people unwillingly and slowly walked away. With a few whispered instructions, the justice followed, and the guards were left alone.

"There is work to do to-night," Eva Scarlet muttered grimly as she saw the guards examine their guns.

Then, like a shadow, she, too, went swiftly homeward.

VIII

FREE BUT NOT SAVED.

"The absent danger greater still appears;
Less fears he who is near the thing he fears."

"But when men think them most in safety stand,
Their greatest peril often is at hand."

WHEN EVA SCARLETT REACHED HOME she found her father there; and, strange to say, sober.

He was eating and talking, explaining how he had joined a second party to hunt for the murderer; how they had seen the man, at the very moment when he saw them, and how, when they ran swiftly after him, he had suddenly disappeared.

Carefully they searched, but the man had disappeared as rapidly and surely as he would have had he sunk through the ground.

Finding it useless to continue the search, they cleverly decided to conceal themselves about the place where the murderer had disappeared, and see how waiting would be rewarded.

Nothing came of it until it grew dark; and then, all at once, as if he had dropped from the clouds, they saw the man where they had seen him before, and a grand rush was made.

Finding that he was fairly caught, he had made no effort to fight, and had pretended ignorance as to the cause of his capture.

So in triumph they led him to the old fort-house, where he was now a prisoner.

"It's well for him as Bill Doty's still livin'," Bill Scarlett added; "we hed intended, if Bill wuz dead, ter hang him ter the fust tree. We are to meet ag'in to-night, an' if Bill dies, there'll be two dead men before mornin'.

No feedin' up people in jails, an' payin' lawyers to keep 'em from hangin' fer us."

"What air you doing' there?" Mrs. Scarlett called crossly to Eva, who was looking over some things in the corner.

Bill Scarlett had gone out again to hear how Bill Doty was progressing, and to confer with his comrades in case of death.

"I'm hunting for my old dress," Eva replied, and at last having found what she was after, she went out, remarking that she was going to bed.

Now Eva's bed was in the loft. The loft was a little hole under the roof, and to get there, Eva had to go outside and climb a ladder and get in through a square, the solitary door or window that opened into this dreary cubby-hole.

She climbed up and went inside, but she did not go to bed. Dressed, even to her hat, she sat there, her busy brain trying to form some plan of escape for the prisoner.

She knew that something must be done, and that at once. If Bill Doty died before morning, the prisoner would never see the light of day.

It did not take her bright brain long to think out a plan. Even while her father talked, one had formed in her mind. She was only waiting now until the hour when she knew the village folks would be in bed to put her plan into effect.

She intended to take desperate chances, but she never considered what would be her fate if she failed. Probably she did not care!

When the lights began to grow less, that marked the location of the different houses, and in consequence the town began to look the darker, she crawled quietly down the ladder, stopping at every loud squeak of the rungs, fearful lest she be heard.

Reaching the ground safely, she crept, a little, dark shadow, along the dark fence. In a corner, made darker by a tree, she nimbly scaled the fence and again ran noiselessly beside the fence, around the fields until she came to the rear of the log fort-house.

This side of the fort was blank, but in front, where the guards stood, was a door and a square, single-pane window that had once doubtless held a gun.

Creeping up to the corner of the building, scarcely breathing in her excitement, she listened. Yes, the guards were still there, she could hear the low murmur of their voices as they talked together.

She smiled, and crept back to where her bundle lay. Taking it in her arms, she got on her knees and crawled under the old log-house. She had been here often. She even smiled in the darkness to think how easy it was.

Feeling softly above her head, unmindful of the cobwebs that swept her face, or the touch of disturbed insects that ran over her hands.

She feared someone else knew what she had known, and had closed the opening she had found accidentally when a child.

Pressing her hands up softly, then using her head for the same purpose, she at last, with the aid of both, slid one of the broad boards of the heavy oak floor aside. It had not been moved for a long time, and it made a sound that to her frightened senses seemed like the loudest thunder.

Stopping for a moment, she held her breath. No one came. Once more she put forth her hands and deftly shoved the board aside.

An instant more and she was in the room where she knew the prisoner was confined.

She listened. She could hear him breathing. If he heard her and called aloud, they were lost!

"S't!" she whispered through her teeth, softly but warningly.

There was no movement, no reply.

"S't!" she dared to utter louder this time. She listened. She could not hear him now, but there was a knowing movement that spoke volumes to her anxious heart.

On hands and knees she crawled about, feeling for him. The room was as dark as a coal mine. She could distinguish nothing—nothing. She dared not call, lest the guards outside the door that was so fearfully near should hear.

At last she was rewarded. Her hand came in contact with something that was not wood, and that made her heart very soft indeed.

"It is your fairy, dear," she whispered encouragingly.

"Don't speak, and crawl on your knees," she told him.

"I'm bound fast to the wall," he whispered in despair.

She put forth her hands with a rebellious despair in her heart, and touched the ropes that bound his hands and ankles.

After all her risk, was she still to fail in saving him?

She took a small penknife from her pocket, and though her heart almost fainted with suppressed excitement, her steady hands opened the blade and deftly cut the binding ropes.

"Softly" she whispered, "it is life or death."

Stiffened from the cramped position in which he was bound, he still managed to keep close to her. They reached the opening in the floor: Thankfully he felt the fresh, damp air of night, and hope lived in his breast again.

Here they stopped with their feet on the earth and their heads in the old fort.

"I have a dress for you," she told him softly. "You must be quick."

She helped him to slip the skirt over his head, and managed in some way to fasten it about his waist. It was her mother's skirt which she had been taking for just this purpose when the former had asked what she was looking for.

There was no waist, but a shawl wrapped about his shoulders answered the purpose even better. Her own old calico sun-bonnet she put on his head as they stood in the opening.

"Free," he whispered gladly.

"But not saved," she answered with dim foreboding as she heard the heavy tramp of feet and the hoarse grumble of angry, desperate men.

She recognized it instantly. Intuitively she knew what it meant.

"What is that?" he asked, a numb, nameless fear shaking him violently.

"Listen! It's the lynchers!" she cried hopelessly. "Bill Doty is dead."

IX

"SWEET, YOU SHALL BE MY WIFE."

*"Thinkest thou
That I could live, and let thee go,
Who art my life itself?"*

*"Oft expectation fails, and most oft there
When most it promises."*

DAZED WITH FEAR, THEY STOOD listening to those meaning sounds.

"Crawl down through the opening," she gasped.

She waited to drop the board carefully back in its place before she followed him, then they stood breathlessly face to face in the night.

"Come," cried Eva, shaking off the hopeless feeling that chained her, powerless. "We must run for our lives!"

Even as they scrambled over the fence, Eva whispered words of caution.

"Don't run across the open field, but keep with me, close in the shadow of the fence. It will make the way longer, but it also makes our chances of escape better.

"Are you giving out?" she asked anxiously, when they, in time that would have put a professional runner to shame, had put several meadows between themselves and the fort-house.

His labored breathing and his awkward tripping in the skirt he wore indicated weariness.

"We must take the public road for a ways now," she continued warningly.

"We are not liable to meet many, if any, persons, but if we do, you keep perfectly still," she said authoritatively. "I will manage them somehow."

"There is some one," he said to her, speaking for the first time after they had walked some distance in silence. They could not run now, fearing to attract attention.

She pressed his arm, which was slipped through hers, encouragingly, and walked fearlessly on to meet the advancing person.

When nearly face to face she went swiftly, dragged her companion with her across to the other side of the road, calling back cheerily:

"Hello, neighbor! You frightened mother coming up so quick in the dark."

Meanwhile she was walking away from the stranger, who continued on his way toward the village.

"Bad time of night fer women folks to be out alone," the man called back in a friendly voice.

"Have to go to see a neighbor who is sick, and mother is timid," Eva called cordially.

The man's hoarse laugh, which greeted this remark, was wafted back to them as they moved on at a more rapid rate.

"Are you able to run again?" she asked tenderly. "It is too bad, but we must, because he will tell the village men, when he hears of your escape, about meeting us, and they will hunt us down.

"Don't be frightened, though," she added encouragingly, as she ran along by his side as lightly as a deer. "It will take those thick-headed people some time to find out that it is possible for a man to wear a petticoat. In that fact lies your chance for escape."

"You are an angel!" he said fervently.

"Where can we run to that we will be safe?" he asked her after awhile.

"I am making for the water tank, which is about eight miles from the village. The trains stop there regularly, and you must go on the first that is going east, so to be carried away from the village, for the men, when they fail to find you, will expect you to hide in the woods or take a train, and they will watch the station."

They talked very little after this. He caught the skirt he wore up around his waist so it would not interfere with his progress, but he did not dare to take it off yet lest they meet someone, so, still burdened with his feminine attire, he walked and ran by Eva's side.

The way was long, but it seemed twice as long to them in their anxiety. Surely the gates of Paradise would not look more magnificent to them than did the outline of a train, with the red-hot coals falling from the engine to the track, as they reached the steep decline above the water tank—nor would a heavenly choir sound sweeter than the escaping steam.

"Come, we must not miss it," he said joyously as they stopped on the edge of the sharp cliff.

"We must," she replied, clinging to his arm. "It is going toward the village!"

"But it may cost us our lives to take any chances waiting for another train," he said dejectedly.

"It will cost your life to take that train," she replied positively, "and you have one chance by waiting."

"I can fix it with the conductor or the porter, and as it is an express train, they will not let it be searched," he told her persuasively.

"They will not refuse to deliver up an escaped—murderer," the girl replied coldly.

And with a muttered curse, the man watched the train go swifter and swifter westward, leaving them alone on the edge of the hill above the road-bed.

"Do you see that?" she asked, holding her arm out in the direction he had watched the train glide away. "Look! Can you see a light that looks like a tiny star? Now, do you see tiny red sparks shooting up like fireworks at a great distance?"

"A train?" he asked happily.

"Yes. A train going east," was the quiet, satisfied answer.

"It does not seem to come any nearer," he said impatiently. "Do you think it has stopped?"

"No; it is coming, but slowly, for it is a freight train."

He watched it moodily. It did not offer much consolation to him, the idea of traveling on a freight train, but he had a dim perception that if it pleased Eva to accept it as a means for escape, it was useless for him to object. So much was he already impressed with the undaunted, determined will of the pretty girl who had saved him from the fate she had unwittingly brought upon him.

"You can take off those garments now," she said with a slight smile, when the labored puffing of the engine sounded very near. "You must keep them, they may be of service as a blanket on your way East. I am sorry we could not bring your hat," Eva said, while folding up the gown.

"I have the entire hat I had with me," he said in a tone of satisfaction. "A soft cap, folded in the pocket of my jacket," as he brought it forth and put it on.

"It is better than a muslin sun-bonnet," said he, laughingly.

"For some purposes," she answered, and then continued:

"There is your train. They will stop for some time. You had better stay out of sight, though we will go down nearer, until is ready to start, then jump on and stay quiet until they find you, because they may want to put you off. If you only had a flask of whisky, you could bribe them to let you ride. They will do more for whisky than they would do for money."

"I have a flask of whisky. I always carry it when I go hunting," he said, tapping his pocket.

"Come, I will go down and stay until I see you safely on the train."

"Why, what do you mean? Surely you cannot contemplate going back among those heathens?" he exclaimed in surprise.

"Oh, yes, I can manage to get out of all blame, somehow," she replied with a brave little smile, though her voice slightly quivered.

"I never considered such a move for a moment. I naturally thought you would go with me. If I had not, I don't think I should have permitted you to take such risks for me."

"Don't think of that. By defending me you brought this trouble on yourself, and it was only my duty to save you from the consequence," Eva answered, somewhat stiffly.

"Come, child, there can be nothing you care for back there," he coaxed, taking her little, cool hand in his as they descended the hill. "Come with me, dear, and learn what it is to be happy and to have someone to love you," he pleaded, tenderly.

"I do not know you, and I cannot afford to run away with a strange man unless—But come, your train is ready to start."

They ran along the train until some distance from the caboose, where they found an open and empty box-car.

"This is your chance," Eva said, and he sprung lightly in just as the wheels began to rub and crack, as they always do when starting.

"Come with me, my darling," he said, holding out his arms to her. "I'll do anything to make you happy."

"If you care enough for me to marry me, I will go," she answered, tossing her bundle into the car; "and in no other way will I go."

"Darling, come!" he cried passionately.

The train was moving. She ran alongside, and, catching her firmly by the arms, he dragged her in, saying, as he folded her to his heart:

"Sweet, you shall be my wife."

X

A RIDE ON A FREIGHT TRAIN.

"Oh, how impatience gains upon the soul,
When the long-promised hour of joy draws near."

"I travel all the irksome night,
By ways to me unknown."

FOR MILES THEY RODE WRAPPED in each other's arms, their bliss-ful silence punctuated only with long, warm kisses.

Both were madly happy. The feeling of rest and security, after a day and a night of intense danger and misery, brought to them a blissful, happy languor that was intoxicating.

Both were busy rummaging through the secret cells of their wakeful brains. Resting snugly in his arms, traveling on to a new life, Eva was living over her old days.

She was at school again, a freckle-faced, thin-legged, ragged, hungry-looking child. She could see the bright sun again, the blue sky; she could feel the soft wind; she could hear the merry shouts of the school-children, and the very wheels kept chanting the old tune:

"London Bridge is falling down,
Fall-ing down, fall-ing down;
London Bridge is falling down,
My fair lady."

She could see Lily Cartwright cast the poor, forlorn child from the merry ranks. She could see that child, with burning eyes and pallid cheeks, stand-ing aloof on the green grass watching the others at play.

Then she could hear the school bell, and see the rank break in confusion and the pupils rush to their classrooms, a few lingering with their leader, who went leisurely toward the building.

She could see her dealt a blow, she could see the warm, red blood, she could hear the frightened cries, she could see the schoolroom, could hear the jeers of the boys, could see the ragged child punished.

Like a panorama stretched before her, she could see her mother nursing the babe at the window, her brother sitting on the door-sill; she could hear her teacher's explanation; she could see the dusty road, and her poor old shaggy dog in her arms; she could see the surrey coming, the man getting out with the whip in his hands; she could feel the stinging blow, and she could laugh again to see her brave dog tearing at the man's arms and face.

Then the scene changed and she could see her poor dog lying dead, his faithful blood staining the dust and forming little pools in the wagon rut.

Last she could hear her father tell of the Cartwrights' success, even as they took his labor and his living from him.

Then she could hear a firm young voice swear revenge, and remember the following years, submerged as they were into one idea, devoted to one purpose, one desire, one object.

"And it has come," she thought gladly. "I'll have revenge at last!"

She opened her eyes and looked up at her companion. It was daylight now; but he, wearied out, was sleeping soundly. She could see the slanting streaks of light that came in where the door was not closed securely, and she fell to wondering where they were.

The train slowed up and at last stopped. Eva was so weary that her eye-lids had begun to weigh down, when the sudden ceasing of the regular rumbling of the cars brought her to a sense of her position. She heard the brakemen running across the top of the car, she heard them rattle the brakes, and her heart beat timidly at every sound. She heard footsteps in the crunching pebbles of the road bed, and in another instant the door of the car was noisily slid open, leaving in a flood of daylight.

"Hello, here! Crawl out of that, now!" a rough voice called as a head appeared at the opening, followed by a form springing feet first into the car.

"Here, out of this! No stealin' rides on this train," he said, crossing over to get a nearer view.

"By the Lord, a girl!" he ejaculated, stopping in intense surprise.

"And you wouldn't put a girl off, would you?" Eva's companion asked persuasively, releasing her and straightening up.

"What are you stealing rides for?" he asked curiously.

"We ran off from home. An elopement. You understand?" the man, who a few hours before had eluded a band of lynchers, answered easily.

"Oh, ho! But you can't steal rides on this train," he said positively.

"Come, now, don't be hard on a fellow. I'll pay you double the rate of fares."

"No, you won't. I can't be paid to neglect doin' my duty," the brakeman said harshly.

"Give him a drink," Eva whispered.

"If you won't accept fares, at least take a drink with me. I'll assure you that it's the best of whisky."

"Thanks. I don't mind if I do," the brakeman said cordially, reaching out for the flask. "It's against the rules for us to carry any of that stuff, and I tell you, a fellow that's up all night, in the night air, need it to warm up his system."

The brakeman took a long drink. Smacking his lips appreciatively, he handed the flask back, saying apologetically, "I haven't anything against anybody ridin', but it's the rule for us to hunt for free riders and put them off. We'd lose our jobs if we were caught letting anyone ride; but if you and your lady stay in here quietly, they mightn't find you. See?"

They said they saw, and he left them alone.

"Are you sorry you came, dear?" he asked tenderly, turning his attention to his pretty companion.

"Are you sorry you brought me?" she asked anxiously in turn.

"How could I regret having you with me?" he said, looking at her fondly. "I had intended, when you left me in the hollow of the tree, to send for you when I reached safety, but you had to save me first."

"You were surprised when you were caught?" she asked, smiling a little.

"Surprised! I was speechless. I waited to give you good time to lead the men off, and then I started out; I had not gone many steps when I saw them——"

"It was not the same crowd that had passed before," she interrupted. "I found them, and kept them searching for a stranger in a swamp for hours."

"I thought it rather strange that they should be coming from the same direction as they had done awhile before, without having retraced their steps. I tell you, they had a glorious search for me," he laughed. "They ran around like dogs about a squirrel hole, but they never thought of looking in the tree. Then, in turn, they surprised me. I waited until dusk, though everything had been quiet hours before. I thought they had given it up. When I stepped out, and in a few moments was surrounded, I was simply speechless."

"Were you frightened?"

"Somewhat. They weren't at all modest about telling me what they would do should that man be dead when they reached the village. I made up my mind my time had come."

"And you didn't expect me?" she asked, feeling hurt that he would not have expected help from her.

"Hardly! How could I, child?"—patting her hand tenderly. "I did not remember that fairies could do the most impossible things."

"There now, don't you know it's again' the rules to steal rides on this here railroad?" a voice called to them, and another man made his appearance.

"Yes, I know. But you won't put a fellow off that's had to steal his sweetheart. Here, wish me joy, and call it square." And out came the flask again, that quickly found its way to the man's mouth.

"I don't blame you for stealin' her," the brakeman said, with an appreciative wink, wiping his uncultivated mustache. "May your life be as fine as that drink. Sorry to intrude myself on you." And with a wide smile, he again went out of sight.

"The first brakeman has given him the tip, and we will not have any peace until the bottle is empty," Eva's companion said with a laugh. "I am getting hungry; I wonder where we are?" he added.

"Don't you think," Eva said, with a bashful blush, "as we are to be married, that I should know your name?"

"It would be the proper thing," he said, teasingly, "to know it before the minister asks you if you will have me for your wedded husband. If you did not know my name, you would not know whether you were taking the right man or not, eh? Well, now, sweet, joking aside, my name is Maurice Vanderfelt, my home, New York, my age, thirty-five, my income, $40,000 a year, and I am yours—all yours."

"I love you very much," she said gratefully, "and I will try to make you very happy."

As she spoke the train stopped again, and two men came into the car. The same proceedings were gone through, the flask was passed around, and all hands were satisfied.

"Where are we?" Maurice Vanderfelt asked when these little pleasantries had been religiously obeyed.

"An hour out from Philadelphia," one of the men answered.

"We lay off here till the express going east passes. If I was in your place I'd get off here and hire some of the farmers to drive you into Philadelphia. We can't let you ride into the city anyway, for some of the inspectors may find you, and it would make us lots of trouble."

"Your suggestion is a good one. Come, Eva, we will change our way of traveling. Please accept the flask. No? Take another drink then, and we will bid you good-bye."

Not far from the railroad they found a comfortable farmhouse where they got food, for which they stood in great need, and made arrangements to be driven into the city. They were artists, Maurice Vanderfelt told the farmer, and had been strolling about the country sketching, their effects having been sent on to the city the day before.

A professional walker, at the end of a seven days' contest, could not have been stiffer in the joints or more bruised up than were these two who had, the previous night, walked and run eight miles to escape the lynchers.

A few hours later, after an uninteresting drive during which they both slept, they entered Philadelphia. Maurice Vanderfelt, being perfectly at home in the city, was driven to a quiet hotel, where he paid and dismissed the farmer.

Leaving Eva in the waiting-room, he went to the office, but soon returned, followed by a bell-boy, who showed them to their rooms.

"Now, Eva, wash up a bit and it will rest you. I have ordered luncheon sent up, and as soon as I get you an outfit, we will go on to New York. Our rather hasty flight and unique mode of traveling does not tend to improve the respectability of ones' looks," he said with a laugh at his reflection in a long pier-glass.

Eva felt very shy and strange, it was all so new to her, and feeling so, she naturally remained quiet.

"Where are we going to be married?" she asked shyly.

"I can't tell yet," he said, with a shadow of a frown on his handsome face.

"You know, dear, we cannot stay here together unless we are married," she said kindly but firmly.

"Let us eat first and talk about marriage afterward," he said lightly, turning to yell, "Come in!" in answer to a knock upon their door.

XI

MARRIED BY A FRENCH MINISTER.

"Take this much for my counsel, marry not in haste."

"What do you think of marriage?
I take't as those that deny purgatory;
It locally contains or heaven or hell;
There's no third place in it."

A MESSENGER BOY ANSWERED THE INVITATION to enter. Maurice Vanderfelt wrote a note and dispatched him with instructions to bring an answer.

By the time they had cleaner faces, and he was resting on a couch admiring Eva as she sat silently by in a large arm-chair, the servant appeared with their repast.

It was all so new to the girl. The presence of the silent, watchful waiter embarrassed her, she was so afraid he would see it was strange to her.

Maurice must have thought that Eva would feel more at ease, for he shortly dismissed the waiter, saying they would ring when he was wanted.

"I have sent around to an establishment to have a woman come here and measure you for some garments. They keep made-up clothing, so that in a few hours they will be able to fit you out with everything you need until we reach New York. Then you can buy everything you please. Do you like to shop?"

"I don't know, I have never done it," she said, smiling at her own simplicity.

"Well, that's one thing a woman doesn't have to learn," he said, with all the mistakenness of a man's opinion.

Another knock, this time followed by the messenger boy and a plump, neat woman, who explained that she was sent in answer to Mr. Vander-felt's message.

He gave her instructions as she went over Eva with a tape-measure, jotting down numbers in a book that was tied to her waist.

"Everything will be just as you wish," the woman said, readjusting her wrap. "In less than two hours Madame will have what you have ordered. If you desire it, I will return with the goods and see that everything is perfect."

"Come back, by all means," he said, closing the door after her.

"Now, darling"—bending over to kiss Eva as she sat again in the arm-chair—"I want you to lie down and take a nap until I return. I am going out attend to some business. You won't be lonely, dear?"

"Don't think of me to let interfere with your business," she said, looking fondly into his blue eyes.

"Come, then, lie down here,"—leading her to a couch.

Going to the inside bedroom, he brought out a robe which he tenderly tucked about her, and with a warm kiss, left her already half asleep.

She had been dreaming all sorts of things when a kiss brought her back to everyday life, to find her handsome lover learning over her and a bright light in the room. It was night.

"Sleeping Beauty, your new grown, and the woman with it has been waiting here for the last half hour." And, lifting her up, he set her gently on her feet,

How exquisitely pretty she was with that warm flush of sleep on her soft cheeks.

The woman took her into the inside room, and in a short time had her entirely clad in fine, scented garments. Eva had never seen anything half so grand before, but she was as easy as if it had been her everyday apparel, though she did look ashamed of the coarse, yellow things that were cast contemptuously aside.

When her dress, a perfect-fitting, plain brown cloth, with short jacket to match, was pronounced satisfactory by the woman, Eva was taken out where Maurice was waiting.

His eyes, but not his lips, spoke his satisfaction, and he carefully watched the trying on of hats until one was found that he pronounced perfect and becoming.

After paying the bill, and giving a generous tip beside, the woman was dismissed.

"My perfect darling!" he said passionately, gazing in rapture upon her increased beauty.

"It is night, dear Maurice. Have you found a minister yet?" Eva asked anxiously.

"Yes, that I have! What a prudish and frightened darling it is. It shows the training of the country," he said jestingly.

"Now, dear, of course you don't speak French? Well, I engaged a French minister. He speaks no English, but I have known him for some time, and he will keep our marriage a secret until we are both in proper trim and ready to meet my friends. Does this suit you?"

"Perfectly," she answered, with a happy smile. "I want a chance to improve my appearance before I am introduced to your friends. When will the minister come?"

"That must be him now," was the answer, and Maurice opened the door.

A young looking man with a high nose, and wearing a long black coat, entered, shaking hands with Maurice Vanderfelt, who introduced him to Eva, with whom he also shook hands, saying something to her in a language she did not understand. Maurice answered him in the same language, and then he called Eva to him. He took her hand in his, and the minister said over some words that had no meaning to Eva, pausing at a place where she thought he mentioned her name.

"Say 'I do,'" Maurice said, and Eva said it clearly, after which Maurice said something and put a plain gold ring on her finger and kissed her. And then, shaking hands again, the minister bowed himself out, accompanied by Maurice, who said he would be back presently.

"You do not speak French, do you, madam?" the woman, whom Maurice had paid and dismissed, said as she returned the moment her husband had disappeared.

"What do you want?" Eva asked curtly. She did not like the scraping, smiling, bowing creature.

"I took a fancy to you, madam, and I made bold to return to ask if you did not want a maid. All fine ladies have maids. I speak several languages and you will find me of service."

"I do not want a maid at present," was Eva's reply.

"I'll leave my address, madam, and if you need a maid, I hope you'll try me. You will find me faithful," and not one whit abashed by the coldness that had greeted her proposal, she bowed herself out.

"Eva, I have decided to go on to New York tonight, if you are rested," her husband said when he returned.

"I am not tired now," Eva made reply. "I am ready to go as soon as you wish."

"I have ordered dinner to be served before leaving, and have bought our tickets and stateroom. I have some business I want to look after, and we might as well be in New York as here—better, in fact, as I don't like this town."

Dinner was served, and with it wine. Eva had never tasted any before, and she sipped sparingly. Maurice, on the contrary, consumed what seemed to Eva a terrible quantity, but she was not bold enough to mention it, especially as he seemed to grow more loving, more devoted as the dinner progressed.

She was very happy. It seemed like a fairy tale to her, it was so unreal.

Here she was, a poor country girl, dining in the loveliest room she had ever seen; in the finest gown she had ever worn; opposite to the handsomest man her eyes had ever rested upon.

There was silver which delighted her eye, fine dishes that lent an additional flavor to the dainty food, a quiet, competent waiter that somehow she found very comforting now.

Her new gown had given her confidence in herself, and since she had put it on she felt perfectly at ease, as if she belonged to the surroundings in which she found herself.

"Husband!" she murmured fondly, slipping her hand under the table, where it was met by his, which she squeezed, all unseen by the waiter, so they thought, at least.

"I dare you!" he said, leaning across the little table that separated them.

Quick as a flash, before he had time to wonder if she would accept his challenge, she leaned over, just as the waiter turned around to get the wine, and pressed a warm, soft kiss on his lips, leaning back in her chair afterward with a low, gurgling laugh.

"Darling!" he whispered passionately, his eyes burning with love.

"The carriage waits, sir, and you have just time to catch your train," a small boy said at the door.

Eva, eager to start, jumped up, laughing as her husband helped her on with her jacket, and buttoned it, stealing a kiss when he had finished.

"Everything goes well," Eva thought, thankfully, when a moment later she was in a carriage on her way to the station. "Eva Scarlett was lost in that hotel, and Eva Vanderfelt, beautiful and rich, goes forth to victory—victory and revenge!"

XII

"DEAR, DO YOU MEAN TO QUARREL?"

"There is not in nature
A thing that makes a man so deform'd, so beastly,
As doth intemperate anger."

"The elephant is never won with anger;
Nor must that man, who would reclaim a lion,
Take him by the teeth."

"I SHOULD BE THE HAPPIEST GIRL in the world, but I am not."

Eva Vanderfelt sighed as she drummed idly on the windowpane and gazed, but without seeing, out at the large, fluffy snowflakes that filled the air, melting as they reached the ground.

"Six months since I was married—six months ago this very day: I have had loads of jewels, fine clothes, a beautiful little home, and a carriage at call, a husband—Heigho! Marriage is not just the thing I dreamed it would be. Maurice is handsome, and almost always loving. He takes me to the theaters, and driving, but he has never introduced me to his friends. He says he wants me to be faultless in manners and appearance first. Well, I have studied, and my instructors praise me. I pay attention to my dress, and my dressmakers praise my taste and figure. Oh, I am sure the gaze of the public proves that I am not unsightly."

With that thought she rushed across the room into one adjoining, when she critically surveyed herself in a long, broad mirror.

"My eyes are good—even Maurice acknowledges that much; my complexion is faultless—Maurice says so; my hair is neither brown nor red, but it does look well when the light falls on it—and Maurice says it is my greatest beauty; my hands are not quite as small as they should be, but my feet make up for that; my shoulders are plump, and my waist is slender, and—Well, I don't see any women any place we go that are better looking; and Maurice has said he never saw any one as lovely—still, I am not perfect enough to meet his friends.

"But why do I want to meet his friends? Why do I want to go into society? It's the same old longing that I have felt for years, the same old thirst for revenge—revenge on the Cartwright's. They are here, right in this town with me, and yet I am as far away from them as if I was in heaven and they were in Hades. Only this morning I read a glowing account of a ball given in Lil Cartwright's honor, while here I, hundreds, ay, thou sands of times prettier, sit alone, unknown. It would not be hard if we were poor, but Maurice has plenty of money—enough to allow me to reign over the Cartwrights, if he would only introduce me into society. It can't be that he is jealous, yet—"

"Well, girlie, what are you sitting in the dark for? Glum, eh?" called a cheerful voice, and Maurice Vanderfelt made his appearance in the room. Still the same handsome, careless Maurice, not one day older than, not as old in fact as he looked on the day he married Eva Scarlett.

"I was thinking, Maurice," she replied gloomily, making no move from the chair in which she was seated.

"Blue, eh?" he said, teasingly, pressing his mustache so lightly to her cheek that in truth it could not be called a kiss nor a caress.

"Somewhat," she assented, passively.

"All women get such spells occasionally," he replied indifferently, "and then the poor men have to suffer."

Eva made no answer to this, and Maurice seated himself before the piano, running his fingers over the key as he asked:

"When will dinner be ready?"

"At six," was the quiet answer.

"I'll dine with you to-night. Then I am going to my club. You need not wait for me."

"Maurice, do you really love me?" Eva asked, coming up back of him and putting her arms around his neck, leaning her head lightly against his.

"Why, certainly, child. What ails you to-night?" he answered lightly, without leaving off his playing.

"I am anxious to know why you never introduce me to your friends?" she said, half timidly. "Surely, Maurice, I have remedied all the faults there were in my looks, and manner, and speech."

"Have I been finding fault with you?"

"No, dear; but you must know that I would like to become acquainted with somebody. I want some friends, if ever so few," she pleaded.

"Then my society is not enough for you?" he said impatiently.

Rising from the piano and shaking off her clinging arms, he stood with his back toward the crackling wood-fire, looking at Eva intently.

"Maurice, please do not evade my question. You know I love you, but you are so often away, to your club, you say, and I am so often left alone! Surely you do not begrudge me one friend?"

"Certainly not. Have dozens of them, if it so pleases you," he said, icily.

"Now you are angry with me!" she said, protesting.

"Not in the least. I only want you to please yourself. I have no fancy for listening to the complaints of a woman. Please yourself, by all means, only spare me."

"You know, dear, I cannot meet any one without your sanction and aid," she said; but he made no reply.

"You are not jealous of me?"

"Ha! Ha! Jealous? I, jealous? Dismiss the thought, my dear," was the scornful reply.

"Then you have some secret motive for not wishing to introduce me to your friends," Eva said positively, a red flush spreading over her face.

"I have made no such assertion," Maurice Vanderfelt said as he turned on the incandescent light.

"Maurice, why evade it? You keep me almost a prisoner. Why? For what reason?"

"My dear, don't drive me too far. Only look about you, examine your jewel case and your wardrobe, recall your carriage and pair, and your visits to the theaters, whenever there is anything to see. If you call that the treatment of a prisoner, very well. I have nothing more to say." And Maurice Vanderfelt shrugged his shoulders as if he had done with the subject.

"Maurice, please don't be angry. Don't think I fail to appreciate your goodness to me. I only ask that you treat me as other men treat their wives."

"You would get heartily sick of it if I did," he interrupted savagely.

"I have no relatives—I have only you," she added plaintively.

"You will excuse me, I am going to the club to dinner," he announced suddenly, as he walked out into the hall. She heard him go into his room, slamming the door behind him, and after awhile she heard him whistling, only stopping long enough to call John to fetch his patent-leather shoes.

"Dinner is served," announced a maid at the door.

"Tell the cook to detain dinner for a few moments, Mr. Vanderfelt is dressing. Probably he may wish to dine at home," Eva said, and the maid disappeared.

She was a very unhappy girl as she went out along the hall, stopping before her husband's door, on which she knocked timidly.

The whistling stopped, and he called out gruffly: "What do you want?"

"It's Eva, dear," she said timidly.

"I'm dressing, and can't be bothered," he answered rudely, beginning to whistle again.

"Please, I won't bother you," she said, like a child on the verge of tears.

"Hang it! Come in, if you will, but cut it short." He stood before his dressing-case in his shirt sleeves, arranging his scarf, and paid no attention to her.

"Won't you stay here for dinner if you have no special engagement?" she asked longingly.

"I prefer going to the club," he said, casting the one tie away and taking up another.

"I am sorry," she said simply, a sob choking in her throat. "Let me assist you?" she said kindly, as he took up his waistcoat and then his coat.

"Thanks, no," was the curt answer.

He put on his Inverness and his high hat, pausing for a moment to survey his handsome, well-dressed figure in the mirror, and to give a final fond twist to his mustache.

Eva took up his gloves, and when he turned to look for them, she silently held them out to him, her lips trembling, and a prayer for love and kindness in her pretty, moist eyes.

Without one word, but with a frown of impatience, he took them from her outstretched hand, never giving her a glance.

"I will not be back tonight," he said, walking toward the door.

"As you wish, dear," she answered meekly.

"Won't you even kiss me good-night?" she asked, with a little forced smile, as she followed him out to the hall door.

"When you treat me properly, I shall kiss you—not until then," was the cold, unfeeling answer.

"Dear, do you mean to quarrel?" she pleaded, half playfully.

"By God, no!" was the savage reply, as he turned to face her. "If you can't be decent and agreeable, and fulfill your share of this bargain, we shall end it, that's all." The brutality of his answer made Eva speechless for awhile, and when she recovered breath he was gone.

She had been used to the hard side of the world so long, that cruelty always awoke in her a savage desire to whip, and not be whipped.

Kindness made her as gentle as a pet rabbit, as devoted as a dog, but harshness made her as cruel as a parrot—she would turn about and bite the hand that fed her.

"Our first quarrel," she cried bitterly; "but not our last. I will know the reason why he will not introduce me to his friends, if it takes my life!"

And with this direful vow upon her lips, she closed the door.

XIII

"THE BRIDE DID NOT UNDERSTAND."

"So, farewell hope, and with hope farewell fear,
Farewell remorse; all good to me is lost;
Evil, be thou my good."

"Woman's honor
Is nice as ermine—will not bear a soil."

EVA MADE NO PRETENSE OF eating dinner. She had no appetite. In some way, she knew not how, she seemed face to face with a great calamity.

Her husband's words had driven the blood from her heart, and she felt a nameless foreboding thrilling through her nerves like a mild electric shock.

She went to bed, but her own depressed feelings made her so unrestful that she left those cozy quarters to seek others.

Throwing a long, loose gown, composed of thin silk and burdened with exquisite lace, over her night-robe, slipping her feet into tiny red sandals, she quietly left her room and went into the alcove next to the drawing-room, in which the light was still burning, just as her husband had left it.

Pulling a big arm-chair up before the solitary window, with the back of it toward the drawing-room, she sat down and gazed out into the dark night.

She was very desolate and unhappy, poor, fated girl!

Her prayer had been answered, and she had gained a husband—rich, handsome and elegant; but she was no nearer the consummation of her plans for revenge than she was six months before, when washing the crockery in her mother's humble home.

She was so wrapped up in her own misery, which brought disfiguring tears to her eyes and cheeks, that she had not noticed the bell, and did not know that someone had come until she heard the maid speak: "Do you wish to see Mrs. Vanderfelt?"

"No; I wish to see Mr. Vanderfelt. I left a note at the club, so if I should pass him on the way he will return. I'll wait for awhile."

Eva heard the maid go out, and she lazily wondered who the person was that had found his way to their home. It was a most unusual occurrence.

"An unpleasant voice he has," she thought; and then she stupidly fell to thinking that it was not altogether unfamiliar to her.

Then she thought, with scorn, how fanciful she was. It was not possible for her to know the voice of any of Maurice Vanderfelt's friends, nor was it possible for any of the people she had known at her home to be acquainted with her husband.

Unable to make her escape unseen, Eva decided to quietly remain where she was until the man, weary of useless waiting, should go away again.

Considerably astonished, she heard a key turn in the latch and heard her husband's well-known voice ask anxiously for her, and on the assurance of the maid that she had retired some time ago, he dismissed her and walked hastily into the drawing-room, closing and bolting the door after him.

She heard the visitor push back his chair, and she was conscious of a fear that her husband would enter the alcove room and find her in hiding there.

"My God! What did you venture here for?" she heard her husband exclaim, angrily.

"I did not know what else to do. It was positively necessary that I should see you without delay," the visitor replied, rather stiffly.

"You haven't seen her?" Eva's husband asked anxiously.

"No."

"Well. I tell you it was an unnecessary risk," he said, in a mollified tone.

"Never mind, I am capable of taking care of that," the man answered, with a laugh.

"That may be. But I don't care to risk the consequences," was the stern answer.

"Say, old boy, don't you think you are getting very chicken-hearted all at once?" the stranger asked jocosely.

"Well, I have taken some very long risks in my lifetime," Maurice said boastingly in return.

"And I suppose you recall the old saying—and a true one, by Jove!—that every dog has his day, and the pitcher that goes to the well too often, and so forth, eh, chappie?"

"Bah! Some dogs never get their day. Some are born for bad luck, and it sticks to them until their dying day. But now to business. You understand my position exactly, and why I should not want you to come here at all hazards."

"Say, look here, my boy, the sooner you deal on a square footing, paying the price for what others have to sell, you will have less pitfalls ahead," the visitor advised.

"Maybe I prefer the danger. Drop it! What do you want?"

"There was a witness to my little amateur performance, enacted at your request, and in your behalf," was the brisk answer.

"Confound it! Who cares?" was the reckless response to the information.

"I do, by gad! State offense, if I understand it right, or a die—a United States dollar die—by gad!"

"Confound you! Speak plainly. How?" Maurice said impatiently.

"The witness intends to make money by me, exempt from the counterfeit law—press it out of me—squeeze it from me—any way you like."

"How did he learn the facts?" Vanderfelt asked thoughtfully.

"He? She, by Jove, watched and listened through the keyhole. Speaks the language like a native. Buried the secret in her ample bosom, and lay for me. Well, she found me, and I handed over fifty cool dollars to last until I consulted with you."

"Chambermaid, I presume?" Maurice said inquiringly.

"No; dressmaker."

"By the Lord, Harry! I wish she may break her neck!" was the savage way in which he answered this last information.

"What will you do?"

"That's what I came to you to learn."

"I don't see what I can do"—savagely.

"By gad, I can't be bled for your scrapes. I got nothing out of it."

"It seems to me mighty queer that you did not bluff her off."

"No bluffing her, old man. I think she has met two or three men in her lifetime. She was onto all the bluffs," laughed the visitor.

"How much does she want?" Vanderfelt asked impatiently.

"Fifty a week during the winter, with a double allowance in the summer to allow her to put up at fashionable summer resorts," the visitor said dryly.

"I'll see her hanged first."

"Just what I said to her, and she replied that she would see us both in stripes, living at the state's expense first, before she hanged," the visitor said gleefully.

"Oh, my God, what horrible trouble has my husband gotten into?" thought Eva, trembling violently where she sat in the dark room, hearing all that was said but failing to understand one word of its direful import.

"Some woman, who knows he killed Bill Doty, has found him out," she thought again, and she sat paralyzed with fear.

"If he was angry with me before, he will hate me now," was her wretched thought.

"It was my entire fault that he killed Bill Doty, and he will remember it, and I shall never be forgiven. Oh, my poor darling."

And Eva smothered the sob that threatened to disclose her presence to the men outside.

"Well, I suppose we'll have to compromise," Eva heard her husband say dejectedly. "I think I had better go over with you and try to bluff her price down. Don't you think it can be done?"

"I don't know," the stranger answered doubtfully. "How is it? Are you still keeping it up?" he added, curiously.

"Don't ask too much, and we will be the better friends," was the warning answer.

"Your affairs don't usually last so long. I only thought if it was all up we could claim blackmail and silence our gay, fat squeezer."

"Does she know everything?" Maurice asked, as if a sudden hope had come to him.

"Everything. She understood the whole game as well as if she had been in on it. I'll tell: you there is no dust on her. She is no antique bric-à-brac."

"She understood what you said?"

"Perfectly. French is as plain to her as the value of a dollar, and I never saw any one who knew its value better."

"Curse her!"

"So say I. She said she heard me say in French that you would not marry under any consideration; heard me ask if all parties were agreed to live together without the permission of a minister, or of a justice of the peace, and if both agreed to stand the consequence, and make no fuss afterward?

"She thought it was all right; sort of an original and unique contract made for mutual benefit, by gad, until she heard you tell the girl to answer in the affirmative, which she *did in English*. That let the hag in on our little game, and when she heard you answer in French, she knew the bride *could not* understand what sort of a contract she had agreed to fulfill—"

"The bride *did not* understand!" Eva repeated slowly to herself, unable to catch the meaning of his words.

"—so she waited outside in order to see me. She knew you by sight, having seen you when she brought the gown—"

"Having seen *him* when she brought the gown!" repeated Eva, as a violent chill turned her blood to ice.

"—and the sly minx was determined to see me, so as to be able to identify us, to her own advantage after ward. When you left your—ahem!—newly-made bride, she—"

"*Left your newly-made bride!* My God! Am I going mad?" the wretched girl thought, as mechanically she repeated to herself his words.

"—waited in the corner of the hall. There was no mistake. She got a good look at me, and what surprises me was that she ever let me escape. She had some other fish to fry first. I'll take my oath, or she would have followed me then and there.

"Why she did not she would not say, but ever since then she has been hunting me down, and she was successful, confound her!

"I told her—" he continued, but what he meant to say was never finished in this world.

An apparition stood before them.

An apparition of the girl they had most bitterly wronged—wronged past all remedy, past all forgiveness.

The sight of her held them powerless.

She clutched the portiere and clung to it for support, trembling in every nerve, with her face as white as the face of those who have found rest in death, with eyes burning like the eyes of a maddened, desperate animal brought to bay, she stood speechless before them.

XIV

STABBED AND TORTURED BY A WOMAN.

"My mortal in juries have turned my mind,
And I could hate myself for being kind.
If there be any majesty above
That has revenge in store for perjured love;
Send, Heav'n, the swiftest ruin on his head,
Strike the destroyer, lay the victor dead;
Kill the triumpher, and avenge my wrong,
In height of pomp, when he is warmed and young,
Bolted with thunder, let him rush along,
And when in the last pangs of life he lies,
Grant I may stand to dart him with my eyes;
Nay, after death
Pursue his spotted soul, and shoot him as he flies."

"**Y**OU ARE LYING!" SHE HISSED at length, frantically.
Dumfounded, the two wretches in man's shape stood speechless before her.

"Tell me you were lying before I tear your vile hearts out!" she cried, a maniacal light in her brown eyes. "What, are you such cowards that you fear to speak?" she scornfully added.

"No, no, my dear; you are excited," Vanderfelt stammered.

"Your dear?"

He cringed under the lash of her insulting tone.

"Out with it—confess you were vilely lying!" she urged.

"Of course it was a lie; a—a joke of my friend's—merely a joke, I assure you," Maurice Vanderfelt said, in a forced, hesitating way.

"A joke! My God! Ha, ha, ha! Weak, blind fool that I am, that I should doubt the truth a moment! There—look on him! See the guilt in his face!" she said madly, pointing her finger at the stranger. "A joke? You name it well. There stands the jester, the prince of fools! He jested; he could not speak English. He carried his joke further—he married us in French. But now this prince of fools, this knave of knaves, stands there, and, in plain, unbroken English, talks with you about deceiving me. He says he did not marry us, and you knew it!

"Oh, you low curs! Look in my face—speak if you dare! I wish the power of God would curse you where you stand!

"Look pallid! Fall back!" she hissed, drawing herself up threateningly. "Well you should shake and lose your color! You are looking on a woman whose soul you have murdered.

"Listen to me," she continued, in that peculiar, low, thrilling voice, "I curse you I and I will never rest until I see you both fill a dishonored grave!

"I saved your life once," she said to Maurice Vanderfelt "I saved it"—with a scornful laugh—"to bring on me dishonor! I'll take it from you! Keep that knowledge with you until your hour comes!"

"Madam, don't let your temper run away with you," the stranger said, making an attempt to break the storm of her wrath, or to face the thing out. "The affair does not justify it—"

"Does not justify it! Oh, Heaven—"

"It is not an unusual thing for women occupy positions such as you hold, as Maurice here will testify. In fact, it is a thing much to be longed for by women with scanty means. I fail to see, judging from appearances, how you have lost anything by it!"

"Lost anything! Merciful God! What more could woman lose?"

"And, by Jove! If you just take time to consider and reason things over, I honestly think you will see that your arrangement with Vanderfelt has been very beneficial to you."

Doubtless the man expressed his honest opinion, for long contact with vice leaves the *roué* unable to see any beauty in purity, as the men who handle decaying hides fail to find any perfume in flowers.

"Oh, Maurice, why did you wrong me so? I loved you, and I was so innocent!" she cried hopelessly, feeling these hardened villains were unable to realize what they had done. "You said you would marry me. You promised faithfully. If you did not want to, why did you not cast me off and let me die, instead of bringing me to this?"

"Don't be a fool, Eva," he said shamefacedly.

When a man can find no excuse for his wrong-doings, he always calls others fools.

"I meant you no harm, and I fail to see that you have been harmed by the transaction in any way."

"But you promised to marry me!"

"You would not come without, and I could not leave you behind to face the mad rage of those country fools," he said in extenuation.

"Oh, my God! It would have been better to leave me bound to a tree at the mercy of a hungry wolf than to have done this!" she cried, holding out her arms appealingly.

"It is only a matter of opinion, Eva. Some would hold, and rightly, that you have been benefited. I have not been unkind to you, and I am ready to do anything for you in the future that I can."

"Will you marry me?" she asked, desperately.

"It is foolish to make such a request. What difference does it make?"

"All the difference in the world. Marry me, only marry me, and I will go away and you shall never see my face again to shame you."

"By Jove, madam! Your face would be your fortune, if you only had proper views on some subjects," the stranger said admiringly.

"I cannot marry, Eva; I never intend to marry," Vanderfelt said, decidedly.

"She's a fool to think of marriage," the stranger said insultingly. "With that face, and that form—"

Even Maurice Vanderfelt's face flushed at the brazen insult, but he made no move to resent it.

With her lips tightly pressed until it crushed out the red, Eva looked at the man she had called husband, and seeing no intention on his part to defend her, she picked up an antique dagger that lay upon a small stand near at hand.

Before they could divine her intention, she rushed at the stranger and stuck the dagger in his breast.

"My God! I am done for," he cried, as the blood spurted forth.

"Woman! What have you done?" cried Vanderfelt, dragging her aside in time to catch his friend. "Bear up, old man, and let me get you out of here and to a doctor," he said encouragingly. "Are you badly hurt?"

"I'm done for!" was the short answer.

"Die!" said Eva, laughing gleefully. "Bleed to death. You stabbed my heart tonight. I have bled to death. But bloodless I shall live to get revenge."

"You are a fiend!" Vanderfelt said, trying to stop the flow of blood with his handkerchief, as he knelt over his friend.

"Yes. Made so by you two. Doesn't his blood flow freely?"

"Have you no pity in your heart?"

"Pity!" she laughed scornfully. "You killed pity tonight. What pity had you, what pity had he, for an innocent, trusting girl? What pity did you have for the soul you were blasting?

"Pity! Yes," she said, in a smooth, cold, cruel voice. "I have so much pity that I want him to last for hours! I have so much pity that I pray he may die by inches, so that his soul may suffer the torments of the damned before he leaves this life."

"Cease your fiendish talk. Go for help!" Vanderfelt commanded.

"Not I," she said quietly, pulling a low chair up close to where her victim lay dying, crimsoning with his warm blood the white fur rug on which he lay. "Who went for help to save my soul—to save my innocence? Let the same help you now."

"He is dying," he said desperately.

"I am glad to hear it. I thank God," she breathed, rapturously.

"Eva, promise me you will not touch him if I go for help."

"Promise, as you promised to marry me?" she asked tauntingly.

"You will hurry his death on if I leave you alone," Vanderfelt said despairingly.

"No, why should I hurry him out of his misery?" she said indifferently. "Run away."

"Bear up, old man; I'll soon bring a doctor," Vanderfelt said, and rushed from the room.

"Don't go—don't leave me!" the stranger cried weakly.

But Vanderfelt was gone.

"How does it feel to be slowly dying?" Eva asked with a smile, holding her dimpled chin in her hand and resting her elbow on her knee as she leaned over her bleeding victim.

"Have mercy!" he gasped.

"Mercy and I are not acquainted," she said softly, as a cat purrs while lazily holding a still living mouse.

"Have you thought of what you will be in a few seconds? A cold, senseless mass of clay," she said, smiling down into his appealing face. "Ah, you groan! Groan more, it is sweet music to my ears. Have you thought what you will suffer, and how you will groan, when your soul faces the Judge that shall pass your sentence? Ah, that cuts deeper than my dagger, doesn't it! Strange, now.

"Probably you had cheated yourself into the happy thought that there is no purgatory. But you realize it now, don't you? You must feel that it yawns for such as you.

"It must be a satisfaction when you remember that damnation for an eternity and the consuming fire that writhes your soul, and still never consumes, has been justly earned.

"Death is coming much nearer," she continued, gloatingly. "Your face wears its seal; your lips are colorless; your pulse grows fainter; even your blood seems to have exhausted its flow. Do you know, I believe the grave is Hell. I believe your mind will live in the grave, and you will be conscious of the worms that slowly—oh, so slowly!—consume your body. Just think what an eternity you will have to lie there, recalling all your evil deeds!

"Ah, you groan fainter! Groan louder. I want to remember that your lost soul went howling into eternity."

"Spare me!" the man pleaded, as large drops of cold sweat stood on his face that was twisted with mental anguish.

"Oh, I can understand why you ask me to spare you. Thoughts of death must be terrorizing even to those who have lived a faultless life. Just think, you are now learning what none have ever come back to explain. Your pulse grows weaker; your heart beats fainter; you feel colder and colder; your breath gets shorter and shorter—ah, you know it, you feel it all; you are conscious that you are dying; your senses reel; you know that you must drift—drift—"

"Vanderfelt—was—more—to—blame," the man uttered in an agonized whisper.

"You cannot save yourself—you cannot save a moment," she continued pitilessly.

"Your dagger—finish me—in God's name—quickly!" he begged in a whisper.

"Never mind; I could not see you escape one pang," she answered with a smile. "Ah, your eyes are glassy and set! Can you still hear me cheering you into death?"

"Monster! Would you torture your victim?" Vanderfelt exclaimed, rushing breathless into the room.

"He is gone," she said with satisfaction.

Maurice Vanderfelt, greatly enraged, caught her by the arm and flung her violently across the room, where she fell to her knees.

"You devil! If you don't leave here instantly, I will hand you over to the police," he said savagely as he bent anxiously over his friend.

"What a nice pair we will make," she said tauntingly as she rose from the floor.

"You are mad! What do you mean?"

"Only this: the police will find two murderers here instead of one."

XV

NOT EVEN MONEY BUYS A REFUGE.

"The price of treason we receive to-day,
Is paid to both of us in evil gold."

"Hell
Has no more fixed and absolute decree;
And Heaven and Hell may meet—yet never we."

CASTING A LOOK OF HATE upon the man she had called husband, and upon the one now lying still and quiet upon the blood-stained fur rug, Eva walked unsteadily away.

Reaching her own room, she began hastily to pack all her belongings.

She stopped for a moment when she heard the bell ring, but returned nervously to her packing as she heard a man admitted.

There was a feverish flush on her cheeks, and a fierce, determined light in her brown eyes, as she took elegant garments from the wardrobe and crushed them into the large trunks, sometimes jumping in on them to make them pack the closer.

"My jewels, too," she thought savagely, going to the dressing-case and taking out the costly ornaments which Maurice Vanderfelt had lavished upon her.

"They are mine," she said bitterly. "They are the price he paid me, and, as they cost me so dearly, I shall not leave them behind."

"Madam—madam! What has happened?" the maid cried apprehensively as she appeared at the door.

She was the only servant that slept in the flat, the others having their rooms on the top story, which was reserved for the servants employed in the house.

"Mr. Vanderfelt's friend is very ill, and I am going away until he recovers," Eva replied hastily, with that self-possession of mind that was one of her chief characteristics.

"I want you to run out and get me a coupe. Tell the driver to bring some one with him, because I want my trunks carried down. Now hurry, Mary, and I'll give you a ring for your speed."

With a mystified look on her face, the maid went out, and Eva heard her close the door.

Then hastily throwing off her silk robe, she proceeded to dress in a black gown, plain but elegant.

Before the maid returned she was ready and waiting impatiently to start.

She had heard the people in the drawing-room move to Maurice Vanderfelt's room, and she wondered in a dazed way why they did not come for her before she escaped.

Even when the maid returned, followed by two men who, without a word, took up the heavy trunks she pointed out and went out again, even then no one made their appearance from the inner room.

Eva stopped at the door as she followed the men out, and looked back at the maid, who stood, stupidly, watching her.

"Here, Mary, I'll make you a present of my ring," she said with a grim smile as she drew off a heavy gold band that Maurice had given her as a wedding ring.

"I don't like that style of wedding rings," she said ironically as the maid hesitated to accept, seeing what it was. "If you do not like it, Mr. Vanderfelt will give you what it's worth in money."

And with a bitter laugh she went on down the stairs. Giving the man on the box orders to drive to a first-class hotel, Eva sunk mentally into a numb, unfeeling state. She had no recollection afterward, except in a dim, uncertain way, of asking for a room, of giving a name and address, and of being told, in a supercilious manner, that it was against the rules of the house to give rooms to women unknown to the proprietors or unaccompanied by men.

Somehow, she did not know whether it was the driver who did it, or whether she knew enough to direct him, she made the rounds of all the reputable hotels she knew of with the same result.

Women were not admitted unless accompanied by men or known personally to the managers.

Stunned at the prospect of finding no place to spend the night, Eva walked out of the last hotel and stood on the sidewalk in an undecided and hesitating way.

"I beg your pardon, miss, but can I be of any assistance?" she heard a voice ask, and turned to see standing by her side a man whose appearance betokened wealth and breeding.

"If you can tell me of a hotel in New York where an unknown woman can spend the night, you will be doing me a favor," she said in a voice of indifference.

"I see you have a carriage. If you will allow me, I will direct the driver and accompany you to a hotel," he said with a smile, which showed his fine white teeth.

"Anything. I am weary and I want a place to rest," she said despondently.

"Are you a stranger?" he asked, getting into the coupe after her and closing the door.

"Yes," she said bitterly, "I am a stranger."

"Did you expect to meet some friends?" he asked curiously.

"No, I have no friends," was the bitter reply.

They stopped at a well-known hotel where she had been refused admittance before.

Leaving her in the waiting room, he returned shortly and took her to the elevator, saying the porter would pay the driver and attend to the trunks. A servant met them at the landing and went on in advance, unlocking the doors and lighting the gas in the rooms that had been engaged.

"I have ordered a light supper to be served. I think you would feel the need of it after traveling, and I should be happy if you will allow me to join you," the man who had befriended her said at her door.

"If it pleases you," she said indifferently.

When supper was served, and the stranger came to her room, he found Eva sitting quietly gazing into the bright fire as if she saw things there that charmed her.

She returned his greetings mechanically, and at his request came forward to the table still with that rapt, absent look upon her lovely face.

She made no effort to eat, and he soon saw that it was useless to urge her.

Just as difficult was it to draw her into conversation, and despairing at last of learning anything definite about the beautiful girl who had so suddenly become his charge, or being able to awaken in her any semblance of interest in his remarks or self, he bade her good night and left the dainty supper almost untasted upon the table.

Eva went to bed, and when she woke again the fire was out and it was daylight.

She lay still, trying to recall the events of the night before.

Her body and mind were tired as if mighty passions had worn them out, and exhausted their energies.

"Everything is done for now," she mused hopelessly. "I have tried to accomplish something, I have done what was right and honest, but Fate is too much for me. Everything conspires to bring me unhappiness. I wonder if there is a God. I cannot see why a God should make my lot such an unhappy one, and make others so blest. Why should Lil Cartwright have a home, wealth and happiness any more than I? Is she better? Has she lived a purer and more honest life? No. It is not that. There is no God, and things happen by chance. I get nothing in life, and she gets all. Even my honor was stolen from me. And now—

"What comes now? The future can give me nothing. It cannot undo the past. I cannot work, I cannot live long on what I have; I have no home or friends. Oh, why am I cursed! Oh, God! Oh, God have you mercy? If there is a God, prove it by lifting me out of this unhappy lot; I am so lonely, so lonely, so wretched, so forsaken!"

She turned her head wearily to the pillow, but no tears moistened her dry, burning eyes.

"I have killed that man," she thought with sudden fear, "and they will hunt me down and hang me. I wonder if it is not better to die now. It would be easier to die now than to hang. It is hard to give life up; not that life gives much, but death is such a dreadful thing. If I only knew what came afterward. The thought of ceasing to exist is maddening, the thought of Hell is terrifying, and thought of the perpetual goodness of Heaven is tiresome. I would rather live and take life as it comes. The very worst is better than death.

"But I must die!" she thought desperately as she crawled out of bed and put on the silken robe which she had brought along in her satchel.

With feverish haste she set to writing a letter on the hotel paper which she found on the table.

It was the story of the rescue of Bill Doty's murderer, with his name and present whereabouts.

"He shall not live!" she said, with bitter hate. "He made me kill that man, and he shall die upon the scaffold for Doty's death, even if I have to lie with my last breath!"

And then she wrote that, while concealed in the wood, she had seen Vanderfelt attack Doty and give him the blows that caused his death.

The letter sealed and addressed, she quietly slid the lock on the door, so that they could come in when all was over.

From the top tray of her trunk she brought forth a little silver-mounted revolver.

She smiled as she looked at it, because Maurice Vanderfelt had bought it and given it to her that, if necessary, she would be able to protect herself in his absence.

"Oh, Heaven, it is hard!" she thought as she looked at the little weapon that was stronger than life.

"Those bits of lead look so small, and yet, the moment I put this to my temple and pull the trigger, that little bit crushes through my head, and I am—dead! Oh, I can't—I can't! But if I can't do this, shall I be able to walk to the scaffold and wait until they hurl me out of existence? No, no! I must do this. Why should I fear? If there is nothing hereafter, I shall not suffer. If there is—I shall not fear to face a God, for if He is all-powerful, it was not the work of a God to make my whole life, despite my endeavors, a cursed existence!"

She lay down on the bed and pulled the trigger, but in her nervousness she allowed the revolver to jerk upright, and the ball grazed her thick, copper-colored hair and embedded itself in the wall.

Before she could pull again the door was hastily opened and closed, and the man who had brought her to the hotel stood over her.

XVI

"MY HEART IS EVER AT YOUR SERVICE."

"Most friendship is feigning."

H E SEIZED THE WEAPON AND wrenched it from her hand.
"What are you doing?" he demanded harshly, his face flushed with excitement.

Before she could reply, a sharp knock came upon the door, which was hastily flung open, and a hall boy entered.

Quick as thought the man whipped a handkerchief from his pocket and began polishing his revolver. He laughed shortly.

"There is nothing the matter," he explained, without waiting to be questioned. "I picked up my pistol to clean it, not knowing that the confounded thing was loaded, and it went off. Order a fire at once!"

"Yes, sir."

The boy did not decline the tip that was thrust into his too willing hand, but retired to give the order to the fireman.

The explanation was an ordinary enough one, but all the matter of fact light died from the man's eyes as he turned again to Eva.

"Don't you know that you are liable to have us both arrested?" he asked savagely,

She sat up, drawing her robe more closely about her. There was a dogged look in the eyes, and a dull flush upon the cheeks, but her manner was surprisingly calm.

"I suppose I ought to thank you, first for saving me from death, and then from arrest. Perhaps I do thank you for the latter, but the former is only a reprieve, and it would have been better had you let me go on."

"What are you talking about?"

"The matter is of no consequence. I meant to kill myself and you interfered. That ends it. Will you give me back that revolver?"

"For you to use again? Certainly not."

"I shouldn't do it again! I shouldn't have the courage. Death is not such a pretty contemplation that one faces it the second time deliberately."

The words were spoken with a certain mechanical force that showed him that she meant them while almost unconscious of having spoken them.

Still, for prudential reasons, he put the deadly toy in his own pocket.

If she intended to remonstrate, her lips were closed by the entrance of the fireman. She watched him as he bent over the grate, her hands lying idly in her lap, her features motionless and emotionless.

The man before her, studying her face, could better have imagined her a stone woman than a creature of flesh and blood.

"She is the most interesting study that I have met in ages," he muttered, rising and ringing for the morning papers. "I wonder who she is, and where she came from."

She did not even turn her head when the boy entered with the papers, but sat staring at the blower after the fireman had gone, as though unconscious of any change.

"Will you have breakfast served here?" the man asked, laying his hand upon her arm.

She lifted her eyes with a slight start.

"If you wish," she replied.

"I will order it while you dress yourself," he said, taking his hat and leaving the room.

She arose in the same listless way and performed her toilet, pausing when she had completed to gaze at herself in the mirror.

Something like a smile, but so bitter a one that it hardly deserved the name, played about her mouth, bringing out a tiny dimple that lay imbedded in the left cheek.

"This is revenge!" she said aloud. "A revenge worthy of Bill Scarlett's daughter. When they hear of this, I know as well what they will say as though I were there listening to them. 'I allers knowed that Ev Scarlett wouldn't never come to no good. She's a chip offen the old block. Murder, is it?'"

The reverie ceased with a shiver.

She sat down, and for a moment leaned her head wearily upon her hand.

She tried to think; but a vision of a scaffold seemed to prevent mental activity.

"I wonder if I shall faint when I see it?" she asked herself. "And I wonder if they would hang me while I am in the faint, or wait until I recover? I think I shall ask that man, if he comes back again."

Her restless eyes began roving over the room, and rested at last upon the papers that were yet unfolded.

She sprung upon them as a half famished wolf does upon prey.

"Suppose he is dead, and they have described me here?" she muttered while she hastily unfolded the sheets and ran her eye rapidly over them column after column.

She found it at last, a short article, without any sensational elements at all, simply stating that Marshall Randall had been accidentally wounded at the bachelor quarters of his friend Maurice Vanderfelt; that it was thought to be serious for a time, but an examination proved it to be a painful but by no means fatal flesh wound.

The article did not say how the accident occurred, and but little else concerning it.

Eva crushed the paper between her hands, threw it upon the floor, and set her small heel upon it, her little white teeth clinched, and something like a snarl upon her lips, that resembled nothing so much as the expression of a hyena in its cage that is being teased.

"He is not dead!" she repeated again and again, as though the greatest evil in life were contained in that thought. "He has wronged me, and I have not killed him. Where is the justice in Heaven or on earth, when I am cheated of my revenge like this! I will have it! I swear that I will live for it alone! What have they made of me? Shall I allow a wrong like that to go unavenged? By Heaven, no! Not if I hang ten thousand times!"

Now that the fear of death was gone, the wild mania for revenge had returned with increased force.

She was no longer the shrinking woman, seeking refuge in suicide, but the same determined one that had leaned above Marshall Randall and taunted him when she believed him to be dying.

Her graceful, tawny Head was lifted, her beautiful eyes blazed with a fire that was entrancing.

So the man who had saved her found her.

"What is the matter?" he asked, his curiosity increasing at each sight of the girl.

She laughed—a little ringing, melodious sound, for all its bitterness.

"Nothing!" she answered. "I was practicing private theatricals. You remind me of the stories Lil Cartwright used to tell to the girls at school when I was a child, about the fairies springing up at unexpected times. Have you ordered breakfast? I am hungry."

"It is being served in the next room. Come!"

She followed him; but for all her affectation of hunger, she ate almost nothing.

She talked, however, with a reckless gayety that, while it aroused his curiosity and astonishment, amused him until he indulged in the most extravagant laughter.

"You are the most extraordinary woman I have ever met," he told her as he pushed his plate away and dipped his fingers in the perfumed water in the finger-bowl. "Beautiful, fascinating, brilliant in repartee, deliciously reckless—there is nothing that gives flavor and zest to life that you are not. Tell me, my dear, who are you? And from when you come?"

She arose from the table, a fierce light glittering in her eyes.

"Who am I?" she repeated. "The existence that was—I mean the woman, the trusting, confiding girl whom my friends, if I ever had any, knew—died with the pistol shot that your hand arrested. What I am to-day is a new creature, with whom I am as yet almost unacquainted. Do you remember the history of the revolt in Heaven when the devil fell? Such a tumult has come into my life, and ended the old existence forever. That is all that I can tell you."

"And you have no friends?"

"I don't know that I understand the word."

"Will you let me teach you its meaning? Will you let me prove to you that there is honesty in the world? There is something about you that attracts me irresistibly, and as no other woman ever has. I know nothing either of your name or your history, and yet I tell you my heart is ever at your service. You need a friend. My dear, may I be that friend?"

He held out his hand, having risen from the table also, and she placed hers in his palm.

She looked into his face without emotion of any kind.

"I am without acquaintances, without knowledge of the city, and will be without funds in a very short time," she said in an indifferent way. "I have not thought of you sufficiently to even know what you look like; yet if you still offer me your friendship, I will accept it, because there is nothing else to do."

His hand closed over hers, and with an expression of extreme satisfaction he drew her toward him.

She did not seem to realize his intention, and therefore, did not resist as he bent over and kissed her lips.

The look of a demon crossed her face.

Her eyes glittered with the fire of burning sulphur; and stepping back a trifle, she brought her open palm against his ear with a force that he would have thought impossible for a woman.

The most stupid astonishment disfigured his face for a moment, but it vanished, and an amused smile took its place.

"I think we understand each other better!" he said ruefully, rubbing the injured member. "The poetry and romance of our friendship is to have something of the thrilling gusto of 'Dante's Inferno.' It tickles my palate—only the next time I think it might be lighter if you took a hammer."

He laughed; but the expression of an enraged animal had not left her countenance.

She turned from him, and entered the room she had left when he told her that breakfast was served.

Once again she gazed at herself in the mirror.

"The beauty of life is gone forever!" she said mechanically. "I live now for revenge alone. I am handsome! I was pure, innocent, trusting—but now—A man did it, and man shall pay the penalty."

The grim expression of the beautiful, pale face was piteous, when one considered its cause.

In her heart was written the old law, "An eye for an eye, and a tooth for a tooth," and the disfiguring letters were printed upon her face:

> "Vengeance is in my heart, death in my hand,
> Blood and revenge are hammering in my head."

XVII

EVA SEES AN OPPORTUNITY.

"If I catch him once upon the hip,
I will feed fat the ancient grudge I beat him."

"The progress of rivers to the ocean is not as rapid as that of a man
to error."

A MONTH LATER EVA WAS COMFORTABLY ensconced in an artistic flat that, to a woman whose heart was more alive to the pleasure of living and less given over to thoughts of revenge, would have been a source of constant delight.

Robert Loran came and went at will. Eva neither requested his presence nor his absence, but in a listless, indifferent way talked to him while he remained and shook hands with him when he left.

That sort of thing was a novelty for a time, but the novelty was wearing off.

Robert Loran was growing tired of it. He was no better acquainted with Eva, if so well, as upon the morning when he had saved her from death.

She made no promise for the future, and, to say the least, the situation was growing monotonous. He was becoming restive under it, like a horse that champs his bit.

But Eva did not observe it. Some plot seemed to be framing in her head, and she was lost to every other consideration.

She was nursing her desire for revenge, hugging it to her heart, and forgetting the man who had asked permission to be her friend.

She had never asked the slightest favor of him, never showed an inclination to know anything of him, either socially or financially.

She accepted his lavish presents with a murmured "Thank you," or, "You are too kind to me," but there was never an offer of a caress, never any intimation that even a little kiss would be tolerated.

At first Loran thought it delightful. It was a new experience to woo a woman so completely in his power; but, when a month had passed and the iceberg that stood between them seemed to be as fresh from the North Pole as ever, the situation seemed to be losing its savor.

His "friendship" was weakening.

Yet perhaps he had done infinitely more than most men of the world would have done, and therefore should not be censured!

He had determined to end it one way or the other, and went there especially for that purpose.

He found her sitting as usual beside the window, her little, dimpled chin resting upon her hand.

Her toilet was, as usual, in delicious taste, and he thought he had never seen her look so lovely as she arose to receive him, contrary to her usual custom.

To his surprise, she gave him both her hands, and smiled as he lifted them to his lips.

"I am glad you have come," she said, pushing him gently toward a chair. "I have something to tell you and a favor to ask."

"Really? You delight me. This is a change indeed! It is granted without the asking!"

"Don't promise until you have heard. Bob, I am tired of living the life of a recluse. I want to know people—I want to go about and see how the rest of womankind live. I am weary of theaters and perpetual *tete-a-tetes*. I want you to bring people here and introduce me to them. Will you do it?"

He looked at her in utter astonishment. If she had asked for the moon, he would have been less surprised.

He gnawed his mustache for a moment in silence. He was intensely embarrassed. "Why, yes, if you really wish it!" he stammered at last. "But you see, Eva—Hang it! I hardly know how to say it—your position and mine are such peculiar ones, that I am at a loss to know what to do. You are living here under my protection, and while our relations have not even been those of brother and sister, I could never convince any of my friends of that fact, and it would place you in a false position. I—"

"I understand that!" she interrupted feverishly. "But it is for me to object to that, not you. You have been very good to me, Bob, and I have never expressed any appreciation. I think I forgot it until to-day, but I shall not do so any more. I seem to have been asleep for the last month, but I am fully awake now. Will you introduce me to people, Bob?"

The man flushed to the very roots of his hair. He thought he understood her, and the novelty of his bondage was returning.

"Yes," he stammered again, seating himself and drawing her upon a couch beside him. "Let me see! What would be the best way to do it? To give you a dinner, I suppose. As well here as elsewhere. Whom shall I ask? Wouldn't you prefer just a few at first?'"

"Yes!"

"Then suppose we say two ladies and two gentlemen? Let me see! I could ask Lettie Steel and Tom Bancroft; then there is Susie Osborne, and I might ask Marshall Randall to meet her."

Eva's hand closed upon his with a power that was painful.

"Marshall Randall!" she ejaculated. "Is he a friend of yours?"

"Yes. Do you know him?"

"Know him!" she cried bitterly. "No! No! But the greatest desire of my life is to know him."

"Why?"

The expression of Robert Loran's face was not good, but Eva did not see it, though she was looking straight at him.

"Because I hate him!" she answered between her set teeth. "Bob, you have been good to me. Add this to your other favors! Bring Marshall Randall here! I promise you that I will be your willing slave ever after if you will do it! Promise me, Bob—promise!"

He gazed at her, first with a frown, then with a smile.

"Was there ever so perverse a creature?" he asked, laughing. "You want to know Randall because you hate him. Are you sure it is not the hatred that precedes love? You know that I should become violently jealous!"

The expression of her face, the loathing, the bitter mockery, was enough. There was no answer required.

"You will bring him?" she asked, her voice not more than a hoarse whisper.

And curiosity prompted him to answer:

"I will!"

In a state of feverish anxiety Eva waited for the night that was to be a memorable one to her. When the evening came she dressed herself in a costume of remarkable beauty—a soft, creamy silk, trimmed with bands of ostrich feathers that touched her marble-like bust caressingly. The copper-colored hair was arranged high and in little, soft, fleecy curls that looked like the abiding place of fairies.

She was a vision of unusual beauty, and so Robert Loran assured her, as she asked his opinion for the first time.

He had been detained and was obliged to hurry to his own apartments and scramble into his dress suit. So he told her as he left her hastily.

He had scarcely reached his room when the bell rang. A moment later the maid threw open the door, announcing:

"Mr. Marshall Randall!"

Eva arose. The vivid color of her cheeks gave evidence of the excitement under which she was laboring, but her manner was as calm as when under the scrutiny of her maid.

She held out her hand with a smile that made her radiant.

"You!" exclaimed Randall, recoiling a step.

She laughed outright.

"Forgive me!" she cried, with an admirable affectation of contrition. "That exclamation was so like the villain in a play that I could not keep from laughing. I wonder if you are going to forgive me for a rather hard thrust I once made in your direction."

"You so utterly surprise me that I scarcely know what to say."

"I dare say. I was an untamed lioness then, but I have learned the world since. You taught me some wholesome truths that were just as well for me to learn then. Suppose we call it quits."

"I am willing, more than willing. Where have you been all this time?"

"Don't ask me"—with a wry face. "Not living on milk and honey, I assure you. When one loves, life is delicious, but when one does not—bah!"

"You are more beautiful than ever!"

"It does not bring happiness. I am weary of barter, utterly sick of sale. I am tired of money; I want love. There"—laughing shortly—"I am speaking to you as if we were old friends."

His face had flushed crimson. "I wish you would let me be your friend, Eva!" he said, unsteadily.

She half turned away, then back again, as though yielding to an irresistible temptation. She put out her hand, and allowed him to press it.

"I have wanted so much to see you," she half whispered, as though the words were wrung from her against her will. "Your face, as I saw it that night upon the rug, I have never forgotten. You will call me a strange creature, half crazy, perhaps; but I can't help it. I despised you then, the greatest desire of my life was to see you die; but the most extraordinary mania has possessed me since. I have lived with but one hope, and those—heavens! What am I saying? You must think me mad!"

"No, no! Go on! I pray that you will. Eva, you asked me to forgive you for what you did to me. You did right. Had you killed me, I surely would have deserved it. Can you forget it? Can you forget that we ever met before, and let our acquaintance date from tonight?"

"Not quite that," she answered, with a pretty shiver. "There are some things that will live forever in one's memory in spite of one. The recollection of your face could never die. As I saw it then, it bears the strongest fascination for me. I am not like others. There is something in my nature that will not answer to the commonplace. I think that I—like you now, because I once so thoroughly hated you."

She had drawn nearer to him, and the perfume of her breath touched his throat. He was about to speak, his eyes were blazing with a passionate light, when a ring at the bell interrupted.

With an upward glance of the eyes that set every drop of blood in his body on fire, she took her hand from him gently and hastily left the room.

Scarcely able to control herself, she rushed without knocking into Loran's room. It was her first appearance there, and he was greatly surprised.

"Your guests are arriving!" she cried excitedly. "You must go at once."

Before he could speak she had gone again, and had locked herself in her own chamber. She stood before the mirror, a wild light of laughter in her eyes.

"I shall not fail," she whispered to the image it reflected. "Oh, how sweet is revenge! There shall be no limit to mine. That fool believed me. I can work upon his vanity, and succeed beyond my expectations. My hour is at hand. There is, after all, something to thank God for."

The curl of her lip made her face almost ugly, but she did not see it.

With head held royally erect, she returned again to the conflict.

XVIII

THE FIRST SKIRMISH IN THE BATTLE OF REVENGE.

"Where most sweets are, there lies a snake.
Kisses and favors are sweet things."

"Like Dead Sea fruit that tempts the eye,
But turns to ashes on the lips."

EVA WAS RADIANT. NEVER, SINCE that fated breakfast that he remembered so well, had Robert Loran seen her in the humor that seemed to possess her.

She jested with that same reckless *abandon* that had so fascinated him at that time. There was nothing bold in her conduct, nothing with which Loran could find the slightest fault, but there was luxuriance, perceptible warmth, an irresistible attraction that no man could withstand.

Even the great beauty of her face and form sunk into utter insignificance when compared with the witchery of her manner.

Marshall Randall sat dumb. He was a man usually of quick perceptions and ready wit. Never at a loss for an answer that would stamp him at once any opponent's equal in a war of words. But beside that dainty, cool woman, with her remarkable flow of spirits, he felt dull and heavy, incapable of remark or of any move. He desired simply to sit and watch her with something of the same sensation that one feels in the first effect of hypnotism.

Occasionally she leaned toward him, and the soft breath intoxicated him more than the really excellent Chambertin, with which his glass was filled to the brim.

Loran looked on with something very like jealousy tugging at his heart.

There was nothing that really justified it, but several times he found himself repeating the most uncomfortable mental question:

"Is that woman using me as a cat's paw?"

But he put it from him as unworthy of himself. Had she ever done anything that indicated a desire of that kind? Never! And yet he watched her!

He was leaning over one of the young ladies in a most cavalier manner, but never losing a tone of Eva's voice as later they were in the parlor, Eva at the piano running her fingers lightly over the keys while she talked in a desultory way with Randall, allowing her eyes to say more than her tongue could do.

"Vanderfelt must have been mad!" Randall muttered heavily, more to himself than to her.

The fingers struck the keys with a discordant sound, the full lips paled for a moment, but it was only for a moment. She leaned slightly toward him.

"I beg that you will not speak of him!" she said, with a little gesture of disgust. "There is nothing that one dislikes to remember so much as an occasion upon which one has acted the fool. There is but one thing that makes the memory of Maurice Vanderfelt tolerable to me."

"And that is—"

She lifted her eyes and allowed them to rest upon his curiously for a single instant, and then they were lowered, while a delicious flush dyed the round cheeks.

"Some time in the future that the present promises, I will tell you!" she answered, so low that the words barely reached him.

His face crimsoned, then paled. He was but a man. He saw no reason why she should care to deceive him. When it came to a question of money, he felt sure that she knew that Loran and had fifty dollars to his one.

He could not see that the cry of her untutored heart for vengeance was forcing her into a course that her innate virtue scorned.

"Do you know that you are maddening me?" he cried passionately. "I think my nature and yours must be identical. That night the expression of your face, as you bent above that rug, appeared to me to be that of a fiend, now it seems that of a siren."

"But they destroyed while they attracted!"

"The illusion will be complete if you fail to listen to me. I—"

She arose hastily, her manner indicating the greatest agitation. She knew well that he had meant to make a declaration of love to her; she knew that the fascination she meant to exert was complete; but she did not intend to allow him to speak then. She wanted to wait until the chain was stronger—she wanted to know that the end of the noose was in her hand by which she could surely lead him to destruction!

There was no one to speak a word of warning to Eva Scarlett, no one to tell her that her nervous hand had closed over a fate whose horror no woman has yet escaped. She drew it to her as Cleopatra hugged the asp.

"Don't leave me," Randall pleaded. "You must not lift me to Heaven to cast me so quickly into perdition. Let me—"

"Not now! You may come again."

"To-morrow?"

"If you will."

"At what hour? Make it an early one, as I shall cease to live until it comes. Are you a sorceress, that you can so completely bewitch one?"

"No," she answered, with a thrill in her voice that set his heart on fire. "I am a woman who loves."

She walked away from him with an unsteady step, entering the library at the rear of the room. He followed her.

"You have maddened me," he whispered, clasping her waist with his arm, and leaning over her until his hot breath touched her bare throat. "You must listen to me! I love you!"

How she prevented herself from strangling him was ever after a mystery. She loathed him with a cold hatred that was startling, yet there was a warm smile upon her lips as she turned to him.

"Yet, until tonight you hated me! No—no! You must prove it. You must prove it so that it will be impossible for me to doubt. You think me pretty, perhaps; the situation is romantic; it appeals to the love of conquest in us all, but it is not yet that giving up of heart and soul, that yielding of self, of life, even of honor that I must have! My nature is absorbent. I give a world of passionate adoration, I must receive even more. Ah!"—with an upward motion of the round, perfect arms—"what is there in life but love, warm, delicious, palpitating love! Neither gold, nor fame, nor social glory can compare with it. This life is all we know. Why not live it to its fullest?"

Her eyes glowed, her face flushed, her voice trembled with the fire of her speech.

Randall would have given all he possessed to have kissed her lips at that moment, but she pushed him from her with a laugh that would have completed his subjugation had it not been complete before.

"Wait!" she whispered, placing a chair between them, but leaning toward him temptingly. "A man never appreciates what he wins too easily. There is as much in anticipation as in realization. Come to-morrow."

"You have not named the hour."

"Twelve."

"No, eleven. Have some pity upon my impatience!"

"I may serve you as I did once before."

There was a smile upon her lips that belied her words, and he laughed aloud.

"I should welcome even that from your hands, my Circe, my Psyche. I am willing to resign life or the world for your sake as you may desire, my Cleopatra!"

"Too much fire burns itself out."

"But it burns out all around it as it dies. A sudden fire is always the most destructive, being beyond control before it is discovered. I—"

"Hush! I will listen to nothing more to-night. At eleven to-morrow."

"You will give me one kiss to live upon until then?"

"Not one! I must know first that there is no chance that you can ever or will ever change. With me this is life or death."

There was a passionate earnestness in her tone that stamped her words with truth. But, as she intended he should, he misconstrued them.

She left him before he could speak again.

"Eva, when is this nonsense between us to end?" Loran asked when they had been left alone.

She raised her eyes coldly. "You asked me to allow you to be my friend, did you not?" she interrogated coolly. "There was never any promise of anything but friendship between us. Goodnight, Bob. I'm sleepy."

She stifled a yawn and left him, locking herself in her own room.

There was not the slightest change in her countenance save a compression of the lips as she undressed herself and went to bed.

"I shall win!" she muttered as her head touched the pillow. "The sun of my day is rising. Now, you who have injured me, beware! I can scarcely wait for the morning!"

XIX

THE QUARREL.

"For I am the only one of my friends that I can rely upon."

"Defend me from my friends; I can defend myself from my enemies."

"YOU ARE TRIFLING WITH ME!"

The expression of Marshall Randall's face was fierce as he stood before Eva the following day, taking leave of her.

Their interview had been one of promises—promises of passionate affection on her part, and of lifelong devotion upon his.

If she was over-acting, he was too blinded by his infatuation to see it.

He had wondered a thousand times if there was ever a situation so romantic as the one in which he found himself placed. But he remembered her ingenuousness upon the occasion when he had performed that false ceremony between her and Vanderfelt, and could not bring himself to believe that she could be anything but truth itself.

And she understood it all as well as though she were dictating his thoughts. She had laughed at his impatience to call again as he was leaving, which called forth his exclamation.

"I swear to you that there was never a woman in this world further from trifling than I am!" she replied with covert meaning.

He crushed her hand in his with a force that hurt her. "Keep that oath," he whispered, "and there is nothing that I will not be to you. In one short hour you won my heart and soul. I cannot understand it myself! I seem to have resigned all to you. It is the strangest thing, under the circumstances, that ever happened to man, but I am your most willing slave! Eva, if you should deceive me, I believe that I should kill you!"

She laughed again softly. "It is the will of Heaven," she said, believing that her own words were true.

"My own!" He endeavored to draw her to him, but she eluded him, and stood back with a tantalizing smile upon her lips.

"Not yet, my impatient Romeo!" she cried coquettishly. "Remember that I have been deceived once and cannot afford to take chances again. I must know that you love me! I must make no mistake—I must be satisfied."

"And you will not allow me to see you until to-morrow?"

She shook her head in the negative.

"Cruelty in a beautiful woman is adorable! Good-bye, Cleopatra!"

He took her hand and was about to raise it to his lips, when the door opened and Loran entered.

The greeting between the two men was exceedingly cool and decidedly strained, Eva looking on with something like a fiendish amusement.

She had been bitterly wronged by a man, and all men were her legitimate prey. That was her theory, in accordance with the old Mosaic Law.

Randall was not many moments in taking his departure and the door had no sooner closed upon him than Loran turned with a heavy frown upon his face to Eva.

"What was that man doing here?" he asked angrily.

"Calling!" she answered coolly.

"What right had he to do so in my absence?" demanded Loran, his temper rising still higher.

She looked at him curiously, her lip curling with irrepressible scorn.

"In your absence!" she repeated, making no endeavor to conceal her sneer. "Do you take me for a child that is not yet out in society, that I must have a chaperon? You must be mad!"

"Not mad, but disgusted with your ignorance, or your willful deception, whichever it may be. You know perfectly well what I had every right to expect when I brought you to this fiat. I have put up with so much nonsense from you that every man of my acquaintance would laugh in derision if he knew it. Now, in my absence, I find you receiving other men. I tell you that I have been used as a cat's paw just as long as I will submit to it!"

He paused and looked at her. She was white to the lips, but her hands did not even tremble as they rested upon her lap, as she sat in the chair that she had taken when Randall made his exit.

"Have you finished?" she asked calmly, a dangerous light flashing in her brown eyes.

"When I tell you that you must make your decision now, I have! Act like a sensible woman, and I am willing to do all I have done and more for you, but this absurdity must end!"

"Bob Loran," she said, with much dignity, "do you remember the conversation we had in that hotel before I came here with you?"

"Yes," he answered sullenly.

"Did I promise to be more to you than I have been?"

"You must have known what I intended!"

"You asked to be my friend. I did not understand you to mean the bitterest enemy that any woman could ever have."

Loran bit his lip for a moment in silence, still his anger did not abate.

"Why did you tell me that you despised Randall?' he asked at last, his blue eyes a sort of greenish hue. "You know that was false!"

"It was true as Heaven! There is no man whom I so thoroughly loathe!"

"Then why were you fawning upon him as I entered?"

There was something so insulting and degrading in the question, as he put it, that all the woman's temper was aflame at once. Her eyes were ablaze with wrath.

"Fawning!" she repeated, the word seeming to issue with a pulsation of the heart.

"Yes!" he cried angrily. "Do you think I do not know what has occurred? You must imagine me to be a most consummate ass! He has been making love to you, even kissing you, and you have been encouraging it! You have played your part very cleverly indeed, but seeing that you cannot pull the wool over my eyes any longer, you are determined to play Randall for all he is worth. I have found the word that applies to your class, my dear Eva. You are nothing but an adventuress!"

Eva threw up her head with a low, savage growl, like that made by a wild animal.

Infuriated with rage, stung to the quick by the insult, she sprung forward, her lips parted by a fierce cry. In that moment she was again Bill Scarlett's daughter, with all the refinements of education forgotten. It was a case of the tamed lioness that turns at a sudden thrust and slays her keeper.

She had forgotten that it was the hand that had fed her, but with the smart of the wound still fresh, she snatched a little gold dagger that she used as a hair-pin from her hair and plunged it, before he could ward off the blow, into his breast.

It dropped from the wound even before Loran had fallen.

White with horror at her own deed, she knelt above him. After all, he had been kind to her, he had not deceived her, for she understood the situation perfectly. Therefore she found no excuse for herself, and sought none.

Even with herself, Eva Scarlett was just!

"I have hurt you!" she exclaimed, her voice trembling over the words.

"You will not believe me when I tell you how sorry I am."

"Not believe you!" he gasped, struggling to his feet and supporting him against the mantel-piece while he pressed his handkerchief above the wound. "No, you infernal tigress, I do not! You think you might have played me for a few days longer, until you had Randall more securely in the toils. But for my own sake I would hand you over to the police, you—"

The odious word that fell from the man's lips would not do to record.

For a single instant the girl looked at him aghast, scarcely comprehending the full meaning of the vile epithet, but when it dawned upon her, the fury of all the demons in Hades could never have equaled hers.

If Eva Scarlett's life was in the balance then, with good upon the one side and evil upon the other, from that moment "good" kicked the beam and "evil" came downward with an awful thud.

With frightful fury, she made a spring in his direction. She felt the strength of a thousand wild beasts and the desire to tear out his very heart.

As she reached him he caught her and hurled her backward, not intending to hurt her, but thinking very little upon the subject.

She struck a heavy antique oak table and fell backward, the force of the fall stunning her.

When she had recovered, her maid was bending over her, and Loran had gone.

She looked about her in a dazed way for a little time, then turned to the girl with her characteristic calmness. "I must have had an attack of vertigo," she said carelessly. "Where is Mr. Loran?"

"I don't know. I thought he was with you, but when I heard the noise of the fall I came in and he had gone. Here is your hair-pin, Miss Scarlett."

"Thank you. It must have dropped from my hair as I fell. Ring for a messenger, Adell, and then you may go out if you wish. I shall not need you."

With lips grimly set, she turned her back upon the girl and walked a trifle unsteadily to her own room.

"It is but another item upon the old score!" she muttered bitterly. "I owe it all to them, to Maurice Vanderfelt and Marshall Randall, and they shall pay for it if I must walk through the mire of every disgrace to be even. Adventuress, am I? Well, be it so! The name is mine. I will learn from words, and that one has taught me my part to the bitter end. Adventuress! Ha, ha! This is my revenge upon Lil Cartwright! But"—and the sneering laugh gave place to an expression of fiercest determination—"everything comes to him who knows how to wait, and my day is at hand!"

XX

THE WORK PROGRESSES.

"Mankind, from Adam, has been women's fools,
Women, from Eve, have been the devil's tools;
Heaven might have spared one torment when we fell,
Not left us women, or not threatened hell."

"YOU ARE QUITE SURE THAT you love me more than any woman in the whole world, my dearest Marshall?"

It was a different flat, with different surroundings and different servants, a different man as master, but in many respects the woman that ruled there was the same one that had presided at Robert Loran's table.

She was gowned more magnificently than she had ever been either as Vanderfelt's wife or the *protégée* of Robert Loran, and yet the man toward whom she leaned with such tender demonstrations of affection, the man who supplied it, was not a wealthy one.

"You are quite sure that no woman has ever touched your heart as you say I have?" she repeated with a little, soft, rippling wave of laughter.

"You know it!" he cried passionately, almost fiercely. "You know that I would sell my soul for you to-morrow if you required it. And yet I seem to be no nearer my object to-day than I was a month ago. Eva, when is this to end?"

"I was to be fully convinced first, you know! Remember how I have been deceived! Listen, Marshall! You have talked about giving your soul for me, you have said that you loved me well enough to die for me, but you have never said yet that you loved me well enough to live for me! You have never mentioned wiping out the wrong you did me by making me an honest wife!"

She was leaning toward him, with one round, bare arm resting upon his knee, her beautiful eyes filled with a passion that had every appearance of reality. Her lips quivered slightly, and an atmosphere of irresistible luxuriance placed about her.

Marshall Randall's brain seemed staggering. He looked at her for a moment as though scarcely comprehending her meaning, and then he pushed her from him and, rising, walked unsteadily to the window.

He stood there for some time gazing resolutely into the street, while she watched the back of his head, as though she could read every thought in his brain through it.

When she thought she had allowed him long enough for reflection, she went to him with that same noiseless tread that characterizes the cat, and standing upon an ottoman, she caught his head between her hands and, drawing it backward, kissed him full upon the lips.

In their month's sojourn together she had never done it before, nor allowed him the slightest liberty, telling him always that she must be satisfied of the truth of his love first.

The act set his blood on fire. He turned and caught her in his arms, his face flushed darkest crimson.

"I sometimes think that you are doing this to repay me for the part I played in that Vanderfelt affair," he said savagely. "That you intend to make me love you until neither honor nor reason are left me, and then cast me away as a punishment. If you did—I should—kill you! You have shown me a way to make sure! I will wipe out the disgrace I helped to put upon you by making you my wife, Eva!"

He held her from him and gazed into the lovely face savagely, as though some evil fate had threatened to take her from him, and so crushing her head backward between the palms of his hands, he kissed her again and again upon the lips, as though he would draw the very soul from her body.

Breathless, half overcome by the suffocating attack he had made upon her, Eva pushed him from her with a short laugh that was soft as the gentle purring of a kitten.

"Monster!" she ejaculated playfully. "Would you eat me?"

"If I could I would, that I might be sure that no other eyes than mine would ever rest upon your face. Oh, Eva, how passionately I adore you! If it were for this that you have been waiting, why did you not mention it before? I would have yielded gladly!"

"Yet you hesitated when I asked."

She said the words looking at him with an arch sweetness that to the infatuated man was maddening. He colored, but reached out his hand and drew her to him as he answered:

"We have all some little thought of the world, my Cleopatra! Forgive me! The hesitation was but momentary. In that single, little instant I saw what a bleak, barren waste life would be without you. Why, my darling, I would commit robbery, or even murder for your sake! I love you—I love you! I wish that I might continue repeating the words forever, if they could but make you understand. Now that we have decided upon it, I am eager that it should be over. Eva, when will you be my wife?"

She laughed again, so softly that it sounded like the tinkling of little silver bells.

"See how generous I can be!" She murmured, passing her hand across his face with tender pride in his love. "Think how I must love you, Marshall, when I have the strength to refuse. Do you think that I will allow you to commit such a blunder as that? You are one of the world's petted darlings. You are of the blood they call blue, and I could never bear to know that I had in any way injured you, my dearest. You say that I am cold. Ah! Marshall, perhaps I have injured you in allowing you to love me, but it was a temptation that I could not resist, dear. I loved you—I loved you so that it seemed to me that every desire in life was encompassed in the one thought of winning your love. I have done it, and in the doing I realize that I have wronged you. But it is not too late, Marshall. I will not allow you to commit a social suicide for my sake, my dearest. Perhaps I have not done just as I should in all things, but you know that, in spite of appearances, I am innocent. I was never anything more to Bob Loran than I have been to you, and I never will be to any man. Marshall"—taking his face between her hands and drawing it down upon a level with, her own—"I wonder if you suspect what I am going to say to you, dear?"

She had become very serious, her countenance drawn as though in pain. Her little white teeth were buried in her under lip, as though endeavoring to force back the tears that would trickle through the dainty eyelids.

Seizing her by the shoulders roughly, he pushed her into a chair and knelt before her, still holding her firmly, his brows drawn into a thick line across his forehead.

"I am afraid I do," he exclaimed huskily. "It is some rot about believing it to be your duty to leave me, but I tell you that you shall not. Do you hear? You shall not! One hour of your society is worth more than the entire world to me. What do I care for the others? I would be glad never to see one of them again, but to live for you, and you alone. Eva, tell me that you will be my wife!"

Any other woman would have feared him, with that expression of fierce passion upon his face, but Eva seemed to revel in it. It showed her the power that she had gained—the power that was to work her sweet revenge that she so earnestly craved. She could scarcely conceal her eagerness.

"You really mean that you would never care to see your friends again if by that you could gain me?" she asked breathlessly.

"A thousand times yes!"

"Then, Marshall, take me away from here. Let us go where no one has ever heard of me and the curse that is upon my life, and I will be your wife. I could not bear it here, dear! I could not endure that any one should look upon you with contempt because of me, as they surely would. But, if you really mean that you would give them all up for me, let us go away together where none will know, and I will make your life one long dream of joy, my darling."

She lingered over the last words, pronouncing them with a delicious languor that seemed to lend them a new meaning.

They thrilled and trembled through his veins like liquid fire.

And yet his face flushed dully.

She watched him as a cat does a mouse, knowing that she had him!

Drops of moisture gradually grew upon his forehead, the veins swelled until they threatened to burst, and still he did not speak!

Then his hands fell away from her lovely, naked shoulders, and he covered his face in her lap, uttering a groan that would have appealed to a heart less hardened by suffering.

"I cannot do it, Eva!" he gasped. "I think it is the bitterness of death to tell you so, but there are reasons why I cannot."

"And you will not tell me what they are?" She said it reproachfully, and in a way that he never suspected that she knew as well as him.

He arose and paced the room rapidly, his breathing audible through stinging unrest. At length he paused before her as a lion does in his walk up and down his narrow cage.

His eyes were blood-shot, his lips pale as death, his hands were clinched as though he were facing his bitterest foe, while drops of icy moisture stood thickly upon his brow.

"Yes, I will tell you and risk all at once," he cried hoarsely. "You believe me to be a rich man. I am not. My love for you has caused me to surround you with the luxury that you see, but it has ruined me. Within a month I have expended upon you every dollar that I possess. I did not realize it until to-day, when I was called upon to settle a bill, and discovered that my account at the bank was already overdrawn. You see now the situation in which I am placed. I love you with all my soul, yet I am powerless to take you away from here, because I am absolutely dependent upon the salary that I receive."

He paused with desperate calm. He did not offer to touch her, but stood there looking down upon her with that strained, hungry sort of expression that would have terrified another woman.

Twenty times in that minute Eva had changed color. Her hands trembled, her lips quivered, her eyes dilated and contracted in a way that made them magnetic as those of a snake.

Slowly, and with the same graceful movement of a serpent, she arose and laid her hand upon his arm, bringing her face so near to his that her hot breath fanned his cheek.

He held his breath, waiting for what was to come! She knew that the whole success of the scheme she had planned lay in the next instant, and her excitement made her thrill and glow like a tropical plant under the influence of a scorching sun.

It seemed to deprive her of voice, and for some time they stood looking at each other with mesmeric influence.

"Marshall," she said at last, not able to force her voice above a whisper, "you know my disposition, you know that I cannot work, you know that I could not live without money—and yet—my darling—my darling—I love you so—that I cannot give—you up! Why should others have all, and we nothing? How sweet—how sweet it would be—if we—"

"Hush!" he cried huskily. "You are maddening me!"

"I cannot hush!" she went on, feverishly. "It is wrong, I know, but so many other things are wrong that we do also. What can it matter, Marshall? They are rich, and coming a little from each one can make no difference to any. Others have done the same thing, and have taken their places afterward in society. Marshall, you are the cashier of that bank, are you not? It would be so easy, so easy! And, oh, my darling, my love, how happy we could be together! You need not work then at all! Day and night we could be together, living in each others' arms, and happy, happy, happy! You do not love me, Marshall!"

He crushed her to him with a mad force that caused her to cry out.

"Not love you!" he gasped hoarsely. "Not love you! I worship you! I would gladly welcome eternal torment, if it brought me you!"

"And yet knowing how to win me, you will not!"

"It would but separate us. I should be detected and thrown into prison. And then I dare not think what would follow."

"Why need you be detected?" she cried excitedly. "Look at the number of men who have done the same thing, and live in luxury and happiness to-day! Canada is not so far but that we could reach it in safety."

Unable to stand longer, Marshall Randall sunk upon a chair.

Eva knew well enough from his manner that that was not the first time that such a thought had occurred to him. It would have come to him with greater horror, and she saw clearly that it was not horror he felt at the act so much as fear.

She sat down beside him, and drew his throbbing head over until it rested upon her bosom.

"Sweetheart," she whispered, "cannot you risk so much for me?"

Once again she pressed her lips upon his in a long dream of ecstasy. He staggered from under it, and drawing her up in front of him, held her where the light fell full upon her face.

"You swear that you will go with, me?" he asked hoarsely. "You swear that you will be my wife?"

For answer, she lifted herself and kissed him once again.

He waited for nothing further. His blood was on fire, his pulses thrilled until he seemed to be going mad. He snatched up his hat, and straining her to his bosom yet again, he dashed out of the house without even an overcoat.

Eva listened until she heard the front door slam behind him; then throwing back her head, she laughed until, from sheer exhaustion, she sunk into a chair.

"At last! At last!" she cried with desperate glee. "You made me an outcast, Marshall Randall! I shall wipe out my score with you this night! It has come sooner even than I hoped for, but Heaven is just after all. You have branded me as a creature lost to virtue. I have branded you as a thief! It is even it is even! If had made you a murderer, it would have been less so. It is honor for honor—honor for honor! This is the first. Oh, Maurice Vanderfelt, your turn is yet to come! This is but the first chapter in the book of my revenge, and, oh, how sweet it is! I must get into the air, or I believe that I shall suffocate under excess of happiness. God, Thou art good! Thou art good!"

XXI

FATE.

"No sooner met, but they looked; no sooner looked, but they loved; no sooner loved, but they sighed; no sooner sighed, but they asked one another the reason."

UNSTEADY FROM HER EXCITEMENT, EVA arose, snatched up a hat and wrap from a chair where she had thrown them on her return from a drive that afternoon, and without even a glance into the mirror, she rushed down the stairs and out into the street.

The wrap fell about her so that it concealed the richness of her gown, but had it not she would have been none the wiser, for she had utterly forgotten it.

Once in the night air, she flung up her head as though with the desire to allow all the cool air possible entrance into her lungs. The realization that her hour of triumph over one of those who had injured her had come was almost too much for her. She seemed to be in a perfect frenzy of joy!

She did not notice in what direction she was going, nor did she care, but went on swiftly, unconscious that she was followed by a noiseless step, while ever and anon a grimy hand was extended as though the owner could wait no longer to seize the sparkling diamonds that hung from the dainty ears.

It was a hideous face, the one that dogged her steps so closely, a face that betokened ungovernable passions as well as greed, and, as suddenly she turned around, attracted by that something that no man has ever yet successfully analyzed, and caught sight of him, a low, terrified cry fell from her lips.

Quicker than thought, his hand was clapped over her mouth, and in a low, hoarse voice he said:

"Make no outcry and I will not hurt you; but even speak, and I will kill you! Quick! Give me those diamonds!"

But Bill Scarlett's daughter was not easily overwhelmed. With unexpected force she wrenched herself from his hand, and delivered him a blow that almost staggered him, then gathering her skirts in her hands, she fled down the street, crying for help.

With a hideous oath, the man sprung after her. But Eva had not lived the greater part of her life in the woods for nothing. On she went like a frightened doe; but the man was gaining upon her.

It was in the very heart of the city, yet not a policeman was in sight, as is usually the case when one is needed.

He was almost upon her when the door of one of the elegant residences opened, and a man with a cigar between his lips came out.

She stopped and cried out imploringly:

"Oh, sir, I beg that you will help me! That scoundrel is trying to rob me!"

Short of breath from her rapid run, she could get no further.

But more was not necessary. The gentleman sprung down the steps; but, even before he had reached the street, the man turned a corner, and a moment later was lost to sight.

With chivalric interest, the latest arrival on the scene took Eva's hand.

"I am afraid he has given you a terrible fright," he said gently. "I should have liked to have caught him and given him the thrashing he so richly deserves. There is never an officer near when one is wanted. May I not see you home? It is rather dangerous for a lady to be alone on the street at this hour, and—pardon me—in the costume that you wear. I think that you know you may trust me."

It required but a glance into the dark, handsome face for her to recognize that fact.

Somehow in that single moment, a desire stronger than life itself seemed to seize her for his respect! Above all else on earth she wanted it!

She did not stop to analyze the feeling, she only knew that it possessed her to a suffocating extent. She must have the respect of this one man, cost what it might!

"I am afraid it would be giving you too much trouble," she stammered. "It was very foolish of me to come out alone, but—my maid was taken ill, and I did not think! I was returning from the drug-store when that man saw me. It was my ear-rings I believe that attracted him. He seized me, but I broke away from him and ran, Heaven knows in what direction. I dropped the bottle, and I think that is all!"

She was trembling, not so much from fright as nervousness at his presence.

With the inborn courtesy of a gentleman he bowed.

"You will not refuse to let me see you home!" he said. "I should not like to know that you were risking another attack from a villain like that. We can call at another druggist's on our way."

"You are quite sure that it will not inconvenience you?"

"Quite sure!" with a genial smile. "You must not risk going into the street at this hour again, even for so humane a purpose as bringing comfort to your maid."

"There was no one else to do it," she answered naively. "I live in a flat, and my maid is the only one of the servants that sleeps there. She and I unfortunately are alone."

"Indeed! I suppose I am very old-fashioned in my ideas, but that seems such a dreadfully dangerous thing to do, particularly for a woman—like you. You will have to tell me the street and number, that I may know how to direct you."

She gave it without hesitation, and as they walked along chatting in a pleasant way, they came to a pharmacy and entered.

Under the brilliant light, after she had given her order, Eva had an opportunity to see her rescuer more clearly.

Every line of his ensemble gave evidence of wealth and breeding. He was the gentleman of culture, from the crown of his high silk hat to the toe of his polished boot.

His face was dark and poetical in its beauty, his eyes velvety in their duskiness, his lips shaded by a mustache that was brilliantly black, with hair the same shade.

A soft crimson in either cheek destroyed anything like swarthiness, and a rare intelligence did away with anything like effeminacy.

They looked at each other, and a vivid scarlet rushed over each face as both pairs of eyes were dropped.

How it would have told the story to an observer! And how the quickened pulsation of each heart told it to those two themselves!

Eva scarcely remembered taking the package from the man's hand, she only knew that her palm rested upon the sleeve of her rescuer, whose name she did not even know.

Both sighed as they left the light, and then both laughed, a nervous ripple of unrest.

"Why do you sigh?" he asked, looking down upon her. "Shall I call a carriage to take you home?"

"No," she answered softly. "I am not tired."

There was a long pause; then:

"Did you ever think what a curious thing Fate is?" he questioned, half unconscious that he had spoken aloud.

"Yes," she answered gently. "It robs so many lives of even hope, and fills others to overflowing."

A dull misery seemed to throb through her voice, and, irresistibly attracted, the man leaned toward her.

"In which list does yours belong?" he asked. "Forgive me! I am afraid my question was an impertinence!"

"Not at all. Mine is of the former. I am all alone in the world, without a relative, almost without a friend. An unprotected woman is the most to be pitied of anything else in this world. It leaves her open to misinterpretation, and insult. She is shunned like an adventuress!"

"Poor little girl!"

"There! I don't know what possessed me to say that to you, an utter stranger, but—I forgot myself that is all. It is the strangeness of our encounter, I presume. After all, what difference can it make? In five minutes I shall be but a shadow to you, and in ten even that will have vanished forever."

"Never!" he answered, more vehemently than he was aware of. "We spoke of Fate just now. Do you not believe that there was Fate in our meeting?"

"I don't think I understand," she stammered.

"I mean the Fate that comes to every life but once. You will think me foolish, romantic insane, perhaps, but do you remember what Marlowe says in 'Hero and Leander'? 'Who ever loved that loved not at first sight?' Did you never think that the passion that rules the world is the one that is perfect from its inception? It is God-given, and therefore has no need to grow. It is the single feeling that can be traced to no beginning, and has no end.

"It is the nucleus of the soul, the exquisite flowering tree of the heart. For every life there is an affinity, a mate for every soul.

"My soul has recognized its allegiance. Forgive me. It sounds painfully like an insult to say this to you the first time that we have ever met, and under such circumstances, but it seemed to be forced from my lips by a power that is stronger than I. I do not know your name; I do not know whether you are married or single, and yet I know that I love you!"

And Eva, who thought her heart had died upon that hideous night when she had discovered the wrong that Maurice Vanderfelt and Marshall Randall had done to her, knew that she loved this man, whose very name was unknown to her, with the first love of her life.

She knew the reality from her experience with the semblance. She knew there was no mistake here, that her heart belonged to the man beside her, and would through all eternity.

She neither knew nor cared whether he was a scoundrel or a nobleman;

she only knew that she loved him, and with that thought she was satisfied.

"Tell me. Have I offended you past all hope of forgiveness?" he asked in his gently, caressing way.

She shivered as she looked into his face. Perhaps it was a premonition of the hideous heart-ache that was to come.

"I will seem lacking in the finer sense of virtue when I tell you that I am not offended," she answered, with a short, nervous laugh that he thought the most musical he had ever heard.

His face glowed with radiant happiness. "And you will let me see you again?" he whispered eagerly. "You will let me teach you to love me? Perhaps I don't know any of your friends whom I can get to perform a formal introduction between us, but you will overlook that, will you not? I am Roderick Hurdis. Here is my card, and almost anyone can tell you who I am."

That was not necessary. She knew the name perfectly from having read it in the paper, from having heard Vanderfelt and Loran both speak of him as one of the wealthiest and most eagerly sought men of the day.

She knew that his income was large—not that she would have cared if he had been a beggar—she knew that there was no better family in the state, that he was spoken of as a man with a future, and it was not necessary that she should have known more.

"Your name is a perfectly familiar one to me," she said, her hand touching his as she took the proffered card from him. "It is introduction enough. You are an honorable man, a gentleman!"

"And you will allow me to call to-morrow?"

"I will."

"I can scarcely believe in my own good fortune. At home so soon? How I wish the hour was earlier that I might ask you to allow me a few moments more to-night. It seems so hard to let you go from me just as I have found you. You have not told me your name yet."

Her face flushed crimson, and her voice trembled as she answered:

"Eva Scarlett. You must let me go now."

"I suppose so. But promise me first that you will not forget me."

She lifted her eyes and allowed them to rest upon his own.

"That has gone forever beyond my power," she answered softly, and she knew she spoke the truth.

He lifted her little bare hands in uncontrollable rapture, and covered them with passionate kisses that had still no sentiment in them not covered by respect.

"Half an hour ago my life contained nothing beyond ambition, a poor thing to live for, but now it is filled to the brim with the hope of a deathless love. Goodnight my little queen, and the God of love watch over you."

She stood in the shadow and watched the handsome, manly form as he walked down the street; then lifting her head with something very like sorrow contracting her eyes, she ascended the steps and entered her own rooms.

"It has come! It has come!" she whispered to herself as she threw herself into a chair and covered her face with her shaking hands. "Oh, God! If I were only worthy! Only worthy!"

XXII

RANDALL'S RETURN.

"Heat not a furnace for your foe so hot
That it does singe yourself."

"Into the wild abyss, the wary Fiend
Stood on the brink of hell, and looked awhile,
Pond'ring his voyage."

FOR THREE LONG DREARY HOURS Eva sat so.

She had forgotten her revenge, forgotten Randall, forgotten everything save her own weary misery. She had met her master, the man who was to rule the universe for her, and it brought her the full bitter knowledge of her own unworthiness.

And as the memory of what she was, of what was within her grasp, and of what honor told her she must not touch was strongest and bitterest, the door opened stealthily and Randall entered.

He set a bag that he carried down upon the floor, and straightened himself as a man does who has taken too much wine. His cheeks were burning, his hair was disarranged, and his hands trembled violently.

With something like a smile, he recognized Eva and approached her noiselessly. He leaned over, and before she was aware of his presence, he had kissed her upon the mouth.

With a half suppressed cry, she sprung up, and as she saw who it was, drew the back of her hand across her lips viciously.

"How dare you?" she gasped.

"Were you asleep, Eva?" he asked gently. "I am afraid I startled you! But I wanted so much to tell you, darling, that it is all done!"

"What is done?"

"Don't you know? It! Oh, Eva, have you forgotten? The money is ours now, my darling! I thought you would be in your traveling dress by the time I returned. You must go at once, dear, and get it on. It is three o'clock and the train leaves within the hour."

Then it all came back to her.

This was the man that had spoiled her life that had made her unworthy of Roderick Hurdis' love, unfit to be the wife of any honest man.

Every fiber of her passionate nature seemed to swell and glow with bitterest hatred. If she could have condemned him to live a thousand years, suffering the tortures of an agonizing death each moment, the punishment would have seemed to her not enough.

The wonder is that she did not burn him to death with the fire in her eyes.

"Do you mean," she asked quietly, "that you have robbed that bank?"

He flushed yet a darker crimson. "I have taken that which gives me you, my darling!" he answered huskily.

She looked at him a moment, then broke into discordant laughter that rang through the room, peal after peal, until it sounded like the raving of a lunatic.

He stood for some time, not knowing what to do, and then he approached her and endeavored to lay his hand upon her arm.

She leaped aside, the wild laughter ceasing as suddenly as it had begun, and an expression of such hatred took its place as he had never seen upon any human face.

"What is it, Eva?" he gasped. "My darling, you frighten me! It cannot be that you no longer love me!"

"Love you! Love you!" she cried, her voice throbbing with desperate loathing. "And you really believed in that farce—that lie? Love you! Oh, God, if I could but tell you how I despise you! If I had but language strong enough to make you understand how I abhor you! You robbed me of my honor, Marshall Randall, you have made my life a curse too bitter to be borne, and I have made you a thief in exchange for it. I thought the score would stand even, but I see that you still have the best of it, and I but hate you the more for it. Love you! I swore that I would have my revenge—I thought that it would be complete when I saw you as utterly disgraced as I am, but I find that it is not. There is more yet to come; but as cleverly as I have planned this, I will plan that, and you shall be even more degraded than you now are. I want to see you so low that even thieves will turn from you with loathing as I do. A thief! Ha, ha! Marshall Randall, the social darling, a thief!"

The stinging scorn of the words had no power to bring the faintest color to the now marble-like face. He stood like an image carved in stone, seeming hot to be able to understand the full meaning of her words.

"Wait a minute!" he said dully, passing his hand across his eyes as though to convince himself that he was not being deceived by some hideous dream. "I don't seem to be able to catch your meaning. Is it possible that you do not mean to go with me now?"

"That is my intention"—mockingly.

"But the money is all there!"—pointing to the bag upon the floor.

"I know it; but I want neither you nor your money. It was not so difficult a thing—even as I supposed it would be—to convert you into a thief. You fell into the trap so readily that I am almost forced into the belief that you were one long before. I suppose there is no doubt but that they will know who did it as soon as the theft is discovered?"

"Wait! I can't seem to—get it through—my head! Is it possible, Eva, that you do not—love me?"

The memory of that hoarse voice, the sight of those bloodshot eyes, looking shockingly like those of a maddened dog, lived with her ever after.

"I have told you that I hate you! Hate you! Hate you!" she cried, putting more force into the words each time they were repeated. "Can you not comprehend when I tell you that it is part of my revenge for the trick you played me when you performed that mock ceremony between Maurice Vanderfelt and me? You blighted my life, you disgraced me, and you robbed me of my honor! Now I have done the same to you. Can't you understand that?"

It would be an impossible undertaking to describe the man's face as she concluded. It was bloodless, and yet his eyes seemed to contain the reflection of a consuming fire. The perspiration stood upon his face in drops like beads.

Feeling that his legs refused longer to support him, he sat down upon a chair and lifted his wild, haggard eyes to hers with a pleading that was piteous.

"Eva," he said gently, "you are saying that to try me! You cannot mean it! You are trying to make me see what my act to you was like, but I know already, my darling. I can't be sorry that I did it, dear, for if I had not, you might now be Vanderfelt's wife, with no possibility of your ever being mine; and, oh, Eva, that would rob life of all the hope or beauty in it. Tell me, my dearest, that it is but a jest!"

She leaned toward him, her eyes filled with a brutal hatred.

"Look at me and see if there is anything like a jest in my face," she said hoarsely. "See if you cannot read tragedy there instead of farce. I loathe—abhor you! There is no disgrace on all God's earth that I would not put upon you if I only could."

He arose slowly, like one who has suddenly grown old. His face was gray, like that of a man after it has been touched with the kiss of death. The veins in his neck seemed threatening to burst.

"You are a brave woman, Eva, that you dare stand there and tell me that," he said, with a meaning that she could not mistake. "Don't you know that I will never allow you to live, now that your love is no longer mine? Oh, Eva, we might have been so happy! Reconsider, dear! Do you prefer life with me to—death?"

"No! A thousand times—ten thousand times no! Come, death, and welcome! Do you think I am such a fool that I have not prepared for this? My revenge would have lost half its sweetness, for I would have thought you did not care. Marshall Randall, leave this house!"

He looked at her in stupefied astonishment, and then the full force of the blow seemed for the first time to strike him.

Some expression of her face reminded him of the time when she thought she had killed him, and leaned above him with taunts and curses. Then there flashed over him that meeting at Loran's which he had believed to be accidental. He recalled with galling distinctness how she had duped him that night by playing upon his vanity, and how she had played with him since as a cat does a mouse that it knows is in its power beyond hope of escape.

And she, watching him, read his thoughts as easily as she might have done a book.

"Eva," he said, with the calmness of despair, "I hope, for your own sake, that you do not mean what you say. I give you five minutes to take back your words, and if at the end of that time you have not done it, you shall at least be mine in death!"

He uttered the words with a slow, ominous intonation that left no room for doubt as to his meaning them. The expression of his face was pleading, and yet threatening as a fiend's. He seemed to be planning his course of action with a calmness that bordered upon lunacy. His eyes rolled, a crimson light making them hideous.

Still there was not the slightest shadow of fear in her manner. On the contrary, her delight in his suffering seemed to approach ecstasy.

"It is better than I thought!" she cried shrilly. "Do you think your words—your threats—cause me the slightest fear? No! They but show me that my revenge is the more complete! But let me tell you this, Marshall Randall, I have not the remotest idea of dying at your hands. I can kill you without the least fear of the after consequences. The proof is all in my favor! You come here to my flat in the middle of the night, after having robbed a bank, you undertake to force me to be a partner in your crime, and upon my refusal you try to kill me! In self-defense I take your life! Is there a court in the world that would not say that I did right and well?"

He did not reply to her words directly, but finding an opportunity, seized her in his arms and pressed his lips upon hers frantically.

"See!" he cried hoarsely, "I am not even angry after all your bitterness. Sweet, tell me that you do not mean it!"

She dashed her hand across his lips with the fury of a fiend. A diamond solitaire that he had given her cut his mouth until the blood poured. She sprung back, her eyes flashing with the sulphurous light of a devil's.

"Try that again and I will kill you!" she hissed, one hand beneath the folds of her dress, closing upon something that he could not see.

The pleading in his face vanished as if by magic. It was white, torn by the rough winds of an uncontrollable passion.

"You have sealed your own fate!" he cried hoarsely. "I tried to spare you, but you would not let me. The result must be upon your own head. Now God help you!"

He started toward her, but with a sneering smile she deftly placed a chair between them, and drew a little silver-mounted revolver—the same that had so nearly taken her life once before—and held it between them.

He stopped short, the coward in him rising higher than his anger.

A bitter, cruel curl curved his bleeding lip.

"You think that you have won, but I see my way to a greater revenge than any you have ever or could ever plan!" he gasped savagely. "I rather thank you than otherwise for balking my intention to kill you. Listen! You think that you have stamped me as a thief! Unless you make yourself a murderess now, you have not succeeded, and I should like to tell you that murder is not a crime that goes unpunished in this state above all others. I am the cashier of the bank, and as such have the privilege of going in and coming out at all hours without being questioned. I am going back now to return the money! Ha! Ha! You see that you have not played your game quite so well as you thought you had! You have lost, but you have made of me a relentless enemy that knows but too well how to hate! Remember!"

Taking advantage of her momentary stupefaction, he sprung forward and seized the bag, and quicker than a flash was out the door.

Rapid as his action had been, however, it had given her time to recover.

He had scarcely reached the hall than with a hoarse, savage cry she was after him. In the dim light of the hall she saw him scurrying along, the bag tightly grasped in his hand.

It was for this, then, to be robbed of her revenge at the eleventh hour that she had worked and suffered such humiliation! The thought maddened her.

Like a swift ball she seemed to spin through the air, overtaking him as he reached the top of the long flight of stairs, at the bottom of which was a marble floor.

With superhuman force, she planted both hands firmly in his back and, never taking time to contemplate, she hurled him forward.

There was a low, quickly hushed cry, a succession of dull thuds then a silence that was intense.

She listened for a moment, a long, dull, miserable moment, then crept back to the door of her own little parlor.

White and trembling, her maid stood there in her night-gown.

"What in Heaven's name has happened, Miss Scarlett?" she asked, breathlessly.

A cold, bitter, cruel laugh fell from Eva's lips.

"Nothing!" she answered in a hard, sneering way. "Mr. Randall came here drunk. He has fallen down the steps, that's all."

"Shall I not go to his assistance?"

"No!"

"But he may be hurt."

"It will serve him right, curse him! If he is only hurt badly enough to keep him there until morning I shall not quite lose all confidence in God. Go to bed!"

XXIII

A NOCTURNAL VISIT.

"Oh, woman, perfect woman! What distraction
Was meant to mankind when thou west made a devil!
What an inviting hell invented!"

HAVING LEARNED TOO MUCH OF her mistress' character in that brief month to disobey even in the smallest particular, the maid retired, leaving Eva pacing up and down the floor of the small, but really magnificent room.

"If I were only sure that there was no chance of his doing as he threatened and restoring that money before morning, I think I could rest in comparative peace!" she kept muttering as she walked rapidly, her fingers clinched in the palm of her hand. "If there were only something that I might do to make it impossible for him to move before morning. But what—but what? I don't want to either kill or hurt him for my own sake, and yet there seems to be no other way. Hold! I have it"

An expression of positive radiance lighted her face, making it intensely beautiful. Her breath came in quick gasps, her white cheeks became crimson, and her lips trembled with excitement.

With hands that almost refused to perform their office, she seized the hat and wrap that she had worn earlier in the evening, and hastily donned them.

"If I could but find a cab!" she cried, her voice quivering with incalculable excitement. "I must succeed! I must—I must!"

With every nerve upon the *qui vive*, she softly opened the door and went again into the hall.

She paused to listen.

All was still as death.

Waiting no longer, she went on swiftly and silently down the stairs.

At the foot she saw Randall still lying there in the shadow cast by the hall lamp. She was forced to step over him in order to reach the door. She shivered ever so slightly.

"If Heaven will only keep him in that condition until my return!" she muttered, setting her teeth hard.

Noiselessly she opened the great front door, and as noiselessly closed it behind her.

"I was a fool not to think of it sooner," she whispered to herself, drawing her cloak more closely about her. "It may be too late now, but it is worth the trial. Oh, Marshall Randall, if I can but outwit you this time."

Her expression was not that of an angel as she flitted along in the darkness, her ungloved hands clasping and unclasping spasmodically.

Under the dim light of a street lamp she paused and glanced about her. The streets were absolutely deserted. Once more she hurried on, stopping at last before the door of a curious looking building.

It had something of the appearance of the office of a livery stable, save that a large but dim lamp upon either side of the door seemed to guard it like sentinels.

She looked at the huge door a moment, then went up the few steps and pushed it open.

The room exposed was dingy enough, uncarpeted, with a large stove in the rear, the bottom of which seemed to have been used for many moons as a cuspidor without cleaning.

Upon one side, inclosed by a railing, was a desk, behind which a man, dressed in uniform, but half-asleep, sat, lolling back in a revolving chair.

He aroused himself as Eva entered, and half arose.

She approached the desk with nervous excitement. "Are you the man in authority here?" she asked, her voice trembling so that her words were almost unintelligible.

"I am for the present!" he answered. "What has happened?"

"The —— Bank has been robbed! I know where the criminal is. Can you send a man with me to arrest him before he makes his escape?"

"The —— Bank? Impossible!" exclaimed the sergeant, ringing his bell violently nevertheless. "How do you know?"

"The cashier, Marshall Randall, is the guilty man. He has been in love with me, and came to my house tonight with the money, to get me to run away to Canada with him. I refused. He started out of the house, and I think he must have been under the influence of drink, for he fell down the steps. I did not want the people to lose their money, and so I left him lying there and came here to you."

She spoke so rapidly, and with such evidently genuine excitement, that the man did not think of doubting her word.

"Reily," he cried to a man who had just entered, "go at once with this lady, and arrest the man whom she will point out to you! He has robbed the Bank. Be sure that he does not escape."

"Come," cried Eva, unable to control herself but seizing the officer wildly by the arm. "He may be gone already. Do not let us lose a moment!"

While the sergeant was still talking and giving the officer instructions, she had almost dragged him from the room.

The man felt the heat of her hand through his coat sleeve. "You are sure there can be no mistake?" he asked, as she was rushing him along pell-mell.

"There is no possibility of it!" she answered, her throat seeming to close over the words and shut them in. "Don't stop to talk. Hurry!"

She gave him no chance to walk, but still holding his arm with a firm grip, pressed him into a run, urging him to greater speed at each moment.

As they turned the corner, where a perfect view of the house was obtainable, she saw the front door swing noiselessly open. A dim light from the hall rushed into the street telling her that she was not mistaken.

Her grasp upon the policeman's arm tightened:

"It is he!" she whispered, her articulation painful under her excitement. "If you let him escape now, all is lost!"

She dashed forward, dragging the officer after her, confronting Randall as he reached the bottom step.

"There is the thief!" she cried, pointing her finger into his blood-stained face. "See, he has the bag of money with him. Seize him!"

The officer needed no second bidding. As he laid his hand upon Randall's shoulder, the latter saw that resistance would be worse than useless.

He glanced in Eva's direction. No words were necessary to express the threat they contained.

"This is your work!" he said, slowly. "We shall meet again!"

She laughed hoarsely, mockingly.

"Yes, it is my work!" she cried gleefully. "All mine! I thank the good God in heaven that you know it is mine!"

He turned and motioned the officer to lead on, with not another glance in Eva's direction.

And she stood there watching him, the same mocking laugh upon her lips, until he was lost to sight.

XXIV

"YOU HAVE MADE ME THE HAPPIEST OF WOMEN."

"Who trusts himself to women, or to naves,
Should never hazard what he fears to lose."

"Be to her virtues very kind;
Be to her faults a little blind."

EVA HAD NOT QUITE COMPLETED her toilet the following morning when her maid entered, bearing a card. She took it from the girl's hand, a sweet, tremulous smile curving her perfect lips.

She knew well enough, even before she had glanced at it, whose name she would read there. But she could not conquer a thrill of delight as she saw the little black letters, for all that. And aloud she read:

"'Mr. Roderick Hurdis!' Say that I shall be in almost immediately, Sara."

The maid departed with a mere bow, while Eva turned to regard herself critically in the mirror.

"I am handsome!" she muttered, in a way that no one would have ever misconstrued as vanity. "Oh, I am glad—I am glad! It has brought me his love, and yet—and yet I am not worthy—I am not worthy! If I loved him as I ought, I would die rather than put upon him the disgrace that I contemplate. What am I to do?"

She was still looking at herself, but did not see the white-faced reflection that her mirror sent back. A nervous trembling seized her, but with the peculiar force of character that had been hers from birth she put it from her, resolutely calling the truest color again to her cheeks and lips.

"Why should I deny myself every delight in life because Maurice Vanderfelt was a scoundrel? The fault was not mine," she whispered to herself, clinching her hands until the delicate flesh was cut. "I will forget it. But, oh—my God! If he should ever discover the truth of the past, I should die. That will be the end. But I shall have lived."

She threw up her head, with the old, characteristic stag-like motion, summoned a smile to her lips that neither dolt nor sage could ever have seen unmoved, and entered the parlor where Rod Hurdis awaited her.

"I was almost afraid that last night had been a dream too beautiful to be real," he said in a sweet, soft voice as he came forward to meet her. "I have lived in those few moments until now, half in delirium at the luxury of loving, half in terror lest they prove but the fabrication of my own brain. Tell me, have you thought of me at all?"

She lifted her eyes to his for the first time, save a fleeting glance on entering.

"I have not slept for thinking," she answered with charming candor.

Still holding her hands, he drew her to a divan and seated himself beside her, looking into her half-averted face with a hunger that demanded satisfaction.

"I have been comparing myself with Cinderella," she continued with a shy laugh. "I think we were very much alike save, perhaps, the ashes and rags; but I have been just as lonely, just as friendless, just as seemingly helpless, until my fairy god-mother sent me out last night to meet—my prince!"

He lifted her hands and kissed them passionately.

"Sweetest, you open Heaven to me!" he murmured, his eyes sparkling with rapture. "I wonder why it was the will of God that all these precious years should have been lost out of my life. Don't you believe in the creation of affinities? I do! You have been near me for months, perhaps, and yet my meeting with you was the result of accident—at least, what the world would call accident. To me it was foreordained. You believe that, do you not?"

"Yes. It was fate, which is about the same thing. I wonder if you think me weak of heart and principle, that I have made no resistance, and that I have been too quickly won?"

"Can you think it? Is there a character in fiction that we admire so much as Juliet? Would we do so if her counterpart in real life would not be lovable to us? Oh, sweet, it is the very essence of love that causes a woman to forget the coyness of her sex and be passion's slave avowed. I would have your brain revolve about the single thought, your lips but frame the words that tell your love for me. Say it yet again, my pretty one, for I dare not trust to the story that I read in your dear eyes."

She laughed softly. "If life were only made up of moments like these, how beautiful it would be to live!" she answered, the smile ending in a sigh. "I can scarcely believe you are serious when I remember that yesterday you did not know my name, and that even to-day you do not know that the one that I have given you is my own."

"But I am so willing to trust to your truth, your honesty. Do you think that there could dwell anything but honesty in the heart that looks through those eyes? There is a voice that speaks from the heart to the eye that will not be silenced. I know that you are true, I know that you are pure!" He dwelt upon the last word as though that contained the acme of all good, even of all living.

She shivered slightly, and an expression of pain contracted her mouth, but it was but momentary, and in his infatuated state did not even reach him.

Hurdis made no attempt to argue with himself. It did not occur to him that what he was doing was the height of folly, or if it did, he put it from him before the thought had time to injure Eva's cause.

It seemed to him that the greatest good that life or Heaven promised was her love. Perhaps it wasn't what those who have reached the zenith of experience in matters of the heart call love, but the term has been applied since the days when Adam spoke to Eve on the same old subject, and will answer the purpose now. At all events he did not know the difference, consequently no one could.

"I wish that I were a thousand times better and purer, for your sake!" she replied, conquering the remorse in her voice by a violent effort. "I cannot realize that what you have said to me is really true! I think that I must be dreaming and that I will wake to-morrow to discover that my prince is but a myth and Cinderella in her loneliness again."

"Never again, pretty one!" he answered tenderly. "I am an impatient Romeo, as you will but too soon discover. Eva, my love, you will never send me from you now? You will be my own, will you not?"

She hesitated an instant, and her face flushed crimson.

In her early girlhood she had dreamed of a time like that to come, when some man like the one that now sat beside her would ask her that question, meaning that she should be his wife, and that she should have so descended that no man would ever ask her that question now cut her to the quick, for she was hard upon herself, and never dreamed that this one could contemplate an act so mad as that.

After all, what was the use in attempting to resist fate?

She leaned a trifle toward him. "I have not a friend in the world," she replied, a trifle hysterically. "I am alone, unprotected, unhappy. Take me, do with me as you will—I love you!"

The speech appealed to all that was noblest and most manly in his nature. He drew her very closely to him, and something like moisture glittered in his eyes.

"I accept the trust," he answered, not without emotion, "and may God deal with me as I with you!"

She glanced at him in surprise, but did not speak.

"Tell me, sweetest," he whispered, after a long pause, "when will you make my happiness perfect by becoming my wife? Do not let me frighten yon by my impatience, but indeed I cannot wait. Have pity upon me and let it be soon."

She had raised herself, and was looking at him with almost terrified eyes.

"His wife!" she whispered mentally. "Oh, God! I had not dreamed of anything like that! It cannot be true! It cannot!"

She was breathing heavily, but at the critical moment her calmness returned, and she covered her confusion by laughing softly.

"I am afraid you have startled me," she said gently.

"One is not accustomed to such haste and vehemence in this lazy age. Besides, I cannot really believe that you think seriously of so rash an act, having not yet known me twenty-four hours."

"Sweet, look at me! Tell me that you are worthy of an honest man's love."

Her lips trembled, but she forced them to speak calmly. "I never did an intentional, deliberate wrong in my life," she answered slowly, believing that she spoke the truth, for she considered that what she had done to Randall was but just.

"And I believe me. You can find out as much of me as you could know in months by applying to men whose integrity has never been questioned. Why, darling, we might know each other for years and gain no greater knowledge of each other. Let us each trust to the honor of the other, and the fate that has guided us thus far. Tell me, dearest, that you will not refuse my first request."

"You have made me the happiest woman in the whole world."

Half an hour later he left her. She watched him from the window until he had vanished. Then with a low groan indicative of anything but happiness, she sank into a chair and covered her face with her hands.

"Oh, God!" she groaned. "What have I done? What have I done? He trusts me, and, merciful Heaven! How I am deceiving him! Would he think of marrying me if he knew the truth? Never! Never! Yet why should I suffer for the sins of another? I love him—I love him, and I will be *his wife* in spite of the hideous blot that Maurice Vanderfelt and Marshall Randall have put upon my life! Curse them. Oh, curse them both! If I could but make them suffer as I have. And I will—I will! But Rod has done no wrong. I must be his wife. The temptation is too strong for me to resist. He need never know. He never shall know. I can make him happy, and I will. He is rich, handsome, respected by all who know him. He is spoken of by men as the young man of the day, and I shall be his wife. It will be the old revenge that I have sought realized at last. I can go back to the old home; I can see Lil Cartwright and all the rest. Oh, it will be so sweet. So sweet I shall forget all the miserable, recent past and Rod shall never know. There is justice in Heaven after all. I am happy—happy! My revenge is gained upon all save Maurice Vanderfelt, and that will come with time!"

XXV

RANDALL SPEAKS.

"Forgiveness to the injured does belong,
But they ne'er pardon who have done the wrong."

"The more we know, the better we forgive,
Whoe'er feels deeply, feels for all who live."

"MY DEAR SIR, I AM *in the very greatest distress! By the memory of the sincere friendship that you entertained for my dead father, and that you were kind enough to transfer to his unfortunate son, I beg that you will come to me at once. I dislike asking you into such quarters as I shall be forced to receive you in at present, but for the sake of the old and honored name, and of my mother, I entreat that you will not refuse.*

"Yours very truly,
"Marshall Randall."

Very carefully Marshall Randall sealed the note that he had written, and then handed it to the messenger boy that the sergeant of the police station had summoned for him.

"Take it to the address on the back and deliver it, if possible, into the hands of Mr. Knott himself, and then see if there is an answer. Return as quickly as you can."

"All right, sir." The boy darted away, the rusty key grated in the lock, the guard retired, and Marshall Randall was left alone again to pace his narrow cell.

His lips were indrawn between his teeth, his brows drawn to a straight, black ridge. His face was gray and haggard, his expression devilish.

"She has ruined me!" he kept repeating savagely. "Even if I can persuade

Knott not to prosecute me, she has ruined me! The whole thing of how I was found with the money upon me will be blazoned in the afternoon papers, the whole world will know, and my name—upon which there has never been a stain before—will be gone forever. Curse her! Curse her! It is all her work, and I will have the longest, deepest, bitterest revenge that mortal ever took. I will not allow my temper to get the better of me, and cause me to act prematurely. I will wait—wait and plan until failure is impossible. Then I will make her live a life of the most fearful torture that any woman has ever suffered. She is capable of suffering as women rarely are, and she shall have the measure full to overflowing!"

But not one word was whispered above his breath. So deep was he in his own reflections that he did not even hear the foul oaths that were leveled at the prison keepers' heads by those in the cells adjoining his.

There was a "drunk and disorderly" in the next room, yelling and cursing like a madman, but it had no power to arouse Randall. He was still pacing the floor with his hands clasped behind him, thinking and dreaming only of revenge.

As composedly as though the earth were made up of a succession of heavens, and he had met only the angels, the sergeant sat behind his desk, lolling back in the revolving chair, with a half-chewed toothpick between his teeth, when the door opened and the president of the —— Bank entered.

The aristocratic old gentleman was a trifle flurried, very red in the face, and decidedly warm. He walked up to the desk and stood there before the Hercules of the law as though he himself were a culprit.

"Good-morning, sir" exclaimed the sergeant in his *basso profundo* voice. "We sent to your house early this morning, sir, but received word that you had not been there overnight, but would doubtless return the first thing this morning. I suppose you received our message?"

"I received nothing except a note from my cashier, Marshall Randall, asking me to come here at once. In Heaven's name, what does it mean?"

"It means that one of our men arrested him last night for having robbed your bank, and—"

"Marshall Randall robbed—you must be mad!" There was such genuine consternation in the man's tone that no one could have doubted his extreme confidence in his old friend's son.

"It is quite true, sir!" exclaimed the sergeant. "The money was in his possession at the time of his arrest!"

"There must be some mistake! Where is Randall? Take me to him at once, and be sure that you don't let this matter get to the public! I tell you that there is not the slightest foundation for such a thing. The man is as honest as—as—as I am, or you, sir."

"I am afraid it is too late to keep it away from the public now, sir. There was a reporter here on another matter when he was brought in, and of course he will not be slow to pick up such a sensation as that!"

"Confound the reporters! Where is Randall? I want to see him at once!"

"This way, sir!"

The officer led the way to the small cell beneath the station-house, a bare and dingy place that contained nothing but a bad-smelling water-basin and a bench that no man could sleep upon, no matter how tired he might be.

Randall was still walking up and down the cramped quarters, his face more drawn and haggard than ever. He sprung eagerly forward as he recognized his visitor.

"What in Heaven's name are you doing here?" demanded the bank president, with a gesture of extreme disgust. Then, turning to the officer: "Is there not some room in which I can take this gentleman for a few moments conversation?"

"The captain will very likely give you the use of his room. I will inquire, if you like," replied the sergeant.

"Well, I do like. Or rather, I don't like, but it is the best that can be done, I suppose.

"And now," he exclaimed nervously to Randall, when they were both seated in the captain's comfortable room, "what in the name of all that is wonderful has gotten you into this box? You need not tell me that you did not rob the bank, for of course I know that. But what were you doing with that money?"

Randall was silent for a moment, leaning his gray face upon his hand. Then he looked up with a wan smile.

"I thank you, sir, more than I can ever say, for the confidence you have placed in me. But I am afraid I do not deserve it!" he said, with a painful effort. "You cannot imagine what it is to a man like me to tell you this, but honesty compels it"—leaping to his feet and walking rapidly again—"I did take that money; but I was returning with it to the bank when I was arrested!"

"You did—" Mr. Knott seemed to be able to get no further. His jaw fell like that of a man suddenly struck with apoplexy.

Randall paused in his walk and looked at him. "Yes, sir," he said, looking from the banker's face to the carpet and back again. "It is the old story—'A woman tempted me and I did eat!' I am ready to make a clean breast of it all, if you are ready to listen!"

There was something exceedingly repentant, and rather manly, in Randall's manner, and Knott made a gesture of assent.

"The cause that led to my disgrace may seem as weak to you, sir, as the fall itself," he began unsteadily, "but many stronger men than I have fallen before the same fire. I do not say that to palliate the wrong that I have done, but because I am infinitely ashamed! I fell madly in love with a woman! For a reason which I need not detail to you now, sir, she hated me, though I never even suspected such a thing, and in revenge for a fancied wrong that I had done her, and of which I was in reality innocent, she determined to make me suffer. God! How she has succeeded! Well, sir, as I have told you, I became madly infatuated with her, blindly in love with her, to such an extent that I ruined myself to give her the luxury that she demanded. At last, in an insane moment, I allowed her to propose to me a marriage, which seemed to me my only hope of holding her, as every dollar that I had saved was gone and I was already head over heels in debt. In the mosy wily way she led to the proposal. God! What a fool I must have been not to have seen it then as plainly as I see it now! Then, when it was made, she declared that she could not and would not do me the wrong to marry me here in this town where she was known, and where the errors of her past would reflect such disgrace upon me! Fawning upon me, caressing me, making me believe that life would be valueless without her, and that anything was welcome so long as she was by my side, she proposed to me that we leave the country together. Then I told her the truth—that I had not a dollar in the world to go upon! That confession was what the she-devil had been playing for! Then she suggested to me that infernal scheme of robbing the bank. I don't know how to tell you, sir, in order to make you understand, for I cannot realize myself how it was done, but the fear of losing her was stronger upon me than the fear of—perdition! In that moment I went stark mad. I forgot honor, forgot my noble old name, forgot my poor old mother, and everything else in this world save just that one diabolical fiend, and listening to her voice, I did—what you know! I realize how flat it all sounds, and that any honest man must think that it required but little to make me a thief, but I cannot describe that temptation to you, sir. It was irresistible! Well," wiping the great drops of perspiration from his brow, "I got the money and went back to her, thinking of nothing but that my sin had bought me her companionship for life and—I couldn't tell you of the scene that followed, sir. Why I did not add murder to my other crime I cannot now understand. Perhaps it was because even under all I loved her too well to do her any harm. Then I told her that her plot had failed. That, as an officer in the bank, I could return the money and no one be any the wiser. I started to do that, but driven desperate by her failure to gain the revenge she had planned, she threw herself upon me as I started down the stairs. I lost my footing and fell. I must have lost consciousness, for I remember nothing further until I came to myself and found myself lying at the foot of the stairs. I got up to go on to the bank, but as I reached the front door she met me with an officer and had me arrested. That is all I have to say, sir. I know that I deserve the punishment that law reserves for cases such as this, but if for my father's sake, and that of the old mother whose heart it will break to know that her son is a criminal, you can find some excuse for me, I can assure you that the lesson has been sufficient! There need be no cause for fear in the future!"

He really looked very manly and extremely penitent as he stood there, a flush of shame dying his cheeks.

And so Granville Knott thought as he looked up from the impatient tattoo he was beating upon the carpet.

He had scarcely heard the words but was thinking of a time in his own life, when, while he would never have committed a robbery for her sake—well, there was a folly that had never come to the world's ears, and "one touch of nature" will generate more sympathy than anything else.

He gnawed his lips for some moments in absolute silence, then when he spoke there was a tremor in his voice:

"I loved your father!"

That was all, but Randall knew the case was won.

"It may be an unmanly thing in me to appeal to that remembrance, sir," he said gently, "in a case like this, but—I don't know what to say! Forgive the wrong, sir, and my everlasting gratitude, my most faithful service shall be yours forever."

And then the answer came, different from what he had expected, but better than he deserved:

"I forgive you with all my heart, Randall. I will not prosecute you. I will get you out of here just as quickly as possible, but I cannot take you back at the bank. That would be out of the question! I should be forced to speak of the matter to the directors, and they would not have it even if I would. The affair has already gone to the papers, but we will hush it up and make as little fuss out of it as is possible—for your father's sake. That is all that I can do, but I will do that much cheerfully."

With a groan Randall sunk into a chair, knowing that the disgrace would be as great as though he served his time in the penitentiary, but knowing that the decree was fixed as fate.

And he owed it all to Eva.

XXVI

THE CURIOUS REVOLUTIONS OF LIFE.

"Senseless, and deformed,
Convulsive anger storms at large; or, pale
And silent settles into fell revenge."

AS IN A DREAM, A sweet, blissful dream that any words might disturb and rudely bruise, Eva passed the month that followed.

She had read with something like a shiver of fear the story of the bank robbery as told in the papers, but after that first headline and column of thrilling sensation, there was little more told, and the matter dropped, at least so far as the public was concerned.

She learned, however, by adroitly questioning Rod Hurdis, that Randall had lost his position; and that he was throwing himself away at a rate that was, seldom equaled.

"I saw him on the street to-day," he said in one of these conversations, "and I don't believe that his own mother would have recognized him. If you ever saw him you will remember what an exceedingly natty fellow he was. His clothing was always exactly correct in shape and perfectly brushed; his hats, boots, etc., flawless; but to-day he was a sight and no mistake. He was disgustingly drunk, his clothes torn and dusty, and his face dirty. Oh, I can't tell you; but it's a confounded shame that such a thing should happen to a man that promised as much as Randall did."

And for some time after that a nameless fear hovered over Eva.

Sometimes it amounted almost to torture, but with a resolution born of despair, she put it from her and hugged her love and her happiness closely to a heart that would ache for all its joyousness and hope.

But gradually it left her! What fear will not fade with time? Randall had not attempted to find her or molest her in any way, and she had come to the conclusion that he thought his punishment but just, and that he did not intend to do so.

With the days that passed, her love for Rod Hurdis became almost a mania.

She loved him with all the strength of her remarkable nature, shivering at the slightest blast that chilled him, tortured constantly lest he discover something of her life that had been.

And she would have sold the blood from her heart, drop by drop, before she would have had him know that!

But she was beginning to lose fear of that also now, and was living in a Heaven of her own creation, with Rod Hurdis as the god.

What mortal was never punished for a fault like that?

And to-day, in her own room, she was dressing for a ceremony! A ceremony that was to make her an honest wife after all her trials and heart-aches.

She had sold the most of her jewels to purchase the dainty, beautiful trousseau, but Hurdis was not aware of that, nor did she intend that he should be.

How happy she was! And yet, into that strange, contradictory head of hers, there came to her, even at that supreme moment, the thought that she would secure her old revenge, the one so long sought, upon Lil Cartwright!

But there was not much time for indulging in reflections such as those.

Her maid entered. "Miss Scarlett," she said, "Mr. Hurdis is waiting!"

Stopping only to gather up her gloves and bouquet, Eva passed from the room.

It was to be a very simple, quiet wedding; just a drive to the church, a few moments in the clergyman's presence, with his wife and Eva's maid as witnesses, a brief visit to the vestry where Eva was to write her name as Scarlett for the last time, and that was all!

It seemed to Eva that it was all done in a whirl! She realized nothing until it was over, even forgetting to be frightened when the clergyman paused after that ominous question: "If anyone knows a reason why this marriage should not take place," etc.

Perhaps she did not even hear it, but Hurdis' voice aroused her in the vestry.

"My sweetheart is my wife now! Are you glad, darling?" he whispered, so low that the words reached her alone.

She lifted her eyes half filled with tears. "Will you ever regret it, Rod?" she asked, wistfully.

"Never, love!" he answered gently. "My wife is pure and true! All is expressed in those words, there is nothing without them!"

That was all, but a chill passed over her, leaving her pale as death. She adored him, but there was little gratified vanity felt at that moment. Her lips were cold as ice as he bent his bead and kissed her.

She responded to the clergyman's congratulations with some appropriate words, and a smile as gentle as an infant's.

Her volatile nature was changing again. She was becoming the Eva of old.

As they were passing from the church, she noticed a man, ragged, unkept, smelling nauseatingly of whisky, leaning against a lamp-post near the carriage door.

Hurdis turned to say something to the coach-man and the wretch doffed his hat. Eva could scarcely control an outcry as she recognized him.

It was Marshall Randall, but the expression upon his face she had never seen there before, not even when she had told him that his crime had been committed for nothing. The sneer upon his lips was horrible.

While Hurdis' back was turned, he slipped a dirty note into the gloved hand that dared not refuse to receive it.

She thrust it into her pocket with a low groan that attracted Hurdis' attention.

"What is it?" he asked tenderly, placing her in the carriage.

"I pinched my hand with the door," she answered with a wan, nervous smile. "Do hurry! I—it has all upset me!"

He laughed carelessly and pinched her cheek. "Do you know," he said softly, "that I am rather glad Dr. Featherston could only give us this hour, which is quite two before our train leaves for California? We can have that much time alone before we must parade ourselves before strangers, and my bonnie bride will have an opportunity of becoming—well, acquainted with me, so to speak. You are too timid, my dearest."

She tried to laugh, but did not reply, and in rather an embarrassing silence they rode homeward.

"You will excuse me for a moment, will you not?" Eva asked as they entered the door of the flat that had been her home.

"Certainly, sweetheart, but not for long." He kissed her with the tenderness of a lover, and watched her as she went from him.

Alone in her boudoir, she quickly locked the door and drew the soiled note from her pocket.

Her hand trembled, her lips were pale as ashes, but neither sigh nor moan escaped her as she read:

Ha! Ha! You thought you had escaped my vengeance! Wait and see! I want you! I command that you leave your husband of a

moment and come to the address that I shall give. I will not detain
you long—only a sufficient time to tell you something that is nec-
essary for you to know. Refuse and Rod Hurdis shall know your
history before your train starts for California. You know as well
as I can tell you what the result of that would be.

> *Him whom you have most cruelly wronged,*
> *Marshall Randall.*

Not once, but twenty times, Eva read the note through to the end. She understood the threat it contained but too well, and the horror of her situation rendered her calm.

"What am I to do?" she asked of herself, again and again. "Rod must not know! He shall not! I swear it, even if I am forced to commit murder to prevent it! Oh, God! Oh, God! What shall I do? The original fault was not mine."

She rung her bell with a violent hand, unlocked the door, and wrote hastily upon a bit of paper:

"Dearest, I have gone to say a word of farewell to an old friend. You will not have missed me until I shall have returned. In my happiness I had forgotten her.

Eva."

"Give that to Mr. Hurdis," she said hastily to the maid who had answered her ring.

She scarcely waited for the girl to leave the room than, wrapping a veil about her face, she slipped down the servants' stairs and out into the street.

With swift steps and countenance fiercely set, she went onward to the place of rendezvous that Randall had appointed.

She rang the bell nervously. It was answered by Randall himself.

"You would have scarcely recognized me, would you?" he asked grimly as he ushered her into a room presumably used as a parlor, as it contained no bed.

"I have not come for sentiment of that kind," she replied coldly. "I want to know what you meant by the threat contained in your note."

"That is true! I am glad you brought me back to a consideration of that, for we have not many minutes to spare and your dear husband may miss you. You were foolish not to have taken me, Eva. I knew all about your past, there would never have been any need to fear discovery, and I loved you! I need not put it in the past tense, for I love you now!"

"Have you brought me here to tell me this?" she demanded haughtily. "For if you have, it is not of the slightest interest to me, and I had as well gone home again."

"I think you are mistaken, Eva. It is of vital interest to you. I tell you that, in spite of all you have done to me, I love you the same as ever, and I cannot bear to have you go so far, leaving me here alone. Eva, you must take me to California with you!"

"Are you mad?"

"I don't know; perhaps I am. I know that many people would call me so for loving you as I do, but it is impossible for me to prevent it. My dear, you must take your choice. Either I go to California with you, or you remain at home."

Eva was too much surprised to reply. A terrible giddiness seized her.

She was not slow to perceive in what a frightful position she had placed herself. She knew that she must either yield to the fiend before her, or have Rod Hurdis discover the miserable truth that she would give her life to conceal.

She stood irresolute for the moment, and, seeing his advantage, Randall placed his hand upon her shoulder.

"It is not necessary that Hurdis should ever know, or even suspect anything," he said slowly. "I do not ask for all, but only a part of what belongs to me by right. You may have your respectability, have the position that comes to you as his wife. I promise that I will help you, even help to protect your secret, if you yield. But you must take me with you; you must let me remain where I can see you in his absence, or he shall know all within the hour. Eva, I am waiting for your answer."

XXVII

"A QUICKSAND OF DECEIT."

"Hateful to me, as are the gates of hell,
Is he who, hiding one thing in his heart,

Utters another."

FOR A SEEMINGLY ENDLESS MOMENT Eva stood staring at Randall, as though she had taken leave of her senses, or thought he had taken leave of his.

She was like a statue, hard and cold as marble. Every sentiment of good seemed to have left her.

She would have murdered him then and there had there been the slightest opportunity to conceal her crime, but she saw with her usual readiness at calculation that she was beneath the lion's paw, with not the faintest hope of rescue.

She did not believe in the very least in Randall's protestations of affection. She felt quite convinced that he hated her even as she hated him and her idea of the infinite was gauged by that but she believed that he was indulging in that little ruse simply to carry out some diabolical scheme against her.

She wound her fingers about each other in a peculiar gesture of self-restraint. "How I would love to kill you!" she said between her teeth.

Randall laughed shortly.

"I have taken the precaution to put all daggers out of your way," he said. "What a curious fondness you had for them, I have never been able to forget. No more has Loran, I fancy. But don't let us recall unpleasant memories, Eva. If you are going to California you have not so much time to spare as you may suppose. I suppose you *are* going?"

"I am!" she answered with dull defiance.

"Then give me the money to pay my fare. Of course I shall go on the same train, but not in the same car if I can help it, as under the circumstances I am not very desirous of being a witness to the billing and cooing of the newly married couple. I think two hundred dollars will do me to start on. If I should need more I can find an opportunity when he is in the smoker or some other time to let you know. You see I mean to be very moderate in my demands."

"And you really think that I will enter into this scheme to defraud my husband?" demanded Eva, her passion at a heat that necessitated calmness.

"I think you will be a very foolish woman if you don't!" exclaimed Randall, not giving her time to finish what she had intended saying. "He has plenty of money, not less than twenty thousand a year. He is handsome, respected, and he loves you. Notwithstanding the fact of his being accredited with being one of the men of intelligence of the day, he would be as weak as ditch water in your hands so long as he believed that you brought no disgrace upon his name. But one suspicion of that, and he would never see your face again. Now what are you going to do? The choice remains with you, and I don't know but that I had rather you would answer in the negative. It would give me even a greater hold upon you."

She flung out her hands helplessly. For the first time in her life she felt like a little child in the firm grip of an adverse fate, without power to battle against it.

She lifted her eyes, endeavoring to conceal their glowing misery. "I have not got the money that you demand!" she answered slowly.

"You can get it!" he returned, seeing that he had won.

"I don't know! I am afraid not. Why will you not allow me to give you the money, if I can, and stay at home?"

"No! I shall never, while you live and I live, lose sight of you! You have only yourself to blame, Eva. You deprived me of my position; I can get nothing else to do, because of the brand that is upon me, and I have no other interest in life than you now. I know that my love is no welcome gift to you, but I am no longer either fastidious or generous. I want what I want and not what others want me to have. I am sorry it does not meet with your approval, but I can't help it. Are you going to give me the money to go to California, or are you going to remain at home?"

"You will make my life a hell!"

"As you have made mine."

The words were uttered so slowly, and with such bitter meaning, that Eva no longer doubted that he would do all and more than he threatened.

She flung up her head defiantly. Whatever she suffered, he should not know. She at least could deprive him of that gratification.

She would yield to his demand, because there was nothing else left for her to do. But she would find a way to rid herself of him, and to have revenge for this last outrage, as well as she had done before.

"So be it!" she exclaimed, coldly. "You have me now where you can demand, and I am powerless to refuse. Take this pin; get what money you can on it, and if it should not be sufficient, you can let me know in some way on the cars. I hope you will have too much sense to kill the goose that lays the golden egg."

She took from her throat a magnificent diamond pin, and dropped it in his palm.

She turned away without a groan, though her heart seemed breaking, and without another word walked through the door and out of the house.

"It has begun again!" she murmured, her set face so perfectly controlled, giving no evidence of how she was suffering. "It is the old misery intensified a thousand-fold. How shall I ever have the courage to bear it now? It will end in something horrible, some disgrace so bitter, so prolonged, that Hades itself will seem less hard to bear. And yet it is too late now to prevent it! God in Heaven! What have I done that I should be so bitterly accursed?"

There was no softening in the beautiful face. She was suffering the torture of death, and perhaps the hardest part was that she knew her lips dared make no outcry, that she must remain dumb to all expression of her agony forever.

With a slow shiver she turned into her own door, summoning a smile to her lips that cost her one of the greatest efforts of her life.

Rod Hurdis met her in the hall.

"Deserted in the first hour of our marriage!" he exclaimed with playful reproach as he took her into his arms. "Where have you been?"

"To see an old friend whom I have sadly neglected of late, since you have occupied so much of my time," she answered with assumed lightness. "My love for you has made me forget so much, Rod, and my life has been such that forgetfulness is denied me."

He noticed the underlying current of bitterness in the voice, but misconstrued the cause. He took her more closely to his heart.

"You have been to see someone who has made you sad upon your wedding day," he said tenderly. "I am afraid I could never like your friend for that. Sweet, you have no more cause for sorrow. I intend that your life shall be a poem, a symphony, from to-day."

She smiled into his face without answering, pitying herself as she might have done had she been someone else whose sorrows appealed to her.

She knew that the happiness of which he spoke was eternally denied to her and yet, knowing that, a great longing took possession of her to feel it and know it. She wanted to feel how it would seem to be happy, as she could have been, had Maurice Vanderfelt and Marshall Randall never crossed her life.

A yearning that had all the pain of a sharp thrust in the heart took possession of her. She lifted her lips and laying them upon, the side of Hurdis' throat, burst into silent, passionless, but bitter weeping.

"Why, little wife!" exclaimed Hurdis, turning her around and taking the lovely face between his hands. "What is the matter? Not tired of your bargain so soon, are you?"

"You know better! You are the only happiness, the only good that God has ever given me. Oh, Rod, if there should ever come a time when you feel that your love for me is on the wane, I beg that you will kill me as the last favor that you can ever do me. Life would be too great a curse to be borne."

"My darling you are nervous, upset!" he said with ineffable gentleness. "There is no power in this entire world that could ever take my love from you!"

"None, Rod? None? You are quite sure of that?" She raised her eyes so wistfully, so anxiously that he was startled.

"No," he answered gravely, "no barrier could ever come between us, save one of your own erection."

"What do you mean by that?"

"I mean an impossibility, my sweetest," he replied, kissing her many times. "There is only one thing that could ever make a difference between us, and that would be deception of any kind upon your part. That is something that I could never endure. I hate it above all earthly wrongs! But there! What a conversation upon our wedding day. One would think that you had done me some terrible wrong, instead of making me the happiest man in existence. Dry your eyes, little wife. See! The carriage is at the door! I am glad the time has come for me to take you away from that horrid old woman who has power to draw to your eyes tears that I cannot control. The new life is waiting. Are you not ready for it, my darling?"

She kissed him without replying and left the room to hurriedly bathe her face.

In all her unhappy life there had never been to her a more miserable day than the one that made her the wife of the man she loved above all the world.

With a heart that throbbed with sharpest anguish, she rejoined him. Almost in silence they entered the carriage and were driven away.

How she would have enjoyed it, had it not been for the knowledge of the terrible incubus that awaited her there, at the end of her journey!

She shivered as she thought of it, and drew the lap robe more closely about her.

They had left the carriage and entered the depot, when Hurdis touched her upon the arm.

"Look, Eva!" he exclaimed; "there is the man in whom you have seemed so much interested of late—Marshall Randall! He is the seediest looking wretch, with the most hang-dog manner that I ever saw. One can scarcely credit the change in him. That is he with the slouch hat on. I think you told me that you had never seen him, did you not?"

"Yes," she stammered. "Poor fellow."

"Why do you say that?" he demanded. "He does not deserve your sympathy. He is a thief a thorough reprobate a scoundrel of the worst kind. I have no patience with him. Come! Don't let us waste time talking of him."

Eva's eyes traveled slowly to Randall. He was looking at her curiously, and by the expression of his face, she knew that he had heard, and that there was another item for vengeance which would be visited upon her head.

She strangled a groan and turned away.

XXVIII

"QUOTH HUDIBRAS, I SMELL A RAT!"

"In the lowest deep, a lower deep
Still threatening to devour me, opens wide,
To which the hell I suffer seems a heaven."

"Yet from those flames
No light, but only darkness visible."

THE BALMY ATMOSPHERE OF SOUTHERN California fanned through the handsomely-furnished suite of rooms in the principal hotel of Los Angeles. Winter was like the soft radiance of gentle June, soothing the heart into delicious languor from which there seemed no awakening. The luxurious perfume of flowers, the tempting odor of luscious fruit came through the window like a soft, delicately ripening pomegranate.

Within the rooms Eva stood, her arms clasped clingingly about her husband's neck.

"Don't be long gone, Rod!" she whispered. "I seem so utterly alone when you are not near me! I—I—"

"Sweetest, one would think that I was going for a month instead of a little half hour," he said with a soft laugh as he kissed her lips. "It is pleasant to be detained like this."

"Then let me keep you always so. Oh, Rod, I think I live only when you are here! Don't go, dear!"

"For only a little while, my darling. Let me go now, that I may return the sooner."

Very gently he unwound her arms from his neck and, placing her in a chair, kissed her again and again before leaving the room.

Controlling a hysterical sob, she watched him go, listening to his retreating footsteps until the last sound had died away, and then sunk back helplessly into her chair.

"I must control myself better," she muttered wearily, brushing the curling hair back from her moist brow, "or I shall betray everything, I cannot bear for him to leave me lest—"

She had not time to complete the mental sentence. The door opened without a knock and Randall entered.

"Hello!" he exclaimed, with brutal familiarity. "What a thundering long time Hurdis stayed! I was about to send him a note to get out. That fellow is growing unbearable! If it were not that he is a necessary evil in the way of supplying money, I should kick him out."

He stretched himself out on the couch as he ceased speaking, and calmly lighted a cigar.

"I wish you would not smoke here!" Eva remonstrated. "Mr. Hurdis never takes his cigars in this room, and the smell of smoke will attract his attention."

Randall smiled as though the assurance gave him infinite satisfaction.

"You must learn to smoke cigarettes," he said calmly. "It will give you such an excellent excuse. Will you have one now? I must have my cigar, and I never could be very particular in which room I took them."

"What have you come here for?"

"What an inhospitable question! Didn't I tell you that Hurdis and I are going pards on this household? Of course"—with a short laugh—"we have not asked his consent to it, but it is all right, particularly as I take second choice. Let me tell you something, Eva, that may surprise you. I am not doing this so much for revenge as you seem to think. I tell you that I am almost as much in love with you as ever, and I am seriously afraid that I am growing jealous of Hurdis. I know as well as you can tell me that we cannot live without him now. We want his money, and we must have it then we must get rid of him."

"What are you saying?"

The woman was bending forward, a light in her eyes like that of a fiend. Ten thousand daggers, each of polished steel, could have gleamed with no more dangerous import.

Randall trembled slightly, but covered it with a laugh.

"Little wildcat!" he exclaimed, with an effort at playfulness, "you may have your pretty toy a little while longer, but you will grow as tired of him shortly as you did of Vanderfelt, of Loran, and of—me."

"You—devil!"

"Names not infrequently turn on one's own head, my dear Eva. I would advise you to avoid them. Act sensibly, my girl, and you and I will get along like two turtle doves. But begin any of the old tigerish actions, and the whole case is dough. By the way! I don't know why it should, but that reminds me that I want some money."

"How much?"

"A hundred will do to-day."

"For Heaven's sake! Take it and go." She flung a roll of bills toward him as she spoke, and turned away with a gesture of disgust.

He looked at her with vindictive hatred.

"Wait until I have finished my cigar," he said serenely. "Come in!"

The latter exclamation was in answer to a knock that had sounded upon the door.

Eva was upon her feet in a moment, but too late to prevent the entrance of one of the hall boys. He looked with surprise at the nonchalant figure upon the couch, then handed Eva a box containing flowers that her husband had sent, and without a word retired.

"Why did you do that?" she demanded passionately, turning to Randall. "Do you want to disgrace me?"

He smiled exasperatingly. "Open your flowers, my love, and see what your dear husband has sent his little tootsy-wootsy!" he said with a slow sneer.

"You are going too far, Randall, for my patience!" she cried, with a bitterness of meaning that he could not fail to understand.

He arose slowly, stretching his long legs indolently. "Let me cut the string for you. I don't think it would be safe for me to lend you my knife," he said with a short laugh.

She was too weak to resist as he took the box and cut the string. He selected a peculiarly rare orchid and fastened it in his button-hole.

As Eva saw what he had done, she sprung at him like a tigress.

With the dexterity of a practiced athlete, he stepped lightly aside and smiled sneeringly.

"You would deny me the privilege of wearing even so small a thing as a flower that the beloved Rod had given?" he asked with exasperating scorn: "My dear girl, don't drive me too far, or I may demand your wedding-ring, and you know but too well that should I, you would not have the power to refuse. I know my ground thoroughly, and I advise you for your own welfare not to tempt me too far!"

"You shall not wear that flower!" she cried, her voice heavy with hatred.

"Shall not!" he echoed, sneeringly. "My dear, all of Hurdis' fortune could not purchase that."

He did not give her time to reply, but seeing that she intended to have it at any cost, he sprung lightly beyond her and threw open the door. He looked backward with a slight, mocking smile.

"*Au revoir!*" he said, tantalizingly. "I shall press it in memory of the occasion, until we meet again." He kissed his hand, and, placing his cigar again between his teeth, lounged down the hall.

Not five feet away he encountered Hurdis returning to his room. With infinite surprise, the latter recognized him.

Randall started slightly; but quickly recovered himself, and, with the faintest sneer curving his lips, raised his hat.

Hurdis watched him as he vanished from sight, a frown contracting his clear brow.

"What was that scoundrel doing in my room?" he muttered. "That was surely one of the flowers that I sent to Eva in his button-hole! And smoking, too, with the privilege of a friend! Eva has told me that she never knew him. What is the meaning of it?"

Turning upon his heel, he entered the room where his wife still stood, her small white teeth clinched in impotent wrath. She summoned a feeble smile as he kissed her.

"My! But this room is full of smoke!" he exclaimed.

"Yes," she stammered. "I am afraid I have been indulging in something of which you would by no means approve. I have been afraid to tell you, but you have caught me now. I have unfortunately become an inveterate cigarette smoker, and I have been smoking."

He looked at her in bewilderment. It had never occurred to him that she would conceal the fact of Randall's having called upon her, but as she had done so, it aroused in his mind vague, but bitter suspicion

"You smoking!" he exclaimed, forcing a laugh. "I can scarcely believe it. Disapprove? Not I. Let me see you smoke one."

"I—I think I have used the last one that I had."

"Then I will send for some"—ringing the bell—"What kind do you prefer?"

"Richmond straight cut," she answered feebly, mentioning a name that she had seen in some advertisement. "I don't think I care for another now."

"But you must smoke with me. Another can't possibly hurt such an old smoker."

He gave his order to the boy who had answered his ring, then turned to her again.

"Ah! I see that you have received your flowers. I ordered the florist to send a certain specimen of orchid"—throwing the flowers about to find it—"I suppose you have not taken any of them out, have you?"

"No," she answered faintly.

"Confound it! The fellow has forgotten. Here are the cigarettes. Let us have them."

He opened the box, and offering her one, took one himself. He lighted

a match and put it to the end of the little white roll that she had placed
between her lips.

She had never held one in her hand before, and as she drew the smoke
through it seemed to fill eyes, nose, and mouth at once. She was seized
with a violent fit of coughing.

Without an endeavor to aid her, Rod Hurdis stood staring down upon
her, his handsome eyes filled with a shadowy trouble.

"Eva," he said quietly when she had recovered, "why did you think it
necessary to lie to me? Did you think that I could not see for myself at
a glance that you have never smoked before? And was it honest to have
concealed from me that you have had a male visitor in my absence? Oh,
Eva! Eva!"

XXIX

"I LOVE THEE AS THE GOOD LOVE HEAVEN."

"And he that does one fault at first,
And lies to hide it makes it two."

"Who dares think one thing and another tell,
My soul detests him as the gates of hell."

THE SENSATION THAT EVA EXPERIENCED while listening to her husband's words was something like that of a person who feels himself falling from a tremendous height with no power to prevent or even break it.

Holding her breath with a curious, long gasp that threatened to choke her, she waited for him to finish, then raised her eyes with the dull misery that touches one in a wounded stag.

Before replying she leaned over and laid her lips upon his hand as though it were the kiss given to the dead. She felt in that moment that, she was taking leave of him forever, and—oh, God, how she suffered.

The act went to the man's heart. He knelt beside her and took her hand gently.

"Have you no word of explanation to give me, Eva?" he asked.

The words gave her hope.

"Yes," she stammered, "but I am afraid!"

"Afraid of me, your husband? Have I ever been cruel to you that you doubt my love or my tenderness?"

"Never!" she cried passionately. "It was only because I dared not risk losing your love that I have not told you. I could not bear that you should know that I had deceived you."

"You have deceived me, then?"

"Yes!"

Hurdis grew deadly white. Somehow he had hoped against hope, but now by her own confession he saw that there was no more room for that. He shrunk away from her and dropped the hand he held.

She felt for a time as Moses must have when he saw the Promised Land and was denied the privilege of entering. Then the determination came that she would have love so necessary to her happiness at any cost, even if it could be hers for but an hour longer.

She threw her arms about his neck with hysterical passion. "You shall not think too badly of me!" she cried, her face quivering with dread and horror. "I could not risk losing you and I deceived you about Marshall Randall. He is my first cousin. We were brought up together from infancy!"

The words were uttered so wildly that it never occurred to Hurdis to doubt them. He looked at her in intense surprise.

"Marshall Randall your cousin!" he exclaimed. "And you thought it necessary to conceal that fact from me? Why?"

"Because he is a thief, a bank robber! Because there is nothing in the whole world that is low and vile that he is not!" she answered fiercely. "I could not endure that you should think that I was in any way connected with a thing so distorted in crime as he!"

"You dislike him, then?"

She forgot herself for a moment, and her face darkened like that of a fiend. He never remembered to have seen such an expression of hideous hatred.

"I loathe him!" she answered behind her teeth.

"Then why do you receive him?" Hurdis inquired in infinite surprise.

The question aroused her to a memory of what she was saying. She pulled herself together upon the instant.

"For his mother's sake!" she answered, almost sullenly, lifting her hair from her brow with a gesture indicative of great weariness.

"And his mother was—"

"My mother's sister."

She hated herself for the lie, she despised herself for the imposition upon a man so gentle and true as her husband, and yet she knew if he ever came in possession of the hideous truth that she would be as dead to him as though the grave had closed over one of them. Strong in one way, she was too weak in another to endure even the thought of that.

"And you really thought it necessary to conceal that from me!" Hurdis exclaimed, with such evident relief as he had rarely ever felt before. "Oh darling, if you knew how I have suffered during the last few moments, you would never have concealment from me again. I love you as the good love Heaven, and any suspicion of the slightest deceit upon your part is like a stab in the heart. I know that you are pure and true as an angel, and I swear to you that I had not the remotest doubt of you until you told me a falsehood about the smoke, and then even it was too shadowy to be called a doubt. Little wife, can you ever forgive me?"

"Forgive you?" The words were uttered vaguely, as though she scarcely understood their meaning.

"You were so foolish not to have told me!" he continued. "Randall may be a scoundrel himself, and undoubtedly is, but there must be a black sheep in every family, and he is the one in his. Whatever he may be, his family is a good one, and it is no disgrace to be connected with it. Sweetheart, tell me that you forgive me for my doubt."

"There is nothing that you could do to me that I would not forgive, Rod," she answered, conquering a sob, "even without the asking, for I love you with all my soul. You believe that, do you not?"

"The greatest happiness in life to me is that I do believe it!" he replied, not without emotion. "If there is a blow that could kill me, I think it would be to discover that I was mistaken in your love, and that your heart had ever belonged to another. I wonder if God punishes us for selfishness like that, my darling."

"I don't know," she stammered. "I only know that I love you, and that to lose your love would be to lose all of Heaven that I shall ever know."

With a grin of diabolical delight upon his hang-dog countenance, Randall walked down the hall after having encountered Hurdis, and entered the elevator to go to the office.

"I would give fifty dollars out of this hundred she gave me to know what lie Eva will tell Hurdis to get out of this!" he exclaimed, strangling a laugh. "She is no novice at the business, and will make up a good one, I am sure. But how she will suffer. By the Lord, it serves her right! I'll bet she rues the day that ever she determined to be revenged upon me! I see the way now to make her suffer most, and I will follow it to the last. When I have tortured her until there is not another drop to add to the measure, I will take him from her. But she must go through it all by slow degrees. Let me see! What will be the next step?"

He had reached the office floor, and as the boy threw open the door, Randall stepped out.

A man drew back to make way, and as he did so Randall glanced in his direction. He stopped short, an expression of demoniacal joy crossing his face.

"Vanderfelt, by all that is wonderful!" he cried, grasping the man's hand. "Where, in the name of Heaven, did you spring from?"

"Hallo, Randall!" replied Vanderfelt, taking the proffered hand with something like restraint. "I hardly knew you!"

"But are delighted to see me as I am you, of course. When did you come to town?"

"Half an hour ago. How did you happen, to be here?"

"One of the nervous fluctuations of my body that is all! Come, let us have a bottle of champagne to celebrate."

"Thanks, no! I am in something of a hurry, and—"

"You are not going to shake me, if that is what you are trying to do, so you may as well come. By the way, you have not heard anything from that little wildcat that stabbed me at your house, have you? I mean Eva Scarlett."

Vanderfelt frowned. "I see you have not gotten over your old desire to bring up unpleasant subjects."

"You wrong me. I asked from interest. You forget that I was almost as deep in the criminal part of that as you, only you had all the benefits."

"I have heard nothing of her since the night she left there."

"No? You got off better than I expected. I suppose you never looked for her?"

"Not I! I would not meet her for a thousand dollars. I have never seen so perfect a specimen of the she-devil as she."

"I have greater cause to remember that than you!" exclaimed Randall with a rueful grin. "You have no idea what has become of her, then?"

"Not the slightest."

"Nor of that French fiend who overheard the whole business?"

"Yes, I have every reason to know her whereabouts, as she forces me to pay her a certain sum of money monthly."

"Where is she?"

The address was given, of which Randall made a careful mental note. Then, with an infamous twinkle in his eyes, he laid his hand upon Vanderfelt's arm.

"Come, old fellow!" he exclaimed, "it is the dinner hour, and I am hungry. Let us feed together. You need not be ashamed to eat with me, because, although those rather unpleasant things were in the papers about me, there is no one here who knows anything about me. And, if they did, would not give it a second thought. So far as your own knowledge is concerned, we each know so perfectly what the other is, that there is no need to fear contamination. Besides, you know it is natural for birds of a feather to flock together. Come, old chap! I feel like a half-famished lion."

There was a nervous hilarity in his manner that Vanderfelt had never seen there before, but to which he attached no importance. It was not a pleasant thing to be forced into such a companionship, but there was no help for it, and, with the best grace he could summon, he allowed himself to be led away.

"Not there!" Randall exclaimed, slipping a dollar into the hand of the head waiter. "I prefer to sit on the other side by the window."

The servant looked somewhat surprised, as the seat preferred now had been refused when Randall first entered the dining room; but it was not for him to question, and without a word, he obediently led the way.

They had not finished giving their order when the head-waiter came slowly toward them in advance of a gentleman followed by a lady.

Randall glanced up. His face flushed crimson, in anticipation of his cruel fun.

It was Hurdis and Eva.

As they stood directly opposite him, he laid his hand upon Vanderfelt's knee beneath the table.

The latter raised his eyes. They rested directly upon Eva's face.

XXX

THE NUMBER OF FALSEHOODS SWELLS.

"The devil tempts us not—'tis we tempt him,
Beckoning his skill with opportunity."

"Peace; sit you down,
And let me wring your heart; for so I shall,
If it be made of penetrable stuff."

"THE DEUCE!"

The word fell with more force than elegance from a pair of very white lips as Vanderfelt's eyes rested upon the lovely face before him.

He was too much surprised and startled to remember that he owed the encounter to Randall, but sat gazing at Eva in open mouth astonishment. And she?

Ay! Verily,

"When sorrows come, they come not single spies,
But in battalions."

She neither fainted nor made any outcry, but Randall, watching her, thought for the moment that the end had come.

He never remembered to have seen such an expression of horror upon any human face. The eyes dilated until they became black as night, the face became livid, and a dull purple settled about the mouth that seemed to indicate death.

He half arose from his chair, but he distinctly saw her, with the same desperation that she might have grasped an object that offered itself while falling from some dizzy height, pull herself together.

He saw that the danger of self-betrayal was over, but he also saw with a smile of satisfaction that she was suffering beyond human expression.

Hurdis, meanwhile, recognizing Randall, felt a most Christian-like desire to place his wife at her ease, and have an amicable feeling exist for his wife's "aunt's" sake. He therefore smiled with great geniality.

"How do you do, Randall!" he exclaimed kindly. "Why, Vanderfelt, is it possible? Not expecting to see you, I did not recognize you at all. By Jove! This is a pleasure! When did you come? I feel as if I had met an old friend in the wilds of Africa. Let me introduce you to my wife. My dear, this is one of my oldest friends. Mrs. Hurdis, Mr. Vanderfelt!"

A broad grin spread over Randall's face from ear to ear. He was simply reveling in the embarrassment of the two people whose secret he had such cause to know. But Vanderfelt had fully recovered himself, and bowed to Eva as if he had never seen her until that moment. She returned it so icily that it was almost imperceptible, but after the first smiling glance, Hurdis had turned to Vanderfelt and was not observing her.

With a sigh that was almost a groan, Eva sunk into a chair that the waiter held for her while her husband was upon the other side of the table shaking hands with Vanderfelt.

If she could but have fainted it would have been something of a relief to her, but even that was denied her.

She tried to think of what she was to do, and how act, but the more she tried to think the more chaotic thought became. Yielding to a magnetic force that she had no power to resist, she lifted her eyes and allowed them to rest upon Vanderfelt's face.

He was looking at Hurdis. "I suppose it is not too late to congratulate you?" Vanderfelt was saying in a voice that was almost composed. "None of us knew that you were married. I fancy it will be quite a surprise to the fellows at the Manhattan."

"Yes, my wife had a horror of a public marriage. Quite an unusual thing in a young woman of this century, is it not?"

"Very! I congratulate you upon it, Mrs. Hurdis. I quite agree with you in your dislike of all the fuss made over a thing of that kind during the present day. I believe that is the reason that the young men have such a horror of getting married."

The coolness that had always been her chief characteristic returned to Eva at that moment.

"I do not doubt it in the least," she replied, looking him straight in the eye. "When one is supremely happy, one prefers that there should be no witnesses of it."

Somehow the speech sent a thrill through Vanderfelt that was by no means pleasant. Looking into her beautiful face, he realized, now that she was removed from him forever, that he had foolishly parted with something that was extremely lovely, and that he could have held in spite of the wrong he had done her, had he cared to do so.

"Then you are supremely happy?" he could not resist asking.

"As I used to picture myself in the fairy dreams of childhood," she answered, with a shadowy defiance in her tone.

Hurdis laughed softly. "Go thou and do likewise!" he said with a teasing glance at Vanderfelt. "By the way, Randall, how is it that you never became a Benedict? There was a rumor at one time that you were about to be married to a woman that the boys were all raving over as a perfect beauty."

"It was quite true," replied Randall. "I was engaged to her for, let me see, about an hour, I think, but she threw me over for a handsome man, and unfortunately I cannot learn to love another. Mrs. Hurdis, are you ill?"

Eva had not even changed color when the malapropos question was asked, and Hurdis turned to her in some surprise.

"Not in the least," she replied, her voice raised a trifle, her eyes stony in their defiance. "From childhood, Marshal! You have been one to ask the most absurd questions of any one I ever knew. Why did you think that?"

Randall was so surprised that he could not reply. If she had thrown her plate at his head it might have been what he would have expected, but to answer so quietly and to call him by his first name was something for which he was unprepared.

Vanderfelt was amazed. Randall covered his confusion with a laugh.

"You change color so easily, that is all," he replied. "By the way, Hurdis, have you seen the 'Twelve Temptations?'"

"No."

"Suppose we make a theater party and go tonight?"

"Would you like to go?" asked Hurdis, turning to Eva.

"I think not," she answered with a cold glance at Randall. "It is not the kind of play that I care for."

"One is enough, without the twelve, eh?" laughed Randall.

"It is not the temptation, but the resistance, or nonresistance, that makes or mars a life," she replied coldly. "I know of no one that should more thoroughly realize the fact than yourself."

Randall was silenced. There was absolutely nothing that he could say without exposing what he very well knew was a necessity that he should conceal.

The conversation had taken a turn that was not agreeable to Hurdis, and he hastened to change it. "Do you remain long, Vanderfelt?" he asked.

"Until Tuesday, I think."

"Then back to New York?"

"Yes."

"How fortunate. Eva and I are going then. We may be quite a merry little party. Will you come for a drive with us this afternoon?"

"I—I am afraid I cannot," stammered Vanderfelt. "I have come on business, you see, and I cannot call my time my own."

"Oh, very well. We are here for pleasure, and can make your time ours. You see we do not mean to excuse you, do we, Eva?" He turned to her to second his invitation, and she was forced to summon a smile and reply in the affirmative.

"Appoint the hour now, any that will suit you, and Eva and I will do the honors of the town," continued Hurdis jovially.

"I don't think I can possibly get an hour to-day."

"Then call the evening ours, and set a time for to-morrow?"

"Very well," stammered Vanderfelt, seeing that he must yield.

They arose from the table at the same moment, and Hurdis, with the same Christian sentiment that had characterized his meeting with Randall, walked out of the dining room with him, leaving Vanderfelt to escort his wife.

With a feeling of loathing that gave her strength, Eva lifted her eyes to the face of the man who had so cruelly wronged her.

"I must see you when my husband is not present," she said coldly below her breath.

He bowed politely. "I am subject to your order," he replied in the same tone.

"Do you know, Mrs. Hurdis," exclaimed Randall, as the four stood together waiting for the elevator, "that I always was under the impression that you and Vanderfelt had met before? It seems to me that I have heard you speak of each other."

Eva knew that her husband's eyes were upon her, and she also knew that the remark had been made simply because Randall knew that it would be the cruelest stab that he could give her.

She summoned all her courage, and raised her eyes with a slight sneer.

"You were always remarkable for your vivid imagination, Marshall," she answered, with perfect composure. "Mr. Vanderfelt and I have never met before." She stepped into the elevator, bowing with cold dismissal to the two men.

"Don't forget that we shall expect you both this evening," called Hurdis cordially as he followed her.

"Curse you!" exclaimed Vanderfelt angrily to Randall when they were alone. "What in the name of thunder ever possessed you to take me to that table, when you knew she would be there?"

Randall could scarcely control his laughter. "I would not have missed it for a thousand dollars!" he answered. "Your faces were better than a play."

"I should like to break your infernal neck."

"Don't doubt it in the least, my boy, but you can't do it! I owe her a grudge that I am obliged to pay, and if you must be a cat's paw on one occasion, you ought not to object for you must remember that it was through you that I knew her. What do you think of the aristocratic Hurdis' wife?"

"That she is a thousand times prettier than ever, and that I have made an infernal fool of myself!" growled Vanderfelt moodily. "A fellow never knows what an ass he is until he sees himself through another man's lens."

Randall looked at him curiously. "You don't mean what you say?" he asked.

"It is none of your business. If you had not have been so smart, this would not have occurred." Vanderfelt walked away in a passion, and with a burst of laughter Randall looked after him.

"Ha, ha! Ho, ho! This is better than I thought. Now the circus begins!" he exclaimed, the expression of a demon curling his thin cruel lips.

XXXI

EVA AND VANDERFELT.

"What then? what rests?
Try what repentance can. What can it not?
Yet what can it; when one cannot repent?
O wretched state! O bosom black as death!
O limed soul, that, struggling to be free
Art more engag'd."

A TAP SO LIGHT THAT HE was almost convinced that he had not heard it sounded upon Vanderfelt's door. He arose and opened it.

Upon the threshold Eva stood, her lovely face drawn with horror at the position into which necessity had thrown her. She loathed herself for the act she was forced to commit, yet she knew there was no help for it.

She entered without an invitation, and Vanderfelt closed the door behind her.

"This is an honor that I scarcely expected," he began, feeling more trepidation than he would have cared to own, even to himself.

"I have not come to speak of either the honor or the disgrace of it," she answered bitterly. "I have come to know why you are here, and what I am to expect of you. I need not tell you, I suppose, that my husband knows nothing of the horrors of my past."

"You disappoint me! I hoped you had come to allow me to tell you how sorry I am for that past, in which I played the part of a dastard and a fool, which is worse. Eva, I would give a good deal to be in Rod Hurdis' shoes to-day."

She made a gesture of disgust. "I beg that you will spare me!" she exclaimed. "You put upon me a disgrace that a long life of the most rigid honesty can never wipe out. You ruined the beautiful, girlish dreams of a pure life, you transformed what was a pure woman into a devil. Oh, Maurice Vanderfelt, there is no more harm to do than you have done. Why, therefore, have you come here to torture me?"

There was such utter wretchedness in her voice that no man could have heard it unmoved. He hesitated a moment, then pushed a chair toward her.

"Sit down, Eva," he said gently. "You are nervous and excited. I have not come here for the unmanly purpose that you assign to me, I swear it! On the contrary, had I known that you were here, I should have remained away. But now that we are together, let us talk rationally and reasonably."

She sat upon the chair that he had thrust toward her, and lifted her weary eyes to his. She looked more beautiful to him than she had ever appeared in the days of her dimpled beauty and gladness, when life had no element but dreams of love and romance.

He took a seat facing her, and leaned toward her, his arm resting upon his knee. There was a flush upon his cheeks that she had not the power to bring there in the old days, and she was not slow to perceive it.

"Eva," he said after a pause, with something very like shame dyeing his cheeks, "I know that in your eyes I am a scoundrel, and yet I solemnly assure you that I am sincerely and at heart your friend! I am not going to offer any excuses for what I did; I don't propose to remind you that nine out of every ten men of the world would have done precisely the same thing and have considered that they were benefiting you; I don't wish to remind you of what your life would have been there in that little village among ignorance, filth, and the lowest depths of poverty, surrounded by vice and even crime. I only want to speak to you of the danger of your position to-day!"

"Do you think you know more of its danger than I do?"

"Perhaps not, but as a man of the world, my vision may be clearer. Did you ever think how many club men in New York know you?"

She lifted her eyes in a quick, startled way. "Know me?" she echoed in a nervous whisper.

"Yes, dear from having seen you with—me! There! Don't look so terrible. I know all you would say well enough. You would tell me that that is more of the curse that I have put upon your life. I know that, but what's done is done and nothing in this entire world can undo it! Don't you know that you will not be in New York twenty-four hours until the whole town will know who it is that Roderick Hurdis has married?"

In her whole life, perhaps, she had never experienced greater suffering than that. "They will know that he has married your—" She could get no further. The horror of it seemed to choke her.

She saw with the same readiness that she grasped all ideas that she had brought an eternal disgrace upon the man she loved, the man who had done her no wrong, and that sooner or later he must know it!

What better was she than the one before her?

He had wronged her as an innocent girl, and she had willfully deceived him who had showered her with every blessing that Heaven had placed within his power.

She sunk back with an awful groan. Try as she would, there seemed to be no escape for her. Why should she censure the man before her, when she had done even worse?

She lifted her eyes again. Their misery was covered with a flimsy recklessness that had no power to keep out suffering. She extended her hand and laid it upon Vanderfelt's.

"I hate you," she exclaimed, "and at the same time I can see some justification for you. You have brought all this misery and sorrow upon me, yet if you had left me there where you found me, perhaps I should have been there to the end of the chapter. With no hope beyond it, and just as miserable in another way as I now am. You did wrong, and so have I! Now wipe out as much of yours as you can by helping me to conceal mine."

"Do you not think the most honorable way would be for you to make a clean breast of it to Hurdis?"

"Undoubtedly, but I have not the courage. It is done now. Let me enjoy the fruit of my sin as long as I can."

"And you think that you can enjoy it with this sword of Damocles hanging forever above your head?"

"Now that I know the end must come sooner or later—yes! So long as I hoped to stave it off forever I was miserable. Now I will throw aside consequences and live while I live. We know that death may come at any hour, yet we dance and sing with an abandon that has nothing in reality but recklessness in its composition; I can do the same. When the end must come, I shall be ready for it and know how to meet it!"

"Would it not be better to tell him?"

She shivered so that her teeth chattered. "No!" she cried shrilly. "Do you know what he would do? He would never see my face again, and I should starve!"

"Not while I lived!" answered Vanderfelt slowly. "Perhaps I was not just what I should have been to you, but it was the knowledge that I was deceiving you that made me so. Now, with a clear understanding between us, we could be happy, Eva!"

She did not resent his words, but shook her head violently.

"No!" she exclaimed. "I will take all out of life that there is in it. I will postpone the knowledge of my past reaching Rod just as long as I can, and then when there is no longer any hope, there is always death."

"Foolish girl! Do you forget what Darley says?

"'Fool! I mean not
That poor soiled piece of heroism, self-slaughter.
Oh, no! On the miserablest day we live
There's many a better thing to do than die.'

"I had a better opinion of your bravery than that, Eva."

She shrugged her shoulders with an affectation of indifference. "I am neither brave nor a coward," she said carelessly. "The world may wag as it will henceforth, I am done with trying! I think there must have been a fiber lacking in my creation. I have suffered until suffering has seared, and now I am incapable of feeling. There is but one desire left—to live in my husband's love as long as I may. A few hours, or days, or months longer cannot hurt him. The wrong is done, and no act of mine can wipe it out now."

"Then you will not come back to me?"

"Not yet! Wait until the end comes. Then, if I have not the courage to die, I may do worse."

"And Marshall Randall?"

She shut her teeth with a wry expression of repulsion. "I shall continue to buy his silence. Now that he sees he can no longer make me suffer, he will not care to taunt me. He played the part of a scoundrel who sinned for the sake of sinning, when he himself was not benefited. Bah! How I despise him!"

"You and I are not to be strangers, then?"

"What need have we? Our not speaking cannot wipe out the past! There is a curious life before me, Maurice. A life that God is good enough not to have repeated often. My single regret now is that He allowed me ever to meet so good a man as Rod Hurdis. I will be as happy now as I was in the days when I taught myself to forget Marshall Randall!"

"You think you can?"

"Think? Wait and see!"

She arose and presented her hand to Vanderfelt. He raised it to his lips.

"You cannot expect me to be sorry when the end that you speak of comes," he said softly, "for remember that it promises me you."

She smiled at him recklessly and left the room.

"Have you been lonely without me, sweet?" Hurdis asked ten minutes later, when he entered the room where she sat alone.

"I am always so when you are not near, Rod!" she answered, greeting him with a smile that was almost too brilliant to be real.

"What have you been doing?"

"Weaving plans for our future happiness from the silken threads of the past," she replied.

He laughed softly, happily, and kissed her. "I sometimes think that there must be some mistake about it all and that you have but deceived me into thinking that you have never loved another man," he said, patting her cheek. "Tell me, Eva, have you never cared for any man but me?"

"Never! Rod, you are my all! Remember that when you are tempted to doubt me!"

"I could not doubt you, my darling! Falsehood never dwells in a face like yours. I would trust you with the world against you."

"You swear that?"

"That and more! I would love you, adore you with the world against you!"

XXXII

A RESOLVE.

"What mighty ills have not been done by woman?
Who wasn't betrayed the capitol? A woman!
Who lost Mark Anthony the world? A woman!
Who was the cause of a long ten year's war
And laid at last old Troy in ashes? Woman!
Destructive, damnable, deceitful woman!"

"A secret at home is like rocks under tide."

"TO-MORROW, EVA, WE LEAVE FOR New York!"

Rod Hurdis had taken the lovely face between his hands to kiss it, and therefore could not see how white it had become.

Before he had released it, it had regained all its sweet, shell-like color, and a pair of dark eyes looked into his reproachfully.

"To-morrow!" she repeated. "Must we go so soon? It seems as if you were anxious to bring our honeymoon to a close."

"I hope that it may never close, my darling."

"But to return there will take you from me so much. Let us stay a little longer. Only one short week, Rod, and then I will not say another word, but go if you wish it. You will let me have one more week, just one little week, won't you, Rod?"

"Was it not just the same last week, dearest?"

"But this will be the last, I promise you."

He kissed her tenderly. "I would yield so gladly, little tyrant, if I only might," he said gently. "But you know how much I belong to the public, and just at present I cannot remain longer. I have over-stayed my time now, and duty calls. I know my little girl would not have me neglect that even for her."

Eva shivered. "And you are sure that you cannot remain another day?"

The voice had grown strangely hoarse, so much so that he took the strained face again between his hands.

"Not after to-morrow, my darling!" he said, thinking that it was a mere whim upon her part. "Do you dislike New York so much then?"

"More than any place upon earth!"

"And yet you met me there."

"I know. It is the one claim that the city has to my affection."

"But things will be so different there now for you to what they were before. You were almost friendless then. Now my friends will be yours, and by and by you will become such a little society woman that I am afraid I shall be sorry that I ever took you there at all, for I shall be quite robbed of my wife and as bad as a lonely bachelor again."

"Then don't let us risk it yet awhile, Rod!" she cried eagerly. "Let us keep our secret! I should so much prefer it! I should, indeed! Then I shall not mind going back at all. Don't tell anyone that you are married, but just let us keep our own secret, live our own life, that none may be the wiser. You will know and I shall know, and that will be quite enough. Promise me, Rod!"

He laughed heartily, taking no notice that she did not join him.

"What an absurd idea!" he exclaimed, still laughing. "I declare, Eva, you are as romantic as a child. What reason could there be in such a foolish thing?"

"None, perhaps. Only that it is my wish, and there is no reason why you should not yield to it. Oh Rod, promise me!"

There was something so genuinely earnest in her tone that he looked at her curiously. "Can you not tell me why you wish it, Eva?" he asked at last.

"No; only that it will seem less like ending the first happy time that I have ever had in all my life. Rod, don't refuse me."

She gave evidence of becoming hysterical, and in order to quiet her he answered:

"Well, dear, if you wish it there is no reason why I should refuse, though frankly, I don't like it. At least you will let me tell my mother?"

"No, not even her, Rod! Remember, I have your promise!"

She kissed him and flung open the door as a knock sounded upon it.

Maurice Vanderfelt stood there.

"Will you come down to Granger's for half an hour, Hurdis?" he asked when he had spoken to Eva. "There's a horse down there that I think of buying, and I want your judgment of him."

"Go, dear!" Eva cried, pushing him toward the door. "I really want to be by myself a little while."

He had scarcely left her presence, however, than, watching her opportunity when she was certain of being unobserved, she ran across the hall and entered a room, the door of which stood ajar.

Randall was seated in a huge arm-chair, the stem of a pipe between his lips, and a glass of whisky-and-water upon a table beside him.

"You honor me," he said carelessly, without rising. "What has procured me the pleasure of this visit? Since you and Vanderfelt became such fast friends I have scarcely seen you. I wonder what Hurdis would think if he knew the circumstances?"

Eva shrugged her shoulders, affecting the most absolute indifference. "I don't suppose that he would be particularly delighted, but there is no reason why he should know," she replied, seating herself without an invitation. "You demanded to know a few hours before our return to New York. I have come to tell you that we go to-morrow!"

"Not really?"

"Why?"

"It seems too good to be true. My wishes do not often turn out so perfectly."

"What can it possibly matter to you?" she asked, not able to conceal the bitterness of her tone. "Wherever you are, you live in idleness upon Rod Hurdis' money. I should think that Greenland would be as good as Florida so long as you have the money to purchase furs enough to keep you warm."

"No, you are wrong there!" he answered coolly. "I have my preferences the same as other people. So you are going to New York to-morrow! Have you persuaded that dolt to keep your marriage a secret?"

He looked at her through a cloud of smoke; but, obstructed as his vision was, he could see how she was forced to bite her lips to keep her anger from bubbling over

"Yes," she snapped shortly.

"Good again! I tell you, Eva, there are not many women in the world like you. You ought to congratulate yourself, my dear."

"No, I congratulate the world!" she returned bitterly.

"You are too modest. Well, my dear, now that you have persuaded Hurdis to allow your marriage to remain secret, have you thought what name you will live under?"

"No!"

"You see how thoughtful for you I am! I have arranged all that. You will bear mine."

"Yours?"—breathlessly.

"Certainly. You told Hurdis that I was your cousin. What more natural thing than that you should take my name under the circumstances."

"I will not!"

"Don't say that, my dear, because it always makes me the more determined. Besides it will greatly simplify matters in another scheme that I have on foot. You must take me to Europe, Eva."

He smoked his pipe calmly while she looked at him aghast.

"Take you to Europe!" she repeated slowly. "Are you mad?"

"Not the least in the world. You see, Hurdis' busy season is coming on now, and he will have to be away from you a great deal. Affairs of state cannot be neglected, even for the sake of a lovely wife, and if your marriage is not acknowledged, Hurdis cannot take you with him. You see, there is much method in my madness. All that time I shall have you to myself; but that will not be quite enough to satisfy me. I want to go to Europe, and you must take me!"

"Do you wish to ruin me?" she cried, clutching the arm of her chair with the same venom that she might have used had the upholstery been his throat.

"No, darling," he replied exasperatingly. "Why will you always forget that I love you? Does not every lover wish to have his amorita to himself without fear of interruption, occasionally?"

"I tell you that it is impossible! Quite impossible!" she cried, endeavoring to control her white heat anger.

"Nothing is impossible to a woman of your infinite resources and finesse," he said lazily, puffing his pipe between the words. "It is quite useless to contradict me, Eva. Either you take me to Europe or Hurdis shall know the secret of your life, and that the man whom you have been receiving as your friend and his, is your former lover. You see, my dear, that unintentionally you have put the strongest weapon possible in my hands. He might forgive you for everything else, in his infatuated state, but never that. Are you going to take me to Europe? And if so, when?"

With the hoarse cry of a demon she sprung out of her chair. Her eyes were burning with a red fire that was strangely wild, her lips the color of dead ashes.

Randall was upon his feet at the same moment, and catching her wrist in a grasp like iron, forced her into her seat again.

"Don't force me to hurt you, darling," he said coolly. "Really, your temper is not improving with age. I think if I were a timid man you would absolutely frighten me. Poor Hurdis! I am tempted to pity him, notwithstanding his having robbed me."

The utter nonchalance of the tone was maddening. With a low snarl, like that of an infuriated dog, Eva sprung up again and fled through the door to her own room.

Once there, she locked herself in, and standing with her hands pressed closely over her bosom, remained there for some moments like a hunted thing that has temporarily eluded its pursuers.

"I shall kill him!" she gasped. "I know that sooner or later it will come. Why not now, and escape the suffering! If I could but think of a way to evade the law. Let me think! Let me think! Conscience? Bah! What have I to do with conscience? I am already a lost thing, beyond hope of redemption. But for him I would be safe and happy. I will do it! I will, I swear it! Only let me find a way to escape the law!"

She paused for a moment, thinking deeply, and then a low cry burst from her lips—a cry so hoarse, so prolonged, that it sounded like nothing human.

"I have it! I have it!" she gasped with a wild laugh. "It will necessitate more deception, more hypocrisy, but it will be the last! The very last, and I shall be free from the hideous bondage. Oh, Marshall Randall, I deceived you once, and little as you think it now, you will be an easy victim again! But this time there will be no future, for the end will be death!"

The laughter had faded from her face, and a deadly white determination that was fiendish had taken its place.

XXXIII

AN UNEXPECTED MEETING.

"Well, thus we play the fools with the time, and the spirits of the
wise sit in the clouds and mock us."

"Who falls from all he knows of bliss
Cares little into what abyss."

RANDALL HAD NOT YET ACCOMPLISHED his purpose of forcing
Eva to take him to Europe, and yet another month had elapsed.

The design that she had so immaturely formed on the last night of her
stay in Los Angeles had by no means been given up. She was only waiting
until the plan of action had been completed, her hatred of him growing
with each day.

Under compulsion she had persuaded Hurdis to allow her to pass under
the name that Randall had suggested, and was known in the handsome flat
in which Hurdis had established her as Eva Randall. How galling it was to
her only her own heart could have told, but she bore it and made no sign.

She was learning in the school of bitter experience to conceal all evidence of her suffering, and while she by no means deceived Randall as to
the state of her feelings, she was a right merry companion upon occasions.

But Randall had also learned by experience! Hurdis was unaware that
Randall ever visited her since their return to New York, and Randall was
biding his time to make the fact known.

While under the strain of the terrible excitement that her position naturally entailed upon her, a desire that was irresistible came over Eva to see
again the home of her childhood, the mother under whose care she had
passed the first years of her miserable life, the little idiot brother who had
been almost her only friend.

She would sit idly for hours going over the old scenes in her mind, the days of her humiliation at school, of the death of her dog, of Lil Cartwright's cruelty, of her childish determination to be a great lady, of the years during which she had striven so hard to accomplish her purpose, of the few weeks of happiness that had followed, and of the bitter, sinful aftertime!

And how she wept!

Then, when she could bear it no longer, she asked Hurdis permission to go there for a little visit.

She did not tell him that it was her mother and her brother whom she wished to see, but only that it was a woman who had been kind to her during her unhappy childhood.

Of course he gave his permission, as he would have she asked for the moon, had it been in his power to give it.

She made her preparations secretly, not wishing Randall to know—and how much childlike pleasure she took in them! There were presents of every description for each member of the family: gowns, wraps, bonnets, gloves and every conceivable thing for her mother, and not forgetting one who had ever spoken a single kind word to her in those old days.

"I will go there under my own name," she murmured, with a smile. "They will know that I have married a great gentleman, wealthy and handsome; and we will see if Eva Hurdis is treated with the same scorn that Eva Scarlett was compelled to submit to. I shall see Lil Cartwright, too, and then..."

She did not complete the sentence, because she had not quite determined what she should do when she did see Lil Cartwright, but even to let her know that Bill Scarlett's despised daughter had married a man of Rod Hurdis' standing was enough.

With tears in her eyes, she kissed Hurdis good-bye and entered her train, thinking more of how differently she had left the village into which she was going, from the way she should return, than of him, dearly as she loved him. And she did love him, more than ever, with all the passionate fervor of her nature.

She was in the drawing-room car, unable to think of anything save her coming triumph, and the fact that she was escaping Randall for a few days at any rate, when, as she sat gazing out of the window, a hand touched her shoulder lightly.

She lifted her eyes with a start. A dark, mocking face was beside her, the man's hat raised with studious ceremony.

"This is a delightful surprise," he said with a slight sneer.

She tried to prevent the hideous pallor that she felt creeping over her face, but it was useless.

"You don't seem overjoyed to see me!" he continued. "I am disappointed.

I thought you would be in raptures."

Before the sentence was completed he had recovered her self-control. "I am not glad," she answered pettishly. "I did not want you, Marshall Randall. If I had, I should have asked you to come."

"I am afraid I should not get anywhere with you often, if I waited to be asked," he said with an easy smile.

"Where are you going now?"

"Home with you."

"But I am not going home."

"Oh, yes, you are. Home where your mother lives. I want to have some fun. I am going there as your husband."

"What for?"

"Fun."

"You don't seem to consider the danger of it."

"To pause to consider danger in war is certainly not an evidence of a good general. My dear, you have not shown any disposition recently to resent my usurpation of your husband's position. I hope you are not going to become squeamish now, just when I am more determined than ever."

For a moment a dangerous gleam came into the brown eyes. There was a stealthy movement in the direction of the innocent-looking sachet at her side that was quickly checked, then Eva turned to her persecutor with a brilliant smile.

"I am not sorry," she announced lightly. "Can't you get this seat next me? It is horribly slow traveling alone."

He bowed with mock ceremony. "That is better than I expected!" he exclaimed, with a grin of satisfaction. "I was afraid you were going to cut up rough, and that I should have to return to the old tactics. You are a wonderfully sensible woman, Eva."

"Thanks!" she drawled, with an affectation of indolence. "I am afraid you are going to become very weary of the village that you will see."

"Not by your side. You are a source of unending interest to me."

Eva did not reply. She had forgotten what he was saying in contemplating the hideousness of her situation.

"Not even for one little hour can I escape from this odious bondage!" she was saying to herself bitterly.

"God cannot blame me if I rid myself of it at any cost. At any cost!"

Then she remembered, with something like self-pity, the little plans she had made for her first visit home. What joy she would bring to the poor, unfortunate mother and the idiot brother, who had loved her in those old days that were happier than these for all her wealth and luxury—and now Randall had come there to spoil all, to make even that little time a curse.

A low sob was choked in her throat, and the dark eyes that looked through the window at the rapidly changing landscape could see nothing that appeared or vanished.

Randall looked at her curiously, and after a moment she became conscious of his gaze.

A frightful anger filled her heart that had all the cunning of mania. A reckless smile hovered upon her lips.

"We will make this a gala time," she said, nodding her head and softly winking the eye nearest him. "I have always held myself in check, and have never had what the boys call a 'high old hilarious,' but we'll do it this time in royal style! Do you agree?"

Not an expression of her rapidly changing face escaped Randall. He leaned toward her with a curious brilliancy in his eyes.

"How foolish you are not to accept life as you find it instead of willfully making a tragedy of it," he said impressively. "Even if you should lose Hurdis, there are other men in the world, and with him removed from your life, you would soon forget him. As a sensible woman, you should accept his favors while they last, enjoying yourself while youth and beauty are still yours, but not making yourself prematurely old by worrying over the day when you will lose him."

She waved her hand, concealing a shiver. "Don't let us speak of Rod!" she exclaimed. "As an honest"—with a curious emphasis on the word—"wife, it does not seem exactly the thing to talk of one's husband to one's—lover! Something of a paradox, I admit, but it suits the case."

And so, with a heart fighting rebelliously over the position that she had no power to change, they went onward to the little village that she had been so glad to leave with the man whom she had believed to be the hero of her dreams. She smiled bitterly as she remembered it, her eyes unconsciously following Randall as he went to order a carriage to drive her to the home of her mother.

She was standing with her back toward the setting sun that cast a red glow over her. The sharp breeze had brought a vivid color to her cheeks, while a heavy sealskin wrap protected her perfectly from the cold. Her skirts and the feathers upon her handsome hat were not moved enough to appear blown, but were fanned into a gentle, graceful movement.

There was rarely ever a more glorious picture of thrilling life than she appeared.

As she stood, forgetting in her disappointment where she was, several men and a few women came upon the platform. It was seldom, if ever, that so elegant a gowned woman was seen in that vicinity, and they stared at her almost rudely.

At length, a child, bare of feet even in that stinging cold, the little dress scarcely covering its small back, approached her timidly.

"Please lady," she said with her finger in her mouth, "Won't you give me something for Christmas? It is coming soon, and we ain't got nothin' to our house."

The little squeaking voice recalled Eva to herself. She looked down at the ragged thing with a start.

How like herself the child was in those old days when she was only Bill Scarlett's brat, the condemned of the village!

Before she could reply to the little one, a rough woman came up.

"How dare you!" she exclaimed to the child, seizing her by the arm and pushing her around. "Don't pay any attention to her, lady. Those brats ain't got no more manners than pigs. I never did see such a lot! Now there was—"

"The child did nothing wrong, madam," interrupted Eva in her sweet, well-modulated voice. "Come here, dear! Indeed I will give you something for Christmas, something that will buy a big, beautiful dolly that will open and shut its eyes, and walk, too, if you wish it. Poor little tot! There! That is for the dolly, and this for a new pair of shoes and a nice warm dress and cloak."

She took from her pocket-book a bill, the dimensions of which caused not only the woman beside her but the others upon the platform to open their eyes as well.

"You aren't a-goin' to give all that to her, be you?" inquired the woman, aghast. "It won't do her no good. That lazy, triflin' Bill Scarlett'll only take it away from her."

"Bill Scarlett!" gasped Eva. "Is that Bill Scarlett's daughter?"

"Lord, yes! I reckin you ain't never bin in these parts before, er you would a-knowed her. They be the toughest lot in this here—"

"Stop!" cried Eva, her voice trembling with mortification. "Perhaps you do not recognize me, Mrs. Stout, but I am Bill Scarlett's daughter myself, and that child is my sister!"

If a cannon-ball had fallen in their midst, the astonishment of the group could not have been greater.

"You—Ev—Scarlett?" gasped the woman.

"Yes," cried Eva haughtily. "But times have changed for me, and with the alteration in my affairs theirs will change as well. I am married now, and—"

Before she could complete the sentence, Randall joined her.

"My dear," he said, "the carriage is here."

Without the smallest hesitation, Eva picked up the little ragged lot in her arms and followed him to the carriage.

"Well, I never!" gasped Mrs. Stout as the carriage disappeared over the brow of the hill. "That Ev Scarlett! A fine lady, with more money than she knows what to do with! Well, I allers said there was somethin' in them Scarletts that folks didn't give 'em credit fur. Well, upon my word! I must go an' tell the folks as she is come. How glad all uv them will be."

And she, who was despised in her poverty, was welcomed as the arrival of a queen would have been.

Verily it is the law of the world.

XXXIV

AT HOME.

"The best laid schemes o' mice and men,
Gang aft agley.
And leave us naught but grief and pain,
For promised joy."

"Now conscience wakes despair
That slumbered; wakes the bitter memory
Of what he was, what he is, and what must be
Worse; of worse deeds worse sufferings must ensue."

THE NEWS SPREAD OVER THE village with the same rapidity that news usually flies. Ev Scarlett had come home!

She was no longer the Ev Scarlett of old, but a fine lady, married to an elegant gentleman who did not know himself how much money he had.

They had put up at the village hotel, and had engaged half the hotel for their own private use, report said, and lived like nabobs.

The hotel proprietor himself opened his eyes in widest astonishment at the prodigality of his guests, and the most marvelous stories, put in circulation by him and the well-fed servants, were afloat that would have put Aladdin to the blush.

The whole town was ringing with it. Mrs. Stout told of how Eva had not recognized little Bess, who was only a baby when she left, and of how, thinking that she was the child of someone else, Eva had given her a whole handful of money that she had not even paused to count.

And as each tongue repeated the remarkable story, it grew and grew until the amount that was placed in the baby's hands bid fair to rival the fortune of Vanderbilt.

"And they do say," wound up Mrs. Stout in one of her remarkable bursts of eloquence regarding Eva, "that she is goin' to buy her ma a house ten times finer than the one that them there stuck up Cartwrights, as used to turn their noses up at Eva, lives in. Lord! I wish you could a-seen Lil yesterday when Ev walked into church with that fine husband o' hern. It was about the bitterest pill she ever swallowed, I recken. She turned green with jealersy. It jist serves her right, fur she used to treat Ev awful mean, and the Scarletts never was as hard a lot as folks give 'em credit fur bein'."

"Wasn't it you, Miss Stout, as said the Scarletts wus light-fingered, and that you knowed none uv 'em would come to no more good than that there red-headed darter o' theirn had done?" asked one of the old women with a malicious twinkle in her bleared eyes.

"No, I never!" cried the other woman, bridling up at once. "I never said nothin' agin the Scarletts in my life, and them as say I did ain't no fonder o' the truth than they oughter be. There is some folks as is allers a-meddlin' in what don't consarn 'em no how."

But while these marvelous stories were in circulation, Eva was not happy.

It was the triumph that she had pictured—greater, perhaps, than she had hoped for—but there was that hideous shadow over her always.

She never moved that Randall was not beside her; she never spoke that he did not say something below his breath that she was in constant terror lest the people beside her should hear. He made remarks that galled her, or demonstrations of affection in public to which she was forced to submit or betray the secret that she would have protected with her very life.

How she suffered! And what fiendish delight he took in witnessing it.

But Randall was growing tired of it all. He wanted to return to New York to make preparations for that visit to Europe that he was now more determined upon than ever. Besides, there was too much money being wasted to please him.

He had agreed to wait over until after the Christmas festival of the twenty fourth, but that must end it, he said. So, with a weary heart, Eva told her mother that her husband was forced, on account of business, to return home, and that she must go with him.

"I ain't seed yer fur so long, Ev, that it's hard to let you go," Mrs. Scarlett whined. But while Eva sighed, she knew that it must be as her master willed.

"I am going to stay for the festival, mother," she said wearily. "But after that I must go, I suppose. I am sorry, but I am glad that you have been the happier for my coming."

"You allers were a good sort uv a gal, Ev! There ain't many as ud keer to recollict their old mammy when they gits to be fine ladies like you. You allers said you'd do it, but I never hardly believed you. I might have been jist like you ef I'd a married Mr. Cartwright instead of Bill Scarlett."

The poor woman wiped her eyes with her apron, and Eva put her arm around the thick waist and kissed the face in silence.

The Christmas festival was the single affair of note during the year in that little hamlet, and rich and poor mingled together, the rich preparing and the poor receiving the presents with bursts of gratitude. And the whole town was talking with one tongue of the liberal donation to it that Eva had made.

This year it was to be a particularly brilliant occasion, presided over by the wife of the governor of the state who was in the village visiting her uncle, the owner of the largest mines in the vicinity. She was a charming woman, dainty and refined, whom the villagers spoke of as they might an angel. But there was no woman in the room who could have compared with Eva as she entered, for either beauty or elegance of costume, though there was nothing either loud or tawdry about her.

The governor's wife advanced with outstretched hands as Eva entered. "I am so sorry, Mrs. Hurdis," she said sweetly, "that I have not been able to call upon you, but my duties have been such that it has been impossible. Friday will not be too late for me to be received, will it?"

"I regret it so much," replied Eva, "but I leave to-morrow."

"Christmas? That is too bad! You cannot remain longer then?"

"I am afraid not."

"I am so sorry. Your husband is a great friend of my husband's, and I had a letter from him to-day telling me that I must be sure to call. He will regret it as much as I."

"My husband is compelled to return home to-morrow," stammered Eva.

"And mine will be here to-morrow. As they are such old friends it is really too bad. Good evening, Miss Cartwright!"

She let go of Eva's hand to take the proffered one of Eva's old enemy, and after a cordial greeting, Lillian Cartwright turned to Eva.

"It is such a pleasure to meet you after all these years, Eva," she said with effusion. "I called at the hotel yesterday to see you, but you were out. Won't you kiss me?"

Half the people in the house were listening. For all the change in her circumstances, it seemed such a strange thing that Bill Scarlett's daughter should be chatting so familiarly with the wife of a governor and that Lillian Cartwright should actually offer to kiss her. But yet a stranger thing happened.

With the dignity of an empress, Eva drew back.

"Pardon me," she said coldly. "I am in no way changed since the time when you had your coachman strike me across the face with a horse-whip and kill my dog for his honest endeavor to protect the helpless. I was an unfortunate child then; I am a fortunate woman now, but the person is the same. Neither position nor wealth can alter that."

Without any apparent desire to attract attention, Eva turned her back upon the magnate's daughter without rudeness and began an animated conversation with the governor's wife.

Sympathizing with her, that lady seconded her efforts, and unable to think of any suitable reply, Miss Cartwright turned away in an unmistakably crestfallen manner and seated herself beside her mother.

As she had cut and insulted Eva Scarlett in the old days, so Mrs. Rod Hurdis had cut and insulted her. It was measure for measure.

The news of it spread through the assemblage like fire. Lil Cartwright was no favorite in the neighborhood on account of her pride and haughty ways among the village folk, and Eva was the heroine of the hour.

"There ain't nothin' stuck up about her!" one old lady said admiringly. "She ain't afeard to acknowledge that she wus poor, even ef she is the wife of a friend of the gov'nor. She jist did right to say what she did to that Cartwright gal, and I fur one glory in her spunk! Who'd 'a' ever thought that one o' them Cartwrights would 'a' got a cut from Bill Scarlett's darter? Well, there ain't no knowin' how things is a-goin' tu turn around in this here world. One minnit the bottom is on top, an' the next it's t'other way."

And Eva's triumph was complete. The governor's wife was one of those sweet, simple-minded women who love worth for worth's sake, and that Eva should have come from poverty to the position that was hers by the right of her being the wife of Rod Hurdis was something very much in her favor instead of against her. And the dear little woman took her to her heart with motherly affection.

And Eva tried to put from her every other thought and remembrance to be happy for that one evening! For had she not routed her old enemy? Had she not humiliated her as she herself had been humiliated in childhood?

She reveled in the thought, and she was happy for that one brief evening. There was not a thing occurred to mar its perfect success, and as she entered the room that served her and Randall as a sitting room when it was all over, she smiled with unfeigned delight that even his presence had not the power to man.

But the morrow! In her unfortunate life there was always the after time.

They were at breakfast, waited upon by an obsequious servant who, when the breakfast had been served, stood behind Eva's chair waiting for orders.

"You lef' a little too soon las' night, Mr. Hurdis," he said, showing his teeth in a broad grin.

"Why?" asked Randall, lifting his eyes from his plate.

"Cause your fren, the gov'nor, come not five minutes after you had went. He wus awful disappointed when his wife told him you had went, and wanted to come right down to the hotel, but his wife persuaded him to wait till this morning."

Eva was more thankful than she could have expressed that the servant was at her back. She lifted her eyes pleadingly to Randall. He could not repress a smile in brutal appreciation of the scene that he could so well picture in his mind.

"I shall be delighted to see him!" he said with a heartiness that was not assumed.

"You may bring the cakes," Eva said to the boy.

The door had scarcely closed upon him than she leaped wildly to her feet.

"We must leave here at once!" she cried. "At once! Do you hear? There is nothing in this entire world that would pay me to have them discover that you are not Rod Hurdis."

He laughed brutally. "This is better than I expected!" he exclaimed, but she interrupted him before he could finish the sentence.

"Oh, Marshall, you have a mother. By her memory I plead that you have pity upon mine! Do not disgrace me here in the place where my childhood was passed. See, I plead with you upon my knees. Save me from this, and I will do anything that you say no matter what it may be. Oh, Marshall, have pity upon me!"

"You have added a new word to your vocabulary, Eva—pity! You did not know it the night that I robbed the bank, did you?"

"I know that you think your hour for revenge has come, but remember my provocation, Marshall. If you will not forgive it, take your revenge in any other way than this. If you kill me, I will not submit to it, I swear to you! I will die first!"

"Get up!" he exclaimed warningly. "The servant is coming with the cakes you ordered."

She arose hastily, chilled to the heart by the fiendish grin upon his face.

XXXV

"MY FRIEND! MY DEAREST LITTLE FRIEND!"

"For nothing canst thou to damnation add
Greater than that."

"O, would the deed were good!
For now the devil that told me I did well,
says that this deed is chronicled in Hell."

SLOWLY, AS THOUGH WITH THE greatest enjoyment, Randall finished his breakfast, knowing but too well that every moment that he detained the servant in the room was a century of torture to the woman before him.

How she endured it she could scarcely remember afterward, but all things have an ending; as had that.

The boy had scarcely closed the door behind him than, with the sudden spring of a panther, she had locked it. She turned to Randall fiercely.

"Now tell me what you intend doing!" she cried. "I am in no mood to endure trifling, and I tell you frankly that I will not bear it! You must decide at once! Are you going to remain here, that my husband's friend may know you are not Rod Hurdis, or are you going away with me while yet there is time to save my reputation?"

She paused, her hands clasped above a heart that was almost audibly beating.

With the same demoniacal grin upon his face, Randall watched her.

"If you knew," he said slowly, "what an exceedingly pretty woman you are when you are angry, you would never be in a good humor."

"And is that the only answer that you have to make to me?" she cried desperately. "Cannot you see that I am in deadly earnest? Do you not understand that my life and the living upon which you depend hang upon your answer? If there is one spark of manliness in you, take me away from here! Release me from the position into which you have placed me!"

He arose slowly, biting the end from a cigar preparatory to lighting it.

"Is it not unfortunate," he said indifferently, "that you cannot release me from the position in which you have placed me? Is it not unfortunate that you cannot erase the disgrace that you put upon my name? It is not the brand of Cain that I bear because of you, my darling, but it is worse! I am an outcast—a thief! Yet I do not murmur. Mark the difference between us!"

"This is no time for marking differences!" she cried violently. "Are you or are you not going to take me away from here before that man has time to call?"

"Are you going to take me to Europe or are you not?" He looked at her coolly, as though her reply were a matter of perfect indifference to him.

She bit her lip for a moment in silence, scarcely able to control her rage, then answered sullenly:

"Yes!"

"Then, my darling, your will is my law." He picked up his hat and left the room.

She looked after him with an expression of fiendish hatred. "Curse him! Curse him! Curse him!" she repeated, the strength of her emphasis almost exhausting her. "I will free myself of this detested bondage. I will! I will! If I am a thousand times a murderess, I will! If I am forced to die upon the scaffold, or kill myself to avoid it, I will submit to this no longer. There is no God that He could condemn me to this hideous suffering when I have done no wrong none! None! No matter! No matter! Oh God, grant me success! I do not even ask escape, but only to *kill him!*"

The emphasis upon the words lent them a horror that would have chilled the blood of a listener, but she seemed to feel none.

She snatched up the satchel that she had carried on the train, and opening it, she took from it a small vial. It contained a preparation that she had procured from an old German physician that he had assured her was deadly poison, but of so subtle a kind that the most eminent chemist could not detect it in the stomach.

She hugged it to her with a smile that was maniacal, then lifted it to her lips and kissed it passionately. "My friend! My dearest little friend!" she muttered as she replaced it.

She had scarcely closed the bag when the door opened and Randall entered.

"There is only one way that we can get away from here before two o'clock this afternoon," he announced, "and that is to take a carriage to the next village. That will help matters so far as my dear friend, the governor, is concerned, but is not particularly pleasant. I concluded, however, that you would prefer it and have ordered the carriage."

She laid her hand upon his arm almost affectionately. "How good of you!" she exclaimed.

"Wasn't it!" he returned, veiling a slight sneer. "Won't you kiss me for it? No? You are the greatest series of contradictions, Eva, that I have ever seen. Well, all right. I'll excuse you until we get to the next town. Let me see. You have just fifteen minutes to get ready."

She was only too delighted that the time was so short, and going into the room that had been hers since her arrival at the hotel, she quickly changed her gown, throwing the one that she had removed into the trunk and mashing the tray down upon it.

Half an hour later they were gone, Eva lying back in the carriage with her eyes closed, nursing the hatred against Randall that had grown to the point of lunacy.

"You are not an entertaining companion," Randall said at last.

Arousing herself to the exigencies of the situation, she opened her eyes and smiled. There was a part for her to play, and if she expected success, she must begin now.

"No," she answered. "I am just trying to recover from the shock of it all. I was picturing in my mind the scene that would have been if the governor had walked in and discovered you masquerading as Rod Hurdis, my respected husband. The tragedy of the situation would have made it farcical. I should have liked to have seen his face, if it had been someone else than myself who was the most interested party." She laughed merrily, and Randall joined her.

"If Miss Cartwright could have only exchanged positions with you for an hour, for instance," he said.

"Yes, then I should have enjoyed it thoroughly. By the way, we must make up something to tell Rod about that, for of course something will be said of it to him, particularly as the worthy governor did not know before that he was married."

"That is a small consideration. When are we to have that high old hilarious that you referred to as we were coming? We have been as demure as two domesticated cats since we have been here."

"Then let us not take the afternoon train but go to the village about ten miles further on. They don't know me there, and we can do as we like."

More astonished than he had almost ever been in his life, Randall readily consented. As they were driving up to the hotel where they were to wait for the train, he stopped the coachman and told him to drive to the next village, but the man could not do it because of the engagements of his employer.

"He would not have sent me this far to-day with any one but you, sir," he said, "and it would be as much as my place is worth to go any further than he said." And though Randall offered any price that might be asked, he would not yield.

Then leaving Eva in the hotel, he went all over the town in an endeavor to procure a conveyance but without success.

"It is no use, we shall have to remain here!" he said when he returned to her.

"I will not!" she exclaimed. "I am going there if I have to walk!"

She went to the window and looked out, but the prospect seemed hopeless enough.

At that moment, a butcher's cart came rattling up the street. She seized Randall by the arm and hurried him out of the room. "Call to that man!" she cried hastily.

"We want you to take us to the next village!" she exclaimed as he paused.

The man eyed her handsome traveling gown and then grinned. "If you want to go in this cart, you are welcome!" he answered, "but it's a butcher's cart and don't smell like strawberries. Besides that, it's greasy."

"I don't care for that, if you will only take us."

Ten minutes later they were being jolted along over the rough roads, the trunk in the rear of the wagon, and Eva jesting with an *abandon* that Randall never knew her to assume before.

Once in the room that he had secured at the hotel, she threw her hat and wraps aside recklessly.

"Now let us celebrate Christmas!" she cried merrily. "Order Pommery Sec, or if champagne is an unknown quantity, get Burgundy. I am going to have a glorious time, to commemorate our escape."

Utterly surprised by her manner, Randall obeyed.

She indulged freely in the first quart of champagne, and as the last of the bottle filled their glasses, she half laid her arm around his neck.

"Get some more!" she cried excitedly. "There is nothing so supremely enjoyable in this entire world as this. Get some more, and let us have a glorious one while we are at it."

There were no call-bells in the room, as she was perfectly aware, and with flushed cheeks and eyes that contained a curious glaze, Randall arose to go for it.

The door had scarcely closed upon him than she had leaped from her seat.

With a hand as steady as iron, she seized the bag that had hardly left her hand, opened it, took out the vial, and poured half its contents in the glass that was before the seat that Randall had occupied.

As she returned it to the bag and took her place, the door opened.

"It will be here in a moment," he said.

"But you won't!" she muttered behind her teeth, the smile never leaving her face, though it had grown strangely metallic. Aloud she exclaimed, lifting her own glass to her lips, "Here is to the European trip, and many more times like the present."

With glittering eyes she watched him lift the glass to his mouth.

XXXVI

"GUILT LIES IN THE INTENT AND NOT THE DEED!"

"A suppressed resolve will betray itself in the eyes."

"Thou tellest me there is murther in mine eyes;
'Tis pretty sure and very probable,
That eyes that are the frailest and softest things,
Who shut their coward gates on atomies,
Should be called tyrants, butchers, murtherers!"

THERE WAS A RECKLESS SMILE on Randall's face as he raised the glass of sparkling amber to his lips, a smile of pleasure that his companion had been converted from the prude into a daring woman, filled with a life that was thrilling.

He was about to drain the glass to the bottom, in response to her toast, when—

What was it?

An indescribable red glare came into her eyes. It looked like sunset on a Western gulch!

Her whole face seemed to fire beneath it, as though the light were incandescent.

He paused an instant.

She dropped her eyes, flipping some imaginary particles from her gown with her finger and thumb. A smile played around her mouth, but a slight, nervous twitching marred it.

Randall watched her curiously. With an assumption of carelessness, he threw himself into a chair.

"Bah!" he exclaimed, with a slight shiver. "When champagne has stood five minutes it grows flat. Then it is positively nauseating."

Eva raised her eyes quickly. The red glow was still there intensified. It had an added touch of triumph that was almost hideous under all her beauty. Her whole face was alight with quivering crimson.

Randall could scarcely suppress an exclamation as he watched her, an exclamation of admiration as well as horror.

She laughed, but there was nothing identical with her usual little, musical ripple in the harsh sound.

"It isn't good, is it?" she cried, her voice hoarse and rasping. "But a new bottle will be here in a moment!"

"How oddly you look, and how curiously your voice sounds," said Randall slowly.

She made a valiant effort to alter it. "You never saw me under the influence of champagne before," she cried, holding herself in check as she might have undertaken to govern an unruly steed.

"Are you now?"

"Yes! Yes! Can't you see?"

"Never mind that! Let us talk of the European trip. When shall we go?"

"Whenever you wish! I am tired of the old misery! I end it this night, Randall, and this is our celebration of it. Here is to the emancipation of a slave!"

She raised the empty glass to her lips and laughed loudly as not a drop moistened their dry surface.

"My suspicions were correct!" muttered Randall below his breath. "God! What a fiend she is!"

"We are to go to Europe, are we?" she continued with hilarious glee. "When shall we sail?"

"Next week."

"So be it! Next week! I wish next week were to-morrow. Oh, Randall, I hope you may enjoy your journey as well as I have this one!"

There was a bitter meaning in the tone that he was not slow to perceive.

He laughed a trifle scornfully. "I have told you before that I shall enjoy anything with you beside me," he said, veiling a sneer. "You go as my wife, remember."

Her fingers caught the woodwork of the chair, almost wrenching it off in her hatred of him.

"Yes!" she cried desperately.

Then mentally she whispered:

"Why does the drug not do its work? It cannot fail! Oh surely it cannot!"

Her hands were trembling, her eyes flashing vivid lightings, her teeth chattering as though with violent cold.

Randall read the expression correctly.

"What an odd feeling I have in my stomach," he exclaimed, drawing his face up in a manner that might have been laughable had there been less of tragedy in her heart. "That wine must be soured."

Try as she would, Eva could not repress a cry of delight. Her fingers left the chair and interlaced themselves in a way that was dangerous.

"I don't notice it!" she said swiftly, as though hurrying the words out of her mouth. "It must be your imagination."

"I think not. There is a curious drawing, a—a something that I cannot exactly describe, but—Oh!"

The exclamation was a long one, as though caused by the most intense pain. He threw himself back in his chair, as though unable to control his writhings, and while there was no perceptible alteration in his complexion, his teeth were set in his lip while his eyes were closed in a heavy frown of agony.

Eva arose slowly to her feet, unable to sit longer, the triumph upon her face illuminating it with the phosphorescent glow of the Inferno. She stood as if chained to the spot.

There was not the slightest horror at finding herself a murderess; there was no effort to undo what she had done. She simply looked on with a smile that was almost delirious.

A knock sounded upon the door. She flew to it, took the champagne that had been ordered from the boy's hand, and closed the door upon him. Then she returned to her contemplation of Randall.

She did not observe that the wire had been cut from the bottle, and as she flung it carelessly upon the floor, the stopple flew from it, the wine spilling over the carpet.

But she was thinking too much of Randall to care for so minor a detail.

He was lying back in the chair breathing heavily, and as she crept closer to him he opened his eyes wearily.

"I believe I am dying!" he gasped. "Get—a doctor—quick! I cannot—move!"

She made no endeavor then to conceal her hideous delight. She bent above him and took his wrist in a grasp that sent her sharp nails deep into his flesh.

"Before you die," she said in a hoarse whisper, "I want you to know that I did it! Ha-ha! You have tortured me, goaded me to desperation and madness, but I have you now! Yes, you are dying! Dying by my hand, and as you go upon your way to Hades, I want you to hear the sound of my voice last, cursing you for the foul thing you have made of me! You have made me a thing so vile that there is no hope of redemption for me in either this world or the next, and I have made repentance impossible for you. Now die! Die like the dog that you are, listening to no words but curses!"

"Eva, have pity! Remember that I loved you!"

"Pity! No! All my pity is reserved for Rod Hurdis, the honorable husband whom you have forced me to deceive and disgrace. If I had killed you before, you coward, you cur, upon that night when I discovered the odious wrong that you had done me, I might have spared myself the ages of suffering that I have endured. But since that was denied me, my revenge comes now. Oh, God is good to grant me this!"

"Eva, a doctor. I ask—it in the—name of humanity!"

"And by the memory of the hideous wrong that you have done me, I reply that you shall die like the dog that you are! Ah!"

She flung the wrist that she held from her with an expression of such loathing that no words could describe it and stood back with folded arms looking at him, a laugh that was wild and horrible bubbling through her lips.

Randall listened, his eyes fixed upon her face, until the sound seemed to chill him to the very marrow of his bones. Then shaking off the feeling as one might the fascination of a serpent, he slowly arose.

The expression of suffering had left his face, and a smile filled with the last degree of scorn rested upon his countenance.

"You were too much excited to know that I was not playing my part well," he sneered. "I suspected you, and if you will look you will find the contents of that glass upon the rug! My dear Eva, guilt lies in the intent and not the deed, so that as you were determined to make of yourself a murderess, the honor is yours. I am sorry that I was compelled to lose the contents of that glass as it might have been an interesting study for a chemist, but perhaps I may find the bottle that contained it in—"

She did not allow him to finish the sentence, but made a spring for the satchel. She had fallen back previous to that, her face white as death. The disappointment was so great that unconsciousness would very likely have overtaken her, but for the sudden thought that he would find the vial.

Like a tigress, she seized it and placed it behind her. "If you take it, you do so after you have taken my life!" she screamed shrilly. "You say I am a murderess; by Heaven! I will deserve the name!"

What might have occurred in that moment only God could have told, for driven mad by his taunting face, and knowing too well the life that was in store for her, the unhappy woman seemed to have the strength of a thousand demons, but the words were heard from without, and the proprietor of the house hastily entered.

She shrunk backward, covering her ghastly face with her hands.

"What is the meaning of this?" demanded the man angrily of Randall.

"My companion has taken too much to drink," answered Randall slowly.

"You must both leave the house at once. Such disgraceful conduct cannot be tolerated in a decent place. You must go at once."

And Mrs. Rod Hurdis was forced to obey.

In the proprietor's presence she was compelled to remove the hands from her shamed, bitterly humiliated countenance, and make her brief preparations.

She had added guilt and shame to deception, yet there was some excuse to be found for her under all!

XXXVII

A NEW DETERMINATION.

"My grief lies all within,
And these external manners of laments,
Are merely shadows to the unseen grief,
That swells with silence in the tortured soul."

"Affliction is enamored of thy parts,
And thou art wedded to calamity."

AFTER HER RETURN HOME, A settled melancholy seemed to come over Eva that she had no power to shake off or even lighten.

During Hurdis' absence, Randall continued to call with the same regularity as of old. He even urged the necessity of the immediate voyage across the Atlantic, but nothing had power to arouse her, until, from melancholy, Eva fell into a slow fever that seemed to be persistently sapping her life away.

She was forced, after a time, to give up all effort and take to her bed, from which it seemed that it would be impossible for her ever to rise.

It was during this time that she met the woman who afterward proved one of her greatest enemies.

It was Randall's mother.

If nature is controlled by the law of inheritance, it was easy to understand how Randall came by the characteristic that led to his downfall.

His father had been one of those rare gentlemen that the world knows so little of, and it was considered odd by those who knew him best where the son had gotten the reckless, almost lawless disposition that had brought him to his present position.

But after one knew his mother, the seeming mystery was explained.

Not that Mrs. Randall was a woman who carried her defects exposed to the light of day! By no means. On the contrary, she had a smooth exterior that very few possess, and while she despised the son with all the strength of her nature, Eva gave to the mother a liking that might almost have been termed affection.

She very soon learned that Mrs. Randall was perfectly aware of all the secrets of her unfortunate life, and it was a time of the greatest relief to the poor, tired heart when she could put her weary head upon a woman's breast and weep out her sorrows.

It was a trying ordeal for Rod Hurdis also.

Compelled to be absent from the side of the woman whom he so sincerely loved, the only relief he found was in knowing that she was cared for by a person for whom she had formed so strong an attachment as Mrs. Randall.

And so the woman came and went at will.

"You know, dearie," she said with a sigh, "that I have as little control over Marshall as you have. Heaven knows I would rid you of him if I only could, but there seems to be no hope of it. There is but one way, and that is for you to obey him, hard as it may be for you to do so. He believes that you spoiled his life, and, while I am convinced that you never did anything of the kind, yet I am powerless to make him believe as I do. You understand that, do you not, dearie?"

"Yes, I understand! You are so good to me," the unfortunate girl would reply piteously, kissing the false face. "But for you, I should never have the strength to endure the terrible trials that are heaped upon me. You must not blame me that I cannot like him, even for your sake, and you will not when you remember that, but for him, I might have been to-day happy and innocent!"

And the old hypocrite would whine and cry over the nervous, sick girl, pretending a sympathy that her heart was too hard to feel under any circumstance. The result would be a beautiful present of some kind, or a passionate pleading upon Eva's part, that Mrs. Randall would accept a sum of money, which, after much hesitation, would be carefully pocketed.

"You must not feel any hesitancy about accepting such things from me," the miserable girl would say to her wearily. "You know that I am aware of the embarrassed state of your finances, and I must have the privileges of a friend to assist you."

After one of these scenes, one day, when Eva seemed to be on the road to recovery, the woman gently took her hand and sat in a chair beside the couch upon which Eva was resting.

"I have something to say to you to-day," she said, stroking the hand she held. "Do you feel strong enough to listen?"

"Yes; go on," Eva answered wearily, feeling sure that something concerning Randall was coming.

"Marshall wanted me to allow him to come with me to-day, but I objected so seriously that he at last consented to remain away if I would promise to deliver a message for him. Will you hear it?"

To reply was an impossibility, but Eva moved her head in faint acquiescence.

"He says," continued Mrs. Randall, "that he has waited for that European trip just as long as he intends to, and that you must get ready to go at once, or—is it necessary, dear, to repeat the threat he makes? Oh child, if I could only protect you from him, but you know how impossible that is. There seems to be but one hope for you, and that is to obey him. You don't know how I pity you, but there seems no other way. Eva, what answer shall I take him?"

Anyone with a heart not made of stone would have pitied the unhappy girl at that moment, but as Mrs. Randall took the wretched head upon her breast, she gazed calmly over it at the gown of some woman passing the window.

"What am I to do?" Eva cried miserably. "Surely you can suggest some means by which I can rid myself of this awful incubus. It hangs over me like a horrible nightmare until it threatens to choke out my very life. In the name of Heaven, tell me, what am I to do?"

"I can see no more clearly than you can! There seems to be nothing for it but to submit to a fate that it seems impossible to avert. Since there is no other hope, Eva, why not try to look upon life as less of a tragedy? Why not endeavor to make the best of it and take what pleasure you can?"

"I have tried—I have tried so hard and failed—failed so miserably that further trial is worse than useless. I love my husband with my whole heart, and to deceive him is the greatest torture to which I could be submitted, and yet I must yield to it to prevent myself from losing him. I know that that day will come. I know that some time Marshall will make a demand upon me to which I will not yield, and then he will go to Rod with the whole horrible story, but I have not the courage to defy him and take the consequences. I must have my husband's love while I may! It is the single space between me and a madhouse. Oh, if there were but some way out of it all!"

"Do you know, dear, I have been thinking for you a great deal of late? My head is, of course, clearer than yours, as, naturally, I have not the burden of your suffering to bear, and it seems to me that there is a way to at least make your chances greater!"

The copper-colored head was lifted with a start of irrepressible excitement. The brown eyes were ablaze on the instant. "A way!" she gasped breathlessly. "What way?"

"Do not allow your hopes to get too high!" exclaimed the old woman soothingly, "for what I have to propose you may reject with scorn. Did you ever think, dear, that it would be a wise thing to make some provision in the event of your husband's ever finding out the story of your past?"

"I don't think I understand."

"Well, think. If he should discover what you have done, how you have deceived him, and most particularly the manner in which you have compromised his name with my son, what will be the result? Why, situated as you are, he will leave you, and if he can avoid it, he will never see your face again. The more he loves you the more sure he will be to follow this course. Is it not true?"

"Yes," replied Eva, in a voice so choked from suffering that her words were almost unintelligible. "Yes, I have pictured how he would look in my own mind until I have been almost mad. It seems to me that, after all, that would be the happier fate—to go mad and forget it all."

"But we cannot lose our minds at will. Memory is the only friend that grief can call its own. It is useless to waste precious time in idle dreaming, Eva. The thing is to think of what is to be done and do it."

"But what is it that I am to do? Heaven knows I will embrace anything that even suggests hope, gladly."

"Then listen. As I said, in the event of your husband's discovering the truth of this unfortunate affair, as matters are, he will never see you again. What you want to do is to make it impossible for him to remain away from you. To force him, under any circumstances, to come to you. Then, loving you as he does, he will in time learn to forgive you."

The brown eyes were brilliant as freshly polished diamonds. "But how could that be done?" cried Eva eagerly.

"The fingers of a little child will hold a man more securely than all the chains in existence." The words were uttered slowly, as though the speaker wished to allow their imprint to sink deeply into the brain of her eager listener.

But the lovely face fell, the weary head sunk back with greater dejection than it had felt before.

"Do you think I have not thought of that a thousand times?" she cried, her voice filled with bitter agony. "I have even prayed to God, wicked as I am, to send me a little child to save me, but He would not hear my prayer, and there is one less for my disgrace to rest upon. It is to those who care not that children are sent, and to those who would give their lives for them that they are denied."

The wrinkled face was placed closer to the youthful one, lovely under all its suffering.

"Would you benefit an unfortunate child, and keep your husband's love, if you could do so with the help of a little deception that could neither harm him nor anyone else?" Mrs. Randall asked, her eyes glittering curiously.

Eva half arose, leaning upon her arm. Her hair had fallen around her shoulders and face, giving her a weird appearance that was added to by the pallor of her complexion and the wildness of her eyes. "I—I—don't think I understand," she stammered hoarsely. "What—is it—you mean?"

"Did you never hear of a woman buying the offspring of some unfortunate when Heaven had denied her the prayer of her life?"

The gray eyes of the old woman were fixed upon the brown ones of the girl with the curious magnetism of a snake.

Unable to remove her gaze, Eva looked on, until the words had sunk into her brain, seeming to burn there. Then with a half smothered cry, she shrunk back slowly, almost imperceptibly, until the wall prevented her going further, when with a quick movement, as though endeavoring to escape some horrible fascination, she covered her quivering face with the drapery upon her wrapper, and lay there exhausted.

Mrs. Randall smiled with supreme scorn, murmuring to herself:

"She who hesitates is lost!"

XXXVIII

EVA'S STORY.

"There are deeds
Which have no form, sufferings which have no tongue."

"Thou art a soul in bliss; but I am bound
Upon a wheel of fire; that mine own tears
Do scald like molten lead."

A SOFT ROSE-LIGHT ILLUMINED THE PARLOR, and imparted a delicate refinement to the room that a glare could so easily have destroyed. It was pleasing to the eye and grateful to the other senses, like the odor of a rare rose.

It was with a feeling of rest after duty well performed that Rod Hurdis entered there.

He glanced about with a quick smile, and went forward even before removing his coat and gloves to kneel beside his wife and tenderly kiss her.

"I felt your presence here even before I saw you, little wife!" he said tenderly. "What a blessing it is to have you here, and how lonely I am when anything takes you from my side. You are feeling better, are you not? You are as lovely as the fairest rose."

He did not notice how she was trembling, too much attracted by the brilliant color in her cheeks that he attributed to the return of health.

"If I did not know that your love for me has made you blind, you would be in a fair way to spoil me with your flattery!" she exclaimed, hiding her face upon his bosom lest he read the secret that her eyes held. "Yes, I am somewhat better."

"It makes me feel like a new man to hear you say so. I have been terribly troubled about you of late, Eva, and it has made me see how little I should be without you now. Darling, you must take better care of your precious health for my sake."

"Sometimes I think it would be better to die now, while I have your love, than to wait until some day in the future when I shall have lost it."

He could scarcely understand the wild trembling in the voice, but attributed it to weakness and kissed her lips to silence.

"You must not say that," he whispered fondly. "Do you think me so poor a thing that I give my love but to take it back again? Why, sweetheart, how you are shaking! What is it? Have I been too rough with you?"

"You could not. You know nothing but gentleness and kindness. Oh, Rod—There! You are making me childish, dear. Get up and take off your coat. I have something to tell you."

When he had obeyed her, she pushed a chair in front of the fire that glowed within the grate; then, when he was seated in it, she placed herself upon a stool at his feet, laying her head against his knee, where she could avert her face by gazing into the crimson coals.

"Now, little woman," he exclaimed, smoothing her hair gently, "go on. I am all impatience to know the secret. I wonder if I could not guess what it is?"

"Try!"

"Try? Well, there has come in to you a great big milliner's bill that is hanging over your poor little head. Isn't that so?"

If he could but have seen the anguish in those dark eyes, he would have ceased his bantering tone upon the instant; but he only saw the pretty profile—that had an additional color.

"No," she said slowly, "that is not it."

"No? Then I suppose I must guess again. That is such a great relief that I shall guess correctly. This time, you must do as the children do, and tell me when I get 'warm.' Will you?"

"I—I am afraid you would never get warm. It—it is something that will surprise you very greatly, Rod, and—and please you, too, I think."

Oh, how much misery might have been spared if he could but have seen her face! But its quivering anguish was resolutely concealed from him, and he was left in ignorance.

"Another relief!" he exclaimed laughingly. "I was afraid it might be the news of a murder, from the lugubrious tone of your voice. What is it, darling?"

"I scarcely know how to tell you. It is all so new and strange to me, Rod, that I don't know exactly how I am to tell you. It is something that I have suspected, but never knew until to-day."

Why was he deaf to the awful shame, the remorse, and the agony of the tone? It would seem incredible that any human creature could have listened to her and not have known. But he did not even suspect.

"You alarm me!" he said slowly.

She turned her face and hid it upon his breast.

"Do you remember," she said, moistening her dry lips, and shuddering at the terrible hush that had fallen upon them, "do you remember a play that we once saw together, in which a wife had a secret to tell her husband, and she adopted the story as told by Dickens—the story of Bella and John? Have you forgotten?"

"Let me see! You mean that Western play, don't you?"

She nodded faintly.

"What was the secret she told him? Let me—oh, yes! It was about the little ship. She meant the ship of a human life, Eva, that was coming to them through a sea of suffering, but was to be the crowning joy of married bliss when it arrived. Someday, my darling, I hope that you will have that story to tell to me, and then I shall know that the greatest happiness of my life has come."

He heard a low, choking sob and tried to lift the face that was still concealed upon his bosom, but it was held firmly.

"Eva, what is it?" he whispered, his voice grown strangely hoarse.

"I have—that story—to tell you now, Rod!" she stammered, seeming to tear the words from her throat as if by force.

"Eva!"

The exclamation was a cry of such ineffable delight that no words could have described it.

It caused her, for the moment, to forget the hideous deception that she was putting upon him, and for the time, her words were as true to her as though the little life to which she referred was hers in reality, and not a fiction.

She sprung to her feet, and was caught in a madly passionate embrace to his bosom.

"My darling, my wife!" he cried, holding her off at arm's length and gazing yearningly into the sweet, crimson face. "Tell me again, that I may be sure that I am not dreaming! Oh, Eva, of all the good that God has ever sent, this surely is the best!"

How she loathed herself! She felt his kisses rain upon her face, and each was a death-dealing stab that she felt must kill; yet she was doing it to secure his love!

And at length, when he had mastered his delighted excitement, he sat again in the chair, with her upon his knee.

It seemed to him that neither Heaven nor earth held a being so happy as he; and she knew that perdition did not hold one so utterly miserable as she.

How she prevented herself from betraying her loathsome secret in that hour she could never remember, but with a desperation that amounted almost to the cunning of madness, she caused her lips to smile, while her heart was groaning with its own anguish.

But there was more yet to be done, and with a feeling of guilt that was never before or afterward equaled, she placed her arm around his neck and laid her hot cheek against his.

"And you are really happy, Rod?" she asked wistfully.

"No king upon his throne was ever more so! It means more to me than you think, Eva, for all my fortune would have gone to a man whom I despise had I had no heir. I had begun to fear that there would be no hope for me, but I would not tell you for fear it might distress you. You must let me make our marriage public now, for, with this honor awaiting me, I could not keep it concealed."

"You shall tell it by and by if you wish, particularly as your friend, the governor, has already discovered it, through my foolish pride, but not just yet, Rod. I—I don't want to frighten you, dear, but—the doctor says that my health is—by no means good, and—oh, Rod, how can I tell you?—he has ordered me to Europe!"

She broke down utterly as the, to her, hideous words left her lips, and sobs that shook her entire frame burst from her.

He strove in every way to comfort her, but the task was no easy one.

"It is not so dreadful a thing, sweet, to cross the ocean," he told her, smoothing the bright hair tenderly. "Can you really be so downhearted when a blessing like this awaits us? It seems to me that I will never again find fault with fate!"

"Then you do not mind my going?"

"Not that, dearest, but I would submit to anything to save your precious health. My single regret is that I cannot go with you without sacrificing the position that I have striven half my life to gain."

"I would not have you do that!" she interrupted hastily. "You must not think of sacrificing anything for me. It would make me utterly miserable if I thought you would. I told—my—aunt my trouble to-day, and—she will go—with me—if you would prefer it!"

"That relieves my mind very greatly, but if you wish it, my darling, I will throw aside everything, and go with you myself!"

"No," she cried, her voice choked with the agony she was suffering. "I should really prefer—that you—should not!"

"That is a dear, sensible, little woman. But it is very hard for me to bear. You will not be gone long, will you, Eva?"

The question was asked so wistfully that it seemed to touch her very heart.

"No!" she exclaimed, an agonized quiver sounding in the tone. "I had rather die a thousand deaths than go there without you, and you may be sure that only death—or—worse could ever cause me to remain one hour longer than necessity demands."

"There could be nothing worse than your death, my wife!"

"You don't know! Oh, Rod, there are so many things in this life that are worse than death, that one can never tell! Oh, my husband, if one could only die while one is happy without the sin of suicide, how much misery, how many lost souls there might be saved! Rod, don't listen to me! Forget what I am saying, but your consent to let me go has taken the one hope out of my life. Oh, my darling, if you only knew!"

And in that moment, with the frightful grief and anguish upon her, she would have saved herself from the odious crime that she was about to commit, had not that adverse fate, that seemed to follow her with such persistency through life, overtaken her.

But Satan advocated Randall's cause—she fainted!

XXXIX

OFF FOR EUROPE.

"Thus woe succeeds a woe, as wave a wave."

"Whom conscience, ne'er asleep,
Wounds with incessant strokes not loud but deep."

IF THERE HAD EVER, AT any time in her life that preceded that moment, have seemed to Eva Hurdis that any pleasure was contained in sin, she was fully convinced of her error when she stepped upon the gang-plank leading to the steamer bound for Liverpool.

If she could but have summoned the courage to have thrown herself into the dark waters that seemed to sough about the vessel like the melancholy swirl of the wind in midwinter, it would have been a happier fate than the one in store for her, but even had she so desired, her husband held her with such tender care that any effort of that kind would but have met with failure. And so she suffered in silence.

For a moment they stood alone in the comfortable cabin that he had engaged for her, his arm encircling her with gentlest love.

"Good-bye, little one," he whispered with a suspicious tremor in his voice. "Remember how necessary you are to my happiness, and take care of your precious health for my sake. You are taking the very heart out of my body to carry in the palm of your little hand until you return, my darling, so do not be longer away than necessity requires. I shall be like a ship in a tempest without a rudder until I have you again. Good-bye, and God bless and protect you, my own."

She dared not trust herself to reply, but with streaming eyes, she watched him as he turned and grasped Mrs. Randall's hand, wringing it earnestly.

"Take care of her," he said, concealing the quiver in his voice under a smile. "She will tell you why her life is of double value now. Bring her back to me in safety, and you may account me ever your sincerest friend."

Then once more he had Eva in his arms, was raining down upon her wet face a passion of kisses. He murmured words that Mrs. Randall did not try to hear, but which lived in the young wife's memory during all the terrible aftertime. Then, placing her in Mrs. Randall's arms, he left her.

With a suppression of grief that seemed bursting her heart, Eva allowed him to go from her as she might have submitted to seeing clods of earth thrown upon his casket, but it is doubtful if even then she would have felt an anguish so poignant.

There are living tortures beside which death seems a pleasure. Her throat ached with sharp pain of a knife thrust, and the throbs of her heart seemed each a separate stab.

She did not call him back, but hiding her face upon Mrs. Randall's bosom, she waited until she knew that should weakness overcome her it would then be too late.

Then she raised her miserable head to encounter the sneering countenance of Marshall Randall.

"What a touching scene!" he exclaimed dryly. "To see you one would never dream that you had wept when Maurice Vanderfelt left you for a single night, or that you had even pleaded with me to remain near you. Ay verily"—with indescribable irony—"there is no constancy like a woman's love."

She did not reply, but lifted her lips and kissed the face of his mother.

Randall frowned. "It is time that you were going!" he said sullenly. "The first thing you know we will be off, and swimming is not pleasant in this weather."

"Must you go?" cried Eva, desperately clinging to her as the last fragment of hope. "Do not leave me! Your presence can make no difference to him, and—"

"It is time that you were off!" exclaimed Randall angrily. "Can't you go before you are thrown off?"

Then silently, Eva yielded. Her spirit was too bruised and broken to resist longer, or to cause any scene. She bowed her head to his will, as a condemned wretch does to the guillotine.

She did not leave her stateroom to see Mrs. Randall off the steamer, but sat like a creature entangled within a maze of anguish that each effort at extrication but entangles the deeper.

Randall looked at her with a sardonic smile. "What a jolly companion," he cried at last. "If this does not improve, I think I shall have to return you to Rod Hurdis with the information that you have suddenly grown too prosaic for my taste. I don't mind your being a termagant, Eva. Not in the

very least. That is rather entertaining and varies the monotony delight-
fully. I can even endure an occasional attempt on my life. But when you
assume Christian airs and graces, when you abandon the manner of a little
savage for that of civilization, it cloys like sweet champagne. Don't do it!
Upbraid me, curse me, do anything you like, but for Heaven's sake don't
sit there in that absurd silence!"

She lifted her eyes into which white heat anger was growing.

"I wonder why God lets a creature like you live?" she said slowly.

Randall laughed. "It is Satan, my darling!" he answered lightly. "And he
does it out of consideration for your pleasure. I thought a few days ago
that you hated me, Eva, but now I am coming to the conclusion that you
love me."

"Love you!" she exclaimed with passionate bitterness. "All the demons
in Hades could not coin words enough to tell you how I hate you! If I
could, even the fear of God himself would not keep me from killing you.
You were the first to wreck my life, and you have followed it up, adding
torture to torture until you have left me neither hope of happiness here
nor chance for salvation hereafter. I am, through you, already a lost thing,
wandering in that chaos that is described in the word 'hell.' Therefore,
what need have I to care? There is one influence that sheds a hallowed
shadow upon my wretched existence—Rod Hurdis! Some day you will
make me forget even him, and in the misery of the moment I shall kill you
outright, without the precaution of concealment. For his sake I shall avoid
that as long as possible, and in order to do so, I shall in future not speak to
you at all. When occasion requires it, in presence of others, I shall do so
to prevent comment, but otherwise not all. You understand me! Neither
persuasion nor threat can move me. Knowing that it is the only way that I
can prevent myself from becoming a murderess, I shall have the strength
to endure your taunts. This is my ultimatum. I have already told you that
nothing you can say will change me."

And try as he would, he could not induce her to break her word. When
threats had failed, he tried to anger her into conversation of some kind.
Then, failing in that, he tried persuasion, equally without avail.

What a time it was to her, only God could have told, and why she did
not return a lunatic she could never quite understand, but so it was. At the
end of the most maddening three months that she had ever endured, they
took the steamer for New York, and if a sigh of relief hovered upon the
poor woman's lips, it was quickly suppressed in the remembrance of the
terrible deception that awaited her there.

"I shall never be happy," she would murmur as she thought of it. "That
child will stand as a living barrier between me and peace, but it is my only
show for retaining Hurdis when the end comes, as soon it must. I cannot

endure this life longer as it is. Then, when Randall tells him the horrible story of my shame, if there is no tie to bind him to me, I shall never see him again. But with the child that he will believe to be his, I can bring him back to me! I will love it for that reason! It will give me my husband back again!"

"One more day!" exclaimed Randall, as he flung a cigar out the window of her state-room upon their homeward voyage. "There is one thing that I should like to say to you, Eva, before our arrival, and I may as well say it now. You have made my trip to Europe an utter failure! I had intended that it should be one gala time, from beginning to end, instead of which I feel as though I were returning from the funeral of my best friend. I want to assure you that I shall not allow an offense like that to go unpunished. As long as you amused me, I was willing to keep your secret, but I shall repay you for this! I hope you will remember what I say!"

She did not reply. She was wondering for the thousandth time how she was to prevent his knowing what she contemplated regarding the child, and how she was to deceive him. She did not care what he suspected, so long as she could keep any proof of it out of his hands that he could ultimately place before her husband.

Therefore, she scarcely heard his words.

He was watching her curiously. "What scheme is she concocting now?" he muttered below his breath. "I have seen that expression upon her face so often of late. I should like to know what in thunder it means. I must watch her, without allowing her to suspect me."

Then aloud, he said sneeringly:

"What a pity you could not let the beloved husband know the time of your arrival that he might have met you! I wonder that you can wait so long! Let me see! I think we shall have to take our next trip back up there among those hills where my divinity was born. I want to see if the governor is still there. I have always regretted that I did not see him! In that instance, I threw away one of the best chances of my life for a lark, and I shall never cease to censure myself for it. You may be sure that it will never occur again. I think that the best thing, however, that I can do would be to tell Hurdis the story that I have to relate upon our arrival in port, and prove by our fellow voyagers how absolutely devoted we have been!"

He could not fail to observe how white she had grown. If he told that story before she had had time to adopt that child, all her suffering and the fearful lie that she had told would go for naught! She would have no chance of holding Hurdis!

"Yes, that will be best!" Randall continued with a grin of delight that he had touched the right cord at last. "I shall tell him!"

And from his tone, Eva was convinced that he meant what he said.

She turned to him with the calmness of despair. "I do not ask you not to do that," she said dully. "But I simply wish to point out to you the fact that in doing it, you destroy the bridge that is carrying you! As for me, I have come to the conclusion that I don't care! Tell it, if you like! There has got to be an end to it all some time, and the sooner it corners, the sooner it will be over. One can only die once, and to suffer the pain of it a thousand times in anticipation as I am doing is foolish. Do as you like, but in the hour that you make Rod Hurdis aware of the shame that I have put upon him, you must be prepared for death, for as surely as we both live, you shall die! Do not think that because I failed once I shall fail again! It will but make my success the next time all the more assured. I hope you understand me!"

He was not slow to do that. He understood her desperation readily enough.

Aloud he muttered, as though intending the words solely for himself:

"I cannot decide which will hurt worse. There is so much horror in constant dread that perhaps the suffering from that would be the hardest to bear, until I am ready for the other. Which shall it be? I cannot quite decide."

And the miserable woman held her breath over the decision, thinking how much the delay meant for her, yet not daring to speak.

XL

ANOTHER LEAVE-TAKING.

"Of this alone is even God deprived—the power of making that which is past never to have been."

*"Dreaming of a to-morrow, which to-morrow
Will be as distant then as this to-day."*

THE MONTH WAS MAY, BUT there was chilliness in the atmosphere that demanded fire.

It glowed in the open grate, shedding a soft radiance through the room. It rested as does a gentle hand upon a bowed head, touching softly a figure that crouched before it upon the rug.

The position indicated enough wretchedness to have delighted the heart of Mephistopheles.

Even the back would have suggested to an artist the wildest dream of despair, without a view of the haggard face that the arms concealed.

Without moan or groan she continued to sit there upon the rug, her head bowed until it rested between her knees, one hand clasped over the back of it.

A woman entered and looked at her curiously, silently put away an article that she had brought, and retired without a word.

Outside the closed door, she paused and glanced back pityingly.

"I wonder what it is?" she murmured. "It is always like this, except when Mr. Hurdis is here. Then she tries to arouse herself, but the effort is pitiable. I wonder if he is blind that he cannot see it as I do. Poor, unhappy girl—for she is no more than that—I—I don't know what troubles her, but I pity her. I am only a servant, but I am a woman, and I have a heart, I believe—"

She seemed to hesitate a moment, then with sudden resolution she opened the door silently and re-entered. The motionless figure upon the rug did not even hear.

Slowly, the woman advanced and stood over the light of a great sympathy, making her plain face beautiful. Again she hesitated, then leaned over and touched her mistress upon the shoulder.

The white face was lifted with a desperate start.

"You—you frightened me!" Eva stammered, summoning a wan smile. "What is it, Anne?

"Nothing, ma'am," the servant answered, controlling an inclination to sob. "I hope you will pardon me, but I could not bear to see you like that day after day and never say a word of sympathy to you. I am only a servant, ma'am, but if there is anything that I can do, any way that I can make the burden you bear the lighter—excuse me, ma'am, but I should be a fool if I could not see how you are suffering. If you would only let me help you in some way, I should be so happy!"

Almost stupidly, Eva gazed into her kindly face.

"You—I don't think I understand," she said hoarsely. "You mean—"

"I don't mean anything, except that one could not be around you as I am and not see that some terrible thing is distressing you until you suffer as women seldom do. I know that the friendship of a servant is a poor thing, but at least I am a woman who can pity the affliction of others from having suffered myself. Is there not something that I can do for you?"

In all her barren life, those were the first words of real sympathy that had been spoken to Eva.

For a moment the experience was so new that she scarcely knew how to receive them, but an instant later her arms were around the woman's neck, and she was sobbing as she had never sobbed before.

What though the breast that sheltered her was that of a servant? It mattered little to her! It was warm with sympathy, the sympathy that is often better than love.

Mistress and maid wept together.

"I am very foolish," Eva said at last, when she had mastered her emotion, "but nervousness has made a child of me. You are very good to offer me your sympathy, Anne."

The woman's face fell. "Then you will not let me help you?" she said wearily. "I hoped that there might be something that I could do."

"I am afraid there is nothing to be done, Anne. You know there are griefs that nothing but death can ever conquer. Mine is one of them. I have dreamed of a healing as one dreams of to-morrow, but, like to-morrow, it never comes, Anne. There is only one hope for me—death!"

"Don't say that! It is the most pitiful thing under God's sun to hear one at your age speak like that. It is surely enough for the old to suffer when life is done. But—don't you think—pardon me, but Mr. Hurdis told me of—"

"Hush!"

The exclamation was a groan of such bitter anguish that Anne recoiled. Then Eva cried, after a moment of painful silence:

"Are you not a woman? Can you not see the lie in it all for yourself?"

The words were uttered before she was aware of it. Then, realizing what she had done, the unhappy woman sunk down again, covering her ghastly face with her hands.

For a moment, the servant stood staring down upon her, a horror that seemed unquenchable filling her eyes; then she kneeled and raised the miserable form in her arms.

"What is it that you are doing?" she cried in a shocked, horrified voice. "Surely not deceiving your husband into believing that he is to be a father, when no such blessing as that is in reserve for him? What has ever caused you to even think of such an awful thing?"

"Hush!" cried Eva passionately, springing from the woman's arms and walking up and down the floor like a mad thing. "In your own security you can prate to me of the evil of a thing; but if your happiness, your honor, your very life were involved as mine are, you would do the same thing, and forget the horror, the awfulness, until the deed was done. You would let repentance follow accomplishment! It is too late for you to preach to me of the sin of it all, Anne! I know it but too well, and have thought of it until the wonder to me is that I still live to think, and it has done no good! There is no help for me! There is but one thing that you can do, and that is to go to my husband and tell him the truth that I have betrayed to you in a moment of weakness."

"Can you think so meanly of me as that? While I condemn the deed, I do not know your temptation, and I am not your judge! My silence might make me considered your accomplice in an act that is called crime by the law; but I know but too well the small chance an unhappy woman has against the world, and I am your friend, if you will accept so poor a thing as the friendship of a servant!"

Once again the arms of the mistress were around the neck of the maid, and Eva was clasped closely to the heart of one honest woman.

"And you will go away with me, Anne?" she asked at last, lifting her head with something very like hope in her eyes.

"If you will take me, you may count on my faithful service through life!" answered the woman, kissing her.

"Why, little woman!" exclaimed Hurdis, entering half an hour later, "that is the first genuine smile that I have seen on your face in ages. It seems like the sun after the deluge. What is the meaning of it all?"

"It means that I have been a very foolish woman, and am sorry for it! Will you forgive me for making you so uncomfortable, Rod?"

"Forgive you, my darling? As if there should ever be any talk of forgiveness between you and me! Where there is perfect love, there should never be any need of that question. But I have bad news for you, little woman! I find that shall be compelled to go to Canada tonight, and it is very uncertain when I can return. I am so sorry, my darling, particularly—"

"Don't think of me, Rod! The separation is hard to bear, but even that will come to an end. You must not fret about my condition, dear, for Anne will take care of me. You go tonight, you say?"

"Yes."

"Then, if you do not object, I think I will go to-morrow, taking Anne with me, to Syracuse. I have friends there, and—if anything should—occur during your absence, I should prefer being with them! You don't mind, do you?"

"Not in the least! On the contrary, it will be a pleasure for me to know that you are with friends who will care for you in the event of an accident. I will leave you my address, and you must telegraph me if anything happens, and write every day if it is but a line! Oh, darling, I am so weary of these separations! I have decided that the best thing for our happiness will be for me to retire from public life altogether, especially now that I am to be"—with a brief but happy laugh—"a family man."

He was holding her closely to his breast, and could not see the sudden, strained look that darkened the beautiful eyes, but he felt her tremble slightly, and drew her closer.

"I hope this will be our last goodbye, sweet, for many years. I shall not let you go again, and I shall not leave you. It seems to me that we have had nothing but partings in our married life."

"Have I made you happy, Rod? Do you ever regret that you married me, knowing nothing of my past? Does it ever occur to you that you might have been happier with another?"

"Why, little woman, what questions! Do you ask them to tease yourself, or me? I would not have our lives changed in the smallest particular, save the partings. There that was the announcement of dinner, was it not? Come, my darling. Put aside fancies, and be the same perfect woman that greeted me on my entrance."

"You are going to-morrow?" whispered Anne, as she found herself alone for a moment with her mistress.

"Yes. Mr. Hurdis proposed it himself—at least, said that he must go. It was a most fortunate thing, as he would surely have thought it strange that I should have desired to leave at such a time. Oh, Anne, it seems that the Devil is always ready enough to assist us in doing a wrong! He always provides the easiest way to place us the more securely in his power."

The bitterness of the tone caused the woman to put out her hand and touch her mistress pityingly.

"It is not too late yet to reconsider," she cried pleadingly.

Eva shook her head.

"It is too late," she said with hollow helplessness.

XLI

THE ADOPTION.

"I am not mad—I would to Heaven I were!
For then 'tis like I should forget myself;
Oh, if I could, what grief should I forget!"

"I cannot weep, for all my body's moisture
Scarce serves to quench my furnace-burning heart."

TWO DAYS AFTER ROD HURDIS' departure for Canada, Mrs. Randall called upon Eva.

The latter was dressed for the street, a tissue veil drawn over the beautiful face that even such suffering as hers had not the power to mar. The sensitive lips were trembling, however, beneath a smile that was a flimsy deception.

"I see you are all ready!" exclaimed Mrs. Randall. "That is well. You have heard nothing of Marshall this morning?"

"Yes; he called," answered Eva wearily, "but Anne told him that I had gone to Albany with my husband. I hope it will keep him away until I can get away to Syracuse. You have not seen the woman of whom you spoke?"

"No; we will go there at once if you wish; then you and Anne can leave for Syracuse tonight, if that is possible, or to-morrow night at the latest."

"How good you are to plan so much for me! But for you—"

"Never mind that now. Some other time I will let you express all the gratitude you like, but we have not the time now. If you are quite ready, we will be off."

The brown eyes glittered with a curious brilliancy as Eva nodded too breathless from excitement to reply in words.

Leading the way, Mrs. Randall went down-stairs and cautiously left through the street-door, as though cleaning to avoid observation.

They had gone but a few feet however, when it became evident to her that she must either assist Eva or she would fall.

"You must bear up," she said encouragingly, taking the girl's arm. "Remember what it promises you, and have courage. I thought it best not to take a carriage—"

"Decidedly!" interrupted Eva. "Don't mind me. I shall get on well enough. Let us hurry."

But though she spoke bravely enough, Mrs. Randall was not slow to perceive that her strength would not last much longer, and stopped a passing car. She almost carried Eva into it, but the rest was beneficial. It enabled her to walk the distance that remained after they had left the car, to a house that seemed to stand remote from the world, though surrounded by it.

Mrs. Randall, still holding the girl by the arm, mounted the stoop and pulled the bell.

A slatternly maid, with not even a pretension at cleanliness, answered.

"Is Mrs. Minturn at home?" Mrs. Randall inquired.

"Walk right in."

Mrs. Randall, still holding Eva's arm in a grasp like iron, obeyed.

They were ushered into a room that looked as though it had never formed the acquaintance of a broom. The dust was inches thick upon everything; the articles of furniture being in utter confusion.

A woman with a greasy black silk apron adorning her person advanced to meet them with a bland smile. "Is there anything that I can do for you to-day, ladies?" she asked insinuatingly.

"Are you Mrs. Minturn?" Mrs. Randall asked, seeing that Eva was speechless.

"I am. Won't you be seated?"

Eva sunk into the chair to which the woman pointed, too much overcome to be fastidious.

"Do you wish my professional services?" inquired Mrs. Minturn, as both ladies were silent.

"No!" answered Mrs. Randall. "We wish to adopt a child, and we want to know if you have any on hand!"

Eva groaned. It seemed a horrible thing to her to traffic in human life in that manner, but the midwife answered in the most nonchalant way imaginable:

"Oh, yes, several! We had one born yesterday and another to-day. You prefer a young baby, I suppose?"

"Yes," replied Mrs. Randall. "Will you let us see the children?"

"Certainly. Letty! Letty!" she cried in a shrill voice. "Bring the two youngest here at once. These ladies want to see them."

There was but a few moments to wait when the same girl who had admitted them entered bearing a baby on each arm. Had it been a bundle of linen, she would doubtless have shown just as much feeling.

With a heart beating almost to suffocation, Eva arose.

Mrs. Minturn took both children upon her knee and unwrapped them, turning the poor little faces to the light that the visitors might be the better able to judge of their respective merits.

"You see," she began in an explanatory sort of way, "that one is a boy and this one a girl. She is the youngest. The mother of that boy is a lovely young thing; her hair is as black as night. She was—"

"I don't care in the least to know their history!" Eva interrupted with a shiver. "The woman who could abandon a little creature like that whom she has brought into the world is too vile to deserve compassion, and her history could never make me care more for the little thing than its own misfortune."

The midwife raised her eyes curiously to the lovely face.

"My dear," she said dryly, "there is one thing that you may learn with years, and that is that there is nothing on this earth that has not its price! There is no honor that either some suffering or hope of some reward will not purchase. There is nothing, even to a mother's love. It is the prerogative of God alone to judge. Now this one," she continued, turning to the children as though they were pieces of merchandise, "is the daughter of a woman not altogether pretty, but well bred and refined."

"But she is ugly!" cut in Eva. "I don't mean that that is anything against the poor little waif, but if I am to adopt a child, I want one that I can forget is not my own. I want a child that I can love just at first, and that will not require time to grow into my heart. I hope you do not misunderstand me. My sympathy for the little one would be great enough to make me always kind, but I want to be more than that. I want to love it! Oh, madam, I can't make you understand, but that child will not do! Have you no other?"

The woman was silent a moment, then motioning to Letty, said something to her in a low tone. The girl retired and a little later returned to the room, bearing another bundle, similar to the first.

"This child is but a few hours old," the midwife said, uncovering its face as she had done the others. "Its mother is dead."

With a sudden impulse, Eva reached out her arms and took the little thing to her breast.

Something in the woman's tone had drawn out all her heart to the tiny waif, and even before she knew its sex or had seen its face, she determined that it should be hers.

Very tenderly, she kissed it and then covered it carefully.

"This baby shall be mine," she said reverently.

The midwife turned briskly to Letty.

"Take the others away," she said in a tone that savored of nothing but business. Then to Eva: "Ten dollars, please!"

Eva stared at her in surprise.

"Do you mean," she said slowly, "that you sell these babies?

"You don't suppose I give them away, do you?" asked the woman with ill-concealed disgust.

Eva was too much surprised and horrified to reply. She therefore took out her pocket-book, extracted a bill from it, and held it toward the woman.

The midwife took it with every evidence of satisfaction.

"If it should die," she said calmly, "I hope you will give me another call."

Feeling a nausea that she could scarcely control, Eva clasped her precious bundle yet closer, and followed by Mrs. Randall, hastily left the house.

What she suffered on the brief homeward journey, only Heaven could have told. But she bore it silently, feeling insensibly that she could hope for no real sympathy from Mrs. Randall, good as she had been to all appearances.

At the door she was met by Anne, Mrs. Randall having gone to her own room.

"You have got it?" inquired the kindly domestic eagerly.

Eva nodded wearily.

"Take it, Anne," she said in a hollow tone that, to the maid, sounded like death. "I have been trying to decide which is the more unfortunate; it or I! Oh, Anne, I pray God that I may do my duty by it! I pray God that my sins may not be visited upon the head of that little unfortunate! I pray God to protect and shield it, whatever punishment may be sent upon me."

"You must not feel like that ma'am. Whatever sin you may be committing, you are harming that child in no way, poor, little, motherless thing!"

With more tenderness, perhaps, than she would have felt toward the offspring of a millionaire, Anne unwrapped the infant, and gently shielding the mite from the glare of the light, turned the tiny face toward the woman who had constituted herself its mother.

"Why, Mrs. Hurdis," the maid exclaimed, "the child is as like to Mr. Hurdis as though it were his own! Look at it!"

Eagerly, the unhappy woman obeyed, gazing upon the little face as though it held every hope in life to her.

The great, dark eyes were staring up at her as though the owner were pleading for her love and tenderness.

With a quickly suppressed, but glad, cry, Eva hugged it to her.

"It is an omen of good!" she exclaimed. "It is an assurance that the curse of Heaven is not upon the deed that I have done! Oh, Anne, I am happy—happy at last!"

But the feeling did not continue.

They left for Syracuse the following morning, but a slow fever, the result of over-excitement, had set in, and upon their arrival there, a doctor was summoned.

The following day, a telegram was sent to Rod Hurdis. It read:

> Laura Roderick Hurdis was born at day-break. Mother and child doing well. Anne Chute.

The answer came back long before either of them expected it.

> God bless you both. Will be with you as soon as possible. Will write. Rod.

"He is coming?" cried Eva nervously. "Oh, Anne what shall we do? What will he think when he finds that I have no friends here?"

"You must not allow yourself to become distressed over trifles. It is easy enough to tell him that your friends had gone before your arrival, and that it was then too late for you to return home! You need not fear. Where there is no suspicion, it is the easiest thing in the world to deceive."

But for all Anne's encouragement, it was a wan face that was lifted for her husband's kiss when Hurdis came at the end of the week, a face that was pale, but more beautiful to him than he ever remembered to have seen it.

"My little one, my wife!" he whispered. "I am the happiest man in all this world. Where is the baby?"

How she pitied him! She could have cried aloud when she saw his eagerness.

"What would he think?" she was muttering to her own heart as a terrible shiver almost overcame her, "what would he think if he knew the horrible truth?"

Then she saw him with the child in his arms, that offspring of a woman of whose very name they were both in ignorance. She saw him bend his head in fortunate delight and press his lips upon the little pink face, she heard him murmur words that a man speaks only to his first-born, the pride of his heart, and with a groan that she could not control, she turned her face to the wall.

This, then, was the happiness of which she had dreamed! It was to purchase this that she had added a crime against the man she loved to the number that she had already committed.

Verily it was:

"Like Dead Sea fruit that tempt the eye
But turns to ashes on the lips."

Then she seemed to awake to the consciousness that he was beside her with the baby still clasped in his arms.

"Eva," he was saying, "this is a combination of our two selves, cementing our love with the seal of Heaven. Darling, let us thank God together!"

And with forced calmness, she was compelled to listen, her heart breaking with the hideous knowledge of her own guilt.

XLII

AN UNWELCOME VISITOR.

"Lo! As the wind is so is mortal life,
A moan, a sigh, a sob, a storm, strife."

"Into what abyss of fears
And horrors hast thou plunged me; out of which
I find no way, from deep to deeper plunged!"

"THERE IS A WOMAN IN the parlor who has asked for you, Mrs. Hurdis."

There was a troubled look upon the honest face of Anne that Eva never remembered to have seen there before.

She was seated in her own boudoir, having returned but a short time before from the drive that her husband insisted upon her taking every day for the benefit of her health and that of the precious child, which was already, at that early age, mistress of the household.

With more feeling than she usually displayed, Eva laid her hand upon her maid's arm. "Has something distressed you, Anne?" she asked, forgetting the words that her servant had spoken.

"I don't like the looks of that woman!" Anne answered, shifting her gaze from her mistress' face to the floor.

"What is her name?"

"Marie Durneo, she said, but there is a curious look about her that don't seem honest. I wish you would not see her, ma'am!"

Eva laughed, a really musical sound for all her trouble.

"What nonsense! Why, really, Anne," she cried with genuine amusement, "you are becoming fanciful. I never heard of the woman before in my life. Why should I not see her?"

"I don't know! Perhaps I am wrong, but I never saw a face like that yet that contained anything of honesty. Somehow I feel that she will bring you trouble!"

"Absurd! I will go to her and prove to you how false your theories are!"

Eva arose, still smiling, and kissing the faithful girl upon the cheek, left the room.

Anne Chute gazed after her wistfully. "I wish she had not," she muttered as the door closed. "I do wish she had not! Whatever wrong Mrs. Hurdis has done, she is a good woman, and I can't bear to see any harm come to her. I wish she had not gone in there."

But it was too late then for wishes to accomplish anything.

Eva entered the room where her unknown guest was waiting. The woman who had given her name as Marie Durneo arose to receive her.

Something in the coarse face struck Eva as familiar, but she could not recall the occasion of ever having met her.

"You wish to see me?" she said in her sweet, lady-like way that was exceedingly charming.

"Yes. You have changed greatly since I had the pleasure last, but your face and the old contrast of your hair is still the same. I recognized you in a moment!"

"Then we have met before! I thought so, but I cannot remember the time or place. No doubt you will enlighten me!"

"I should not think that you would have forgotten me! There was a time when I might have been your friend, when I offered you my services, but you repulsed me with scorn. Your manner has changed since then."

"You puzzle me!"

"I have come to offer you my services again."

"Indeed? No doubt you intend to be most kind, but I am not in need of any servants at present. Still I should like to know where I have seen you before."

"And when you do, I think you will change your answer. Will you allow me to recall a scene to you?"

She paused with her eyes upon Eva's. There was something in them that had a greasy appearance that was the most extraordinary thing that seen ever remembered to have seen, and yet they were familiar.

A sensation came over her that was far from pleasant. She seemed suddenly to have come in contact with a lump of ice that had thoroughly chilled her.

She motioned to the woman to speak, but felt that she could not have done so herself.

"Will you allow me to sit down?" Marie Durneo asked smoothly. "And will you not sit yourself? I am afraid our conversation may be a long one."

She did not wait for permission to be accorded her, but seated herself in one of the luxuriant chairs, and waited calmly for Eva to follow her example.

"When I saw you before," she said leisurely, "you were younger than you are now, but less beautiful, less cultivated, less, in short, of the *grande dame* than you are to-day. You were beautiful, but it was the beauty of the peasant and not the princess. That beauty won you the love of a man who could not raise you to his rank by presenting you with his name, whereas this beauty has placed you upon a level with the best in your own land. By the way, have you learned yet to speak French?"

There was no need for more. With a thrill of horror, Eva remembered all. The scene was too appallingly distinct.

She could see the room in the Philadelphia hotel, she could see Maurice Vanderfelt, the hero of her girlish dreams, she could see herself as the deceived maiden who had been so supremely happy for the moment, she could see the woman whom she had regarded at the time as fairy god-mother, clothing her in the most gorgeous gowns that to her could ever be fashioned. And then when that scene had faded, she remembered how, after that hideous mockery of a ceremony was over, the same woman had come to her asking to be engaged as maid, and how she had refused.

And this was she! There could not be any doubt of it. It was clear as day.

Then she remembered how, in that memorable interview between Randall and Vanderfelt that had wrecked her whole life, the former had told the man whom she believed to be her husband, that the dress-maker understood French and knew the whole thing as it had occurred.

And this was she.

The madness of despair came over her. Was she never to escape from the frightful consequences of that time, in which she was the dupe and not the criminal?

As she gazed at the woman, the form began gradually to fade, and Eva realized that she was fainting, but by a masterful determination she over-came it.

Not an expression had escaped the French woman's keen eye.

"I see you have not forgotten!" she said quietly but with meaning. "I believe I am to congratulate you upon the possession of a husband and a child since then. Mrs. Hurdis, have you told your husband the history of that time?"

She paused.

Eva opened her lips to utter a falsehood which the woman expected, but Marie Durneo did not give her the opportunity.

"After all!" she exclaimed, "why should I ask you a question to which I know the answer so well! I know that like a sensible woman you have not!

I know that to-day you are purchasing the silence of others, and I have come to sell you mine."

And Eva knew that she was caught in a net from which there was not a chance of escape unless she wished Rod Hurdis to know the truth, and that she was just as anxious to conceal as before the coming of little Laura.

She half arose from her seat, clinging to the back of her chair for support. It required a second effort before she could force any words through her dry lips, and even the ones that she had framed refused to fall.

"What is it you demand?" she asked so hoarsely that even Marie Durneo started.

"It is that you take me as the nurse of your precious child," answered the woman complacently. "You see, I am fond of children, and that will give me time to know exactly what it is that I demand."

"You wish to be my baby's nurse?"

"Yes. Strange, isn't it, when I might live without work? But I wish it so."

"But—"

"There must be no 'buts' in the case, my dear Mrs. Hurdis. Either I come at once, or your husband shall know the truth. I do not wish you to feel that I am coming here as your enemy—far from it! I am coming as my own friend. I have no wish to harm you or make any demands that it will be even difficult for you, but I want to see for myself, and know what I can do. If you wish, we may be the best of friends. I have no desire to use my knowledge against you, unless you force me to it."

She paused again, but seeing that Eva only stared at her as though her words had been unintelligible, she added:

"What is your answer, Mrs. Hurdis?"

The brown eyes were lifted wildly.

"The coils of the serpent are drawing more closely about me!" she cried in an agonized undertone. "There is neither hope nor escape for me! I will yield until the demand upon me breaks my heart, and then the end will come! Well, I am ready for it. It will find a willing victim."

And then the tired heart found relief in insensibility.

XLIII

AS WEAK AS HIS BROTHERS.

"A man's a man for a' that."
"Why, he's a man of wax."

"Men have died from time to time, and worms have eaten them, but not for love."

MATTERS WERE SWINGING ALONG IN the old unvaried monotony in the Hurdis household.

Marie Durneo was installed there as the nurse of Baby Laura, Marshall Randall came and went with the same maddening regularity, Mrs. Randall was as persistent as ever in her smoothly veiled demands for money, which would have been outspoken enough had there ever been a refusal upon the part of Eva to grant her requests, Rod was just as tender and considerate, Anne as faithful, and Eva just as miserable.

Days, weeks, months brought no change, not even reconcilement to fate.

At the end of the third month after the installment of Laura into the family, Randall became again more loud in his demands. He felt that he was allowing Eva to fall too far away from his influence, and therefore decided that they must take another trip, such as they had indulged in upon one or two occasions before. And, unable to defy him, the unfortunate woman was compelled to submit.

She could not afford to have Marie Durneo know more of her affairs than necessity required, and as that worthy individual refused to allow Laura to leave her protection, the two were left behind, and so Roderick Hurdis found them upon his return from Albany one evening.

"Has Mrs. Hurdis gone?" he asked of Marie as he lifted the baby in his arms to kiss it lovingly. "She telegraphed me that she was going, but I thought I should get here in time to see her before she left."

"She left on the four o'clock train, sir."

"Taking Anne with her?"

"Yes, sir. But she ordered dinner for you before leaving, so that you need not go down-town unless you wish."

"That is good, as I am not in the least humor for the club to-night."

Marie did not wait for him to ask, but with thoughtful kindness went to the wardrobe and took from it his dressing gown and slippers, placed his chair out of the draught but where a delightful air could circulate around him, placed his paper within reach, then stood back as though waiting his pleasure to surrender the child.

He thanked her with a pleased smile, but retained the baby until supper was announced, ate alone—not a delightful thing for a man at any time—and returned to the library for his after-dinner smoke.

"Give me the baby, Marie," he said kindly, "while you have your dinner."

"And have her little eyes and lungs filled with cigar smoke?" asked the nurse with a light laugh. "I think it would be better not. I am accustomed to eating with her, sir, and shall not object to it."

"No, give her to me! There is nothing that does one so much good as an uninterrupted dinner. I will postpone my smoke until you return."

Nothing loath, though with seeming reluctance, the baby was given to him, and half an hour later, when the nurse returned, she found Laura fast asleep.

"It is wonderful, sir!" exclaimed Marie. "Her mother has never been able to do that. It is really extraordinary, considering how little you are with her, that Laura should take to you so much more than she does to her mother."

"You think she does?"

"Think, sir? I know it. She really seems rather to dislike Mrs. Hurdis, but then she sees very nearly as little of her as she does of you."

Hurdis frowned. "Do you mean that my wife neglects the child?"

"By no means. Mrs. Hurdis seems absurdly fond of her, on the contrary, but Mrs. Randall and her son occupy so much of her attention that she really does not have the time. Then she knows how devoted I am to the baby, and that there is no danger of her being neglected."

"Does Randall come here, then?"

"Oh, yes, sir. Every day and sometimes oftener."

Hurdis bit his lip for a moment.

"Won't you let me take the baby, sir?" Nurse Durneo asked, after a slight pause.

"Bring her crib here. I see so little of her that I want her near me.

Besides, it is cooler here and more pleasant."

Very readily the nurse obeyed, and with his own hands Hurdis placed the little one in its bed, covered it carefully with a diaphanous material, then, turning out the light, drew his chair nearer to the window and sat down.

A cool wind was blowing through, and as though fearful of his taking cold, Marie drew the curtain so that he was more shielded, while still getting the benefit of the breeze.

"That was thoughtful of you, Marie," he said, settling himself back comfortably. "Women always seem to know the best way to do everything."

She responded with a smile, then brought him a cigar and a match.

"I think you may venture to smoke now, she said, still smiling. "You are too near to the window for the smoke to disturb the baby."

"Thank you. That is delightful. I shall insist upon my wife's leaving you whenever she goes away hereafter. Sit down, Marie, until I am ready to have the baby go. I suppose you have not a husband, have you, Marie?"

The woman hesitated for a moment, then answered as though endeavoring to control some strong emotion:

"I have been married, sir, but like marriages generally, it was a tragedy of heart. I married a scoundrel."

"I must ask you to pardon me for having made an inquiry like that!" exclaimed Hurdis. "I had no idea that I was touching upon a truth. It seemed to me that you would make a very comfortable wife for some man, and that was the cause of the question."

"I don't know, sir," returned Marie sadly. "A woman is not a comfortable companion for a man unless she loves him. I sometimes think that perhaps Paul Durneo was not so much to blame, after all. But there! I beg your pardon, I forgot that you could not possibly be interested in the affairs of a servant, but the kindness of your tone betrayed me into speaking."

"There is no apology necessary. I am interested. Go on, and if there is anything that I can do for you, you may count on me."

"It is not often that a woman in my position hears words like those from her employer, sir, and you will never know how I appreciate them. I have not always been a servant, and the position is a galling one to my pride, but I hope I shall never forget my place, or impose upon the consideration that may be shown me. I was at one time, Mr. Hurdis, in a social position that half the girls in America would have envied."

"And yet—" He paused, too polite to complete what he had intended saying.

"And yet I am to-day a servant" she exclaimed bitterly, finishing the sentence for him. "Very true."

"Was there nothing else that you could do? Your education does not seem to have been neglected. You speak French, your grammar is not bad. It seems to me that you might have preferred to be a governess to a nurse."

The eyes of the woman fell. A crimson blush crossed her unlovely face; she seemed for the moment intensely embarrassed; then, when she spoke, there was a curious tremor in her voice that attracted him.

"Perhaps it was not because I—could not—do better—but—Oh, in Heaven's name! What am I saying? You should not have spoken to me as you have. Have you never heard of how the ice about a woman's heart is melted by a single word of kindness? Have you never, watched a little moth flit about the dangerous flame in comparative safety until some sudden flicker of the flame would suck the helpless thing in and destroy it?"

If he had but let her go then!—if he had but allowed her to take the child and leave him, how much bitter misery might have been spared them all.

But the kindness of his heart was their undoing. He saw her suffering, and as he had raised a bird with a broken wing from the ground to heal its agony, so he approached her.

The gas was not lighted in the room, and a faint glow from a distant electric light imparted the only radiance. He could scarcely see her face, but the eyes were brilliant as diamonds.

Her hands were clasped in her lap, as he could dimly see, and by the tone of her voice, modulated to suit her surroundings, he knew that her lips were trembling piteously.

He was intensely sorry for her.

"What is it you mean, Marie?" he said gently. "You must not speak in metaphor, but tell me your trouble clearly, and if I can, I will help you!"

She lifted her eyes to his face and allowed them to rest there a moment in silence, then she covered them with her hands and sobbed.

"I am a fool!" she cried hoarsely. "Worse than a fool! I have allowed myself to love a man as high above me as the stars are above the earth! I have allowed myself to love him until the very hope of Heaven has sunk into insignificance beside it. I have given up everything in life to be near him, if only in the horrible capacity of a servant. I have watched him ignore me, I have known that he despises me, and yet I am content, so that I am near him. It is madness, I know; but like madness, I am powerless to prevent or even control it. Oh, God I what have I said? How you must abhor me—" She could get no further.

It was a consummate piece of acting, faultless in detail.

Overcome by astonishment, Hurdis half fell into a chair. If she had made a murderous attack upon him, it would have surprised him less.

In a moment she was upon her knees beside him, her face bowed upon his hand that was clasped between both her own.

"Speak one kind word to me!" she cried wildly. "Say that you do not utterly despise me—tell me that you will try to forget what I have said, and I will, go—go where you shall never be distressed with the sight of my face again! I have made all my suffering useless. I might have gone on living near you, happy in knowing that I could sometimes put my hand out as you passed and touch you; but by a single moment of weakness I have made that impossible. Oh, speak to me—tell me that, you can find some degree of pity in your heart for one so miserable as I!"

"I do pity you, Marie," he answered softly. "From the bottom of my heart I do. But you will forget it in time. When you can no longer see my face—"

"The thought of eternal perdition is contained in those words!" she interrupted hoarsely. "Oh, God in Heaven, am I different from other women that I must be denied for all time the only craving of my soul? Forget what I am saying, and bid me go. I am mad to speak such words to you, but where the whole soul is bound in one thought there is no other escape from death. Bid me go, and I will obey you, but before you do so, I entreat that, as the last hope of a life, as you might grant the request of a dying woman, you will kiss me!"

He could not see her face; he forgot there in the darkness that she was ugly; the romance of the moment overcame him, and, bending his head, he touched her lips with his.

In an instant her arms were clasped about his neck, her lips were pressed against his—the wild passion of her nature transfused itself to his own.

He was like wax in her hands. He forgot himself, forgot his wife, forgot his child, and forgot everything—not even remembering who it was that clasped his neck so fiercely.

He returned the kiss as ardently as she had given it.

XLIV

AFTERWARD.

""The storm is past, but it hath left behind it
Ruin and desolation."

"Blow, wind; swell billow; and swim, bark!
The storm is up, and all is on the hazard."

THE TIME HAD COME FOR Roderick Hurdis to suffer.

He scarcely realized the calamity that had fallen upon his life until the following morning, but when it did come there was no mistaking the genuineness of his grief.

The duties that required his attention were forgotten, and even the child that had been his idol was put aside.

He had remained in his room something like four hours, thinking of what was to be done, but unable to arrive at any conclusion; he rang his bell violently, and requested that Nurse Durneo be sent to him.

She came almost at once, her coarse face coarser and uglier than usual.

He turned away from her with a gesture of abhorrence at his own mad folly.

"You wish to see me, sir?"

It was she who broke the silence, and the voice had a curious ring in it that somehow startled him. There was a note of defiance that was jarring, not to say ominous.

He turned to her with more sternness than he often assumed.

"Marie," he said, "I am very sorry, but I think the best thing that can be done will be for you to leave before the return of Mrs. Hurdis. I will take care of you until such time as you can succeed in securing another position, but your own good taste will make you understand how impossible it will be for you and my wife to live beneath the same roof."

He paused, glancing at the woman with some well concealed trepidation.

A calm smile that contained an unveiled sneer had crossed her face.

"Were you foolish enough to believe in that theatrical scene last evening?" she inquired coolly. "I have always found that the best thing that a domestic can do is to gain control over her employer. My dear Mr. Hurdis, you must excuse me if I decline to leave your employ."

Hurdis was white with anger. "What do you mean?" he demanded, going a step nearer to her.

She stood her ground with perfect composure. "I mean that I do not propose to be dismissed," she replied, folding her arms with greatest nonchalance. "I came here to stay, and I shall do so. I hope you understand that clearly."

"But I tell you that you shall not! One more word like the ones you have spoken and I will throw you bodily out of the house, forgetting that you are a woman. Will you go?"

"No, I have already told you, and I see no reason yet why I should change my mind. Mr. Hurdis, do you take me for a fool?"

"No, an adventuress!"

"You honor me with the little. Very well, then. I am an adventuress. Do you think, being an adventuress, that I have so little sense that I do not know perfectly well the power that I hold over you?"

"You infernal—"

"Names are so useless. If it pleases you, however, to call them, do so by all means. I am not in the least thin-skinned. But let me tell you frankly that they will do no good."

"Do you think I am insane enough to allow you to blackmail me in this manner?"

The woman laughed sneeringly.

"How absurd you are!" she exclaimed, with seeming good-nature. "One would think you were a boy, not yet out of the puling state. Would you like your wife to know the truth of what occurred here last night? Would you like her to know that you took her nurse into your arms and kissed her? Would you like the scene described to her as it was when I was clasped so tenderly in your arms?"

"Do you think she would believe you?"

"The chances are that she would, particularly after she had seen this."

The woman drew from her pocket a paper, neatly folded, and handed it to him. There was a smile upon her face of amusement as well as scorn as he opened and gazed upon it.

Every particle of color faded from the man's face, leaving him pale as death.

The paper was a blue print, taken by flashlight. It represented the library in his flat, every article brought out with unusual distinctness. Upon one side his baby laid asleep in its pretty crib, the face showing plainly; from over the mantel a crayon of his wife looked down; and in the center of it all was himself, with Nurse Durneo clasped in his arms, his lips meeting hers.

There could be no mistake as to the identity of the two. It was as plain a likeness as any he had ever had taken.

He remembered the flash of light that had half-blinded him for a single instant, but he believed it to have been the foolish prank of a boy in the street, and had forgotten it the second after its occurrence.

This then was its meaning!

A low oath fell from his lips, and with a hand that he felt could have destroyed giant, he tore the paper into a thousand pieces.

Nurse Durneo only laughed.

"How fortunate that is not the negative," she said with a sneer. "Had it been, the world might have lost a wonderful piece of art. I wonder what your opponents would think of that, Mr. Hurdis, at the next election? No doubt I could sell it for a much larger sum than it would require to take care of me until such time as I can succeed in securing another position. By the way! Do you still wish me to leave your house?"

There was only one way for Hurdis to prevent himself from strangling her, and that was to leave the room. Putting a mighty restraint upon himself, he turned his back upon her and stalked out. He was utterly in the power of his wife's servant, and he knew it!

Two days later Eva returned. Nurse Durneo was present at the meeting between husband and wife. Nurse Durneo sat at the table during the dinner hour with baby Laura upon her knee. Nurse Durneo remained in the sitting room, hushing baby to sleep long after the child was soundly sleeping, occasionally bearing part in the conversation, contradicting both Eva and Hurdis with the familiarity of a privileged friend instead of a servant.

More than once Eva looked at her husband in amazement that he did not rebuke her to silence, and more than once find Hurdis frowned as his wife allowed some familiarity to pass unnoticed. The restraint upon them was anything but pleasant.

With the morrow matters did not alter. She refused to allow Eva more than a passing glance at the child, whom the unfortunate woman had grown almost to worship, lavishing upon it all the heart that was not in the keeping of Rod Hurdis, and even that passing glance the nurse seemed to grudge her.

When Hurdis returned in the evening, it was still the same.

Unable to bear at longer, Eva turned to her.

"Marie," she said, speaking as gently as her rising temper would allow her, "give me the baby. Mr. Hurdis and I would like moment alone."

"Excuse me!" replied the woman. "I can't do anything of the kind. You don't care anything about the baby. You never notice it when Mr. Hurdis is not here, and you don't know how to take care of her. You don't love her and I do!"

Eva's dark eyes blazed with wrath. And yet, to her intense astonishment, Hurdis was silent.

"How dare you say that?" she exclaimed indignantly. "You know that it is not true. Give me the child and leave the room at once."

"I shall do nothing of the kind! You are a fine creature to command me!"

The sneer in the tone was all the threat that Eva required. She knew that the woman had been drinking, and that she really would prefer telling Hurdis the truth if she were to follow her inclination, and therefore Eva knew that to preserve her own secret, she must be silent.

Miserably enough, she turned to Hurdis. "I suppose one ought not to mind her!" she exclaimed, her lips trembling piteously. "She has been drinking."

"No, I've not been drinking, either!" Marie cried, rising to her feet and holding the baby close to her breast. "I am as sober as you are and that is not saying much as a general thing. You think that I don't know when you are half full of opium and—"

But before she could finish the sentence, Hurdis had taken her by the shoulder and hurried her from the room.

Once outside the door, he closed it securely. "For God's sake be silent!" he exclaimed in a hoarse whisper. "Do with me as you will, exact what you like, but spare my wife such scenes as that! One more such and your power will vanish. Do you understand me?"

"I understand that you would shield her at my expense, and I tell you that I will not have it! You have a noble old name. You do not want to see it dragged through the gutter. Very well. In order to avoid that, you have got to obey me. Let me alone. I tell you that your honor lies in the palm of my hand, and it is all according to the manner in which you treat me whether I shall use it or not.

"Remember the photograph will keep! I will not have that woman commanding me! You must think of that the next time that you are tempted to thrust me from the room in the manner in which you have done tonight. I shall do as I like, and you have got to force her to submit to it, or it will be the worse for you and her also. This household belongs to me. If you don't want to be forever disgraced, you have got to obey me and not I you. I hope that is clear enough."

"But, Marie—"

"There are no 'buts' in the case. Remain quiet and you are safe, but lift a finger against me and you are lost. Don't think that you can frighten me in any way I have absolutely nothing to lose, while you have all. I am not a star in the social firmament, I am only a nurse, but with such proof as I have in my possession, if you think you can afford to defy me, it is your privilege to do it."

He turned from her wearily, knowing that his wrath was impotent, and entered the room where he had left his wife.

Knowing that her battle was won, that the surrender of the enemy was complete, Marie retired, the baby still clasped in her arms.

Eva lifted to her husband's a face that was pale with flight.

"You must not let Marie annoy you," he said, patting her cheek, "She is a good-hearted thing, and adores the baby. We could scarcely get along without her; but she has been drinking, as you said. They all have their fruits and I supposed we could not do better if we should discharge her. There! Don't look so frightened. It is nothing. They all drink more or less, and we should not do any better if we sent her away, particularly as she is so attached to the child. You agree with me, do you not?"

"Yes!" answered Eva, in a hollow voice. "I suppose we could not do better."

XLV

THE WAY OF THE TRANSGRESSOR.

"Farewell, happy fields,
Where joy forever dwells. Hail horrors! hail."

"Temple and tower went down, nor left a site—
Chaos of ruins!"

IF SHE HAD IMAGINED THAT she was suffering all the agony of which she was capable at the hands of Randall, Eva had yet to learn that a woman can concoct more ways of torture in one half hour than a man, no matter how great a fiend he may be, could think of in a month.

Nurse Durneo was the ruling power of that household. It was she who gave the orders, she who discharged and engaged the servants, she who used the carriage which she had ordered from the stable, she who directed everything, making Eva less than a stranger in her own home.

And to it both husband and wife submitted in silence.

But the most galling part, perhaps, to Eva, was the calm manner in which her husband was appropriated.

Nurse Durneo never showed herself in his presence unless she was dressed with the most scrupulous care, and on more than one occasion she had refused to carry some message to him for Eva because her hair was in curl-papers.

How exasperating that was to the wife, only a wife could ever know.

Then she usurped Eva's place in every way possible. It was she who placed his gown and slippers in their proper position for him in the evening, she who always saw that his cigar-case was filled in the morning, she who looked after his socks and attended to his buttons, doing it in a demonstrative way that was maddening.

During his absence she did almost nothing. She sat in an easy chair in the sitting room or parlor, reading her newspaper or a novel, and leaving the child to Eva's care, or she went out in a carriage to do some shopping for her. Perhaps those were the only bearable moments of the day to Eva.

Once in a moment of desperation, she told the story to Randall, actually seeking his sympathy in her affliction. Such is the leaning of a woman's heart upon sympathy.

And bad as he was, Randall did feel some disgust that the woman could carry her fiendishness so far as that. Perhaps the disgust that he expressed made Eva feel more kindly toward him than she had ever felt before.

July was well along, and Hurdis was growing weary of the city. He therefore proposed a trip to Elberon that was to continue through the month of August, to which Eva but too gladly acquiesced. Any change would have been welcomed as Heaven, but if she expected to have matters altered so far as Nurse Durneo was concerned, she was reckoning without her host.

The latter part of July found them snugly ensconced at Elberon, in a charming vine-clad cottage that over-looked the sea. They were boarding, and for some time it seemed to Eva that the rest for which she had so earnestly prayed was to be hers.

Nurse Durneo was not well, and while in that condition Eva had more freedom, more comfort with her husband than she had had for months past. Randall, too, was allowing her a time of rest from his persecutions.

It was the calm that always precedes the storm.

More than one of the neighbors asked another who the charming woman could be who went every evening down the street so regularly to meet her husband as he returned from the city.

It was the same daily; the same charming toilets, the same winsome smile as she wheeled the baby along in front of her, always the same affectionate kiss, not too demonstrative for public eyes, but loving; and people grew to watch the clock that they might not fail to see her.

Then they began to whisper that it was Rod Hurdis and his wife. Few had heard that he had a wife, but all agreed that she was a most beautiful and charming woman.

The residents began to call upon her, and, in her own delightful way, with every evidence of gentle breeding in her manner, Eva cordially welcomed them. They saw no shadow of the tragedy in her life in the lovely face, and with one accord they pronounced her perfect.

But the success she was achieving was not pleasant to Marie Durneo. She watched it with feelings of envy that boded Eva no good.

At last, unable to endure the sight of it longer, her obstreperousness broke out afresh. She was more marked in her attentions to Hurdis than ever, and, by constant threatening, forced him into a line of conduct utterly abhorrent to him.

He dared not remain away, because upon his return she would be more demonstrative than ever, sickening him with her show of affection.

And yet to Eva he spoke of her good qualities, and urged the necessity of her services.

It never occurred to the young wife to doubt her husband, far less to be jealous of her servant; but any woman given to that sort of thing would have seen evidence enough in his conduct to have condemned him a thousand times.

Blind as she was, however, it required but a single act to most effectually open her eyes.

The child's room, that was shared by the nurse, communicated with the one that was occupied by Mr. and Mrs. Hurdis, and into it Nurse Durneo would summon Mr. Hurdis upon the slightest pretext possible, a summons he dared not disobey. Sometimes it was to see a new accomplishment of the baby's, sometimes it was to ask his opinion concerning something that she should or should not eat, again it would be to see some article that she had made for the mite, detaining him each time as long as she could find a pretext for doing so, and even after decency required that she should let him go.

One day he returned on a train earlier than was his wont, to find that Eva had gone for a walk upon the beach with the child, an airing that she took daily, though Nurse Durneo was careful that Hurdis should not know it.

The woman was in Eva's room when he entered, seated in a huge chair that was reserved for Hurdis' express use.

She arose, with a bright smile, giving him no time to question her.

"Your wife has gone out," she explained, pushing the chair toward him. "She did not expect you so early, but left word that she might be detained a little longer than usual. Let me get your gown and slippers. You look so worn and tired. Are you?"

The question was asked anxiously, as though she was really concerned regarding his health, and Hurdis was forced to reply.

"Yes, I am worn and tired," he said, peevishly. "It is this kind of life that I am forced to lead that is telling upon me. I am wearied to death of it. Look here, Marie. Suppose we make a bargain. I have stood this sort of thing just as long as I can. I am willing to give you any reasonable sum that you may name, if you will deliver into my hands that accursed negative and all the copies that have been made of it, and leave my house forever. What do you say?"

"That I cannot do it, Mr. Hurdis. You do not seem to take into consideration that my heart is in the affair."

"Did you not tell me that it was not? Did you not say that what you had done was simply to gain supremacy?"

"I said it because you angered me into it by your references to your wife. How little you know of a woman! You cannot realize now that I would be your slave, that I would crawl upon my hands and knees to the ends of the earth, if by it I could purchase the smallest atom of your love. But I know that I cannot. I know that if I left here to-morrow you would never see me again, and I purchase the happiness of being near you at any price that I must pay."

Like the mole that he was, he was blind to the fact that she had another object to attain. His own supreme vanity was too great for him to see that she was playing with him as a cat might play with a mouse. If she could have her own jewels, her own carriages and horses, her own house and her own servants, would it not be better than to be the servant of his wife?

And Hurdis? He had an object in view also. If he could by any means, fair or foul, get that woman to deliver up that negative and those pictures, if he could get her from under the same roof with his wife, would it not be well?

Then when she was in his power, as she would be, he could snap his fingers in her ugly face and defy her. She had obtained the power she held through fraud, therefore would he be censurable if he wrested it from her through fraud?

He saw a plan clearly enough! He would play upon her love for him and persuade her to follow his wishes. It was like gall upon his palate, but there was nothing else for it.

"I am afraid, Marie," he said slowly, "that you and I have been playing at cross purposes all this time, have believed that what you did was simply the ruse of the adventuress, and you have believed that you were hateful to me for the part you played. I think we were both wrong. There is no reason why you should remain here in this house as a servant. I will provide a house for you as handsome as you could desire, and there you will be happier than you have ever dreamed of being."

"But I should never see you."

"On the contrary, the most delightful hours of my day will be passed there. You will never accuse me of neglect, so long as you love me as you do now. Marie, is it a bargain?"

She threw herself between his knees upon the floor, and repulsive as it was to him, he leaned over and placed his arm about her.

"You do not mean it!" she cried with well simulated eagerness. "You do not love me."

"Why do you torment yourself with doubts like those?" he asked, endeavoring to assume a passion he was far from feeling. "Is it hard to realize that you are a woman whom any man could love?"

"But your wife—"

Hurdis shuddered. He was about to drop his arm from her, then remembering the object that he had in view, he tightened his hand upon her waist, that was by no means slight.

"Never mind her!" he exclaimed, commanding his voice by an effort. "Only tell me that you love me well enough to do as I ask, and all will be as you wish it."

Her coarse face was raised to his, his arm still encircled her his lips were almost meeting hers, when a low cry from the doorway attracted their attention.

Hurdis turned.

He did not speak, but the pallor of death overspread his face. He arose, trembling like one with palsy.

Upon the threshold stood his wife, their little child clasped in her arms.

If he could but have died of the shame, it would have been a blessed relief, but the wages of sin are not always dissolution.

XLVI

THE STORY TOLD AT LAST.

"Oh, jealousies! Thou art nurst in hell:
Depart from hence and therein dwell."

"Oh, she is fallen
Into a pit of ink! that the wide sea
Hath drops too few to wash her clean again."

PERHAPS THE MOST COMPOSED ONE of the three was Marie Durneo, yet even she grew white to the lips as she realized the horrible thing that had occurred.

If the salvation of his soul had depended upon it, it is doubtful if Hurdis could have spoken.

And Eva? She stood there like a statue, unable to realize the hideous calamity that had fallen upon her.

She had believed in Hurdis as it had never occurred to her to believe in God, and that he had betrayed her trust she could not bring herself to realize, even under the evidence of her own sight. She stood motionless, apparently unable to think or even breathe.

And so the trio remained, until Marie Durneo broke the uncanny silence by an odious laugh. Eva started as though she had struck her.

"There is no use in making this matter public!" exclaimed the nurse, with an assumption of careless indifference. "It was something that was never meant for your eyes, but since you have discovered it, I hope you will have sense enough to keep your mouth shut and say nothing."

Even Hurdis gasped! He never remembered to have heard anything so utterly cold-blooded in his life, and that it should be said to his wife was something hideous.

Yet what was he to say? Was he not in the woman's power, past hope of salvation, so far as his world was concerned? He was silent!

Eva looked from one to the other; then, with the calmness of despair, she placed the baby upon her tiny cushioned chair and tied her there with the delicate silken cord that they used for that purpose.

Nurse Durneo advanced to take it.

As she placed her hand upon the child's arm, Eva tore the hand away, and with the strength of an angry lioness, flung the nurse to one side.

"How dare you touch my child!" she panted, her dark eyes blazing with wrath, a cold perspiration forming upon her upper lip.

Her lovely, tawny head was lifted like that of an infuriated tigress, her body was curiously erect, and her teeth were set so that her breath came through them with an audible sound.

Nurse Durneo laughed again. "Melodramatics!" she exclaimed scornfully. "The stage has missed an ornament. My dear Mrs.—Hurdis, your sympathy for me should be so great that you should forget that you know how to censure!"

The words, but more particularly the hesitation before the name was pronounced, was intended to convey a threat, but Eva did not even hear.

"Leave this room!" she cried in a low vibrating voice. "Each moment that you remain you are running the greatest chance of death. Go! And never dare show your face here again!"

But the sneer upon Nurse Durneo's face only deepened. "You are making yourself ridiculous!" she said scornfully. "I warn you for your own good—don't tempt me too far!"

Had she been capable of hearing anything, Eva might have heard the warning in the voice—she might have understood the danger to herself; but she had utterly forgotten herself, and was thinking only of the horror of her discovery—if she were thinking of anything, which is doubtful.

Again Marie made a step in the direction of Baby Laura, but it was only a step. She took warning and remained out of the reach of the woman in whose eyes she read but too plainly madness!

With a density about her tone that was alarming, the perspiration standing upon her face like rain, Eva turned to Hurdis. "Will you tell her to go now and forever?" she said slowly.

The man was nonplused. If his wife had asked him to kill the woman who had betrayed him into such a fearful position, he could have done it with a relish; but to tell her to go, and forever, was quite a different thing! There was that horrible negative, and those dreadful blue prints to be considered.

He gasped, like a man that is strangling.

Again Nurse Durneo laughed. "He might tell *you* to leave and forever!"

she exclaimed tauntingly; "but never me. I wonder that you have the courage to stand there and talk to me like that, knowing so well what I know
of your past!"

But before she had concluded her speech, Hurdis had regained something of his manhood. He could not, even to protect himself, have his wife
submitted to such indignity as that. He turned to Marie sternly.

"You are going too far!" he exclaimed, his eyes ablaze. "Will you be good
enough to leave the room?"

All the scorn left Nurse Durneo's face, and a white-heat anger took its
place. Her entire rage seemed to be directed toward Eva, leveled with a
force that neither Eva nor Hurdis had the strength to combat.

A stream of oaths that were loathsome fell from her foul lips. She
seemed to shake like a tree under a midwinter blast from anger.

"You order me to leave this room because of her?" she cried shrilly. "I
would see both of you dead first. What is she that you should command
me to go because of her! She is nothing but a—"

"Will you force her to leave the room, Rod?"

The question came from Eva with a tensity that expressed volumes. Had
Hurdis not been blinded by his own danger, he might have understood the
terrible situation in which she was placed, he might have seen that there
was nothing short of murder in the dark eyes.

To Bill Scarlett's daughter was added a wild, raging jealousy that converted her into a tigress! There was a crimson glow in the face that was
transfused to the eyes, lending them a scarlet brilliancy that was horrible.

Rod Hurdis advanced toward Nurse Durneo, but she sprung aside and
warned him back.

"Don't you dare to lay a hand on me" she cried fiercely "If you do, as
surely as there is a Heaven I will expose the pictures that I hold to the
world."

Hurdis paused.

"Are you going to make her go?" demanded Eva, her voice unrecogniz-
ably hoarse.

"For Heaven's sake, Eva, be reasonable," he exclaimed fretfully. "I will
explain everything to you."

"There is no explanation needed. Are you going to send her away, or are
you not? That is the only question that requires an answer.

"Then let me answer it for him!" exclaimed Nurse Durneo, her voice
raised almost to the screaming pitch. "He will not send me away, because
he dares not do it! And he will not, because he loves me better than he
does you. Does that satisfy you? Are you content to let matters remain as
they are?"

With a low growl, Eva made a spring in her direction; but as though accustomed to such situations, Nurse Durneo stepped lightly aside.

Hurdis caught Eva around the waist, holding, her firmly.

"For God's sake, think what you are doing!" he gasped. "Have a little patience, and you shall know all; but—"

"Then send that woman away!" cried Eva, scarcely conscious of what she said. "I cannot breathe with her in the room. Send her away, and—"

"Neither you nor he have the power to send me away!" screamed Marie Durneo. "You are a fine thing to talk of any one else. Rod Hurdis need not feel so mortally ashamed of what he has done. You are not his wife, and you know it as well as I do. Why have you kept me in this house? Because you knew I should tell him the truth about Maurice Vanderfelt—that you lived with him long enough to make you his wife under the laws of New York. Because you knew that I should tell him that after you quarreled with Vanderfelt, you went to live with a man named Loran, and that at the time that mockery of a ceremony was gone through, you were living with Marshall Randall, whom you have pretended was your cousin. Because you knew that I should tell your poor dupe how you have supported Marshall Randall out of his money, that he has lavished upon you; and also who was your companion during your voyage to Europe, and how you and Marshall Randall were registered in every hotel you visited as man and wife. Why don't you tell Rod Hurdis that that is why you have not sent me away long ago, and then ask him why he has not done the same!"

The taunting voice ceased.

For a time after she began speaking, Hurdis held Eva closely, but at the conclusion of the nurse's remarks his arms fell away from her as though death had struck him. And Eva felt it with paralyzing horror.

The hideous truth was out at last. That which she had sold her soul to conceal was told. And in face of his own guilt, Rod Hurdis had turned from her.

The thought was maddening.

The woman before her had robbed her of every hope that life held. She had stolen her husband's love first, then robbed her of his respect. She had made the whole world a barren waste. There was nothing left—nothing.

And then everything—time, place, people, circumstance—all seemed to become a blank. A consuming fire licked the poor girl's brain, she saw though a crimson haze that seemed to her like blood. She felt that insensibility was overtaking her, but instead she had never been more active.

All the tigerishness of Bill Scarlett's daughter was upon the surface, backed by a madness that for the moment was as genuine as any contained in Bloomingdale.

Upon the bed there lay a hunting knife that Hurdis had taken from his trunk that morning for some purpose, and without realizing that she saw it, Eva seized it.

Hurdis was looking straight at her, but could not realize her horrible intention.

With the quick spring of a lunatic, she reached Nurse Durneo, and with the frenzied strength of madness, plunged the sharp knife into her about two inches below the waist.

With a cry of indescribable horror, Hurdis dashed forward and caught his wife's wrist—too late to save her from the crime that she had committed.

For a moment Nurse Durneo reeled; then, summoning all her strength, she clasped both hands over the terrible wound the knife had made, and staggered from the room.

A wild cry of "Help!" and "Murder!" rung through the pretty cottage, clarion-throated, and mingled outside with the weird slush of the sea.

XLVII

THE ARREST.

"Though some of you with Pilate wash your hands,
Showing an outward pity; yet yon Pilates
Have here delivered me to my sour cross,
And water cannot wash away your sin."

THE KNIFE WITH WHICH THE terrible deed had been accomplished fell slowly from Eva's hand, and without cry or moan she turned her eyes upon Hurdis.

The anger had faded out of them like a suddenly quenched fire.

"What have you done?" gasped Hurdis, snatching up the knife and flinging it, all stained with blood as it was, into a closet. "In the name of God, what have you done?"

With every evidence of calmness, from her inability to feel, Eva answered slowly:

"I hope I have killed her!"

Hurdis shuddered, though the gruesome words seemed to have no effect whatever upon his wife. She still looked at him in that same stony sort of way that seemed to chill his blood. He went to her and took her hand. She neither repulsed him, nor made any response.

"Oh, Eva!" he cried desperately, "why in Heaven's name could you not have trusted me? You might have known that I could have explained away everything; even with this damning proof against me. Do you hear that woman groan? God! Come! Of what have I been thinking? You must leave here *at once!* There is not an instant to lose!"

Still he had not aroused her from that frightful stoniness that had fallen upon her.

"Leave here!" she repeated drearily. "What for?"

"Can you not see how impossible it is for you to remain here? Eva—Oh, darling, you do not seem to realize that you have killed that woman!"

A slow, mocking laugh fell from the blue lips, a laugh that seemed to chill him with terror.

"I have not killed her!" she said scornfully. "Heaven has been against me always, or I should have done so. I regret that more than all the mistakes of my terrible life."

"Hush!" he cried, chafing the hands he held in an endeavor to impart some warmth to them. "You must not speak like that. Come! Let me take you away. If they find you here they may—hang you!"

There was awe and horror in the tone of the man's voice, but it had no power to reach her. She sat down quietly.

"There is nowhere that I could go to escape from myself and memory," she said dully. "It would be a useless journey."

"Then you mean that you will disgrace me?" he asked, thinking to move her in that way.

Her lip curled scornfully. "Do not allow fear to disturb you," she answered slowly. "No word shall ever pass my lips by which the world shall ever guess the truth of what I discovered here to-day."

"Eva, I swear that you misjudge me!" he cried desperately. "As there is a God, that woman was nothing to me—nothing! If you will only listen, I can explain everything! She was—"

"She was my servant," interrupted the unhappy woman in the same stony voice, "and I saw her in your arms. I don't ask for any explanation, Rod. Perhaps I don't deserve any, but the end is here now, and it is useless to endeavor to postpone it."

"But, Eva—"

"You are only making matters harder for us both. If she has me arrested, I shall be sorry, because it will be your name which I must bear, but you may be sure that I shall screen you all that lies in my power. If they hang me, my lips shall remain closed."

"I can save you, if you will only let me."

"No; salvation is denied me. It has been always so. The whole world has seemed to close in around me, leaving but one road before me, and that leading to destruction. I was born with the shadow of eternal damnation upon me, and it has pursued me relentlessly. Let me alone. That is all I ask."

Down-stairs the groans of Nurse Durneo were frightful. With her hands still locked over the deep and jagged wound, she fell upon a sofa, alternating her groans with hoarse curses leveled against Eva. Attracted by the calls for help, a man came up to her.

"What is the matter?" he asked, touching her shoulder with his hand.

Marie Durneo raised her blurred eyes to his face. "Eva Hurdis has stabbed me!" she cried. "Get an officer and have her arrested at once."

It was not a doctor that she wanted, but an officer.

The man smiled. "I guess you are not much hurt, are you?" he asked.

"Not much hurt!" she repeated savagely. "Look there!"

She removed her hands from the place where she had torn her clothes away, and a sickening spectacle met the man's astonished eyes.

With a shiver of horror, the man bounded away for assistance.

As he went on his way for a doctor, he passed an officer of the law.

"There has been a murder committed at Mrs. Rupert's cottage," he panted. "The murderess is still there, and not under arrest. You'd better go up at once."

He was off again, almost before he had ceased speaking, and the officer hurried away in the direction he had indicated.

The news spread like lightning! The words: "There has been a murder committed at Mrs. Rupert's cottage, and Eva Hurdis, the wife of Roderick Hurdis, is the murderess," went from lip to lip, but no one attempted to even suggest a cause. That was buried in mystery.

When the officer arrived upon the scene it seemed to him that half the residents and visitors at the little city by the sea had gathered in front of that vine-clad cottage. Rich and poor, aristocratic and lowly alike yielded to the common characteristic of mankind—curiosity.

Pushing his way through the throng, the officer went up to the woman who still lay curled up on the sofa, groaning dismally.

"What's the matter?" he asked, without any great show of sympathy.

The eyes, in which death seemed to lurk, were raised to his, but even in death Marie Durneo was the same harridan that she had been in life.

"I'm dying, can't you see?" she gasped. "She cut me! That woman upstairs did it, and I want her hanged higher than Hamen, curse her. Why don't you go and arrest her? I only wish that I could live to see her upon the gallows for what she has done!"

The officer turned away from the sickening spectacle, unable to summon any pity for the woman under all her suffering, and as he started in the direction that Marie Durneo had indicated, the man who had informed him of the murder entered with a doctor.

"I am afraid you are too late, doctor," he said, lifting his helmet. "It seems to me to be a case for the corner instead of the physician."

And then, in response to the call of duty, he ascended the stairs.

The low hum of voices told him which door to knock upon. He did not wait for permission after the single tap, but walked in.

Eva was sitting in a chair facing the door, quieter than she had been for weeks. Her beautiful blonde head was lifted, while one shapely white hand clasped the arm of the chair firmly. Her eyes were lifted bravely, fearlessly. What she suffered was concealed beneath an exterior of ice.

Hurdis had turned, burying his face upon one arm that rested upon the mantelpiece. The very droop of his shoulders seemed to express humiliation and despair.

"Are you Eva Hurdis?" the officer inquired, advancing toward one of the loveliest women he had ever remembered to have seen before.

"I am!" The words fell distinctly, icily. There was neither hesitation nor tremor in manner nor voice.

"There is a wounded woman down-stairs who claims that you cut her," the officer said, somehow feeling that his words were unsuited, though he was unable to change them.

But he need not have paused to consider them. The woman before him was like flint.

"Yes," she answered indifferently, "I did it! Is she dead?"

"No."

"I am sorry. I regret that I did not finish her at one blow."

The officer shuddered. "Will you come with me?" he asked. "You are my prisoner!"

She arose at once. She had not removed her hat since her walk upon the beach with Baby Laura. By a gesture she indicated to the officer that she was ready to accompany him.

Only once did she glance in the direction of the man with his head bowed upon the mantelpiece; but as he did not move, she heaved a low, short sigh, and motioned to the officer to lead on.

The noise of the opening door attracted Hurdis' attention. He turned. His face was strained and ghastly, his eyes wild as those of a madman.

"Eva!" The single word burst through his white lips in a cry of agony. His arms were outstretched.

For an instant she forgot everything but her passionate love for him and that she had torn herself from him. Unable to control herself longer, she sprung back, and was folded fiercely to his breast.

Then remembrance returned. She lifted her lips and pressed them, ice-cold, upon his own.

"Do not fear!" she whispered. "All that I can do to save you I will. Good-bye and God bless you, my darling!"

Without an order, she tore herself from his arms and signaled to the policeman to go on.

At the foot of the stairs they met the doctor.

"You will have to hold your prisoner for murder," she said solemnly. "The woman cannot live."

Roderick Hurdis heard! He crept back to his room, while his wife faced that curious throng alone, crept along as one suddenly stricken with blindness and there in the silence that had fallen over him, he faced the first grief of his life.

And what a grief it was!

Perhaps it was the straying of baby fingers over his hair that saved his reason, but it was spared for greater suffering, a humiliation that few men have ever shared.

XLVIII

HOW THE NIGHT WAS PASSED.

"My heart is drowned with grief.
My body round engirt with misery."

"Had I but died an hour before this chance,
I had lived a blessed time."

INTO A CARRIAGE EVA WAS thrust, and accompanied alone by the officer, taken to Long Branch, where the jail was situated.

It was a broad, old-fashioned building, situated upon the corner of the street, perhaps less dreary than such places usually are because the upper portion was used as a courthouse, but the cells were lonely and barren enough to please the heart of the hardest law-maker.

Into one of these Eva was placed, her beauty and her suffering purchasing her small courtesy from those men, accustomed as they were to crime and criminals.

Like one in a dream, she heard the key turned in the lock, and knew that she was alone.

For hours she sat dully, listening to the wash of the sea upon the shore, hushed to quiet by the weird, mournful sound; she watched the little stars twinkling in the heavens as though they had been asleep when her heart had broken.

Then, with that same curious calm upon her, she began going over the scenes of her life again, as she had a habit of doing when any new calamity befell her.

It was the same thing—from the ragged child, whipped and insulted, to the young woman betrayed and disgraced, through the miserable months that had followed, until the morning of her marriage—afterward through the months when she had been the bond-slave of the man whom she loathed—the coming of Marie Durneo, and—

Was it not a fit ending? Could she have expected Heaven to have sent aught else?

Then there arose in her heart a terrible rebellion.

Why had Heaven selected her as the one upon whom to heap all its horrors? Had the first fault been hers? Had not all that had followed been forced upon her through a necessity to conceal the wrong that another had put upon her? Would she not have been a wife of perfect truth and fidelity, had fate allowed her?

An anger that was horrible filled her heart. Yet she neither moved nor spoke.

Gradually it faded, leaving the same misery, the same hideous longing for a death that would not come at her bidding.

She glanced around her with apparent calmness, but it would have meant suicide, had there been an object near with which it could have been committed. But she knew before she had looked as well as she did after that no such object would be found.

She thought of Hurdis, wondering why he had treated the story that was told by Nurse Durneo so lightly.

Then it occurred to her that he did not believe it.

Why did she not think, and allow him to take her away before the arrival of that officer? If it had once occurred to her that he doubted the nurse's words, that is what she would have done, and possibly she might have saved herself, and retained his love.

The thought had scarcely presented itself than she put it aside as absurd.

"He had already ceased to love me," she said without a tremor in her voice. "It will be a relief to him to be rid of me, even if he must purchase his freedom at such a cost. I wonder—oh, God! How I wonder, how I shall ever have the courage to walk up on the gallows? Shall I faint, or—"

She did not complete the sentence, but fell to thinking of the night when she had thought that she had killed Marshall Randall and had tried to end her own life because she was afraid to live.

"If Loran had but let me alone!" she exclaimed without a shiver. "How much suffering I might have been spared, and how much shame I might have saved Rod. If I but had a pistol now. There is never anything remembered against the dead, and even I might escape, and spare him all the frightful humiliation that he must endure. But there never has been any hope for me. From birth to death I have been accursed!"

She paused a moment, then after a time, a slow smile came about the beautiful, tender mouth, a smile that contained nothing of mirth, but only the bitterness of most wretched memory.

"I wonder what the governor's wife will think?" she muttered. "And Lil Cartwright? After all, the entire failure of my life dates back to the cruelty of that girl when I was a helpless, innocent, ignorant child. It is to her that the curse belongs, not to me. But she will live her life out in ease and plenty, loved by those whom she has not the heart to love in return, while I—I shall be 'hanged by the neck until I am dead.' I wonder how I shall ever have the courage so bear it?"

She arose and began to slowly pace her narrow cell. Then, as the day was breaking, she lay down, and a few moments afterward was peacefully asleep.

It is the holiest provision against suffering.

Meantime Hurdis was engaged in a task that was pitiful. With his own hands he was removing the little garments from the person of his child, preparing it for bed.

The baby looked in his face curiously, its great eyes wandering about, as though puzzled that the mother whose tender touch it seemed to miss, was not there.

With a groan of anguish, Hurdis lifted it and pressed a kiss upon the little mouth.

"Mamma is not here, my darling," he whispered brokenly. "Thank God, you are too young to know why. But we will save her—we will save her, if there is any pity in Heaven! Pray with papa, my darling! Pray that the good God may, after all, spare that woman's life, that we may have our own again. Oh, my baby! My little, pure, my holy one, how can we live without her? Surely God will not curse you like that. He will let us save her, for your sake!"

Then, kneeling there with the child in his arms, he prayed for her—prayed Heaven to spare the woman who had blighted his life through love.

But God helps only those who help themselves, and Rod Hurdis was weak!

As tenderly as a man can, and with the same awkwardness, he gave the child its bottle of milk, watched it with a half-breaking heart as it nursed itself to sleep, then arranged it in its own bed for the night.

As he raised his head from the task, he stood looking down upon the sleeping infant.

"I wonder if your poor mother is thinking of us now?" he muttered sadly. "I wonder if there, in her lonely cell, she is not breaking her heart because of this hideous separation? I will go to her to-morrow and comfort her in every way that mortal can, and I will find a way to save her!"

He kissed the baby once again, then approached the window, through which the loud horn of the sea sounded like a death-wail, sat down and leaned his chin upon his hand, his elbow resting upon his knee.

The breaking day still found him there, helpless in his terrible grief.

His wife, the wife of Roderick Hurdis, to be tried for murder! That was the horror of it, and what man could contemplate the situation without a chill of mortal terror?

As the sun arose, shining with unwonted brilliancy into the room, as though in mockery, he left his chair, his legs stiff and cramped from long sitting. Scarcely conscious of what he did, he approach the mirror and looked in.

He recoiled with a cry of bitter astonishment. His face was sallow and pale to ghastliness, his eyes were sunken and shadowed by deep rings, his jaw seemed to have fallen, and his hair was streaked with gray.

He had suffered during that night as even he could not realize, but the reflex of misery was stamped there in a manner that no one could have read without understanding.

As he looked, he recalled the scene of the night before with hideous distinctness, and for the first time the words of the nurse came to him with startling force.

He heard them even more clearly than he had heard them then. He knew that his wife was accused of having lived with Vanderfelt, whom she had allowed him to receive and entertain as a friend; that she had been over Europe with Randall, and that she had lived with Loran.

He remembered also that up to the time of the telling of that by Marie Durneo, that Eva had remained comparatively quiet, but when that was told she stabbed the woman who had uttered the words.

He remembered that his wife had made no denial. He remembered hearing the governor, upon his return from the country, playfully abuse him for running away just when he had arrived, and he could see now that Eva's remarks upon the subject would have aroused a jealous man's suspicions, but he had never thought of suspecting her.

He stood there thinking of those things, unconscious of the passage of time, deaf to all sound, until he was aroused by a touch on the shoulder.

It was Mrs. Rupert, the landlady of the cottage.

"Excuse me, sir," she said, "but I heard the baby crying, and I came to see if there is not something that I can do for you?"

He turned and looked at her, all intelligence seeming to have left his face.

"Yes," he exclaimed, hoarsely, "do anything you like. It is all one to me now. Will you keep her until I return?"

"Certainly. But where are you going?"

She knew that her question was not a polite one, but the expression of his face was frightful.

He did not reply, but picked up his hat and strode from the room.

Down the street he went, his head bowed, his hands clinched in his pockets, his eyes rolling fiercely. He strode through the gate leading to a cottage, up the walk, on to the balcony, and with a nervous hand pulled the bell.

"I want to see Marshall Randall!" he said to the servant who answered his ring.

"I will tell him, sir, but he is not yet out of bed," the servant replied.

"Then show me to his room! I only want to see him for a moment."

"Are you a friend of his, sir?"

He hesitated a moment, then with a look that might have made the girl understand had she been capable of understanding anything, he answered: "Yes!"

She led the way and he followed. She knocked upon a door at the head of the stair; and in answer to Randall's "Come in," he entered alone.

The man was standing there with one leg thrust into his trousers, the band between his hands. He was expecting his own servant and barely glanced up at the interruption to his toilet.

That glance was sufficient.

Hurdis closed the door carefully behind him, and then advanced toward Randall with such an expression of countenance as he had never seen upon any face before.

"I have come," Hurdis said slowly, "for a simple answer from you. Is it true that you were my wife's companion upon her recent tour in Europe, and that you were registered there as man and wife?"

The words were ominous in their awful quiet.

Randall was silent a moment, looking at the man in a dazed, horrified sort of way, then in the same way he asked:

"Who, told you that?"

"The woman who has nursed my child."

"Cursed fool. I never meant that you should know from her!"

"Then it is true?"

"Your wife can answer you better than I."

"But I demand to know from you."

Randall looked at him another moment in silence, then replied slowly: "And I decline to answer!"

For a moment Hurdis stood there as if striving to decide whether to kill the man or not, simply by closing his long, slim fingers over the cursed throat. Then he turned around, and as quietly as he had entered the house, he left it.

Randall gazed at the door through which he had vanished for some time, the band of his trousers still caught between his hands, then, with great deliberation, he thrust the other leg in and drew them on.

A slow laugh rippled from between his teeth.

"There is a storm brewing off the Cape of Good Hope!" he muttered. "I should like to strangle that woman for getting ahead of me, and I did not intend that it should be known just yet. I would have—Pouf! My revenge is great enough. Henry, get me a darker tie. The colors in that thing are not becoming to me."

Very calmly he whistled "Rock a Bye Baby" while his servant obeyed.

XLIX

THE VISIT TO THE PRISON.

"The sun, too, shines into cesspools and is not polluted."

"What man dare I dare!
Approach thou like the rugged Russian bear,
The arm'd rhinoceros, or the Hyrcan tiger;
Take any shape but that, and my firm nerves
Shall never tremble."

THE FOLLOWING DAY, PRECEDED BY a journalistic blaze from all parts of the world, Eva was removed from Long Branch to Freehold and placed in the dingy prison in that place.

She was beginning to suffer cruelly.

At first it had been something after the order of a wound that is terribly lacerated—sensitiveness to pain seems for the time to be destroyed, but with returning life comes the agony of suffering—the bodily anguish that seems beyond endurance.

She had looked without hope for the coming of Hurdis, but she was forced to follow the officer of the law without even a message having arrived from him.

Believing herself to be deserted by every friend, she bowed her head to the yoke from which there seemed to be no escape, but even in dreams she had never thought such grief possible.

The child, too, that had grown so dear to her, was denied her. But she knew but too well that pleading was useless, and so she held her peace, feeling that her heart had already broken, though yet enduring the most acute anguish.

It had never occurred to her to inquire as to the condition of Nurse

Durneo. She believed her to be already dead, and believing so, of what avail was it to ask?

She obeyed her director in silence, a fact that the unfeeling reporters construed as careless indifference to the terrible crime that she had committed.

Left in her dismal room with no occupation, and not even a view of the world to distract her, the old apathy seemed to again settle over Eva that threatened lunacy.

Her hands were clasped idly to her lap, her eye gazed vaguely at the opposite wall, her chin had fallen, as though from coming death.

Breakfast and luncheon were alike left untouched; she had simply forgotten her food the moment it had been brought.

It was while in this condition that the door was opened by the warden of the prison.

She glanced up slowly, but as she saw who passed him and come forward into the room, a sudden color suffused her cheeks, her eyes grew wildly bright, and a low, glad cry fell from her lips.

"Rod, my darling!" she gasped, flinging herself upon his breast.

Only a moment thus, then she realized that they were not alone.

She could not endure for even that short space of time that there should be a witness to their meeting. It was too sacred to her for that.

Without thinking what she was doing, she turned excitedly to the prison-keeper, and laid her hand upon his shoulder. "Leave us alone!" she cried. "Let me see my husband alone!"

With lugubrious expressions of countenance, he went without a word.

Then Eva turned to Hurdis.

"You have not abandoned me!" she exclaimed tearfully. "I can bear anything now. Let them hang me if they will. I can ascend the scaffold with composure."

She paused. Something in his face replied her. There was no answer to her caress, no response to her gladness. She felt like a fire that has received a douche of iced water.

She staggered back from him, the arms that had been extended falling inertly at her side. A dazed horror seemed to take the place of her recent joy.

"Rod," she cried hoarsely, "what is it? Have you come here—"

She could not complete her sentence; she scarcely knew herself what she had meant to say; she only knew that the hardness the deadly coldness of his face had frightened her.

He lifted his hand to his brow and wiped it, as though the perspiration were annoying to him, while none could be seen. He waited a moment, his lips seeming to be unable to frame the terrible words that were in his mind.

"Eva," he said at last, "I have come to ask you a question. Your answer to it will decide my whole future life. You heard the hideous charges that woman, Marie Durneo, made against you. Were they true or false?" He paused, waiting for her to speak.

It would have been less cruel if he had thrust a knife into her heart and let the blood out at once. She stood staring at him for a long minute, and then turned away, with a short, dreary sigh.

He caught her by the shoulder and turned her where the light fell full upon her cold, gray face.

"Answer me," he exclaimed, his voice containing not one note of sympathy.

She looked up at him again. There was nothing of life or animation in her eyes. They were as cold and expressionless as they could ever be in death. Her stiff, blue lips managed at last to frame a single word. It was:

"Yes."

He neither fainted nor moved. There was a sudden tightening of the lips, a suppression of the breath that was but momentary, then very slowly he lifted his hat.

"That was all I wished to know," he said briefly, turning toward the door.

She watched him until be had reached it, watched him unconsciously. There was nothing to her either in life or in death and she felt absolutely nothing as she saw him going. A stone woman might have felt as much.

At the door he paused and looked back.

"If," he said, slowly, "there is anything that I can do to assist you, you may call upon me. My purse is open to you to its last farthing. Good morning."

"One moment!" she cried dully, extending her hand with a detaining gesture. "In common humanity you have no right to leave me until you hear what I have to say in my own defense!"

"There is nothing that you can say to lighten the load of disgrace that you have put upon me. There is nothing that you can say that would wipe out the humiliation with which you have cursed my life. I had not injured you. I loved you!"

"And I swear—"

He lifted his hand deprecatingly. "Do not!" he exclaimed. "It is all useless—all! You have broken my heart, while I was showering you with every blessing that lay in my power. You have dragged my name through the gutter, while I was shielding you with its honor and its love. I do not mean to reproach you. I should have said nothing had you not forced me to it. I regret even now that you have done so. Again, good morning!"

As the turnkey answered his call, he once more turned his head in the direction of the unfortunate woman. "You might like to hear," he said slowly, "that Marie Durneo is not dead. There is even a chance of her recovery."

She did not reply, but stood there with her hands clasped in front of her, her eyes following him. She saw his form disappear, she heard the door closed and looked, she listened to the retreat of the footsteps down the hall until the last echo had died away, and then, without sigh or moan, she sunk down.

She was sitting upon the floor, her hand supporting her chin, the elbow resting upon her knee. She might have said with King Richard:

> "Here I and sorrow sit:
> Here is my throne—bid kings come bow to it?"
> for sorrow is the hand that levels this world.

She may faintly have heard the door swing open again, but it is doubtful; certainly she did not look up until a hand was laid lightly upon her shoulder.

She raised her head listlessly. A man was standing there, a man whom she had never seen before—a man whose face seemed to glow as though the radiance of a halo were falling upon it.

Eva did not alter her position, but sat there staring at him as though waiting for him to break the almost uncanny silence.

"You are Mrs. Hurdis, are you not?" he asked, in the most commonplace of tones.

Eva nodded.

"I have heard that you are in trouble, and I have come to see if there is not something that I can do for you!"

He paused for an answer, and very slowly Eva staggered to her feet.

Her eyes were fixed upon him curiously, her lips half parted.

"Who are you?" she asked, in a voice so altered from its usual musical ring that even she would have failed to recognize it. "And what interest can you have in me?"

"I am Ralph Hoyt, and I have in you the interest that common humanity demands for suffering. You have few, if any, friends, and I have come to offer you any assistance that lies in my power."

"Do you know of what I am guilty?" The question was asked without emotion, in a hard, stony way that might have repelled a man less in earnest.

"Yes, I know. I never saw you before, but I know a great deal of the history of your life, and from the bottom of my heart I pity you."

"Who has told you?"

"You had a servant who was in my employ for years—in fact until the death of my wife, when I went abroad. I refer to Anne Chute. She called upon me this morning, and told me the story of your life as far as she knew it. She felt convinced that there would be few of those with whom you had been connected who would offer you their sympathy and protection at this time; and I am here to provide whatever you may need in the absence of any other."

"Do you know why I stabbed that woman?"

"Yes; Anne Chute heard all."

"Did she tell you of what Marie Durneo accused me?"

"Yes."

"But she could not tell you, because she did not know, that I am guilty of all she said and more! She did not tell you that I did live with Vanderfelt for months, that I deceived Robert Loran, that I played upon the weakness of Marshall Randall, in order that I might have revenge for a terrible wrong that he had done me, until I robbed him of his honor and made of him a thief. She did not tell you that I married Rod Hurdis with that secret upon my conscience, wrecking his life and my own as well, loving him so selfishly that I sacrificed both him and my own peace of mind to it. I do not deserve your sympathy, I am not worth it. They will hang me, and except that I shall be forced to ascend the gallows bearing his name, I shall not care. You are very kind, sir. As much as the deadness of my heart will allow me to appreciate anything, I appreciate the offer that you have made, but I do not deserve it. My husband was here to-day; he has left me to my fate. If there had been any extenuating circumstances he would have seen them, for he—loved me!"

There was not the slightest break in the voice as the last words were uttered, only a faint pause; but there was something of unutterable woe that sent a thrill of indescribable sympathy through the man's heart.

He gently took her unresisting hand.

"If he has abandoned you, you need my friendship all the more!" he said softly. "I do not ask you to accept it. I simply thrust it upon you. Anne has told me how you have suffered, and the good book tells us that there is no sin that suffering cannot expiate. We are not all Gods, that we can resist temptation. I was tempted once myself; I yielded to a great wrong; and because the world never discovered it, was no reason why the misery of it should not have kept sympathy alive in my heart forever. The greater the sinner, poor child, the more my friendship is yours. The righteous, you know, do not need to be saved."

L

HURDIS HEARS THE TRUTH ABOUT BABY LAURA.

"Yes, this is life, and everywhere we meet,
Not victor crowns, but wailings of defeat."

"All is confounded, all!
Reproach and everlasting shame
Sit mocking in our plumes."

A WEEK LATER HURDIS SAT IN the room that he and his wife had occupied together, his worse than motherless child upon his knee.

He had read all the articles that the papers had contained, he had seen himself disgraced and humiliated, but he had not tried to refute any of the charges against either himself or his wife. He maintained a quiet that seemed killing him.

During this time Baby Laura was his only consolation. He held her upon his knee, he played with her he dressed her with his own hands, and would scarcely allow any other the privilege of touching her.

In the pretty room that answered as parlor, that he still retained in Mrs. Rupert's cottage, he sat in a large chair, crooning a song to her, and watching the baby hands that were lifted sleepily to grab vaguely at the mustache that was just a little beyond its reach, when a soft knock sounded upon the door.

It was opened almost immediately. "A gentleman sees you, sir," announced the servant.

Before Hurdis could ask the name, a man stepped by the girl and entered his presence. The servant retired.

"I beg your pardon, Mr. Hurdis, for comparatively forcing my presence upon you in the manner in which I have," the man said, drawing a card case from his pocket, "but I was afraid you might decline to see me if I sent you my card first and it was necessary that I should see you. I am Henry Ormsby of the——" The name of one of the largest of metropolitan papers was mentioned, and the gentleman's card handed in support of his statement.

Hurdis arose in considerable embarrassment. He had no desire to be taken for a sentimentalist, and most of all, wished to conceal from the press any of his feelings upon the subject so near his heart.

He started to lay the baby into its crib, but the child set up such a lusty cry that he was forced to lift it in his arms.

"My nurse has gone out, sir," he explained to the reporter. "You will have to pardon me if I must perform that office for myself. Will you not be seated?"

Ormsby bowed, seating himself upon a chair where he could watch the young father in his awkward efforts to manage the child. It was pitiful in the extreme to him.

He did not speak, and Hurdis broke the silence. "You say that it was necessary that you should see one?"

"Yes. I wanted to know if there are any points in this case that have not been given to the public that you would like to make known?" he said with some hesitation.

"No," replied Hurdis curtly, "I have nothing whatever to say. So far as justice is concerned, it has all the points that are necessary in the case immediately before it, and I do not see why the public should interest itself in my private affairs. I have no statement whatever to make."

He half arose from his chair as though in dismissal, but the reporter continued to stare at him curiously as though he had something to say, and was striving to find the most humane way to say it.

"There is something more?" questioned Hurdis. "If so, I beg that you will state it briefly. I am not well."

"Mr. Hurdis," the reporter began, "there are many people who are taking interest of this affair actuated by curiosity alone, and there are others whose business it is, in the interest of the law, to discover all they can relative to the antecedent and past history of a—pardon me—criminal. Some such reason as that has caused our inspector to inquire into the former history of your wife—"

"Excuse me, sir," interrupted Hurdis, his face crimson with shame, "I have read all that story in the papers. I have no denial to make."

"But more has been discovered to-day that the papers have not yet produced. Mr. Hurdis, are you acquainted with that section of the law that relates to the counterfeiting of an heiress?"

"What do you mean?"

"Will you allow me to read you a copy of it that I have made?" Ormsby took from his pocket a note-book, and turning to a page that he had marked, read slowly and with strong emphasis:

"'A person who fraudulently produces an infant, falsely pretending it to have been born of a parent whose child is or would be entitled to inherit real property, or to receive a share of personal property, with intent to intercept the inheritants of such a property, or the distribution of such personal property, or to defraud any person out of the same, or any interest therein, or who, with intent fraudulently to obtain any property, falsely represents himself to another to be a person entitled to an interest or share in the state of a deceased person, either as executor, administrator, husband, wife, heir, legatee devisee, next of kin, or relative of such person, is punishable by imprisonment in a state prison for not more than ten years.'"

The voice ceased, the book was closed and replaced in the reporter's pocket.

Hurdis lifted his eyes, his hands straying with a soothing caress over the soft hair that rested against his breast.

"Well," he questioned, "what has that so do with me?"

"Nothing to do with you personally, sir," replied Ormsby solemnly. "But perhaps a great deal to those who have been, if they are not now, very dear to you."

"I don't think I understand."

"I am sorry to tell you, sir, that there have been some very sensational developments in the case that so nearly concerns you to-day. The inspector has suspected this, but has been unable to get all his proofs together until to-day, when Mrs. Randall voluntarily told all she knew upon the subject."

"Mrs. Randall told—I beg that you will not speak in conundrums, sir. If there is anything that you wish to tell me, do so without any effort to spare my feelings. What is it that Mrs. Randall has told?"

"She declares that your wife is amenable to the law, for having palmed off upon you a spurious child—a child that is neither yours nor hers!"

Hurdis' face became white as death. Slowly he arose from his chair, clasping the child closely to his breast, his eyes blazing with wrath.

He threw his head back with a gesture, that iron animal indicates danger, and uttered in a voice that was terribly distinct:

"That is a lie!"

The reporter arose and faced him. "Will you look at the proofs that I bring, sir?" he asked. "I have copies of all the sworn statements that furnish irrefutable testimony. I am sorry to tell you that it is undoubtedly the truth, sir. We have even the testimony of the woman who sold to Eva

Hurdis the baby which you hold to your breast now, and for which Mrs. Hurdis paid her the sum of ten dollars."

Had not Ormsby caught the unfortunate child, it would have fallen to the floor. It fell from Hurdis' inert arms as he dropped into a chair.

But he was not long in recovering himself. "Will you allow me to look over the papers that you have brought?" he asked.

Ormsby handed them without a word, and while Hurdis was examining them, the reporter sat there playing with the child that was never to know the secret of its own parentage. The man's heart ached for the little innocent, but there was nothing that he could do.

When Hurdis had finished the perusal, he handed the papers to their owner.

"What do you intend to do about it?" the reporter asked.

"Nothing," replied Hurdis dully. "I have done all that I can or shall. I still have nothing to say."

The reporter arose, and offered him the child.

A shudder shook the man from head to foot. "Would you have the kindness to place it on that sofa?" he asked.

The whole story was told in the request. He knew what he had read to be the truth; his love for the child had been killed by the blow; the last tie that had held him to the woman who had been his wife was snapped; he was as much a stranger to the case as the hideous disgrace that chained him to it would allow him to be.

He had forgotten his own yielding to temptation; he had forgotten that, to a great extent, he was the cause of his wife's being in the situation that she then was; he had forgotten everything except himself.

He scarcely knew when the reporter left him, but was recalled to himself by hearing the cry of the child.

He started toward it, put out his hand to raise it, then recoiled with a shiver of horror.

With a muttered curse he snatched up his hat and dashed from the house.

Eva was, indeed, left to her fate!

LI

GUILTY, OR NOT GUILTY.

"That is the bitterest of all—to wear the yoke of our own wrong-doing."

"Never morning wore
To evening, but some heart did break."

"NURSE DURNEO WILL NOT DIE!"

Those were the words of comfort and good cheer that were brought in to the prison by Eva's single friend, Ralph Hoyt.

He had expected her to clasp her hands and utter a cry of delight, but she only turned from him with a weary groan.

"It is too late!" she moaned. "Too late to bring me back my husband's love. Too late to restore to me my innocence. The fault is not mine that she did not die!"

"But think, dear, what it is that it promises you."

"Nothing! Escape, perhaps, from the gallows, immunity from death; but that is all, and that is worse than nothing! What does the hope of the world offer to me? A hearthstone that is deserted by every human creature, a home that knows no presence save that of a broken heart, a conscience that has branded me across the face with a mark that is worse than the one that afflicted Cain. You are very good to me, you are my only friend, you mean to comfort me. But there is no comfort for such as I. Why do you not leave me to my own misery?"

A week before, Ralph Hoyt would have answered:

"Because you have a soul to save, and I wish to add it as a jewel to the crown that I shall wear in Heaven;" but now he lowered his eyes, and was silent.

He could not have answered, because he was struggling against something that was nameless even to him. He toyed with his watch-chain and held his peace.

"Mrs. Hurdis," he said, after a long pause, speaking in as commonplace a tone as he could force, "have you received an answer to the message you sent your husband?"

She shook her head wearily. "No," she replied. "Since he heard the truth about the child, he will listen to nothing! Anne went to him, she told him all that I had to say; she repeated to him the story of my life; she pleaded my cause as I should never have had the courage to do; she even pointed out to him the bitterness of my temptation, and that, while appearances were so terribly against me, I was, after all, not criminally guilty. He listened in silence, but when she had finished, he raised his head from his hands and looked at her.

"'I suppose Mrs. Hurdis has sent you herewith this message to me,' he said. 'Tell her that I have no answer to make. I was her dupe once, I can never be again! Whether she is innocent or guilty of the charges to which you refer, the confession that she made to me would render it utterly impossible for me to ever see her again voluntarily.

"'Should she force her presence upon me, I shall find a means to rid myself of it. Where I once loved, I now despise her. I have no sympathy to offer in the position in which she finds herself.

"'I make no reference to the hideous disgrace that she has put upon me, but the silence that is between us must be preserved forever! Tell her that, and then never mention her name to me again. I have listened to you simply that she may not think that I have not heard the lie with which she is striving to deceive me again.'

"That was all."

She had told it coldly, stonily, as though all the feeling had been frozen from her heart by his cruelty.

Ralph Hoyt's eyes flashed fire. "The cursed—"

She silenced him by a gesture.

"You must not say that!" she exclaimed. "He is right and I was wrong! I hoped that he might have some mercy, but I see now how foolish I was to expect it. He could never trust me again after the manner in which I have deceived him. He is right to think of his own interests first."

If Ralph Hoyt was unconvinced, he said nothing, but went on, day after day, working in her interests, doing all he could to secure her acquittal at the trial that was then progress, hoping against hope, and striving all that lay in his power to cheer the drooping spirit.

But there was not much hope.

She bore up astonishingly well with the whole world against her, but it was the courage that proceeds from despair.

He tried to save her upon the day upon which Hurdis was called upon to testify. He tried to induce her to remain away from the courtroom, but she saw through his kind maneuvers, and gently, but firmly, declined to remain away.

She saw the man whom she had loved ascend the witness-stand, she listened to his words through a roar comparable only with Niagara, she heard him without understanding, she knew vaguely that he had said nothing of the scene that had led to the stabbing of the nurse, that part for which he was responsible, and she bowed her head and wept silently as he left the witness-stand.

She tried to shut it out, she tried to convince herself that he did right, but something very like contempt filled her heart to overflowing as he passed her without even a glance in her direction.

She was braver than ever as she ascended the stand to testify in her own behalf. Her lawyers had told her what she was to say, and what not.

She had told them nothing of the opening cause of the quarrel with Nurse Durneo, thinking it time enough to have that come out when Hurdis should have told it himself. And now! A smile that was half cynical curved her dainty lips.

She answered the questions that were put to her, she never lost her perfect self-possession, her sweet eyes were lifted occasionally and then lowered, but there was no word that implicated Hurdis that passed her lips.

The guilt was hers and hers alone, and she alone would bear the entire burden.

It was a generous sacrifice, but she made it without considering that she had done more than any other would have done. There was no ostentation in her manner, and less in her heart.

When she had finished, she was led from the room. She did not hear the charge of the judge to the jury. Neither did Ralph Hoyt, who was beside her.

She sat near a window looking out, and he leaned over the back of her chair, saying nothing, but allowing her to feel the encouragement of his presence. She was incapable of feeling much. Her heart was dying, and it was dying hard.

How long she had been there she could not recollect, when an officer came to conduct her back to the court.

She was placed in the terrible seat facing the curious crowd, and then the awful enforcer of the law turned to the twelve men who sat so solemnly upon his right.

"Gentlemen of the jury," he said solemnly, "have you agreed upon a verdict?"

The foreman arose, seeming to feel the dignity of his position to its fullest extent. "We have!" he answered.

"Have you found the prisoner at the bar guilty or not guilty?"

A silence that was frightful fell upon the room. Every neck was craned forward; every ear was strained to catch the words that would follow.

Ralph Hoyt seemed to be choking. His fingers were caught in the collar of his shirt, but he was the least observed, perhaps, of any one in that well-filled room.

Eva was like marble. Not a muscle of her beautiful face moved; her respiration stopped for the moment, but that was not observable. The hush was awful.

The voice of the foreman sounded like a clarion. Slowly, steadily he uttered the words:

"Guilty of assault with intent to kill!"

Instantly the room was in utter confusion. Everyone had expected it to be acquittal, and the greatest excitement prevailed.

The gavel was brought down upon the desk with great force, and "Order!" imperatively demanded. Then the judge's voice was heard again. Others may have listened to his words, but they reached neither Eva nor Ralph Hoyt.

In some vague way she knew that she had been condemned to serve a term of two years in the penitentiary, from which she knew there was no hope of escape.

She was stony in her calmness. She knew that some hand had been reached forth to her; she knew that someone had assisted her from her chair; she felt that she was going from the room in which those dreadful words had been spoken, but she was doing it as a somnambulist might. Yet there were those present who could not understand.

The breaking of a heart was called indifference!

LII

TO THE PENITENTIARY.

"There she stands
Childless and crownless in her voiceless woe."

"Eating the bitter bread of banishment."

IN THE CENTER OF HER plainly-furnished room Eva stood, a light wrap encircling her shoulders, a hat of dark blue pressed closely over her copper-colored hair, awaiting the coming of her escort for that enforced journey.

In front of her Ralph Hoyt stood, his hands tenderly holding her own. She was like a piece of marble, while he quivered and trembled beneath the strongest emotion of his life.

"You must have courage," he whispered. "Remember that you have friends whom no misfortune—however great—could cause to desert you. The time will end as all time must, and then—"

"Don't!" she interrupted. "It is the 'and then' that would kill me, if anything had power to do that. I must be made of granite that I cannot die. If I but had the means—"

"Hush! You would but condemn yourself to an eternity of suffering, instead of a few months that will not seem so long, after all. God is waiting to comfort you, if you will only listen. We have but a few moments now. Tell me, dear, is there not something that you would have me do? Is there not some message that you wish delivered—some commission that you can give me by which I shall know that you trust me?"

She raised her eyes to his. There seemed to be the light of Christianity in the confidence they expressed.

"Trust you!" she exclaimed, with her first show of emotion. "It is only because of you that I have not lost all confidence even in God. What do you think my life would have been here but for you? I should have been exhausted with the struggle and have died long ago. I know that there is hope for me with God, since He has sent me a friend so noble, so sincere, and as true as you! I will leave you a commission, the holiest one that I can give. There is one who has suffered innocently through me. I have disgraced her at the very beginning of her life, when she was defenseless. I would make to her what amends lie in my power, and since I am helpless, I leave her to you, my single friend. I mean Laura, my baby. See that they are kind to her. Do not let her suffer, and if I cannot reward you, surely God will."

"I accept it as the most sacred trust." He lifted her hands to his lips and kissed them in silence; then, after a long pause, his voice hoarse and broken, he said:

"It is—good-bye, now, dear. If I could bear your burden for you, I would do it with gratitude to God for allowing it, but you know that is impossible. As often as they will allow me I will visit you there, but—"

He could not finish his sentence for the trembling of his voice, and Eva glanced at him in surprise. She, who had been so perfect in the art of reading the hearts of men, had no power of knowing the struggling that was going on in his.

"You must not let it grieve you," she said calmly. "You must look upon me from this hour as dead. I am dead to the world, dead to those who have loved, as well as those who have hated me, dead to my own heart, alive only to the hope of God! It is good-bye, indeed, my friend, a long and eternal farewell! I do not say God bless you, for the palm of His divine hand is resting upon your head at this moment. You are a god yourself!"

"You must not say that. It sounds like blasphemy! Eva, before the guard comes, will you kiss me once?"

Even then she did not understand. Her suffering seemed to have taken all worldly knowledge from her, as it had robbed her of the power to feel.

She lifted her head and allowed him to press his lips upon hers, but they were cold as the lips of the dead, and he shuddered as the contact ceased; it had chilled instead of thrilling him, and with bowed head, and eyes that could not see, he stood back as the guard entered.

"All ready!" the custodian of the law cried briskly.

Hoyt did not lift his head—he did not see the backward glance from the eyes of the unfortunate woman, but he heard a low, suppressed sob, the first she had uttered since that dreadful day. It gave him hope.

And she followed the man who was conducting her to the home that the law had provided for such as she. She bowed her head again in shame as she remembered it, and clasped her hands closely over each other. It was her single exhibition of feeling.

In silence she went onward, doing as he directed, yielding to a fate that had seemed to overpower her from the beginning. In a deep reverie from which nothing seemed to have the power to arouse, she sat until they reached Trenton, then she was taken from the train and placed into a carriage.

The drive that followed was not a long one, and she lifted her eyes only when the officer of the law offered his hand to assist her to alight. Then she gazed upward.

The massive brown stone loomed above her, seeming to stretch out its hungry arms for an embrace. The huge, solid walls, rising unbroken, save by the massive columns in front, seemed to impress her with but a single idea—that it was a mammoth sepulcher in which thousands of human souls were entombed alive.

She shuddered.

The hand that she extended to the guard was icy cold, even through her glove; her lips were blue. Still there was no outward demonstration, and the heart of the man was touched to pity.

"It will not be so bad when you are used to it!" he said encouragingly. "Besides, you know, your sentence will be commuted for good behavior. Don't you let those people in their persuade you into trying to escape, or any act that is against the rules, and you'll get out full three months sooner."

Eva tried to answer—she tried to thank him for the courage that he had meant to give, but the words stuck in her throat. She could think of nothing to say. The thought of the hideous sepulcher had overcome her.

She felt the man take her by the arm—she managed to walk up the steps leading to that terrible door—she heard the clang of a bell, hollow and hideous, sound through the silence of the great stone building, and then the heavy iron door swung open.

A man with a pleasant face, but ominous brass buttons, answered the summons.

"You!" he exclaimed. "We were not expecting you for a half hour yet. Come in."

But Eva scarcely heard the words. She was looking beyond him at the great piles of stone wall, the hard, cruel stone of the floor. Stone everywhere, even to the hearts of the men.

And yet she was treated courteously. She was too much dazed and horrified to realize that. As she was taken into the office, a man in red and brown stripes passed her—a man with a face as hard and brutal as the stone that surrounded her.

She shuddered again. Were these people to be her companions during her stay in that awful place?

Then the apathy came again. She was glad that it was so, glad that her brief suffering was over, glad that she was dead to emotion.

She scarcely remembered what happened after that, until she found herself in a narrow cell, more cheerless than the one at Freehold. She looked around helplessly at the bare walls, the iron bed, and then at herself, clothed as she was in a plain dress that left no shapeliness to her rounded, beautiful form.

But even that, could she have seen her face, she would have realized, had no power to destroy her loveliness. Nothing could obliterate that, when the bitterness of the grief through which she had passed had not the power to do so.

She sat down upon the edge of the little bed, her eyes fixed upon the opposite wall. A hard, cold smile curved the corners of her mouth.

"It has come at last," she muttered. "They all said at home that I would come to no good. Bill Scarlett's daughter, who scorned her own father, finds herself in a position in which even he, bad as he is, has never had the misfortune to be. Perhaps it is justice, but I cannot see it! I am wrong to say that, but there are others who should suffer with me! I am not a martyr to wish to take all the wrong-doing upon my own shoulders, and there are others that have sinned even more than I have. But all this is useless. There is no hope for me. I shall stay in this place until the time expires and then I shall leave it; leave it an adventuress, would-be murderess, an ex-convict! Where can a creature like that find a place to hide her head? I shall be like a fox run to earth but to be torn to death by dogs! It is a fitting ending to a life that contained no desire but for revenge!"

She was still sitting there when they came to take her to supper.

And what a supper it was! In all her dainty life since those days in the little village that had once been her home, and perhaps not even then, had she been called upon to partake of such fare.

She lifted her eyes but once, and beside her she saw a negress, black as ink. A coldness that seemed to threaten death seized upon her. That she should be forced to submit to an indignity such as that.

Then she remembered that the law knows no distinction in its treatment of criminals. They are all brutes, dogs, that deserve nothing but black bread and the lash!

She tried to force her food down her throat, but it would not yield. She seemed choking to death.

The coarse food was left untouched after the first unavailing effort, and when she was permitted she retired.

The morning following the prison physician was summoned.

"No. 98 was in delirium!"

And for many days she lay so, worn to a shadow by the violence of her ravings—ravings in which the name of Lil Cartwright was oftenest heard, ravings in which she seemed to be moaning over the death of a dog, her only friend, the one thing that loved her.

It was the beginning of her undoing, and to it she went back with persistent force.

The name of Marshall Randall was rarely called, that of Hurdis but once, and that in piteous entreaty.

And then a constitution of remarkable power asserted its supremacy. The fever left, and a weakness from which it seemed impossible for her ever to rise came upon her, but that, too, diminished with time, and she was restored to health once more, restored that she might endure the greatest blow that had yet come upon her, when she was to realize more fully than ever before the horror of the position in which she had allowed misfortune to place her.

LIII

LAWYER RAMSEY.

"Inhumanity is caught from man—
From smiling man."

"Why, courage, then! what cannot be avoided,
'Twere childish weakness to lament or fear."

A BRISK MAN OF BUSINESS, WITH traces of kindness and gentleness in his manner for all his brusqueness, was ushered into the presence of Mrs. Hurdis, when all others were denied her.

A smile that brought out the pretty dimple in her left cheek played over Eva's face as she half arose from her chair to receive him; but weakness caused her to sink back again. She put out her hand and grasped his cordially.

"I am too weak to rise," she said, "but not too weak to be most delighted to see you. I see so few, outside of the—prison, that it is a most welcome change. You seem to bring me a breath of the fresh air that one cannot get near this building—this sepulcher. How good you are to come, Mr. Ramsey!"

"Not at all! Not at all!" he exclaimed, pressing the hand he held. "You are not looking so well as when I last saw you, but the smile is better, much better. I tell you, Mrs. Hurdis, I had rather see a woman smile and be a fit subject for engagement by Barnum as a living skeleton, than weigh three hundred and look as you did the last day you were in that courtroom. If they had told me that you had gone mad, I should not have been surprised."

"That would have been a happier fate, Mr. Ramsey; but madness and death are only vouchsafed the fortunate."

"Tut! Tut! Child. You must not say that. You are young yet and the world holds many happy days for you. If we should all despair because of misfortune, there are very few of us that would not become suicides, if nothing worse. This is not going to last forever."

"I believe I could bear it with greater fortitude if it were. It is the thought of facing the world with this load of disgrace and shame upon me that is unendurable. Tell me! Did you come to see me to-day because your heart was touched by my loneliness and isolation, or have you brought me news?"

"Well—ah—you see"—rubbing his chin until his hand upon the day's growth of beard sounded like rubbing bristles—"it was partly one, and partly the other. I wanted to see how you have borne your illness first. To know that you are on the high road to recovery. And you are, are you not?"

"Yes. I am almost well again."

"I thought so. That is good. There is nothing like looking on the best side of everything. Every cloud has a silver lining, you know, and there was never a trouble yet that time could not heal. I tell you it is a great healer—time! Never was anything like it! Did you ever notice how quickly one recovers after a death that has seemed to take every bit of the heart out of one at first? Why, it's marvelous!—Marvelous! That is the way you will do! If you don't have anything to remind you of the old life when you leave here and go into the world again, you will recover from the sting of it all the quicker. Don't you think so?"

"I don't know that I quite follow you."

"No, of course not. I mean, if when you leave here, you have cut loose from all the association of the past, you will the sooner forget it all. Isn't that true?

"Perhaps."

"I knew you would see it in a sensible way. It makes my task a much easier one. You always were a wonderfully sensible woman, Mrs. Hurdis. I have taken a great interest in you, though I have not been very successful in the management of your affairs, but I like you, and I don't want to see you suffer any more than you must. That was the reason that I hesitated to tell you, but now that I am sure you will see things in their proper light, I need not hesitate any longer."

"You are very good, Mr. Ramsey, and I appreciate everything you say, but I do wish you would tell me what you are talking about."

"I am coming to it right now. The fact is, Mrs. Hurdis, Hurdis has made an application for a divorce"

"What?" The woman was upon her feet, her pale face ghastly. For a moment things seemed to swim before her eyes; then all turn dark.

She put out her hand and groped in the blackness of her misery for a moment; then Ramsey sprung to her side and caught her.

"Do not let me distress you!" she stammered hoarsely. "I shall recover in a moment. There. It is passed now. What was it you said?"

She sat down again, and lifted her eyes to his face. He had never seen such a change in any human countenance in his life. She had borne the trial and her condemnation stoically, but this was a death-blow.

He stood beside her with his hand resting upon her head.

"I wish you could see it in the proper light!" he cried. "Believe me, it is much better so. Even if Hurdis should ever live with you again, there would be no happiness for you. Confidence would be destroyed, and the family that is not united by confidence is the basis upon which purgatory is planned. You would grow to hate him in a short time for his continued jealousies, and he, however much he might love you, would grow to hate you from the humiliation that you would necessarily bring on him. Every slight that he received from that world that had fawned upon him, he would visit upon your unoffending head, and you yourself, when you saw it, would loathe yourself for the shame that you had caused him. And so it would go. I am very sorry for you, little woman, but as a man who has seen much of and every side of the world, I tell you it is the only hope that is offered either to you or to him."

"But a—divorce? Surely he could have been happy never to have seen me again without—that!"

The tone of her voice made him shiver, but he answered quietly:

"Believe me, that is the only way out of the difficulty. Until that divorce is granted, you and he are still husband wife, and it is that tie you want broken! Would you like to see him go through life miserable and alone, because you and he had had the misfortune to meet? I am sure you would not! Come! Think of it rationally and with your usual good sense. Do you want Hurdis to gradually forget the wrong with which you have cursed his life, or do you want him to live to loathe the very mention of your name, to feel that the bond that holds him to you is the one that is dragging him to destruction? I tell you again, and believe me, I speak truly, that if he loved you enough to forget the past and take you back, there would be nothing but destruction in his future. It could promise nothing but degradation and shame to both of you. You know that however much the world may sympathize, it never forgives! When the doors of society are once shut in the face of one of its members, it never again opens. It is hard for me to say this to you, but cruelty is often kindest after all. Child, if you will let me direct you, me, an old man who knows the world, you will yield in silence to this divorce, and you will try never to see Rod Hurdis again. You will do it for his sake as well as for your own. What have you to say?"

"Nothing. What is there left for me to say? What has there ever been that I could say? From the beginning there has never been but one way open to me. I was compelled to follow that or none. Suppose I should fight this case, what could I hope to gain? What would there be for me in justice, with the shadow of the penitentiary surrounding me? There is nothing that I can do; I am in the hands of fate, and however adverse it may be I can only yield."

He never forgot the bitterness of her tone, the terrible anguish of her face.

He took a chair near her, and stroked her hand gently.

"You are yielding, but not in the right spirit," he said almost tenderly. "You are yielding in a manner that will break your heart."

"It would break were it not already broken, but I am a fool, a fool! I might have foreseen this from the beginning and have been prepared, but one never is prepared for calamity such as that. Perhaps somewhere, deep down in my soul, there was an unvoiced hope that someday he would learn to forgive me; and seeing so clearly now that you are right and that I have been wrong is the bitterest blow I have had to bear. He said that he loved me, yet he has never made an inquiry concerning me, he has never shown that he was conscious of my existence until now, and then—oh God!—in what a way. Perhaps I deserve it; but loving him as I have done, there is no wrong that he could have done me that I would not have forgiven. But I am an erring woman—I can expect nothing—I *do* expect nothing."

"There may be a glorious future in store for you, a future given to God."

A half cynical smile flitted over the cold face. "It seems a sacrilege to offer to God that which none else will have. To give one's self to Him, because there is nothing else to do with the useless gift. I cannot thrust myself into Heaven simply because the devil refuses to receive me. For all I am a convict, there is something more honorable in my nature than that."

"You think of it incorrectly. Heaven has received some of its most loyal subjects through the highways of adversity. My child, work will not end for you when you leave the prison walls; it but begins."

"You wish to offer me consolation, and I thank you for the good intent, but tell you frankly that there is none. I shall not cry out, I shall not beseech the sympathy of the people. I shall hold my tongue and suffer until the end comes, but to the last day of my life I shall never forget the blow that Rod Hurdis has struck this day. Not that I blame him. Please do not understand me so. Perhaps I should have done the same myself. Why should he be tied to a woman with the odor of a prison clinging to her? He was always a thousand times too good for me. Many a night before I married him I have lain awake all the night through striving for the courage to tell him the truth, praying for strength to save him from myself. But I loved him too well. I could not do it. And this is the result—this!"

She seemed about to break down, and the brusque but good-hearted lawyer hoped she would.

But the weakness was but momentary. She folded her hands in her lap with a resignation that was pitiful.

"Have you any message for Hurdis?" he asked, after a long pause.

"None, except that his will is my law. A thousand divorces could not more utterly divide us than we are now, but I am willing to do anything that will release him from the bondage that must have grown hateful to him. Tell him that from the very bottom of my heart I am sorry for the terrible wrong that I have done him. Of course that cannot lessen the harm that I have done, but I should like him to know. Tell him that, for his sake, I hope we shall never meet again, but that I shall never cease to pray that God may bless him and wipe out the stain that I have put upon his name. Beseech him to think of me as seldom as he can, for that is the only way that he can ever forgive me. Tell him that I submit to anything that he may see fit to do, and that I shall never lift my voice against it. That is all. And now, dear friend, I must ask you to leave me. My strength is gone and—"

She could not complete the sentence.

Lawyer Ramsey was more touched by her manner than he ever remembered to have been before, and hardened lawyer though he was, he pressed her hand to his lips and left the room in silence through inability to speak.

When he had gone she crawled back to bed again. She drew the covers up about her, shutting out the view of the mocking sunlight, and fought out the last battle of her life with suffering such as that. She surrendered at last to a foe that was more powerful than she and yielded the last hope of a misdirected life.

LIV

INTO THE WORLD AGAIN.

*"Long is the way
And hard, that out of hell, leads up to light."*

*"So spake the seraph, Abdiel, faithful found
Among the faithless, faithful only he."*

THERE IS NEVER AN ILL, however meekly or rebelliously borne, that time will not end.

So Eva Hurdis found upon the day that her term in the penitentiary expired.

She did not welcome the change that was promised—there was no joy in her heart; on the contrary, she seemed to feel some sorrow that it should be so. She dreaded to leave the walls that had shielded her from the public, she dreaded to face the eyes of the world that had so cruelly condemned her.

"Good-bye!" she said to the matron, with tears in her eyes. "I suppose I am about the first one that ever left prison walls that did not do so joyfully; but there is no promise in the world to me! You have been kind to me, and there is nothing to hope for where I am going. I leave you to face scorn and derision that I am not sure I have the strength to endure."

"You must not feel so cheerless. You have one thing to lean upon that you knew nothing of when you entered here—your trust in God!"

"That is my single hope; but it is very hard to go again into a world in which I have not a single friend. I will try to be brave, but I am afraid I am a great coward, after all. Good-bye! And God bless you for your kindness to me. When I feel that my spirit is fainting I shall come to see you, if you will let me. Remember that I have not one friend in all this world.

I leave here to-day, not knowing where I shall seek shelter to-night, and with the shadow of the penitentiary upon me. Good-bye, and pray God to have mercy upon me!"

There were tears in the sweet, dark eyes, a trembling of the lips that was pitiful.

The matron kissed her with real affection. "Good-bye, dear!" she whispered. "I am glad that you are free, but I shall miss you more than you think. I hope life contains for you a greater joy than any of which you have ever dreamed. Don't forget me; and come to see me as often as you can."

With her own hands the good woman drew the veil over the lovely, quivering face, fastened the glove that Eva had just drawn on, and turned away that Eva might not be overcome by the sight of her emotion.

A messenger entered the room. "There is a gentleman waiting for you in the office, Mrs. Hurdis," he said.

Thinking, of course, that it was a guard waiting to conduct her from the prison, Eva drew her veil yet more closely, and suppressing a slight sob, she followed her guide.

She did not lift her eyes when she entered the office until some one advanced toward her, and she felt both her hands taken in a firm grasp.

Then she looked up. It was Ralph Hoyt that stood before her, speechless under his emotion.

"Mr. Hoyt!" she exclaimed brokenly.

"Yes," he answered. "I have come to take you away, if you will let me."

"How can I thank you for this kindness? The hardest trial of my life was in thinking that I should have to leave this place alone, to go again into the world absolutely friendless. And now you have come to help me. You are the only one who has remembered me, and you come to this place to take me by the hand. Oh, it is good of you! Surely Heaven will bless you for it."

"It is enough to see you safe at last and well. I am quite content. Come, let us go."

He drew her hand through his arm, he watched her as she said a timid farewell to those around her, then led her down the steps to the street to where a carriage was waiting.

She was silent from excess of emotion. For nearly two years she had remained inside the walls of that terrible building, and now she was free again. There were no words that could describe it; it was the bursting of the heart, the wild thrill of joy that one could only feel.

She did not know where he was driving her, and she did not ask. What mattered it—were not all places upon the earth alike to her? And then—she trusted him!

She knew that he had been her one friend through all, the one who had come to her through a Christian love for any of God's creatures that might be in distress and had stuck by her through everything. For the first time in years, a feeling of perfect repose, of sweetest rest, came over her.

Even when he took her from the carriage and placed her in the train, she asked no questions, but remained silent, happy in the thought that she possessed one friend that was staunch and true, who knew the circumstances of her wretched life and yet was not afraid to trust her.

And he was content to watch the changes in the lovely face, thinking how few traces there were of the suffering through which she had passed.

Only necessary conversation passed between them, and then, in short, quick sentences, commenced and ended with a glance of trust and affection.

When they reached New York she was placed in another carriage and driven up-town. He took her from it and led her up-stairs. At the door of a flat he paused and rang a bell.

Only a moment of silence; then the door was thrown hastily open, and Anne Chute rushed out—Anne the faithful.

With a glad cry Eva flung her arms around the girl's neck and burst into a passionate sobbing.

Anne half carried her into the room and closed the door.

"It seems too good to be true that you are really here!" exclaimed Anne, her own eyes streaming with tears as she smoothed the bright hair. "I can hardly realize that it is all over at last and that I have you again. Oh, Miss Eva, are you not glad that all the concealments and fear are through forever? Are you not glad that the end has come? Even this is better than the old life with all its hideous suspense and torture. Don't you think so?"

"When I have found two such friends as you, and—"

She did not complete the sentence, but turned and placed her hand in Ralph Hoyt's, her cheeks dimpled by a tearful smile.

As she turned to Anne Chute, her eyes fell upon a little figure in the corner, a little dainty, airy creature that had retired sulkily because she had been forgotten. She stood there with a frown upon her dimpled face, her finger between her rosy lips, her tiny gown a dream of beauty.

From her to Anne, then to Hoyt, Eva glanced quickly, half questioningly; then she threw herself upon her knees in front of the child and clasped it to her bosom.

She did not move for so long that they thought she had fainted, and Anne lifted her gently.

"How can I ever thank you both enough for this?" she cried, holding the child to her breast. "It is the single thread from the old life that was necessary to make this complete. But she is mine, is she not? They will not take her from me?"

"No one shall take her from you," replied Hoyt. "She is yours now forever."

"How good God is to me—I, who have deserved it all so little! Surely it cannot be that the night has passed and the day has come at last!"

"Trust in Heaven that it is so," returned Hoyt reverently.

Then, after a time, he took the child away and left her there alone with Anne, because he knew that, although they were mistress and maid, there would be many things that they would have to say to each other that they would prefer to have no third ear hear.

"It seems so good to have you back!" cried Anne, falling upon her knees at Eva's side. "I cannot tell you how we have missed you, nor how long the last few days have seemed. They have seemed to have a hundred hours each, and each hour an age."

"And I was despairing so that the time had come for me to go into the world alone. Oh, Anne, if one could always remember to trust God in all things, how much unhappiness there might be saved! Tell me. What has become of them all? You know who I mean. Marshall Randall and his mother and—the others?"

"Nothing! Nothing ever does happen to people like those. Marshall Randall has gone more to the dogs, if that were possible. He is always drunk. Some people suspect him of being in the 'confidence' games, but I don't think drink has left him sense enough for that. I don't know you would know him, he has changed so."

"And his mother?"

"She is the next thing to a beggar, as she richly deserves to be. The truth about Laura would never have been known but for her, and she only put you up to doing it to get you into her power more securely. Her son knew all about it all the time. She was the one who told Marie Durneo where you were, and put her up to coming to you. I tell you, Miss Eva, it was a case of 'like mother, like child,' only in this instance the mother was the meaner of the two."

"Where is Nurse Durneo?"

"I don't know. If she had her just desserts she would be on the scaffold, but I suppose she is somewhere putting up more jobs on innocent families. By the way, Maurice Vanderfelt is married."

"Indeed!"

"To one of the wealthiest girls in New York. Is not that an evidence of how the world will 'stone the woman and let the man go free?' I went to the church to see them married. She is a beautiful girl, but I fancy it was the twenty millions that her father has that he married and not the girl, for I never saw him look worse."

"And Mr. Hurdis—have you heard nothing of him?"

The melancholy of the tone cut Anne to the quick. She toyed with one of the shapely hands as she answered, softly:

"Yes, I see him often in the street. He looks older and much graver, but that is all. His hair is gray in the temples, but I think he is better looking by it. I have never read his name in the papers as being at any of the society affairs that are given in the city, but I am quite sure that he is not shunned, for I saw him standing at the carriage door talking with Mrs. Roosevelt the other day."

Eva sighed. It seemed to make her realize that she had done him one service in allowing him to have that divorce that had so nearly killed her. She did not regret it now.

After a moment of silence she exclaimed, more brightly:

"Now, Anne, you and Mr. Hoyt seem to have planned everything else—how have you arranged that I am to make my living? Of course, you know, I cannot be dependent. I have had quite enough of that."

"Yes, I thought of that. I was thinking one day what we should do, and I remembered what beautiful embroidery you used to do. I told Mr. Hoyt, and he went down-town to see a friend of his about it. He has got you enough embroidery and decorative art work to do to keep you constantly employed, and to make all the money that you will need. You can do it at home, too, so that the world need not know anything at all about it."

Perhaps that was the most touching thing that had occurred to Eva during that day.

She bowed her face upon the head of her faithful friend and wept again, but they were only tears of thankfulness and peace.

The way had been long and hard, but she was beyond the walls of perdition at last.

LV

HURDIS.

"For 'tis sweet to stammer one letter
Of the Eternal's language—on earth it is called Forgiveness!"

THE WEEKS THAT FOLLOWED WERE filled with a peace that seemed eternal. How grateful the woman was who had suffered so much and so long, only her own heart could have told.

There were no more thoughts of revenge, no more longings to be wealthy and powerful that she might humiliate another, no more desire to make others suffer for the wrongs that they had done her.

She was willing now to leave their punishment to God, and even prayed Him to spare them all!

She did her work with a song in her heart. She worked early and late, but it was a labor of love, it was food for the soul.

Ralph Hoyt passed almost every evening in her company, and she had grown to look for his coming, to watch the hands of the clock, and if he were detained beyond the usual hour, there was a nervous anxiety until he came that she could not control.

Once she chided him for being more than an hour late, and was surprised at his happy laugh as he kissed her hand apologetically.

"It was a lady that detained me," he said lightly. "You know how inconsiderate of one's engagements they are."

Her face flushed dully, and a slight anger crept into her eyes. "I hope," she answered, stiffly, "that you will never allow an engagement with me to cause you to lose a moment's pleasure. After all, it is no engagement. I simply look for you because you have been accustomed to coming."

Hoyt laughed again. Was it possible, he asked himself, that she was jealous?

"Indeed it is an engagement," he replied. "You will soon find out how angry I should be if you were the one to break it."

She smiled then, and leaning toward him, placed her hand upon his.

"Forgive me!" she exclaimed. "I am very ill-natured to-day. I am afraid I was rude, but you have no one but yourself to blame. You have given me so much of your time, that I have grown to look upon it as mine by right. I am afraid you have spoiled me."

He bit his lips to keep back the words that rose to them. He meant to tell her some time how he loved her, he meant to ask her to be his wife; but he did not want to think in the years to come that he had forced her inclination in any way.

He did not want her to come to him through gratitude—but love. He wanted her to be thoroughly independent when he asked her; he wanted her to know that she was not dependent upon him for her livelihood, and it was for that very reason that he had obtained for her the employment that he had.

Under circumstances like these, it was very hard for him to wait. But bravely he pocketed his impatience, and with a smile upon his lips watched the white hands as they pulled the needle in and out with such artistic care.

She was very happy, happier than she had ever thought it possible to be.

There were times when the memory of her love for Rod Hurdis returned to her; there were times when she fancied she heard his footstep in the hall, and every drop of blood seemed to forsake her heart. But even that had not the power to rob her of her sweet content.

She had loved him—she loved him yet, she told herself persistently. But she would bear her pain philosophically, knowing that it was all for the best.

She was thinking of it all one day as she dressed herself to go to see an art display that was open to the public in the private house of a lady, who had generously opened her doors to all lovers of fine art in the decorative line.

It was the first time that Eva had ventured out except at night, and then with a veil across her face. She hesitated about going, but she knew that it would help her in the work she was doing, and knowing that she could not live all her life in the seclusion in which she was, she determined to brave the danger of recognition and go.

She wore a costume all of black, that against the whiteness of her skin and the reddish-gold of her hair, was exceedingly becoming.

She did not realize how lovely she was as she tied on her veil and left the house; but there was scarcely a man in the rooms to which she went who did not see more of the beautiful, sad face than of the decorative art they had been invited to admire.

She noticed at last what observation she was attracting, and unable to bear it in her fear of recognition, she slipped away to another room where the crowd had not yet gathered.

There was but one man present, and she did not even glance in his direction. With her lorgnette raised to better see the pieces upon the walls, she stood there, outlined against a drapery of pure Persian, that made a picture of her of rare loveliness.

So absorbed was she in the purpose for which she had come that she did not see the man turn to notice who his companion was—she did not see his closer look, nor how pale he became; but it was the low groan that fell upon her ear that attracted her.

He had fallen into a chair, covering his face with his hands.

In common humanity she approached him. "Are you ill, sir?" she asked in her sweet, musical voice.

He lifted his head and looked at her.

For a moment the objects in the room seemed to swim before her, then all turned dark, but she did not faint. With a valiant effort she recovered herself.

"I—I—beg—your pardon," she stammered hoarsely. "I—did—not know—that it was—you!"

She bowed slightly, turned away, and started toward the door.

Her heart was beating so, that she did not hear a step behind her, and was unconscious of an approach until he laid his hand upon her arm.

"Eva," he cried, his voice rasping in its hoarseness, "have you nothing else to say to me? Are we to meet and part as utter strangers?"

She raised her eyes sadly to his white face. Of the two, she was by far the more composed.

"Is it not better so, Rod?" she asked, half bitterly. "Life holds nothing in common between you and me. There is just one thing that I should like to say, and that is that if you can find one word of forgiveness in your heart that you can say to me for the terrible wrong that I did, God will bless you for its utterance. I know it is a hard thing to ask, Rod, but it all ended now, and perhaps freedom from the old life, from every chain that bound you, has taught you in some sense forgetfulness and forgiveness. If so, I pray that you will speak it!"

"And you can refer to it all so calmly?"

"I have tried to teach myself to think of it calmly, but it has been a terrible struggle, and only the knowledge that I have made my peace with God has brought be any rest. Rod, I ruined your life. I wonder that you can look at me ever again."

"I thought I could not! If any one had told me this morning that I was to meet you here to-day, I would have gone a thousand miles to have avoided you. But the moment I did see you, all the old feeling rushed back with the same fervor—God! What am I saying?"

"Nothing but madness!" cried Eva, half wildly. "I beg that you will not! I beg that you will let me leave you! Oh, Rod, my strength is so frail. I am but a woman who has loved you with all her heart and soul—with such desperation that madness came of it, and I dared anything, even to murder, to retain your love. Think of that, Rod, and let me go while I can."

His hold upon her arm grew firmer. "It is of that that I am thinking, and it is because of that that I have not the courage to let you go!" he said huskily. "I thought that I had forgotten, and that I was happy, until I say you to-day, but the old infatuation is too much for me. Eva, I don't ask what you have been, I don't ask what you are now, but—come back to me! Let the world go. What care I for it when it no longer cares for me? We shall get our own happiness out of life, and after all it is enough."

There was a dogged determination in the voice—a fierce expression in the eyes that showed her he meant what he said; but it showed her another thing at the same time—that the words of Lawyer Ramsey were true.

She shivered and drew back. "No, Rod, no!" she cried miserably. "There would be no happiness in it for either you or me! You would grow to despise me worse than you have done, and I should loathe myself for allowing you to yield to an infatuation. When you are once away from me, you will see the truth of what I say, and thank me that I have had the courage to refuse. Perhaps that act upon my part may teach you to forgive me, but you must believe me that it is wisest and best for us both."

"I am not asking you what is wisest and best, I am asking you for what is mine by right. You love me! Deny it if you can!"

Suddenly the face of Ralph Hoyt came up before her, less handsome than this one, less aristocratic, but so noble, so faithful, so true.

She shrunk back, and Hurdis caught her to his breast.

"You see, you cannot deny it!" he exclaimed fiercely, his face close to hers. "You cannot remember those old days that we passed together without a thrill of joy. You must yield to me—you shall!"

She broke away, and stood there before him, panting for breath. What the temptation was to her, none but herself could ever have told. All the memory of those old days had come back.

But she resolutely put it from her.

"Hush!" she cried. "You are tempting me beyond my strength, and for your sake I must not yield. I wronged you once—a wrong which, by the grace of Heaven, you have outgrown—and I will not add to it another that would be greater than the first. I am not of your world—I never was—and am less so now that the shame of the penitentiary is still upon me!"

"Do not say it! That shame is mine! Had I come forward like a man, you might have escaped; but I concealed my guilt, and put all the blame upon you. Do you think I have not felt it? Do you think my conscience has allowed me to rest? I will never give you up now, do not think it! There can be no talk of forgiveness between you and me; for if we should despise each other to the end of our lives, we belong to each other, and no power can set us free."

"You are wrong—all wrong. You do not see it as I do, because of the infatuation of which you spoke. It was a correct word—it is infatuation! Oh, Rod, let me go! When I am gone—when you can no more see my face—you will overcome this madness, and forget me. You will thank me that I have had the courage to resist; and some day you will marry some good woman who will make you very happy, as I never could. From the bottom of my heart I pray that it may be so! If I were worthy of you, Rod, I would sacrifice my whole existence to make you happy. But the thought of what you would be forced to give up for my sake would kill me. And then when I saw it all turning to hate—when I saw you rushing on to destruction through yielding to a folly like this, I should commit suicide, if nothing better offered. For more than two years you did not see my face, and you were as happy as the wrong that I had done you would allow you to be, and you will happy again when I am gone. Will you not say good-bye, dear, and let me go?"

He did not reply, but with folded arms and bowed head he allowed her to pass.

She turned and looked at him as she walked through the door, then with eyes blinded by tears, and a great sob that stuck in her throat, she let the portiere fall between them.

LVI

REST AT LAST.

"Let the dead past bury its dead!"

"The great world's altar-stairs
That slope thro' darkness up to God."

A FIRELIGHT GLOWED FITFULLY UPON THE hearth, flashing up, and then half falling from sight, as though making a last strong endeavor for life.

Before it upon the rug, curled up like a beautiful, shining kitten, Eva rested, forming pictures in the fast dying embers.

Whether her dreams were those of pleasure or sorrow, her countenance did not indicate, but a peace that nothing had the power to destroy, the peace of God, dwelt there.

The day of her poignant suffering had now passed forever.

She did not move as the door opened, but became conscious at last that some one had entered, that some one was leaning upon the mantle-piece looking down upon her, and without a start she lifted her eyes to the some one's face.

It was strange, but Ralph Hoyt might enter there whenever he would, and she would never feel the slightest sensation of surprise at his presence, he never startled her in any way. It seemed as a matter of course that he should come and go at will.

"You are half an hour early," she said, without a greeting.

"How do you know? You have not looked at the clock."

"But I know just the same. It was so good of you to come early. Did you know that I wanted you?"

She had risen and was standing beside him, but she did not offer her hand as was her custom.

"I don't think I knew it!" he answered with a smile. "Did you want me?"

"Yes; I wanted to tell you something. I want to feel that I have your approbation in something I did to-day. Will you sit down?"

He did so, drawing her down beside him. "What is it?" he asked. "The seriousness of your manner frightens me."

She was silent for some time, then without removing her eyes from the smoldering embers she spoke. "I saw—Rod Hurdis to-day."

She was not looking at him, but she felt the awful start that he gave, she knew from his quickened respiration that he was putting a terrible restraint upon himself, but when he replied his voice was as still and quiet as usual. "Did you—speak to him?"

"Yes; he said that he would forget all the past, if I were willing to begin life again."

"And you! What did you say?"

"I told him"—still gazing dreamily into the coals—"that it could not be! That I had never been worthy of him, and that I was still less so now, with the stain of the penitentiary upon me. He persisted, but I—declined."

"Did you—do that, Eva, because you believed that in the years to come he could censure you even more than he does now, or—because you had—ceased to—love him?"

"I don't know! I would to Heaven that I could answer your question with satisfaction to my own heart, but I cannot. While I was there with him, I tried to force myself to believe that there was no happiness for me in this world where he was not, but since I have left him, since I know that it is all over between us forever, I cannot help but feel a sort of relief that is startling to me. It is because I suffered so much during the short season that I was his wife, I suppose. Since I have been here I have thought of him so many times, longing, yet dreading to see him, half praying God for a glimpse of his face, without myself being seen, and now—I don't know what it is, I don't understand myself, but it is all changed. I could never go back to Rod Hurdis because I loved him, for I think that must have died when my heart broke, that heart that lives now through God."

The voice died away, not as one's does at the conclusion of a sentence, but it seemed gradually to fade into stillness.

For a long time there was silence between them, then Ralph Hoyt leaned toward her, and laid his hand upon hers.

"Is your heart dead, Eva?" he asked with tremulous earnestness. "I have prayed that God would cause it to turn to me. I have hoped that you might learn to lean upon me for the rest and peace that you have never know. Is your heart dead, Eva, or is it only exhausted from the struggle that has been too much for it to bear? If you will think I don't believe that I shall have to tell you how I love you! You must have seen it in my every act. Eva, have you nothing to say to me?"

She had turned and was looking at him in amazement.

"You love me!" she whispered. "You love me, knowing all the story of my shameful past?"

"Don't, dear. I shall not try to excuse you to yourself. You know your own temptation, therefore I have no plea to offer for you. If you have not sinned too much for God to forgive you, should I place myself beyond Him in the scale? Eva, will you be my wife?"

She was silent another moment, then answered slowly:

"It will be a poor way to pay the debt of gratitude that I owe you."

He shrunk back as though she had dealt him a blow where he expected a caress.

"If you have nothing but gratitude to give me, Eva," he cried, as though in bodily pain, "I beg that you will refuse. The marriage that is consummated without love as its basis is worse than perdition. I will take back my request that you be my wife, and ask only: Do you love me?"

She hesitated a moment with her eyes fixed curiously upon his, then almost in a whisper she replied:

"It is the strangest thing in all this world, but I believe I do."

He caught her to his breast, and held her there fiercely. "You must not believe—you must know!" he exclaimed vehemently. "You must be sure that you prefer me above all the world. I don't ask you for the passionate enthusiasm of untried youth, but I must know that the tenderness of your very soul is mine. I must know that I occupy your heart to the exclusion of all others except your God.

"Can you say that to me, Eva? If so, you will make me the happiest man upon the earth. You know that I am in the world, but scarcely of it! Your misfortunes cannot injure me in any way. My life is absolutely my own, and into your hands I place it. What is it to be?"

A slight noise attracted them. Slowly she drew herself from his breast, and to her utter surprise, found herself face to face with Rod Hurdis.

How he had entered there, or how he knew that she lived there, she never knew.

As she looked at him in utter bewilderment, he came slowly forward.

"Eva," he said hoarsely, "you have heard what that man has said, and you know that I am willing to take you back to my heart to-night. Now make your choice between us!"

She stood there between them, her face white as death, her hands clasped before her. "I beg that you will not put it like that, Rod!" she cried out miserably. "You know if there were anything that I could do to wipe out the stain that I have put upon your life that I would do it if it required the last drop of blood out of my heart; but what you wish would but make it deeper. Do not ask me to add sin to sin!"

"You will not, then?"

"I cannot. There would be only destruction and death promised to either of us, and not one hour of the happiness that you crave. Go away, Rod! I entreat that you will not distress yourself or me again. For your own sake I must not listen to you."

"Answer me and truly! Do you love that man who has just asked you to be his wife?"

She hesitated a moment. It hurt her to cause him pain, but she knew that it was wisest after all.

She turned to Hoyt and placed her hand in his; then, dropping her eyes from Hurdis' white face, she answered dully:

"Yes."

He did not speak again, but turning away, passed through the door and out of her life forever.

She crept up to Hoyt slowly as the echo of the closing door reached her, and hid her face upon his breast.

Poor girl! Sin had brought its just punishment, but the halo cast by the forgiveness of God encircled her head and heart at last.

Adieu, Eva. May

> "Silken rest
> Tie all thy care up!"

THE END.

AFTER WORD

The most "ripped from the headlines" novel Bly wrote, *Eva the Adventuress* takes events and relationships from the real-life scandal of Eva Hamilton, a scandal that was all the rage in the fall of 1889.

New York State Assemblyman Robert Ray Hamilton—great-grandson of founding father Alexander Hamilton—had been seeing Miss Eva Steele for two years when, in 1888, she told him she was expecting. When, after months in seclusion, she introduced him to his daughter, Hamilton did the honorable thing and married Eva. Leaving public life, the couple journeyed to California.

Eight months later Eva was charged with attempted murder of the baby's nurse.

The story tumbled out. Eva Steele was really an "adventuress" named Eva Mann—aka Eva Parsons, aka Eva Brill. Already married to one Joshua Mann, she'd carried on with both men for years before convincing Robert Ray Hamilton that she was carrying his child.

There was no evidence, however, that she had ever been pregnant. She apparently purchased a child, who died. So she bought another, who also died. She bought a third, but that baby didn't look enough like the first one, so she sent it back. She then bought a fourth child, and passed this off as Hamilton's.

Once married, Eva supported Joshua Mann with her "pin money" of $6,000/year, a full third of her respectable husband's income. In August of 1889, while staying at a resort in New Jersey, Hamilton tried to cut some of her pin money. The couple quarreled, and the child's nurse intervened. Eva fired the nurse, who then got drunk and came back to tell Hamilton the truth about Eva and Mann. A fistfight broke out between the two women, and Eva was apparently badly beaten. Eva then snatched up a dagger and stabbed the nurse in the abdomen.

Eva was arrested and charged with attempted murder. Before the trial the story about the baby (babies) came out, and Robert Ray abandoned his defense of her. The nurse survived, so the charge became Aggravated Assault and Battery. Eva pled self-defense, but ended up convicted, with a maximum sentence of ten years. Given the fight, however, the judge sentenced her to two. The verdict was unpopular partly thanks to the coverage of *The World*.

The following year, Hamilton was in process of annulling his marriage to his incarcerated wife when he was reported to have mysteriously drowned in Snake River in Wyoming. But wait—was he *truly* dead? Rumors said he faked his own death to escape the annulment with Eva. Reports came of him in Japan, Australia, and eventually a raving panhandler in Mexico. Then, almost a decade later, his former partner was charged with his murder!

The death of Robert Ray led to long legal court fights between the Hamilton family and Eva, who used the fact that the annulment had never been completed to extract money from the Hamilton family.

By this time Eva had been released early from prison, pardoned by the governor. She took to the stage, re-enacting her story for people's entertainment, in a play cleverly entitled *The Hammertons* (a title changed before opening night). Her victim, the nurse, took up life in a freak show, displaying her scar from Eva's dagger for money. Her ersatz husband, Josh Mann, sued for divorce, only to have the complaint withdrawn when he went mad. Eva remarried yet again, this time to a fellow calling himself Frederick Hilton, who was in reality named—I kid you not— Duke Gaul. In 1895 she was part of another scandal when it was revealed she had been released through a pardons-for-bribes scheme.

Meanwhile the Hamilton family disavowed the memory of Robert Ray, even to the point of opposing a memorial fountain in the district he had ably represented before his fall from grace. They wanted to erase him as if he had never existed. All because he had loved "not wisely, but too well."

In writing her novel just as Eva Hamilton was being tried, Bly had to invent an ending after Eva's incarceration. Had she known how strange things would get, she probably would have kept her ending, as no one would believe the truth.

Yet the strangest part of this whole story by far is this line from the *New York Times* article quoting the annulment complaint:

"In the complaint, which is verified by Mr. Hamilton, it is stated that the marriage of Robert Ray Hamilton to Evangeline L. Steele was performed by the Rev. Edson W. Burr of Paterson, N.J., on Jan 7, 1889."

A Hamilton got into a scandal over a woman, and it was a Burr that married them. Truth is far stranger than fiction.

As noted in the Introduction, this novel changes how we understand a small but significant piece of Bly's history. She interviewed Eva Hamilton in early October, 1889. A month later she was on the high seas, making her dash around the globe. The novel had to have been completed by then, because it started appearing in the pages of the *New York Family Story Paper* in mid-December. One of her longest novels, Bly must have felt real inspiration—especially as this is the point when Bly began to complain of crippling headaches. One hopes that she found relief in penning this story, which tries to make Eva as sympathetic a figure as circumstances allow.

Most of the elements of the novel are taken from a lengthy account of Eva's life that appeared in the pages of the Sunday edition of *The World* published September 22, 1889 (found on page 340). The factual elements Bly used were:

- Eva's birth in a small mining town in Pennsylvania
- Her disabled brother
- Running away with a stranger, who then wronged her
- The living with and draining dry of a kindly older man
- Eva's relationship with an unscrupulous man
- The secret marriage to R.H. and the trip to California
- Eva's purchase of a baby (just one)
- A trip to Europe with her lover
- Eva supporting her lover and his mother with her husband's money
- The nurse revealing Eva's tryst to the husband
- Eva stabbing the nurse
- Eva going to jail
- Reports of her husband wanting her back

Bly, however, turns all of these into things that happened *to* Eva, rather than things she planned to do. Even the buying of the baby seems thrust upon her. Either for the sake of making her protagonist less reprehensible or from honest sympathy for Eva Hamilton, Bly sets out to offer the very best motives for Eva's terrible behavior.

This is in complete opposition, as you will see, to the reporting of the Hamilton case. Eva is slut-shamed and vilified as a scheming "adventuress" who played upon a good man's "infatuation," a word used constantly to describe the feelings of Robert Ray Hamilton, who comes off as a credulous dupe who left himself open to blackmail because he couldn't control his libido. There seems to be agreement that he was fine when he had her as a mistress, but marrying "the woman" was tantamount to lunacy.

The story was front-page news from Chicago to Los Angeles, from St. Paul to Topeka. When the verdict was handed down, headlines reading "Jezebel's Tears" and "A Siren's Fall" covered 5 O'CLOCK EXTRA! editions in Philadelphia and Boston.

I have collected the high points of the reporting narrative here, choosing when I could from Bly's own paper, *The New York World*.

Initially *The World* lumped the story in with two other tales of infidelity under a banner headline MISERY OF HUSBANDS AND WIVES. Yet even at the first, Eva is labeled an adulteress and a "hopeless victim of the morphine habit." It is fascinating to read her (maybe) mother-in-law's account of the whole affair in two separate newspapers, both for how the account was treated and for the fact that she clearly sold her story to several newspapers at once—the *New York Times'* and the *World's* versions were nearly identical, though the *World* was slightly—*slightly*—more sympathetic toward Eva (for brevity, I have included only the *World* version here).

It was the attempted murder combined with Hamilton's fame that initially made the story worthy of the front page. Then came tales of bigamy, of purchased multiple purchased babies, of plots and schemes. For Colonel Cockerill and Joseph Pulitzer, it must have felt like Christmas had come early that year. The moment the trial began, the *World's* reporting tone altered. Whoever Cockerill had sent to the New Jersey courthouse was decidedly against Eva, and the reporting was relentlessly negative. The September 22 story that Bly undoubtedly used as her guide for the novel referred to Eva as "this creature," describing her as "tigerish," "diabolical," and, significantly, "an adventuress."

Then Nellie Bly stepped in.

When the Hamilton story broke in late August 1889, Bly was writing a dismal version of what might today be called a puff piece, a review of what to do in Newport (in typical Bly fashion, she asserts that Newport is fine, so long as you are rich). Returning to New York, she dove into the Hamilton case with gusto. She wrote three stories on Hamilton, each one demonstrating different aspects of her own career: the undercover reporter, the friendly interviewer, and the describer of social conditions. Together, these three stories encapsulate Bly's reporting in a nutshell.

The first story is the obvious one, given the Hamilton saga—"Nellie Bly Buys A Baby." This story was also the perfect sequel to her 1887 piece, *What Becomes of Babies*, in which she'd posed as a young mother trying to dispose of an unwanted child (a story I made use of in my novella *Charity*

Girl). Here, she plays a wealthy prospective buyer, and tracks down a woman who claims to have sold one of the babies to Hamilton.

The second is, of course, Bly's blockbuster interview with Eva Hamilton herself. It was a major scoop, as up to that point no one had gotten a statement, much less an interview, out of Hamilton herself.

There is one major frustration, however. Only the first half of Bly's interview with Hamilton exists today. That first half appeared in the morning edition of *The World* on October 9, 1889. The piece ends promising that the second half would appear in a later edition that same day. But it does not appear in the *Evening World*.

Yet we know it *did* appear at some point on the 9th, because on the 10th excerpts from the second half of Bly's interview with Hamilton are quoted in papers all across the country. This means there was likely a midday edition of *The World*, one that no Bly scholar has yet been able to locate. Like everyone else, I've searched, but was unable to track it down. The best I was able to do was draw upon excerpts published on the 10th to convey at least a little of that explosive second half of their momentous interview.

It was in that lost second half that Eva leveled the accusation that she had twice found her husband in the Nurse Donnelly's rooms, intimating the true cause of the fight was not Eva's infidelity, but her husband's with the nurse. Bly clearly seized on this for her novel.

Her third piece is a follow-up to the interview, with added details from the prison, painting a picture of prison life in general.

In curating these articles, the most of any of this series by far, I have tried to keep an eye both on narrative and flavor. For pure fact, I could have included fewer articles. But the biased, sexist, sensationalist journalism of the era is on magnificent, horrific display here, and I simply could not resist sharing them.

I have transcribed these articles myself. Any errors or infelicities not belonging to the era are entirely mine. However, if I were to mark period spellings or newspaper errors, I'd've been putting *sic* into every third line. Unlike the novel you just read, here I have deliberately left in typos, differences of capitalization or hyphenation, and other curiosities in order to display how inconsistent the quality of journalism was at the time, and also how in flux the language was (being a fan of Shakespeare's First Folio, I am forever fascinated by how words change over time). So if it's odd, assume it's the era. If it makes no sense whatsoever, assume it's me.

So, now that you've read Nellie Bly's version, you can explore the real-life true-crime saga of Eva Hamilton.

A brief word about the chapter quotations Bly employs. While not the only novel to use literary quotations at the start of chapters, this novel has the most. I do not mean to impugn Bly in any way when I say that, though she was likely a voracious reader, outside of Shakespeare most of her literary tastes were likely on the pulpier end of fiction (though a storyline in a later novel makes me wonder if she read *Les Misérables*). For this novel, I imagine she did what I do when searching for the perfect quote: turn to her copy of Bartlett's *Familiar Quotations*. Published in 1855, in Bly's day it was a popular staple among households. I got mine in my late teens and have never ceased using it.

That said, she was a regular theatre-goer, and quotes from plays or musicals would have been at her fingertips. Her favorite work to quote seems to be *Macbeth*—making her a woman after my own heart.

For those looking for more about Nellie Bly, allow me to direct you to two nonfiction examinations of Bly's life. The first is *Nellie Bly: Daredevil, Reporter, Feminist* by Brooke Kroeger. This is an exhaustive and amazingly researched work, examining every aspect of Ms. Bly's life, making all kinds of connections between the professional and the personal.

The second is Matthew Goodman's *Eighty Days*, an examination of Nellie's trip around the world. It is a wonderfully compelling read, giving much color and detail to Bly's work and world.

Both Ms. Kroeger and Mr. Goodman were of direct help to me as well, graciously sending newspaper clippings that were missing from various library collections, and being generally encouraging about my work.

I must thank Syed Asad Nawazish for doing the first pass at transcribing this novel, and Cathy Hunter for her fabulous covers for this series.

This has been the second volume of *The Lost Novels of Nellie Bly*. If you enjoyed it, you can do something to help other readers: leave an honest review on the platform you got it from, or else on Goodreads or any other review site. Any author will tell you that even a five word review is deeply appreciated. Thanks!

Next up, Nellie Bly's best detective story, as a handsome millionaire and a girl reporter set out to solve a diamond heist in: *New York By Night*.

Cheers,
David Blixt

THE
Eva Hamilton
Scandal

EVA MANN.

FALSE TO HER MARRIAGE VOWS, MRS. R.R. HAMILTON STABS HER CHILD'S NURSE.

SHE IS DETECTED IN A LIAISON.

A TERRIBLE SOCIAL TRAGEDY IN AN ATLANTIC CITY COTTAGE.

FOLLOWED BY AN OLD MAN.

MR. AND MRS. HAMILTON UNDER ARREST—AN ADROIT THIEF ENTERS THE ROOM OF THE TRAGEDY AND CARRIES OFF $2,000 WORTH OF DIAMONDS—STORY OF A MARRIAGE WITH A DISREPUTABLE WOMAN— THE NURSE HOPELESSLY CUT.

[SPECIAL TO THE WORLD]

ATLANTIC CITY, N.J., AUG. 26.— As the guests were seating themselves about the dining tables at the fashionable Noll cottage, on Tennessee avenue, at noon to-day, the cries of a woman and the smashing of furniture on the second floor threw them into a panic and attracted a large crowd of excited men and women about the building. The noise came from the private apartments of a couple known in the house as Mr. and Mrs. Robert R. Hamilton, of New York City. A waiter hurried upstairs and, kicking in the door, discovered a fine-looking middle-aged man struggling desperately, in the centre of the apartments, to overpower a wild-eyed blonde woman, who was striking out in all directions with a blood-stained dagger. Another woman lay upon the floor of the handsomely furnished room in a pool of blood; and on a bed near by the crowed a six months' old infant, much diverted by the excitement.

THE PARTIES TO THE TRAGEDY.

The man was cool and resolute. He was Mr. "Hamilton." The desperate, hysterical woman was his wife and the infant was their only child. The wounded woman, who lay writhing in agony on the carpet, suffering from a horrible knife-thrust in her abdomen, from which the intestines protruded, was Mary Donnelly, a New York nurse who has been with the child since its birth. She is hopelessly wounded, though alive at midnight to-night.

A WICKED WOMAN'S CURSE.

A jealous quarrel led up to the awful tragedy. Joshua Mann, of No. 111 West Fifteenth street, New York, an old lover of Mrs. Hamilton, had been following her all Summer wherever she and her husband travelled. Mr. Hamilton did not know the man, did not suspect that the lover's mother was the keeper of a disreputable house in New York, and that Mann's relations with his wife had been of the most intimate character. He has been seen driving with her, they have been known to stop at road-houses together to get drinks, and last night the wife and her lover met in a beer garden, where they passed some time together.

THEY ARE DISCOVERED.

Mr. Hamilton was ignorant of the liaison, but yesterday he met Mann face to face and recognized his as a countenance he had seen in every city and fashionable resort visited since his marriage. He had the man watched under the impression that he was a thief following his movements to steal Mrs. Hamilton's jewels. Last night the realities of his position dawned upon him. Mr. Mann had grafted a neat pair of horns upon the husband's head; he completely possessed the wife's love. Mr. Hamilton passed a sleepless night, but said nothing. This forenoon, the wife and mother announced that she was going to New York for a visit, to return in a few days. It was then that the husband's indignation overcame him, and, grasping the woman by the shoulder, he said:

"You are my wife, and you remain here. Let 'Josh' Mann take care of himself."

AFTER ADULTERY, MURDER.

The name of her lover pronounced by her husband astounded Mrs. Hamilton. She became madly, viciously desperate. She ran to a bureau, snatched up a Mexican dagger and made a lunge at her husband. He grappled with her and pushed over a chair. The nurse, Mary Donnelly, hearing the noise, rushed into the room. The wife no sooner saw her than she dashed at her with the dagger raised, and hissed these words from between her gnashing teeth:

"You she devil. You are the cause of this. You have exposed me. You'll never talk about me again." (She) plunged the weapon into the poor girl's abdomen, and felled her to the floor.

Mr. Hamilton and his wife are both in custody, and the excitement in this city to-night over the affair is intense.

AN HONORED NAME.

The only Robert Ray Hamilton known to New Yorkers is he who was for eight years a member of the New York Legislature from the Murray Hill district, New York City, is a son of Gen. Schuyler Hamilton, one of the leaders of New York's 400; a grandson of John C. Hamilton, author of a "Life of Alexander Hamilton," and a great-grandson of Alexander Hamilton, the Secretary of the Treasury under Washington, who was killed in the duel with Aaron Burr. He is a member of the New York Bar, the possessor of an income of $18,000 a year, and was, until a few years ago, a prominent figure in society in the metropolis.

The story of his courtship and marriage is as romantic as the story of to-day's tragedy is thrilling.

Hamilton is about thirty-seven

years of age, and his wife about ten years younger, and a hopeless victim of the morphine habit. About two years ago they were clandestinely married in New York. Six months ago he took his wife to Southern California with the intention of locating permanently. Mary Donnelly, the nurse, accompanied them. He returned disgusted and stopped at Atlantic City two weeks ago. Here Mrs. Hamilton's display of diamonds and magnificent costumes at once created a sensation, and the movements of the couple were noted with interest.

HAMILTON'S SYREN.

SHE SMILED UPON HIM FOR MONEY FOR HER FAVORITE TO SPEND.

HE SUPPLIED A WHOLE FAMILY.

A YOUNG NABOB WHO ESSAYED THE PART OF THE CHEVALIER DES GREUX.

PARTNER IN LOVE WITH "JOSH" MANN.

THE TRAGEDY AT ATLANTIC CITY THE CLIMAX TO A LONG CAREER OF A RECKLESS VILLAGE BEAUTY WHO CAME TO THE METROPOLIS TO ENSNARE MEN OF WEALTH AND HONOR—WONDERFUL INFATUATION OF THE MAN WHO NOW CLAIMS TO BE THE HUSBAND OF THIS PRETTY "MANON LESCAUT"—HE FOLLOWS TO THE CELL WHERE SHE AWAITS A PROBABLE CHARGE OF MURDER.

I.

It is the story of a beautiful, passionate, reckless, unscrupulous woman. It begins in the annals of a quiet neighborhood, borders upon the bagnio, revolves about a violent attachment wherein the want of money is the one source of discontent, and ends in the disgrace of the man of family, of reputation and of millions, who fell into the net spread for him. To tell all of its details would take one to the beginning of the nation, recalling honored names of the last century and a tragedy which startled New York when it was scarcely more than a village. There is embraced every trait of character. There is portrayed every human passion. There is proof that human nature does not change with the ages and that the way of the transgressor is hard now as ever. The forces long have been in operation which resulted in the tragedy at Atlantic City Monday.

"I can only say that I am astonished. Mr. Hamilton is the last person in the world I would have suspected of such an entanglement. That he should have yielded to it,

ROBERT RAY HAMILTON.

as he seems to have done, appears incredible."

So say the most intimate friends of Robert Ray Hamilton. He is a man of refinement—a cultured, studious man. He has not even enough of the manners of the man of the world to suggest the idea of his being a politician. His name and his fortune, together with his attainments, made him naturally a conspicuous figure in society; but he was not regarded as a "marrying" man nor as one who was reckless in his pursuit of pleasure. He was, even to his intimates, socially a quiet bachelor and an honor alike to the name he bore and the district he represented for eight years in the State Assembly. There is no other explanation than the weakness of human nature for his relation to the scandal of the day which brings him in an hour to appear the wreck of his former self.

II.

EVA PARSON'S DAGGER.

Just around a corner, only three or four blocks from the Marshall Flats, where Robert Ray Hamilton last resided in this city, is the shop of a tradesman who has more than once trembled before the dagger of "Eva Parsons."

"I am married now," he said yesterday to a World reporter, "and in telling you that I know of the woman in this case I do so in the belief that I am not to be reinvolved with people and places I only knew as a young man too careless to appreciate the penalty. Ten or eleven years ago a man was shot in Waverley, N.Y. It was a lover's quarrel and the woman's name was Eva Parsons. Somehow she escaped punishment for her deed and a few months later I met her in Elmira, where I resided. She was a most attractive woman, but already lost to regard for reputation. She had taken the name of a man with whom she had lived in her native town, a small place in Pennsylvania near the New York line, the name of which I have forgotten. I was clerk in a store at a small salary and was without the means to take her from her surroundings and give her such an establishment as I should have been glad to give her. So I left Elmira and came here. She followed me. We lived together in this city and it was on account of my infatuation for her and her pursuit of me that I lost two good situations. Finally I managed to get into business for myself and we lived a year or so very tranquilly."

Here the tradesman paused and gave a little shudder as though he had called to mind some incident of his life with Eva Parsons that was not so happy.

"What happened then? The dagger?"

"That's it exactly—the dagger. Somewhat literally and a good deal figuratively. The first time we quarreled seriously I found that her temper was terrific and her profanity something indescribable. I stood my ground in spite of her profanity, but when she whipped out a bright little dagger and jabbed at me with even more energy than she had put into her oaths I beat a retreat. I made up my mind it was time to get clear of the woman. I left her and discovered soon after that my immediate successor was 'Dotty'—Joshua Mann."

"There is some mystery about the manner in which she fell in with her supreme affinity. You didn't bring forward 'Dotty' to occupy the vacuum which you were about to create, did you?"

"No, I did not. She left me to lead a reckless life with a Mme. Fairfax and in other places. I cannot say where she met Mann."

"Were you ever troubled by her afterwards?" the reporter asked.

"Yes. I had to appeal to the police for protection. One day I got desperate and called in Capt. Williams. He had a conversation with her and I haven't seen her since."

III.

THE FAMILY OF "DOTTY."

"I have known for some time of the Swintons, who were so intimate with Robert Ray Hamilton and the woman who is said to be his wife," said a gentleman yesterday to a reporter of The World, "and it was at Mrs. Swinton's that I first saw Eva Hamilton, or, as she was then known, Eva Mann.

"Mrs. Anna T. Swinton, who is now a woman over sixty, was living at the time, about four years ago, in Waverley Place. Her maiden name was Dryden, and she came of a good family in Baltimore, where her father was known as Major Joshua Dryden. He got his title, I think, from being a chaplain in the army during the war of 1812. Mrs. Swinton was married three times— first to a Dr. Kyrie, by whom she had one daughter, now an actress. Upon Kyrie's death she married a Mr. Mann, a member of Julian's Band, which was a famous organization in this city forty years ago. But this marriage she had a son, Joshua, who now figures in the affair at Atlantic City. Mann died and then she was married to Frederick Swinton, who was connected with the office of the State Printer at Albany. Mrs. Mann became Swinton's housekeeper and in time he married her. After living some time in Albany the couple moved to Philadelphia, where Swinton committed suicide—for what reason I cannot say, though I know he was a man of intemperate habits, and he probably ended his life while in his cups.

"When old Major Dryden died he left some property to his daughter, Mrs. Swinton, which she soon squandered. When I first met her she was making dresses for a living, at the same time pushing a claim she had in court against the Swinton estate on Staten Island, a claim which her late husband had left. At Mrs. Swinton's I first met Eva, known to some in the house as Eva Brill, though others spoke of her as Eva Mann, the wife of Joshua Mann, the son by the second husband. Joshua was known as

"Dotty." I have tried often to learn something of Eva's early life, but always without success, as she kept her early history to herself. I was given to understand, however, that her home had been somewhere near Port Jervis, N.Y., and 'Dotty,' who had once visited that part of the State, spoke of the kind treatment he had received from Eva's father and mother.

"All during that time Eva was known as Dotty's wife. They did not live in the Waverley place house, but somewhere uptown, Eva living in one place and 'Dotty' in another. Eva claimed that she had been married to 'Dotty,' though the young man's mother doubted it. Whether they were married or not, Eva seemed to hold something over his head. However, they had the appearance of being man and wife. 'Dotty' had been a salesman in a Philadelphia woollen-goods house, but Eva made him give it up, and ever after she kept him well supplied with money. Eva also gave money to Mrs. Swinton, but she made the old lady pay it back by making dresses for her."

"Where did Joshua, or 'Dotty,' as you call him, first meet Eva?" asked the reporter.

"I think they met in Philadelphia, and they came to this city to rooms on the west side, where they began housekeeping," was the reply.

"Though I never met Robert Ray Hamilton," continued the reporter's informant, "I knew from the date of my first meeting

with Mrs. Swinton, 'Josh' and Eva that he was supporting the young woman. He lived uptown, and I was told that when he called upon Eva, 'Dotty' found it convenient to be absent. As long as Hamilton kept 'Dotty' supplied with money the other young man was content. Mrs. Swinton often told me of the infatuation that Hamilton had for the young woman, but when I told her how disgraceful the relations were between them she said she was afraid of Eva, and so was 'Dotty.' Eva seemed to know something about 'Dotty,' for she said one day that if he did not do as she wished him she would have him arrested.

"Once the family went to live in a flat in West Fifty-fifth street, Hamilton still supplying the funds. While they were living together there Mrs. Swinton's daughter by her first husband had a quarrel with her husband, and she left him and went to live with Eva and 'Dotty.' In order to recover some valuables the husband claimed that his wife had taken, he had his wife and Eva brought before Police Justice Patterson, in the Yorkville Police Court. In the court-room the husband yelled out that "Eva was the mistress of Robert Ray Hamilton!" Judge Patterson at once committed him in default of $700 bail and, after keeping him in prison for three days, he was sent to the Island, where he was kept for four days, until released by friends. It was said at the time that Hamilton and Patterson, who are of the same political organization, had conspired to punish the husband for the charge he had made in court by sending him to the Island. Since that time I have never seen any of the parties."

IV.

THE RETREAT IN JERSEY.

The Mann crowd, as known to the people of Passaic, consisted of Joshua J. Mann, as he called himself; Evangeline E. Mann, Matilda Gurney, a Scotch servant, and William Cameron, the Scotch coachman. An examination before the Passaic Police Court brought their affairs into such notoriety that they were forced to leave the town. The examination occurred before Justice Norton June 23, 1887, when the coachman, Cameron, having been terribly beaten and kicked, making him a sorry sight, made a complaint against Joshua Mann for assault and battery. Against Evangeline Mann he preferred two charges—one for assault and battery and one for assault with a deadly weapon.

The Justice, after hearing Cameron's story, sent a policeman in quest of the accused parties. The officer had a great deal of trouble in trying to persuade the woman to go with him, and he says that several times he thought his life would be pounded out of him. However, he succeeded in lodging her safely in the Justice's Court. Upon hearing the charges read by the Justice she flew into a frantic rage and threatened to tear him to pieces

unless he stopped the delivery of the same. The Justice says that in all his experience he has never seen such a human tigress.

The examination resulted in every step in bringing out damaging testimony. Cameron testified that he had been beaten in a most brutal manner by both Joshua and Evangeline. The subtle servant strove to screen her mistress and swore in direct contradiction of the coachman's testimony, but enough was drawn from her to corroborate Cameron's statement, and also to show what a very respectable gentleman in New York, who was a frequent visitor, kept up the establishment. It appeared also that Joshua man was not the husband or brother of Evangeline.

Joshua's mother lived with them part of the time. From her it was gleaned that Joshua was no relative of Evangeline, but that he had been fascinated by her a long while ago, and in his blind devotion was a slave to her whims and fancies. The old lady also admitted that a gentleman of great wealth in New York supported Evangeline and paid her bills wherever she went. Evangeline lived in superb style at Passaic. She had horses, carriages and almost every evidence of wealth, her diamonds being the talk of the town.

The prisoners were released on bail, Henry Burger becoming their security. Shortly after their release Evangeline struck up an acquaintanceship with a rather handsome young man of Passaic, named Doll. The two for awhile were inseparable and spent money extravagantly. When the time came for the Grand Jury, at Paterson, to deal with Cameron, Mr. Doll accompanied Evangeline to the jury-room. She was a fine looking woman and must have made a good impression upon the Grand Jury, for the Cameron case was thrown out. Soon after Evangeline left Passaic and Doll, and never was seen there again.

The neat cottage occupied by the Manns in Passaic is said to have been rented by Robert Ray Hamilton, who, after the Police Court scandal, ordered the house to be closed. Before they returned to the city "Eva" and "Dotty" went sleighing one night, and when they came back "Dotty" was found to be badly bruised on one side of the head. "Eva" said that he had fallen out, but in this city it was believed that she beat him and threw him out. However, he was in a very bad way and Hamilton went to the cottage and attended his beside for weeks. After the Manns came to the city again they went to Europe for a short time.

V.

WAS HAMILTON MARRIED?

ATLANTIC CITY, N.J., AUG. 27.—Mrs. F.J. Swinton, at the request of THE WORLD correspondent, submitted to an interview this afternoon, in which she gives away the secret of the whole affair.

"I have been twice married," she said. "My first husband's name was Mann. I have two children—Joshua Mann, who has been connected with the affair by the published reports, and a daughter sixteen years old. I afterwards married Prof. Swinton, who was for many years and until his death the paleontologist of the Smithsonian Institution and the United States Geological Survey at Washington. He died in the Government service in 1875, leaving me in comfortable circumstances. Time took our little fortune away from us and I became housekeeper for one of the leading families in New York's world of fashion on Fifth avenue. I left their service and went to live at No. 111 West Fifteenth street, depending for a livelihood upon my son and my dressmaking trade.

"It was while there, about four years ago, that I met Mrs. Hamilton, who was then Miss Evangeline Brill.

She was residing at a fashionable uptown boarding-house and was supported, she said, by her parents, who were very wealthy and resided at Passaic, N.J. My son undoubtedly was Miss Brill's first and most devoted lover. I knew he was with her frequently, but whether their relations were more intimate than what I supposed they were, from what I saw myself, I cannot say. He was not the man to hold up his end against Hamilton, however, in a battle for a woman's heart. Hamilton had both good looks, wealth, and influence behind him, and for his wealth, more than anything else, I suppose she married the man she did, although she has to-day the warmest feelings for my son.

"The first I knew of Hamilton's marriage to Miss Brill was about four months before the birth of their child. She came to me one night and said:

"'Pshaw, granny, there is no use keeping this from you any longer. We are married, and that's the end of it.'

"Hamilton was a member of the Legislature up to May 15 last, and used to come down from Albany every Friday night and stay until Sunday with his wife. After the session adjourned he concluded to go West. His friends made too much sport of his marriage, and he concluded to put an end to it by getting away. They were disappointed in the climate of California and returned to Atlantic City eight weeks ago. They first registered at the Windsor and then at another big hotel, but did not like hotel life and went to the cottage where the affray occurred. During their absence from New York Mrs. Hamilton lost forty pounds of flesh, and when they came to Atlantic City they wrote me to come here from New York and take charge of her wardrobe and alter her garments to fit her. I came down two weeks ago with my son Joshua, and all of us have been on the most congenial terms since our arrival. We all went to the opera together Saturday night, which shows that

Mr. Hamilton had nothing against my son. Sunday night a week ago Gen. Schuyler Hamilton visited his son and daughter-in-law in Atlantic City. He registered at the Chalfonte and left for home after having persuaded the couple to locate again in New York, where they were to go last Sunday. The day after the General left he sent his daughter-in-law a very affectionate letter, showing that neither she nor her husband had been cast off by the General's family."

Mr. Hamilton was seen by the correspondent in company with Lawyer Samuel E. Perry. He was under great mental stress, and was totally unnerved. Lawyer Perry had enjoined upon him not to say anything for publication, and when the correspondent accosted him he refused to talk.

"You have nothing to say, then, Mr. Hamilton?"

"No, sir."

"It is reported that you are not the same Robert Ray Hamilton, of New York, who was for eight years a member of the New York Legislature from the Murray Hill district," said the reporter.

"That is a base lie!" exclaimed Hamilton, who momentarily lost his head. "I am Robert Ray Hamilton, of New York, and did represent the Murray Hill district in the New York Assembly."

Lawyer Perry then interfered.

"Let me alone," was the answer. "I do not want to allow any chance of misrepresentation."

Perry again expostulated. Then the correspondent asked: "Were you legitimately married to Mrs. Hamilton?"

"I was," answered Hamilton.

"Have you received any dispatches from your New York friends?"

"I have, and they contain proof of my identity."

VI.

THE TRAGEDY AND THE TRIAL.

ATLANTIC CITY, N.J., AUG. 27.— The trouble between Hamilton and the woman he calls his wife began at 3.30 Monday morning, at which hour both happened to awaken, when they began discussing their financial affairs. An expressman was due at 7 o'clock to remove their baggage preparatory to their going to New York. Hamilton had promised her $6,000 a year for pin money and to defray her expenses at home, he being in Albany for a great part of the time. This amount she has received in regular installments to the present time, but as she was more anxious to return to New York he suggested that if they located there and he remained home her endowment allowance would no longer be forthcoming. Quick tempered and passionate, she began to quarrel with him, and threatened to leave him forever. Hamilton was very stubborn and the battle began. After half an hour's war, at 4 o'clock, the nurse appeared and endeavored to step between them, but was ordered to leave the room. She left and did not return for several hours. She went to the

Verona and had Mrs. Swinton go over to the Noll and endeavor to pacify Hamilton.

At 7 o'clock an expressman came, but was ordered away by Hamilton. His wife then insisted on sending for Gen. Hamilton to settle the affair and have her allowance assured before he left. Mrs. Swinton pacified them finally, and left at 9 o'clock, at which time Mrs. Hamilton was sitting on her husband's knee. They then began drinking whiskey punches, and soon were in each other's hair. At 11.30 Mary Donnelly, the nurse, returned, and was upbraided by Mrs. Hamilton for having gone away and for leaving the child. A discussion ensued, and Mary was discharged. She then, in the presence of Mr. Hamilton, denounced Mrs. Hamilton as a woman of the town and said that she cared more for "Josh" Mann than for her husband, to whom she was unfaithful. The two women then indulged in a fistic encounter, in which Mrs. Hamilton received the worst of the battle, being cut on the cheek and having her left eye blackened by a blow. Mary was strong as a bull, and had the fight lasted much longer Mrs. Hamilton would have been beaten insensible. The latter was enraged, and, picking up the dirk, she plunged it into her assailant.

She said as she struck the nurse:

"You she-devil, you have abused me enough and you'll never strike me again You are a drunken hound."

The husband, hearing the noise,

rushed into the room and jumped between the two. He was cut in the right leg and left arm in the tussle. The bleeding nurse ran downstairs and fell helpless on the sofa in the parlor.

The first witness called in the crowded courtroom was the husband of the woman in custody. On being examined by Justice Irving he testified under oath as follows:

"My name is Robert Ray Hamilton. I am a native of New York City, but for five months I have not been living there. I have no city address at present. I am a lawyer by profession and a member of the New York Bar. I am thirty-eight years of age. I am the husband of the prisoner at the bar."

"How long have you been married to her?"

"That question I refuse to answer, by advice of my counsel."

"Were you present when this assault occurred at the Noll cottage yesterday afternoon? If so, please state what you know about it."

"I was present at the time the stabbing was done with a dagger in the hands of my wife. The victim, Mary Donnelly, has been employed by us as a nurse for the past eight months. She accompanied us to California and back, but was discharged by my wife at 9 o'clock yesterday morning, about three hours before the affair occurred. The reasons for her discharge I am advised by counsel to reserve for the present."

"How long has Evangeline Hamilton been your wife?"

"That question I refuse to answer."

"Have you any children?"

"One child eight months old, of which she is the mother."

Samuel E. Perry, counsel for Mr. and Mrs. Hamilton, then arose and said:

"I have no cross-examination to make, inasmuch as the defense to be set up by the two prisoners is a good one and should not be given away until the last moment. When the case is called for trial it will assume an entirely different phase, and the assault will prove to have been justified by the circumstances surrounding the case."

William Biddle was next called and testified:

"I am an officer of the Police Department of Atlantic City. About noon yesterday I was called to No. 135 Tennessee avenue. On reaching the second floor I saw Mrs. Hamilton in her room. She seemed very much incensed and excited, and there was blood on her hand. The moment she saw me she threw up her right hand and in a tragic expression of countenance and attitude she said:

"'I sent for you. I want that woman downstairs arrested. She is Mary Donnelly, and I will appear against her at the police station.'

"I went downstairs and into the back room, where this other woman was lying on a cat, her clothes covered with blood and her face pale as death. I sent for a physician, but before he arrived I asked her who had stabbed her. She yelled to me as if frantic with rage:

"'You know who did it. It was that —— upstairs. I want her arrested, and if I live I'll cut her stomach out. If I die she'll hang for this.'

"I went back upstairs and found Mrs. Hamilton putting on an overgarment to cover her dress, which was stained with blood. I asked her if she did the cutting, and she said:

"'I did it, and I'm sorry I didn't finish her.'"

"Did she say why she wanted the nurse arrested?" asked the Court.

"Yes; she said that the girl was drunk and had been making trouble and was a dangerous character."

Dr. Crosby, who has been attending Mary Donnelly, testified:

"About 1 o'clock yesterday afternoon I was summoned to dress the wounds of Mary Donnelly. The wound was rather deep and might have caused her death had it been an eighth of an inch deeper. As it is her condition is dangerous and decidedly critical. She might live a week, but her death in less than an hour would not surprise me."

Mrs. Elizabeth Rupp was sworn and testified that she knew nothing of the people or the trouble further than hearsay. She helped to separate the two women with the assistance of Mr. Hamilton, but her knowledge of the case would justify no further testimony. She stated that Hamilton and his wife registered at her cottage about two weeks ago.

Sergt. Loder, of the Central Police Station, testified that Mrs. Hamilton admitted having dealt the blow when she was brought to the station-house. She said that she did it in self-defense, but regretted having done it.

Mrs. Hamilton was remanded to jail at May's Landing without bail to await trial Sept. 10. Hamilton himself and Mrs. Rupp were placed under $600 bail each, to secure their attendance as witnesses.

VII.
CARRIED TO A CELL.

ATLANTIC CITY, N.J., AUG. 27.—At 2 o'clock in the afternoon Constable Williams called out "Time's up" through the bars of Mrs. Hamilton's cell. The tearful prisoner sprang from her hard couch in a nervous tremor and piteously exclaimed:

"Oh, must I go to jail?"

Her husband, who was out on bail, had been devoted in his attention to her all morning, not leaving the cell-door even for an instant. A colored porter had brought her a valise filled with articles of apparel, and when she stepped from the cell she was arrayed in a striking costume, consisting of a natty white sailor hat, trimmed with dark-blue ribbon; a rich skirt of striped blue and white satin and a dark blue directoire coat. She leaned heavily on her husband's arm and walked through the rear door of the police station, accompanied by Constables Williams and Pettit. When she reached the platform of the depot, she suddenly turned to her husband

and impulsively embraced him.

"Good-by, Ray," she sobbed, and he held her in his arms and wept bitterly.

It was not his intention to go with her to the jail, but his heart failed him and he hurriedly procured a ticket and joined her on the train. The constable allowed him to sit by her side and he put his arm around her neck and whispered in her ear.

"You know I told you before I left New York that if you did not discharge that nurse there would be murder committed," she said, and then in a forgiving vein, "but don't worry about me, Ray; they'll not keep me in jail long."

Her husband then suggested that he had time to run over to the doctor's office and learn the condition of the wounded woman, but the prisoner seized him by the sleeve and prevented him.

As the train began moving slowly from the depot Lawyer Perry and Mrs. Swinton, who were in the group, hurried from the cars. Hamilton and his wife were targets for the curious glances of the many passengers in the cars; but they were oblivious to all their surrounding, not even

paying heed to the two constables. When they reached the portals of the county jail at May's Landing and Sheriff Johnson conducted them along the gloomy corridor Mrs. Hamilton's sobs were most distressing. She bid her husband an affectionate adieu at the cell-door and dropped heavily on the bench. She will have the best treatment possible while in jail and will be surrounded with all the luxuries which her husband can procure.

Additional material from the NEW YORK TIMES story:

Mrs. Swinton, who has figured so conspicuously in the case, is an elderly woman, small of stature, and having much the appearance of a housekeeper. Her son, Joshua Mann, is an ill-favored person of perhaps thirty-five years, and at first glance would hardly strike one as the sort of man to capture the affections of a woman of Mrs. Hamilton's only too evident predilections. His mother says that a year ago he received a severe blow on the head and has never been quite right in that important part of his make-up since.

A MAD INFATUATION.

THE STORY OF A CAREER WRECKED BY A WICKED WOMAN.

The astonishing story concerning Robert Ray Hamilton which comes from Atlantic City, N.J., has set on foot an investigation into the life of that gentleman during the past three years and it has revealed so many extraordinary details as to make the whole tale almost an incredible one. That a man of Mr. Hamilton's character, his abilities, and his position in the world could have done the things which he has been found to have done, could have sacrificed his whole career, could have lived the sort of life he has led for three years—and all for an object so utterly worthless—is a matter which creates the most profound astonishment. Now that the secret is out and the whole world has it, only sorrow for the man and an earnest desire to help him in his extremity are the feelings which animate his friends.

The woman who has done him such irreparable harm is now in the neighborhood of thirty years old. She is very pretty, but absolutely devoid of the qualities which make up decent women. Her first appearance in New York, as nearly as a Times reporter could ascertain the facts, was made about eight or nine years ago. She was even then a woman without moral stability, and came to this city with the definite intention of living at the expense of her virtue. Her youth and beauty made the road she traveled an easy one. She obtained admittance to a house of unquestioned reputation in the Nineteenth Precinct, and shortly after her arrival she made the acquaintance of a Mrs. Swinton, who induced her to become an inmate of a resort kept by her in Jersey City.

This woman had a reputed son, whom she supported, and who is the Joshua Mann alluded to in the dispatches from Atlantic City. With this worthless fellow the girl who was then known as Eva May hell in love, and he, more it is presumed for financial gain than any feeling of affection for her, permitted her to love him and to assist his mother in his support.

From Jersey City Mann's mother, after a time, came to New York, and took up her residence in West Thirty-first-street. Eva, about this time, left her for a period, living in a flat on upper Sixth-avenue, and nightly frequenting the notorious resorts further down that thoroughfare. Her intimacy with Mann was kept up, however, all the time. For four or five years the life led by this young woman was most disreputable, and then, in a house which she had selected as her abode—most probably one over which Mrs. Swinton presided—she first met Robert Ray Hamilton, three years ago.

That young man's infatuation for her began that very night. He wept continually to see her, gave her presents, and finally proposed to take her away from the house in which she lived, provide a home for her, and support her in a fashion of which she had only hitherto dreamed. Her acceptance of the proposition was immediate, and within a week she was mistress of a handsome suite of apartments which the rich young man provided for her. From that time until the unhappy dénouement at Atlantic City the woman was cared for by Hamilton. Her intimacy with Mann, however, was not broken off—only it was not so apparent to people as it had been.

Evidently she cared for her wealthy lover only in a financial way, for she let slip no opportunity to be with the fellow Mann. Mr. Hamilton was of necessity out of town much of the time, and when he was away she and Mann were constantly together. It was Hamilton's money which enabled Mann to live, and it came to him through the woman. Hamilton knew Mann, but only as the woman's brother, and he knew Mrs. Swinton as her mother. He provided for all their wants.

About this time, too, the woman appears to have managed to spend enough time in New Jersey to make herself notorious in the district about Passaic. At any rate,

there moved into a handsome but secluded house in Franklin-avenue in that city a woman who called herself Evangeline Mann, and a man who was known as Joshua Mann. Their doings were soon brought to the attention of the authorities, for on July 23 William Cameron, a Scotch coachman, went to Justice Norton with a complaint that he had been terribly beaten by the woman when he had asked her for the wages due him. She turned upon him like a tigress, he said, beat him savagely, and shot at him twice, and when he fled from the house he was knocked down by Joshua Mann. Then the woman jumped upon him and kicked him furiously as he lay on the ground. He feared that in her fury, which was simply ungovernable, she would kill him.

The woman was brought before the Justice after a scene with the constable sent after her. When she arrived, all ablaze with diamonds, the Justice says he never in all his life saw such a perfect she-devil for temper. He would not have been surprised if she had drawn a revolver upon him. She was "a dreadful way ahead of Sarah Althea Hill," he says. The examination before the Justice elicited the facts that the man calling himself Joshua Mann was no relation to the woman. Despite the frequent beatings she had given him while under the influence of liquor, he was her most devoted slave, and his own mother said that nothing could induce him to leave the woman. It also appeared that a wealthy gentleman from New York was a frequent visitor at the house, and seemed to support the establishment.

The woman had horses and carriages and spent money lavishly. She afterward fascinated a young man named Doll living in Passaic, and for a time he was her constant attendant. The Grand Jury dismissed all the complaints in the case, and soon after she left Passaic and the Justice heard no more of her until her appearance in the rôle of Mrs. Hamilton at Atlantic City.

In May last Mr. Hamilton gave up his bachelor apartments in The Alpine, and actually went to live with the woman as her husband in a flat at 117 West Fifteenth-street. He was not known in the house or in the neighborhood as Robert Ray Hamilton, nor in fact by any other name. The woman with whom he lived, and who then called herself Mrs. Mann, arranged, either herself or through her friends, for the rent of the apartment, and Mr. Hamilton went there and lived with her, associating with none of the people of the neighborhood and having no questions asked him. Mrs. Swinton and her son before that time had gone to live in rooms a few doors from Mr. Hamilton's flat at 111 West Fifteenth-street. "Mrs. Mann" was frequently a visitor there, and while she was there acted like the commonest of common women. She drank heavily, ate morphine, had a frightful temper, and vented it harshly upon Mann and Mrs. Swinton. Even her conduct in her own apartments, often while Mr. Hamilton was with her, was most violent, and her habits were none the more temperate.

All this time Mr. Hamilton seemed to be blissfully ignorant of the part he was playing in supplying the money for the support of the Swinton-Mann establishment and of the relations which existed between Mann and the woman. Early in the Summer, however, his suspicion seems to have been aroused. He and the woman went out one evening, and when they returned the woman called upon Mrs. Swinton and told her that she and Mr. Hamilton had been married, and that they were immediately going West. She wept at the prospect of leaving Mann, but said that she would not long be away. In a few days they left New York and went to Southern California, it is believed, because of Mr. Hamilton's desire to separate the woman from Mann.

They did not stay in the West, however. About a month ago "Mrs. Mann" appeared one night at the house, 111 West Fifteenth-street. She was radiant with joy, said that she and her husband were living at Atlantic City, and insisted upon Mrs. Swinton and Mann's coming down there to live with her. Leeches as they were, this precious pair were installed in the woman's seaside home within forty-eight hours. What happened after that unfortunate time has already been told. Mr. Hamilton had one child by the woman.

The story that Mr. Hamilton had an unfortunate liaison was not a surprise to many of his more intimate social and political friends, but that the woman was his wife—that he had been legally married to her—was a crushing one. So incredible did the fact appear that no one believed it, even after the assertion had been made by Mr. Hamilton himself. That he should have lived with such a woman was shameful enough, but that he had married her was preposterous. It is not now believed that any ceremony was ever performed, but the impression prevails among Mr. Hamilton's friends in this city that that gentleman had publicly acknowledged the woman as his wife out of a mistaken sense of chivalry to save her reputation—as if anything human could do that in the light of the facts revealed.

Within a few months after Mr. Hamilton's infatuation for this woman began, the fact became known to some of his friends. In fact, he seemed to take no very great pains to conceal it. While he never talked about the woman, he had no hesitation in being seen with her in public places, at the theatre, in the Park, and other resorts, where he was morally sure to meet some of his friends, and to have attention attracted to him because of his companion. And, after a time, he came to notice that he did not have so many cordial friends as he once had had. His political associates, many of them, began to evince less pleasure in his society, and his family did not regard him as affectionately. However, the infatuation was absolute, and nothing seemed able to relieve him of the unfortunate passion. It must have been a species of insanity.

No event which has occurred in recent years has created such a sensation in New York as has the revelation of this most deplorable episode. Everywhere yesterday it was talked about and discussed in all its bearings. The social standing of the man and his political position—a man of most temperate, quiet habits, whose life had seemed as calm, happy, and prosperous as any man's life could be—made it appear impossible that he could by any human means come to be the actor in such a tragedy, and the wonder of it all was in every man's mind.

Not many Americans have a better line of ancestors than has Robert Ray Hamilton. Alexander Hamilton was his great grandfather, his grandfather was John C Hamilton, and Gen. Schuyler Hamilton is his father. He has an independent annual income of from $35,000 to $40,000, which he got from his grandfather on his mother's side, Robert Ray. He is a member of the Union League, the University, and Tuxedo Clubs. He was graduated from Columbia College and the Columbia College Law School, and is a lawyer, but rarely practiced his profession. Politics was more to his taste and, wishing to be known in politics, he gratified that desire.

Mr. Hamilton's political career was begun, rather disastrously, in 1879, when—he was then twenty-eight years old—he ran for Alderman in his district and was defeated by the Democratic candidate. Two years later he ran on the Republican ticket for the Assembly in the Eleventh Assembly District and was elected by a creditable majority. During his term he served on various important committees, and was very favorably regarded by his constituents until the bill taking the power of street cleaning out of the hands of the Police Commissioners and creating the Bureau of Street Cleaning came to a vote. Public sentiment was strongly in favor of the bill, for the power possessed by the Police Commissioners was used solely to further their political advancement. For some reason Mr. Hamilton was induced to vote against this bill, and his action in so doing put him out of politics until 1885.

In that year he ran again in the Eleventh Assembly District and was elected to the Assembly, and since that time he has been re-elected each year, having served in the last Legislature. Up to the last session his record was a very clean one. He was one of the representatives of the respectable elements in politics and was always on the "right" side of every measure upon which he voted. He assisted Ernest H. Crosby in the latter's fight for high license

in this State, and his own great but unsuccessful struggle was in the effort to reduce telephone rates in New York. His bill was killed. In the fight in 1886 of Allen Thorndike Rice against "Mike" Cregan Mr. Hamilton was Mr. Rice's personal representative.

Last Winter, however, the Cable Railway grab came up in the Legislature, and, to the astonishment of his constituents, Mr. Hamilton was earnest in his support of the bill. He did all in his power to pass it. At the close of the last session he announced that he was definitely out of politics, but it was known then that it would have been impossible for him to get the nomination for the Assembly again in his district. The Cable Railway matter had killed him. On Feb. 13 last a meeting of citizens of the Eleventh Assembly District was held at 455 Sixth-avenue to protest against Mr. Hamilton's action, and the following was passed unanimously:

Whereas, The Hon. Robert Ray Hamilton, representing this district in the Assembly, has introduced a bill to revive the Cable Railway Company at the dictation of George Bliss, counsel for the company; and

Whereas, While we have faith in the honesty of our representative, yet the weakness he displays in truckling to the interests of an individual as against his own better judgment and that of the press and the public should merit our condemnation and the rebuke of his constituents; therefore, be it

Resolved, That we protest against the policy adopted by our representative in representing the interests of an individual as against those of the people of his district and of the city on matters of great public importance, and we warn him that the lesson of 1881, when an outraged and indignant constituency refused to return him to the Legislature, will be repeated in the future if he continues to serve his present master, George Bliss.

By many people to whom Mr. Hamilton's conduct in the Legislature last Winter was inexplicable, this revelation is regarded almost as a complete explanation. It involves the belief, however, that a marriage between him and the woman has actually occurred. Mr. Hamilton's personal demeanor during the Winter had undergone a change. He was quieter than ever, inclined to melancholy, and seemed ever burdened by something that never left him. Had he been married, and had the fact become known to the men who control legislation at Albany, it is argued, the knowledge could have been brought to bear as a powerful means of influencing his action toward any measure his support of which would be of value to its promoters. The fear of exposure—for disastrous exposure it would have been—would have been a powerful factor in guiding his political decision.

IN THE GRASP OF A HARPY

MORE PROOFS OF THE WAY HAMILTON WAS BLED.

RECORDS OF SALES OF HIS BROOKLYN PROPERTY—IS HIS SELF-PROCLAIMED "MARRIAGE" LEGAL?

SAYS SHE IS A BIGAMIST.

A RUMOR THAT MRS. HAMILTON WAS MARRIED TO MANN WHILE ABROAD.

THE WOUNDED NURSE MAKES THE STATEMENT—MRS. HAMILTON'S COUNSEL WILL NEITHER AFFIRM NOR DENY THE REPORT—THE PRISONER IS COOL, BUT NOT YET ADMITTED TO BAIL—HER VICTIM IMPROVING.

[SPECIAL TO THE WORLD.]

ATLANTIC CITY, N.J., AUG. 31.—There is only one story in connection with Robert Ray Hamilton and his alleged wife, Evangeline, that is worthy of significant mention to-night. It is to the effect that Mrs. Hamilton is a bigamist; that she was married in Europe to Joshua Mann; that the latter is not the son of Grandma Swinton, and that the little girl is really the daughter of Mann. This story was privately circulated a few days ago, but was scarcely given any credence. It appears, however, that the wounded nurse, Mary Donnelly, has reiterated it and that possibly it may have some foundation.

Counsellor Samuel E. Perry, who represents the defense, was seen to-night after he returned from the May's Landing jail, and asked as to the truthfulness of this statement of the injured woman. He positively refused to say anything about it. He said his duty as legal advisor of both Mr. and Mrs. Hamilton precluded him from giving for publication any of the material facts bearing upon matter now in his possession. To the point blank question if Joshua Mann and Evangeline had passed as man and wife in London and Paris, and if, as is again reported, there was a marriage certificate in existence showing that they had been wedded, he merely laughed, but in a moment emphatically said that he would not divulge anything bearing upon his side of the case, neither would he talk regarding the report that Mrs. Hamilton had pawned the family jewels of Robert Ray, which he gave her at the time of his first infatuation, and that she had used the money to meet alleged blackmail demands of Joshua Mann.

He said that during his visit to Sheriff Johnson's house at May's Landing to-day, he found the prisoner cool and collected. Every effort has been made to save her from mental prostration. It had not been found necessary at any time to call for the services of a physician, and her lawyer seemed to believe that if she was brought to trial she would be equal to the occasion.

Prosecutor Thompson was also seen to-night and asked if he had yet ordered an official examination of the wounded nurse. He said he had done nothing further in the matter since his talk with THE WORLD correspondent last evening and that he did not propose to take any steps until Dr. Crosby, who is in daily attendance upon the nurse, is prepared to give him a certificate saying that she is absolutely out of danger. Then he would ask County Physician Reilly to make an official examination. In this connection it can be stated that Mary Donnelly is steadily improving. Her temperature is regarded as perfectly proper, and her pulse normal. It is even said that if the wound were congealed a physician would pronounce her in good bodily health. County Physician Reilly says he is not prepared to state when he will make the examination that devolves upon him as an officer of the county.

As regards the matter of bail, THE WORLD correspondent has the positive assurance that no application will be made by Mrs. Hamilton's counsel, at least before Tuesday morning. Mr. Robert Ray Hamilton himself went to Jersey City this morning for the purpose of consulting with an eminent legal friend who practices both in that place and New York. During his absence it is understood that a dispatch was received here from Mrs. Hamilton asking him to come to May's Landing.

The startling rumor of last night, that there might be a remarriage in the jail to-day, has not been borne out, though there is some ground for believing such a proceeding was at least contemplated. There was a great expectation during the course of the afternoon regarding the rumored preparation of a statement by Mr. Hamilton; but if such a document is in existence it is being carefully kept from the public.

A VILLAINOUS CONSPIRACY.
ROBERT RAY HAMILTON THE VICTIM OF A PLOT.

HE IS MADE TO BELIEVE THAT HE IS THE FATHER OF AN ILLEGITIMATE
CHILD BOUGHT BY EVA MANN.

A story was told in Inspector Byrnes's office last night which places three conspirators—Robert Ray Hamilton's wife, Mrs. Swinton, and Joshua T. Mann—under a caesium light. It establishes the fact that the child which Mr. Hamilton believed to be his offspring came from a midwife's, and was foisted on him basely and heartlessly. It gives more of the shameful history of Swinton, Mann and company, and is so convincing that Mr. Hamilton is said to have come to his senses and will endeavor to atone for his folly by allowing the law to proceed against Mrs. Swinton and "Josh" Mann for palming off the child on him and for conspiracy.

It appears that a counter-conspiracy against Mr. Hamilton was gotten up by friends who thought too well of him and his name to allow them to be any longer sullied by contact with the creatures who got him into their clutches. Among these friends were Elithu Root and Charles A Peabody, Jr. Thursday last Mr. Root called on Inspector Byrnes and asked him to meet him at the residence of one of Mr. Hamilton's friends to discuss his associations with Mrs. Swinton, Eva, and Mann.

Inspector Byrnes met Mr. Root, his partner, Mr. Samuel B. Clarke, and others, and, at their request, consented to "sift fine" Mrs. Swinton, Mann, and Eva. He started in with the belief that Mr. Hamilton was forced to marry Eva by her statement that her honor and the child's were at stake; in other words, he believed her and acted like a gentleman. Learning that she said that she gave birth to a girl in Elmira on the 17th of December, 1888, and that she was attended by Dr. Burnett Morse, a physician of good repute, Mr. Byrnes sent Detective Sergeant McNaught to Elmira. He reported that Eva lived in Elmira in a hotel and in boarding houses with Josh Mann and that they passed as a married couple. Dr. Morse remembered that he attended her for cramps of the stomach, but he was sure that she did not at that time give birth to a child, and there were no indications that she was likely to become a mother.

McNaught went over the evidence carefully, and finally procured affidavits to establish what he had learned. As soon as Inspector Byrnes had these affidavits he, as had been arranged with Messrs. Root and Clarke, who probably had an understanding with Mr. Hamilton, telegraphed to Mr. Hamilton to come on from Atlantic City.

Mr. Hamilton responded at once. Friends and detectives met him Friday night at Jersey City, and he went unrecognized to Mr. C. A. Peabody's, at 13 Park-avenue. Inspector Byrnes saw him there, proved to him that Eva lied in her story about her confinement, and promised to show him that he had been basely deceived in regard to the child which he believed to be a Hamilton. Mr. Hamilton was greatly agitated, but he said firmly that, although he loved his wife dearly, if he had been deceived he would not hinder in the punishment of all who were in the plot.

Mrs. Swinton evidently felt uneasy, for on the same evening that Mr. Hamilton went to Mr. Peabody's she and "Josh," as Mrs. J.W. Brown and son, registered at the St. Charles Hotel in this city and occupied one room. Inspector Byrnes had by this time learned enough to warrant him in arresting mother and son, but he waited until Sunday night, when he sent Detective Sergeants Hickey and McNaught to the hotel with instructions to "bring them in." They were not in their room, but had left word that they would return for letters. At noon on Monday Mrs. Swinton came to the hotel, dined, and left under surveillance. She went to 335 West Twenty-ninth-street, a flat house, and, as word had been sent to Police Headquarters that Mann would turn up during the day, she was arrested by Hickey and Detective Sergeant Crowley, taken to the Central Office, and put in a cell to

ponder. Three hours later "Josh" fell into the clutches of the detectives at the West Twenty-ninth-street house, and he was put in another cell. The chief detective, as he puts it, does not worry smart prisoners by questioning until they have had an opportunity to reflect and examine the place in which they are locked up. Yesterday, after they had been remanded at the Tombs, their situation was explained to them, and they were given an opportunity to make a statement.

Both made confessions, and part of Mrs. Swinton's was read to the reporters. She said, in substance, that about the 10th of last November Eva told Mrs. Swinton that she wanted a layette and that it must be as fine as money could buy and ready by the 14th or 15th of December. She explained that Josh and she were going to Elmira, and that a friend of "Ray" had got a girl into trouble and that when the child was born it would have to be taken care of until a home could be found for it. Eva did not return from Elmira until about Christmas. Mrs. Swinton then lived at 51 East Thirty-first-street and Eva went there with "Josh." The layette was incomplete and Eva was angry. No shops that they usually patronized were open, but they (the women) hurried to the Bowery, and in a store kept by a Hebrew bought what was lacking, including a cap and a cloak. The purchases were given to Mrs. Swinton, and Eva left her, saying, "You hurry home and I'll go and get the baby." Eva appeared at the house with a girl four of five days old. It was fair and wrapped in a green shawl.

On the same day in the evening Mrs. Swinton engaged board at 105 East Twenty-eighth-street for Mrs. and Mrs. Mann and an infant. "Josh" and Eva went there with the child and remained there a week. Meanwhile Eva furnished a flat at 208 East Fourteenth-street and they moved into it. A day or two after the infant was sick and died under the care of Dr. Kemp of 263 West Twenty-third-street. It was buried as Alice Mann, the child of George and Alice Mann, and Dr. Kemp certified that the cause of death was inanition, due to lack of nourishment. On Jan. 4, before the child was buried Eva went to a midwife and got another baby girl and took it to the East Fourteenth-street flat. It became sick like its predecessor, and Mrs. Swinton remarked that "it would not do to send for Kemp," so it was carried to 51 West Twenty-third-street, and Dr. Gilbert of 401 West Thirty-third-street was called in. It died on the 14th of January, and was buried as Ethel Parsons, twenty-five days old, child of Walter and Alida Parsons. Adair & Aldred of 359 Fourth-avenue buried both children.

Eva was in despair over her "luck" and hastened to get a third child. She had to have "an order" for one at a midwife's, and when it was brought she was in a rage because it had dark hair and "looked like a Dutch baby." She remarked that "Ray" had even

(sic—"seen"?) the first child, and it would never do to "spring this one on him as he knows the difference between a blonde and a brunette." Besides, Eva had an aversion to the babe at first sight, couldn't like it, and couldn't kiss it. It would have to "go back." Next day it was stowed away in a cradle and Eva went to hunt for a fourth child. She found one that suited her and that could be used to hoodwink "Ray," but she had to pay $10 for it. This is the child that came with Mr. and Mrs. Hamilton to Atlantic City. When Eva got to the house with child No. 4 the "Dutch baby" was crying, and Eva got in a passion. She compelled Mrs. Swinton to take it back to the midwife and told her to say that she had no use for it, as the lady who adopted it had died. Mrs. Swinton had a war of words with the midwife, who did not believe her story, but they finally came to an understanding on Mrs. Swinton's paying $5.

So much for the legitimacy of the child that Mr. Hamilton believed to be his, and which was the main link between him and the adventures and the main cause of their marriage. The marriage, according to Inspector Byrnes, took place at Paterson, N.J., on the 7th of last January. Mrs. Swinton's statement is that Hamilton believed that he was the father of child No. 1 and listened to her tearful entreaties to legitimize their offspring. The certificate was not at Police Headquarters last night, but the witnesses were

Edward Dryden, an insurance agent of Broadway, Paterson, and Mrs. Swinton's brother. The child was christened in a New York church, and "Josh" and his mother were godfather and godmother. Mrs. Swinton has evidently thrown Eva overboard, for she tells how "Ray" hugged Eva and kissed child No. 1 when he first saw it at 208 East Fourteenth-street. Mrs. Swinton goes on to say that for the past four years Eva represented that she was married to "Josh." Early in March Eva gave him a check for $2,000 on the Union Dime Savings Bank, and "Josh" opened an account with it at this bank in his own name, but in April Eva learned that he had down out a large sum. She went into one her fierce tantrums, got a cab, was driven to the bank, demanded to see the President, and made an affidavit that "Josh" was her husband and that he was demented and incompetent. It was, however, discovered that the story was unserviceable, as "Josh" had only a few dollars to his credit. Mrs. Swinton made the statement that before going to Elmira "Josh" obtained $500 from Eva, and that when she married "Ray" she was merry had having fooled him, and said that as soon as she got her hands on the jewelry and place left by his mother, which he promised to her, she would turn them into money. Although it is hardly necessary, Mrs. Swinton felt constrained to say that since 1885 "Josh" and Eva's relations were those of man and wife.

"Josh" comes out in a statement which is characteristically vile and cowardly. It has the sole merit of being brutally frank. He says he first met Eva in 1881 in a house in Thirty-first-street. He describes her attractions. He admits that he was favored while she was protected in a flat by another man, and that they "quarreled and fought and quarreled and fought, but always made up." During the last year he had bled her to the tune of $3,000. He knew of the imposition practiced on Hamilton and that the child at Atlantic City was neither his nor Hamilton's.

Inspector Byrnes says he has verified all the statements in this horrible story, but he is mute on the question of bigamy. He says, however, that when Eva and "Josh" were at Elmira last year her brother was arrested for larceny at Towanda, Penn., and they went there to try and release him. They testified at his trial, and swore that they were man and wife.

Dr. Gilbert has made a statement to the effect that when he attended child number two both Eva and Mrs. Swinton urged him to do his utmost to save it, and Mrs. Swinton said a large moneyed estate depended on its life, and it would be worth $100,000 to Eva if it lived. Inspector Byrnes can produce the mother and midwife for every one of the four children, and he states that Robert Ray Hamilton has done with "the gang" and will let the law take its course, but does not hint what his future attitude toward Eva will be.

Mrs. Swinton was allowed to leave Police Headquarters yesterday afternoon with two detectives to go for letters and transact private business. She was recorded as a dressmaker and "Josh" is put down as a salesman. It is probable that they will give little trouble to the courts by pleading guilty to charges of conspiracy and substituting children.

Mr. Charles A. Peabody, Jr., the lawyer who represents Mr. Hamilton's interests, as well as being one of his best friends, was seen last night at his home, 13 Park-avenue. Mr. Peabody did not wish to talk about the case, but intimated that the action against Joshua J. Mann and Mrs. Swinton was largely owing to Mr. Hamilton's friends. The former were arrested, he said, for having formed a conspiracy against Mr. Hamilton. When asked what Mr. Hamilton's intentions were in regard to the adventurers now in May's Landing jail, Mr. Peabody said he did not know, and if he did, would not feel at liberty to say.

Mr. Hamilton slept last night at Mr. Peabody's house. To the pedestrian passing by the residence gave the appearance of being closed for the warm season. The Summer doors were still up and the front was well darkened. Undoubtedly Mr. Hamilton has been spurred up to take decisive steps against the two conspirators by his friends in the city, who feel that his infatuation for the so-called Mrs. Hamilton made him blind to the little scheme that was being worked to get possession of his property, and that they finally succeeded in persuading him to fight the thing through and appear as the complaining witness against Mann and Mrs. Swinton.

MRS. HAMILTON SEES THE BABY.

ATLANTIC CITY, N.J., SEPT. 3—Mrs. Hamilton was made happy to-day in her prison at May's Landing by having the baby, Beatrice, brought to her. Mrs. Rupp of the Noll cottage, accompanied by S.E. Perry, took the little one over to May's Landing. Mrs. Hamilton evidently anticipated their arrival and spent fully an hour at the barred window looking anxiously toward the station. She manifested great joy when she pressed her child in her arms and kissed it rapturously. She had also a warm greeting for Mrs. Rupp and made eager inquiries about the wounded nurse's condition. Mrs. Rupp brought the baby back to Atlantic City to-night.

It was learned to-night that Mrs. Hamilton's physician has expressed considerable alarm at her nervous condition. She daily becomes more irritable and has fits of melancholy, and he is of the opinion that she will soon succumb to nervous prostration and be confined to her bed.

The wounded nurse, Mary Donnelly, was found at the Noll cottage at 11 o'clock to-night. She was averse to talking at first, but when she was informed that Mrs. Swinton and Joshua Mann were in the custody of Inspector Byrnes at New York, she said:

"They went there, did they? It is

about time that their schemes were nipped."

The baby, Beatrice, she said, had been represented to her as the offspring of Mrs. Hamilton. She was engaged as wet nurse when the child was but three months old, and went to California in that capacity.

On one occasion she admitted she heard Mrs. Hamilton say to a friend from Passaic that the child was not hers. As far as Mrs. Donnelly knew, the child Beatrice might be Mrs. Hamilton's, but she felt "purty certain" that Robert Ray Hamilton was not its father.

A TALE OF WOE.

Troubles of the Hamiltons Ventilated in Court.

THE ROW THAT LED TO THE CUTTING

Nurse Donnelly and Eva Had
a Very Lively Time.

ROBERT RAY HAD HIS SHIRT TORN OFF

Whisky Bottles and Parasols
Whizzed in the Air.

BABY BEATRICE HAD A CLOSE CALL.

The Millionaire Testifies in His
Wife's Favor.

EVA REFUSES TO TALK ABOUT THE BABY.

Its Paternity Left for the Jury to Guess.
Its Birthplace Not Revealed.
Mrs. Hamilton's
Weeping.

EVA ASKED FOR MORPHINE.
MRS. ROBERT RAY HAMILTON VERY NERVOUS.

HER HUSBAND APPARENTLY INTENDS TO LEAVE HER TO HER FATE—HE
ORDERS AWAY HIS TRUNKS.

ATLANTIC CITY, N.J., SEPT. 5.—The Noll cottage to-day furnished another important link in the new phase of the strange and sensational Hamilton case. A young New Yorker visited it shortly after 11 o'clock and handed Mrs. Rupp, the proprietress, a note of which the following is a copy:

> LAW OFFICES OF ROOT & CLARK - NO. 34
> NASSAU-STREET- NEW YORK - SEPT. 4- 1889.
> Mrs. Howard Rupp:
>
> Please let the bearer, Mr. Edward R. Vollmer, have my personal property in your possession, including trunks, clothes, gun case, and box of saddles, &c. Yours truly,
>
> ROBERT RAY HAMILTON

When Mrs. Rupp received this note she refused to honor it, and referred Mr. Vollmer to Judge Irving. The latter gentleman gave his official sanction, and then began a thorough search of the rooms formerly occupied by the Hamiltons. All the wearing apparel and other personal effects of Mr. Hamilton were quickly packed in a trunk, and even the large photograph album was stripped of his pictures. Mrs. Hamilton's trunks were carefully searched and every article belonging to her husband taken out, the young man, who was armed with a detailed list, being careful not to take anything belonging to the imprisoned woman. He left on the 3 o'clock express this afternoon taking with him two trunks, a valise, and a large box all filled with the personal effects of Robert Ray Hamilton. Judge Irving said to-day that this latest move on Hamilton's part means that he will probably never set his foot in this county again. "We can do without him at the trial," he said, "and would rather have his $600 bail than himself." The removal of Hamilton's personal effects is another conclusive proof that he means to desert the woman at May's Landing.

It was learned to-day that during Mrs. Rupp's visit to May's Landing on Monday Mrs. Hamilton entreated her to send over six morphine pills for the purpose, as she stated, of allaying her nervousness. The guileless Mrs. Rupp promised to gratify her wish, but when she returned to Atlantic City was dissuaded from doing so by Judge Irving, with the injunction that she herself would be likely to occupy a prison cell if she aided Mrs. Hamilton in her "suicidal plans." The question now is, "Will the forsaken and deserted woman attempt to take her own life?" and while that query is unanswered the May's Landing authorities mean to take extra precautions to frustrate any such desperate move.

The visit of the two New York detectives to May's Landing last night has been prolific of much trouble at the county jail, and as a result Deputy Sheriff Frank Moore was summarily discharged from his official position this morning by Sheriff Johnson. The Sheriff was in Atlantic City last night when the New Yorkers were seeking admission to Mrs. Hamilton's apartments. She was not averse to their seeing her, and after a consultation between Mrs. Johnson and the Deputy Sheriff, the strangers were shown up to the attic. They were accompanied by the German midwife and a little girl whom she represented to be her daughter. They both failed to identify Mrs. Hamilton as the woman who had purchased the foundling which is now known as Beatrice Ray. The detectives spent the night at May's Landing and left this morning for New York. Sheriff Johnson returned to the county jail this morning, and when he learned what had taken place in his absence he immediately ordered his deputy, Frank Moore, to quit the premises, which he did. Mr. Moore says the Sheriff's wife gave the detectives permission to see Mrs. Hamilton, but she shields herself by stating that the deputy advised her to admit them, as they were not reporters, and it would therefore be all right. Sheriff Johnson puts his side of the case as follows: "I have all along refused the Atlantic City reporters, some of whom are my personal friends, access to the prisoner's presence. And here was a lot of perfect strangers who in my absence and in direct violation of my positive orders were allowed to see and talk to the woman."

The Sheriff was decidedly out of humor, and talked in a very positive vein. He has not yet selected a deputy, but as Mr. Moore has held the position for a number of years, and has always been faithful and upright in the discharge of his duties, it is generally expected that he will be reinstated. He is very popular in the county, and was strongly urged to accept the nomination for Sheriff at the last election. Counselor Perry went to May's Landing to-day and stoutly upbraided his client for submitting to an interview with the New York detectives, and enjoined her to secrecy until the day of her trial. He reports that Mrs. Hamilton is still very weak, but that her nervous condition is somewhat improved. Nurse Donnelly was able to move her limbs to-day without any pain, and will no doubt be able to enter the witness stand when the case is called for trial. Prosecutor Thompson has ordered an extra guard placed on the Noll cottage, and has otherwise taken hold of the case in good earnest. With reference to Mr. Perry's part in the coming trial, a legal authority said to-night: "On the first day of the trial he [Perry] will probably go before the court, state the peculiar circumstances under which he was retained in the case, and then ask to be relieved from further participation in it. Hamilton has paid him his retainer, and even he has since then notified him that his services were no longer necessary. In view of the first fact, Mr. Perry's position as counsel for the woman whose husband has not only deserted her but is endeavoring to make her one of a guilty trio, would be a very embarrassing one." The same authority gave it out that Prosecutor Thompson would take hold of the case in his usual vigorous way, and as New Jersey juries are not noted for sentimentality, Mrs. Hamilton would, beyond a doubt, be sentenced to a long term of imprisonment, and that thus Jersey justice would play into the hands of Robert Ray Hamilton and his influential New York friends. Then when her term would be up, she would be wanted in New York as an accomplice of the conspirators, Swinton and Mann, and probably end her days in prison.

Inspector Byrnes, in order to establish a perfect case, questioned "Josh" Mann again yesterday, and he repeated his statement that at no time was Eva enceinte. He said that after Eva married Mr. Hamilton she brought him "Ray's" will. It left all his property, jewelry, and plate to Eva and the child and Eva was to manage the estate for the child until she came of age. Eva, after reading the will, tapped it with her finger and remarked, "Now, that's a good thing to have. 'Ray' is reckless and might get killed, and if anything does happen I'll marry you."

Inspector Byrnes does not believe that Mann and Eva were ever made man and wife by a clergyman of any sort. He has probed every phase of the case, and has not a scintilla of evidence that there was ever any plot to kill Mr. Hamilton suggested or discovered. A friend of Mrs. Swinton was a Police Headquarters yesterday, and said that he was going to get a criminal lawyer for her, but last night she had not consulted any legal advisor.

EVANGELINE MUST ANSWER.
THE GRAND JURY FINDS TRUE BILLS AGAINST THE HAMILTON CONSPIRATORS.

EVA ALSO INDICTED IN NEW JERSEY.

SHE MUST ANSWER FOR ATROCIOUS ASSAULT ON MARY DONNELLY—
ROBERT RAY AT MAY'S LANDING.

If any one ever doubted that Robert Ray Hamilton had decided to sever all connection with the woman Eva, who bears his name, let the doubt be quickly dispelled, for yesterday, on complaint of Hamilton, the Grand Jury found two indictments against Eva Hamilton, Joshua J. Mann and Mrs. T. Anna Swinton. One of the indictments is for conspiracy, and the other for grand larceny in the second degree. At the same time, at May's Landing, where Eva is imprisoned, the Grand Jury was preparing to hear her case. And so, in two States, the machinery of the law is slowly closing around the miserable woman and her accomplices.

The papers in the case were sent to the Grand Jury yesterday morning by Assistant District Attorney Lindsay, who drew up the indictments. Robert Ray Hamilton was not present as a witness, as his presence was necessary at May's Landing, where the Grand Jury was preparing to consider the charge of the attempted murder of Nurse Donnelly by the woman Eva. It is likely that the woman's conviction for assaulting Mrs. Donnelly and confinement in prison will be the basis of an action for divorce by Robert Ray Hamilton.

As Mrs. Hamilton was in the jail at May's Landing she could not be arraigned on the indictments in General Sessions, for New Jersey justice has a prior claim. In order, however, that there could be no possible hitch in the criminal proceedings Judge Martine yesterday signed and issued two bench warrants for Mrs. Hamilton's arrest, and they will be sent to May's Landing and there lodged with the warden of the jail as detainers in case Mrs. Hamilton should be acquitted or discharged.

The Grand Jury filed the indictments in court at 1.30 o'clock. Joshua J. Mann and Mrs. Swinton were soon after brought up from the Tombs and were arraigned before Judge Martine. Both pleaded "not guilty," and were taken back to the Tombs to await trial.

ATLANTIC CITY, N.J., SEPT. 16—Robert Ray Hamilton came down to May's Landing this morning, accompanied by young Edward

Vollmer. The September term of the court, which has been delayed for a week on account of the storm, was opened this morning promptly at 10 o'clock, with Judge Reed, of the Supreme Bench, presiding. The Grand Jury was impaneled and went upstairs to deliberate. They filed into the court-room again shortly after 4 o'clock, and were discharged for the term by Judge Reed.

Among the true bills found was that of Mrs. Evangeline Hamilton, who was indicted for "atrocious assault upon Mary Ann Donnelly." Capt. Perry, her counsel, expects the case to be called for trial to-morrow afternoon.

Hamilton said to-day that he was not here in the interest of Mrs. Hamilton and would take no part whatever in her defense. She could suffer the penalty of her crime and it would give him no concern. He simply came to May's Landing to fulfill a promise he had made to Judge Irving. Hamilton chatted pleasantly with his acquaintances and did not seem to give a thought to his wife, who is confined to her bed with nervous prostration in the attic room of Sheriff Johnson's house. Although the little court-room was crowded, there were few women present.

HE WILL BE EVA'S WITNESS.
ROBERT RAY HAMILTON SUMMONED TO APPEAR ON HIS WIFE'S BEHALF.

THE CASE WILL BE CALLED TO-DAY.

MRS. HAMILTON BEGGED HER HUSBAND TO SEE HER, BUT, ACTING UNDER THE ADVICE OF COUNSEL, HE DECLINED—NURSE DONNELLY'S HEART BELIEVED TO BE WARMING TOWARDS THE WRETCHED ADVENTURESS.

[SPECIAL TO THE WORLD].

MAY'S LANDING, N.J., SEPT. 17.— Robert Ray Hamilton will appear as a witness in his wife's behalf in the trial which is set for to-morrow morning at the County Court-House. He was served with a subpoena this afternoon at the insistence of Capt. Samuel E. Perry, counsel for the accused woman. This step, while unexpected, was not taken until after consultation between Hamilton, the Sheriff and the lawyer.

To-night the strangely deceived husband sleeps in May's Landing, within a stone's throw of the jail and within full view of the attic in which his wife is imprisoned. He has shown no signs of relenting and will probably follow out the course he has evidently determined upon, which is to renounce completely and utterly the woman who has brought his name into such scandalous notoriety. Hamilton had an interview this morning with the wife of the Sheriff, but the subject of it can only be surmised.

There have been strong efforts made, especially during the last three days, to surround the case with mystery. Any question concerning Mrs. Hamilton, her condition, her hopes, her fears, is met with a blank stare. The questioner is referred to the Sheriff, who seems to have placed the entire village under a ban of impenetrable secrecy. When this official is approached he refuses point blank to say a word. Indeed, it was not without some difficulty that the information was gained as to the time set for the trial, and that was given with injunctions that the source should not be divulged. Hamilton himself is more courteous, but positive in his refusals to make a statement.

The fact that Prosecutor Thompson discharged Mr. Hamilton as a witness for the State and that Counselor Perry immediately secured him to testify in favor of the defendant is the first indication of the probable policy to be pursued by the defense. THE WORLD correspondent learned from an undoubtedly authentic source in Atlantic City this morning that the child Mamie, on whose testimony the defense rests with a good deal of confidence, is not the only witness whose story is valuable. A lady living in Philadelphia was in the Noll Cottage when the nurse entered and made threats against Mrs. Hamilton and started upstairs with the avowed intention of doing up her mistress. Immediately after the fracas occurred the lady left for her home in Philadelphia, but not until she had told Mr. Hamilton what had taken place. It is believed that the statement was made in the presence of the defendant. If so it will be competent testimony and will have a significant bearing on the case.

The plea will in all probability be self-defense, and the defendant's counsel will attempt to prove that Mrs. Hamilton was in such imminent danger from her drunken assailant that she seized the dagger to defend herself. Robert Ray Hamilton will therefore be placed in the rather paradoxical position of helping to shield a woman whom he has already abandoned.

On the first train from Atlantic City this morning there came a bandbox addressed "Mrs. Robert Ray Hamilton, May's Landing Jail. "It contained a lot of toilet articles and underclothing, and was addressed in the unmistakable angular handwriting of Nurse Donnelly, and underneath were the words: "Beatrice is nine months old to-day." Whether the wounded woman had done this out of pity for the wretched condition of her mistress, or whether she simply wrote the address at the request of Mrs. Rupp, the proprietress of Noll Cottage, nobody knows. If the former it shows that the nurse's heart has softened and that she will not be a willing witness for the prosecution.

Notwithstanding the vigilance of the Sheriff, it leaked out to-day that Mrs. Hamilton passed the day principally and making cigarettes. She read nothing, because she had nothing to read. She managed to have a message conveyed to her husband, who sat on the hotel piazza, begging him in terms of endearment to call and see her. Hamilton declined, sending back word that he was acting in accordance with the instructions of counsel, who advised him to hold no communication with her pending trial. There is one thing that excites some little pity for the adventuress and that is her distress when she was unable to obtain morphine. Mrs. Hamilton has long been a confirmed victim of the morphine habit. Without the drug, like all fiends, she is utterly miserable. It was this propensity that led to the unthinking sensation-mongers to assume a couple of weeks ago that Mrs. Hamilton contemplated suicide.

THE NEW YORK WORLD
THURSDAY, SEPTEMBER 19, 1889

EVA HAMILTON AT BAY.

THE LATEST CHAPTER IN THAT MOST EXTRAORDINARY OF DRAMAS TOLD BY THE WOMAN HERSELF.

ARRAIGNED IN A JERSEY COURT.

ROBERT RAY ALSO TESTIFIES AND TRIES TO SHIELD HIS WIFE.

BUT HIS LOVE IS PLAINLY DEAD.

THE WOUNDED NURSE DESCRIBES THE CIRCUMSTANCES LEADING TO THE ASSAULT—EVA HAD QUARRELED WITH HAMILTON AND TORN THE CLOTHES FROM HIS BACK—SHE WANTED TO HAVE HIM ARRESTED, AND CALLED MARY VILE NAMES—THEN THE TWO WOMEN FOUGHT AND MRS. HAMILTON USED THE KNIFE—THE HUSBAND'S STORY.

[SPECIAL TO THE WORLD].

MAY'S LANDING, N.J., SEPT. 18.— With all her tigerish nature in check, cunning, crafty, and alert Mrs. Robert Ray Hamilton appeared in the Atlantic County Court-House to-day to answer a charge which, while of no great significance itself, brought to light one of the most astounding stories of conspiracy, of turpitude, of plot and counter-plot, ever revealed outside the realms of improbable fiction. The overacting that she did in real life was duplicated on the witness-stand to-day. As cleverly and successfully as she played her first parts in the drama which so nearly resulted in a tragical dénouement, she missed her lines when it came down to a cold recital of facts as they were told before a relentless judge, a persevering prosecutor and twelve unsympathetic arbiters.

MRS. HAMILTON IN COURT.

Until Mrs. Hamilton undertook to testify in her own behalf the prospects for her acquittal, or virtual acquittal through jury disagreement looked bright enough. Her distinguished husband was her best witness. True to his chivalric instincts, he came manfully forward and told a story, not altogether to his own credit, it is true, but one that helped the cause of the woman who bears his name. The wet-nurse, too, Mary Ann Donnelly, State witness though she was, helped the defense more than she did the prosecution. The physician who attended the wounded woman, the policeman who made the arrest, and the policeman who searched the cottage after the assault, all contributed in a measure to the fabric woven by the attorney for the defendant. It was practically a matter of compulsion for Counselor Perry to put the accused understand. Had that step not been taken it would have given the State the opportunity for an argument that is invariably convincing with a Jersey jury, namely—that the defendant feared to injure her case by testifying.

Mrs. Hamilton was a disingenuous witness. While she had an intuition of the purpose of the questions put to her, she could not avoid the inevitable chain of circumstances that led surely to the point that the prosecution sought to reach. To combat this she assumed a modesty and reticence strangely at variance with the testimony given by her own witnesses. A naïveté that was altogether unbecoming and perfectly transparent did not help the story she told, and it was with an apparent air of relief that her counsel saw her drop the active part as a witness and take up the positive rôle of a prisoner.

NURSE DONNELLY.

There were three or four petty cases of minor crimes to be disposed of before the principal case of the day received consideration. The plain little court-house, with its whitewashed walls and rare old bits of bric-à-brac, called tipstaves, was filled with farmers and farmers' boys, who strolled leisurely in a few minutes after the clanging bell had announced the opening of court. Presiding Judge Alfred Reed and Lay Judges Byrnes, Scull and Cordery were on the bench before half the audience had been seated. Assistant Prosecutor Clarence Cole busied himself with clearing up the desks for his principal, while Capt. Perry engaged himself with a bundle of papers. Prosecutor Thompson sharpened a lead pencil with the dagger with which the assault had been committed, and at 11 o'clock moved for the trial of the cause "The State versus Hamilton."

Judge Reed, who wastes no time and sentiment, immediately ordered the Sheriff to bring the prisoner into court. Mrs. Hamilton was waiting in the parlor that adjoins the jail and came out in a few moments escorted by her lawyer, who had gone to meet her, and the Sheriff. Close behind followed Nurse Donnelly and Mrs. Elizabeth Rupp. Mrs. Hamilton wore a blue cloth coat, which enveloped her graceful figure completely, and a Gainsborough hat trimmed in black ostrich plumes. The nurse looked shabby. She had on a rusty black coat and a dress of dark stuff that hung in limp folds. Pretty Mrs. Rupp wore an ordinary waterproof that came down to her heels.

The defendant's face looked pinched, and her eyes, which are wonderfully bright and expressive, showed perceptible traces of tears. Without looking at the Judges she seated herself in a chair at a table next to her lawyer, and between him and the jury-box. Her lips were compressed and an unfeigned nervousness was betrayed in the clasping and squeezing of the dainty handkerchief that she held in her gloved hands. Mrs. Rupp took a chair inside of and next to the railed inclosure set apart for lawyers a newspaper representatives. Mr. Hamilton sat down beside her.

SOBS FOR THE JURORS.

Then, in accordance with the quick, sharp command of the Presiding Judge, the selection of a jury was begun. As the fourth man took his place Mrs. Hamilton put her handkerchief to her eyes and began to sob. Mary Ann Donnelly's face was impassive as a piece of marble. She looked at Mrs. Hamilton's swelling neck and the merest suspicion of a contemptuous curl came to her lips. When the eighth juror had answered that he had neither formed nor expressed an opinion on anything in general, and the Hamilton case in particular, Mrs. Hamilton began to sob more violently than before. The cords in her neck swelled out and her ostrich-plumes trembled. After that she became more composed, and her conduct from that time forward ceased to be natural.

The sprucest-looking man on the panel was Charles Evans, the proprietor of the Seaside House. He declared frankly that he had formed an opinion and the defense challenged him. Judge Reed asked Mr. Evans whether he could render a just verdict on the evidence presented and the answer being in the affirmative the challenge was overruled and the juror took his place in the box. At 11.30 o'clock the twelve men were in their places, and after being sworn Prosecutor Thompson presented the facts, as he expected to prove them, in a five-minute speech, relating substantially the version of this the assault as already published in THE WORLD.

Dr. Howard Crosby, the physician someone to attend Nurse Donnelly immediately after the stabbing, was called by the State to explain the nature and possibilities of the wound. The witness found the nurse on a sofa in the Noll Cottage, bleeding freely from an incised wound in the abdomen. The membrane covering the intestines had been lacerated, but the intestines had not been punctured. A two-edged dagger with a sharp point and a bone handle was shown to the doctor and he said that such a wound could have been made with such a weapon. In response to a query as to Nurse Donnelly's present condition, Dr. Crosby said he considered her well and out of all danger. The cross-examination did not discover anything important. Counselor Perry tried to add emphasis to the constant improvement in the condition of the patient, which led the Court to dryly remark:

"Had the improvement not been made this defendant would have been held for murder instead of assault."

THE NURSE TELLS HER STORY.

While the physician's testimony was an important part of the case, it did not excite a great deal of interest in the audience. The buzz and murmur of comments ceased instantly when the prosecutor called Mary Ann Donnelly to the stand. The witness glanced at Mrs. Hamilton, who had again covered her face with her handkerchief, walked up to the clerk of the court and swore to tell the truth. There was a gleam of defiance in the nurse's eyes as she grasped the sides of her chair with both hands and braced herself for the ordeal. After telling that she was

in the employ of Mrs. Hamilton at the time of the assault the witness went on as follows:

"On the day that I was stabbed I first saw Mrs. Hamilton in the morning, about 5.30 or 6 o'clock. Both she and Mr. Hamilton were up. Mrs. Hamilton came to her door and called me to come up and unlock a trunk. I went into the room and then went out again. She commanded me to come back. I did go back. Mr. Hamilton was naked. She had torn the clothes off his back and"—

The defense objected to this last statement as not being the personal knowledge of the witness, and the nurse was cautioned.

WANTED HAMILTON ARRESTED.

"When I went back," she continued, "he had the bed-sheet around him, and Mrs. Hamilton was abusing him. I unlocked the trunk and went out, returning in about fifteen minutes. She told me to go out and get an officer to arrest Mr. Hamilton. I went out and although I saw plenty of officers I told her I couldn't find one. I didn't want to disgrace the house. Meantime the expressman had come for Mr. and Mrs. Hamilton's trunks. Mr. Hamilton didn't want his to go. Mrs. Hamilton insisted that it should go, but Mr. Hamilton was firm. The expressman went away, came back in fifteen minutes, and went away again without either trunk. "

Nurse Donnelly's tone was hard. She kept turning her head to look at Hamilton, who had his eyes fixed on the floor in front of him. He never saw the glance that asked for approbation.

"I had asked Mrs. Hamilton's permission to go out," continued the nurse, "and I went over to the Verona cottage to tell Mrs. Swinton and Mr. Mann that Mrs. Hamilton was quiet, for she was on the bed with the baby when I left the house. When I came back I picked up a silver cup which she had thrust at Mr. Hamilton. I had bought a bottle of whiskey by her orders and was putting it in the closet where she grabbed me by the head when she grabbed me by the head."

Judge Reed became impatient at this point and suggested that the history of the assault be reached as quickly as possible.

A REGULAR ROUGH-AND-TUMBLE.

"Well," said the nurse, looking hard at Hamilton again, "when I came in for the third time Mrs. Hamilton was in the middle of the room and Mr. Hamilton was sitting down in a rocking-chair. This was between 12 and 1 o'clock. After striking at me with the whiskey bottle, which only gave me a slight touch on the nose, she called me out of my name and I pushed her on the bed to make her take it back. Before that she had tried to hit me with the baby's bath-tub. Mr. Hamilton jumped up but she pushed him between the bed and the wall. Then she gave me the knife. 'Look,' I cried to Mr. Hamilton 'she has stabbed me.'"

"Was this the knife used?" asked

the prosecutor, holding up the dagger.

"I don't want to look at it," replied the nurse, turning away her head. The squeamishness was only of a moment's duration, for she looked again and continued:

"Yes, that's it. She took it out of the bottom of the trunk which I had packed."

A torn coat and a pair of trousers slashed in the upper part of the right leg were shown to the witness and identified as Mr. Hamilton's.

The cross-examination was conducted in a quiet conversational tone, and the concluding statement of the nurse as she left the stand injured her case materially.

"Are you married?" asked Counselor Perry.

"Yes, I married."

"Husband living?"

"Yes."

"When did you last see him?"

The witness bridled up instantly. "I won't answer you," she replied hotly, but upon being pressed she admitted that she had seen him in May, but had not lived with him as a wife for over a year.

"You were a wet-nurse for Mrs. Hamilton, were you not?" asked the lawyer.

The witness instantly saw the implication in the question, and when asked again about her husband refused flatly to answer. Then the lawyer questioned her rapidly as to whether she had ever fought with her husband and whether she hadn't once struck him in the face with a hatchet and whether she had not been discharged from service at one time for fighting. To each of these queries a sharp denial was given. Gradually it was wormed out that Mrs. Hamilton had given the nurse a five-dollar bill to buy a bottle of whiskey, and when she stopped at the Verona House to see Mrs. Swinton she took a drink out of another bottle with "Josh" Mann.

"It was a half wine-glassful," explained the witness spitefully.

A QUESTION OF MONEY.

Questioned further as to what was going on when she went back to Mrs. Hamilton's room, the witness said that the husband and wife were quarrelling over the question of allowance. She was asking Mr. Hamilton if he was willing to give her $5,000 a year, and, when he said yes, she jumped up and said she wanted $6,000 a year; that he had an income of $18,000, and that $12,000 was enough for him. Robert Ray began to chew the ends of his mustache when he heard this, and kept his eyes fixed on Mrs. Rupp's shoulder.

Capt. Perry then asked a series of questions concerning Mrs. Hamilton's diamonds and their custody, which the court ruled to be irrelevant. Then came the clincher for the defense.

"What did Mrs. Hamilton say after you had struggled with her?"

"She hollered, 'Murder, police.' I guess she thought I was going to murder her."

"Going to what?"

"I guess she thought I was going to murder her."

Policeman Biddle was called to settle that he found Mary Donnelly on the porch of the Noll cottage. She cried: "My God, I'm stabbed," as soon as she saw the officer, and he in turn exclaimed, "My God, woman, who did this?" The answer was returned: "That —— upstairs."

A physician was summoned (Dr. Crosby) and Mrs. Hamilton was arrested and taken to the City Hall. "I cut that nurse in self-defense," was all she said. Sergeant of Police Samuel Loder was asked by Mrs. Hamilton why her husband couldn't be with her, and then when he asked why she cut Mary Donnelly, she told him it was none of his business. He asked where the knife was and she said it was either in a closet or on the bed.

Charles Boggs, another policeman, told of making a search of the Noll cottage for the knife, and after the dagger had been offered in evidence the State, at 2.20 o'clock, rested.

HAMILTON CALLED TO THE STAND.

The presentation of the case for the defense was equally as brief as it had been for the prosecution. Counselor Perry said, in substance, that he expected to prove that his client was not guilty as charged in the bill of indictment, but that she had acted in self-defense, believing herself to be in great bodily danger. Dr. Crosby was called to prove that Nurse Donnelley was under the influence of liquor when the physician was called in to attend her, and that inferentially she was quarrelsome and dangerous. The doctor said the nurse was under the influence of some sort of alcoholic beverage when he saw her and his testimony evidently made the impression that it was intended it should.

"Robert Ray Hamilton."

The call was a sudden one, and the interest which had been growing every minute became more intense. Mr. Hamilton arose slowly from his chair. His head was bent; his eyes were half closed as he walked slowly to the witness-stand. Mrs. Hamilton covered her face with her handkerchief and put her black fan in front of that. The witness was sworn and he then dropped into the chair behind him. The man looked ill. His face was sallow and his eyes dull. Nevertheless he betrayed no nervousness and answered the questions put to him frankly and without any apparent attempt at concealment. It was clearly evident, however, that he made the best possible showing he could for the accused. Albeit, perfectly truthful, he got in quick replies where he saw an advantage or delayed answering where the cause of Mrs. Hamilton might be injured.

HE SHIELDS HER, BUT HIS LOVE IS
DEAD.

In speaking of his wife Mr. Hamilton almost invariably referred to her as "the defendant in this case." It was only where he could not avoid it by reason of the nature of the question that he spoke of her as "Mrs. Hamilton," but never during the entire examination as "my wife."

Prosecutor Thompson plunged into the subject at once by asking the witness to relate so far as he knew the circumstances connected with the stabbing.

"I remember the day of the cutting," said Mr. Hamilton, in a low but audible tone, "because I was there that morning. Nurse Donnelly had been in our employ for several months. She was given to being rather abusive and was quarrelsome."

"Did you see any evidence of this disposition before the affray in Atlantic City?"

"Yes. One night, in New York, I came home about 7.30 o'clock and found the defendant in a great state of excitement. She said the nurse had gone out early in the day with the baby and had not yet returned."

"What has to do with the cutting?" asked Judge Reed, who was

AS THE HUSBAND TESTIFIED.

pacing up and down behind his brother judges.

Counselor Perry explained that it was intended to show that the nurse was rather a dangerous character.

The witness told of the defendant's avowed intention of discharging Mary because she was abusive and got drunk, When the judge again interrupted and ruled that if the nurse made any threats it would be competent to offer evidence of that fact. "But," he said, "get down to the threats." Mr. Hamilton then confined himself to a history of the assault.

AS THE HUSBAND SAW IT.

"The nurse came to the room about 6.30 o'clock to say that the expressman had come for the trunks. I saw her again shortly afterwards when she brought up coffee. At 11 o'clock she brought in two letters; she handed one to me and one and kept the other. Mrs. Hamilton was then on the bed with the baby. She got up and asked Mary what had become of the other letter, and what she meant by retaining it. The nurse became abusive, and the defendant told her that she was discharged. I said: "Come, Mary, go out now. You must leave. You must leave this afternoon." The nurse squared off and said: "I won't leave for both of you." Then she made a rush for the defendant and used abusive language. She grappled with Mrs. Hamilton and got her fingers in Mrs. Hamilton's mouth. Mrs. Hamilton got her fingers in Mary's mouth. The defendant then got hold of a bottle and Mrs. Rupp came up and took away the baby.

"Mary called the defendant a vile name and said she had seen her marriage certificate, and announced her as a disreputable woman before her marriage. She followed this by exclaiming, 'let me at her.' Mrs. Hamilton went to the window and called 'police, help, murder.' Mary was then out of the room. She came bouncing back in a few minutes very much excited and drunk. She used the same kind of language and added 'let me kill her, let me kill her,' and she grabbed the defendant by the wrists. Then, with Mrs. Rupp's assistance, Mary was put out. Mrs. Hamilton called to Mrs. Rupp to get the police. The nurse rushed up and passed me, going over to where the defendant was standing, aiming a blow at her with her left hand, striking her in the head. Then the defendant struck with the knife and the police came up soon afterwards."

Mr. Hamilton was exceedingly vague in describing the actual assault, although minute and specific in his preliminary statements.

"I didn't know that Mary was cut," he went on. "I couldn't keep her away from the defendant."

"What sort of language did Mrs. Hamilton use?" asked the prosecutor in his cross-examination.

Robert Ray look thoughtful for a moment, paused and then answered, slowly:

"She called her a d— —."

"Were you dressed?"

"I had on my trousers," replied the witness, boldly.

"How was your coat cut?"

"The defendant tore it." The answer came with great reluctance. "It was during the dispute about the trunks. I said I wouldn't let might be sent to New York. She insisted that it should. We quarrelled about the railroad tickets."

"Did the defendant strike you?"

"No, she tore my night-shirt."

Here all the tipstaves rapped for order with their staves.

"Did Mrs. Hamilton beat you with an umbrella?"

"No, she struck me with a parasol."

"Did she say she would make a lively day for you?"

Robert Ray parted his lips in a smile. "No," was his answer.

"Why did she tear your night-shirt?"

"She said if I wouldn't get up she would fix it so I couldn't stay in bed."

THE DAGGER WAS HIS.

The defendant covered her face with her fan, and tried to look shocked. Mr. Hamilton denied that his wife had spat in his face, and shielded her again when he told how he had knocked the portable bathtub out of her hand. Then he explained how the dagger—which was his property, and which he had bought in Norway—came to be out of his possession. It had been removed with other articles, and was thrown on the bed. This little bit helped to prove that Mrs. Hamilton had not taken out the weapon

for the express purpose of using it on the nurse

In his redirect examination the witness said he had seen bruises on Mrs. Hamilton's body which could've been inflicted by no other person except Mary Ann Donnelly. Then Robert Ray stepped down, and, without as much as a glance at "the defendant in this case," took his place again beside Mrs. Rupp.

Dr. D.B. Ingersoll was called corroborate the latter part of Mr. Hamilton's statement as to the bruises on Mrs. Hamilton. He did so with painful particularity, even to describing the defendant's skinned thumb. He prescribed liniment for her.

Comely Mrs. Rupp, in a low and gentle voice, told what she knew of the fracas, giving the same story, in substance, as told by Mr. Hamilton, but adding what his unwilling ear did not hear, the remark made by the defendant: "Ray Hamilton, you will have me on the gallows yet."

AS SHE TELLS IT.

Then came a witness that did more harm to the defense than all the others had done good. It was Mrs. Hamilton herself. She assumed the air of an ingénue, but she didn't do it well at all, and before she got back to her seat she had been considerably embarrassed by the prosecutor, who insisted on asking her whether Baby Beatrice was her own flesh and blood, and asked her to tell all about her first acquaintance with Mr. Hamilton. The witness began to speak in a low voice. Occasionally she would lift her dark eyes and

THE JUDGE.

look at her counsel or the Judge. She never turned her head in the direction of her husband or of the jury. She began by telling of the visit of Mrs. Swinton to the Noll cottage and of the impudence of Mary Donnelly, who asked her (Mrs. Hamilton) why she didn't let Hamilton alone and cease "deviling him."

"I was always afraid of Mary," said Mrs. Hamilton in a tearful voice. "I never could say that my soul was my own, and Mr. Hamilton upheld her." The witness put her handkerchief to her eyes and sobbed. Hamilton never moved a muscle. "She said," continued Mrs. Hamilton, "that she would cut my heart out and show it to me. The reason I told her to get an officer that day was because I had discharged her and if she made any trouble I could have her taken away."

Then coming down to the assault, the witness described how she had heard "my baby" crying, and knew

that Mary had neglected it. This testimony was given in a dreamy voice and with an air of weariness. "I was pasting a letter in a scrap-book when Mary came in and lifted me out of the chair by the hair. We called up Mrs. Rupp and with her assistance got Mary out. Yes, I had that white wrapper on (when a torn garment of fine texture was shown) and that is where it was torn by Mary.

"Was the skirt torn too?" asked the lawyer. There was a very audible titter all around as this remarkable knowledge of women's wear was displayed.

The witness admitted that she had struck at Mary Donnelly with the whiskey bottle. "I picked up the knife and ran to the baluster crying for Mrs. Rupp to bring up my baby. 'It's not the baby, it's you I mean to kill!' cried the nurse. With that she came rushing at me. She threw me on the bed and grabbed me by the throat while she put one knee on my stomach. Then I knew she meant to kill me. Mr. Hamilton was between us, with his back to me, trying to push her off. I cut her with a knife. I didn't know that she was cut at all, for when the policeman came I said I wanted her arrested."

"When did you first meet Mr. Hamilton?" was the Prosecutor's first thrust.

The defense objected, but the Court admitted the question. After twenty seconds' pause Mrs. Hamilton replied:

"I met him at a friend's house."

"What was the name of that

friend?"

Silence for half a minute. Question repeated.

"Mrs. Brown, I think. I went there with a friend—a Miss Craycraft."

"Was Mrs. Brown a married lady?"

"Yes, sir."

"When did you meet Mr. Hamilton again?"

"On the street, I think."

"And next?"

"At my boarding-house on East Twenty-first street. I don't remember the number."

"Are your father and mother living?"

The witness gets red in the face. "No, sir," she replied.

"How were you supposed before you met Mr. Hamilton?"

"By money left by my father."

"Where did your father live?"

An appealing look to counsel. Objection overruled.

"Sullivan County, Pa."

"How long have you lived in New York?"

"Two years before meeting Mr. Hamilton."

"Before that where did you live?"

Another long pause. Then: "In Scioto Vale. I moved thence to New York. "

"What relationship does Mrs. Swinton bear to you, Mrs. Hamilton?"

"None. She's not related to me. I met her six or seven years ago in a boarding-house. No. 10 East Twenty-eighth street. She had a child or grandchild (with a yawn) and a young man with her. Don't

know whether he is her son or not."

"What is his name?"

"Joshua Mann."

"When were you married to Mr. Hamilton?"

"In January, 1889, at Patterson, N.J."

"How old was that baby when Mary Donnelly came to you as a nurse?"

"Three months."

Tacitly admits the imposition.

"Where was the child born?"

"Northern part of Pennsylvania."

"What town?"

Mrs. Hamilton became very much distressed, and asked Capt. Perry whether she must answer. Hamilton was listening with all his ears. The Court ruled that if the answer tended to criminate the witness she need not answer, and she reluctantly admitted that her answer would tend to criminate her.

"Are you the mother of that child?"

This was a deeper thrust even than the other. Mrs. Hamilton's assumed artlessness left her instantly. Again she appealed with a look, and again her counsel came to her rescue. She was excused from answering on the same ground as before. Robert Ray never lifted his eyes.

Officers Biddle and Loder were recalled on an unimportant point and the defense rested. The Court will charge the jury to-morrow. Mr. Hamilton and his friend Vollmer went to New York tonight. The probabilities are that Robert Ray will never see his wife again until he meets her in a divorce court.

PUT AWAY FOR A TIME.

ROBERT RAY HAMILTON'S ADVENTURESS-WIFE SENTENCED TO TRENTON PENITENTIARY.

TWO YEARS IN CONVICT'S GARB.

CALMLY SHE HEARD HER FATE, BUT WEPT BITTERLY IN HER CELL.

SHE DENOUNCES HER HUSBAND.

WHILE TRYING TO MAKE A STATEMENT TO THE WORLD SHE WAS LED AWAY BY THE SHERIFF—THE JUDGE BORROWED A LESSON FROM THE MAYBRICK TRIAL AND ARGUED AS WELL AS CHARGED—ONE OF INSPECTOR BYRNES' MEN WAITED WITH A WARRANT TO ARREST THE WOMAN, HAD SHE BEEN ACQUITTED.

[SPECIAL TO THE WORLD].

MAY'S LANDING, N.J., SEPT. 19.—"Two years in state prison at Trenton."

Evangeline Hamilton, wife of the representative of the Murray Hill district, heard her doom pronounced this afternoon by a cold-faced Judge, without the slightest semblance of emotion. Indeed her countenance was so thoroughly impassive that the natural sneer which has always hovered about the corners of her Cupid-arched mouth was plainly perceptible. There were undried tears in her eyes, and her hands were clasped nervously over her handkerchief, as they were yesterday, while she listened to the testimony of the man who sought to shield her while he held up before the whole world the evidence of his most peculiar and unaccountable infatuation. The assumed artlessness which the defendant had shown up on the witness stand during the examination, which so prejudiced her cause, had entirely deserted her. Albeit she did not show in her outward demeanor that her spirit had been broken, nevertheless it was patent to the most ordinary observer of human nature that she had cried quits.

She was laboring under a strongly suppressed emotion when she was brought into court by the surly Sheriff of Atlanta County. It has been generally expected by the gossips and newsmongers assembled to hear the verdict that the judgment would be "Not guilty." But it was pretty clearly foreshadowed in the WORLD to-day, that the testimony of Mrs. Hamilton herself, its disingenuous presentation, her assumption of a modesty which her previous course of life did not bear out, her affectation of the rôle of la grande dame, would result to her disadvantage.

A temporary delay of travel on the West Jersey Railroad between

Atlantic City and May's Landing, caused by the derailment of a freight car, prevented the appearance of either Judge or jury until 11 o'clock, an hour after the time set for the winding up with the case. Like auditors in front of a slow curtain, the farmers in the whitewashed Court-House showed some signs of impatience—not by stamping of feet or clapping of hands, as the gallery gods in a Bowery theatre would give to show approbation or disapprobation, but by whisperings, nudgings and guttural sounds peculiar only to the residents of South and West Jersey. When he did arrive, following out the procedure of the preceding day, Presiding Judge Reed lost no time in getting to work and directed the Sheriff to bring in the prisoner.

SHE DECLINED TO GO TO COURT.

Capt. Perry arose and with a bland smile said:

"The defendant says that she doesn't want to be here."

There was a pause of ten seconds and Judge Reed wrinkled his brow. No further order was given and Mrs. Hamilton was not brought into court. It had been arranged that counsel for the defense and legal representative of the State should each occupy thirty minutes in summing up. Judge Reed believes in expediting justice in whatever circuit he may sit. Capt. Perry, understanding this thoroughly, started immediately after the Judge had given his favorite command, "Proceed." The attorney for the defense made a good speech. "My work," said he,

MRS. HAMILTON'S COUSIN.

"is about done; the last of this sad occurrence is about finished. I am here for the purpose of defending Mrs. Robert Ray Hamilton against one charge alone, as specified in the bill of indictment—atrocious assault and battery. That is all. Whatever else may have come before you should not enter into your minds. You are to be the judges of the facts and the law."

Judge Reed has been in the anteroom part of the time Attorney Perry was making his speech. He came in just as this sentence was completed, and Judge Byrnes whispered something in his ear. The brow the presiding Judge became corrugated again.

THE JUDGE TAKES A HAND.

"Do I understand you to say, Mr. Perry," said Judge Reed, "that the jury is to be the judge of the law in this case?"

Counsellor Perry slid very gracefully out of the position in which he had unwittingly placed himself and continued the argument. He reviewed the evidence exhaustively, putting special stress on the threats of Nurse Donnelly when she said, according to the testimony of Mr. and Mrs. Hamilton: "I will kill her. Let me at her. I will kill the——." Then, as a peroration, the counsellor quoted from the speech of Portia in "The Merchant of Venice." "The quality of mercy is not strained," etc.

Even those rare old bits of bric-à-brac, the tipstaves, look preternaturally solemn as the eloquent counsellor finished his half-hour's speech. Prosecutor Thompson's presentation of the case for the State was not marked by any extraordinary brilliancy. He did not appear to have studied the circumstances of the assault thoroughly. At times his review of the evidence was altogether faulty, but he was helped out

A GROUP OF JERSEY CONSTABLES.

a good deal by the charge of Judge Reed.

FOLLOWED JUDGE STEPHEN'S EXAMPLE.

It would be fair to say that the charge of the presiding Judge, like that of Judge Stephen in the Maybrick case, partook more of the nature of an argument that it did of a simple laying down of points of law and a review of the evidence. Mrs. Hamilton looked glum enough when the jury left the box in the charge of a constable, who was sworn, according to the old English formula, to see that the twelve men should have "neither meat nor drink excepting water until they should have arrived at a conclusion concerning the guilt or innocence of the accused." Capt. Perry had made one good point in his summing up which the prosecutor had attempted to combat, but failed, and Court stepped in and smashed it. Perry

THE PROSECUTING ATTORNEY.

INTERIOR OF COURT-HOUSE.

asked why the State had not called the husband of Mrs. Hamilton as a witness.

"Oh," said the Prosecutor, "I would not put a husband up as a witness against his wife. The law does not permit it."

"Well," retorted Capt. Perry, quickly, "you put him under $600 bail as a witness and then discharged him. I then subpoenaed him as a witness. Why did you hold the man by surety if you did not intend to use him for your side?"

It was here that the Court took a hand.

"I would not have permitted him to testify, anyhow," said Judge Reed.

In his charge the Judge defined the elements of the defense of self-defense and explained the difference between the grades of atrocious assault and simple assault as defined in the statute. At 2 o'clock the jury was ready for deliberation. Counsellor Perry asked the court to instruct the jurors more fully as to the alleged threats made by Nurse Donnelly immediately preceding her third entrance into Mrs. Hamilton's bed-chamber. Judge Reed complied with this briefly, and then, when the defendant's attorney asked for further instructions, the Judge said:

"I've charged all I'm going to charge."

Pending the return of the jury trial to test the ownership of a dog was argued, and its amusing features relieved a good deal of the monopoly of the morning's work. The Hamilton jury had its verdict ready at 3 o'clock, while the dog case was still on. The defendant, pale, nervous and trembling, came into the court-room at 3.15 o'clock.

"Gentlemen of the jury, have you agreed upon a verdict?"

There was just as much solemnity in the clerk's tone, and just as much of a hush in the court-room, as though the cause were a capital one and a woman were being tried for

BROUGHT INTO COURT.

her life. The jury, too, looked solemn and two of them almost tearful. The foreman announced when questioned according to the form: "We find the defendant, Evangeline Hamilton, guilty as charged in the bill of indictment."

Mrs. Hamilton sat perfectly still as the foreman spoke. She did not betray even by movement of a facial muscle whatever emotion she may have felt.

"In that dog case," said Judge Reed, suddenly, "we find for the plaintiff in the sum of $25."

It was rather a prosaic interjection and the corners of Mrs. Hamilton's mouth twitched just perceptibly.

The defendant was then directed to stand up and Judge Reed in a very few words reviewed the offense of which she had been convicted, and sentenced her.

"The judgment of this court is," said he, "that while the penalty could have been ten years imprisonment for the crimes of which you have been found guilty, the behavior of the nurse Mary Ann Donnelly was such that it is regarded as a mitigating circumstance. The sentence of the Court is that you be imprisoned in the State prison at Trenton for the term of two years and that you will stand committed until the cost of this prosecution are paid."

LISTENING TO THE VERDICT.

Mrs. Hamilton looked as though she were dazed. She glanced around the room and beckoned to THE WORLD correspondent and attempted to make a statement to him.

SHE WOULD MAKE A STATEMENT.

"My husband," said she, "was too fond of Nurse Donnelly. Mrs. Swinton is not guilty of any conspiracy, as charged in the city of New York. I"—

At this moment the autocrat of Atlantic County, Sheriff Smith Johnson, came out of the ante-room in the rear of the Court-House and peremptorily ordered Deputy Sims to remove Mrs. Hamilton instantly and lock her up. She was taken out and put in the attic under the roof of the Sheriff's dwelling. There she begged and pleaded but she might be permitted to make a statement for publication in THE WORLD, inasmuch as her husband had received extraordinary consideration in the public print. The Sheriff refused to grant the request.

Mrs. Hamilton had not been back in her upstairs prison for more than half an hour before she broke down and wept bitterly. Then her mood changed if she began upbraiding and denouncing her husband and his friends. About 5 o'clock she had calmed down considerably and was composed enough to go back to her favorite dissipation—smoking cigarettes.

Detective Sergeant McCluskey, of Inspector Byrnes's staff, waiting with two warrants at May's Landing until the verdict was rendered. His intention was to arrest Mrs. Hamilton, in case of acquittal, on the charge of conspiracy with Mrs. Swinton and Joshua Mann to palm off on Robert Ray Hamilton a bogus heir to his estates.

Counsellor Perry has not yet determined his future action as to his convicted client. He took no exceptions during the trial and cannot apply for a writ of error. The court adjourned to-day for the term. The only recourse of the defendant's lawyer is to apply for a writ of certiorari in the Supreme Court. Whether he will do this or not he declines to say.

THE KNIFE.

The New York World
Saturday, September 21, 1889

SHE IS TIRED OF THE COUNTY JAIL.

MRS. EVA L. HAMILTON IN GOOD SPIRITS AND READY TO GO TO THE STATE PRISON.

[SPECIAL TO THE WORLD].

MAY'S LANDING, N.J., SEPT. 20.— The sensational rumor was spread about the village to-day that Mrs. Hamilton had attempted to commit suicide. It was utterly without foundation. Instead of being depressed, Mrs. Hamilton was in unusually good spirits, much better, in fact, than at any time during her imprisonment. She was disappointed because she had not been permitted by Sheriff Johnson to make a statement to the World. The discourtesy of the pig-headed official has made him a laughing stock among sensible people. He does not know, apparently, how to answer a question civilly, and his foolish display of anger in discharging his deputy because the deputy acted like a man has lost him several of the few friends he possessed.

The law permits the convicted woman to remain in the county jail for ten days before being taken to Trenton to begin serving her term. It is hardly probable, however, that she will avail herself of this privilege, but she will ask to go within a day or two. She smoked cigarettes incessantly to-day, and was supplied with the usual quota of morphine. It is said now that her seemingly assumed air of ennui on the witness stand was not to impress the jury but was due to the fact that she had taken an extra large dose of the drug to brace her up.

Mrs. Hamilton has not given up hope and expects that her lawyer will make further efforts in her behalf in the near future. Capt. Perry said to-day that he had not yet determined fully what his future course in the case would be.

THE NEW YORK WORLD
SUNDAY, SEPTEMBER 22, 1889

FROM HOVEL TO WEALTH.

WHAT AN EXTRAORDINARY STORY THIS IS OF ROBERT RAY HAMILTON AND HIS WIFE.

THE WOMAN'S EVIL HISTORY.

IT HAS NOT BEFORE BEEN TOLD, AND THE LIKE OF IT PERHAPS NEVER WAS BEFORE.

NOW TWO YEARS IN CONVICT GARB.

A FRECKLE-FACED CHILD IN A PENNSYLVANIA LUMBER CAMP— PRACTICALLY WITHOUT EDUCATION, BUT WITH REMARKABLE SHREWDNESS OF INTELLECT—WHAT WAS IT THAT FASCINATED A MAN OF ROBERT RAY HAMILTON'S REFINEMENT, CULTIVATION AND SOCIAL CONNECTIONS?—PHOTOGRAPHS OF THE WOMAN AT VARIOUS STAGES OF HER CAREER—HER FATHER, MOTHER AND UNCOUTH COUNTRY BROTHER—FOUR ACTUAL ATTEMPTS AT MURDER AND PERHAPS TWO MORE CONTEMPLATED—THE MEN SHE HAS RUINED AND HOMES SHE HAS WRECKED—SEE WHAT ANTECEDENTS THIS UNUSUALLY SUCCESSFUL ADVENTURESS HAD!

[SPECIAL TO THE WORLD].

WILKESBARRE, PA., SEPT. 21.—While Eva Hamilton was in the little attic-room of the jail at May's Landing, waiting for the trial which ended the other day in her sentence to the State Prison to Trenton, she said to the Sheriff's wife:

"Let me see Ray Hamilton for twenty minutes and I'll win him back, with the world against me!"

It was the belief of all the newspaper correspondents who reported this trial and the events that led to it that the woman's boast was well-founded. There seems no doubt that Mr. Hamilton's infatuation for the depraved creature remains almost as strong as when he married her. His better judgment fought with this infatuation and won, but he obviously did not dare to risk a personal interview with her alone. The friend who accompanied him acknowledged all this to be true.

As described to her intimates by the Sheriff's wife there was a ring of defiance in the tone and a glitter in the eye of this wife of the representative of the most noted political district in the United States as she made this challenge. She knew her power and she asked for an opportunity to exercise it. In a moment of frenzy she had marred the success of one of the most remarkable plots ever revealed in actual life.

The vicious thrust she made with that double-edged hunting-knife not only laid bare the vitals of her intended victim, but cut the bonds that bound up the history of the most infamously clever conspiracy—a conspiracy complete and its details and diabolical its intention.

The extraordinary attraction which so depraved a creature had and has for a man of Robert Ray Hamilton's antecedents and social connections and personal refinement of mind and manner is a curious psychological study. It was worthwhile to trace the woman's history to her infancy, and this the correspondent has done at her birthplace, some sixty miles from this town.

In one of the lumber camps of Northern Pennsylvania this woman was born in May, 1860. It was in a log house in Bradford County, about eight miles northwest of the village of Wyalusing, which is on the banks of the Susquehanna River and a station on the line of the Lehigh Valley Railroad. Her father, who is still living, and, old as he is, the terror of the village when drunk, is named

THE STEELE CABIN.
(From a Photograph taken for THE WORLD.)

William W. Steele. Her mother's name is Lydia A. Steele. At the time of the child's birth the father was engaged as a wood-chopper and bark-peeler in the wilderness. The babe was named Eva Lydia Steele. There was no christening, because the Steele's "didn't believe in such tom-foolery."

The family consisted of the father and mother and six children—Joseph L. Steele, who is married and resides in the lumber woods of Michigan; Thomas W. Steele, who resides at Lacyville, Wyoming County, Pa.; Samuel T. Steele, who is about twenty-three years of age, and Benjamin E. Steele, who both remain under the paternal roof; Alice, who married Eugene Foote, cousin of Supt. Foote, of the Delaware and Hudson Canal Company's coal mines near Wilkesbarre, and Eva Lydia.

Eva was just like the rest of the children in the camp—dirty, unkempt and spindle-shanked. When she came to the age of nine her parents removed to Bernice, a coal-mining hamlet in the forests of Sullivan County. The father obtained employment in a sawmill, and the children were sent to the little log school-house at the foot of Tyler Mountain. For three years the child appeared to be stupid enough. She had one half-witted brother, and the folks about the village thought that Eva "wan't goin' to be bright" Entering her thirteenth year, Eva seemed to brighten up with a great suddenness. She developed a knowledge of human vices and follies far beyond her years and astonished her teachers at times with her shrewd conclusions. The outside world was a vast fairyland to the girl. She had never been ten miles from home and her imaginings of what life in great cities was like, framed in words, kept her companions interested for hours.

At the age of fifteen the freckle-faced, lanky child had developed into an astonishingly graceful woman, symmetrical from her high instep to her well-poised head, and it did not take her long to discover that her charms were the envy of her less fortunate sisters and the admiration of the rough miners of the town. With the physical development grew a mental fungus—a violent, unreasoning temper, blind to consequences when once aroused. When in one of these frenzied moods Eva Steele was the terror of the town, young as she was.

One day there came a handsome commercial traveler from Williamsport. He saw the village belle, and, being the first man from that fairyland of which she had dreamed so often, captured Eva's heart without half trying. Perhaps she had been a virtuous girl until then. With the salesman she fled to Oswego, N.Y., where she remained for four days, and was then deserted.

Her mother said to the correspondent: "I never knew a better behaved girl than Eva was while she was at home." The old woman has a picture of the girl sent back to the Sullivan County cabin just after she had

EVA STEELE AT SEVENTEEN.
(The New York photograph.)

reached New York after two years of wild dissipation. She was seventeen when it was taken and here it is:

After her betrayal and desertion the usual result followed. She entered a house of ill-fame and, perhaps stung by the knowledge that she had been conquered and then scorned, gave her fiery temper full play. This ended in being driven into the street. With the few dollars she had in her pockets she made her way to Waverley, N.Y., and became an inmate of a notorious resort kept by Mrs. Washburn. Exhibitions of that temper which seemed to grow more murderous with its growth again set her adrift and she sought refuge with a Mme. Meade in South Waverley.

A married man and a prominent

figure in that little town became infatuated with her. Refused a pecuniary favor by this lover, who had been drained dry, she shot at him. The bullet narrowly missed his brain. It sliced off a goodly portion of his left ear, however, and his cries of murder brought half a dozen inmates, who disarmed the infuriated creature before she could fire a second shot. Again she was driven forth and her trunk was held for an unpaid board bill. Eva had no notion of leaving her effects behind, and she returned, battered down the door and demanded her property. The landlady capitulated.

WAS THERE A MARRIAGE?

From Waverley, Eva returned to Bernice, the home of her parents. There she fell in with Walter Parsons, the twenty-year-old son of C.A. Parsons, Superintendent of the Bernice Coal Company, of Boston. The conquest was an immediate one, and two days later she ran off with him to Elmira. The family of the young man heard of his escapade and every effort was made to bring him to a sense of shame, but without avail. Then came a report that the couple had been married. This set the boy's mother to work, and the filial love, which had not been altogether smothered, brought him back to Bernice—and alone.

Meantime Eva had by some means or other managed to reach New York. Her stay in the metropolis on this, her first visit, was brief. She went to Tawanda, Pa., and was arrested there for stealing a pair of gold bracelets from a jeweler named Hindleman. Eva appealed to Walter Parsons, the young man mentioned above, who induced his father to compromise with the jeweler, and the scandal was hushed up. From that time until 1882 Eva went from one small town to another, living in bagnios, until a quarrel and an attempt to shoot or cut would result in her dismissal. Her wretched temper seemed to increase with her beauty.

The latter part of the year named found her in Elmira. She was accompanied by a pretty girl who called herself Katie May. Eva gave her surname as Parsons. The two girls were expensively attired. The adventuress had developed a strong liking for liquor. Many was the wild debauch in that house, with Eva the central figure, and the slaves around her men prominent in business and

AS MRS. EVA PARSONS.
(From a photograph.)

politics in Chemung County. The brother-in-law of the proprietor of the big dry-goods store in Elmira met her one day while she was shopping. Like scores of others, he was instantly smitten. Eva nearly ruined him. About this time the married lover who had had a piece of his ear shot off appeared on the scene, and became obtrusive. He was tolerated while his money lasted, and then Eva shot at him again.

Her aim this time was bad, and the ball went wide of its mark. She had aimed a second time and was about to fire when she was disarmed by the proprietress of the place, who approached her from behind.

It was then discovered that this female fury carried, as an ornament in her hair, a keen stiletto. She tried to use it one day on one of her frail sisters and she was given notice to leave.

With the young man who met her in the dry-goods store she came to the city and lived with him in apartments on East Thirty-first street until her demands compelled him to make an assignment for the benefit of his creditors. Then he was dismissed. Following this came a liaison with an elderly New Yorker, who lavished the most costly present upon the hovel-born adventuress, and remained completely under her power until his home was broken up and his wife died of a broken heart.

WAS HER HAMILTON MARRIAGE BIGAMY?

It was shortly after that she met Robert Ray Hamilton; but, before that, the fellow Joshua Mann, whom,

true to her birth and unique characteristics, she preferred to the gentleman who loved her so well that he married her. Here is an episode that illustrates just what she was and what were her home surroundings, and it was the events that happened at this time which the grandson of Alexander Hamilton may use to break the bonds that bind him in marriage to this creature.

Shortly after her reported marriage to Parsons, thirteen years ago, her parents removed from Bernice to Michigan, where the son was working in the pine forests, and after a few years spent there returned to where they had formally lived in Bradford County. It was while her parents resided near Wyalusing in 1885 that Eva, accompanied by Joshua Mann, visited them. Mann quarrelled with her brother Thomas, committed an assault upon him, was arrested, and is now under indictment in Wyoming County.

Her sister, Mrs. Eugene Foote, resided at this time in the suburbs of Wilkesbarre, in a locality called the "Five Points," and received a visit from her sister Eva and Joshua Mann. The sisters quarrelled and accused each other of various unmentionable offenses. Until August, 1888, little had been heard of her until she came to visit her parents who had removed from Bradford County to Dallas Township in Luzerne County about two and a half miles from that beautiful summer resort, Harvey's Lake. The house in which her parents reside is built of boards with battens over the crack, of which a cut is given above, taken from a photograph.

Eva and Joshua Mann spent two weeks at the home of her parents, and passed as man and wife. On the Saturday they were to depart they went for a drive around Harvey's Lake—Joshua, Eva, Mrs. Steele and Mr. Steele, whom Joshua called "Pap." When the party arrived at the north corner of the lake, instead of returning home they continued their ride to a small village about four miles from the lake called Slabtown. Here they stopped at the Rock Hotel and drank freely of liquor, carried into the room by Josh Mann, and to pay for which Eva handed him the money from a large roll she carried. While they were drinking at the Rock Hotel a butcher's wagon driven by the local butcher, Mr. Charles Johnson, drove up in front of the hotel. Rather as a tipsy joke,

THE FATHER.
(From a photograph.)

perhaps, than out of regard for her parents, she purchased a leg of lamb and a large beef roast for them. After paying the butcher Eva invited him to "take something," which invitation the gallant butcher accepted. Josh and Eva subsequently, while at the hotel, hire Johnson to take them and the trunk, to Dallas; Johnson replied, when first asked to take them, that he had no vehicle other than the butcher wagon, but if they were satisfied to ride in it he would be pleased to accommodate them. Johnson was evidently taken aback when they wanted to ride in the meat-wagon, for he saw that the woman was richly clad. But he drove them home the whole four miles, the trunk was hastily packed and placed in the meat-wagon, the man and woman took their places on the seat, Johnson mounted to the wagon-tongue, resting his back against the dashboard, and away they started for Dallas. Eva and Joshua had intended to remain at the tavern in Dallas until Monday, but after they had had more liquor, which was paid for by him, Eva handing him the money, the landlord, Mr. Phillip Raub, concluded they were not fit for him, and told them the house was full. They had said to him that they were man and wife. Then they told Johnson he must take them and the trunk four miles further down the "pike" to the Forrest House, better known as the Ice Cave Hotel, kept by Joseph Harter. There they registered themselves as Joshua Mann and wife, and secured quarters until Monday.

Meanwhile old man Steele had also got drunk, and, pistol in hand, had started for the home of the Johnsons, half a mile distant. He had somehow persuaded himself that his daughter had been robbed. Reaching the Johnson house he stopped in the middle of the road, and, flourishing his weapon, declared that he had come to kill the butcher. The female portion of the household were much frightened, but Mr. Peter Johnson, father of Charles, went out to the front gate, and demanded to "know the meaning of such conduct and language which he was not accustomed to." Steele said that Charles Johnson had stolen $180, and a trunk from his daughter, Eva.

"If Charles has stolen anything," replied Mr. Johnson, "go and have him arrested. You needn't talk about shooting, and get away from here."

MRS. STEELE AND SAMUEL.
(From a photograph taken last week.)

The old man started towards home, and then drove Mrs. Steele, his wife, out of the house in her nightclothes and closed and locked the door. The poor woman made her way to Neighbor Johnson's and there was provided with clothing. Charles Johnson had meanwhile returned home and heard of Steele's charges. He drove over at once to Dallas, went before C.H. Cook, a Justice of the Peace, swore out a warrant, found a Constable, told him to arrest Steele, bring him before Squire Cook on Monday morning, as the Squire wouldn't wait up that night, and also to subpoena Mr. and Mrs. Joshua Mann, who were at the Ice Cave Hotel, as witnesses. At the hearing of the case the question of the relationship existing between Eva and Joshua Mann came up. Eva declared in court that they were man and wife. This declaration on the part of his daughter brought old man Steele to his feet, and he denied in the most positive language that they were married, where upon Eva said: "Joshua and I are as much man and wife as are my father and mother." The case was finally disposed of on a payment of the cost by the defendant Steele, the money being furnished by his daughter. After the trial Mrs. Steele returned home with her husband, and Joshua Mann and Eva boarded the next train for New York.

Eva's mother says that Eva was "a handsome woman and a good woman if she had a mind to be." When asked if Eva had ever sent her any of the large sums of money received from Hamilton, she replied that Eva had not, though sums which Eva could very well have spared out of all the money she squandered would've done her parents a world of good. The mother adds that Eva kept up a running sort of correspondence with her since leaving home, having written from New York, while she was in Europe, and from California, but that no letter had been received since she left California. The first they knew of her return East was when the papers published an account of the assault in Atlantic City and her arrest. Mrs. Steele says she never knew that Eva had a baby, and did not hear of her being in Elmira last Winter. She says that when Eva and Joshua were at her home last August (1888) there was no evidence, as far as she knew, that Eva was in a delicate condition. The child was supposed to have been born to her in the following December.

A few months ago while drinking at the Rock Hotel, at Slabtown, the old man Steele became thoroughly drunk and fired several shots from the road into the bar-room. For this escapade he was arrested and placed under bail to appear at the Quarter Sessions Court of Wyoming County, to be held in Tunkhannock, on Nov. 14, when he will be tried.

That the attempt to take one life in Atlantic City saved two other lives admits of very little doubt now. The vulgar brawl between two women prevented the consummation of a double diabolism, the

ROBERT RAY HAMILTON.
[From a Recent Photograph.]

doing away with Hamilton first, and the puling babe that had been imposed upon him as bone of his bone and flesh of his flesh next. All the evidence points that way. All the circumstances surrounding the scandal substantiate it.

The fraudulent heir to the Hamilton estates given its quietus, the conspirators could enjoy the rich fruit of the cunningly contrived and almost successful plot. But the frenzy of a mad moment destroyed in a flash all the planning of three years, and gave to the world a tale so strange, so horrible, that it would be altogether incredible were it not supported by cold, incontrovertible facts.

It is true that it took Hamilton some time to realize that he had been in such imminent peril, but when the truth came to him in all its hideousness he was staggered. Nevertheless he feared to trust himself within the range of the charms of the woman who had so enslaved him. Hers was no idle threat.

"Let me see Ray Hamilton for twenty minutes, and I'll win him back, with the world against me."

The victim dared not trust himself. A caress, a kiss, a dozen soft words, and he would again be completely in the toils as ever the Chevalier de Greux was with the fair and fickle Lescaut. The revelation of the plot would have had no weight. His former danger would have been looked upon as a dream. Under the magnetic influence of those soft, velvety eyes he would have forgotten self, reputation, honor itself. Let the tigerish enchantress but once wind her arms around his neck, and the real past would have been forgotten in the contemplation of the false future. Robert Ray Hamilton knew this and by a strong effort kept aloof. To strengthen his determination he had a trusted friend constantly by his side, a man of more resolution than himself, who watched him like a hawk and had a wet blanket ready to throw whenever the slightest symptoms of yielding became apparent. He won the battle with self unwillingly and was saved.

Is it not an extraordinary drama?

Take the story in its entirety, now that it has been dovetailed together and is complete, and see if Dumas, or Sue, or any of the weavers of the ingenious fabric of French fiction, have ever produced a stranger story. From prologue to dénouement it bristles with startling situations, dramatic coloring,

and the essence of perverted human nature. It opens, as the French playwright would have opened it, in a gilded palace of sin. An adventuress, rich in those physical charms which attract men of certain temperament, lay in wait there for a victim. This woman, like all of her class, has a lover on whom she lavishes a wealth of genuine affection. He is a loutish, ignorant fellow, all animal, and with low intellectual development. Back of the lover stands the old woman of the play, the hag, "the cunning, cozzening queen."

She is the master planner. It is her active, scheming brain and her accurate judgment that are appealed to when a bold stroke is to be made or a critical situation considered. Then enters the principal character, about which all the others revolve—the scion of a noble house, the representative in legislative halls of an aristocratic constituency—a man of wealth, refinement, culture. Directly in contrast he stands with the low-browed chap, who acts the part of the villain. This is the prologue.

Then the play begins. The adventuress, shyly coy, evinces a regard for the distinguished stranger, and he, poor dupe, feels a gratification that he should charm such a woman. He finds her bright and entertaining. She artfully conceals her ignorance, and her superficiality is palmed off as depth. A week's acquaintance and the fair-faced schemer confesses with blushes and tears that she is in love, madly in love with her newly found friend.

She bewails her fate and threatens self-destruction because her passion is a hopeless one. The pinnacle she seeks is too high, and she must go on living and loving without hope. Better the grave than this. Better death than loveless life.

For two days the victim basks in the smiles of the siren. For two days the spell is woven about him, and when the parting time comes his whole nature is changed. Infatuation has taken the place of sober judgment; enslavement the place of independence. From that time on the principal character plays a dual part—a Jekyll with the enchantress and her kind, a Hyde with the people in his own class and station.

The next scene shows the stately halls where the lawmakers for the people gather. The man with two characters is there, the champion of morality, the upholder of the good, the denouncer of the bad. He seeks to promote morality by statutory enactment. The social evil receives his condemnation and vice in every form his stern disapproval. Then the scene shifts, and the conspirators are discovered. The loutish lover is being fondled and caressed by and the master planner looks on with pleased satisfaction.

The second act brings the stars of the play together again. The enthrallment is then complete. Demands have been made and complied with. Wild whims have been gratified and the adventuress, finding her power limitless, makes preparations for her first coup.

With honeyed words and passionate kisses Robert Ray Hamilton is asked to make Eva Brill his wife. Thoroughly under the control of the stronger will he consents and bestows an honored name on a miserable creature all unworthy to bear it. Then another shift and the conspirators are together again. This time there is no caressing, no fondling. There is a whispered consultation lasting far into the night. When the human harpies part they laugh and rub their hands together gleefully.

THE PURCHASED INFANT.

A new character appears in the third act. It is a babe end—a whining, miserable thing—that is presented as the offspring of Ray Hamilton. Public duties call the man away, and during his absence the child gasps out its life. A second babe appears. It, too, goes the way of all flesh. And then comes a third substitute. It is at this point that the interest becomes intense. The deceived husband is almost at the door. The third child is so unlike the first that it cannot take the part, and so a fourth is procured and just in time. The doors swing open and the husband and father enters. The screeching infant is thrust into his arms, and he is made to believe that it is his own flesh and blood, and the identical child that he kissed good-by when he left his home. The deception is successful, and then preparations are begun for the master stroke. Another character is brought on—the nurse. Mistress and made intuitively recognize in each other the same characteristics. The one forgets her assumed dignity, the other her menial station. They rail at each other like very drabs. The servant discovers the secret of her mistress, and holds it as a weapon of offense and defense.

The time is almost ripe for the carrying out of the principal plot. The scene has changed from the metropolis to far-off California. The loutish lover has, through the influence and power of the siren, been permitted to form a part of the household. So has the beldame, and the husband who has become under complete control, permits the usurpation of his rights without a protest. Another shift to a city by the sea. All the characters are on the stage at once. It has been determined that the husband shall die, and the manner of his taking off is discussed and settled upon. Poison is to be the means, and with her own fair hands this modern Borgia is to administer it.

THE ATTEMPTED MURDER AND TRIAL.

Then comes the overthrowing of vice and the elevation of virtue. Could anything in the mimic stage have been brought to a cleverer climax? Has the fictitious light behind the foot-lights ever shown a stronger situation? Mistress and servant quarrel. There comes the flash of the glittering blade, a shriek of agony, and the conspiracy is laid bare.

A court-house, a stern judge, a weeping woman, a deceived but still infatuated husband. Banishment for two years closes the set. The dénouement has not yet been presented. The scene will be in a divorce court, and then the characters will speak their last lines, make their bow and retire and the drama will be ended and the curtain rung down.

Are not all the elements of the play there?

Evangeline Hamilton's remarkable deception in seeking to palm off four separate children as her own when she never gave birth to a baby in her life, is without parallel in any country. The nearest approach to it is the famous case of Lady Gooch in England some years ago, and that of Mme. Tischki in St. Petersburg in 1854. The English gentlewoman had prayed in vain for children. She had journeyed to Smyrna and eaten the seeds of the sacred pomegranate that are supposed to make women fruitful. The most famous physicians of the day were consulted without avail. The husband of the barren wife began to grow cold and indifferent.

He was anxious that his name should not die out, and that there should be an heir to his estates. One day, after he had given up all hope and a grown almost cruel in his indifference, he received the welcome intelligence that his desire would in all probability be gratified. A doctor—not particularly eminent and, as was afterwards discovered, not particularly truthful, corroborated the intelligence, and strongly urged the temporary separation of husband and wife. This advice was followed, Lord Gooch taking a trip to India.

On his return he was overjoyed to

find a male heir awaiting his coming. It had been born to lady Gooch, he was told, three weeks before his arrival. The physician who was a party to the deception demanded an extra fee of £500 from the pretended mother, in addition to the £1,000 he had already received. He received it, and extorted large sums thereafter regularly for a year. One night in his cup he betrayed the secret. The deceived husband was informed and frightened his wife into confessing her crime. Disgrace and divorce followed, and in six months the nobleman died of a broken heart.

Mme. Tischki played a similar trick that was followed by the most deplorable consequences. When her husband discovered how he had been deceived he stabbed his wife to the heart and strangled the bogus heir in its cradle.

There is nothing, however, in any of these that approaches the strange romance of Robert Ray Hamilton's life. The descendent of the most notable figure in American history—a figure that stood on the same intellectual plane with William Pitt—it surpasses belief that he should have been duped as he was. Not one bogus baby, but four of them! Think of it. See the incredulous smile of every matron in the land as she reads these lines. Deceive a man as to approaching maternity, and that man constantly in the company of the woman who is fooling him?

"Impossible!" exclaims even the youngest mother. Preposterous

bosh! says the mother of half a dozen. Nevertheless it was accomplished. Robert Ray Hamilton was made to believe that his wife had become a mother and he a father, and it was not until he had received the positive assurance of a physician, who was alleged to have attended Mrs. Hamilton during her confinement, that his services were required to overcome a fit of indigestion and not too superintend the birth of a child that the husband consented to recognize his own credulity.

What makes the whole story stand out in bas-relief, a study by itself without a counterpart, is the life history of the adventuress herself. Born in a hovel of parents so ignorant as to be almost barbarians, and reared in an atmosphere which gave no opportunity to gain even the most commonplace culture, it seems strange indeed that this freckle-faced, angular, flat-breasted child should have developed into a dangerously attractive woman, who, from a pallet of straw and a diet of

AN ATTITUDE IN COURT.
(Sketched by THE WORLD artist.)

black bread and molasses came to swan's-down pillows and partridges stuffed with pearls.

THE WOMAN'S LIFE IN PRISON.

Life in the May's Landing jail has been prosaic enough for the convicted woman. Her time was spent principally in reading whatever newspapers the Sheriff's wife permitted her to see. On the fourth day of her incarceration a Bible was sent to her from an unknown and passages were marked in Deuteronomy, chapter vi, and Matthew, chapter x, for her to read.

While she turned over the leaves of the sacred volume Mrs. Hamilton calmly rolled a cigarette, and, placing it between her lips, lighted it and began to smoke. She did not become interested in either the old or the new dispensations, for she soon put the book aside and read and reread the newspapers she had gone over so many times. From the day she entered her attic prison she dosed herself with morphia. Dr. Ingraham, of Atlantic City, who attended her immediately after her arrest, was the first to discover that she was addicted to the habit. Her distress because of the temporary deprivation was so great that he prescribed for her, and regularly thereafter she obtained it from his drugstore through Mrs. Elizabeth Rupp.

When Dr. Denman B. Ingersoll visited Mrs. Hamilton to examine the bruises alleged to have been inflicted upon her by Nurse Donnelly, he tried to induce her to reduce the dose. After a good deal of persuasion he convinced the prisoner that she could get along on two grains a day—enough to kill a strong man—and that had been her quantum ever since.

HUSBAND AND WIFE.

For the anthropologist it was an interesting study—those two characters in the quaint old Court-House, as they sat within touching distance of each other and yet kept their eyes averted—these two who had been so close and once so loving. Mrs. Hamilton is not now a pretty woman as the word goes. Her features are sharp, lips thin and bloodless and her jaw is too square for feminine beauty. It is her habit to keep her eyes downcast, but when she lifts them they are wonderfully expressive. The pupil is large—extraordinarily large for an opium eater, and were it not for a shrewd squinting at the corners they might be called beautiful. Her figure is well-proportioned and slightly inclined to angularity. She has a long slender waist, and the bust below the throat is not as full as it was when she posed as Mrs. Eva Parsons.

Mr. Hamilton weighs about 130 pounds. His complexion is dark almost to sallowness. His hair and closely cropped mustache are jet black. A 6 7/8 hat will fit his head. His face is thin, chin weak and eyes small and dark. He has about 5 feet 8 inches in height and is of a delicate physique.

There is little likelihood of a stay of sentence, and within eight days she will doubtless be dressed in the prison garb at Trenton.

THE EVENING WORLD
FRIDAY, SEPTEMBER 27, 1889

SHE'S A FREAK NOW.

NURSE MARY CONNELLY IN A BOWERY DIME MUSEUM.

SHOWING THE WOUND MADE BY EVA HAMILTON'S KNIFE AND THE WHISKEY BOTTLE WHICH RAY HAMILTON'S WIFE DRANK FROM.

Nurse Mary Donnelly, who was so nearly carved to death by Mrs. Eva Hamilton at Atlantic City last month, has joined the noble army of freaks.

A museum on the Bowery has allured her, she alleges, for two weeks' engagement at a salary of $150 a week, with the privilege of a renewal, and she will begin to hold "daily receptions in Curio Hall," from 10 a.m. to 10 p.m. on Monday next.

She arrived in town from Atlantic City this morning in company with Manager Hoffman, of the Globe Dime Museum, who has been hard at work for two weeks past trying to induce her to accept his offers for her services.

At first she would have nothing to do with the proposition, but finally she yielded to the persuasion of Mrs. Rupp and her sister, and accepted the engagement which she is now confident opens for her a brilliant career upon the stage.

Nobody would have suspected the short, stout, middle-aged woman, plainly dressed in black, who was wandering around the museum this afternoon, as the woman who had played so prominent a part in the Hamilton scandal.

She talked freely with the reporter of the evening world and seemed to be quite elated at the prospect before her.

At her daily receptions she will sit between Dolly Lyons, the Circassian girl, and Maida Kennedy the albino, and will be ready to answer any questions in regard to the domestic affairs of the Hamilton family that may be put to her.

She told the reporter all she knew, and even went so far as to show him the wound in her side made by Mrs. Hamilton's hunting-knife.

It was originally purchased, she said, by Mr. Hamilton from a Norwegian sailor whom he met on his travels. Mrs. Hamilton had always taken a great fancy to it.

The management of the Museum has also secured the whiskey bottle from which Mrs. Hamilton imbibed so freely on the morning of the tragedy, and it will form a part of the exhibit.

The telegram sent from Atlantic City by Manager Hoffman announcing the engagement of Nurse Donnelly, together with her picture, is pasted up in front of the Museum, and is stared at by crowds.

That Robert Ray Hamilton is cured of his infatuation for Mrs. Swinton's protégé is evidenced by the fact that he has begun a suit in the Supreme Court to have his marriage to her annulled on the ground of fraud and the existence of a previous marriage. Judge Patterson, in Supreme Court, Chambers, yesterday granted a motion made by Mr. Hamilton's lawyers, Root & Clarke, to have the service of the summons in the case made on Mrs. Evangeline L. Hamilton by publication. It will be published for six weeks in two newspapers and a law paper, and copies of it will be mailed to Mrs. Hamilton at the county jail at May's Landing and at the State prison in Trenton.

In the complaint, which is verified by Mr. Hamilton, it is stated that the marriage of Robert Ray Hamilton to Evangeline L. Steele was performed by the Rev. Edson W. Burr of Paterson, N.J., on Jan 7, 1889. The story of the deceit practiced by Eva Steele in palming off Baby Beatrice on Hamilton as his own child is fully told, and Mr. Hamilton declares that the woman knew he would not marry her unless he believed her representations to be true. As a second cause for the annullment (sic) of the marriage it is charged that at the time the marriage between Mr. Hamilton and Eva Steele took place the woman was already married to another man. About this previous marriage Mr. Hamilton can give little proof, but he asks leave to present such evidence as he may discover in the future.

Mrs. Swinton and her son "Josh" were taken to the Central Office from the Tombs yesterday, and Inspector Byrnes and District Attorney Fellows talked with them for half an hour. They were taken back to the Tombs, and neither Mr. Fellows nor the Inspector would say why they wanted them.

THE NEW YORK WORLD
SUNDAY, SEPTEMBER 29, 1889

HAMILTON AGAIN A VICTIM.

HE ELUDES HIS FRIEND AND SUCCUMBS TO THE ADVENTURESS.

HE VISITS HER CELL AND SHE MAKES GOOD HER WORD TO "WIN HIM BACK IN TWENTY MINUTES"—NOT EVEN HER CONFESSION OF THE FRAUD OF THE BABY CHILLS HIS INFATUATION—HE WILL ATTEMPT TO FREE HER.

[SPECIAL TO THE WORLD].

MAY'S LANDING, N.J., SEPT. 28.—The hovel-born adventuress in prison has made good her boast: "Let me see Ray Hamilton for twenty minutes and I'll win him back again." She has captured what she has never lost, the heart of the man she has deceived so basely. She owns him body and soul and his enthrallment is as complete to-day as it was when he first came under the magic of Eva Steele's spell. Hamilton actually has promised to use all the influence that money could exert to have the sentence of the convicted woman lightened, and, if possible, have her pardoned. In addition to this, so completely is he in the toils, he has promised that his political power shall be used with as much freedom as his money. He has pledged himself, in the event that Leon Abbott is elected governor of New Jersey, and this seems probable, that he (Hamilton) will leave no stone unturned, will neglect no opportunity, to gain for the woman who has disgraced him her freedom. The utterance made by Mrs. Hamilton and published in the World Sunday as the text of the remarkable story of her life was founded on a knowledge of her power. Hamilton read it in New York City while in company with his friend Vallmer. It is said that his face flushed and he cast the story aside. He avoided Mr. Vallmer's society after that, and Thursday he came down here without his friend's knowledge. He was accompanied by Lawyer Clark, and his coming was a secret as possible.

Mr. Hamilton appeared to be half ashamed of himself at first and didn't show a disposition to call immediately at the Sheriff's house. Finally he swallowed half a tumbler of whiskey and with the lawyer crossed the road and entered the jail. The Sheriff's wife was surprised at first at the visit, but she led the two men upstairs without a word, and, turning the key in the lock, threw open the door. Mrs. Hamilton had seen her husband crossing the road and she was prepared to meet him. No sooner was the door of her prison opened than she was in his arms, or rather he was in her arms, for she wound herself about him like a serpent. She smothered him with kisses. She cooed and cried and laughed by turns. Hamilton was completely overcome. He returned the caresses half shyly at first, but in a few moments with much fervor. Then the couple sat down. Mrs. Hamilton gave her victim one long, earnest look, then she got up and kissed him passionately. That settled. Only ten minutes had a elapsed, but the woman had made good her word.

Lawyer Clark waited until husband and wife had returned to earth, and then asked them to get down to business. Mrs. Hamilton was disposed to be capricious at first, but she was convinced that her husband's counsel would stand no nonsense. His first inquiry was as to what the putative mother proposed to do with baby Beatrice.

"Why care for her, of course," was the reply.

"Is that child the child of Mr. Hamilton?" asked the lawyer.

The prisoner did not like the blunt directness of the question and evaded it.

"Are you the mother of the child?" persisted the questioner.

To this Mrs. Hamilton offered another evasion, and this resulted in her being informed that unless she consented to talk business and tell the truth further consideration of her case must cease. Then came the admission that corroborated what has been told already of one of the strangest intrigues of the century. She admitted that baby Beatrice was neither hers nor Mr. Hamilton's child. She went further than this,

confiding to the lawyer the name of the woman from whom the child had been bought and the amount paid for it. She did not appear anxious to cast any blame on either "Josh" Mann or Mrs. Swinton, and as excuse for her deception she pleaded her passionate love for her husband and the fear that she might lose him. Turning to Robert Ray at this moment she cast herself on his neck and again burst out:

"Why did you leave me, Ray? Oh, why desert me?"

Hamilton, who had been sitting like a man stupefied while the shameful admissions were being made, did not reply, but wound his arms more closely around the woman's waist. It was decided that the infant should be cared for temporarily by Mr. Hamilton until its final disposition should be decided upon. This discussion seemed to interest Mrs. Hamilton intensely, and she was solicitous lest the little one should not receive every care and attention. Robert Ray informed his wife that while the trial had been an expensive one, he was prepared to go still further to assist her. This remark lead to a partial clearing up of the mystery surrounding the disappearance of the $3,000 worth of diamonds which were said to be missing a short time after the assault.

"Those diamonds," said Mr. Hamilton, "are in safe keeping. They are in the hands of Capt. Perry, the lawyer, of Atlantic City. I have sent him $1,000 for his services, and he will now return the stones." Following this Robert Ray is said to have made the declaration that in the event of Leon Abbott's election he would apply for executive clemency. Both Hamilton and his lawyer left with the same secrecy that characterized their arrival. They went to Atlantic City and held a consultation with Capt. Perry. Neither of them would talk for publication, but it was intimated pretty plainly that even should Mrs. Hamilton be released before serving out her term of imprisonment her husband would not live with her again; that he was only acting from a sense of duty and not because of any infatuation. This hardly seems plausible, especially when the parting between the two was considered. It was even more passionate and clinging than the meeting. Mrs. Hamilton embraced her husband again and again and rained showers of hot kisses upon his face. He took these evidences of affection without a protest. His own manner was not particularly demonstrative, because he is not a demonstrative man, but he did not seem in the least displeased.

EVA HAS HER DIAMONDS.

THEY WERE RETURNED TO HER YESTERDAY— THE WOMAN'S FAITH IN RAY.

[SPECIAL TO THE WORLD].

ATLANTIC CITY, N.J., SEPT. 29.— Mrs. Robert Ray Hamilton has her diamonds and counselor Samuel E. Perry his $1,000 fee. The gems were returned to the convicted woman at 8 o'clock this morning without having been given into the custody of Lawyer Clark as originally intended. The ten days' interval prescribed by law between the day of conviction and conveyance of a prisoner to the State prison expired to-day; nevertheless, Mrs. Hamilton will not go to Trenton to-morrow, but will probably make a start early Tuesday morning.

The prisoner passed a comparatively quiet Sunday. The only visitor was Capt. Perry, who found her asleep when he arrived at the jail. She ate a late breakfast, and then, lighting a cigarette, read a part of an old newspaper. When visited by the Sheriff's wife she expressed an ardent desire to see a New York newspaper. She expressed surprise that the meeting between herself and husband should have become public property. Her manner all day was such as to indicate that she had full faith in her husband's promise to look after her interests.

It comes out to-day that Robert Ray offered his wife, between hugs and kisses, a liberal sum if she would disclose the real paternity of the baby Beatrice. Mrs. Hamilton was either unable to do this or else she would not, for she protested that she knew nothing, and although the amount of the bribe was increased she refused to divulge what knowledge she possessed on that point, if any.

After that last kiss Mrs. Hamilton's face, which had been wreathed in smiles, became clouded. She complained about being separated from her husband, and inside of an hour had worked herself into a frenzy. This she relieved by a generous dose of morphine and then took further solace in her inevitable cigarette. She seemed regard her conquest with a good deal of satisfaction for, when Mrs. Johnston came to see her again, she said with a smile:

"I told you so."

The friends of Robert Ray Hamilton were surprised to learn that he had visited his wife in the May's Landing Jail and the accounts of the visit, as printed, caused them serious anxiety, which will not be relieved until Mr. Hamilton, or someone authorized to speak for him, disproves the inference of a reconciliation drawn from his visit and Eva's previously reported boast that she could with him back in twenty minutes if an opportunity were afforded her. None of his friends were able to throw any authentic light upon the rumored reconciliation and it was asserted by a legal associate of Samuel B. Clarke, Mr. Hamilton's counsel, that none of them knew the object of the visit to May's Landing.

IN CONVICT GARB AT LAST.

EVA HAMILTON BEGINS HER TWO YEARS' TERM IN TRENTON PENITENTIARY.

Removed from May's Landing Before Daylight and Taken to the State Prison by a Circuitous Route—She Breaks Down at the Threshold and Weeps Bitterly—To Be Put to Work Monday.

THE NEW YORK WORLD
WEDNESDAY, OCTOBER 2, 1889

SHE HAS NOT WON HIM BACK.

NO RECONCILIATION HAS TAKEN PLACE BETWEEN HAMILTON AND EVA.

"The friends of Robert Ray Hamilton can safely dismiss all apprehensions arising from reports of a reconciliation with Eva," said Samuel B. Clarke, Mr. Hamilton's counsel, yesterday. Mr. Clarke returned to the city yesterday, but denies that he was at May's Landing with Mr. Hamilton. He says he knows all about the visit, however.

"I can assure you," he continued, "that no reconciliation, or anything approaching it, has taken place. There is no foundation whatever for the report that Mr. Hamilton promised to use his influence either personal or political to secure a pardon or commutation of sentence for Eva. The plain facts are that Mr. Hamilton has been fairly deluged with letters from Eva appealing for an interview. She assured him in the most positive terms that she had been maligned; that there was a plot against him of which she could furnish the proof, and that she could also, if given a chance, show him conclusively that his friends had entered into a conspiracy against her. The woman's appeals were so earnest and persistent that Mr. Hamilton finally concluded it was only just that she be given an opportunity of explaining, and he, accompanied by Mr. Knuzman, went to May's Landing solely for that purpose. The explanation and pretended proof of her innocence did not amount to even a respectable pretense, and they had no effect whatever upon Mr. Hamilton.

"The jewelry and clothes alluded to in the telegram from May's Landing were not returned to the woman at Mrs. Hamilton's solicitation. All he did in the matter was to give notice that he had no claim on them and there was nothing to do but return them to her. None of Mr. Hamilton's family jewels are in the collection.

"On Mrs. Hamilton's behalf we, some time ago, wrote Mrs. Rupp that he would pay for the babies care until some permanent arrangement was made for it, and it has been cared for under our letter, but he has not signified any intention of adopting or even providing for it permanently, although he will do so until it is placed in good hands. I think the matter is definitely ended so far is the joint affairs of Hamilton and Eva are concerned and he will not see her again. He feels he has given her every reasonable chance to clear herself and she has failed."

THE NEW YORK TIMES
THURSDAY, OCTOBER 3, 1889

WANTS A DIVORCE.

ROBERT RAY HAMILTON BEGINS SUIT TO HAVE HIS MARRIAGE ANNULLED.

That Robert Ray Hamilton is cured of his infatuation for Mrs. Swinton's protégé is evidenced by the fact that he has begun a suit in the Supreme Court to have his marriage to her annulled on the ground of fraud and the existence of a previous marriage. Judge Patterson, in Supreme Court, Chambers, yesterday granted a motion made my Mr. Hamilton's lawyers, Root & Clarke, to have the service of the summons in the case made on Mrs. Evangeline L. Hamilton by publication. It will be published for six weeks in two newspapers and a law paper, and copies of it will be mailed to Mrs. Hamilton at the county jail at May's Landing and at the State prison in Trenton.

In the complaint, which is verified by Mr. Hamilton, it is stated that the marriage of Robert Ray Hamilton to Evangeline L. Steele was performed by the Rev. Edson W. Burr of Paterson, N.J., on Jan 7, 1889. The story of the deceit practiced by Eva Steele in palming off Baby Beatrice on Hamilton as his own child is fully told, and Mr. Hamilton declares that the woman knew he would not marry her unless he believed her representations to be true. As a second cause for the annullment (sic) of the marriage it is charged that at the time the marriage between Mr. Hamilton and Eva Steele took place the woman was already married to another man. About this previous marriage Mr. Hamilton can give little proof, but he asks leave to present such evidence as he may discover in the future.

Mrs. Swinton and her son "Josh" were taken to the Central Office from the Tombs yesterday, and Inspector Byrnes and District Attorney Fellows talked with them for half an hour. They were taken back to the Tombs, and neither Mr. Fellows nor the Inspector would say why they wanted them.

ATLANTIC CITY, N.J., OCT. 3.—Mrs. Hamilton will remain at May's Landing Jail to-night and it is probable Sheriff Johnson will take her to Trenton to-morrow morning. Should this be the Sheriff's determination, although not definitely known, he will drive from May's Landing to Egg Harbor, reaching there in time to take the express train via the Camden and Atlantic City Railroad, which leaves the city at 8:25 A.M. Capt. Perry visited Mrs. Hamilton this afternoon and expects to see her early in the morning. The visit to his client was with the object of talking over her business affairs; also the disposal of the child Beatrice. What disposition will be made of the child is not known here this evening.

The New York World
Thursday, October 3, 1889

MRS. HAMILTON IN A BAD WAY.

ILLNESS ATTACKS HER IN HER ATTIC CELL AT MAY'S LANDING.

[SPECIAL TO THE WORLD].

MAY'S LANDING, N.J., OCT. 2.—Mrs. Robert Ray Hamilton is a sick woman. She has not dangerously ill, but she is certainly in a very miserable condition. Influenza has a pretty firm grip on her, and she suffers considerably. Sheriff Smith Johnson still maintains his policy of silence and refused to say when or how he will take his prisoner to Trenton. The probability is that he will spirit her away in a carriage and drive to Egg Harbor, taking a train there for Camden, and thence over the Pennsylvania Railroad to Trenton. He has been away from May's Landing all day and had not come home up to 11 o'clock tonight.

Baby Beatrice was with her pretended mother only a few hours during the day. The little one is fretful and peevish and does not seem at all contented with Mrs. Hamilton, but is perfectly good-natured when in charge of the Sheriff's wife. During the last three days the prisoner has received a number of letters from managers of dime museums in various parts of the country offering a liberal some for the privilege of putting the child on exhibition. None of these has been considered, and the future of the waif is still uncertain.

Dr. Crosby, the Atlantic City physician, would like to adopt it, it is said. It is expected that Mr. Hamilton will be here again before his wife is taken to prison to have her re-transfer some personal property of his still in her possession.

THE NEW YORK WORLD
SUNDAY, OCTOBER 6, 1889

NELLIE BLY BUYS A BABY.

AN INNOCENT CHILD SOLD INTO SLAVERY FOR TEN DOLLARS.

THE APPALLING TRAFFIC IN HUMAN FLESH IN NEW YORK.

HEARTLESS MOTHERS AND GRASPING MIDWIVES WHO BARTER HELPLESS CHILDREN FOR MONEY—SHOCKING INDIFFERENCE OF THE SLAVE-DEALERS AS TO WHAT BECOMES OF THE LITTLE ONES— NO QUESTIONS ASKED—A VISIT TO THE MIDWIFE WHO SOLD THE BOGUS HAMILTON BABY—STARTLING FACTS WHICH WILL APPEAL TO EVERY LOVING MOTHER IN THE LAND.

I bought a baby last week, to learn how baby slaves are bought and sold in the city of New York. Think of it! An immortal soul bartered for $10. Fathers—mothers—ministers—missionaries, I bought an immortal soul last week for $10!

We had a war not many years ago—a long and bitter struggle, which cost many millions of lives and many millions of dollars, and it was supposed that slavery had ended when the armies disbanded.

But it did not stop slavery. Slavery exists to-day in New York in a more repulsive form than it ever existed in the South. White slaves, baby slaves—young, innocent, helpless baby slaves—bought and sold every day in the week—bargained for before they are born—sold by their parents! The negro slaves had a John Brown to start their march to freedom. Who will start it for the baby slaves of New York?

For several days before I bought a baby I advertised in a number of newspapers for a baby to adopt. I received no reply. Why? Because people who adopt babies for good purposes and in a legitimate way do not expect to buy them. Those people who have babies in the market expect to sell them, and they will not give them away.

I went first to see Mrs. Dr. Dimire, as her sign reads. She lives in a comfortable house in West Forty-eighth street. A neatly dressed maid ushered me into a very homelike and artistic parlor. The floor was softly carpeted, the windows were hung with real lace curtains, and there was some valuable bric-à-brac about and handsome jardinières and pictures. Large, rolling glass doors shut off a small room in the rear. When the door opened to admit Mme. Dimire two Skye terriers troubled over each other in their rush to get in first. Mme. Dimire is a large, fleshy woman, with a double chin and dark eyes. She wore a loose wrapper of some thin material that was as white as the spotless cat which lay snuggled up in the window.

"Are you Dr. Dimire?" I asked.

"Yes," she replied, motioning me to be seated.

"Did you advertise a baby for sale?"

"Yes," she replied again, smiling still broader. "Do you want a baby?"

"Yes. Have you the baby still?"

"Well, you are the eighth person that has called for that baby to-day," she replied complacently, folding her arms across her ampleness. "It has gone now to the doctor's with a lady who wanted a baby. She wanted a boy, though, and a fair one. She said her doctor could tell how babies will turn out, so she has taken the nurse and the baby to the doctor to see if it will be fair. I am expecting her every moment now with an answer, but there is another woman upstairs who is very anxious for it. She wanted a boy, but this girl baby is so beautiful that she will take it if the other woman does not. How old do you want the baby to be?"

"Quite young," I said slowly, for I had not thought much about age. I expected, however, they would at least be several weeks old.

"Well, this baby was born at 7 o'clock Saturday morning. That is old enough if you are going to pass it off as your own. Are you married?" she asked suddenly.

"Is it necessary for me to tell about myself in order to buy a baby? I thought not," I answered evasively.

NOT INQUISITIVE.

"I don't want to know anything about you. I never remember ladies I have business with" she said, with a laugh. "When I am paid and a child is taken out of here that is as far as I am concerned. You look so young that I could not believe you wanted the baby for yourself."

"I supposed you never asked where the baby was going or what use was to be made of it?" I said stiffly.

"I don't," she answered quickly. "I never tell who its parents are; I never know who takes it. The moment it is born I send it to my nurse, who does not live here. There it remains until somebody takes it. The children born here are all of aristocratic parentage. I never take common people in. Just now I sent a woman to my nurse's for care, because she did not belong to the class that patronizes me. What did you expect to pay for a baby?"

"I did not know, as I never bought one." I replied hesitatingly, "How much do you charge for one?"

"I don't sell babies," she replied, "but people are expected to pay me something. How much are you willing to give?"

"Ten dollars!" I said, remembering the price paid for the Robert Ray Hamilton baby.

"Oh, my, no!" she said scornfully. "I never get less than $25. The woman who has the baby this afternoon said she would give me $50 if she took it. If she does not take it will you give $25? Hurry, for there is a woman waiting now who is anxious to take it."

"If it suits me I will give you $25 for it," I replied.

Mme. Dimire then said that she would see the woman who was waiting for the baby and, if possible, persuade her to buy the one that was expected to arrive at the house inside of forty-eight hours. If the woman consented she would then give me the address of her nurse and I could go to see the baby. The woman consented, with the proviso that if I did not like the baby I would come back to Mme. Dimire's, where she would wait for my report.

SUSPICIOUS OF DANGER.

"Now, before I give you this," said the madame, indicating a note which was to be my key to the baby slave's presence. "I want you to give me your word of honor that you are not a lady detective."

"Why!" I exclaimed, with an injured air, "what a dreadful idea! How can you imagine such a thing for a moment?"

"I must protect myself," she said apologetically. "If you had come alone and then published what I have said, I could swear that you lied; but as you have a witness," indicating my elderly companion, "I could not do it; so I want your word before I trust you with my nurse's address."

"I don't see how you can imagine such a thing," I said sadly. "I am just as anxious as you are for secrecy."

"You evade my question," she said suspiciously.

"I am not a detective," I said positively. This satisfied the woman, and she gave me the sheet of paper on which was written the nurse's name and address, with this below it:

"Please show the little girl and tell what that lady has decided."

In a tenement-house in East Fifty-second street I found the nurse. She lives in three rooms on the second floor.

"Don't ask for her in the halls or let anyone know what you go to see her about," cautioned Mme. Dimire.

Still, I did ask one woman I met in the hallway. When I was leaving she came into the same flat, so I suppose she was a member of the nurse's family. The flat was small and dirty. I asked for the nurse by name. A woman, with ample shape, greasy dress and a great space between the eyes, who met me at the door, claimed the name as hers. She was very gruff and suspicious, and when I told her I had come to see the baby she never moved a muscle and wanted to know what baby. Then I gave her the note madame had given me.

OUT IN THE RAIN.

"I just got in with the baby," she said, snappishly, "I've had it out most all day with a common sort of a woman who made believe she wanted her doctor to tell if it would be fair or dark. It caught a cold, I guess, and I have just done givin' it some oil."

She took us into the tiny front

room of the flat, but before we sat down she invited us to return to the kitchen. Two small, dirty girls, who in nowise resembled each other, followed her about.

"I guess you can see her here better than in the front room," she said.

In one dark corner was a small cook stove. Near it was a window. Almost touching the stove was a rocking-chair. On a pillow in that chair and covered with a shawl was the baby slave. The nurse pulled down the shawl and I leaned over to look at the tiny mite, the little slave, who was but two days' old, and had been handled and examined by many with a view to buying it. My heart ached for that poor slave. A two-days'-old baby out on a rainy day for many hours!

But it stretches itself. Its little face is awfully red and it has such dark hair and such heavy eyebrows and such a straight nose, which the nurse tells me is a wonderful thing for a two days'-old babe. But its tiny hands are whiter than the pillow it rests on. It works its little fingers feebly, almost as if it wanted to put them in its little mouth. It moves

THE BABY.

again and strange cries come from its tiny throat.

"She caught a cold to-day," the nurse explained in answer to my startled question. "She cried all the afternoon. I made a long trip and I guess she was cold. That's what makes her hoarse now. I gave her a big dose of oil and I think she will be all right to-morrow. Do you want me to undress her?"

OPEN TO INSPECTION.

"Oh, no; please don't. What would you do that for?" I said, all in a breath.

"Most everybody that buys a baby makes me undress it a dozen times before they're sure it's all right. This is a lovely girl though, big for its age," she said as she lifted it out of the chair. The poor little slave twisted up its tiny face, then it opened its tiny dark eyes and blinked just as if it wanted to ask me to buy it. I could not stand it. I turned my back and asked her to put it down.

Hurrying from the house, I returned to Mme. Dimire's. I left my companion in the coupé this time, for I only intended to make my report.

"Madame, the woman took the baby to her doctor's and then sent the nurse home, saying she would come over to see you. The baby has a dreadful cold and even if the woman does not take it I would be afraid to after it was so exposed. I am dreadful afraid of death and I don't want to buy a baby that is going to die."

"That woman has treated me badly," she replied sternly. "This is the second time I have fussed with her. If she doesn't take this one she will have to go somewhere else the next time."

"I would rather wait and take my chances on the next you have for sale." I said pleasantly.

"I cannot keep a baby for you unless you give me a deposit," she said cunningly. "The reason I asked you so many questions" going back to our former interview, "was because you looked too young to be married and wanting a baby. You had a lady with you who looked very smart. She wouldn't say a word, so she could say she wasn't guilty if anything happened. I am not responsible if a woman gets a baby from me and then pretends to her husband it is her own. I nearly got in trouble, and may yet, by giving a baby to a woman who came here accompanied by another woman just as you did to-day. I was the one who furnished the Hamilton baby."

"Robert Ray Hamilton's baby!" I exclaimed in surprise.

SHE SOLD THE HAMILTON BABY.

"Yes, the very same. Mrs. Hamilton came here with Mrs. Swinton for a baby. Mrs. Hamilton looked as if she was in good circumstances; she was dressed expensively and Mrs. Swinton looked respectable enough, though awfully cunning. I didn't like to give a baby, when there was a witness, just as I felt to-day in your case, so I said to Mrs. Hamilton, 'Does your husband know that you are going to adopt a baby?' She

laughed and said, 'Oh, yes, he knows I am going to get one,' and Mrs. Swinton said, 'You don't need to be afraid to give us the baby, for my son is her husband!"

Mme. Dimire asked a flood of questions about my domestic affairs. She wanted to give me advice about the way to deceive husbands, as she said she understood things much better than I could; she had had so much more experience. My replies showed my ignorance in many respects, and though she laughed at it, she was completely disarmed by my feigned frankness.

I afterwards visited a number of places, always with the same result. There were babies to be had for the money. Still, I must make two exceptions. Dr. O'Reilly, of West Forty-ninth street, was very sharp. He is a tall man, with smooth face, stubby gray hair and a stutter. He occupies an entire house, as does Mme. Dimire, and, like hers, it is always filled with high-priced patients. "This is the hi-hi-hi-highest priced place in New York," he said proudly, as he looked at me with an impudent, suspicious look. "I cha-cha-charge $100 entrance fee, and everything else accordingly. This is the only place, the only place where aristocratic children can be found. W-w-when I take a patient in her offspring is signed over to me to do as I like with it."

"You ask no questions of those who take the babies?" I asked.

"N-n-never," he answered giving me an evil look. "I don't want to know who or what they are or what becomes of the baby. Th-th-that's nothing to me."

The other exception was a woman on the east side who said she had no babies, and never had. She claims that she always makes the mother take her child away with her and does her utmost to persuade all the women not to part with their children. Her house, she says, is always open to any officers of the law who may wish to inspect it. As she carries on a legitimate business she has nothing to conceal, so she says.

Mrs. Schroeder lives in East Fifty-eighth street. She runs a large establishment and always has babies for sale. She is very cunning. Nobody has ever learned who her nurse is. As soon as a baby is born in her house it is wrapped in a blanket and taken to the nurse's. Then she advertises "babies adopted," which means she both buys and sells. She buys the baby from the mother, according to an agreement made on entering her house, for some sum not exceeding one dollar! She sells for what she can get.

PRICE-LIST OF BABIES.

"I have no baby here now," she said to me. This is her regular plea. "If you set an hour for coming back I will get a baby for you. How much? Oh, now, I don't dare sell babies; but, of course, you will expect to pay me for my trouble. Say $15. No? Well, then, $10. You can't expect much of a baby, nor one of good, respectable parents, for $10!"

I did not return. If she would not send me to her nurse's I had no interest in returning. There had been a baby born in her house the day I was there.

Mrs. White, in East Forty-ninth street, buys and sells babies. She has a fine private house, and claims acquaintance with a number of society men and women. She sells a baby for what she can get, but she expects to get a good price.

"I have babies every day," she told me. "A lady from Brooklyn secured one here this morning. If you wait an hour or so I will have one for you."

"A boy or girl?" I asked sarcastically.

"Oh, now, you wouldn't expect me to tell that," she laughed. "If you don't want to wait give me a deposit and I will keep it for you."

"It is quite too new for me. I want to see the baby before I buy it," I said, and I went elsewhere.

"You can never get a baby from more desirable people than this will be," she said, at the door. "The girl belongs to wealthy people. Her mother brought her here, and when she recovers she will go back home and someday marry. Her father doesn't know anything about it. He thinks she is visiting friends. It's an easy thing to do, and is done every day in New York."

Mrs. Eppinger lives in East Eighteenth street. She is a short woman with a shrewd face, and wears a nurse's cap and apron. Mrs. Eppinger furnished two of the Hamilton babies, both of which died.

A FINE GRADE OF BABIES.

"You can get babies of good parents from Mrs. Dimire and myself, but no place else," she said, boastingly.

"How much do you charge for babies?" I asked boldly.

"I don't sell them, but I always get something for my trouble. The lady who bought the baby I have at my nurse's now gave me $20 for it. She put the money in my hands. I thought it was a silver dollar, but it was a twenty-dollar gold piece."

"Don't you keep the babies here?"

"Indeed I don't. The moment they are born I send for my nurse and she takes them away and keeps them until they are taken by somebody."

"You never ask any questions of the persons who buy the babies?" I asked.

"Indeed I don't. I don't want to know anything about them."

Sold to the highest bidder, let them be what they may, let them buy for any purpose they please! Sold by their parents and by the female slave-masters!

Every physician is required, so I believe, to make a report of every birth, with the names and ages of the parents, to the Board of Health. These dealers in baby slaves acknowledge averaging a birth a day, yet they make no report. This enormous birth-rate in these houses alone must make considerable difference in a year in the census of New York.

I bought my baby from Mrs. Koehler, of East Eighty-fourth street. She is about four feet high and three feet wide. She has been in trouble several times, but by some means she always manages to escape punishment. If she stole a loaf of bread she would be imprisoned, but as she only deals in human flesh she goes free.

"Mrs. Koehler, have you a baby to sell?" I asked, as I sat down in her well-furnished parlor.

"Yes, I have—one born at 2 o'clock this morning," She answered quickly. It was then 3 in the afternoon. "It is a girl. I will bring it to you," and the slave-dealer went out the door to get the baby slave.

I think probably there was a death in the house that day; at least a vase of tuberoses on the centre table suggested such an idea to me. Their perfume was very heavy and oppressive, and I moved nearer the darkened windows in a vain effort to gain a breath of fresh air.

ONLY HALF A DAY OLD.

"Here is the girl," she said, re-entering the room with a bundle in her arms. She took it to a dark corner of the room for me to examine. Her excuse was that the light would hurt its eyes. In reality she wanted to prevent my seeing any blemishes there might be about the baby slave.

It was thirteen hours old, and I bought it. I had no nurse as yet, so I told Mrs. Koehler I would call for it the next day. The woman had been in difficulties before, as I have said, and she fixes up a dummy—a woman to represent the mother—whom she introduces to the buyers, so she may give her consent. Mrs. Koehler also gives what she pretends is an agreement. This also is to prevent the law from getting its clutches upon her; but it is perfectly worthless, so far as legality is concerned.

"How much do you want for the baby?" I asked when I returned the next day.

"Well, now, I can't set a price, I do not sell babies," she said.

She brought the baby into the room. She had been feeding it and the milk seemed to have such a peculiar tinge that it suggested ideas of drugs and such things. It is well known that babies are often drugged and live but a few days after leaving these slave-dealers' hands. Mrs. Eppinger sold Mrs. Hamilton two babies. They both died. Mrs. Koehler sold Mrs. Hamilton one baby. It died. None of these slave-dealers, with the exception of the one who did the business, knew what woman sold baby Beatrice who lived.

"Will you give your word that the baby is healthy and perfect in every respect?" I asked the slave-dealer.

"Yes, it is a beautiful baby. Now, if you will pay me, we will go up to see the mother. She has never seen the baby yet."

I gave her $10. She looked at the money, then, holding the baby in one hand, she held out the other, saying:

"Please give me more. That is a very little price for such a baby. Won't you pay me more?"

"Not another cent now," I replied. "If the baby turns out well I will send you a present."

I send her a copy of the SUNDAY WORLD containing this article, with my compliments.

A DUMMY-MOTHER.

On the third story, in a front room, lay a fair young woman. She had been talking to a friend who was visiting her.

"Here is the baby," the slave-dealer said. "This is the young lady who wants it."

I knew the dummy-mother trick, so I asked the pretended mother what hour the baby was born. She turned to the slave-dealer for answer. She was handed the baby. She undid the shawl. The little slave, which I had just paid for, opened its tiny blue eyes, as if striving to see for the first and last time—its mother. It rolled its little head feebly; it worked its tiny hands. I felt my throat fill and Hood's cry enter my heart, "O God! that human flesh should be so cheap!"

"It's little, isn't it?" the woman remarked indifferently as she handed the slave back to the dealer, without one kiss, without one glance, without one prayer. If she was its mother her own baby was going from her forever. Where? She did not know. With whom? She did not ask. For what purpose? She did not care.

I took the badly written paper

Mrs. Koehler handed me. This is what it said:

"In consideration of the sum of one dollar the party of the second part surrenders to the party of the first part her child, and it is agreed that the party of the first part may dispose of the said child in any manner."

The mother sold it for $1. I bought it for $10 from the slave-dealer. This on the 2nd of October, in the year of our Lord 1889.

The inhuman, barbarous transaction made me heartsick. I wanted to get away from the slave-dealer and her patients. Tenderly my companion wrapped the blue-eyed, day-old babe in a soft, warm shawl and we left the house as the slave-dealer called after me:

"Don't forget to send me more money for that baby. It's worth it."

NELLIE BLY

THE NEW YORK WORLD
WEDNESDAY, OCTOBER 9, 1889

MRS. EVA HAMILTON'S STORY.

SHE TALKS FULLY TO "NELLIE BLY" IN TRENTON STATE PRISON.

REMARKABLE STATEMENTS, IF TRUE, OF HER LIFE BEFORE AND AFTER MARRIAGE.

SHE SAYS SHE DIDN'T WANT TO MARRY HAMILTON, AND TELLS WHY.

THE FIRST TIME SHE HAS BEEN ABLE TO SPEAK FREELY WITH A REPORTER AND TO GIVE HER SIDE OF THIS EXTRAORDINARY SCANDAL AND ROMANCE—HOW SHE MET ROBERT RAY HAMILTON, MARRIED HIM AND WAS BLACKMAILED BY "JOSH" MANN AND HIS MOTHER—THEY KNEW HER PAST LIFE AND THREATENED TO TELL HER HUSBAND—HE DID NOT BELIEVE HER ALTOGETHER BAD—SHE WAS AN ACTRESS FOR A YEAR, AND FOR A TIME WAS WITH THE FLORENCES—UNTRUTHS ABOUT HER BIRTH AND CHILDHOOD—HER MARRIED LIFE AND HER EXPLANATIONS ABOUT HER BABY AND THE OTHER BABIES—WHY SHE DIDN'T TELL THIS STORY ON HER TRIAL—HER DIAMONDS.

[SPECIAL TO THE WORLD].

TRENTON, N.J., OCT. 8.—I interviewed Mrs. Eva Hamilton late this afternoon in her prison cell in the Trenton Jail. Everybody has heard Robert Ray Hamilton's side of the story. It seemed only fair that the woman be given a show. I have seen her. I have talked with her, and I write her story as she gave it. She has been judged in more ways than one. I smooth over nothing in the telling of what she told me.

The sun came faintly in the high windows, lighting the cells of Trenton State Prison where the women are confined, and heard the low hum of a sewing machine, and looking down the corridor I saw seated along the spotless walls blue-clad women sewing. Forgetting the peculiarity of dress they resembled nothing so much as a society sewing for charity purposes. I excepted the dress; I should also except the quiet. No one ever saw a quiet sewing society. But these women-prisoners were so quiet that I could hear low, despairing sobs, that came not from among them, but from the topmost tier.

I went up the three flights of stairs to this top tier, and, walking along the narrow balcony, I came to a door that was closed and locked. I looked in and saw a woman lying on the narrow cot. Her face was hidden in her hands, and she was crying bitterly.

The door was opened and I stepped inside.

"Mrs. Hamilton," I said, as the woman jumped to her feet. "I come to you from THE WORLD to state justly and exactly whatever you choose to say to the world in your own defense."

Without a word, without one question, the desolate woman flung her arms around me and sobbed so terribly that I almost feared she could not be quieted.

"Have you seen my husband?" she replied as she became more calm and drew back to look at me.

"No," I replied. "I am Nellie Bly, of THE WORLD. I have come to you to give you the same chance that has been given to Mr. Hamilton and the Swintons. If you have any story to tell I will faithfully report it."

"I know of you," she said, "and I will tell you the truthful story. It has never been told. They have told so many untruths about me."

We sat down sat by side by side on the cot. I looked about her tiny cell. On a little table were the remnants of a meal. The cot was extremely simple, but was furnished with two mattresses. There was a wooden stool in the cell and nothing more excepting a framed motto, which was printed in colored letters:

I believe in God my Father,
And in Jesus Christ, my Saviour,

And in the Holy Spirit
Who Comforts Me, and Leads Me
into All Truth.

I looked at Eva Hamilton also. All her finery had disappeared: still she has a pretty face, but a weak one. She looked so much younger than I had expected. In the simple blue gown, plain waist and straight skirt, with a black and white breakfast shawl pinned about her throat, her bangs combed smoothly back, and her soft, reddish-brown hair hanging in one braid down her back, she looked not more than twenty years old. A pretty, slender girl.

HER CHILDHOOD.

"To begin at the first," she said, holding my hand with her white, cool, slender one; "I am not the child of the Steeles, as has been said. I was only their adopted child. My mother died whom I was born, and when I was three years old my father died of consumption. I was born in Tunkhannock, Pa. The Steeles adopted me and I never knew any other people but them.

"When I was fifteen years old I moved to Towanda, Pa. I went there to learn to earn my own living. I was with Mrs. Marsh, who kept a millinery store on Bridge Street. I learned the trade and there I met Walter Parsons, who was then superintendent of a railroad.

"We were married," she continued, releasing my hand and absently pulling single hairs out of her long braid. "My folks and his folks fought about it. It made a great deal of trouble. I had one child, a daughter to Walter Parsons, and then things went so badly by others interfering that we separated."

"What became of your daughter?" I asked.

"I don't like to bring her in this," she said plaintively. "She is thirteen years old now. I have her at school and she does not know anything about this. I don't want her to, and it is not right to drag Walter Parsons up, for he is married again."

"Then tell me what you did next," I said.

"I went to work for Durling & Pratt, in Elmira, N.Y. I was their ribbon counter. When I was eighteen I received some money which was left to me by my father. I then went back to the Steeles, and lived there quietly for some months."

MARRIED AND DIVORCED.

"In 1879, I think it was, Father Steele and the Parsons arranged to get a divorce to free Walter and myself. This was all done by them in Elmira, N.Y. After the divorce was granted I went to Elmira, where I lived for three months. Then I went to New York. I immediately got an engagement with a dramatic company and went on the road."

"Tell me what company?" I said.

"Don't ask me," she said again, "I do not wish to drag the names of people before the public who have so far escaped. While I was travelling with this company I met Joshua Mann. The company was stopping at the West End Hotel, Philadelphia, and Josh Mann was there. One of the girls in the company knew him and she introduced him to me. I was two years with this company and then I was out for nine months with Billy Florence. Then I went to New York to stay.

"I first got board at Mrs. Dean's, No. 252 West Twenty-first street. She was the wife of a captain whose trip was to Brazil and back. Of course you know the rest of it and how I met Mr. Hamilton?" she said, with a long-drawn breath.

"I do not," I answered. "Tell me the story."

HER MEETING WITH HAMILTON.

"A friend of mine took me to a home one night. Mr. Hamilton and two friends of his [she gave the names] were calling there at the time. We were all introduced and Mr. Hamilton and I became the most intimate friends from that time. That is five years ago this coming spring.

"We cared for each other," she said, as she hung her head sorrowfully. "I mean by that that he paid all my expenses and was with me all the time he was in New York, which was usually from Friday night until Monday morning, coming down from Albany. He was a member of the Legislature then.

"Twice during that time I was going to be a mother. I told Mr. Hamilton and he was very angry. Both times he compelled me to consult a doctor and he gave me $300 each time to pay expenses. Once he gave me the money and the other time he sent the money in a registered letter to me to the Passaic Bridge Post-Office in New Jersey.

"All this time," she said, getting off the bed and pacing nervously up and down her tiny cell, "I was friendly with the Swintons. 'Dot,' as we called Joshua Mann, had introduced me to his mother, Mrs. Swinton. Josh lost his position and they were hard pushed, so I began to lend them money. I liked them; they treated me kindly, and I didn't miss what I gave them. After I met Mr. Hamilton I tried to keep it from Grandmother (Swinton), but she found it out, little by little, and then my trouble began."

SAYS SHE WAS BLACKMAILED.

"Every time they wanted money they came to me. If I refused they would threaten and then I would give up."

"What would they threaten?" I asked.

"They threatened to tell my people and they threatened to separate me from Mr. Hamilton, so I gave them money to buy their silence and my own happiness. Mr. Hamilton knew I supported them, but he never made any objections."

"Why did you not get rid of them?"

"You ask me that," she said scornfully, with a hard, short laugh. "I couldn't. I was afraid of them. They followed me everywhere and they threatened until I was glad to get peace at any price. They somehow found out everything I had ever done in my life and they held my own deeds over me.

"Mr. Hamilton claims he gave me $10,000. That is not true. I will tell you how it happened. He and a friend of his went out the road with —— —— (she again gave the names). They stopped at a road-house and they all drank too much wine, and when Mr. Hamilton came back, he told me all about it and what had happened, which was something dreadful. I got angry and we had a quarrel, and I threatened to go to —— ——, the husband of the lady (giving his name) and tell him the whole thing. Mr. Hamilton begged me not, and said if I promised never to tell he would give me $10,000. I promised. He gave me $9,000, which I intended to pay for a house I had bought at Passaic Bridge, N.J. In a few days he asked me for $6,000 back. I gave it. Afterwards he borrowed $4,800 of my own money and still again $3,250. He had never paid the other he borrowed back, so this time I said to him: 'Ray Hamilton, you will promise to-day to pay this, but to-morrow you will deny every word of it, so I won't give you a cent unless you give me a receipt to that effect.'

"He wrote out: 'I owe Eva Hamilton borrowed money, &c,' This receipt is with my papers in the Atlantic City Bank. At three different times after this he borrowed $150, $100 and $150 from me. He never paid one cent back, and they have all been saying I was taking him money from him."

HER DIAMONDS AND PROPERTY.

"My diamonds they talk about

are only worth $1,500. The majority of them I owned. Mr. Hamilton gave me very few. Besides, I have $2,700, all of which is in bonds and mortgages except $900, which is a deposit in a bank.

"Mr. Hamilton, as I have told you, never raised any objections to my giving money to the Swintons. I kept Mrs. Swinton, Josh Mann, Mrs. Swinton's granddaughter (Carrie Swinton, or Collens, as her right name is). I kept them all, because they threatened me. At last Kate Collens, Mrs. Swinton's daughter, found out about Mr. Hamilton and she also made me pay her money. When I went to Jersey they all went along and lived with me, and Mr. Hamilton knew it and did not object. Josh Mann got knocked down with my horse, which was very vicious, while in Jersey. He struck on the back of his head and lay insensible for almost twenty-four hours. When we returned to New York I took him to Dr. Bull, Dr. Paine and half a dozen other doctors. He has never been right since that, and should not be held responsible for what he says.

"One year ago last spring I told Mr. Hamilton I wanted to go to Europe. He gave me $1,000 to go on. I told him I wanted to take Josh Mann for company, and he said it was all right. I went in May. When I left Mr. Hamilton I knew I was going to be a mother. I did not tell him then because I knew he would make me go to a doctor's again and do as he had me do before. I returned from Europe sooner than I had expected and went up to the mountains, still taking Josh with me. Sept. 1 I returned to the city and took a flat in West Fifty-seventh street. Then I told Mr. Hamilton I was about to become a mother. He was very angry and wanted me to go to a doctor's. I told him it was too late then and so matters rested. He was very angry, though, and we fought over it."

MR. HAMILTON'S KNOWLEDGE OF JOSH.

"Just at that time Mrs. Swinton became high in her demands on me. I told her I could not give her money then, as I had been to a great expense all summer travelling (sic) about and keeping Josh. She threatened me, but for once I would not yield. I went to my flat and Josh went to hers for the trunks. He was to come back to take dinner with me. The trunks came, his with them, but he did not come. The next morning I sent down to find out what had become to him, and Mrs. Swinton said she thought he was at my house. For several days we did not hear of him, and Mrs. Swinton was at me all the time to advertise in the papers and offer a reward for him. She seemed to be in such distress about his disappearance that at last I consented and advertised, offering $100 for any information as to his whereabouts. Mr. Hamilton knew this, and one day, as we were together, the negro janitor from the house where Mrs. Swinton lived came in and said he would tell me where Josh Mann was for $50.

Mr. Hamilton said, 'Give the nigger $50 and see if he can tell you.' I gave him the money and he told me that Mrs. Swinton had Josh hidden in Edward Driden's flat. I went there. It made a big fuss and I did not find Josh, so I made the nigger give back the $50. Then Mother Swinton said she had Josh, and she wanted the $50. I gave it to her, and in a few days she came back for $75. I was ashamed to tell Mr. Hamilton how they had 'worked' me about Josh, so I just told him he had returned and we dropped the subject.

"After this Kate Collens threatened me until I gave her $25 a week. Then her husband got in a fight with her and Judge Patterson gave him three months on the Island. Kate went off with the Rockwell Dramatic Company and I haven't seen her since. I had a chance to go with the same company, but Mr. Hamilton coaxed me to stay with him."

THE CHILD.

"I kept very quiet about the fact that I was going to become a mother. Mr. Hamilton knew it, and he knew I didn't want Mrs. Swinton to know it because it would be something more for her to threaten me about. She accused me several times but I always denied it. I slipped off to Elmira, to my brother's, a Mr. Steele, who lives in Third Street. Mr. Hamilton gave me $200 to buy baby clothes, and $150 for myself before I left. He also sent me a check for $500. My brother knew what was wrong with me. I had not been at his house three days until Josh came. He followed me up. On Nov. 15 I slipped away and went to some good, honest people in the country. On the 19th my baby was born. On Dec. 1 I returned to Elmira, and on the 24th of December I returned to New York, leaving my baby at the house where it was born.

"Mrs. Swinton was the first one to see me on my return. She told me Mrs. Jennings wanted her to buy her a baby: that Mrs. Jennings offered her $500 for the right kind. In the mean time Mrs. Swinton had taken a family named Priestman in to board, and she was trying to get rid of them.

"On the morning of Jan. 2 I had my baby brought home. Mrs. Swinton got a baby somewhere, and as her boarders had not gone out she asked me to keep it for a few days at my house. The colored servant I had (Celia Dickson) knew all about Mrs. Swinton's child. Mrs. Swinton of course saw my baby and she accused me of being its mother. Mr. Hamilton helped me make up a story to tell her that the baby belonged to a friend of his who had it by some girl, and we were to care for it for a few days. Her baby got sick and died. She was sick herself, so she persuaded me to go to some house and get another baby she had engaged. This I did, and brought the baby to her. At this time Mr. Hamilton and I quarreled."

THE MARRIAGE.

"I found out about him and —— ——, —— ——, and —— —— being off on a spree and with women. We had a terrible quarrel and I said I was going to leave him. He begged me not to, but I was determined, so he said for me not to leave him and he would marry me. We had never thought or spoken of marriage before, and at this moment our child was not thought of. Mr. Hamilton had been wishing she would die from the time he knew it was to be born. So we did not have much to say on the subject. This fight was on the night of the 8th of January. The next day Mrs. Swinton brought her two babies down to my flat and looked after the three while Mr. Hamilton and I went to Jersey and were married. That night and the next day Mr. Hamilton and our baby and myself were at the flat. I got a message from Mrs. Swinton that hers had died and I went up, but did not even see it.

"When Mr. Hamilton asked me to marry him I said I would not. I would not marry him to take his people's abuse afterwards for having lived with him before we were married. He said if I would only marry him we would keep it secret until after the Legislature and then we would take a trip to Southern California and he would say he met and married me there. I loved him and with these promises I consented.

"While Mrs. Swinton was at our house she sent out for a doctor to see her baby. She told him it was mine, and I let it go because she was afraid of getting into trouble if he knew she was nursing babies, as she was in one case. The nurse Marie Canfield warned me not to have anything to do with Mrs. Swinton and her babies or I would get into trouble. She nursed both babies while Mrs. Swinton was at our house.

THE "BOUGHTEN" BABIES.

"Still there were more babies. After the second died, she got another, but it was so ugly the woman wouldn't have it. I went with Mrs. Swinton to—"

(EDITOR'S NOTE: Here the first edition ends. The rest is reconstructed from other versions printed on October 10th from THE SALT LAKE HERALD and THE ROCHESTER DEMOCRAT AND CHRONICLE)

She laughed at the recollection and began again her nervous pacing.

"When I got home Mrs. Swinton was there with the baby. She was in a terrible temper and tried to coax me to take it for her back to the woman from whom she bought it. I would not do it, but I said I would go with her. So we bundled the poor child up again and went down to the woman's, somewhere on Second street. The woman said she would take the baby if she was given $10 with it. So I told Mrs. Swinton to drop the baby and a $5 bill into her lap. She dropped them and we both ran, with the woman after us. I jumped on a Third avenue car and Mrs. Swinton on a Second, but we both got home all right. All this time my own and Mr. Hamilton's child was at the hospital, where they have a swinging basket. My nurse said we could drop it in the basket and leave it there, but the watchman caught us and made us take the baby out again. I was terribly frightened. He said if she left it on the steps he would watch her leave and have her arrested, and when he went to look for an officer, we both started to run.

"We lost each other," she said with a smile which brought a dimple into her cheek. "I got to an elevated station somehow, and as I started up stairs I looked back and saw a policeman come running as hard as he could. He came up stairs back of me, two steps at a time. I ran, thinking of course he was trying to catch me, and when I got to the top of the stairs, fainted."

She laughed a really melodic laugh, amused at the recollection of the adventure. "Next day Mrs. Swinton came in with a roll of money; $300 she said it was, and that she had at last found a baby, and a woman had taken it. I afterwards learned that it was not Mr. Jennings who bought the baby. Who it was I do not know."

Mrs. Hamilton has a very sweet face and a most affectionate manner. Her eyes are dark blue but a very beautiful shape and have round, innocent, confiding expression. She is really very attractive. She has thin lips but a tiny mouth beautifully curved; there is a pretty dimple in her round chin and one in her cheek, when she forgets her trouble and she is very fair even in prison garb. They came to warn me

it was time to go.

"I must go, Mrs. Hamilton. Is there anything more you would like to tell me?" I asked, as I rose to go.

"I want to tell you that I never struck Nurse Donnelly. I had discharged her several times, but Mr. Hamilton would always tell her not to go. Twice I found Mr. Hamilton in her room. That is the secret of the fuss. After the fight, when I had called for the police, one came up stairs and said the nurse was cut.

"I said: 'Ray, you go down stairs and see if it is true.' He went down and when he returned he said 'she was.' He said she accused me and advised me to say, 'I did it.'

"'There can be no trouble, and it will end sooner if you just say you did it,' said he. So when the officers asked me I said, 'I did it.' The knife was never mine. I never saw it before, and if it was hidden I knew nothing about it. After they took me to jail Mr. Hamilton wrote me several notes, in which he said for me to 'bear up,' that he would have me 'freed,' but that 'the innocent had to suffer with the guilty.' Whether she cut herself or Mr. Hamilton cut her I do not know, but I do know if I had a knife I surely would have known something about it. I did not even see a knife during the fight.

"I have those notes to show what Mr. Hamilton wrote me as you know. All my diamonds and money disappeared. I had to let things take their course. No one helped me; no one to do a thing to make my case lighter. I was kept away from reporters, so that I had no possible way of letting my story be known. Then see, the moment I am convicted and sentenced my diamonds, which disappeared when I needed money, suddenly reappeared, but they could do no good then."

"Good bye. I must go," I said as I was invited outside and the iron-barred door was closed between us. I held her hand, her lips trembled, and her pretty blue, round eyes filled with tears. I pressed her hand. "Don't forget I am deserted, I have no friends," she said, huskily, holding to my hand as if she could not be left alone. "Help me. It is so hard to be alone." And so with that I took myself away.

Signed,
NELLIE BLY.

EVA RAY HAMILTON said: "Give me but twenty minutes with RAY HAMILTON and I will win him back with the world against me." The question now is whether, since her interview with NELLIE BLY, she will win RAY HAMILTON back with the *World* for her.

THE NEW YORK WORLD
FRIDAY, OCTOBER 11, 1889

MRS. HAMILTON'S "OWN" BABY.

HER QUEER STORY OF HOW AND WHERE IT WAS BORN—HER LIFE IN PRISON.

BY NELLIE BLY

In my interview with Mrs. Robert Ray Hamilton published in THE WORLD Wednesday last I did not tell the reasons Mrs. Hamilton gave me for the non-appearance in the case of the people at whose house she said her baby was born.

I have before quoted her as saying that Mr. Hamilton not only knew of her approaching maternity, but urged her to resort to unlawful means to get rid of what promised to be a burden to both. Finding it impossible to follow this alleged advice, Mrs. Hamilton says that Mr. Hamilton became very much enraged and never ceased his maledictions upon the unborn child. That it should never breathe the breath of life was the mildest curse he asked for it.

"Finding that I could not escape Josh Mann in Elmira, N.Y., as he had followed me there, and being determined to keep my secret I began to plan to elude him," Mrs. Hamilton said in explanation.

"On the pretense of visiting I managed to go to the country, where I made arrangements to be cared for. The people who consented to take care of me are honest, respectable, quiet country folks. On Nov. 15 I eluded Josh Mann and got away.

My brother was aware of my intention and my purpose. I went after night, travelled a short way by rail, was met at the station by the people whose services I had engaged and was taken to their house unknown to any one outside of their own household. On the 19th of November my baby was born. There were six people in the house at the time who can swear to the truth of my statement."

"Why did they not do so then?" I asked.

"Because there was no necessity of it before this trouble in Atlantic City, and now they dread being brought into the scandal. I wrote to them from May's Landing," she said wretchedly. "I begged them to come forward and tell about my stay at their house and the birth of my child, but they wrote back that it could do no good now to make a statement, and to do so would make things very unpleasant for them, so, in view of the facts, they refused. I wrote them again that I must save myself, but they replied that telling about the child could not aid me now; that if I did not keep quiet they would deny the whole affair before they would bear the scandal. They promised, though, that if I did not tell to the public where my baby was born they would go to Mr. Hamilton after things got quiet and prove to him the truth of my story. I trust them. They will tell Mr. Hamilton and he will help me to prove that the baby was my own. Why, he knew it all the time. Kate Collens, Mrs. Swinton's daughter, knew it and on the strength of that knowledge made me give her $25 a week. She could tell all about it if she would. My colored girl and my nurse could also tell. Why do you suppose they have not come forward to clear me? Do you think they have been bought over? Has everybody turned against me?" she cried bitterly.

"People say it was a strange thing for me to try to do. But do you think so under the circumstances?" she asked sternly. "Mr. Hamilton knew it as well as I did. He knew what were my reasons for the secrecy and fully approved of them. He knew what were my reasons for the secrecy and fully approved of them. He knew when the baby was brought to our house and he was there all the time to see and know that it did not die or leave there. He knows the truth and why does he deny it, unless he wants an excuse for deserting me?"

Mrs. Hamilton will not be put at the washtub, as has been stated. Mrs. Paterson, the jailer's wife, reports Mrs. Hamilton as remarkably gentle and obedient. She has none of the indulgences accorded to her at May's Landing and she asks for none. New clothes are being rapidly made for her. At the present time she wears a blue gingham dress that hides the beauty of her form.

In a cell almost under the one occupied by Mrs. Hamilton, but on the first tier, is a woman who has been incarcerated for seventeen years. Her face is unusually pale, her smile is wistful, and her manner is hopeless, but still she has hope.

When she was fourteen or fifteen years old she committed murder—child murder, I inferred from what was said. She was sentenced to hang, but her sentence was afterwards commuted to life imprisonment. Her name is Libby Garrabrant. She has never given up the hope that she will be released some day and greets every visitor as her savior. Many people have interested themselves in her behalf, but her pardon will probably never come.

She will be one of Mrs. Hamilton's companions for the next two years.

NELLIE BLY

EVA HAMILTON.

GETS THE NEW JERSEY LEGISLATURE INTO A FIRST CLASS ROW.

TRENTON, N.J., APRIL 7.—Eva Hamilton seems bound to make a sensation, even behind prison bars. She has gotten the State Legislature into what promises to be a first-class row. It is said she enjoys champagne, Manhattan cocktails and imported cigarettes. It has even come to the ears of the members of the Legislature that she has roast duck and ice cream, and, in fact, anything she wants, and is willing to pay for it, and there is going to be an investigation. There are good reasons for the suspicion that these investigations are prompted by spite, whatever the facts as to the woman's treatment in the prison. Tonight Speaker Heppenheimer will appoint a committee of five Assemblyman to begin a thorough investigation of the management of the state prison, and the Hamilton case will be the first one taken up, so it is said.

THE WASHINGTON EVENING STAR
SATURDAY, AUGUST 16, 1890

EVA HAMILTON'S TRUNKS.

THE SHERIFF OF ATLANTA COUNTY SENDS THEM TO HER IN STATE PRISON.

Sheriff Smith E. Johnson of Atlantic County, N. J., has sent Mrs. Robert Ray Hamilton three large Saratoga trunks, which were stored in the little attic in which Mrs. Hamilton was confined before she was taken to the state prison. Mrs. Hamilton is serving a two years' sentence for atrocious assault on Nurse Mary Donnelly at the Noll cottage, Atlantic City, in August last. Mrs. Hamilton wrote to Sheriff Johnson, thanking him for his kindness in keeping the goods for her and asked him to send them at once. Two of the trunks are nearly new. These two are marked Eva L. Hamilton, and the other, which is an old one, is marked Eva Mann, the name under which she lived with Joshua Mann. The trunks are filled with costly wearing apparel.

Sheriff Johnson was asked if Mrs. Hamilton was soon to be pardoned, but the only reply he gave was that "I shipped her clothes to her, and you know she cannot wear them in prison." Capt. Daniel Gifford, who drove the sheriff and Mrs. Hamilton on their midnight ride when the latter was conveyed to the state prison, says that he believes Mrs. Hamilton will be released some time next week, and, as the captain is the sheriff's most intimate friend, significance is attached to his statement.

DEATH HAS DIVORCED THEM.

ROBERT RAY HAMILTON DROWNED IN SNAKE RIVER.

HIS BODY FOUND AND IDENTIFIED BY A FRIEND FROM THIS CITY— THE END OF A TROUBLED LIFE.

Helena, Mon., Sept. 14.—J.O. Green, son of Dr. Norvin Green of New York, who started for New York last night, gave the first particulars that have been received here of the drowning of Robert Ray Hamilton in Snake River, near the south end of the Yellowstone Park. The region is remote from any settlement or telegraph station, and Green, who identified the body, has communicated the fact only to the family in New York.

Early in August, Green and a party of friends went on a hunting trip to Beaver Cañon, on the Idaho line, and from there followed Snake River to a ranch in which Hamilton had purchased a half interest, intending to make it an outfitting station for hunting parties from the park. He had been in the country several weeks, and was making arrangements to live there.

When Green and his friends arrived they found that Hamilton had been missing four or five days. He had started with a horse and dog on a hunting trip, and not returning it was supposed he had continued his journey further than he at first intended. Mr. Green and his friends started on his trail, following Snake River for thirty miles. They found a fallen tree across the river, and in its branches was Hamilton's dead body. It had been in the water several days.

In the pockets of the clothes were several letters, some from attorneys in Mr. Hamilton's divorce suit and others relating to the closing of his business affairs in New York. His watch had stopped at 9 o'clock.

Further down the river his horse was found grazing, with part of an antelope tied to the saddle, which was reversed. The dog which was with the horse had eaten part of the meat. Green took the body of Hamilton to the ranch and left immediately for the park. Thence he came to Helena and started East. No further particulars of the accident can be gleaned here.

The news of the sad death of Robert Ray Hamilton was a great shock to his friends in this city, and his aged father, Gen. Schuyler Hamilton, was almost prostrated by the blow. He was seen at the Windsor Hotel yesterday by a Times reporter, and said he had been advised of the occurrence on Saturday, though he had been made acquainted with none of the details.

"I have not heard from my son," said he, "in some time. He left for a hunting trip in the West with some friends in May last, I think, and I had expected that he would reach home about this time. In fact the friends with whom he made the trip are now on their way back. The news of his death was communicated to me on Saturday, but I am told that it took place eighty miles from a telegraph station, and I am as yet uninformed of the circumstances. I expect my other son, Schuyler Hamilton, Jr., here to-morrow, and when we receive the details we will be able to decide what to do."

Until he became the victim of an adventuress, the career of Robert Ray Hamilton was bright with every promise that wealth, influence, and opportunity could bring to a man of his decided taste for political life, and who had already made his mark as a member of the Legislature, where for four terms he represented the Eleventh District of this city.

ROBERT RAY HAMILTON IS DEAD.

HIS FAMILY IS ENTIRELY SATISFIED THAT THAT IS THE FACT.

THE BABY GETS AN ANNUITY.

PROVISIONS OF THE WILL MADE BY ROBERT RAY HAMILTON.

The will of Robert Ray Hamilton was presented at the Surrogate's office yesterday for probate. It was executed March 17, 1890. The witnesses are Edward R. Vollmer and D.W. Couch, Jr., and the executors are Gilbert M. Speir, Jr., and Edmund L. Baylies. Evangeline L. Mann, the woman with whom Mr. Hamilton became so unfortunately infatuated, is not mentioned in the document, but the baby, Beatrice Ray, which she attempted to palm off on him as his, it is directed, shall receive $1,200 a year.

In regard to Beatrice, Mr. Hamilton says:

"I give and devise to the child, my adopted daughter, christened Beatrice Ray at Atlantic City in August, 1889, an annuity of $1,200 a year, to be paid to her by my executors in monthly installments during her natural life, and I hereby charge the same on my property in the city of Brooklyn. I hereby appoint Edmund L. Baylies guardian of the person and estate of the said Beatrice Ray."

It is directed that all the property except books belonging to Mr. Hamilton in the house of Mrs. Nathalie E. Baylies, 369 West Twenty-eighth Street, be taken by Mrs. Baylies. All his books, silverware, and jewelry are to be received by his cousins, Edmund L. Baylies, Walter C. Baylies, and Cornelia P. Lowell. His friend, Gilbert M. Speir, Jr., is to have his guns, rifles, boats, and dogs, and a share in the Monroe Marsh Company. Mr. Hamilton's brother, Schuyler Hamilton, Jr., is to receive the income from the Prescott Building, Broadway and Spring Street. The residue of the estate is to be received by the children of his brother Schuyler. The executors are authorized to give the city $10,000 for the erection of an ornamental fountain, provided it be placed in a street, square, or other public place. (Ed. note: This fountain was erected in 1906 and exists to-day, at Riverside Drive and West 76th Street. Its construction was opposed by the rest of the Hamilton family, who seem not to approve a monument to the black sheep of the family. It is topped by an eagle, and bears the inscription "Bequeathed to the people of New York by Robert Ray Hamilton.")

It is also provided in the will that the executors shall have Mr. Hamilton's body cremated, in case his death "should occur at a place not inconveniently distant from a proper crematory."

THE ADVENTURESS RELEASED.

EVA HAMILTON PARDONED AFTER SERVING EIGHTEEN MONTHS IN PRISON.

TRENTON, N.J., Nov. 25.—Eva Hamilton, the widow of Robert Ray Hamilton, was released from the State prison at six o'clock this evening. She left the prison with her counsel, ex-Speaker Hoppenheimer and Col. Charles Fuller. It is presumed that she will remain in seclusion in Jersey City, not daring to venture into New York on account of an indictment pending there.

Mrs. Hamilton's application for pardon was filed last spring, and the petition was signed by 2,228 prominent citizens of Atlantic City and county. The petition being made before the death of her husband, it gave reasons that are now obsolete, mainly that her confinement in the prison was jeoparding (sic) her interests, inasmuch as her husband had charged her with fraud, and was seeking an annulment of their marriage. The application also stated that nurse Donnelly, who was assaulted, speedily recovered and was able to give her testimony in court and afterwards go on exhibition in a dime museum. The board unanimously voted in favor of the pardon.

The pardon proved a surprise to Mrs. Hamilton, and it took three hours before she had completed the preparations for her departure. She was profuse in her thanks to the jail officials for their kindness and courtesy to her during her incarceration. Her two years sentence would have expired next May.

EVA HAMILTON'S SECRETS.

THE STORY TOLD BY
VAGRANT MAY THATCHER.

NEW YORK, Nov. 28.—May Thatcher, young and frail, was on Wednesday last, by Justice Power, in the Tombs Police Court, sentenced to six months on Blackwell's Island as a vagrant. May publicly declared that she was put away so that she would not reveal secrets of Eva Hamilton's past life.

She says: "I knew her long before she met Ray Hamilton, and lived in the same house with her for several months."

She tells a rambling story of her knowledge of Eva Hamilton, Josh and Mrs. Mann, but gave the impression that her facts had been derived from reading newspapers.

Eva Hamilton has hidden herself in her room, No. 90 at Taylor's Hotel, Jersey City, where she is registered as Mrs. A.T. Henry, and no amount of persuasion will induce the hotel people to ask the lady to give an interview to anybody. The only visitors to Eva yesterday were her counsellors, Col. Charles L. Fuller and ex-Judge Wm. T. Hoffman.

It was learned late last night that Mrs. Hamilton is gradually recovering from the effects of her confinement in the Trenton Prison, and that her old time lively manner and volubility are returning to her. She was confident, it was further stated, that she will win her law case.

EVA WILL CONTEST THE WILL.

Evangeline L. Hamilton is not satisfied with the will of Robert Ray Hamilton, which provides an annuity of $1,200 for Baby Beatrice Ray, but contains no provision for her (Mrs. Hamilton's) direct benefit. She will therefore

EVA HAMILTON NO LONGER UNDER INDICTMENT.

Judge Martine granted, yesterday, in the General Sessions, District Attorney Fellows's motion that Mrs. Eva Hamilton, Mrs. T. Anna Swinton, and Joshua J. Mann, who were jointly indicted in January, 1889, for conspiracy to defraud Robert Ray Hamilton, be discharged upon their own recognizances and that the indictment be dismissed. The motion was also considered to apply to the indictment for grand larceny in the first degree filed at about the same time. Judge Martine handed down this memorandum:

"The District Attorney recommends the dismissal of these indictments. I have carefully examined the case, and I am satisfied that no case of conspiracy can be made out without the testimony of Mr. Hamilton. There is a question whether a conviction could be obtained even if Mr. Hamilton's testimony were available. The motion to dismiss is granted."

Mrs. Eva Hamilton may now come to this city whenever she likes to press her contest of Robert Ray Hamilton's will, in which she was not mentioned.

BUFFALO EVENING NEWS
MONDAY, DECEMBER 29, 1890

EVA HAMILTON'S NEW LIFE.

SHE IS AT HER CHILDHOOD'S HOME AND SEEMS TO BE A HAPPY WOMAN.

WILKESBARRE, PA., DEC. 28.—Eva Hamilton seems a happy woman now. She is at her step-father's home at Dallas, this county. "Bill" Steele, her step-father, is about 60 years old, but the neighbors say he looks 20 years younger since Eva came home. After the Atlantic City assault on Nurse Donnelly he started to walk to the seaside. He fell by the wayside before he had gone far. When he made known his mission a man paid his fare to Atlantic City, where he remained for some time.

When Eva was released a month ago Mr. Steele went to Jersey City and accompanied her to Pittston. She remained there with a friend for a day or two and then went to Dallas, where she joined the family. For many years Farmer Steele eked out a miserable existence on a small patch of land he called a farm. He had one cow, and the stable was an old rickety affair which let in the wind from all sides. Since Eva came home, however, things have changed wonderfully. There is a new gate in front of the house, and there is also a new stable. Instead of one cow, there are two. Eva has discarded fine feathers, and now dresses like all the other women in the neighborhood. Last week was the first time she left home since she came from New Jersey. She went to Scranton on a shopping to her.

It was 18 years ago when Eva left this part of the country. For 10 years nothing was heard of her. Then one day a man who was acquainted with the family and who knew Eva very well, brought the news that while traveling in California he had met her in company with her husband. That was the last heard of her until the Atlantic City incident. It is said to be her intention to make her home permanently with her own people in Dallas.

EVA HAMILTON'S HOME.

SHE IS NOT LIVING IN LUZERNE COUNTY, THIS STATE.

WILL NOT TELL WHERE SHE STOPS, AND WANTS NO MORE NOTORIETY.

NEW YORK, JAN. 1.—Mrs. Eva Hamilton visited the office of her counsel, Colonel Charles W. Fuller, in Jersey City yesterday, on business relating to Robert Ray Hamilton's estate. Her manners were reserved and dignified. She was attired in black, and wore a widow's bonnet, with a long crape veil. Her complexion is clear and youthful, her features mobile and expressive.

"I do not wish to see reporters and I have no desire for newspaper notoriety," she said to a reporter. "All I desire is to be allowed to live quietly and privately, yet only last Monday one paper contained a statement purporting to come from Wilkesbarre which contained much that was untrue and uncalled for. It states that I have been living at Dallas, a place in Luzerne county, Pa., since I left Trenton, and that I had been there continuously since I left New Jersey; that I had never left there since that event until last week, when I went to Scranton to do shopping.

"Except for two or three days after I left Trenton, when I was in Philadelphia, I have not been in any part of Pennsylvania. That effectually disposes of that story. The truth is that I am living quietly at the home of a friend and I do not wish to have my address known at present. Every one who has business with me knows the address of my lawyer, and those who have only curiosity to gratify should have more consideration.

"There have been a great many persons who have written to me offering aid, advice and sympathy. During the time I was imprisoned there were a good many letters received by the prison authorities for me. They were retained until I was liberated and given to me in a bunch. I thought it was too late to answer them. One lady, a stranger, collected $700 and brought it to me after the trial at May's Landing, but I declined to receive it. My husband was defraying my expenses then, and I had no need for outside aid. There have been a good many letters sent to my counsel expressing sympathy. For them I am grateful, but I cannot answer them at present.

"Fortunately, I am not well known and I have no special annoyance in going about the city, though I had an experience that was very amusing," and a merry smile spread over her face as she recalled it. "I was in an elevated train a few days ago in New York when a young widow came in and took a seat across the aisle. She was quite good-looking and attracted the attention of two men who were sitting in the next seat to mine. I overheard one of the men say, 'That is a young-looking widow.'

"'Yes,' answered the other, 'and quite pretty. I wonder if that is Eva Hamilton.'

"'I would give $10 to see Mrs. Hamilton,' said the other.

"I turned and looked out the car window during the rest of my journey, but it is very unpleasant to feel one's self an object of public curiosity.

"I am awaiting a settlement of my husband's estate, but I do not wish to talk about my private affairs. It would not do me any good to try my case in the newspapers, and it will probably be considered in court before too long. I think the public will learn all about it then that is of interest.

"The only thing I would like to state is that I have not been in Pennsylvania, and I am not going there."

Mrs. Hamilton firmly refused to answer specific questions about her case, but did so in the most courteous manner, alleging as her reason for refusing that she desired to avoid notoriety and to obey her counsel, who had requested her to avoid reporters until her case was out of the courts.

FIGHT FOR A FORTUNE!

Eva Hamilton's Attempt to Claim Her Dower.

WAS SHE "JOSH" MANN'S WIFE?

Strong Evidence to That Effect and a Great Deal of It—Robert Ray Hamilton's Relatives Making a Determined Effort to Defeat Eva's Shrewd Game.

EVA'S STORY NOW.

OPENING THE CASE FOR THE ALLEGED WIDOW OF ROBERT RAY HAMILTON.

COUNSEL ARGUES THAT SHE IS NOT PROVED TO BE MRS. MANN.

THE FAIR CONTESTANT FAINTS UNDER LAWYER ROOT'S DENUNCIATION.

The proponents in the contest of the will of Robert Ray Hamilton having presented all their proofs that Evangeline L. Steele, the contestant, was the wife of Josh Mann at the time of the ceremony of marriage to Robert Ray Hamilton, at Paterson, Jan. 7, 1889, and that therefore she was never the wife of Mr. Hamilton, the contestants were given the floor in Surrogate Ransom's Court to-day.

The court-room was crowded, a hundred spectators standing back of the seats and filling all the available space in the chamber.

There were more than a score of citizenesses in the audience—young, old and middle-aged. There is no other phase of human experience that has an interest so deep for women, apparently, as that of marriage and its various vicissitudes.

Women crowd the churches at weddings, though a majority of them will solemnly affirm that marriage is a thraldom for women.

Women gather boldly to listen to the marital woes of the parties in divorce trials. Breach of promise trials always draw the fair sex, and the Hamilton will contest presents a charming mixture of these things, with a widow in weeds who must establish her wifehood, and a baby girl heiress who has neither father, mother nor name thrown in for makeweight.

The female auditors whisper together, sometimes with blushes, again with eager curiosity that forgets the blush that the testimony should bring to modest cheeks, and again with smiles and giggles.

EVA COMES INTO COURT.

The court-room is filled, but there is one vacant chair at the front. Ever and anon the waiting throng turns its gaze expectantly towards the entrance door, and presently there is a suppressed murmur like the buzzing of bees, and every eye is bent upon an advancing figure. People who chance to be seated where one of the granite pillars obstructs their view, crane their necks, and others in distant corners arise from their chairs to gaze at the figure advancing, like one who is tardy, with a quick step toward that empty chair.

Ordinarily that figure would pass unnoticed anywhere. It is the figure of a woman of medium height, of graceful carriage, with shapely shoulders and well-poised head.

The step is that of a young woman, a vigorous woman, a woman accustomed to act for herself—not the movement of a timid, weak or modestly unobtrusive woman.

But that is all that the eager spectators see, for the figure is closely shrouded in deepest mourning. Not a scrap of white or color relieves the folds of sombre crepe.

It is the figure of Evangeline L. Steele. She is in mourning for Robert Ray Hamilton, who indicated by leaving her that he had discovered that he was her dupe. She is either Robert Ray Hamilton's widow, or else she is a heartless jade who played fast and loose with his affections, while she had a husband in the person of Josh Mann, who spent the money that Robert Ray Hamilton gave her.

This young person would surely be called as a witness to-day.

OPENING FOR THE CONTESTANTS.

But not now. Col. Fuller, of her counsel, opened the case in her behalf, by a motion for the dismissal of the answer of the heirs, under the will to the objections presented against the proof of the will.

Col. Fuller argued long and exhaustively. He insisted that the proof that Josh Mann and Eva had lived meretriciously together as man and wife did not make them man and wife, and that the Paterson ceremony made Hamilton Eva's lawful husband.

Col. Fuller cited a host of modern instances from musty law books to show that a man and woman might pass as man and wife for years, yet shake off the relation and take unto themselves other marital partners.

Of course, all of these cases were full of suggestions, but every detail was drink in eagerly by the women present.

THE SURROGATE INTERFERES.

Surrogate Ransom begged pardon for interrupting the learned counsel, but he called attention to the fact that these cases differed from this one, where "Eva L. Steele told the minister who married her to Hamilton that she had never been married before, while she had told her relatives and all her friends that she was the wife of Joshua Mann. The evidence establishes that fact in this case, and the presumption, too, that she was the wife of Joshua J. Mann at the time of the ceremony with Hamilton.

"I interrupt only because this case is not before a jury, and we might as well get on with it as fast as we can without wasting any time," concluded the silver-gray Surrogate.

The iron-gray Colonel was not crushed, though Gen. Schuyler Hamilton, father of Robert Ray Hamilton, nodded his approval of the Surrogate's views.

"I insist, sir," said Col. Fuller, pointing every clause of his insistence with his right index finger—"I insist, sir, that every scintilla of testimony that has been offered here is evidence only of a meretricious relationship between this plaintiff and Joshua J. Mann, and not of a marriage between them."

DEFINING A COMMON LAW MARRIAGE.

Then Col. Fuller read another decision that when a couple had lived together for thirty years as man and wife, then separates, and then each of them within a year married somebody else, neither was guilty of bigamy, and the Court would not say that a common law marriage existed where such decision implied bigamy by each of the parties.

There was no shutting Col. Fuller off. One by one pugnacious Morrison transferred book after book from a big stack on the floor to the hand of the reading pleader, and after the reading of the case in point in each book it was laid gently on a pile before him on his table.

This went on drearily for an hour or more, and there were more than a score of calf-bound law books on the table, though the supply on the floor was far from exhausted.

After each reading the weary surrogate repeated, at first considerately, then tenderly, then in pitying tones, then testily, then disgustedly, and then for half a dozen times languidly, resignedly, the words:

"Each case rests on its own evidence. In this case a marriage by agreement and common report and declaration seems to be indicated, prima facie, by the evidence."

MADE THE SURROGATE TIRED.

"Mr. Fuller," said the Surrogate, finally; "this woman stated over and again that she was the wife of Joshua J. Mann. That is not by reputation, but by common report. That establishes fact. She must be held responsible for her declarations. If she were on trial for bigamy under the common law those declarations would convict her."

Col. Fuller succumbed, but pugnacious Morrison leaped into the breach. He called attention to the fact that the Court might decide that Evangeline was Mrs. Mann, but that would not, could not bind Josh Mann, if he did not intend at any time to be the husband of Evangeline.

MR. ROOT TAKES A HAND.

Mr. Root begged pardon for making a formal reply to the opposing learned counsel. He briefly reviewed the testimony, showing that Eva had taken Josh to her home and introduced him to her father, mother and brothers as her husband—"as near to a ceremonial marriage as man and woman could go, and in no wise the introduction to a meretricious relationship."

Mr. Root continued in a long and quite impassioned speech.

EVA FAINTED AWAY.

Evangeline listened but made no sign during this plain, unvarnished statement by Elihu Root, but at its conclusion, in response to a sign from her, she was assisted to her feet and led into the stenographer's private den, wither she was followed by several goblets of ice-water, and attended through a fainting spell by the tender-hearted Underhill and a court attendant.

The Surrogate decided in the negative the motion of Eva's counsel that Eva's status as the widow of Hamilton be established without controverting the testimony offered by the proponents.

A SETBACK FROM THE SURROGATE.

"If—I see no other way of designating her—'the contestant' was the wife of Mann by presumption under the common law, when in Jan., 1889, the ceremony of marriage to Hamilton was gone through with, then she was never the wife, is not now the widow, and has no standing in this court as a claimant and heir to Robert Ray Hamilton's estate.

"The testimony takes the case out of the realm or probability, presumption and public reputation. It satisfies me that Eva L. Mann was the wife of Joshua J. Mann until such proof has been controverted."

The Hamilton contingent looked happy, while Eva's lawyers were slightly crestfallen, and their assistant gathered up and carried away the mountain of law books with the same hilarious air that marks the undertaker's man while engaged in gathering up the camp chairs after the funeral cortege has set out for the graveyard.

This left the contestants slightly disfigured, but still in the ring. After fifteen minutes time was again called and Col. Fuller began the work of establishing affirmatively that Eva is the Widow Hamilton and was only Josh Mann's affinity, never his wife.

Mrs. Esther Blake, of 54 East Twenty-fifth street, was the first witness.

A VERY DELIBERATE WITNESS.

Esther wasn't quite sure whether it was yesterday or the day before that she was in court. She wasn't sure, in a stately, dignified and painfully haughty way.

She recognized Evangeline, and said that Eva lived with her at 65 West Ninth street in 1885, and that she knew the bleached-blonde young woman as Mrs. Brill.

After sparring by counsel, this was ruled out by Surrogate Ransom.

Witness Esther was permitted to say that Eva offered Robert Ray Hamilton as her reference when she engaged her room, and that Hamilton called on her during the time that she lived with Esther.

HAMILTON WAS EVA'S VISITOR.

"He came twice—three times a week. Mrs. Brill moved with me to 67 Twelfth street, and lived with me there two months," said the stately Mrs. Blake, in full tones.

Evangeline was brought in to be identified, and afterwards she sat with her veiled head in her black-gloved hand.

Mrs. Blake said that the next time she saw Eva the fair one visited her house with Robert Ray Hamilton.

MRS. HAMILTON THIS TIME.

"What was her name then?" asked Col. Fuller.

"Am I at liberty to answer that interrogation, may it please the Court?" asked the stately witness.

On being assured of her liberty

she said, slowly and solemnly, and with the air of one who confidently looked for a collapse of the four walls of the temple of justice, when they heard her answer:

"Mrs. Ro—bert—Ray—Ham—il—ton!"

MR. ROOT OBJECTED.

Mr. Root smiled, and formally objected to this line of questions, whereat the Court declared his inability to see what bearing it all had on the case.

The witness proceeded:

"Mr. Hamilton done the talking, and he asked me if I possessed any apartments which would be suitable for him and his wife.

"I replied: 'No, sir; my apartments are all occupied, but I can direct you to a very reputable and highly respectable party.'

"They went. I do not know whether they did or did not engage apartments. The party is now dead."

A recess was taken.

EVA HAMILTON.

EVA HAMILTON SUED!

"JOSH" MANN BRINGS ACTION FOR DIVORCE.

HE SAYS THAT SHE WAS HIS WIFE.

NEW AND SENSATIONAL DEVELOPMENTS ANENT THE WOMAN'S ATTEMPT TO CAPTURE A DOWER INTEREST IN THE ESTATE OF THE LATE ROBERT RAY HAMILTON.

NEW YORK, JANUARY 16.—Another chapter was opened yesterday in the romantic career of Evangeline L. Steele, sometimes known as Evangeline L. Parsons, Mrs. Mann and Mrs. Robert Ray Hamilton. The prologue began Friday night last, when an old woman called at the residence of Lawyer William Howe, on Boston avenue and One Hundred and Sixty-ninth street. She introduced herself as the mother of Joshua J. Mann. "My son desires a divorce," said Mrs. Mann, Sr. "You know he is married to a woman who claims to be the widow of Robert Ray Hamilton."

"JOSH" MANN'S DEPOSITION.

The lawyer made an engagement to meet "Josh" Monday, but the latter was too ill to leave his home in St. Mark's Place, and a clerk went there and took his deposition.

He says he met Eva in April, 1881; that they agreed to be man and wife, and they lived together as such in various places in this state and Pennsylvania. They visited together the homes of Eva's relatives, and Joshua was everywhere recognized as her husband. Even never questioned the relationship, but instead, on certain occasions, insisted on Joshua's declaring the fact of their marriage.

SHE HAD MARRIED HAMILTON.

This continued until January, 1889, when Joshua learned that Eva had married Robert Ray Hamilton, and he told Eva that he thought it a "practical joke," and that the marriage certificate had been procured solely for the purpose of "playing a joke" upon him. Joshua seeks a divorce on the statutory grounds.

HE PUT IT UNDER HER ARM.

Louis B. Allen, of Howe & Hummel's office, was yesterday detailed to serve the summons on Eva, and he kept her in view in the Surrogate's court. When the recess was taken Allen followed the heavily veiled woman into a Third avenue elevated train. She got off at Fourteenth street and entered number 203 of that street. Allen slipped into the hallway after her.

"Oh, Mrs. Mann!" said he, and Eva turned about impatiently.

"I have a little present here from your husband, Mr. Mann," said Allen softly.

"Well, what is it?" asked the lady with acerbity.

"Only a summons for divorce," and Allen held it out, but Mrs. Mann refused to take it. Allen then put it under her arm, and left as quickly as he could, without waiting to hear what she said.

NOT HAMILTON'S WIDOW.

Col. Charles W. Fuller, counsel for Mrs. Hamilton, began the proceedings in the will contest in the surrogate's court with an argument in favor of declaring the contestant's status as the widow established. "There is not," he said, "even a hint that she and Mann ever intended to marry, or that they lived together for any length of time. There can be no presumption of marriage. Joshua Mann was in the jurisdiction of the court, and could have been called to give partial evidence of a marriage between him and the contestant, if there had been a marriage."

Elihu Root answered on behalf of the proponents. The woman's conduct and the fact that she carried on business as Eva L. Mann, signing checks on bank books and such, was alluded to.

This closed the argument, and the surrogate said that Eva's statements and declarations were evidence of her marriage, and she must be held and bound by those declarations. The motion, therefore, to declare her status as the widow of Robert Ray Hamilton must be denied.

EVA SOBBED VIOLENTLY.

Colonel Fuller then called several witnesses to prove the marriage of the contestant and Hamilton. During this time Eva wept and sobbed violently. Elihu Root was himself placed upon the stand to identify Hamilton's signature.

Maj. Gen. Schuyler Hamilton identified the contestant as the woman who had been introduced to him by his son as his wife. An adjournment was then taken.

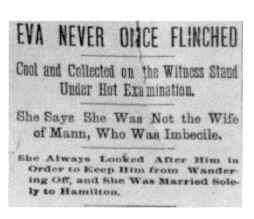

EVA NEVER ONCE FLINCHED

Cool and Collected on the Witness Stand Under Hot Examination.

She Says She Was Not the Wife of Mann, Who Was Imbecile.

She Always Looked After Him in Order to Keep Him from Wandering Off, and She Was Married Solely to Hamilton.

EVA IS A WITNESS.

ROBERT RAY HAMILTON'S ALLEGED WIDOW TESTIFIES FOR HERSELF.

SHE DENIES SEVERAL OF HER OWN PREVIOUS SWORN STATEMENTS.

JOSH MANN COMPLICATES HER CASE BY SUING HER FOR A DIVORCE.

When Evangeline Steele smiles, two hard little lines crease her cheeks almost in the very middle, and the effect is anything but pretty.

These creases appeared in the otherwise smooth and solid cheeks this morning, when an evening world reporter asked her lawyer, Mr. Morrison, what he proposed to do in the matter of Josh Mann's suit for absolute divorce from Evangeline begun yesterday afternoon by the thrusting upon the alleged widow of Robert Ray Hamilton, as she entered a hallway in Fourteenth street, a summons and complaint, in which Mann alleged that he and Eva had lived as husband and wife since 1881, and had held out to the world that they occupied this relation Jun. 7, 1889, when Eva "pretended to marry" the New York Assemblyman.

"Do? Why," said Mr. Morrison, "we don't know whether we shall accept the service of the paper and go on and defend it or not. Of course, you know Josh Mann has been suffering with paresis for two years and has been under the care of his mother."

In the formal complaint on which Josh Mann seeks an absolute divorce from the fair Evangeline, he makes affidavit that he is thirty-six years old; is the son of Mrs. T. Anna Swinton, and husband of Evangeline L. Mann, formerly Evangeline L. Steele, and sometimes known as Evangeline L. Parsons.

"I met my wife, Eva, about the 19th day of April, 1881," says Joshua in his affidavit. "After some preliminary acquaintance we agreed to be man and wife, and, therefore, lived together as such in New York and in various places in Pennsylvania."

Then he relates that he and Eva visited "her folks" and that they were recognized everywhere and by everybody as husband and wife.

Eva conducted herself as a dutiful wife till about Jan. 7, 1889, when she pretended to marry Hamilton, of which Josh says: "I thought it was practical jokes, and said to Eva, 'I don't believe it is true.'"

Lew Allen, of Howe and Hummel's office, served the papers on Eva. She refused to receive them, and that is why they were tucked under her arm by the imperturbable Allen.

Eva's counsel in this will contest have over and over again called attention to the fact that even if the Court should decide that Eva was Mann's wife it would not find him, and he would not be her husband unless he chose to be.

They have repeated the legal maxim that a marriage is a contract, and a contract implies a meeting of minds. Eva could not agree all alone that she and Josh were man and wife. Josh must be consulted in the matter. Eva might sign the name Evangeline Mann a thousand times and tell ten thousand people that she was Mrs. Mann, but that would not be true unless Josh so considered her.

Therefore when Josh came forward and sued for divorce the milk was spilled. It implied that Josh considers himself the lawful husband of the woman who has said so many times that she is his wife, and who lived with him for seven years.

The only defense, practically, is that suggested by Mr. Morrison, that Josh is suffering with paresis and only imagines the existence of marital relations between him and Eva.

Dr. Frank H. Rice, a Passaic physician, was called to the stand when the Surrogate's Court was opened, to repeat a statement made to him by Eva, but it was not allowed, and the witness only succeed in showing that he knew her than as Mrs. Mann.

Then Col. Fuller called importantly, "Eva L. Hamilton."

(Editor's note—I have threaded testimony from two separate articles into the following exchange. The additional material is from a similar article the following day, Saturday January 17, 1891)

MRS. EVA ON THE WITNESS STAND.

The contestant arose with a quick, nervous air, threw back her long veil and advanced to the witness-stand She looked the Surrogate full in the face as he administered the usual oath, pressed her full lips to the Bible and then sank back in the witness-chair as comfortably as possible.

"Do you know Joshua J. Mann?"

"I do," was the contemptuous reply.

"Do you remember being in Pennsylvania in January, 1886, when Joshua Mann and your brother met?"

"Yes, sir."

"Did you introduce Joshua Mann to your brother?"

"No, sir; I think my uncle did."

"Did you ever enter into any contract of marriage with Joshua J. Mann?" asked Col. Fuller.

"No, sir; I never did," replied the fair enslaver of Robert Ray Hamilton.

Her voice was a half falsetto, not at all musical, but rather harsh and grating at times. It expressed no passion of any kind.

"Did you ever introduce him to any one there as your husband?"

"No, sir; not to any one."

"Did you visit your father's home, as stated by your brother on the stand?"

"Yes, sir; I went with Mr. J.J. Mann."

NEVER SAID MANN WAS HER HUSBAND.

"Did you introduce him to your people as your husband or ever say that you had been married to Mr. Mann?"

"No, sir; I introduced Mr. Mann and told them he was a friend and that I resided with his folks in New York."

"Did you ever tell any one that he was your husband?"

"No, sir, I never did in my life."

Elihu Root smiled, and Col. Howard looked disgusted.

"She is going too far," he whispered to his nearest neighbor. "They have broken their back."

If Eva was telling the truth, then her father, mother, brother, sister-in-law, Mr. and Mrs. Adams, the hotel-keeper and his wife, Justice of the Peace and Towards lawyer all perjured themselves on the stand—perjured themselves wantonly and for no reward.

HER STAKE A FORTUNE.

A fortune was at stake for Evangeline. She testified in a cold, dispassioned way, and her face expressed nothing of what was going on within her breast.

Evangeline identified a letter as one she had received from Josh Mann, Aug. 25, 1889, after much wrangling by the lawyers, and while every person in the great gathering in the court-room strained every muscle to get a view of the roman who comes forward to claim the fortune of the man whom she duped with a bogus baby heir, and who is defendant, in a suit for divorce, by another man who claims to have lived with her as her husband for seven years.

Those of the spectators who are habitual court attendants, gazed askance at the nonchalant woman who ventured to proclaim a dozen citizens perjurers, and the clerks, criers and other court attaches paused in their work to take a look at the immobile face haloed in the widow's weeds that she was seeking to establish her right to wear.

OTHER WITNESSES CONTRADICTED.

But she was not done. Having disposed of her Pennsylvania relatives and acquaintances with one wave of the hand, she now proceeded coolly to stamp the mark of "false witness" upon the heads of the Eastmans, Chas. S. Wright the real estate agent from whom she and Josh rented a flat; Mrs. Julia Everson, who housed her and Josh for a time; Dr. Ammidon and a half dozen other New Yorkers who had testified that either she or Josh introduced themselves as "Mr. and Mrs. Mann."

It was all false. She had been very much interested in Josh, but they had not occupied one room in common at Mrs. Everson's, nor anywhere else. She was awfully interested in Mann because, poor fellow, he was sick as the result of being tumbled out of a carriage.

THE LACYVILLE EPISODE.

"Did you ever stop at a hotel in Lacyville, Pa., with Mr. Mann?" asked Col. Fuller.

"Yes, sir; one night."

"Did you know what Mr. Mann wrote on the register?"

"No, sir."

"What was Mr. Mann's mental condition?"

"Well, I went there to the hotel at about 5 o'clock in the afternoon and asked the clerk, or whatever he was, to register for me, as Mr. Mann was not in a condition to do it. The clerk registered, I don't know what, and I took Mr. Mann up to his room and he went to bed.

"I went down to dinner and when I got back he was gone. About nine o'clock I went out to look for him and found him very drunk. He had not been right after the accident."

The crowd in the corridor had got wind of the fact that Evangeline was on the stand, and inch by inch they forced their way into the Court-room, shoving those already standing in the aisles further forward till they almost reached the bar.

SHE ASKS TO EXPLAIN.

Evangeline asked to explain why she took Josh Mann to her room that day.

"I took him to my room because he was in a dreadful condition and unfit to take care of himself. He always needed a guardian to look after him."

Dr. Kemp was the next witness to be slaughtered. She declared that Mrs. Blake introduced her to Kemp incidentally, and that afterwards she called the doctor professionally and never corrected his idea that she was Mrs. Mann.

"Was Dr. Kemp introduced to you as the wife of Mr. Mann?" asked Col. Fuller.

"No, sir," replied the impassionate Evangeline.

"Was Joshua J. Mann ever introduced as your husband?"

"No, sir."

"Where were you born?"

"Tunkhannock, Luzerne County, Pa."

"What is your age?"

"Thirty."

"Up to what time, Mrs. Hamilton, was you know known as Mrs. Brill?"

"Up to the time I purchased that Passaic property—I think it was 1887."

IN THE NAME OF MRS. MANN.

"In what name was that Passaic property?"

"Evangeline L. Mann."

This woman made the answer with the utmost nonchalance—though she had been denying right and left that she was ever known as Mrs. Mann.

"Why did you not take the title to that place in the name of Brill?"

"Because Mr. Hamilton did not wish me to. That was the first time that I ever went by the name of Mann."

Evangeline said she lived in the Passaic house for a few months with Mrs. Swinton, Carrie Collins, Josh Mann and her servants.

"Did you occupy the same room with Josh Mann?"

"No, sir; I did not."

"Give me the names of your visitors there."

"Mr. Hamilton visited me there, and the brother of Mrs. Swinton."

"Did you ever say to any one in Passaic that you were Mrs. Mann or that J.J. Mann was your husband?"

"No, sir, I never did. I stated that he was my cousin."

HER FIRST MEETING WITH HAMILTON.

"When did you first meet Robert Ray Hamilton?"

Evangeline answered readily enough, with the flippancy of one speaking of the most ordinary occurrence:

"Oh, I don't know; may be about six years ago—might be seven."

Evangeline said she moved from Passaic to Fifty-eighth street, where she lived alone with her servant. Mrs. Swinton was a frequent caller, in fact was there most of the time. Josh called also, and Hamilton was attentive.

"When you became acquainted with Hamilton by what name did you know you?"

"Mrs. Brill."

"Did he ever know Joshua J. Mann?"

"Yes, sir; I think in January, 1886."

"Did Mr. Hamilton call on your regularly after January, 1886?"

"Yes, sir; up to January, 1889."

"He was a member of the Legislature, and much at Albany during that time, was he not?"

"Yes, sir. He used to come down Friday night and stay with me till Monday."

"Did he contribute to your support?"

"Yes, sir; he paid it all."

UNDER CROSS-EXAMINATION.

"Your witness, Mr. Root," said Col. Fuller, and then Elihu Root arose and began the cross-examination with the austere air of a judge and the voice of one who felt outraged.

"When did you last see your parents?"

"At Elmira—at my house in West Third street."

"Who lived there?"

"Myself, Mrs. Swinton, Joshua L. Mann,"—

"Under what name did you rent the house?"

"Evangeline L. Mann, I guess"—

Evangeline paused and said she wasn't quite sure.

"Oh, you're quite correct, quite correct," Mr. Root assured her. "By what name were you known in Elmira?"

"Evangeline L. Mann."

The cross-examiner touched next on her assault upon Mary Donnelly, the nurse who had charge of Baby Beatrice in 1889, but Evangeline declined to answer on the ground that it would tend to degrade her.

"Were you a witness in a trial in a New Jersey court, Sept. 9, 1889?" persisted Mr. Root.

CONFRONTED BY HER OWN OATHS.

He got an affirmative reply, and while Eva's lawyers squirmed and her blue eyes were more expressionless than ever, read a bit of testimony in which she swore that her parents were dead; that they died a great many years ago, and had lived in Sullivan County, Pa., and that she subsisted on money left her by her dead father.

Eva declared that she had no recollection of the questions nor the answers.

She was no longer nonchalant. Color came to the smooth, hard cheeks, and when Mr. Root followed up with the question:

"Were those answers, if made, true?"

She blurted out in a shrill, cutting voice:

"I tell you I can't remember. I won't say whether they were true or false."

Mr. Root persisted.

Eva was perplexed. She sought the face of her lawyer, but got no sign. Then she replied faintly:

"I do not understand anything about it. I may have and I may have not understood on that trial in New Jersey."

HER HANDWRITING IN QUESTION.

Mr. Root asked her to examine a bit of paper and say if the writing thereon was hers or not.

"Well, it looks like it and again it don't," was the Police Court witness style of evasion that Eva resorted to.

"Look again!"

Eva scanned the writing closely and then replied slowly:

"It looks very much like my handwriting"—then she added hastily,

"but in other was it is very unlike my writing."

Mr. Root showed several checks on the Union Dime Savings Bank, drawn in 1886 and bearing the signature, "Eva L. Mann."

Evangeline faintly admitted that the signatures were her own.

This was a year before the purchase of the Passaic house, the transaction by which Eva fixed the date of her first appearance under the name of Mann, but an appeal to the stenographer's minutes showed that Eva in her testimony had qualified that statement, saying faintly and audibly to the stenographer only:

"I first became known as Mrs. Mann in 1887, except for banking purposes," was her answer on the record.

WHEN SHE SWORE SHE WAS A WIDOW.

Mr. Root next produced the jurat attached to the deed of the Passaic property from Mr. and Mrs. John Scott to Evangeline L. Mann.

In it Eva swore that she was a widow, her husband having been dead eight years.

"Were you a widow at that time?" asked Mr. Robb.

"No, sir."

"Had your husband been dead eight years?"

"No, sir."

"Is that your signature and did you swear those statements?" demanded Mr. Root in a voice from the cellar, and with fierceness bristling his mustache.

Evangeline said:

"It is my signature I've no doubt. But I do not remember that part of the affidavit."

"Let's look at this bank business again. When you opened that account in 1885 at the Union Dime, what name did you give?"

"I don't remember."

"The bookkeeper has sworn that you said you were the wife of Joshua J. Mann, is that true or false?"

"I tell you I don't remember. I think—I am not positive, you know; but I think—Mr. Mann accompanied me to the bank. I'm not sure."

"Do you remember opening an account at the Bleecker Street Bank? Of signing the signature book? Of telling the attendant who you were?"

REMEMBERED, AND WAS SORRY FOR IT.

Evangeline remembered all these things in a tone that indicated that she wished she had not.

"I told them that I was Eva L. Mann," she replied, faintly, resignedly.

"Well, but you told him also that you were the wife of Joshua J. Mann, didn't you?"

"I suppose I did," replied the witness so faintly that it was necessary for the stenographer to repeat it.

"What do you mean when you say that you never lived with Joshua Mann as his wife?" demanded Mr. Root.

"I mean that we were never known as man and wife," came the shrill reply.

EVANGELINE HAD ASSUMED A DEFIANT ATTITUDE.

Other questions were asked, but she declined to answer, on the ground that so doing would tend to degrade her, and the Surrogate ruled that she need not answer.

After some further questions the Surrogate announced a recess. Evangeline took refuge in the stenographer's room, but the crowd held their places.

The contestant was half an hour late to the afternoon session, and the Surrogate did not attempt to conceal his impatience at her tardiness. Mr. Root began by inquiring into her trips to Pennsylvania. He asked her what was the purpose of her visit to Laceyville.

"Must I answer?" asked Eva, turning to the Surrogate with an appealing glance.

"Will the answer tend to degrade you?"

"No no, it isn't that." Then, turning to Lawyer Root again:

"I got a letter that Thomas Steele's wife was sick and in need, and I went there to attend her wants."

"Why did you take Joshua Mann as your escort?"

"I had no particular reason."

"You say he was almost an imbecile?"

"I didn't say almost. He was and is a complete imbecile."

"Then why did you take him?"

"Oh, to take care of him and relieve his mother."

"Why did you say on your direct examination that he was incapable of registering?"

"Because any drunken man would be incapable."

"Was he drunk when you left New York?"

"Well, he wasn't sober. Then he drank on the train. It only took one or two drinks to make him drunk."

"Is it true that Dr. Kemp attended a child at your house in this city in January, 1889?"

"It is."

"Is it true that you were introduced to him as the wife of Joshua J. Mann?"

"Do you mean as the wife of or by the name of Mann?"

"Both."

"As his wife—no; whether I was introduced to him by the name of Mann I cannot say."

"Don't you consider being introduced as Mrs. Mann in Joshua's presence as equivalent to an introduction as his wife?"

"No, I don't consider it so."

Mr. Root then went over the ground of all the contestant's movements with Joshua Mann and the different places in which they lived and visited. He inquired particularly as to her visit to Sciotadale, Pa., whither she went alone in November, 1888. Mr. Root wanted to know who was there, what she did while there, and finally asked her why she went there. Eva refused to answer on the ground that a reply might tend to criminate or degrade her.

About this time she leaned over and whispered to the Surrogate. The latter then told the counsel that the contestant was ill and unable to proceed. Court was therefore adjourned till Monday morning.

Eva's sudden illness possibly may have been due to the pertinacity with which Mr. Root was inquiring about the Sciotadale trip. It was there, in November, 1888, that baby Beatrice Ray is supposed to have been born.

ANOTHER DAY OF TORTURE

EVA WAS OVERCOME BY MANY SEARCHING QUESTIONS.

THE SURROGATE ALLOWED HER TO LEAVE THE STAND—SOME DAMAGING ADMISSIONS WRUNG FROM A MOST UNWILLING WITNESS.

EVA SHOWS HER TEMPER.

IN SUCH A MOOD, PERHAPS, SHE STABBED NURSE DONNELLY.

SHE SHRIEKS AT THE SURROGATE AND DEFIES THE LAW OF CONTEMPT.

SO FAR THE CASE LOOKS DARK FOR THE HAMILTON WILL CONTESTANT—AT LEAST SURROGATE RANSOM INTIMATES THAT THE EVIDENCE THUS FAR PROVES THAT SHE IS THE WIFE OF "DOTTIE" MANN.

The officers attached to the Surrogate's Court had a hard time yesterday morning keeping back the crowd which clamored for admittance to the Hamilton will contest. It was an eager and persistent crowd, and despite the positive instructions of Surrogate Ransom that none but lawyers, witnesses and reporters be permitted in the court-room, scores of people who had no other motive than curiosity succeeded in forcing their way inside. As a consequence the room was filled when the proceedings began and many were glad to obtain standing room only.

The contestant, Eva, who is invariably referred to as Mrs. Mann by the proponents and as Mrs. Hamilton by her own lawyers, was in the witness chair promptly at 10.30 o'clock, ready to again submit to Elihu Root's searching cross-examination. She wore her widow's weeds, and her face was paler than usual. The mental strain to which she has been subjected while on the stand was apparent by her features. She looked Languid and weary, but occasional flashes of fire lit up her gray eyes when Mr. Root asked her some particularly disagreeable question, and once or twice she lost her temper completely and snapped back replies, which evidenced more of anger than distraction. She held her own well, however, and persisted in her refusal to answer certain questions even when Surrogate Ransom, with sternness depicted in every lineament of his face, threatened to send her to jail for contempt of court.

The Surrogate also intimated plainly at one stage of the proceedings, when the giving of testimony was temporarily interrupted by the arguments of counsel, that the legal presumption up to that time was that Eva is the wife of Josh Mann. This was a very significant straw, inasmuch as the impetuous contestant cannot be the widow of Ray Hamilton if she is the wife of Joshua Mann. If the Surrogate holds that opinion now the chances are that his decision will be rendered accordingly, as all of the contestant's evidence is practically in.

Mr. Root began his cross-examination at that point of Eva's career where he stopped last Friday. This was in October, 1888, a period of more than ordinary significance. It was then that Robert Ray Hamilton was receiving letters from Eva informing him that he would soon become a father. The child Beatrice Ray was supposed to have been born about that time. It was when Mr. Root touched upon this subject last Friday that Eva suddenly became too ill to continue on the stand and requested the adjournment which was granted.

EVA'S LITERARY EFFORT.

A register of the Delevan House in Elmira was shown to the witness. Under the date of Oct. 3, 1888, it bore the names of "J.J. Mann and wife; J. Steele and wife." Eva identified the first signature as that of Joshua Mann.

"Did you take Joshua to Elmira to take care of him?" asked Lawyer Root.

"I didn't take him there at all," came the ready answer. "We all went there together."

"Was he an imbecile when you took him there?"

"He was."

"What is your idea of an imbecile?"

"Oh, I don't know. He wasn't right in his head."

Continuing, Eva said that Joshua was known to the members of his family as "Dotty." She herself called him by that name. She also admitted that she addressed his mother, Mrs.

Swinton, as "Grandma."

Then Mr. Root started on a new tack. He asked about Eva's trip to Europe in May of the same year. She admitted that she had made the journey with Josh Mann. After an ebullition of anger she further admitted that they occupied the same stateroom on the steamship. Mr. Root produced a letter written by the witness under date of May 24 and read it in evidence. It was as follows—punctuation, spelling and all:

> *Liverpool, May 24*
> *My dear grandma. We have arrived all safe after our long journey and we are very tired indeed. We was ten days out of sight of land. We are as well as can be expected. I was sick on board very little. Dottey was not all. The trip was not pleasant it was so long. We shall not go back on the City of Bostin. We do not like her. The Saturday she left she run on a sand bar, and was stuck all day & they say she hurt herself then and that was the reason she was so long crossing. We had nice weather all the way except Sunday and then we had a terrible storm and could not get out at all. We will stay in Liverpool a day or so then go to London from London we shall go to Paris and from there to Carlsbad in Austria and I cannot say where we shall go from there. We met very nice people on board. Dotty seemed to enjoy the trip untill the last few days then he got tired of it too. I hope you are*

all well do not worry about Dottey I hope and believe it will do him good. remember us kindly to Mr. Dryden and all who ask about us. I shall not write to Mrs. Dixon. She got angry with me that night because I laughed at her when the seats went down. So I suppose she won't care to hear from us. Kiss that dear baby for me, for I love it very much. take good care of dear little Fan for me. the weather here is not at all warme. It is now three o'clock in the morning but I cannot sleep so I thought I might as well do my writing now. Dotty is sleeping like a good fellow. I suppose you are all asleepe in New York. we hope to get a letter from you as soon as we reach London. Dotty wrote you a letter three days ago but we did not stop at Queenstown so I suppose you will get booth at once. we will write again from London. take good care of yourself untill we return so I will say good morning with much love and kisses I remain yours,

Eva and Dotty.

HER TEMPER SWAYS HER.

Underneath the signature are ninety-six "o's" closely written on three lines and presumably representing kisses. Another letter was introduced, written by Josh to his mother and dated in London. It was a commonplace letter, describing the voyage and the weather, and announcing that the voyagers would sail home on June 2. It concluded thus:

Don't tell any one that we are coming home so soon, for Eva doesn't want it know. She got a letter from Mr. Hamilton dated May 18. Eva joins me in sending love.

"Why did you want nothing said about your return home?" asked Mr. Root.

"I didn't want it kept quiet."

"Then Josh wrote what was not true?"

"No," petulantly.

Mr. Root persisted. "When why did Joshua ask his mother not to mention your return to any one?"

Eva's weary air disappeared, and she straightened up in her chair and glared wrath at her inquisitor.

"Well, I don't remember!" There was defiance in very syllable.

"If you don't remember, how do you know you didn't ask him to write as he did?"

Eva's face became a study. She wriggled in her seat, grasped the arms of her chair convulsively and her rage knew no bounds. Her lips got ready for action, but she sank back in her chair without replying. For the instant words couldn't express her thoughts. She was too angry to speak. Then she fairly shrieked:

"I said I don't re-mem-ber!" A dozen exclamation points wouldn't represent the outburst adequately.

A letter was produced from Josh to Mrs. Swinton, dated Elmira, Dec.18, in which a message was conveyed from Eva, asking if she had got "those things" done and cautioning Mrs. Swinton not to disappoint her.

"What is meant by 'those things?'" asked Mr. Root.

"A wardrobe." Storm center over the witness's chair.

"What kind of a wardrobe?"

"An infant's wardrobe." Cyclonic outburst.

"Whose infant?"

SHE DEFIES THE LAW.

Eva again reached that stage where her anger lapped over itself and subsided from sheer exhaustion.

"Mine," after much hesitation.

"Was that infant living Dec. 18, 1888?"

"Yes, sir."

"Where was it born?"

"I refuse to answer that question."

"Why?" inquired the Surrogate in apparent surprise.

"Because it would tend to degrade me."

Surrogate Ransom declared that the question was permissible and directed the witness to answer. Eva persisted in her refusal.

"You must," declared the Surrogate. "Now, Mrs. Hamilton, or Mrs. Mann, it is the ruling of the Court that you answer the question. I direct you to answer."

Eva turned upon the Surrogate and promptly but firmly replied:

"I refuse to answer any questions about my baby case."

"It is proper," rejoined the Surrogate, "that I instruct you that in refusing to answer you render yourself liable to be put I the common jail until such time as you consent to comply with the direction of the Court."

Still Eva declared that she would not reply to any such question. Lawyer Morrison asked the Surrogate to instruct the witness that she might refuse to answer if it would tend to incriminate her. The Surrogate did so, and after a great deal of expostulation and argument Eva based her refusal on that ground, though with extreme reluctance.

She afterwards admitted that the child was born in Pennsylvania on Nov. 19, 1888.

"That is information," exclaimed Elihu Root triumphantly, "which we have been vainly trying to get since last Summer."

When Court reconvened after adjournment Eva told the Surrogate that she was too ill to continue in the cross-examination. The afternoon session was accordingly taken up with the evidence of two Elmira witnesses, who gave cumulative testimony to the effect that the contestant and Josh Mann lived as man and wife in that city in the Fall of 1888. The case will go on Wednesday morning.

EVA CONFESSES THE FRAUD.

AFTER LYING FOR MONTHS EVA OWNS BABY BEATRICE A SHAM.

THE IMPOSITION ON ROBERT RAY HAMILTON ADMITTED IN COURT.

CHARGES THAT SMACK OF PERJURY IN THE TESTIMONY OF THE CONTESTANT—HER RELATIONS WITH JOSH MANN—THE SCENE IN THE SURROGATE'S COURT YESTERDAY WAS A CURIOUS ONE.

Harassed and worried almost beyond the limits of a woman's endurance by three days of torture on the witness-stand, wrought to a pitch of intense nervous excitement by the pitiless inquisition of cross-examination, the contestant of Robert Ray Hamilton's will practically confessed yesterday the stupendous fraud perpetrated upon that unfortunate young man, by which she became his wife through the instrumentality of a baby bought from a midwife (for) $10, which he was made to believe was his own child.

The confession came reluctantly, and would not have come at all, despite the agony of the witness-chair, only for the fresh trouble heaped upon the contestant by the news of the death of her mother. Anxious to attend the funeral in the little Pennsylvania town where her parents reside, and only too glad to escape at any price from the rack of Elihu Root's insightful questioning, she said sat before the Surrogate with bowed and colorless face and acknowledged that she was not the mother of the infant, Beatrice Ray, and that the man for whose estate she is fighting was not its father.

This meant that Eva Hamilton, by which title her own lawyers address her, or Eva Mann, which her adversaries contend is her rightful name, stood before the court a self-confessed adventuress, conspirator and blackmailer. The admission concerning the parentage of the child came from her own lips in a court-room where curious crowds stood with mouths agape to hear her words.

ALL DOUBT IS DISPELLED.

Whatever lingering doubts might have remained that Robert Ray Hamilton was duped into marrying Eva through false pretenses is now dispelled. The woman he made his wife has, until now, persistently refused to break (her) silence regarding her alleged child. Last Friday she went so far as to boldly declare that she would not answer questions concerning the birth of the infant, even after the Surrogate commanded her to reply, with a warning that he would commit her to the common jail if she disobeyed the mandate.

The story of the $10 baby first came from Inspector Byrnes. When the reports of the Nurse Donnelly shooting affray in the Rupp cottage at Atlantic City were published in the newspapers a year ago last summer the services of the Inspector were enlisted by Robert Ray's friends in this city. The careers of Eva Mann and Josh Mann and Mrs. Swinton were investigated by detectives. Hamilton at first refused to believe the astounding revelations they made. They furnished him with the proofs of their discoveries. He learned that the first baby which Eva secured died a few days after; that another was obtained, which Eva repudiated and sent back because, she averred, it was cross-eyed and wasn't pretty enough; that a third was finally bought for $10 which pleased her fancy and seemed to fill all the requirements.

This third baby is Beatrice Ray.

Eva looked the picture of despair as she entered the Surrogate's Court yesterday morning with a quick, nervous step and took her accustomed seat. Never before have such crowds sought admittance to a will contest in this city. Every day the number of women who clamber for seats increases. Nearly fifty of them were in yesterday's assemblage. There were stately matrons and girls in short dresses, handsomely dressed and plainly clad, and what a buzz of whispered comment went around the room as Eva appeared!

All through the day men, and

women too, came to the doors, which were locked after the room was comfortably filled, begging the court officers to let them in "just a minute," long enough to catch a glimpse of the contestant's face.

Around the big table just outside the railing sad the usual array of lawyers and attorneys. Behind Mr. Root, in the same seats they have occupied ever since the contest began, were Gen. Hamilton and his wife, the father and mother of Robert Ray, and young Mr. and Mrs. Schuyler Hamilton. A few of their friends sat around them.

While Eva toyed nervously with her long crêpe veil, artfully concealing her features behind its folds from time to time, her counsel, Col. Fuller, was reading to the surrogate a dispatch announcing the death of Eva's mother in Dallas, Pa. Mrs. Hamilton wished to attend the funeral, he said, but could not reach there in time unless she departed on the 1 o'clock train.

Meanwhile Eva stared into vacancy, her foot beating Staccato time on the raised floor underneath her seat, and her whole body quivering with nervous excitement.

"I informed Mr. Root of this dispatch," continued Col. Fuller slowly and impressively, "and in a very manly way he offered to make some concessions. Mrs. Hamilton has told me that she is physically unable to go on and testify, and Mr. Root has offered to suspend her cross-examination upon our agreement to make certain admissions."

An instant's hush fell upon the court-room, while the spectators looked expectantly at one another, wondering what the admissions would be. Then Mr. Fuller read from a paper these words:

It is admitted by the contestant that the child, which the contestant testifies was born in Pennsylvania on Nov. 10, 1888, was not the child of Robert Ray Hamilton. It is admitted by the contestant that the child known as Beatrice Ray, and christened such Atlantic City, N.Y., and a respondent in this proceeding, is not the child of Robert Ray Hamilton.

Even the stern-faced Surrogate looked astonished while a sup-pressed murmur of voices and a rustle of dresses throughout the audience indicated the effect of the announcement. Eva's brow contracted, her full lips were pressed more firmly together, while her foot beat even quicker time than before, and she permitted her veil to conceal one side of her face.

"You heard what was read," said the Surrogate, looking at the contestant over his spectacles. "Do you admit that the infant is not the child of Robert Ray Hamilton?"

"Yes," replied Eva, in a low tone.

Few except those very near to her heard the answer.

Not Robert Ray Hamilton's child! True, it was known before, and he himself asserted the fact in the suit for an annulment of the marriage,

THE SCENE IN THE COURT-ROOM WHEN EVA CONFESSED THE FRAUD.

which was pending at the time of his death. The police authorities have told it and the newspapers printed it, but it came with a peculiar significance from the lips of the contestant.

That whispered monosyllable told that Robert Ray Hamilton, a man of culture and education, a member of the bar of New York and of the Legislature of the State had been in trapped, deluded and hoodwinked by the woman who uttered it—an ignorant woman, hardly able to write her name.

After the excitement had subsided Eva was asked whether her brother, Joseph Steele, and Josh Mann had or had not written the entries "Joseph Steele and wife" and "J.J. Mann and wife" on the register of the Ochs House in Tawanda, Pa., on Oct. 28, 1888. The witness declared that she could not remember. The hotel keeper, Joseph Ochs, was in court waiting to testify that the signatures were written by Mann and Steele.

Col. Fuller then began his re-direct examination. Another sensation in court was speedily occasioned. The contestant had previously testified that she never lived with Josh Mann, but occupied the same room with him at times for the purpose of nursing him, as he was an imbecile and could not take care of himself.

"Where did you first meet Josh Mann?" asked Col. Fuller.

"In Philadelphia." Eva was now holding a bottle of smelling salts to her nostrils.

"When?"

"In 1881 or 1882, I think."

HER RELATIONS WITH JOSH MANN.

"Where your relations with him proper or improper?"

Again the black veil fluttered and the witnesses eyes were cast upon the floor.

"Improper."

"How long after your first meeting did these improper relations begin?"

"About a week."

"What were your relations to Josh Mann?"

The crowd in the court-room acted surprised at such a question from the contestant's own counsel. There was another bustle and an expectant stir as Eva, with the faint suggestion of color in her cheeks, turned to the Surrogate and whispered something to him.

Another look of surprise came over the Surrogate's face.

"The witness replies," he said, "that she was his mistress."

Eva bit her lips and rocked slowly back-and-forth in her chair. The admission was an unexpected one, and entirely at variance with the contestant's previous declarations.

"Who paid for the property you bought at Passaic?"

"Mr. Hamilton."

Not the least surprised listener in the court-room was Mr. Root. His turn soon came to cross-examine again.

"Why," he demanded, "have you made these changes in your testimony?"

A flash of the old-time fire came back into the witnesses' eyes.

"Oh," she replied in a tone which was meant to be icily polite, "I don't consider that I have made any changes in my testimony."

"Have you not been told that you would have to change your testimony if you wanted to win this case?"

"No, sir," in a slightly louder tone.

"Why did you previously testify that you had never asserted yourself to be the wife of Joshua Mann?"

"Oh, I don't know," snappishly. "Everybody is liable to make a mistake. I didn't think."

"Why didn't you think?"

"Everybody forgets to think sometimes." Evidences of rising anger were apparent.

"Why did you not testify on your first examination that you were the mistress of Joshua Mann?"

"Because I thought I might be spared the humiliation of telling what I was in the presence of my relatives in this room."

"Why did you testify that you took Joshua Mann to Pennsylvania with you simply as an escort?"

"I took him along because I wanted him. (spitefully.) I don't know whether it might be called simply as an escort or not."

"Do you still say that while you were staying at all of these different hotels with Joshua Mann he was a complete imbecile?"

"No, not all together." The witness had now sunk back into her chair

again. "I say that he was helpless and had to be watched continually, because he could not control his appetite for liquor."

"When you testified on Friday that you stayed in the same room with Mann simply to take care of him you made a statement which was not true, did you not?"

"I do not consider that I did." Another petulant outburst.

"Do you not understand that you have made a radically different statement to-day concerning your relation to the Joshua Mann from what you made previously?"

"I did not wish to speak out plainly then. I thought it could be inferred."

"Then you did not intend to tell the truth?"

"I did intend to tell the truth."

"That's enough," ejaculated Mr. Root.

EVA AND HER FAMILY.

Then the Surrogate reminded Eva that she had sworn that she was not on good terms with the members of her family. He asked her with which of them she was on bad terms.

The angry look faded out of Eva's face, and with a flirt of her long veil she replied in a much softer voice then she had accorded Mr. Root:

"I am not on good terms with my brother, Thomas Steele, nor with my sister, Mrs. Foote, nor with my father."

This concluded the contestant's testimony and she immediately left the court-room, having just about time enough to catch the 1 o'clock train.

Col. Fuller next called Harry Spencer to the stand. Mr. Spencer is a sallow-complexion man with a gray mustache and positive style of uttering his words. He said he lived at No. 148 West Tenth street and had known Eva Hamilton since 1885.

"Are you in any way related to Mrs. Swinton?" asked Col. Fuller.

"Unfortunately, yes," replied the witness.

"What is that relationship?"

"I married her daughter Kate."

"Did you ever hear the contestant in this case addressed as Mrs. Mann?"

"Never!"

"Was it ever understood by you that the contestant and Joshua Mann were man and wife?"

"It was understood that they were not."

"What business was Joshua Mann in in 1886?"

"Not any."

"Who supported him?"

"Eva."

The witness declared that he had heard Joshua and Eva both declare that they had never been married. He had expostulated with Josh, he averred, for living with her.

Elihu Root was eager for the cross examination.

"Is your real name Spencer?" he demanded, sternly.

"It is the name I have been living under for three years."

"Answer my question, sir!"

After considerable evasion the witness admitted that his right name was Harry Collins.

"Were you ever in prison?"

"I was locked up in the Yorkville prison once?"

"What was the charge against you?"

"I was held in bonds to keep the peace. I had been too demonstrative with my wife in the police court."

NOT AFFECTIONATE DEMONSTRATIONS.

"Demonstrations of affection, do you mean?"

"No, quite the contrary."

It was then brought out the witness and his wife were not on terms of friendship.

In reply to a question Spencer or Collins admitted that he had been in the employee of Root & Clark obtaining evidence for them against Eva in the conspiracy case, which has since been abandoned. For this work he received $150.

"Did you call at the office of Root & Clark yesterday?" demanded Mr. Root.

"I did."

"Did you inquire for Mr. Clark?"

"I did."

"Did he refuse to see you?"

"He did."

"And then did you not go to the office of Col. Fuller, the lawyer on the other side?"

"Yes, sir."

"And now you are testifying for him. That's all."

After recess Josephine Johnson, a colored woman, who was who in 1887 was janitress of the flat house

No. 225 West Fifteenth street, where Eva resided, was called to the stand,. The witness swore that Eva received frequent calls from Josh Mann. The latter did not live there, but with his mother, Mrs. Swinton. While in conversation with Mrs. Swinton on one occasion, the witness testified, she referred to Eva as Mrs. Swinton's daughter-in-law.

"Don't call her my daughter-in-law," she said was Mrs. Swinton's reply. "She has never been married to my son."

On another occasion, continued the janitress, Josh and Eva had a quarrel in the house while Mrs. Swinton was there. The latter ran downstairs and requested the witness to go for a policeman. She did so, and upon the officer's arrival Joshua, who had been drinking, requested the policeman to lock him up. The witness swore this dialogue followed:

"I can't lock you up," said the policeman, "unless your wife makes a complaint."

"She is my wife," promptly rejoined Joshua.

"No, it isn't likely to be," added Mrs. Swinton.

On cross-examination Mr. Root showed that the witness had served a term in the penitentiary for larceny, and also succeeded in obtaining many contradictory statements from her.

Col. Fuller took the stand himself to introduce a letter which Joshua Mann had sent to Eva in Trenton prison. In the letter Joshua admits that he and Eva were never man and wife. Col. Fuller also testified that Joshua had made similar statements to him.

"If he was at all clear-headed," added Col. Fuller, "I would have had him here to testify long before this."

J. Andrew Wilk and William Maxwell, both Towanda lawyers, stated that Eva heard Joshua testify in that town in the trial of William Steele for larceny that he was her husband. Eva denied, in her examination, that she was in court at that time.

This concluded all the evidence on both sides. This morning counsel will some up before the Surrogate.

EVA IS WIFE, NOT WIDOW.

SURROGATE RANSOM HOLDS THAT SHE WAS MARRIED TO MANN.

THE WOMAN HAS NO STATUS AS A CONTESTANT OF HAMILTON'S WILL.

HER TESTIMONY IN COURT FORMALLY PRONOUNCED UNWORTHY OF BELIEF—HER COUNSEL ANNOUNCES THAT HE WILL APPEAL THE CASE—PROOF OF HAMILTON'S DEATH STILL IMPERFECT.

Evangeline Hamilton, or Mann, has lost her suit for recognition in the courts as the widow of Robert Ray Hamilton. Surrogate Ransom decided yesterday that she had no legal standing upon which to contest the will and obtain a dower right in the estate. The decision was rendered immediately after the lawyers had concluded their arguments.

All the evidence in the case had been submitted Wednesday, and nothing remained yesterday morning except the summing up by counsel. Eva had departed for Pennsylvania to attend her mother's funeral, and did not hear the Surrogate declare that she was Joshua Mann's wife and not Robert Ray Hamilton's widow. The court-room was crowded, as usual. Gen. Schuyler Hamilton was the only member of the Hamilton family present.

Elihu Root began by recalling the ceremonial marriage between Robert Ray Hamilton and Eva on January 7, 1889. He spoke slowly and deliberately, with no attempt at oratorical effect. That marriage, he admitted, no one could deny. Six months afterwards Mr. Hamilton began an action to annul the union on the ground of fraud. The status of Joshua J. Mann in this case, Mr. Root asserted, was perfectly clear. He first tried to help the woman's cause by a letter placed in evidence, and then turned against her with his suit for divorce. The evidence to show that Mann and Eva were married was briefly reviewed.

"I want your honor to believe that they were man and wife," declared Mr. Root, "and not simply to think that it is a presumption from the evidence. This woman watched over and cared for him when he was ill and nursed him when he was drunk; he transferred money to her as his wife, and she told the bank officers that she was his wife; they lived in the same house and passed before the world as husband and wife. Not until recently has the other monstrous assumption been put forward. An illicit intercourse could never bring about these close relations. With a louder tongue than any protestation or any oath there speak from the record the voice of a sister and Eva's own brother. They have tried this question and decided it. The testimony of Evangeline is the most astounding tissue and fabric of falsehood I have ever listened to. Your honor can never award a widow's share to this woman on such evidence as this."

When Mr. Root sat down Mr. Fuller arose. He referred to his client as a woman friendless and alone, struggling for her rights against an array of counsel who had scoured the States for witnesses, while she had been unable to procure any. She had been compelled to sit and listen to what other people thought of her conduct. Mr. Fuller admitted that Joshua Mann and Eva had on different occasions represented themselves as man and wife, but such a relation, he contended, never existed in fact. It was her misfortune to have ever met this apology for a human being, Joshua Mann. But afterwards she met Hamilton and loved him, and their union was legal in the eyes of God and man. Eva was the only one who could testify as to a marriage contract with Joshua, and she had denied it. Mr. Fuller wanted to give the Surrogate a list of precedents for the latter to consult.

"It will be useless, Mr. Fuller," replied the Surrogate, "for I am going to decide this case as soon as you conclude with your argument."

In his decision the Surrogate said that the law in the case was plain, and that it was his duty only to apply the facts.

"Whether or not the contestant at the time of her marriage to Hamil-ton was a woman worthy to be the wife of an honorable man is not a question for me to decide," he continued. "Assuming that the relations between Mann and this woman were in the beginning meretricious, I think the evidence would satisfy any reasonable mind that they afterwards became matrimonial. I regret that duty compels me to say anything in criticism of this contestant. I think her evidence is unworthy of belief. I do not believe her. I hold and decide that on January 7, 1889, the date of her marriage with Hamilton, she was a lawful wife of Joshua J. Mann and that the marriage was void, and that she has no standing in this court to contest Robert Ray Hamilton's will."

Col. Fuller said afterwards that the case would at once be taken up on appeal.

After recess formal proof of the execution of the will was put in, preparatory to admitting it to probate. Gilbert M. Spier, jr., one of the executors, testified as to Robert Ray Hamilton's death. He and C.D.R. Moore left this city on invitation of Mr. Hamilton to visit his ranch near Yellowstone Park. When they reached Moffat Lake, in Idaho, they heard for the first time of Hamilton's death. They pushed on to the ranch and upon their arrival learned that Mr. Hamilton had left it on Aug. 22 to hunt and fish at the foot of the lake. He did not return the next day, and two days later searching party was organized. On Sept. 1 Hamilton's body was found in Snake

River. Mr. Spier saw the grave but did not see the body. He produced a gold watch which, it was declared, had been found on the dead body and which he identified as Mr. Hamilton's. The witness had also seen the decedent's saddle, torn in water soaked.

Mr. Moore corroborated Mr. Spiers testimony. Surrogate Ransom said the factum of the will had been established, but it seemed to him as if Hamilton's death had not been proved. He reserved the case until conclusive evidence of death could be presented. Mr. Root said that two men could give such testimony, having both seen the body. One was John D. Sargent, who is now on the ranch, and the other is a son of Dr. Norvin Green. Young Mr. Green is in Europe. An order for a commission will have to be issued in order to take the testimony of one of these two witnesses.

ABOUT BABY BEATRICE

Eva Says the Child Was Not Hamilton's.

HER RELATIONS WITH JOSH MANN.

he Admits That They Were of a Very Questionable Character—There Was No Marriage and None Was Ever Mentioned—Eva's Fight for Her Dower.

IS HE DEAD OR ALIVE?

THE STRANGELY ROMANTIC CAREER OF ROBERT RAY HAMILTON.

DID IT END IN A TRAGEDY, OR WAS THE STORY OF HIS DEATH A FICTION?—SOME OF THE PECULIAR STATEMENTS MADE IN REGARD TO THE BODY FOUND IN THE IDAHO STREAM.

The story of Robert Ray Hamilton's downfall is a strange romance. It has not yet been proved that it is a tragedy. Perhaps it is not!

Nothing in the pages of fiction surpasses the startling truth regarding his career, says the New York Sun. Born of the best blood of New York, inheriting a fine estate, a member of the highest social circles, well educated, refined, and intelligent, he sought in politics diversion as well as duty. Believed to be incapable of accepting a bribe and marked as the soul of honor, he was foremost among the Republican leaders in the legislature, and challenged admiration by his devotion to every reform measure that had public favor and party support.

Suddenly a press dispatch in the newspapers recited Mr. Hamilton's narrow escape from death at the hands of a mistress frenzied with drink. Within a day, the world knew the sad and disgraceful story of his liaison with a vicious woman of the lowest type, a liaison that ended with marriage, and that was said to have borne fruit in the birth of a daughter.

Dragged into court to protect his alleged wife from the punishment she deserved, the proud-spirited man broke down. He found his only refuge in silence and seclusion. The conviction and imprisonment of his mistress for assaulting her nurse followed, and Mr. Hamilton was no longer heard of. He dropped completely out of sight until the press dispatches again made a startling announcement, that the death of Hamilton while on a ranch in Idaho, which it was said he had recently purchased, though he had never manifested the slightest interest in ranching.

The briefest possible announcement of his death was made, and it came from intimate friends of the family. The news, when borne to his venerable and affectionate father, sad as it was, did not fall, apparently, like an overwhelming blow. It seemed almost as if it had been anticipated. To newspaper inquirers the father simply remarked that he had no further facts to impart. The body was not brought home, the house was closed to all questioners, and no funeral notice was published until October 6, thirty-four days after the report of death, for the reason, as alleged, that Gen, Schuyler Hamilton had been ill for some time, and had not had an opportunity to have the notice published.

Under the pressure of constant inquiry, it was finally disclosed that in March last Mr. Hamilton had made a will in this city, and that late in the summer he had invited Mr. Gilbert M. Speir, Jr., one of the executors named in his will (the other was his cousin), to visit him at his far-away home in the wilderness of Idaho. When Mr. Speir arrived with another friend, Mr. C. D. R. Moore, on the 5th of September, he learned, as he said, that Hamilton's body had been found in the Snake River three days before.

It was reported that Mr. Hamilton had left his ranch in the absence of his partner, Mr. Sergent, on the 22nd of August, taking his horse and dogs, and gone hunting and fishing, going alone, though he was unfamiliar with the region, having resided there only a few weeks. Strangely enough, he took with him on this sporting trip his valuable gold watch and a number of letters and papers regarding his litigation with his mistress or wife. When, on Aug. 27, his partner came back to the ranch, he was told that Mr. Hamilton had gone hunting and had not returned. A searching party was organized, and on Sept. 1 Mr. Hamilton's horse was found, with the hams of an antelope upon its back, and his dogs were discovered wandering aimlessly about. The next day Mr. Hamilton's body was

discovered, and it was at once taken to his ranch and buried, because, as Mr. Sargent says, "He once told me that he would rather be buried here if anything should happen."

It is a remarkable fact that the body was found, not by Mr. Sargent, but by Mr. J. O. Green, son of Dr. Norvin Green, of the Western Union Telegraph Company, another friend of Hamilton. On his way to Yellowstone Park he made a detour to visit Mr. Hamilton's ranch, found he was missing, and joined in the search for him. According to Mr. Green's story, while looking along the Snake River he noticed Hamilton's body hidden under the overhanging branches of a tree. It appeared as if it had been in the water for five days, but Mr. Green says he was able immediately to recognize it; yet he particularly identified the watch and papers. Mr. Hamilton's horse, which had been wandering around for many days, was comfortably grazing, and the dogs, apparently, had been feeding on the antelope meat, and were also in excellent condition.

Mr. Green notified Hamilton's relatives at once, according to the statement telegraphed in the dispatches of Sept. 14 last, and then quietly went on and continued his hunting sport. Although, according to the statement, the body was found on the 2nd of September. Mr. Hamilton's father in this city received his first notice of his son's death on the 13th of September. This was brought to him by another son, and he was so little interested in it, according to the interview printed at the time, that he could not remember the signature to the dispatch. Two letters were forwarded to Sing Sing, giving what purported to be the fact in the case. One was sent by Mr. Sargent to the attorneys in Mr. Hamilton's suit to annul the marriage with Eva Hamilton, a marriage which his death annulled! The second was sent to Mr. Hamilton's brother by Mr. Moore. It was brief, but it urged that Mr. Hamilton's body be not removed. Mr. Moore said he knew that "Ray had expressed a wish to be buried here," in Idaho. Why this strange wish?

It is certainly most remarkable that Mr. Hamilton's father did not receive prompt and full information of his son's death, and that a friend of the family should have waited two weeks to notify him and then sent no particulars excepting by letter. It was strange that Mr. Speir happened to be in the vicinity at the time, and that just at this time Mr. Green, another friend, made a detour to visit Hamilton's ranch in the wilderness. It is also quite significant that Mr. E. R. Vollmer, of this city, who had charge of Mr. Hamilton's confidential business matters, disappeared and went West, according to the newspapers of last fall, just before the discovery of the body. It is peculiar, to say the least, that instead of hastening home to tell the shocking story to the bereaved family, both Mr. Speir and Mr. Moore decided to remain some time at the ranch, and Mr. Moore, in writing to the brother of Mr. Hamilton, said they stayed because "Mr. Sergent seems to want us to."

It is also noticeable that Mr. Hamilton, who had only been in possession of his ranch for six weeks, should have gone out alone in the wilds of the West to hunt and shoot, at a time, too, when he was expecting visitors who had notified him of their coming and who wished to participate in the sport. Moreover, according to the dispatches, Mr. Green expressed surprise, when he returned to Helena after his shooting expedition to Yellowstone Park, that the public had heard nothing of Mr. Hamilton's fate, though, if Mr. Green's first statement was accurately reported, the dispatches had been forwarded more than ten days previously.

Neither Mr. Hamilton's father nor his brother hastened West to bring the body home, leaving it to be buried at the ranch. His death annulled the marriage from which he had been trying to escape, and it only remained to determine the settlement of his property and to put the claimant for a dower interest to the trouble of contesting for herself. As soon as Mr. Hamilton's death was announced, Mr. Vollmer returned from the West and produced the will, which was immediately presented for probate. As it made no provision for the woman claiming to be his widow, she began her contest on her release from prison. Without the slightest difficulty the lawyers retained in behalf of the estate drew out from the unfortunate creature the evidence of her shame, wrung from her the admission that she had sustained marital relations with a drunken vagabond before she met Mr. Hamilton, and that therefore her marriage with the latter was illegal, and finally obtained her confession that the child she had presented as Hamilton's was neither his nor hers.

Her case was thrown out of court at once, and the Surrogate decided, finally, conclusively and absolutely that she had no claim on Mr. Hamilton's name or fortune. Then came a suggestive proceeding. Mr. Hamilton's will was again presented for probate, and the astonishing statement was made by the Surrogate that the evidence of death was insufficient. Neither of the two men who said they had seen the dead body and recognized it, was present. One of them, Mr. Hamilton's partner in the ranch, was sad to be snowed up in Idaho; and the other, Mr. Green, was in Europe. A commission was ordered to take the testimony of these two persons, and the end is not yet.

If Mr. Hamilton is not dead, he can now with safety return to his home. The woman who crossed his path has no longer a claim upon him. The child that he felt himself called upon to support, and to whom he left as his adopted daughter an annuity of $1,200 a year, is confessedly of another's blood. His estate is free from entanglements, as it was left mostly to his brother, who can pass it back and let Mr. Hamilton start in life anew. There are those who knew Robert Ray Hamilton well who have never believed for a single moment the story of his death. Taciturn, secretive, self-assertive, adroit, skillful in expedients as they ever knew him to be, they believe he foresaw that his only and readiest way of escape from a most distressing situation was by hiding behind the shelter of an invented death. Should he return, he will find himself now under no compulsion to appear in court, to face a judge or a jury, to hear and perhaps tell the story of his shame, or to meet his tormentor face to face. The tangle has been skillfully unraveled, the judgment given, and, if living, the way of life for Robert Ray Hamilton is once more straightened out before him.

Whether or not the veil of mystery will ever be lifted from the case, it stands as one of the most sensational in these sensational times, and sadly recalls the philosophic poet's couplet:

"The open, wayward life we see;
The secret, hidden springs we may not
know."

IS RAY HAMILTON ALIVE?

A STARTLING AND SENSATIONS STATEMENT.

REASONS FOR HIS ACTIONS.

ONE OF HIS WARMEST FRIENDS CLAIMS TO HAVE HAD
LETTERS FROM HIM RECENTLY—THE ALLEGED DROWNING A
PRE-ARRANGED SCHEME.

NEW YORK, FEBRUARY 8.—A.O. Howard, until recently an officer in the coast survey, and who was the playmate, schoolmate and college mate of Robert Ray Hamilton, in an interview with a Times reporter on Tuesday, January 27th, used this language: "Robert Ray Hamilton is alive and in good health. He is beginning life anew there under an assumed name. He has cast behind him the past and is looking hopefully forward to the future."

At Mr. Howard's request his name was not used in connection with the interview. At a subsequent meeting with the reporter he said:

"I have here in my pocket" (producing a bundle of letters) "several letters from my old friend Ray Hamilton. They were written after I went West. The last one I received from him is dated at San Francisco, Cal., Friday, October 3, 1890."

Hamilton was supposed to have been drowned on August 21.

"In this letter Mr. Hamilton appraised me of his intention of going to Japan and then to Sydney, New South Wales. I have received no communication from him since that time, but, allowing for leisurely traveling, delays, sight-seeing, etc., I would say that he has reached Australia by this time. His adoption of an assumed name is only to avoid notoriety and to keep his whereabouts secret."

"Would you object to my reading the letter?" asked the reporter.

"I most assuredly would. When I first mentioned the fact that Mr. Hamilton was alive I had no idea that you would print what I said or that the interview would provoke so much controversy. The letters that I have in my pocket are of a personal nature and were written solely for my eyes. Robert Ray Hamilton and I have been friends for years. I am the custodian of many of his secrets, to reveal and publish which would result in no good to him and would be of no public interest."

"Will Mr. Hamilton make Australia his permanent home?" was asked.

"The settlement of that matter rests solely with him," was the answer. "He may or may not. I cannot say positively, but I think that before many months he will return to New York."

Mr. Howard asked that this interview be withheld from publication until his return from New York. This morning Mr. Howard passed through this city on his way West. His destination he refused to disclose. By appointment the reporter who interviewed him met him at the Broad street station, and in response to numerous questions he made this statement: "When I said in the latter part of January that Robert Ray Hamilton was alive and in Sydney, New South Wales, I only partly spoke the truth. Mr. Hamilton is alive and well. He is not in Australia, however, and if it matters which are of vital importance to him move along in the groove which he has marked out, he will return to New York within three months. His exact location I cannot make public. At least six of Mr. Hamilton's friends know where he is and are in constant communication with him. My visit to New York was to arrange some matters of business in which he is interested.

"During our previous interview you asked me why Robert Ray Hamilton would feign death and under an assumed name bury himself in the antipodes. In answer to that question it will be necessary for me to go back several years, beginning with his first acquaintance with the cunning and unscrupulous woman who is in a great measure responsible for his social, political and moral downfall. I think I made the acquaintance of Eva Steele, Brell, Mann or Hamilton at the time that Mr. Hamilton

first met her. Hamilton seemed to be infatuated with the woman. She accompanied him to Albany and they lived together. Hamilton introduced her to his legislative friends, and their house was the resort of many of New York's leading statesmen. They were frequently disgraceful orgies enacted there. When men are under the influence of liquor they say things which would otherwise remain unsaid. Eva Mann became acquainted with many state secrets and, being a scheming woman, she hoarded up this knowledge to use for her own advantage. Eva Hamilton had in her possession letters and other documentary evidence which, if made public, would humble to the dust the heads of many New Yorkers. I know she use this information to coerce Hamilton into making her his wife. It was because of the threat of Mrs. Hamilton to make certain disclosures that would affect the prospects of a prominent New York politician that Ray took to Lower California the February after they were married.

"No man knows how keenly he felt the disgrace that was brought upon him, and it was to seek oblivion that he went to a lonely ranch in Nez Perces county, Idaho. While he was there he was, of course, in constant communication with his friends and with his attorney. Through them he learned that Eva Hamilton had threatened to make things hot for him and certain others high in New York politics as soon as she was released from the

New Jersey State prison. It was in a moment of desperation that simulation of death was thought of and carried out. Of course, his friends and relatives were prepared for the thing beforehand. It was the fact that they did not show the surprise nor evince the grief that would be natural under the circumstances that first led newspapers and afterward the general public to question the fact of Mr. Hamilton's death.

"The purpose for which he simulated death has been accomplished. He was afraid that when brought face to face with Eva Hamilton in court she would either make a startling revelation herself or have questions to put to him when he should take the stand that would add further to his own disgrace and bring disgrace upon others. He desired to save his friends. He has done so, and they know it. It is probable now that the whole wretched scandal will die out. Arrangements have been made within the last few days which will eventuate in a settlement of the difficulty to the satisfaction of all parties. It may be possible that Mr. Hamilton will for some time remain in his present hiding place. He may come back to New York, mingle with his friends and trust to time to live down the scandal."

"It is said that Mr. J.O. Green, son of Dr. Norvin Green, of the Western Union Telegraph Company, who is now in Europe, will make an affidavit that the body found by him in snake River, Idaho, was Mr. Hamilton," said the reporter.

"He will do nothing of the kind," was Mr. Howard's emphatic reply. "Mr. Green is a gentleman of the very highest character, and he would not perjure himself. I am sure that he never said that he had positively identified the body as that of Robert Ray Hamilton. Anyway, you can say from me that it was not his body."

"Whose body was it?"

"That question I decline to answer, but it was not Robert Ray Hamilton's."

Eva Hamilton's Story.

WILKESBARRE, March 19.—Eva Hamilton left for New York to-day. She said that Robert Ray Hamilton's family had offered her $60,000 to settle all matters, but she wants $75,000.

NEW YORK, March 19.—Eva Hamilton's counsel and the counsel of the Hamilton estate deny having made any negotiations with her.

THE NEW YORK WORLD
TUESDAY, MAY 19, 1891

EVA AS AN ACTRESS.

RAY HAMILTON'S ALLEGED WIDOW TO GO UPON THE STAGE.

HER CAREER AND THAT OF HER VICTIM WILL BE DEPICTED.

A DESPERATE SCHEME FOR MONEY AND MORE NOTORIETY.

FOR TWO MONTHS SHE HAS BEEN RECEIVING INSTRUCTION FROM A DRAMATIC TUTOR — NEW AND HITHERTO UNSUSPECTED FEATURES OF THE HAMILTON CASE PROMISED IN THE PORTRAYAL.

Following the dramatic developments in the mysterious case of Robert Ray Hamilton comes the announcement that his alleged widow Eva is about to make her debut in the role of an actress. Coupled with this announcement comes the one, even more surprising, that the play in which she is to appear will set forth with great power and effect the dramatic life story of the unfortunate man who is supposed to have met his death among the tangled weeds at the bottom of Snake River. Again the skeleton which has disturbed the serenity of one of the most historic families in this country is to be dragged forth from its charnel-house and exposed to public view. It is promised that the stage portrayal will bring to light new and hitherto unsuspected features in this remarkable case. Eva will appear in a conspicuous rule.

The play in which Eva will appear is entitled "The Hammertons." In the opening act she will appear as Nadine Brenn, and in the subse-quent three act she will assume the rôle of Mrs. Hammerton, which is a palpable play upon Robert Ray's family name. The surprising revelations are promised for the fourth and last act, but the character of the alleged disclosures are being carefully guarded, and will not be revealed by either Eva or her manager until the scenes are enacted upon the stage. As yet the cast has not been entirely arranged, but it will be in part as follows:

NADINE BRENNAN/MRS. HAMMERTON....
Mrs. Robert Ray Hamilton

MR. HAMMERTON.............................——

MRS. VINTON.............................——

JOSH DANN (MRS. VINCENT'S SON)....——

LAWYER HOWELL, ALSO A DETECTIVE...——

NURSE CONNELLY.............................——

BABY HAMMERTON.............................——

There will be fourteen characters in the cast. The company has not as yet been engaged, but promise is made that it will be a strong one. The scenes of the play will be laid in New York and vicinity and Atlantic City, where the stabbing of Nurse

Donnelly first revealed Robert Ray's unfortunate marital complications.

In the initial act will be portrayed the first meeting between Mrs. Hamilton and Nadine Brenn and their subsequent marriage. The second and third actual will deal with their married life. The climax in the third act will be the stabbing of the nurse in Atlantic City.

In the fourth act Mrs. Hamilton declares that she will disclose "startling revelations" concerning her married life. To bring her production in touch with the realistic tendency of the day, the latest aspirant for histrionic honors will appear in one of the acts seated upon a saddle horse which she rode during her intimacy with Mr. Hamilton in Central Park, and at Passaic Bridge and Atlantic City. Her manager, in due time, will bring out his proofs that she is a graceful and daring equestrian.

A TALK WITH THE FUTURE STAR.

Mrs. Hamilton was found yesterday at her temporary country residence by a reporter for THE WORLD. She was dressed for the street and said she was about to start for a rehearsal. She was attired in deep mourning and her features were particularly hidden behind a thin black veil which she subsequently removed, disclosing a pretty face, mightily flushed, with a dimple in the chin. She is tall and possesses a slender and graceful figure. Nothing in her appearance is indicative of her varied and eventful career, which has repeatedly been made public. Regarding Mr. Hamilton she would say nothing. She complained, however, of the way the newspapers had commented upon her and consented to say that she has keenly felt her position before the public.

"I do not care to speak of the past," she said, "it is too full of sadness. Yes, I have not only decided to go on the stage, but have been in training for that purpose for more than a month. I have signed a contract with a well-known and wealthy gentleman, outside of the theatrical business, who has in turn arranged with an old and experienced theatrical manager to assist him in the details of booking and arranging the routes. They will also arrange for the company. It is our intention to have a strong supporting company and to play only in the best theaters. I shall open with a two weeks engagement at the Broadway theater in November. I am unable to say just now what our route will be after leaving the city. I have some litigation on hand, which will be so arranged in a few days that I should be able to tell positively when my presence will be required here to attend to it. Then the route will be arranged accordingly. I have adopted the stage as a means of earning an honest livelihood, and at the same time preparing a truthful portrayal of the incident of my married life, which were so terribly distorted by the newspapers and my husband. I am studying hard and I know I shall like the stage very much. I appreciate all the hard work and the many obstacles that are in my path, but I am determined to push ahead and feel now that I shall be fairly successful. Another thing, my life recently has been very lonely. Of course I have numerous friends, but I don't let them know where I am, especially since I began preparing for the stage, because they would only interfere with my studies.

"When did I make up my mind to go on the stage? Only within the last two months. I had constantly been receiving letters through my counsel from theatrical managers making me most tempting offers, to all of which I paid little or no attention. I finally realized, however, the necessity of doing something for a living, and after careful study of the matter, decided to go upon the stage.

She continued by saying her health was excellent, and that she felt able to withstand the hardships of an extended tour of the whole country.

(Editor's note: here the copy I have becomes illegible. I have cobbled together the rest from parts of this article and an Associated Press story that ran across the country, specifically in the Independent-Record of Helena, Montana and the Star-Gazette of Elmira, NY)

Mrs. Mann, or Hamilton, comes to New York every day to take lessons from a well-known dramatic teacher. The World reporter also had an interview with the gentleman who had undertaken to prepare her for the stage. Both he and Eva's financial backer insisted that for the present their names be withheld.

A gentleman outside of the theatre, who has loosened his purse-strings to see Eva before the public, was confident as to her future.

CONFIDENT OF HER SUCCESS.

"Mrs. Hamilton has great dramatic force in her," he said, "and the scenes of the play are well suited to her. I understand the substance of the play are true, am familiar with some details of her married life. I don't see that it can be anything else than a hit that way. The curiosity of the public for Mrs. Hamilton, and the story of her life portrayed by herself, promises large audiences."

The dramatic teacher, with apparent reluctance, admitted that he was giving Eva lessons in acting.

"She is to appear in a play written expressly for her, and which will embody many of the startling episodes in her eventful career."

"Do you think she will be successful?"

"Why not? She has been as extensively advertised as any woman in America. The stories of her past life which have appeared in print from time to time will not be very quickly forgotten by the public. Neither will the principal scenes enacted by her and those surrounding her in the trying ordeals. The court proceedings and the famous Hamilton will case were watched with keen interest from Maine to California. No prosecution of modern times, probably, has attracted so much attention as the case against her in New Jersey.

"True, public opinion was divided, with the preponderance against her, but even many of those who condemned her saw that it was a struggle of a lone, friendless woman against power and wealth. No matter whether she was guilty or innocent, or about the wrongs she may have caused or endured, there is a spirit of fair play which exists among us that will always show itself."

The conversation then turned to the death of Robert Ray Hamilton.

NEEDS MONEY TO FIGHT HER SUIT.

"There are many well-informed people," continued the tutor, "who do not believe that Robert Ray Hamilton is dead. Within three weeks a daily newspaper has printed in a half-column article an argument, based on many incidents known to be facts, to prove that he was still alive. Do you suppose that any sane man, a man of education and refinement such as Hamilton was, would do all the things attributed to him? Eva does not believe that he is dead. She does not express herself, but she sees before her a long and expensive litigation with a rich and powerful family. There is no better way for her to obtain the necessary funds to meet the inevitable expenses than to go upon the stage. When the general public understand this case as I do, they will flock to see her, in my opinion, and the largest theatres will be too small to accommodate the thousands who will want to see presented in dramatic form the principal incidents connected with the life of Mr. and Mrs. Hamilton. Many details will necessarily be omitted, but their first meeting, two acts of their married life, and many incidents which thus far have been made public only in a garbled and disjointed form will be shown in their true light, while the last act will be a revelation even to those who think they have nothing more to learn.

"Eva has a great deal of dramatic ability. She is a veritable tempest when aroused, as her career has disclosed. In some of her strong scenes she surprises me, and I look at her in amazement. I guess the people who saw her at times in the court-room will not question her dramatic force and power. She will surely make her mark on the stage. She is a genius, and her talent will be quickly recognized when brought before the public. Besides all this, she has a great deal of feeling in this matter. She considers herself the victim of a conspiracy, and means to contest the decision of Surrogate Ransom that she is not Mr. Hamilton's widow to the bitter end. She also thinks that the stage life will be congenial, the surroundings thoroughly agreeable and her natural ability sufficient to give her a fair standing in the profession. There is no doubt that every theatrical manager will be anxious to secure her as an attraction, for there can be no question about the drawing powers of Mrs. Robert Ray Hamilton in a play which is virtually the story of her life."

THE VISIT OF EVA HAMILTON.

The passing of Eva Hamilton was of little moment, save in the revival of the old stories of the scene at Noll Cottage, the arrest, the trial, conviction and sentence. You were told of her movements in the daily dispatchers. She came almost wholly unobserved, except by those who could not fail to recognize her, and who told The Inquirer correspondent and one other newspaper representative, and she has gone with even less show of interest. If she sought retirement from public gaze and kindly treatment as well, she could not have chosen a more secure or more hospitable shelter than the cottage of ex-Sheriff Smith E. Johnson. Mrs. Hamilton had reason to know that she would find a friend in the even-tempered, sympathetic disposition of her ex-jailor's wife and in his own robust, bluff, good nature. She had been treated by the one at May's Landing as some women will not treat others in distress and she had been as leniently indulged as duty under the law would permit by the other. She was spared officious annoyance on the part of some of those who she knew or thought had hounded her before and though she complained bitterly of treatment by some of the newspapers, yet she conceded that others had prior to and during her trial endeavored to do her justice.

That she will need money in the upcoming litigation to obtain what she regards as her due if she should be the widow of the son of the old General Schuyler Hamilton brooks no doubt. It will be a long and most stubborn fight, where wealth and position will have vantage over blackened reputation and worse and meagreness of purse. What Colonel Fuller, her counsel, came here for that demanded her presence also has not been specifically made known. It is the lawyer's secret of a client's hope that must be divulged to none lest the resisting force meet it and defeat its purpose. The Prosecutor of the Peace, whose searching cross-examination broke down her case before a judge and jury—Joseph E. Thompson—has no theory, because the record is clear in sustaining her conviction. As for her theatrical venture, she is, it is believed, doing her best to attain success. The abandonment of the original intent—the production of the "Hammertons" with the plot worked up upon the occurrences here and elsewhere that culminated in the stabbing of the after dime museum freak, Nurse Donnelly—is taken by those who know the strength and weakness of her character best as evidence that she caught, of herself, or by impression of her teacher, the fear of failure and was easily induced to make the change. Mentally, she is less excitable, less morose than two years ago, and physically she is said to be in the best health. So you will not have heard the last of Eva Hamilton, though she'll be gone from here and be living down on a Connecticut farm.

WILKESBARRE EVENING LEADER
WEDNESDAY, SEPTEMBER 2, 1891

EVA AT THE FOOTLIGHTS.

STARRING IN NEW JERSEY AS MRS. ROBERT RAY HAMILTON.

THE PLAY IS "ALL A MISTAKE."

THE PLOT OF HER SENSATIONAL PIECE IS FOUNDED UPON HER AFFAIR WITH HAMILTON, BUT SHE FIGURES AS A HEROINE OF HIGH CHARACTER—JOSH MANN THE VILLAIN.

BOONTON, N.J., SEPT. 2.—That curious woman who calls herself Mrs. Robert Ray Hamilton, but whom the courts decided to be Mrs. Joshua Mann, has once more shuffled the cards and has made a new deal in the entertaining if uncertain game of adventure which she began so many years ago. In this small New Jersey town she made her debut as an actress last night in a play embracing and centering about the incidents of her life with Robert Ray Hamilton. Months ago it was known that some one had written a play for her which was to be called "The Habbertons," and it was also known as that Habberton was selected because it would suggest to the public the fact that the play would deal with the Robert Ray Hamilton episode.

"ALL A MISTAKE."

Eva has been spending the months of retirement in restoring her shattered nerves and in developing that histrionic talent which every adventuress is confident she possesses. That she studied assiduously and with some intelligence was shown by her performance last night.

During the last two months rehearsals have been frequent. Among the first moves Manager Gardiner made was to change the title of the play. He decided that "The Habbertons" was not as attractive as it might be, and substituted "All a Mistake," relying upon the publishing of the name, Mrs. Robert Ray Hamilton, in big black type just under the title, to put people in mind of what was "all a mistake."

HER STYLE OF PLAYBILL.

There's not been any great amount of money back of the enterprise. For the past week various small New Jersey towns have been billed with posters reading like this:

THE SEASON'S SENSATION.
MRS. ROBERT RAY HAMILTON,
UNDOUBTEDLY THE MOST FAMOUS
WOMAN IN THE LAND,
FOR ONE NIGHT ONLY,
IN HER BEAUTIFUL, REALISTIC AND
PRETTY ROMANTIC DRAMA, ENTITLED
ALL A MISTAKE.
SUPPORTED BY A COMPETENT COMPANY
OF METROPOLITAN PLAYERS.
EVA AS A HERONE.

About 250 people came out to see her in the evening. The plot of the play follows the incident known to the public, but it follows them in a distorted way. Eva Mann is made out to be a heroine and a martyr. Robert Ray Hamilton as a weak but noble-hearted man of the world. Both are victims of the wiles of a character who is supposed to be Josh Mann and of another character, a cast off mistress of the hero, who never appeared. Robert Ray Hamilton is masquerading under the name of Roland Livingstone. Josh Mann is called Ivan Vanteck. Eva Mann is called Nadine, a friendless orphan, surrounded by low and vicious persons. Nurse Donnelly may be strainedly discovered in a Mrs. Preston, who is a drunken housekeeper for the Livingstones.

THE PLOT OF THE PLAY.

To strip the characters of their names in the play, Robert Ray Hamilton is made to meet and love Eva Mann, thereby enraging his bosom friend, Josh Mann, and his cast off mistress. The wicked Josh hires a man to personate a priest, and thus when Robert Ray and Eva think they are married, they are not. Eva finds out the truth through the drunken housekeeper, thinks Robert Ray has deceived her, and prepares to fly. She is prevented, and a second and genuine marriage takes place. They go to the seashore, followed by the machinations of the same villains.

The drunken housekeeper comes in with a knife and tries to stab Eva; Robert Ray interferes and accidentally stabbed the drunken housekeeper. Crowd rushes in.

EVA TAKES THE BLAME.

Eva takes the blame and Robert flies—which is a new and much revised version of the story of the crime for which Eva did time in the Trenton penitentiary. The last act does not pretend to follow the facts, unless it is intended as a sort of prophecy, for in it Eva is about to marry Josh because she thinks Robert Ray is dead, and would wish her to marry his bosom friend. But Robert Ray comes back just in the nick o' time, and villain Josh sneaks away exposed, while the castoff mistress takes poison and dies.

SHE MAKES UP WELL.

Eva certainly makes up well. Her stage presence takes ten years from her life and much of the hardness from her face. Considering the fact that she never acted before on the stage, her poses and her stage walk are quite good. Her form shows to advantage, and her bare arms are round and white and tapering.

But when it comes to reading the lines Eva Mann is not there at all. If ever a play demanded tragedy of this sky piercing sort this play requires it. Eva Mann expressed a tremendous passion in her gestures, while her voice had about as little excitement in it as a glass of rain water. The contrast was highly entertaining.

THE STAR WAS OVERSHADOWED.

When she said, "oh, that Roland

were here in spirit," she waved her arms and body frantically, but maintained an even tone set aside in good society for observations about the weather. When she cast up her eyes and try to blush it was a cause for a far from polite titter in the Opera house. The company is about of the barn-storming average with one or two exceptions, who are a trifle above it. Mrs. Mann's gowns would not create a sensation on a city stage. But in her costume in the last act she won great applause, her neck and arms showing to fine advantage. The lady who played the cast off mistress did very creditably, acting far better than the star.

EVA MANN ON THE STAGE.

BILLED THROUGH NEW JERSEY AS MRS. ROBERT RAY HAMILTON.

Her Debut Made Last Evening in the Opera House in Boonton — The Play Gives Her Version of Robert Ray Hamilton's Ruin—Her Style of Acting.

THE DEMOCRAT AND CHRONICLE
WEDNESDAY, SEPTEMBER 9, 1891

A DESERVED FAILURE.

EVA MANN'S ALLEGED THEATRICAL COMPANY BROUGHT TO GRIEF.

SHAMOKIN, PA., SEPT. 8.—The collapse of Mrs. Eva Mann's theatrical enterprise has been complete. The people didn't care to see her parade her disgrace and the show did not draw. The company was discharged here after the performance Saturday night. Eva paid the hotel bills out her own pockets. The receipts of the performance were very small. In all about 300 persons, mostly men, attended the show and they made it very unpleasant for Eva. They made derogatory remarks about her acting, her appearance and her character loud enough to be heard on the stage. Mrs. Mann once fell back into the arms of her leading man out of sheer nervousness. Her manager said she did not even make a pretense of acting. She relied entirely on her bad character to draw. She never attended rehearsals. Instead, she remained at her hotel, drinking wine and smoking cigarettes. While here she gave an exhibition of temper. She was called on in her room by an enterprising boy, who begged permission to sell her photographs to the audience in the evening. The adventuress flew into a rage and drove the boy from her room. She said that the newspapers had paraded her face entirely too much to suit her.

EVA SEEMED ASHAMED.

They Thought That She had a Right to be After the Play.

EVA MANN IS BACK AGAIN.

THE NOTORIOUS WOMAN RETURNS AFTER HER ATTEMPT AT "ACTING."

When Eva Mann, the notorious woman with whom Robert Ray Hamilton became entangled, was released from Trenton prison, where she was confined for stabbing Mrs. Donnelly, the nurse of the bogus Hamilton baby, she began to prepare for the stage.

Charles R. Gardiner, a theatrical manager who lives at Norton, Conn., wrote a play for her built upon the incidents in her career and her connection with Mr. Hamilton. He engaged a company to support her. It wasn't a large company now was it an expensive one. Mr. Curtiss, the theatrical agent, said yesterday the salary list footed up about $325 a week.

According to Eva's contract with Gardiner she was to furnish her own wardrobe and get half of the net profits. Alas for her dreams of wealth and fame! She said Sunday night that she was out of pocket fully $600.

Eva and the "All a Mistake" combination came back to town Sunday night. The Eva Mann company, in addition to the star, consisted of Edward Warren, Harry W. Mitchell, C.R. Patterson, J.E. Sheehan, Ella Wieman, Mrs. Edward Clifford and Florence Mirrill. Warren was the leading man. He was the Roland Livingstone of the play, and stabbed the nurse. Nadine, his wife, though, took the crime upon herself. That is where the mistake was made. The Josh Mann of the play was called Ivan Vanteck.

The company played just five nights and went to pieces at Shamokin, Pa., last Saturday night.

"We broke up because we refused to play any more," said Mr. Warren yesterday. "I was to be paid my salary every night. I didn't get it on Friday and Saturday. Besides, we had no paper, not even a lithograph of the star. There was a lot of half-sheet and three-sheet posters in the express office, but Follansbee, the advance agent couldn't get it out. It was sent C.O.D. and the bill was $15. Follansbee didn't have beer money. Gardner started him out with $5."

"How did the star act?"

"Very well for a beginner. Yes, she knew her lines, but she didn't speak loud enough."

"Did she tell you what she had had enough of the stage?"

"No. I think she will continue in the profession. She did not get a cent, but she helped pay the railroad fares home. I parted from her on the ferry, and haven't seen her since."

Eva Mann is somewhere in New York, but she evidently does not want to talk of her starring tour of five days in Jersey and Pennsylvania towns.

NO TIGHTS FOR EVA.

ROBERT RAY HAMILTON'S IDOL AS A BOWERY BURLESQUER.

A BIG AUDIENCE OF TOUGHS.

DISAPPOINTED BECAUSE SHE DRESSED MODESTLY AND IN EVERY WAY APPEARED OUT OF HARMONY WITH HER DIZZY SETTINGS SURROUNDINGS—IS BILLED AS "FAMOUS" AND DRAWS $400 PER WEEK.

NEW YORK, SEPT. 30.—Evangeline Steele, who claims to be the widow of Robert Ray Hamilton, yet who is claiming in a suit for divorce by "Dotty" Mann, has reached the pinnacle of one variety of ambition.

She has made her debut before a metropolitan audience. And what an audience!

The London Theatre, in the Bowery, the inner construction of which is such that the seats rise, tier on tier from the stage clear to the roof at the back of the auditorium, was crammed, packed, jammed full of people last night.

It was a typical Bowery audience. There were gamblers and gutter-snipes, newsboys in east-side merchants, with here and there an ill-advised woman.

The doors opened at 7:15. In five minutes every seat was occupied. Half the men lighted cigars and the other half sighed, because pipe-smoking is against the rules of the house.

On the big mirrors that adorn the walls of the theater was artistically painted in red, white and blue soap the announcement that:

> The Famous
> EVA RAY HAMILTON
> will appear this week.

In four places on the programmes distributed at the door was the announcement in black letter that Eva Ray Hamilton would appear in the burlesque, "looking for O—," and the last name on the programme was that of the woman who hoodwinked New York's young statesman, befooled him with a borrowed baby, run riot with his immense income, stabbed Baby Beatrice's nurse in a fit of ungovernable temper and served a year in Trenton prison, posed as the stricken widow of the descendent of the great secretary, whom she had dishonored, and confessed to Surrogate Ransom a series of appalling sins covering a period of years; capping the climax on being thrown out of court denied a participation in the Hamilton millions, by offering her undesirable self to New Jersey audiences in a play purporting to rehearse the story of her life with Hamilton.

Everyone in that smoking, shirt-sleeved, perspiring audience waited in feverish expectancy for the appearance of Eva, but they waited till after 10 o'clock.

Then the burlesque came on, and with it Eva.

About a score of wonderfully developed women were prancing about the stage of the London in lurid costumes, when four Vassar girls in knee-high skirts, brilliant tights, frizzled hair and mortarboard hats suddenly missed "Minnie."

"Why, where is Minnie, Daly?" one asked, and another answered: "Oh, here she comes."

That was the cue for the appearance of the new star of the evening. The audience held its breath, and there sidled in from the wings a tall, rather angular female, with a deep blush, that she brought down to the theater in her reticule, on her rather pleasing face.

Then there was a hush—then a little, rather doubtful murmur of applause. Eva bowed like a grammar school recitationist, but the audience was disappointed and there was no more applause for her.

There was no anatomical display at all. The supposed shapely limbs of the siren who won Ray Hamilton's heart and turned his head were invisible. They were draped in a gown of soft pink stuff, embroidered and beflowered. It was cut low in the neck, but there was a lace filling. It came down to the ankles,

showing only a bit of pink stocking in a silvern shoe. The long, rather elbowish arms were bare, save for diamond bracelets, and at least a dozen diamond rings were distributed over the fingers of both hands.

There were solitaires in Eva's ears, and manager Tom Miaco whispered in almost awe-stricken tones that Eva's diamonds cost him $10,000.

Eva's brown hair—it was sunny yellow in the old Hamilton days—was combed Boston fashion, straight back from her low brow, and it was covered up by a tremendous big hat of white leghorn.

Eva trembled. She was clearly abashed by the sloping walls of pug-nosed faces before her. She said her few lines in a half-audible voice, like a schoolgirl.

She looked at her slippers and picked at a rich lace fan till she nearly tore it to pieces. Then she exchanged it for a less expensive lace handkerchief.

The half dozen lines were read in a stammering, halting way that inflicted deserving suffering upon her auditors, and a sigh of relief actually went up as she hurried from the stage at her cue.

Eva is not a histrionic success. She has a way of nodding her head as if she might say "Uh-huh!" in expression of her understanding of the remarks of the other characters.

"I had a hard time getting Eva at all," says Tom Miaco. "I pay her $400 a week. Our contract is for six weeks and I have the privilege of continuing it. But she insisted on an iron-clad cause in the contract that she would not wear tights and stipulating that her gowns must come down to the ankle and must not be decolette. She has her carriage that brings her from her hotel just in time for her act and takes her back again."

Studying a Play.

DEAD BEYOND DOUBT.

THE END OF ROBERT RAY HAMILTON IS A MYSTERY NO LONGER.

AN INQUEST IN WYOMING WILDS.

EVIDENCE WHICH MADE THE IDENTIFICATION OF THE BODY COMPLETE.

THE ROUGH MANNER OF HIS BURIAL.

MARKET LAKE, IDAHO, OCTOBER 14.— Coroner Henry Code, of Evanston, Unitah county, Wyo., arrived here to-day after a journey of two weeks' duration to Jackson's Lake, in what is known as Jackson's Hole, in the northwest corner of Wyoming, where he held an inquest over the body of the late Robert Ray Hamilton, of New York, who drowned more than a year ago. The story of the last days of Mr. Hamilton, already partly known to the public, is now complete.

There were curious facts about the death, and the public very soon connected them with another interesting fact. Hamilton's death, if he was dead, not only annulled his marriage with the wife, Evangeline, but threw upon her the burden of proof in the legal squabble over the estate. If she were to share the estate she must needs prove she was a widow of the deceased man. The advantage which the Hamilton family obtained through the death of Robert Ray in the contest with Evangeline was apparent.

Then Henry Strong, of Green, Chenango county, N.Y., who had been in the Yellowstone Park, came East and declared that he had seen Hamilton alive in the Park, having recognized him by his voice as well his features.

LETTERS FROM A DEAD MAN.

Later came A.O. Howard, of the coast survey service, who said he had been a schoolmate of the deceased man, and that he had received letters later than August from Hamilton, who is supposed to have been drowned in the latter part of August in the year. While there were inconsistencies in the full statements of these men, they were not without their weight.

Finally a reputable young citizen of Idaho, who had been in Jackson's Hole with a party of mining engineers, returned home after having been some time in the mountains and reported that events the residents of Jackson's Hole doubt it very much the identity of the body. An investigation which would forever settle the matter was then instituted.

As The Dispatch correspondent, in his journey to the Fenton region, drew near to his destination he found the public interest in the case growing stronger, and the belief that Hamilton was alive was more firm. Leaving Market Lake, the nearest railroad station, he went back 22 miles to a village called Rixburg by the Mormons, who outnumber all the other inhabitants, and Kaintuck by the postoffice authorities.

SURE IT WAS HAMILTON.

Here he called upon Roman Safert, one of the workmen who had testified to the identity of the body found in Snake river. Mr. Safert was still sure that the body was that of Hamilton, but when asked to describe the body he said among other things that the upper front teeth had been filled with gold in a most conspicuous fashion. As a matter of fact the upper front teeth of Robert Ray Hamilton were noticeably large and perfect. This fact seemed to confirm the belief prevalent throughout the community.

The most intelligent and influential men here were confident not only that Hamilton was still alive, but that a man resembling him had been sent to Jackson's Hole to personate him, and had there been put out of the way by John Delaney Sargeant.

Indeed, when one considers the extraordinary fact that no effort had been made to remove the body to a suitable resting place, and that no inquest had been held over the body by the Coroner, it was impossible to escape the conclusion reached by the citizens living nearest the region where Hamilton was alleged to have been drowned.

THE CORONER FORCED TO ACT.

Accordingly the following affidavit was filed with Coroner Code, of Evanston, Wyo., who had jurisdiction over the district:

State of Wyoming, county of Unitah:

The affiant John R. Spears, after having been first duly sworn, deposes and says that there is buried in the said county and State the dead body of a man reported to be Robert Ray Hamilton, and that the said body of the person so buried was interred at or near what is known as Jackson's Hole, and that affiant is informed and believes that person so buried came to his death by unlawful means and by violence, and that said body was buried without any inquest having been made thereon.

Thereat, Coroner Code, with W.A. Hecker, an experienced surgeon of Evanston, joined a party organized by the correspondent, and on Thursday, October 1, left Market Lake Station in a blinding snowstorm for Jackson's Hole. Their adventures in crossing the plains and Teton pass and in following the Sheridan trail to their destination, were at times quite thrilling. One week later, October 8, they camped on Jackson's Lake, a quarter of a mile from the Hamilton lodge, and the next morning the body was disinterred and carefully examined for such marks as would identify it were it really the body of Robert Ray Hamilton.

MARKS FOR IDENTIFICATION.

One of these marks was simple and easy to distinguish. Mr. Hamilton had glossy black hair, his upper front teeth were noticeably perfect while those in the lower jaw were crowded and overlapped. Further than this he had, while riding in Central park one morning, fallen from his horse and had fractured his left leg below the knee, an injury that kept him in the hospital for eleven weeks. When this fracture healed the growth of the bone formed a prominent projection on the front of the shin. There were still other marks of identification as the following statement of Dr. Hecker made when testifying before the jury shows:

"On October 9, 1891, I was called on by a Coroner's jury to examine a body supposed to be that of Robert Ray Hamilton. I made the examination, and as marks of identification found the first molar tooth in the right lower jaw filled with gold, the second molar on the same side and jaw filled with silver or some composition, the last molar on the same side and jaw filled with gold. The second molar on the left side of the lower jaw were gone, and I presume had been extracted, as the bone had filled up and absorbed in a way to show that the tooth had been gone quite a time. I also found the left tibia had been fractured about the middle and the leg a little shortened as a result of the fracture. I have also heard all the testimony of the witnesses examined before the Cor-

oner's jury, and I'm satisfied that the body examined by me to-day is that of Robert Ray Hamilton."

SETTLING AN IMPORTANT POINT.

Partner Sargent said that these teeth have been filled and the one extracted by a dentist in New York during the month of May proceeding Hamilton's death. He probably told the truth, for he had a memorandum book in which were noted in Hamilton's hand the charges made by the dentist. The other witnesses were Mrs. Sergent and John H. Holland, J.P. Cunningham and Edward Hunter, who were of the searching party. They testified of the details of finding the body, which have already been published. The jurors were Robert E. Miller, Andrew Mattson and C.F. Hamm. They rendered the following verdict:

"State of Wyoming, county of Unitah. We, the Coroner's jury, empaneled to inquire into the cause, time and manner of the death of the person whose body lies before us, do find the name of the deceased was Robert Ray Hamilton, a native of the United States, aged about 39 years, and then he came to his death in the State and county or force it, by being accidentally drowned while attempting to cross snake river, below Jackson's lake. According to the evidence furnished by his watch, which had stopped when he entered the water, and by a note which he left on a tag at the south end of the lake, Robert Ray Hamilton was drowned at 9.30 O'clock on Saturday night, August 24, 1890."

The picture presented to the little group of spectators when the cover of the rude box in which the remains were found had been removed was pitiful and shocking. Here lay the body of one who had served his constituents well—legislative, assembly—and who was, moreover, a great grandson of one of the most distinguished statesmen.

A VERY HASTY BURIAL.

It was crowded into a box too shallow to allow the feet to remain upright. It was clothed in a rough woolen coat, waistcoat, and shirt, and in trousers that had been cut off below the knee into the semblance of knickerbockers. Thick leather leggings and leather shoes were on the bare extremities and a pair of heavy spurs were strapped over all. Around these were twined long shreds of water grass. The kindly face and graceful form his friends had known were gone with his gentle spirit.

Strangers found his body, and those who could not appreciate his worth knocked a few boards together for a coffin, wrapped the body in a dirty and ragged tarpaulin, loaded it into the box and so, without a tear or prayer, dumped it into a hole on a desolate hillside, under the shadow of the barren, forbidding tetoes—and there it was allowed to remain, marked only by rough pine headboards, on which someone had scrawled with a lead pencil a tribute of praise that, when viewed in the light of all the facts, is an exasperating mockery.

A loyal friend, a true gentleman and a brave man was Robert Ray Hamilton; but hundreds of dogs have been more decently interred by their masters than was he by the friends to whom he was loyal.

Eva Mann's Manager Dying.

Arthur M. Cole, who represented C. R. Gardiner, the backer of Eva Mann in her brief tour as an actress, is dying of consumption in St. Vincent's Hospital. Cole was left without money when the Eva Mann company disbanded, and Secretary Gurney of the Actors' Fund found him sick and destitute at the Americus Hotel in Fourth avenue. Charles Gardiner, whom Cole represented, lives in Connecticut and is said to be wealthy.

EVA MANN SKEPTICAL.

SHE DOES NOT BELIEVE ROBERT RAY HAMILTON IS DEAD.

THE STORY OF THE INQUEST ON HIS BODY RIDICULED BY HER—GROUNDS OF HER DISBELIEF CLEVERLY PUT—SHE HOPES TO SEE HIM YET.

ALBANY, OCT. 15.—[SPECIAL.]—Eva Mann, or Mrs. Eva Hamilton, as she prefers to be called, who is here with a burlesque company which is performing at the Gaiety Theatre, was to-day asked to read the article verifying the report of Robert Ray Hamilton's death. After reading it she explained: "It seems as if this trouble will last forever." When asked if she still doubted the death of Hamilton, she said emphatically:

"I have always doubted it. I did not believe the former stories, and I do not believe this one. I am quite confident that Mr. Hamilton is alive. Is it not proof enough that it is not Ray's body that they make no endeavor to have it brought here to rest with the others of his family. It is not proof, I say, when they let him lie there, buried like a dog. They say they cannot bring the body on without my consent, yet they have never asked my consent."

"You don't, then, believe in this inquest?"

"No. Why should I, or why should any thinking person believe it? Why did his family wait a whole year before they had this inquest made? Is it likely that at this time a decomposed body can be recognized? Not at all. If his family had wanted to prove his death they should have had the body disinterred and examined right away. There was no sense in this waiting a year, unless it was in the hope that decomposition would destroy all evidence that would lead to identification."

"What about the marks, such as the filled teeth?"

"They are nonsensical and untrue. Mr. Hamilton had very sound teeth. Not one was filled or decayed and not one removed. He never had a bit of trouble with them, and there were no gold or silver fillings in his mouth."

In conclusion Eva declared her belief that Ray was still alive, and that she would yet see him.

PITTSBURG DISPATCH
SUNDAY, OCTOBER 25, 1891

STUDYING THE PLAY.

BILL NYE INVESTIGATES MATHEMATICAL ACCURACY UPON THE STAGE.

NEW YORK, OCT. 23.—Recently I went to the London Theater for an afternoon of pure and innocent delight. The London Theater is not so English as I had expected to find it from its name. It is an American theater where one can see a play that is mathematically and dramatically accurate.

Friends of mine told me to go there and study the mechanism of a play so that when I write another border drama I can see how to put the border on without puckering the drama. I can never be thankful enough that I did so. I put in the entire afternoon studying the construction of a play that has been thrilling the Bowery for a long time. In this play a maid with a feather duster is seen at the beginning of the first act dusting the parlor and trying to think of her peace. This is well done and dramatically accurate. The plot now proceeds to unfold itself. In the second act a villain appears with pink whiskers made for a smaller man. He moves about the stage to melancholy music.

IMPRESSIONS OF EVA HAMILTON.

The piece all the way through is so dramatically accurate that I could go out for an hour I know exactly where they would be when I came back. But I went there mostly to see Eva Hamilton. I wanted to see how she would succeed as an actress. I thought that if she acquitted herself nicely I could write a play for her next year. But she did not do very well. She wore yachting clothes and a scared look, but her voice was as devoid of emotion as that of John L. Sullivan, and her statements were as devoid of sympathetic effect as those made by the man who calls trains in the Union depot in Pittsburg.

Go home, little Eva. Go back to your old life, whatever it may be. Do not attempt to be emotional when an Eastside audience frightens you and your lines light out like a scared jack rabbit at the early dawn. It is high time you called a halt. Go not to the quiet grave of that deluded man whose name you are pasting on the deadwalls in order to get new clothes and bait the old deadfalls for new victims. I am glad the press united on this evil angel of a soft hearted man whose life was ruined by her. Such women discourage a young dramatist like myself from writing the great American play. Let us change the play.

CAMDEN COURIER POST
TUESDAY, NOVEMBER 3, 1891

EVA HAMILTON NON EST.

BREAKS HER STAGE CONTRACT.

HER MANAGER DOESN'T WANT HER BACK, BUT DOES WANT HIS MONEY.

BROOKLYN, Nov. 3.—A good sized audience that expected to see Eva Mann or, if she calls herself, Eva Ray Hamilton, appear at Hyde and Bahman's Theatre, Brooklyn, yesterday afternoon, did not have its morbid curiosity satisfied. Eva did not appear. Her failure to do so was not explained to the audience, and, indeed, even the management could not assign a clear reason for her action. What followed his best told in the words of H. M. Miaco, one of the managers of the company:

"I went around to the Clarendon, where she was stopping," said the manager, "and found her reclining on the bed, smoking a cigarette. She told me that she would not appear anymore. I asked her why, and she said: 'Ask that object over there.' The 'object' was Edward Warren, an actor who has been traveling with her, and who was sitting at the other end of the room. I asked Warren what the trouble was and he told me not to ask him. The woman would give me no satisfaction at all, although I had already paid her for the week in advance. She simply said she proposed quit and that was all there was about it. As I had given her $200 for the week's work I naturally wanted to know where I came in, but she had made up her mind and that settled it.

"I went away and when I returned a short time after I learned she had packed her trunks and started for Jersey City. Warren was sitting in the hotel office with his valise, and he assured me that he was glad she was gone. According to her statement she paid Warren $75 a week to travel with her. I won't try to get her back, but I want my $200. Why, during the five weeks she was with me I almost ran my legs off attending to her. She's a terror, I tell you. Nobody who has not had dealings with her can imagine what she is. She boasts, though, that she is one of the Four Hundred."

Manager Behman, who was present, suggested that Miaco might engage another Eva who had occupied a large share of public attention by outdoing the famous Darby Doyle, who swam from Cork Harbor to Quebec. "I've had one Eva," replied Miaco sententiously, "and one is enough for me."

EVA HAMILTON'S AFFAIRS.

THE FAIR SIREN AFTER A SHARE OF ROBERT'S MONEY.

Ever since Eva Mann Hamilton was living in Carbondale she has been making a quiet effort through her attorney, Colonel Fuller, for a share in the Hamilton estate, and the Colonel says that the case will now be pushed with renewed vigor. A motion to dismiss the appeal to reverse the refusal of Surrogate Ransom to permit Eva, who claims to be Robert Ray Hamilton's widow, to enter his court as such and sue for her alleged right in his estate, was to have been heard on March 7th, but owing to illness of counsel it went by default. Gossip was busy, and it was said that underlying the default was the fact that the celebrated case has been compromised at last. In order to show cause why the dismissal should not be set aside and the appeal reinstated has been granted.

"Eva does not deny that offers of settlement have been made," continued Colonel Fuller. "On the contrary she has had $20,000 and the custody of her child proffered her, but that she declined the offer without a moment hesitation. She is so confident, moreover, of winning a fortune that she announces her intention to soon leave the stage for good. The tidy sum of $400,000 represents the amount of Robert Ray Hamilton's estate in New York and Brooklyn. The bulk of it is comprised of houses about Ninth avenue and Twenty-fourth street. Of this sum Eva wants nearly $100,000 as her right of dower, and has perfect confidence that she will get it. It is asserted that title guarantee companies have repeatedly refused to give titles upon certain portions of Robert Ray Hamilton's estate until the release was signed by Eva, thus virtually recognizing her power of dower. It would not seem from this that the Surrogate Court proceedings had had much effect with these institutions."

EVA MANN'S MEMORANDUM.

BASIS OF HER SUIT AGAINST ROBERT RAY HAMILTON'S EXECUTORS.

The suit of Eva Mann against the executors of Robert Ray Hamilton, which has been referred to ex-Surrogate Daniel G. Rollins as referee, is dragging because of engagements of the various persons concerned. There was another postponement on this account yesterday.

Suit is brought on a memorandum written on a leaf of a pocket pad which belonged to Mr. Hamilton. The leaf did not come from the top of the pad, but from the centre. It is in evidence and contains these words:

I intend to pay you, Eva, thirty-two hundred and fifty as soon as I can.

R.R.H.

On the strength of this alleged promise Miss Mann wants $3,250 from the executors. The defense is that the paper is a forgery. The writing is so faint that at a little distance the leaf seems to be blank. There is no appearance of blurring, however, for on close inspection the letters are clear enough, though they seem to have been made with a light hand using a hard pencil.

Hamilton's Body Taken to New York.

By Associated Press.]

NEW YORK, July 27.—The body of the late Robert Ray Hamilton, a descendant of Alexander Hamilton, is on its way to this city from the west, for interment. Hamilton drowned while attempting to cross the Snake river, below Jacksons Rake, Wintah county, Wyoming, nearly two years ago.

MANN SAID TO BE INSANE.

A COURT PROCEEDING RECALLING THE FATE OF ROBERT RAY HAMILTON.

Eva L. Mann, who figured in the misfortunes of Robert Ray Hamilton, is again brought to public attention by the somewhat unusual motion before Judge Patterson in the Supreme Court yesterday of A.H. Hummel, attorney for Joshua J. Mann, the woman's husband, in his action for divorce. Mr. Hummel asked that the case be stricken from the calendar on the ground that his client was suffering from dementia and unable to appear in court. Affidavits were presented in support of this statement from the insanity experts Drs. Carlos F. Macdonald and E.F. Macdonald. The defendant's attorney, Charles W. Brooke, has until to-morrow to file affidavits to show why the case should proceed to judgment.

Mr. Hummel told a New York Times's reporter that Mann is suffering from a mild form of dementia, the result of a blow on the head; that he is not under restraint, but is living with friends in this city. The suit was brought originally by Mann when the woman was attempting to establish her right to bear the name of Hamilton. She was anxious that the case should be settled, and through her counsel resurrected it.

Early in the Summer of 1889 it became known that Robert Ray Hamilton had become the dupe of a woman, who had induced him to go through a marriage ceremony with her, averring that he was the father of her child. Investigation showed that the baby was not her own.

Eva served a term in State prison in New Jersey for an assault upon her nurse. Hamilton clung to her until it was proved that he had been duped as to the child, when he brought suit to annul the marriage. After setting up his affairs and making provision for the baby, he went to a ranch in Montana, where he was drowned in August, 1890, while fording the Snake River. The woman attempted to obtain a share in his estate, but without success, it being proved that she had married Mann before she ever met Hamilton.

EVA MANN AGGRESSIVE,

She Wants to Have Joshua's Suit for Divorce Tried and Done With.

EVA HAMILTON MARRIED.

THE CENTRAL FIGURE IN THE BOGUS BABY SCANDAL NOW MRS. HILTON.

NEW YORK, SEPT. 12.—It has become public that Eva Mann, the leading figure in the Robert Ray Hamilton bogus baby scandal, has been married for the past six months. Her husband is Edward Hilton.

Hilton is a young Englishman and keeps a boarding house. He said that he had been in the country only a few months. Hilton refused to talk about the marriage. He denied that the Surrogate had decided that his wife was the wife of Josh Mann.

Lawyer Charles W. Brooke, who was the lawyer for the woman in the case, admitted the marriage.

Mrs. Hilton had signed her name as such for an affidavit in a supplementary proceeding against her late husband's estate three months ago involving a $200 note given her by him.

"Discovered" Again.

Robert Ray Hamilton, the degenerate scion of a famous New York family, who was drowned in the Snake river, in Yellowstone Park, is brought to life every few months with the same regularity as Bill Dalton. The latest report declares that Hamilton has been seen in Mexico in a demented condition. As Hamilton's body was identified by near friends, and as all the details of his death were brought out by patient investigation this Mexican tale is evidently a canard.

THE NEW YORK TIMES
SUNDAY, JULY 8, 1894

EVA MANN COMPROMISES FOR $10,000.

SHE RELINQUISHES ALL CLAIMS ON THE ESTATE OF ROBERT RAY HAMILTON.

For the consideration of $10,000, Eva Mann-Brill-Steele-Gaul-Hamilton has relinquished her claim to the estate of Robert Ray Hamilton, whom, it is alleged, she enticed into marrying her by means of a bogus baby which was palmed off him.

The woman is more familiarly known to the public as Eva L. Mann. Her other names are Evangeline L. Hamilton, Evangeline L. Steele, and Lydia E. Gaul. The quit claim which she signed in consideration of $10,000 was filed in the Register's office Friday. The paper is dated July 5, 1894, and is drawn between Lydia E. Gaul, mention of her various other names being made, and Edmund L. Baylies and Gilbert M. Spier of this city.

The $10,000 has been paid by the executors of the estate, and the document states that Lydia E. Gaul, in consideration thereof, "agrees to dismiss all claims to dower, and agrees that she will cause all actions so pending to be dismissed."

THE NEW YORK TIMES
WEDNESDAY, MAY 1, 1895

EVA HAMILTON'S PARDON.

THE JERSEY INVESTIGATING COMMITTEE SHOWS HOW IT WAS OBTAINED.

GOV. ABBETT HAD COUNSEL CHANGED.

LAWYER HEPPENHEIMER GOT $1,000 FROM MRS. HAMILTON, AND THEN THE PAROLE WAS GRANTED BY THE COURT.

TRENTON, N. J., APRIL 30.—Counsel Corbin of the Voorhees committee this afternoon, after an interesting day's session, shifted the trend of evidence to Eva Hamilton's famous case, and, despite the efforts of Senator Daly and Allan McDermott to save the name of their dead friend, Leon Abbett, the committee probed deep into the facts surrounding her pardon.

Mr. Corbin gave a history of the Court of Pardons. The proceedings of the court were mostly secret until 1887, when, by legislative enactment, they were made matters of public record. Rumors, the council said, had been current that there were scandals connected with the court.

Executive Clerk Fox, who has been in that position for so many years, and served so many governors that the date of his appointment is almost forgotten, and who holds more secrets of the inner workings of the State executive departments for a quarter of a century than any other man, was the first witness called. He said the petition of Eva Hamilton for apartment was pre-sented in 1890. It was passed over at the March term. The June term passed and it was not taken up, but at the November term it was granted.

John H. Patterson, head keeper of the State prison, was asked if he remembered being sent for by Gov. Abbett in regard to the pardon. He said he did.

"Mr. Corbin, does this apply to anything between this witness and Gov. Abbett?" asked Senator Daly.

"It does," replied Mr. Corbin.

"Then, gentlemen," said Mr. Daly, "I want to enter an earnest protest. I don't want to besmirch the dead. I do not feel we should go into the grave for scandals."

"Proceed, Mr. Patterson," said Mr. Corbin. "You were sent for to come to the executive chamber, and on going there met Gov. Abbett—"

"Hold on a minute," came in a loud tone from the body of the chamber, as Allan McDermott strode to the front. Mr. McDermott said:

"I may be interrupting the proceedings of this committee, but I desire to ask permission at this time, if it is the intention to assail the memory of my dead friend, one who was a dear friend, that I be allowed to cross-examine all witnesses who may testify in this matter."

"The rule was laid down at the outset of this committee that no counsel will be allowed. However, any questions you may want to ask will be put by Mr. Corbin," said Mr. Voorhees.

"Proceed, Mr. Patterson," said Mr. Corbin.

"I came to the Governor," said Mr. Patterson. "He said he understood Eva Ray Hamilton sought a pardon. I said yes. He said he understood she had engaged Counsel Hoffman and Fuller. I said she had. 'You had better tell her,' said the Governor, 'that she had better retain Colonel William C. Heppenheimer. I don't believe she will be successful with a present counsel.'"

"What did you do then?"

"I declined to tell her."

Mr. Patterson said that when he returned to the prison he found Mrs. Hamilton appeared to know what was expected of him.

A few days later Mrs. Hamilton requested him to draw on her money, of which he, as keeper, was custodian, to the extent of $1,000, and give it to Mr. Heppenheimer. The witness said he did it she desired, and paid the money to Mr. Heppenheimer. The money was paid by check.

Colonel W.C. Heppenheimer testified that his first knowledge of the case was when Col. Fuller called on him. He was asked to become counsel in the appeal for a pardon, and named his retainer as $1,000. He admitted having spoken to Gov. Abbett, both before and after he had been retained. He neither visited nor communicated with his client before the pardon was granted. He did some work for her in New York afterward. Before the pardon he saw the Judges of the Court of Pardons. The thousand dollars was all for his own use, and he gave no one else any of it.

Col. Fuller admitted that he had been told by Judges Brown, Smith, and Whittaker to change counsel in the Hamilton case, because the Governor was a stumbling block, and would be so, unless Heppenheimer was retained.

Mr. Corbin then left the Hamilton case and called witnesses from the Secretary of State's office to show that, by Gov. Abbett's direction, unsigned certificates of parole for the Hudson County ballot-box stuffers were filled up before the Court of Pardons took any action in their cases. Mr. Corbin characterized the paroling of these men as a general jail delivery of men who had committed the greatest crime possible against the state.

BEATRICE HAMILTON LOSES.

ROBERT RAY HAMILTON'S WILL CONTESTED BY HIS RELATIVES.

There was handed down by the appellate division of the supreme court yesterday a decision in the action brought by Nathalie E Baylies tease for the partition of property at Broadway and Spring St., Street, Manhattan, part of which belonged to Robert Ray Hamilton when he died. The questions involved in the suit relate to the construction of Mr. Hamilton's will, and one of the defendants is Beatrice Ray Hamilton, who was adopted by him after the unsuccessful attempt to impose the child on him as his own. Mr. Hamilton's will provided for her annuity of $1200 a year for life, chargeable upon certain property in Brooklyn. The lower court had decided that this annuity was a charge upon the remainder of the estate after the death of Schuyler Hamilton, Junior, Robert Ray's brother. The appellate division holds that the annuity is not a charge upon the remainder. The Brooklyn property referred to is not sufficient for the production of the annuity, so that the child whose protection was the cause of so much anxiety to Mr. Hamilton, will not profit as he intended from his estate.

EVA A BOARDING HOUSE MISTRESS.

Robert Ray Hamilton's 'Once Famous Companion Accused of Holding Trunks Belonging to an Actress.

ELMIRA STAR GAZETTE AND FREE PRESS
WEDNESDAY, NOVEMBER 1, 1899

MURDER CHARGE.

THE FORMER PARTNER OF
ROBERT RAY HAMILTON ARRESTED.

The sensational death of Robert Ray Hamilton and the contest over his property made by Eva Mann, a former Elmira woman, and at one time inmate of a resort here, will be well remembered by Elmrians, because of the great interest taken in the case at the time.

Another chapter in the long list of events connected with his death has been added, according to a dispatch to a New York paper from Cheyenne, Wyoming. The dispatch states that J.B. Sargent is in jail in Cheyenne for alleged wife murder. Sargent was a partner of Hamilton when the latter was mysteriously drowned. His home is in Machias, Maine, and he was placed under arrest last week at Jackson's Hole in Cheyenne.

FORFEITED HER BAIL

NOTORIOUS EVA RAY HAMILTON COMES TO THE CENTER OF THE STAGE ONCE MORE.

Eva Ray Hamilton temporarily occupies the center of the Stage once more. Wilkes-Barre, Pa., is the scene of her actions this time.

Mrs. Hamilton visited her father, William Steele, of Monroe township recently and succeeded in getting in a fight with him. She was arrested and gave $100 bail for appearance for trial. She has "skipped" and the money has been forfeited.

Eva Ray, Man, Hamilton, or whatever her name is, is well known to Elmirans. Years ago she resided here. She was a claimant for a portion of the estate of the late Robert Ray Hamilton.

THE NEW YORK TIMES
THURSDAY, DECEMBER 28, 1899

JOHN I. SARGENT INSANE.

HE WAS SUSPECTED OF KILLING ROBERT RAY HAMILTON— INDICTED FOR KILLING HIS WIFE.

EVANSTON, WYO., DEC. 27.—John B. Sargent of New York, who is suspected of the murder of Robert Ray Hamilton, the New Yorker whose body was found in Snake River in 1891, is incurably insane.

Sargent and Hamilton established a ranch on Snake River and lived there for some time. Later Hamilton was drowned, and Sargent was accused of the crime.

Sargent is now under indictment for the murder of his wife, and is also charged with assaulting his four-year-old daughter. He fled to New York after the latter crime was said to have been committed, but returned last summer to stand trial. The confinement in jail caused him to become a physical wreck and to lose his mind, consequently he has been released.

A LYNCHING AT JACKSON'S HOLE

The Notorious Sargent Is the Reported Victim.

IS PURSUED BY CITIZENS.

Was Charged With Assaulting His Little Daughter.

Was Also Accused of Responsibility For the Death of His Wife—He Was a Partner of Robert Ray Hamilton, Who Was Drowned In the Snake River in 1891—Report of the Lynching Brought In by a Ranchman.

EVA HAMILTON DIES A PAUPER.

WOMAN WHO BECAME NOTORIOUS BY ATTEMPTING TO PALM BOGUS BABY ON ROBERT RAY HAMILTON VICTIM OF HEART DISEASE.

BOUGHT INFANT FOR $10; GOT $10,000 FROM ESTATE.

HAD BEEN LIVING IN ENGLAND SINCE DEATH OF HAMILTON AND BUT RECENTLY RETURNED TO THE UNITED STATES.

It is just been learned that the woman who died in the charity Ward at St. Vincent's Hospital on Nov. 23 under the name of Eva Hamilton was the famous Eva Ray Hamilton, whose career was strangely linked with that of Robert Ray Hamilton.

The body was buried in the common plot in Mount Olivet Cemetery, there being but one mourner present, a "Mr. Hamilton," who acknowledged that was not his name and who said he had known her intimately for eight years. He declared that the woman was the original Eva Ray Hamilton, and that he has letters and papers to prove it.

OBTAINS BOGUS BABY.

Robert Ray Hamilton was the son of Gen. Schuyler Hamilton and a descendent of Alexander Hamilton. He was a young man with a brilliant future and had been elected to the Assembly when he met a woman, then known as Eva Mann. In 1889 he surprised his friends by marrying her. It developed some time after that she had fooled him into the belief that she had given birth to a baby. It was later established in the court that she had purchased the child for $10, and that several infants had been sent to her before she selected the one which she represented to be a descendant of the Hamiltons. The child was a girl and was named Beatrice.

In a quarrel at their country home in New Jersey Mrs. Hamilton stabbed a nurse girl, a Miss Donnelly, and was sentenced to two years in the Trenton Penitentiary. Hamilton began an investigation of her past and discovered her long connection with the blackmailing gang that had helped her to deceive him regarding the child.

GETS $10,000.

Hamilton went to Wyoming to work on a ranch and forget, if possible, his troubles. Word came to New York in 1891 that he had been drowned while fording the Snake River. His partner, John D. Sergent, was arrested on the charge of murder and was afterward sent to an insane asylum.

It developed that Eva Ray Hamilton had little claim to the title she wore, as it was shown that at the time of her marriage to Hamilton she was really the wife of Joshua Mann. Her marriage to Hamilton was annulled. She sued the estate and got a settlement of $10,000. She left this country for England in 1893.

On Nov. 22 she developed signs of heart failure and Dr. O'Connell, of No. 116 Waverley place, advised her removal to St. Vincent's. She was in a state of coma when taken to the hospital and died there the next afternoon at 5 o'clock.

No information regarding her parents is given in the records of the Health Department, the man having been unable to supply it. A sister living in Pennsylvania has been notified.

EVA RAY HAMILTON DEAD IN POVERTY AFTER EVENTFUL LIFE.

EVA HAMILTON

ABOUT NELLIE BLY

Nellie Bly was born Elizabeth "Pink" Cochran. Her father, a man of considerable wealth, served for many years as judge of Armstrong County, Pennsylvania. He lived on a large estate called Cochran's Mills, which took its name from him.

Being in reduced circumstances after her father's death, her mother remarried, only to divorce Jack Ford a few years later. The family then moved to Pittsburg, where a twenty-year-old Pink read a column in the *Pittsburg Dispatch* entitled "What Girls Are Good For." Enraged at the sexist and classist tone, she wrote a furious letter to the editor. Impressed, the editor engaged her to do special work for the newspaper as a reporter, writing under the name "Nellie Bly." Her first series of stories, "Our Workshop Girls," brought life and sympathy to working women in Pittsburgh.

A year later she went as a correspondent to Mexico, where she remained six months, sending back weekly articles. After her return she longed for broader fields, and so moved to New York. The story of her attempt to make a place for herself, or to find an opening, was a long one of disappointment, until at last she gained the attention of the *New York World*.

Her first achievement for them was the exposure of the Blackwell's Island Insane Asylum, in which she spent ten days, and two days in the Bellevue Insane Asylum. The story created a great sensation, making "Nellie Bly" a household name.

After three years of doing work as a "stunt girl" at the *World*, Bly conceived the idea of making a trip around the world in less time than had been done by Phileas Fogg, the fictitious hero of Jules Verne's famous novel. In fact, she made it in 72 days. On her return in January 1890 she was greeted by ovations all the way from San Francisco to New York.

She then paused her reporting career to write novels, but returned to the *World* three years later. In 1895 she married millionaire industrialist Robert Seaman, and a couple years later retired from journalism to take an interest in his factories.

She returned to journalism almost twenty years later, reporting on World War I from behind the Austrian lines. Upon returning to New York, she spent the last years of her life doing both reporting and charity work, finding homes for orphans. She died of pneumonia in 1922.

Books by Nellie Bly

JOURNALISM

Ten Days in a Mad-House

Six Months In Mexico

Nellie Bly's Book: Around the World in 72 Days

NOVELS

The Mystery of Central Park

Eva the Adventuress

New York By Night

Alta Lynn, m.d.

Wayne's Faithful Sweetheart

Little Luckie

Dolly the Coquette

In Love With a Stranger

The Love of Three Girls

Little Penny, Child of the Streets

Pretty Merribelle

Twins and Rivals

ABOUT DAVID BLIXT

David Blixt is an author and actor living in Chicago. An Artistic Associate of the Michigan Shakespeare Festival, where he serves as the resident Fight Director, he is also co-founder of A Crew Of Patches Theatre Company, a Shakespearean repertory based in Chicago. He has acted and done fight work for the Goodman Theatre, Chicago Shakespeare Theatre, Steppenwolf, the Shakespeare Theatre of Washington DC, and First Folio Shakespeare, among many others.

As a writer, his STAR-CROSS'D series of novels place the characters of Shakespeare's Italian plays in their historical setting, drawing in figures such as Dante, Giotto, and Petrarch to create an epic of warfare, ingrigue, and romance. In HER MAJESTY'S WILL, Shakespeare himself becomes a character as Blixt explores Shakespeare's "Lost Years," teaming the young Will with the dark and devious Kit Marlowe to hilarious effect. In the COLOSSUS series, Blixt brings first century Rome and Judea to life as he relates the fall of Jerusalem, the building of the Colosseum, and the coming of Christianity to Rome. And in his bestselling NELLIE BLY series, he explores the amazing life and adventures of America's premier undercover reporter.

David continues to write, act, and travel. He has ridden camels around the pyramids at Giza, been thrown out of the Vatican Museum and been blessed by John-Paul II, scaled the Roman ramp at Masada, crashed a hot-air balloon, leapt from cliffs on small Greek islands, dined with Counts and criminals, climbed to the top of Mount Sinai, and sat in the Prince's chair in Verona's palace. But David is happiest at his desk, weaving tales of brilliant people in dire and dramatic straits. Living with his wife and two children, David describes himself as "actor, author, father, husband - in reverse order."

WWW.DAVIDBLIXT.COM

THE MYSTERY OF CENTRAL PARK

A rejected marriage proposal and the corpse of a dead beauty confound Dick Treadwell's hopes for happiness, until his beloved Penelope sets him a task: she will marry him if he solves— *the Mystery of Central Park!*

EVA, THE ADVENTURESS

Nellie Bly's ripped-from-the-headlines novel of a poor girl determined to revenge herself upon the world, only to find that, in the battle between love and revenge, only one can triumph.

NEW YORK BY NIGHT

Setting out to solve the bold diamond robbery, millionaire detective Lionel Dangerfield finds himself in competition with Ruby Sharpe, daring young reporter for the *New York Planet*. Will "The Danger" solve the case before Ruby can steal the story—and his heart?

ALTA LYNN, M.D.

A prank goes awry and Alta Lynn finds herself wed against her will. Leaving love behind, she throws herself into the study of medicine, only to find that love has other plans for her!

WAYNE'S FAITHFUL SWEETHEART

Beautiful Dorette Lover is rescued from poverty when she finds work as an artist's model. That same day she witnesses a seeming murder. To protect the man accused, she agrees to become his bride—only to fall desperately in love with him!

LITTLE LUCKIE

Luckie Thurlow longs to be accepted by society and gain the man she loves. But she harbors a dark secret—she is the daughter of the murderous Gypsy Queen, who plans to use Luckie to gain her own revenge!

IN LOVE WITH A STRANGER

Kit Clarendon is in love! Trouble is, she doesn't know her love's name. But she is determined to track him down and force him to love her! A wild pursuit filled with disguises, desperate deeds, and declarations of love as Kit determines to go through fire and water to win him!

THE LOVE OF THREE GIRLS

An heiress in disguise, a factory girl with dreams of wealth, and a sweet child of charity are forced into rivalry when they all fall in love with the same man! Murder, fever, fallen women, and a desperate villain conspire against—
the love of three girls!

INTO THE MADHOUSE

Never before collected! "Who is this insane girl?" asked other papers, completely taken in by Nellie Bly's plan to infiltrate Blackwell's Island. The complete reporting surrounding her daring expose, including details not included in her initial accounts and her scathing rebuttal of the doctors' excuses!

NELLIE BLY'S WORLD - Vol. 1
1887-1888

Bly's complete reporting, collected for the very first time! Starting with the stunt that made hers a household name, Nellie Bly spends her first year at the New York World going undercover to expose frauds, sharpsters and boodlers, interviewing Belva Lockwood and Hangman Joe, and tackling Phelps the Lobbyist!

NELLIE BLY'S WORLD - Vol. 2
1889-1890

Bly's complete reporting, collected for the very first time! Nellie buys a baby, has herself followed by a detective and arrested, interviews Helen Keller, champion boxer John Sullivan, and convicted would-be killer Eva Hamilton, all before setting out on her greatest stunt of all, a race around the world!

COMING SOON:

NELLIE BLY'S WORLD, Vol. 3 & 4
NELLIE BLY'S DISPATCHES, Vol. 1 & 2
NELLIE BLY's JOURNALS, Vol. 1 & 2

ALL FROM SORDELET INK

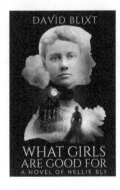

WHAT GIRLS ARE GOOD FOR
A NOVEL OF NELLIE BLY

Nellie Bly has the story of a lifetime. But will she survive to tell it?

Based on the real-life events of the tiny Pennsylvania spitfire who refused to let the world change her, and changed the world instead.

CHARITY GIRL
A NELLIE BLY NOVELETTE

Fresh from her escape from Blackwell's Island, Nellie Bly investigates the doctors who buy and sell babies in Victorian New York. Based on real events and her own reporting, Nellie Bly asks the devastating question—what becomes of babies?

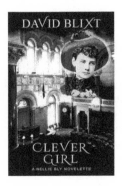

CLEVER GIRL
A NELLIE BLY NOVELLA

A blizzard has frozen all of New York, and Nellie Bly is going stir-crazy when she and Colonel Cockerill plot out her most daring undercover assignment yet: she's going to trap the most crooked man in politics, Edward R. Phelps, the self-styled "King" of the Albany lobby.

COMING SOON:

STUNT GIRL

A NOVEL OF NELLIE BLY
BY DAVID BLIXT

MORE FROM SORDELET INK

PLAYSCRIPTS

ACTION MOVIE - THE PLAY BY JOE FOUST AND RICHARD RAGSDALE

ALL CHILDISH THINGS BY JOSEPH ZETTELMAIER

CAMPFIRE BY JOSEPH ZETTELMAIER

CAPTAIN BLOOD ADAPTED BY DAVID RICE

CHURCHILL BY RONALD KEATON

THE COUNT OF MONTE CRISTO ADAPTED BY CHRISTOPHER M WALSH

DEAD MAN'S SHOES BY JOSEPH ZETTELMAIER

THE DECADE DANCE BY JOSEPH ZETTELMAIER

DR. SEWARD'S DRACULA ADAPTED BY JOSEPH ZETTELMAIER

EBENEZER: A CHRISTMAS PLAY BY JOSEPH ZETTELMAIER

EVE OF IDES BY DAVID BLIXT

FRANKENSTEIN ADAPTED BY ROBERT KAUZLARIC

THE GRAVEDIGGER: A FRANKENSTEIN PLAY BY JOSEPH ZETTELMAIER

HATFIELD & McCOY BY SHAWN PFAUTSCH

HER MAJESTY'S WILL ADAPTED BY ROBERT KAUZLARIC

IT CAME FROM MARS BY JOSEPH ZETTELMAIER

THE LEAGUE OF AWESOME BY CORRBETTE PASKO AND SARA SEVIGNY

THE MAN-BEAST BY JOSEPH ZETTELMAIER

THE MAN WHO WAS THURSDAY ADAPTED BY BILAL DARDAI

THE MOONSTONE ADAPTED BY ROBERT KAUZLARIC

MY ITALY STORY AND LONG GONE DADDY BY JOSEPH GALLO

NORTHERN AGGRESSION BY JOSEPH ZETTELMAIER

ONCE A PONZI TIME BY JOE FOUST

THE RENAISSANCE MAN BY JOSEPH ZETTELMAIER

THE SCULLERY MAID BY JOSEPH ZETTELMAIER

ANTON CHEKHOV'S THE SEAGULL ADAPTED BY JANICE L BLIXT

SEASON ON THE LINE BY SHAWN PFAUTSCH

STAGE FRIGHT: A HORROR ANTHOLOGY BY JOSEPH ZETTELMAIER

A TALE OF TWO CITIES ADAPTED BY CHRISTOPHER M WALSH

WILLIAMSTON ANTHOLOGY: VOLUME 1

WILLIAMSTON ANTHOLOGY: VOLUME 2

WWW.SORDELETINK.COM

CPSIA information can be obtained
at www.ICGtesting.com
Printed in the USA
LVHW011413190122
708831LV00002B/74